WHENCE, SIMULACRUM?

Whence, Simulacrum? by Ryan Finch
Copyright © Ryan Finch, 2020

Cover art by Vladislav Orlowski

This is a work of fiction. It is entirely the product of the author's imagination. Any resemblance to actual persons, events, et cetera is coincidental.

All rights reserved.
The moral rights of the author have been asserted.
No part of this book may be reproduced in any manner without the express written consent of the author.

Typeset in Crimson Prime

10 9 8 7 6 5 4 3 2 1
First edition, first printing.

Visit the author's website at: **ryanfinchwrites.com**

Print ISBN 978-1-83853-289-5
eBook ISBN 978-1-83853-288-8

For Samantha
I'm yours forever

CHAPTER ONE

5:47 PM. SEPTEMBER 2ND.

Erin was, in fact, no longer quite present.

Sitting with her legs crossed on the window-seat, she had become transfixed. She was placidly marvelling at the strangeness of what lay beyond the glass. And her enthrallment was *total*. Undisturbed by thought, she just *saw*. It felt like her consciousness was seeping out of every pore of her mind like tiny tendrils, straining to reach out and meld with the sight. She didn't resist or embrace the experience, but merely permitted it to unfold. For that fleeting dissolution of self was not unpleasurable. Indeed, it produced a serene lightness of being, somewhat akin to a... kind of neuroses-anesthetic, and the freedom which resulted was one she only very rarely felt.

She held her body perfectly still, so as not to inadvertently dispel what was happening. Her head drooped languidly to one side, pressing her temple against the frigid windowpane. And her eyes, defocused to absorb the view in its entirety, appeared vacant and unseeing. All of this combined to imbue her, disquietingly, with the semblance of a posed mannequin, a well-made stand-in. Only by paying close attention to the occasional blink or her soft breathing could one detect some telltale indication of life.

Positioned beneath her was a large, plush cushion, needed to lessen the discomfort which always set in after a few hours. This was one of several such tricks she had come up with. After all, she often ended up whiling away much of the day in this very spot. She couldn't help but do so. Its lure was intense. From this perch she could watch the outside world and its people as an unseen observer. And there was just something so gratifying about peering, from such a distant omniscient vantage, into a realm she had quit. It granted her a sense of power, which lay in self-aggrandizement. She belittled the city by making it a mere plaything of her gaze.

This had not always been the case, however. When she first took up the pastime, she beheld what she saw wistfully, just as when the memory of a childhood home flashes before the mind's eye. At that time, she was oppressed by a sense of loss. She could not shake, let alone disprove, a suspicion of having relinquished something of great intangible value. But as the weeks passed, it gradually became apparent that this inclination to mourn was not to be trusted. The more she examined it and dissected it, the less it seemed to be genuinely her own. She realized that there was a certain nebulous sadness which she simply felt she *ought* to feel. Such that her psyche, having not yet settled on what would be her real reaction, just acquiesced to manifesting this stopgap instead. It did so quite convincingly too. But when she finally wised up and countermanded this, all ersatz traces of heavy-heartedness and regret faded away like a dissipating smokescreen.

Then came the clearheaded anger, which she welcomed. The only problem was that it does not play well with others. And as such, it quickly sought to monopolize her. Just as surging magma erases all that lies in its path, the anger indiscriminately purged whatever else she may have genuinely felt about her past life. Standing atop that wide swath of scorched-earth, she knew not what seeds of unbloomed emotions, now shrivelled and dead from the heat, may have lain just beneath the sod. But, of course, she still had the anger. And she made good use of it. Its power, as millennia of the lost and the damned have well discovered, is to make everything seem so very simple. So she would glare out of her window, seething with hostility and resentment. She hated that world for having proven so inhospitable to her. And she begrudged its inhabitants for having found a way to survive what she had to flee. All else was unimportant.

Yet, eventually even the anger, that ficklest of allies, deserted her. From that point onwards, things shifted in a manner she could never have anticipated. The cityscape, having only been seen from afar for so long now, seemed to become something else, something new. It at last assumed the deeply unfamiliar and uncanny aspect which had been steadily unfurling over it. She wondered that she had *ever* stepped foot in it before. And she started to regard it with, above all, an intense curiosity. Unfortunately she had no idea what it would mean, or take, to understand the outside world anew. So many idle moments were spent studying it, trying to dismantle its air of impenetrable alienness. This obsessiveness itself was, oppositely, rather easy to explain. The mystery she faced seemed to contain the faint, taunting promise that some crucial personal insight would be the reward for unravelling it. Even though her understanding of the world may have rotted away, *it* still somehow understood her, and kept what it had discerned hostage like a landlord bitterly clinging onto a collateral deposit when a tenant ups and leaves without warning. She hadn't realized the cost of her escape would be surrendering these traces of abstract self-knowledge she'd left behind as though an imprint. Nor did she now accept it. Her hope was that if she could just fathom (and decipher) her erstwhile home once more, she'd be snatching back whatever it was withholding from her. But, no matter how hard she tried, it was no use. There was just an unspannable gulf of incomprehensibility. She might as well have been scrutinizing the newly-unearthed ruins of some vanished civilisation, squinting at its hieroglyphic graffiti and fingering its gaudy relics.

A shiver suddenly shook her body for a split-second: the cold air of the room finally eliciting a reaction from her. She frowned in annoyance and huffed at her watchful reverie being broken. She looked across the large-ish room, which constituted the whole of her studio apartment, to the temperature control on the wall. This was definitely not the first time she had found it being located over by the front door irksome. Getting up and going all the way over there was *obviously* out of the question. She tried to make out what number was presently displayed on its little blue screen. This was made impossible by the fact that, as was her preference, the room itself was only very dimly lit. And it was now even dimmer than before because most of the candles dotted around had depleted their wax and self-extinguished. Rolling her eyes, and not about to grant circumstance an easy victory, she picked up her phone. She opened the camera app and zoomed all the way in on that faraway digital readout. As soon as she hit the shutter button, the software's low-light optimisation did its best to brighten and

3

sharpen everything. Then, once the finished photo was presented to her, she was just about able to ascertain the two numerals.

She tilted her head side to side and pursed her lips as she pretended to herself that she was actually deliberating.

Finally, she mumbled under her breath, "eh, it's... fine."

Several feet away on the bare wooden window-seat was her sweater. After leaning over to snag it, she pulled it on. This movement had the side-effect of, slightly painfully, revealing to her just how dead her legs were. So she roughly massaged some feeling back in to them and re-crossed them the other way. Next she shifted around on the cushion, turning to face the window head-on. She also picked up the open laptop sitting just beside her and rested it in her lap. It had been on for quite a while now and, honestly, she really just wanted to warm herself with the heat emanating from its underside.

With all that taken care of, she eagerly returned to staring out of the window. It only took a few minutes before she absentmindedly raised her hand to her mouth. The laptop screen splashed its anemic glow across her face, illuminating the minute movements of her jaw as she bit her fingernails. She would occasionally pause just to pluck a tiny nail fragment off her tongue and flick it away, but quickly resumed afterwards.

The late afternoon sky was darkened by a vast and awe-inspiring armada of grey rain-clouds that had been slowly drifting overhead throughout the course of the day. At several points Erin had been mesmerised as she witnessed the foreboding majesty of their unhurried arrival. It was really something. And the fact that they had ventured here and gathered above her, seeming to have answered a summons, made it even more affecting. For, in her mind, she *had* issued just such an invitation to whatever nimbus fleet might heed it. It pleased her to think that her whims had such power. Still, it pleased her even more that her morose mood today should have such a fitting visual accompaniment.

At the moment, just a mild shower persisted. It really wasn't much at all, being so fine as to resemble an ever-replenishing descending mist. But she was no rube. Others may have been beguiled by the feebleness of this opening move, whereas she knew it served only to probe the target of attack. One only had to glance at how swollen and dark these waterlogged clouds were to realize that this drizzle was merely a prelude. They were not gravid with such a heavy payload for nothing. The main bombardment was yet to come, of that there could be no doubt. And Erin was downright tingly as she envisioned it. How dearly she wished to stand beneath the downpour, to be cleansed by nature's disinterested fury.

Alas, this was no longer her lot. It just wasn't. No matter how desperate she was to have all her accumulating flaws and maladies and mistakes be washed away. And the frustration she felt at being separated from this absolution by a mere pane of glass was indescribable. She would have even settled for being able to reach her arm out of the window and touch the rain as it fell. But, *of course*, the window itself did not open, due to her being near the top of this high-rise apartment building. (She did have to at least concede that on several occasions the fact it was not openable had proven very, very fortunate...)

She mentally scolded herself as she felt aggrieved by these thwarted desires once again. What was the use in pining after the impossible? It was sheer masochism. And she needed a lot less of that in her life, not more. Besides which, not only was it a waste of time and energy, it also threatened to rob her of such voyeuristic pleasures as *did* still remain to her. These offered only meagre satisfaction in comparison, but being all she had, they were to be coveted and protected. So, taking her own advice, she stopped dwelling on all that foolishness, and re-focused on the rainfall's beauty. And she really tried to savour the delicious aching tension which swam along her body as she anticipated the might of the full deluge being unleashed.

As she waited, she distractedly pushed her fingertips through her short, shaggy brown hair, ruffling it in one direction then the other. It was probably time to cut it again; she couldn't stand for it to get too long. Thankfully, this was a quick enough chore. And she had, in her own opinion, become fairly adept at trimming it wholly by feel. Now, granted, kitchen scissors were not the ideal tool for the job, but what did it matter? She didn't care how uneven or messy the finished haircut ended up being. After all, no-one was going to see it...

Abruptly piercing the silence and snatching Erin's attention, her laptop began to chirp. A string of new messages materialized on the screen in quick succession. Upon looking down at it, she squinted and blinked and winced at the harshness of the unnatural light assaulting her eyes. Decreasing the brightness setting and pushing the hinged screen back to improve the viewing angle both helped. She then watched the messages pop up one by one.

[18:37] Alabaster&Freckles: Alright I'm back, honey.

[18:38] Alabaster&Freckles: And woah, just saw the time. Sorry about that! Took way longer than I expected!

[18:38] Alabaster&Freckles: Where were we?...

[18:38] Alabaster&Freckles: Oh okay, yeah. So, what about your eating then?

[18:39] Alabaster&Freckles: I know the last week's been particularly trying in that regard... But has there been *any* improvement today?

[18:39] Alabaster&Freckles: I promise I've been sending good vibes to you all day long!

[18:39] Alabaster&Freckles: I'm talking prescription-strength medicinal good vibes.

[18:40] Alabaster&Freckles: Like, you can't even get them over-the-counter at your pharmacist, don't even try.

[18:41] Alabaster&Freckles: And definitely not those mail-order homeopathic knock-off ones you see in the ads at the back of weird magazines!

[18:41] Alabaster&Freckles: (Hopefully not dating myself with that reference! Ha!)

Erin appreciated the upbeat tone and the humour, as a gesture at least. But she nonetheless found it uncheering. For the question this tried to palliate, like a hand-puppet distracting a child getting a shot, still glared at her starkly. And it served as an unwelcome reminder that she still needed to face another meal this evening. She grimaced and gnawed at her jagged fingernails even more fervently. A competing swell of anxiety kicked up inside her as she thought over how to formulate her response. She was painfully aware how similar it was going to seem to those she *always* gave. But there's only so many ways to phrase the same answer. Still, she really wanted to articulate things honestly. Otherwise she would be wasting this sole chance to disburden herself of the day's vexations, which was a continual fear she nursed. So, with all this in mind, she set about replying. With her dominant hand still held hostage by her nervous habit, she clumsily began pecking away at the keyboard with the other.

[18:43] PluckingPurgatory'sPetals: Uh, nope, afraid not.

[18:44] PluckingPurgatory'sPetals: Funnily enough, this morning seemed... unusually promising. Well, I was fairly hungry at least.

[18:44] PluckingPurgatory'sPetals: Then I'm halfway through my breakfast, trying to keep my mind distracted with other things. And suddenly I'm gagging, out of nowhere.

[18:45] PluckingPurgatory'sPetals: The switch had flipped without me even realizing it. And food once again seemed like the most revolting thing in the world.

[18:45] PluckingPurgatory'sPetals: I was hoping this would... well... revert back. Even started making a sandwich thing just in case it did. I guess maybe even thinking that might stimulate things.

[18:46] PluckingPurgatory'sPetals: But then afternoon rolled around and still no dice. So I just eventually forced myself to speed-eat a granola bar.

[18:46] PluckingPurgatory'sPetals: And I know this is, what? The millionth time that something like that has happened. But it was somehow extra, extra frustrating this time.

[18:47] PluckingPurgatory'sPetals: I thought it over for a while. And I think it might be because that hunger made me naively hope that things would be different today. That I might genuinely be able to break the recent streak.

[18:47] PluckingPurgatory'sPetals: It gets hard to not start viewing hopefulness as just the precondition for disappointment, you know?

[18:48] PluckingPurgatory'sPetals: Anyway... I know I'll need to eat something soonish. Really not looking forward to that. Will perhaps try and get some bland rice dish down.

[18:49] PluckingPurgatory'sPetals: Sure would be nice to turn things around and get to salvage the day, but I'm not holding my breath...

Once she had started typing, it all just rapidly spilled out of her, like liquid escaping through a funnel. This was a common occurrence for her. So too was the fact that upon sending the last message, she had to re-read them all to really grasp what she had actually said. She did this quickly and then nodded to herself. Upon review, she had been a little dour but nevertheless acquitted herself adequately well. This verdict quelled the anxiousness in her chest. It had long since stopped seeming odd to her that she obsessed over her messages in this nerve-wracking cycle of trepidation and then (possible) relief.

Tilting closer to the windowpane now, she pressed her forehead against it and relished its pleasant coolness upon her skin. Time to check in on the ant-farm. With downcast eyes, she scanned the streets far below. A long row of cars was held immobile by a traffic jam. So her gaze flitted from one hurrying pedestrian to another as idle whim dictated, watching them scurry along the pavement. Some shielded themselves from the rain with umbrellas, some held newspapers or briefcases aloft as makeshift cover, but they all shunned it in their own way. Their deep-seated urban instincts convinced them that inclement weather was just a nuisance. They resented nature boisterously interfering in their lives. This was amusing, in a way. But it was also sad. And Erin knew exactly what explained the stark difference in attitude which separated her from them. They were just far too close to the thing. Whereas she, being at an impenetrable distance, was able to see the matter clearly. That was the galling catch-22. *She* knew that in the brief, pristine moment inbetween moisture being expelled by the sky and then drunk by the earth, the wretched could be alleviated by it. However, she could not avail herself of this knowledge. *They* received the boon, but were oblivious to it, worried only about preserving their clothes from getting damp and their hairdos from being disturbed. This was just yet another example of fate's twisted sense of humour. But, given it so closely mirrored her own, Erin struggled to really sustain too much animosity towards it. It also helped that even with the punchline coming at her expense, she found that she could still abstractly appreciate the ingenious sadism of the joke.

Instead of just endlessly jumping about from one to another, Erin started zeroing in on certain tiny figures and following them for a little while. She tried to get some sense of who they were, what they were like, where they might be going. Peculiarly enough, she was glad when she found that she could not deduce anything of the sort. When viewed from this high up and through the window's everchanging overlay of downward-racing droplets, they all more or less looked the same. Literally all that could be discerned was that they were human-sized, clothed in human garb, and darting along with bipedal locomotion. All of which testified only to them being... human beings. Or convincing enough anthropoid impostures, at the very least.

The swirling, enveloping fog of anonymity which these faraway passersby were wading through was fascinating to Erin. Indeed, so much more so than whatever their actual mundane identities might be. Because the fact that these nameless, faceless strangers were unknown and unknowable had a transformative effect. Each of them became a sort of charismatic enigma. And this new guise they donned was itself rather magical. It wasn't simply that they could now potentially turn out to be anyone. Suspended in a sublime state of flux, they *were* anyone. She was extremely jealous of this. To have to be someone in particular, and only them, was so rigid, so suffocating. It was just a costume to wear and a role to play. But to shed the obligation of this facade? How ennobling it would be to lose oneself in the aura of infinite possibility which Erin's thwarted observation had conferred.

It suddenly occurred to her that a telescope would be a weapon of absolute lethality here. To magnify one of these people and examine them closely would trap them like a specimen on a skewer. And the ethereal silhouette, precisely their shape and size, which had been airily trailing behind them would finally seize upon its quarry. It would overlap them and definitively stamp all the precise details of their personhood back onto them. This would constitute a sort of death, and one made so much more appalling by happening without the victim even noticing. Erin tried to tell herself it was silly, but couldn't stop herself being moved by the overlooked tragedy of it anyway. And it seemed to her that to knowingly inflict this was, in its own way, heinous. She could not imagine herself doing such a thing. Besides, how much better it was to glimpse the intermingled crowds below only in the dignity and brilliance of their indeterminacy.

Another series of shrill little chirps issued from the laptop's tinny speakers and interrupted her rumination.

Erin was loath to pull away from the window having now stumbled upon such an engaging spectacle. So she waited for the chirps to finish. And then, without even needing to glance down, she just held down a certain combination of keys. Instantly, a soft, accentless voice began reciting the new IM messages aloud. The underlying code worked hard to very nearly replicate the flow of someone actually speaking. But that small gap which remained might as well have been a yawning chasm. The ear was just too discerning. If it was not wholly tricked, it scorned the attempt. And this imitation lacked the familiar, prettifying flaws of real speech, which were much missed when absent. Still, despite all this, Erin just found it nice to be spoken to sometimes. Solitude has a way of making certain sounds seem like rare, sumptuous delicacies. Having somebody talk to you out loud was one of those. Even if this substitute could occasionally be jarringly wooden, it served that purpose well enough.

"New messages from *alabaster ampersand freckles*. **Six fifty-two PM.** Aww, sweetheart, I'm so sorry it went down like that! That sucks! **Six fifty-two PM.** I know it's worse when it toys with you! Damn you appetite, what *is* your problem?! **Six fifty-two PM.** Hopefully you will be able to eat something substantial tonight. **Six fifty-three PM.** But either way, please don't let all this dishearten you too much. Like we've talked about, you just gotta remember that tomorrow is another day! A bonafide well of possibilities! **Six fifty-three PM.** Also, if you don't mind me asking, you still keeping up with updating your eating diary thing? **Six fifty-four PM.** Like, how are these past few days shaking out in terms of your caloric minimums?"

Erin winced, and stopped her nail biting.

The 'Food Journal Pro' app on her phone had, in point of fact, been neglected for some time now. She had even exiled its colourful little tile to the very last page of the home screen, where it languished alone and unseen. It was just... better that way. Otherwise she felt a little pang of displeasure whenever she saw it. An unwelcome reminder of having once resolved to diligently fill it in each day. It now seemed unbelievable that she had ever done that. But this resolution was the foolish product of an incredibly unusual moment of optimism and can-do spirit, which she now blushed to recall. And it had also been in that tizzy that she had told *A&F* all about this plan, overconfidently meaning to cement the commitment. What happened then was very predictable. She unhappily made herself scribble down a week or two of entries. But it soon just got so depressing to constantly be repeating the scant few variations of 'five bites of X' or 'half-eaten Y'. So the exercise had quite frictionlessly fallen to the wayside.

Yet, even without tallying things up in the app, she always managed to have a rough sense of her daily calorie consumption. With so few figures to add up, the math wasn't exactly hard to do, sometimes without even meaning to. The mind just seems to love keeping track of whatever it can. She hated this, but there it was nonetheless. It was just her reality. The banal numerical tyranny which inescapably lords over the lives of those who eat too much and too little alike.

And so she found herself not really wanting to answer either of *A&F*'s questions.

But she also couldn't lie.

After all, wasn't the entire point of these conversations that she *didn't* have to lie? There was no pressure, no repercussions. It was hard to see how the stakes could possibly be lower. And yet, explicitly admitting, to herself too, the dire calorie deficit she had been building this week was an... unpalatable option. Perhaps a middle ground then. Some blend of limited disclosure and evasion to signal that she didn't want to discuss it right now. It was going to be a delicate balance to strike. Half-truths always are.

Again she blindly pressed several keys at once. Hearing the beep, she began to dictate her response in a croaky, faltering murmur.

"Well... right now. *Comma.* I don't... really... like to type out the day-to-day totals. *Period.* Too... disheartening... to dwell on... given how little control I have over my eating patterns anyway. *Period. Send message.*"

She paused and anguished over how best to phrase the next part. This was harder than she had expected. It somehow really hammered home the weaselyness when articulating it aloud, as if actually conversing with the other person. She tried to ignore this uneasiness, very aware that if she hesitated too long before shooting off the follow-up, this may arouse suspicion, may hint at its difficult construction.

"Better to... worry about that stupid shit..."

Another lingering pause, another calculation.

"*Erase* 'worry about that stupid shit'."

She pushed her knuckles hard into the other palm to stifle her nervous jitters.

"Add it all up... weekly... or even every two weeks... and review it then really. *Period.* So fingers crossed... but only time will tell. *Period.*"

Good god, this was painful. Could it please just be over already?

"Until then. *Comma.* Just gonna... keep my chin up... and try to stay positive and... keep on... keeping on. *Period. Send message. End dictation.*"

As soon as it was done, she shuddered at the cringeworthy quality of this effort. She had just gotten too flustered and shot from the hip towards the end. Who *was* this platitude-spouting moron she was trying to pass herself off as there? As mad as she was at herself for this lapse into driveldom, she at least had some sense of why it had happened. There was a good reason why moments like these were so emotionally reminiscent of being hauled before a schoolteacher to answer for something. Here, she was answering not only to *A&F* but also to *herself.* And it was daunting to try and simultaneously direct her excuse-making to these two very different recipients. Especially while also trying to pretend to herself that she wasn't doing so. Juggling all this was bound to lead to some discombobulated stumbling.

She blew out a long, weary exhalation with inflated cheeks. There was nothing to be done about the slip-up now, and no point in beating herself up about it any longer than necessary. It was wiser to try and just move on. And, to that end, she was keen to put this discomfiture firmly behind her by distracting herself with something else.

The rain had not forsaken her before, would not forsake her now. It again gave her exactly what she needed.

In the last couple of minutes, what had been a faint pitter-patter rose to a steady, emphatic din. Fatter raindrops were now pelting the windowpane hard and fast. She focused in on this blissful noise. What was even better was that, with her forehead still pressed to the glass, she *felt* the rain's impact too. The subtle vibrations resonated through to her skull and were a sensual delight. Quite inadvertently, she synced her breathing up to the arrhythmic fluctuations of the peltings. All of this combined to give her a sense of connection to the rain itself, which she had often chased. The thrill of it now trickled down her spine with exquisite slowness, discharging the tension that had been built up inside her as it went. Her eyelids fluttered and drooped halfway closed. Her mouth fell open as a wavering breath danced up her throat.

Outside, the true cloudburst had indeed begun in earnest. It was that aggressive sort of shower which seems like colossal sheets of rainwater being flung at the ground over and over in quick succession. Although the visibility through the window was even further diminished, she could still just about make out the quickened streaks of motion down below on the sidewalks. This was the soaked crowds scampering for shelter. She fixated on them now. As she watched their mass exodus to whatever cover presented itself, she couldn't help but picture their faces awash with indignant shock and dismay. Something about this image elicited a slight chuckle from her. The rainstorm had surely been loudly forecast by all the weathermen around, but these people probably still somehow felt caught off guard by it. They had been so sure that they would of course get home before the really bad rain hit. Then it came, just as predicted, and they felt the perceived injustice of getting drenched with doubled intensity. All because they had subconsciously assumed they were certain to escape it. The universe had not been specially cooperative to them - as, naturally, it never was for anyone - and they childishly resented this fact.

Erin knew this form of self-deception well. It amused her when exhibited by others. However, she despised it in herself, and unfortunately had had ample opportunity to do so. For she habitually tried to ignore the reality of foreseeable, inexorable hardships and miseries. She did it as if they might dissipate by dint of this stubborn refusal to acknowledge them. And when they arrived perfectly undiminished, they seemed to afflict her even worse. This was maddening. She had even tried and tried to stop doing it. She really had. But there was an inescapability to this folly which was as undeniable as it was infuriating. After some consideration, she came to suspect that it must just be some fundamental cog in the great machinery of human psychology. And the mind's irreducible complexity made any attempt to simply pluck out this one unwanted part a futile endeavour.

This truth did little to dull her itch to do so though. She often fantasized about how profoundly satisfying it would be to defy the instinct whenever it arose. Because in the instances where she tried to, she could feel a corresponding battle raging inside her, as she tried to fight against her own nature. And when she inevitably failed in emphatic fashion, this also felt just like being defeated by an enemy. This really got under her skin. She *hated* that feeling of having been beaten, of having been victimized. It made her feel so weak and helpless. So she desperately longed to know what it would be like to finally win, even if only once. When the enemy charged, she didn't want to cower and tremble, awaiting the landing of their blows. She wanted to charge right back at them head-on. And when the collision came, she wanted to be kicking and punching and bellowing a guttural warcry. Oh wouldn't that be something?! The pride she would feel! It was such that she hardly cared whether she was doomed to suffer greatly to achieve the victory. As long as the victory finally came! What a glorious moment that would be. Mid-leap and hurtling forward with the due pugnacity of someone intent on being their own master.

Sighing, she put this daydream out of her mind. She wondered what it really profited her to indulge in this gung-ho cant. Why was she always stupidly dreaming about being more than she could be, doing more than she could do?

The answer was glaringly obvious. She craved control in these smaller matters because of the freedom she lacked in a much larger, more important one.

As she pulled back from the windowpane, she noticed a sizeable patch of condensation had formed from her breathing. She reached out and dragged the fingertips of both hands down through it, like an animal pawing plaintively at something. As she regarded the array of vertical lines traced in the fogged-up glass, it reminded her of something she couldn't quite place. She held her chin and stared at it hard. What was it?...

And then the tiniest flicker of a mirthless, self-loathing smirk twitched the corners of her mouth. How fitting, she dolefully reflected, that it should be her own breath and her own flesh that had ended up depicting the prison bars which might as well be there. After all, she was the unwitting architect of this *de facto* cell she found herself trapped in. The whole thing had come about quite insidiously. At first she had voluntarily retreated to her apartment, as a refuge from society. It was safe and private and her own little domain. Everything she had wanted, and needed. The problem was that it took a good long while for her to fully realize the bargain she had actually struck. And by then it was too late to renege. For though she was indeed hidden away and protected from all that she found abominable in the outside world, there could be no re-emerging.

She was rather conflicted about this. She definitely didn't *want* to go back out there, not at all. And she very much struggled to imagine how that urge would arise anytime soon. Yet, to have even the choice itself revoked was disquieting all the same. And to be regularly reminded of this fact by her view through the window needled her in a subtle way. It made her want to in turn remind herself that she still agreed with her decision. Not only was there a certain indignity in having to do this, but by the thousandth time the re-affirmation began to sound noticeably rote and hollow. Despite all this, the matter did have to be kept in perspective. It was, she told herself, such a tiny niggle compared to how glad she was to have escaped the outside world's harsh tumult. She even tried to cultivate a sense of schadenfreude towards its denizens. Wasn't it true that they were caught in a woeful existential confinement so much more severe and profound than her own? Had she not indolently ogled at them carrying out the same clockwork motions day after day, as though affixed to the tracks of some motorized diorama? The whole thing, from her vantage, might as well have been enclosed within the glass case of a museum exhibit. It was a performance which was mesmerizing and magnificent and so very depressing. For what soulless automatons they seemed.

And yet, some contrarian voice inside her piped up to say, how much *freer* they were than her anyway. They still walked through the wide world, gazing at its varied wonders and breathing its fresh air. Whereas she had only this little space, this stale air, this same old view. Though that latter limitation, at least, was not totally without remedy. For seeing only the exact same limited range of sights each day had caused her mind to kick into an imaginative overdrive. To compensate for the external monotony, she had had to perforce cultivate a rich inner life. And having always had a very visual mind, it now took every opportunity to translate her thoughts and her observations into phantasmic scenes which played out in her head. This meant she now tended to actually *think* in vivid, elaborate metaphors.

A chirp-chirp-chirp broke in and, as it tended to do, derailed her train of thought. She gave the laptop her attention once more.

[19:04] Alabaster&Freckles: I can understand that. Might well be smarter to adjust things from an overview than to drive yourself crazy micro-managing.

[19:06] Alabaster&Freckles: Just let me know how the numbers end up working out at the end of the week, would you kindly?

[19:06] Alabaster&Freckles: And I'm heartened to see you're taking my advice about trying to stay optimistic about it all!

[19:07] Alabaster&Freckles: Two steps forward, one step back still ends up with you moving in the right direction, right? That's what matters, that's the bigger picture.

[19:08] Alabaster&Freckles: Now, if you don't mind me moving on, could we talk about the cutting? What's the current status of that?

[19:08] Alabaster&Freckles: Have you felt any temptation since we last spoke?

Erin's eyebrows raised.

It was to be a full check-up then.

And how like *A&F* it was to make these inquiries with such naked frankness, like a doctor with a clipboard going down a list of her problems. This only managed to be endearing because it was coupled with equally guileless compassion. And, when it came down to it, Erin was grateful to be routinely prodded into conducting this sort of self-review. She knew she would otherwise endlessly demur from doing so. That would not at all be a healthy outcome. The rot of neuroses and denial amassing in her psyche festered even faster in the dark. Whereas the spotlight of introspection could halt its growth, sizzling it under an intense glow, if only temporarily. That was still much better than nothing and, if she was being pragmatic, about all she could really hope for anyway.

Now, as she mulled over how to answer, Erin instinctively looked over at her freezer. It was hard not to. Tucked amongst containers of frozen food neglected so long that they were nigh-antique, there were a few blocks of ice a bit bigger than a man's fist. And suspended within each one was a razor blade.

This set-up had been easy enough to enact. It required only an oversized novelty mug of hers - ironically, this was emblazoned with a cutesy panda saying a cheery slogan - and a good long while for the water to freeze solid. But she was proud of her little invention nonetheless. It was a basic but effective solution. For this was the *time-lock* she placed on her access to self-harm, and the only key was patience. Smashing the thick ice would reliably damage the straight line of the blade's edge, rendering it unfit for its purpose. She had learned this the hard way. Alternatively, it was at least possible to cheat and speed up the melting process. But even being forced to delay cutting for just a few extra minutes could sometimes be enough. That surging, swelling vortex of emotion which gave her the impulse to seek something sharp with ill intentions always subsided with time. The question was simply how much time. If it faded quickly, whilst the ice was still unlocking drip by drip, then calmer deliberation could occur. This is why the whole thing was worth doing. It couldn't always work, but it had spared her scars on several occasions.

However, she knew that despite its utility it was, at heart, also somewhat of a self-indulgent half-measure. It just created a barrier, not a remedy. And, worse, it may just be formalizing and cementing the ritual, which would lend further difficulty to stopping altogether. There was a part of her which wondered whether this even mattered though. Perhaps it was necessary to concede that ridding herself of all the things related to her self-harm was just a pipedream. It did seem absolutely unthinkable to her. And plus, counterintuitively enough, it was far easier to stifle the urge to cut when she knew she had the means to do so. If there were no razor blades in the apartment, the urge, when it arose, became a hundred times stronger. So maybe 'good enough' was actually pretty good after all.

She went on weighing up how to phrase her explanation so as not to seem too brusque or condescending. As she did so, she was lightly stroking her palm back and forth across the keyboard, feeling the rows of keys brushing against the sensitive skin there. She thought it was best to just be direct and clear. And throwing a little solemnity in there too would help avoid underselling the matter.

Having settled upon this tact, she began typing.

[19:11] PluckingPurgatory'sPetals: I totally get why you used the word 'temptation'. But I gotta tell you, it's really not a good way to measure things.

[19:12] PluckingPurgatory'sPetals: To one degree or another, I'm almost always tempted. That's the point. That's the problem.

[19:12] PluckingPurgatory'sPetals: What really matters is whether I've actually cut or not. And, recently, I haven't.

[19:12] PluckingPurgatory'sPetals: I know I should feel good about that, but I just can't.

[19:13] PluckingPurgatory'sPetals: I try to just keep my mind off cutting as much as possible, even when I've been doing well.

[19:13] PluckingPurgatory'sPetals: It's like... hmm... it's hard to explain.

[19:13] PluckingPurgatory'sPetals: Well, you know how when the cartoon coyote runs off the cliff, he somehow keeps going and going?

[19:14] PluckingPurgatory'sPetals: At least, right up until he stops and looks down, seeing it's just thin air he's treading on...

[19:14] PluckingPurgatory'sPetals: So I try not to examine this stuff too closely, because I'll notice I'm doing the impossible.

[19:15] PluckingPurgatory'sPetals: Then I'll fall too.

[19:16] PluckingPurgatory'sPetals: Besides, if I dwell on it too long, I will just get myself so damn worked up about how much I hate cutting.

[19:16] PluckingPurgatory'sPetals: Which, irony of ironies, sometimes makes me *want* to cut, to make myself feel better.

[19:17] PluckingPurgatory'sPetals: Really not good, I know. It's a vicious self-reinforcing cycle.

Erin had become well acquainted with how steering clear of *dangerously* bad moods was a very delicate endeavour. To find herself in even a half-decent mood was generally the most she could aspire to. And even that was as fragile as a bubble floating on an errant wind: anything it encountered was liable to burst it. Dealing with the constant background anxiety from knowing that this emotional crash could come at any moment was the real torture. She was basically just waiting for it to happen. In turn, the effect that had was to make her subconsciously want it to just finally happen. If for no better reason than simply to be free of the dreadful anticipation. And so the cutting itself became imbued with an enticingly multilayered form of relief. Not only would it satisfy her craving for pain and self-mutilation, it also silenced her incessant worrying about when she was going to cut next. Blade in hand, she didn't exactly have to fret about that anymore.

It was only upon retracting her fingers from the keyboard that she realized her heart rate was a little elevated and her hands were clammy. Being so focused upon typing out those messages as fast as they would come, she'd been scarcely breathing. She had experienced this same weird adrenaline rush when making these sorts of difficult disclosures before. Even though it was satisfying to unburden herself, there was always the fear. And she was afraid because she was unsure. Was there, she often pondered, a line which she should not cross? Some new aspect or nuance of her craziness which when exposed to *A&F* would finally scare them off for good? It seemed distinctly plausible. Everyone has a threshold beyond which things become just... too much to deal with. For *A&F*, it had to be said, this bar did seem to be set quite high. Yet, if Erin was certain that she was exceptional in any way, it was this: her crazy was world-class.

One day she was going to reach into the bag for show-and-tell with *A&F* and pull out a real doozy. Something which would make her seem so irreparably, insufferably broken that it would ensure her abandonment. It just felt like an inevitability. Conversation by conversation, admission by admission, she was granting ever more insight into just how stupendously defective she was as a person. Eventually some new facet of the hopelessness of her condition *would* arise and make it, in its totality, seem overwhelming. At that point, she wasn't sure she could even blame *A&F* for fleeing. The healthy shun the leper when he bears his weeping sores; that's just what they're programmed to do. To begrudge someone else their self-preservation instinct was nothing short of preposterous.

Be that as it may, the risk still had to be borne. Erin needed this outlet. It was the only one which worked. What she had to vent, the pages of a journal could receive with only a maddening deafness and muteness. That just wasn't enough. It could never be enough. There had to be another human being out there, somewhere, who knew about her struggles. A living breathing person who heard and registered what she whispered through the wires. This may seem paradoxical, given that she cloistered herself in this tower of isolation partially because she couldn't bear to be engulfed by humanity anymore. But, in fact, it was not. There is a form of aloneness an order of magnitude worse than just withdrawing from the presence of others. For nobody to know that she existed and, moreover, how she struggled to even exist... that threatened to induce a loneliness of unbearable profundity.

This had not been an easy predicament to resolve. Erin was no longer in contact with any friends, and had long been estranged from the few living members of her immediate family. So she had had to seek an *unorthodox* solution. The internet, panacea that it is, offered to furnish her with a sympathetic ear. She found a strictly pseudonymous service which paired those who needed to talk with those who wanted to listen and perhaps advise. This opportunity to purge her woes without having to disclose her identity seemed too good to be true. But, not exactly flush with other options, she decided to give it a chance. It did not go well at first. She trialled and quickly rejected more than a few boring, semi-literate duds, the type who would scarcely pass the Turing test. And so she started to think her original skepticism was being proved right. If worthwhile conversational partners in the pool of 'listeners' were such rare anomalies that she might as well be hunting unicorns, what was the point? Yet, then, as these things often go, she was matched up with one. It was almost instantly obvious that *A&F* was precisely what she had been looking for, even if she hadn't known it.

They had been talking for about nine months now. She had no idea what *A&F* got out of being a 'listener', or how one could even have the requisite selflessness. But then how could she? They were each at their respective poles for a reason. All that mattered was she had a really good rapport with *A&F*, having built a sense of trust and familiarity. And they had progressed, Erin liked to believe, into an actual friendship. This was, it had to be admitted, a strange sort of relationship however. For one thing, they both studiously avoided mentioning their real name or age or location or any other identifier which could pinpoint them. Although Erin had worried that this restriction would always be awkwardly circumscribing their discussion, it soon became clear that this wasn't so. That trivial biographical info was completely irrelevant. For another thing, there was the purposely lopsided nature of their talks. It meant that *A&F* knew so many intimate details about Erin and her issues. Yet, oppositely, she knew almost nothing about *A&F*. There were probably some general facts Erin could infer if she really wanted to, but she actually tried not to. She didn't want to know them, or even think she did. That would defeat the whole point. All she wanted was to throw a tether, consciousness to consciousness, from herself to someone out there in the world. Everything else was just a superfluous and potentially detrimental distraction.

Presently, Erin had taken to staring intently at the screen, as if willing the reply to come faster.

Her anxious impatience was making her very restless and fidgety. She shifted her weight again and again on the cushion underneath her, trying to get more comfortable. When she peered down at it, she saw that it had once again become flattened from prolonged use. Some tough-love upkeep was required. She cradled the laptop in the crook of her arm and, leaning forward, pulled her butt up off the cushion. Then she reached back with her free arm and went about punching it into renewed plumpness. It was undeniably satisfying to let off some steam by pounding away at it. She even continued for a little while after having achieved the desired improvement. Right up until the fabric of the cushion's case started to chafe her knuckles.

Having resettled herself, she grabbed the nearby glass of water and gulped down a couple mouthfuls. She felt several fingernail shards which had escaped retrieval slide down her throat too. Immediately she grimaced with an expression of distaste. It really bugged her whenever this happened. On a practical level, the stomach did not seem meant to digest something like that. And, philosophically, there was something about autocannibalism - negligibly minor though this example was - which felt so antithetical to the natural order. Creatures are supposed to consume other things, and try to avoid being consumed themselves. Those were two of the core laws which underpinned the very economy of life. So, to eat a part of oneself was to totally flout both of them at once. The sheer *wrongness* of it made Erin uneasy, made her shiver in her mind.

Several more nervous minutes elapsed. She tried to get lost in watching the still unflagging rain again. But she found she simply couldn't get back into the flow of concentration.

Just as she was trying to come up with some other way of distracting herself, new messages began to arrive. They were heralded, as always, by the untiringly enthusiastic electronic chirps. Ostensibly annoying though they were, Erin had now become wired to get a little boost of happiness at hearing them. She seized upon these incoming replies with great relish. Almost without blinking, she read and re-read and re-read each one in the brief span before the arrival of the next.

[19:25] Alabaster&Freckles: Thank you for explaining that distinction to me, I'll really try to keep it in mind.

[19:25] Alabaster&Freckles: And yep, gotta say, you hit the nail on the head: 'not good'.

[19:26] Alabaster&Freckles: Obviously, I'm not gonna pretend I know what it's like to be in that predicament. For real, honey, I can only imagine how frustrating it must be.

[19:26] Alabaster&Freckles: I do know, however, that it is really good you're so self-aware about it!

[19:26] Alabaster&Freckles: Recognizing the sneaky psychological mechanisms which fortify your unhealthy behaviors against resistance is SO important, I can't even tell you.

[19:27] Alabaster&Freckles: We need to comprehend a problem before we can try to fix it, and that's sometimes really difficult. So please try to give yourself some credit for doing it!

[19:27] Alabaster&Freckles: I remember you said if you're not making permanent gains in countering these compulsions, it can really dishearten you.

[19:28] Alabaster&Freckles: But if you set the bar that unreasonably high, it will just lead to a quagmire of inaction. And that doesn't help anything.

[19:29] Alabaster&Freckles: That's why I think you'd really benefit from bearing in mind that progress comes in a lot of different forms.

[19:31] Alabaster&Freckles: Building your stockpile of self-understanding is just as crucial as the moments spent fighting the urges themselves. It's the ammunition which HELPS you fight them.

[19:31] Alabaster&Freckles: And the more prepared you are, the more likely you are to prevail the next time you're put to the test.

It was a fine, rousing sentiment. And yet another instance of sagacious counsel from *A&F*. That was all secondary, however. Most of all, Erin was just so relieved that *A&F* somehow went on unfazed after these latest revelations.

This was not a perfectly unadulterated relief, alas. Somewhere deep inside, Erin noticed a bizarre little twinge of dissatisfaction which distorted the way she wanted to feel. Exasperatingly enough, it wriggled away whenever she tried to pin it down, like a parasitic worm evasively burrowing around in her emotional core. But its effect was unmistakable: it made her feel both guilty and confused. The problem was that some irrational, self-destructive part of her secretly wanted *A&F*, as someone whose opinion she valued, to finally just lose all patience and all civility. That is, to finally scream at Erin that her whining was pathetic and she ought to just grow up already. Getting berated like that would vindicate the self-pitying belief in her own worthlessness which plagued her during the most trying times. And to a masochist this was the bittersweet jackpot. There would be such a finality to it. For it would give her the perfect reason to just give up on everything at last. Give up trying to dampen the pain, give up trying to fix herself, give up trying to see tomorrow.

She hadn't quite yet worked up the courage to talk to *A&F* about this worrisome dimension of her difficulty receiving kindness. It wasn't that she didn't want to. She really, really did. But something always stayed her hand when she went to type it out. Despite having not shied away from sharing so many (at least nominally) embarrassing personal stories before, this managed to somehow still feel... different. It was a confession which seemed sure to thoroughly infantilize her in *A&F*'s eyes. Thinking about that prospect made her cheeks preemptively burn at how mortifying it would be. The real exacerbating factor was that she had been in solitude for long enough to lose all built-up tolerance for enduring others being party to her own humiliation. And this would be a huge bodyblow to take with none of that particular armour-plating against shame intact. Because it was one thing to seem crazy, but it was another thing entirely to apparently reveal yourself as being akin to a bratty child. The former may elicit sympathy, the latter is just unbearably obnoxious.

[19:33] PluckingPurgatory'sPetals: Hmm, always little steps in the interim, always conserving momentum. I really like that idea.

[19:34] PluckingPurgatory'sPetals: It's so true that I have a really oppressive fear of tumbling back to square one all the time. I don't think I quite realized the paralyzing influence that has until you put it like that.

[19:35] PluckingPurgatory'sPetals: But the way of thinking you suggest sounds like it could combat that. Help me to stay motivated and push me onward.

[19:35] PluckingPurgatory'sPetals: Okay, so I'll try to reframe my perspective towards that, wherever possible. And see how it affects things.

She often tried to acknowledge *A&F*'s suggestions, sensible and welcome as they were, in this kind of upbeat manner. After all, Erin wanted to genuinely feel that way. And... possibly it was even true that if you fake the smile long enough, you suddenly find you're happy. Anyway, this well-meaning pretense was surely no more untruthful an account of herself than the alternative. That was to merely relay whatever deceptive nonsense her pessimism and defeatism were hectoring her with. Such comments were just idiotic propaganda from the part of herself which didn't want her to get better and be better. She refused to allow that to speak for her. It didn't reflect who she was, not really. The voices warring inside her head, despite having such disparate messages, all vied to convince her that *they were her*. But she got to choose which of them to believe, which to honour as her internal monologue. That was the all-important ongoing act of self-realization. And there was, in point of fact, a particularly quiet voice she could sometimes just about make out underneath the babel. This timid, ineloquent little pipsqueak was *hope*. Though a radically undersized constituent of her psyche, she was trying to foster it, to help it develop some brawn. Maybe one day it would be able to shout down the rest of the rabble. Until then, she figured it was okay to sometimes kind of pretend as if it had. This was just like taking an advance on the future she was seeking to ensure.

It was, perhaps, conceivable that some cynic would say that this was nothing but a self-serving, fastidiously unexamined fiction. Erin told herself it was just a clever little mental workaround.

Either way, it was certainly not the only one she entertained.

[19:36] Alabaster&Freckles: That's awesome, I'm so glad to hear it!

[19:37] Alabaster&Freckles: I truly think it's a change which is gonna benefit you greatly. Just stick with it and you'll see.

[19:37] Alabaster&Freckles: I'm super-duper excited to see it help you be who you want to be!

[19:37] Alabaster&Freckles: Seriously, you got this! Those stupid little urges are no match for you!

An honest little smile came onto her face quite unconsciously. *A&F* was pleased, and this in turn really pleased Erin. This warm glow of satisfaction was why she felt so justified in taking these slight liberties with the truth in its most priggishly rigid form. All she was doing was... benignly moulding her own interpretation of her feelings. And just look at the utility of this compromise! It gave *A&F* a strengthened impression that they were actually helping Erin, actually getting through to her. And she had intuited that *A&F* needed to feel like that, for her own sense of accomplishment. So what did it matter that she wove a little bit of theatre into very specific parts of their back-and-forth? She was being empathetic, accommodating. Just doing something nice for someone she cared about. It was preposterous to think that could somehow be bad.

[19:38] Alabaster&Freckles: Alrighty, on that happy note let's pause things there, if that's okay with you.

[19:38] Alabaster&Freckles: Gotta shift my tushie and go deal with something again.

[19:39] Alabaster&Freckles: Be back in like 20-30 minutes.

These unexpected follow-up messages instantly stripped the smile from Erin, and elicited a pouty huff. How quickly the rug had been pulled out from under her.

It occurred to her that she had probably better get up and stretch her legs to stave off cramping. This would also allow her to attend to some practical matters, in turn helping to pass the time. So, pushing the laptop aside, she slowly swivelled her legs around and draped them over the window-seat's edge. Her nose wrinkled in frustration as she tried to will herself to actually get up. She knew she should. But she didn't want to. And she really felt she shouldn't have to. Things were so delightfully simple and easy on her perch. The rest of the apartment was just a minefield of potential annoyances.

Too bad, she told herself. Her palpably full bladder was going to draw her away sooner or later anyway. Time to stop stalling and just get on with it.

She impetuously thrust herself off the ledge and landed with cat-like lightness. The hardwood flooring was so cold it seemed to sting the sensitive soles of her feet. Briefly, she scanned the room for her tattered slippers - they were somewhere, always somewhere - but could not spy them. They had perhaps been kicked amongst all the junk underneath the bed, but who could be bothered with excavating for them? Fortunately then, littered here and there across the floor were haphazardly abandoned socks. She scooped up the closest two, which were not only different colours but very different thicknesses, and pulled them on. This was better than bearing the barefoot discomfort, at any rate.

With a drawn-out sigh, she traipsed across the apartment to the toilet. And she winced as she sat down to pee, the toilet seat proving no less frigid than the floor. Her elbows dug into her knees as, leaning forward, she lazily propped up her head in her hands. After flushing and walking away, the noise of the sloshing, draining water resounded around the room. Its grating loudness irritated Erin just like it always did. Some noises penetrated the silence very much unwelcomely.

Midway towards the kitchen sink, where she intended to wash her hands, she stopped in her tracks. Something had caught her eye and caused an expression of panic to flash across her face. The folded blanket duct-taped over the bathroom mirror on the wall was sagging down again. She darted over to it, rearranging the material's hanging weight and pressing down hard on the strips of tape to re-adhere them. In point of fact, this was the only mirror in the apartment. She actually very badly wanted to shatter it and dispose of even the shards. But the prospect of jeopardizing the exorbitant security deposit she had paid was too powerful a deterrent. So she had settled on simply keeping it covered at all times, the better to pretend it didn't exist at all.

This was necessary because of a nearly pathological aversion Erin had developed. She did all she could to avoid beholding her own appearance, and *had* done so for quite some time now. Even the thought of seeing herself made her feel ill. She did not understand why this was the case, nor had she sought to. It was just so much easier to make some... palliative adjustments. There were, after all, mercifully few reflective surfaces to deal with. The windowpane was already impregnated with a subtle anti-solar tint which shielded the apartment from becoming a hotbox in the summer, also rendering it non-reflective. And the shower cubicle over in the corner was entirely frosted glass. Thus, after hiding the mirror, all that had been left to do was applying a matte anti-glare film to the screens of her phone and laptop. How easy these few changes were helped reassure her that the mission they advanced must be harmless.

Yet, banishing her reflection from the apartment had produced a worrisome consequence. Over time, and quite unnoticed, her mental image of herself was gradually supplanted by some distorted phantom. The process was really very simple. As the memory of what her face looked like began to fade, it became foggy and... malleable. And starved of error-correcting visual data, her mind settled for an untrustworthy substitute: touch. Whenever her fingers explored her face, she registered only the gaunt contours and edges, visualizing them in an exaggerated form. This then became the blueprint to craft a false and unflattering mask for her self-image to wear. Of course, her body was a different matter, the sight of it being so impossible to evade. But this did not stop Erin from trying her best anyway. She braved nakedness only when showering became absolutely imperative. And even then she tried to stare straight ahead, averting her gaze, but a few accidental glimpses were inevitable. These were combined with what she felt as she washed herself: the ridges of her rib cage or the thinness of her limbs, for example. Her subconscious eagerly seized upon this habitual glut of 'evidence' for all her perceived flaws and moulded it maliciously. The delusory doppelganger which was then drawn up for her was a twisted masterpiece of self-loathing. Medieval sketchers of the repulsive untreatables kept in hospital dungeons could hardly have done better. But now this was all she could see when she pictured herself.

She left the cabinet and treaded over to the nearby dimmer switch. With the trepidation of a safecracker, she minutely shifted the dial around, increasing the room's meagre lighting a correspondingly minute amount. And, as she looked around to survey the change, she noticed all the spent candles dotted around. In anticipation of nighttime, she promptly went around and replaced them. Just as she could not stand for the room to be too bright, so too she rather feared getting trapped in darkness when the sun went down. Things had to be just so.

Just as she was putting the bag of candles down again, she remembered how she had originally been going over to the sink. She blinked in amazement that she had completely forgotten this intention so quickly. But, no matter, she went over there now and washed her hands.

Afterwards, she repeatedly splashed cupped handfuls of warm water against her face, hoping to wake herself up a bit. She just stood there for an extended moment, feeling the wetness drip ticklingly down along her throat as she tried to recenter herself. It was hard to discern how well she was doing at this, which perhaps actually testified to its lack of success.

Cutting her losses, she went over and grabbed one of the big fluffy towels from the rack besides the shower cubicle. As soon as she pressed it to her face and neck, she made the unwelcome discovery that it was damp. This was very weird. Her last shower had been... what? Two days ago? Maybe three? It was hard to say. She strained to remember. But all she could vaguely recall was inadvertently soaking that towel with the shower at one point. She shook her head in exasperation. This scatterbrain tendency seemed to be encroaching more and more. But, at any rate, even if she *should* have changed the towel, she still found it aggravating that it had stayed wet for this long. It just didn't seem right. Was this the universe once again taking special pains just to fuck with her? Or was this just how towels worked? Perhaps that's all it was. She felt she should know that, if so. Weren't adults supposed to have amassed a wide store of these lame, but obviously useful, domestic facts? Yet, even at twenty three years old, she strangely still didn't *feel* like an adult. And she still definitely regarded boring info like the moisture-retention timeline for bath towels with disdain. She didn't want to clog up her brain with stupid crap like that.

She threw the offending towel at the overflowing laundry basket by the bed, where it landed half in and half out. Picking up another towel from further down the rack, she went about patting herself dry again. Then, as she passed by the fridge on her way back to the window-seat, she considered trying to force herself to eat something. Maybe half of that little ham and cheese baguette she had dejectedly given up on making earlier. Maybe even just nibble some crackers. But, recoiling as she envisioned the ordeal, she decided that... it just wasn't an opportune moment. This was never an easy decision to make. Eating was awful; not eating was also awful. To abstain was merely to prolong the torture. For the hunger pangs, as she well knew, were going to build and build until they reached an agonizing crescendo. Then her hand would be forced. And what that hand would be forced to do would likely not be pretty. The dehumanizing

29

indignity of *pushing* morsels down one's throat just to stop the stomach pain was not out of the question. At that point, very little would be really. She wouldn't wish this conundrum on anyone. Whereas the body, being but a dumb superintendent, has no compassion for the person trapped inside it. It cared only about a set of biological demands being met. And the irony was that this was ostensibly intended to preserve her well-being, yet she was made to comply by means of coercive suffering. To say the very, very least, she resented being 'helped' in this way. It was a profoundly exhausting cycle to find oneself trapped in.

She pulled herself back up onto the ledge and resettled herself on the cushion. Using her laptop, she checked which day her next twice-monthly delivery of food and other essentials would fall on. As with many things in Erin's life, the simple act of receiving this delivery was way more difficult than it needed to be. This was because for some time now even opening the door to someone had become just... too much for her. She couldn't do it. She couldn't bear even that minimal face-to-face human contact. Obviously, this could have snowballed into a very dire problem indeed. But, thankfully, she had somehow just ended up in a quasi-unspoken arrangement with the apartment building's concierge, a friendly old man. The first time her inability had presented itself, she phoned down to him with some excuse about being too unwell to get to the door. He had been very sympathetic. Quite unprompted, he offered to sign for her packages at the front desk, and have them left outside her door for her to retrieve as soon as she was able. (Of course, in truth, that came about thirty seconds later when the hallway was once again empty.) And then he simply went on doing this, unasked. She figured that most likely, as time passed, he came to suspect what kind of sickness she *really* had. So an even greater pity must have induced him to go on helping out the pathetic shut-in woman. Much as some part of her raged against being pitied by anyone, she also knew how badly she needed this special accommodation. Accordingly, she made sure to get a christmas card sent to his desk with a remarkably generous 'tip' enclosed inside, to signal her appreciation... and, in all honesty, to further ensure his ongoing kindness.

Next she logged into her bank account. She wanted to make sure that the automated payments for rent and utility bills were still going out on time. In practical terms, this was an unnecessary exercise. There had never yet been a problem since she had set this payment system up. Despite that, regularly double-checking it had become something of a tic for her. Seeing all the numbers lined up exactly as they were meant to be granted her peace of mind. For the possibility of some weird computing error causing her bills to go unpaid terrified her. *Really, really terrified her.* She would gladly overpay them threefold than miss the payment window by even a single minute. Because in the semi-rational recesses of her mind, two scenarios took turns playing out on a constant loop. In the first, an unintentional non-payment of something important would absolutely require her to go down to the bank to rectify the situation. Most people would consider a quick errand like this a negligible hassle. Erin viewed it like an expedition into the abyss. Slotting the second scenario's reel into the projector was reserved for when she needed a backdrop for some truly hardcore catastrophizing. In it, some string of equally unlikely and unforeseeable events lead to her rent going unpaid for a few months, causing her to be evicted. This was unbearably nightmarish. Contemplating it for too long was a surefire method for summoning a crippling panicked-thoughts spiral, and one far worse than the usual variety which plagued her unbidden. The sort of thing where you sit fully clothed in the inexplicable safety of the shower cubicle and just... shake, and stare dead-eyed at your feet. Therefore, she had to stop herself gawking at these personal disaster-movies in the first place. Which is why she applied such meticulous, repetitive oversight to her bill paying apparatus. It reminded her that the basically-impossible outcomes were indeed basically impossible.

The money itself, at least, was not really an issue. As a teenager, Erin had inherited a sizeable sum of money. It came from a doting aunt who she was close with right up until the cold earth cruelly closed over her. These funds were, by request, kept inaccessible until Erin turned eighteen. And even then, for a good while, they had sat largely untouched. She had quite unexpectedly developed a sentimental attachment to their existence, as though they were a memento of her aunt's affection. Yet this had to be put aside once they became her sole means of supporting herself. Now she guarded the money even more intensely, but in a very different way. Knowing that no other windfalls were on the horizon, she meant to make this one stretch as far as it could possibly be made to. After all, when it was gone, it was gone. And pennilessness would spell certain doom for such as her. So she utilized her money with a miser's restraint. This included her apartment, which although located in a decent enough apartment building was so much smaller than she could technically afford. Fortunately, this sacrifice, such as it was, did not pain her at all. She was just so glad to have this long-sustainable sanctum. To fret about the square-footage or the quality of the furnishings seemed laughable in comparison.

Just as the mind-numbing effect of surveying one's finances began to set in, new chirps interrupted and pulled her back to reality. The sound of them had become so laden with positive connotations in her mind that it unfailingly elicited the same response. Frisson whirled like an eddying gust down the nape of her neck. Her breathing became heavy and open-mouthed at her single-minded eagerness. And she fumbled as she sought to speedily bring up the chat window again.

[20:15] Alabaster&Freckles: And... I'm back again!

[20:15] Alabaster&Freckles: So, sugarplum, sugarplum, don't be glum!

[20:15] Alabaster&Freckles: What shall we discuss next?...

[20:15] Alabaster&Freckles: How about the masturbation?

[20:16] Alabaster&Freckles: I know you didn't really want to talk about it last time I asked for an update.

[20:16] Alabaster&Freckles: But with this conversation having already been so wonderfully productive, I'm just curious if maybe you feel differently today?

[20:17] Alabaster&Freckles: I remember you saying you did want to open up about it more. And I really think that would help you.

[20:17] Alabaster&Freckles: It's not good to let anything become a blindspot. That happens so much faster than we ever expect.

[20:18] Alabaster&Freckles: Also, the struggle always *feels* worse and worse the longer we keep it trapped in the pressure cooker of our own heads.

[20:18] Alabaster&Freckles: Just a thought.

[20:18] Alabaster&Freckles: It is, of course, totally fine if you would rather not discuss it.

Erin's fingers had been hovering, and twitching almost imperceptibly, just above the keyboard as she started reading. They were preemptively raring to respond, to get her back into the discussion. But once she had finished, she slowly withdrew her hands and interlocked her fingers behind her head.

This was not a favored subject. The admissions called for here were oftentimes particularly humiliating or gross. And, moreover, it irked Erin that this marked the third time that masturbation had been included in *A&F*'s customary checklist of her problems, which essentially cemented it as one. She was not about to sign off on this surreptitious re-categorization, not by a long shot. It was in conflict with her desire to deem the frequency of her masturbation as a merely benign, if unseemly, quirk of her situation. This, perhaps, constituted wishful thinking. But it was born out of necessity. From her perspective, she already had way too many problems to cope with, to try and fix. So even a single new addition to that list had to be fought against: excessive straw and the unpredictable weight-bearing limit of camels' spines and all that. Besides, there was also the fact that it seemed rather damning to have managed to *problematize* something as innocent as her own masturbation. What would that say about her?

Nevertheless, protest as she might, Erin knew that she ought to at least talk the whole thing out. Her hands were even kind of tied, in truth. Because, otherwise, wasn't *she* the one aggrandizing it, by letting her reticence imbue it with more power than it warranted? But whilst talking about it, she could make her case for why it didn't at all deserve the 'problem' designation. If masturbating could still be clawed back from that toxic semantic dumping ground, she certainly had to try. And, quite possibly, she might succeed in putting the matter to bed for good, sparing her a repeat of this irritation. Yes, that was an enticing enough reward.

[20:20] PluckingPurgatory'sPetals: Ah... that. Sure. We can go into that again, if you want.

[20:22] PluckingPurgatory'sPetals: Well, look, I haven't been noting down each time I do it or anything. But I'd maybe guess that

33

the frequency has stayed about the same over the last week or two.

[20:23] PluckingPurgatory'sPetals: Hard to really foresee any change to that unless something disrupts my daily routine.

[20:23] PluckingPurgatory'sPetals: And to put it plainly I'm not sure that's necessarily a bad thing.

[20:24] PluckingPurgatory'sPetals: I know that doing it... this much isn't strictly 'normal'. But my life isn't normal. I'm not normal.

[20:24] PluckingPurgatory'sPetals: Like, what if this is just an inevitable byproduct of how things are for me? A sort of harmless vice?

[20:24] PluckingPurgatory'sPetals: I mean, there is a proportionality to the thing.

[20:25] PluckingPurgatory'sPetals: I have nothing to do all day. So I've got a LOT of boredom and numbness and sadness to assuage, somehow.

[20:26] PluckingPurgatory'sPetals: And to me it's obvious that out of all my... *options* to do that, masturbation is surely the safest, most innocuous one. I thought that you of all people would see that too.

[20:27] PluckingPurgatory'sPetals: So, yeah, damn right I use masturbation whenever I need to!

[20:27] PluckingPurgatory'sPetals: I think I ought to be allowed that indulgence. And no one has any right to judge me for it.

[20:28] PluckingPurgatory'sPetals: Like, whatever. As far as I'm concerned, anyone who would sneakily try to pester or shame me about it is just being a dick!

Literally the moment after Erin irately mashed the send key for the final time, she re-read it all and felt a sickening sense of regret creep over her. She fixated on the particular wording which was so telling. No matter how hard she tried to imagine ways it could be parsed to render it less mortifying, it was to no avail. It was like the mere act of shooting it into the electronic ether had stripped away, as if by wind resistance from the velocity, some outer facade of reasonableness which had camouflaged it as she wrote it. So that now it lay before her, bare and shameful. And this realization came, of course, altogether too late. The message had already zipped away and was now exasperatingly impossible to recall.

In her brusqueness, she had let slip way more than she meant to. The truth had ended up embedded in the midst of her threadbare, half-hearted attempt at justification. She had revealed that she actually did grasp the deeply dysfunctional aspect of it after all. And that wasn't even hidden away in the subtext. It was right there, plain as day. She 'used' masturbation, did she? God, how she wished she could unsay that. But there it was, immortalized in all its unambiguous glory. Her frustration at her own stupidity was volcanic. She clutched the sides of the laptop screen tightly and, bringing her face close, growled through gritted teeth at it. A fine mist of saliva sprayed across the screen. Hers was an anger that waxed all the hotter for being so impotent. That didn't stop her fantasizing though. She imagined herself armed with an icepick and, reaching right through into the virtual plane, chiselling each tiny black letter out of that plasterlike white digital-substrate which bore them.

The lid was slammed down and the laptop was shoved away. Something was hardening inside of her, or trying to at least. She folded her arms defiantly, a visual declaration of intent despite there being no observers. She hated this feeling, and repudiated its right to afflict her. If there was a way to *think* her way out of it, she was going to. It had to just be a matter of reframing things. Getting the story straight in her head and sticking by it. Then that could function as an amulet of denial, held up to ward off all these unsettling misgivings.

First things first. When it came down to it, she did 'use' masturbation, knowingly and gratefully. There was no getting around that. So if there was any usable ethical wiggle-room to be found, it was going to be in the crevices of the *why*. Her mentality about it revolved around one crucial conclusion. She thought of the body as no more than a machine, helmed by the computer nestled in the brainpan. Given this, the trick was figuring out how to manipulate the former to input certain commands to the latter, or vice versa. That was everything, the only art which mattered. And someone in Erin's position was not about to scruple against employing a few quick-and-dirty shortcuts here. Masturbation was just one of the most effective ones.

Press the right buttons in the right sequence and the reward was guaranteed. The flesh was granted pleasure and, afterwards, the mind was buoyed by a heavenly influx of endorphins. A perfectly incentivized *quid pro quo*. Knowing that she could feel good, improve her mood and kill some time all at once via an act with no downsides, how could she not? And even if it was the fifth or sixth time that day, what difference did that make? Moderation was just an ideal born out of affectation. She was all alone, so who exactly did she have to impress with a show of self-restraint? Considering the stakes, that whole notion was ludicrous. Was a drowning sailor to be scolded for again grabbing the rope thrown to them because, washed overboard several times already, they had availed themselves of it beforehand too? Really, *who would* lecture them on the dangers of maybe overdoing the ol' rope-grabbing as they sunk sputtering beneath the waves? Erin felt the implications of these questions very acutely. For she was at sea too. Adrift on a pitilessly heaving ocean of malaise and radical unhappiness. And when she was knocked off her little raft, it fell to her to save herself. This meant that she had to find a way to be both rescuer and rescued. The difficulty of this feat can hardly be overstated. Especially when it has to be repeated daily.

Naturally, she wasn't proud of how this sometimes had to be done. She was made uneasy by the almost de-sexualised form her habitual pick-me-up masturbation took. But what choice did she have? Sure, ideally she would only do it when actually in the mood. This was a capricious impulse, however, and could not be relied upon. If she had to wait on that arising to legitimize the decision, she would be in trouble. Once a day just wasn't nearly enough, given its role in helping her to cope. She needed control. That was precisely why she often had to decide to masturbate despite being stone-cold unaroused. Now, sometimes, she would be pretty desensitized by that point in the day, making the stimulation itself only vaguely palpable. But wasn't something better than nothing? Even if that meant a dispassionate race towards the expected payoff, that jolt to her brain chemistry. Of course, Erin could still appreciate how, to an outsider, this might seem fucked-up. But the healthy of mind have the luxury of being squeamish, of sentimentally declining to exploit their own biology. They got to be precious about things like masturbation. She did envy them that. It would be nice to just keep it as an occasional self-indulgence, enjoyed in its most delicate and sensual and patient form.

A lot of things *would* be nice.

Yet, she did what she had to do. There was no way to prettify utilitarianism, but if it worked there was also no need to.

She pulled the laptop back over to her. Telling all this to herself had helped, a little. But only in the way that a repeated mantra can brute-force quiet the mind. And this was not quite the effect she had been hoping for. She had wanted to re-strengthen her convictions, not merely smother their potential criticisms with mental word-vomit. She tentatively poked the lid upwards and used her sweater sleeve to wipe the screen dry. Through the fading streaks of moisture, she saw the responses which had had their chirpy announcements silenced. That they had tiptoed in without a sound somehow made them more imposing. It was like waking up to find a message written on your pillow.

[20:29] Alabaster&Freckles: Sweetie... I hope you won't resent me pointing out the undertone of defensiveness there.

[20:30] Alabaster&Freckles: I really do appreciate that this is kind of a sensitive topic.

[20:30] Alabaster&Freckles: It's just that you've mentioned how it can be helpful if I prompt you sometimes, so I thought you'd want me to try bringing these things up.

[20:31] Alabaster&Freckles: But if it's not something you want to discuss, that's okay. There's no pressure for you to do anything, ever.

[20:31] Alabaster&Freckles: I truly NEVER want you to feel like you're being made to talk about something you don't want to.

[20:32] Alabaster&Freckles: We go at your pace, that's always been your right. And I always want to respect that.

[20:33] Alabaster&Freckles: I'm really sorry if I upset you and if I overstepped that boundary without realizing it.

Look what she had done.

This wasn't right. *A&F* was not some antagonistic interrogator. They were a friend, and a good one at that. They were also her *only* friend.

Given all that, was this really how she intended to treat them? And for what? What motive had caused this petty behaviour?

She ashamedly turned her face away from the screen and scrunched her eyes shut as it all became so painfully clear to her.

Here she was trying to downplay her own... questionable habit - or whatever the hell it ought to be called - and apparently she was willing to stoop to childish *fingers-in-ears and la-la-la-ing* to do it. Did she really want to be the type of person who does that? Being rude to somebody trying to help her was bad enough by itself. But desperately trying to pretend that a problem didn't even exist was for cowards and simpletons. And even on her worst day, she aspired not to be counted among the ranks of either camp. This was what made this lapse in judgment so galling. She already knew better. She understood, far more acutely than most, that things like this didn't just go away because you turned a blind eye to them. She wished they would, but they simply never did. The proverbial head-burying ostrich is destined to, when finally daring to steal a quick glance above-ground, discover that, *yes*, the snarling hyenas are even closer now and, *yes*, it is still today's meal. And Erin knew how lucky she was that *A&F* was merely like a really kind hyena with a high emotional intelligence and well-meaning persistence. She should be dropping to her knees and thanking the heavens that someone like that even gave a damn about her.

Yet, she had instead taken her conflicted feelings, all that unconfronted self-doubt and frustration, and spewed it out. This was a sordid, deformed sort of catharsis. For she had misdirected all this negative emotion towards *A&F*, even subconsciously sought to push them away. But in the end, there was no having it both ways. She couldn't treat *A&F* like both a punching-bag and a friend. This mess had to be fixed, right now. She had to show she knew where the line was, and that she had crossed it.

She took a deep breath.

Her fingers were already fervently tapping away at her mea culpa before she finished exhaling.

[20:42] PluckingPurgatory'sPetals: God, you don't need to apologize, I do! And I *am* really sorry!

[20:43] PluckingPurgatory'sPetals: I should *not* have talked to you that way. I never want to seem cold towards you, in any way.

[20:43] PluckingPurgatory'sPetals: I was being a total idiot, taking my own shit out on you.

[20:43] PluckingPurgatory'sPetals: Barely fifteen minutes of hindsight and I can already see that, and even why.

[20:44] PluckingPurgatory'sPetals: I guess I didn't fully realize that it was such a sore spot. I think I'm kinda just still working things through in my head about it.

[20:45] PluckingPurgatory'sPetals: Part of me really doesn't want to acknowledge that my mindset towards it is growing problematic, because I've managed to use it to my advantage.

[20:45] PluckingPurgatory'sPetals: I'm... scared of having to give that up.

[20:47] PluckingPurgatory'sPetals: It's kind of hard to explain... but eventually you get so rabidly protective of the little makeshift tools you've amassed to help you cope.

[20:48] PluckingPurgatory'sPetals: Not only because the process of finding each one was so lengthy and hard-fought, with success seeming so unlikely.

[20:50] PluckingPurgatory'sPetals: But also because you still remember what it was like way back at the beginning. When you were defenseless: easy prey for all the demons plaguing you. And you *never ever ever* want to go back to that.

[20:51] PluckingPurgatory'sPetals: The tricks that help with getting through the day are all that really separate this you from that you. Meaning that the idea of giving any of them up just feels so... unwise.

[20:52] PluckingPurgatory'sPetals: So all I can really say is that for the time being, this particular thing is working for me, just about.

[20:52] PluckingPurgatory'sPetals: If and when it isn't, I'll reassess, you know?

What made Erin's conversations with *A&F* so powerful, so worthwhile, was that they made her want to be better. For *A&F* had become the avatar of some nebulous figure who Erin respected, whose approval she longed for, who she wanted to impress by showing she could fix herself. And this encouraged her to uncover her own truth, that unparalleled healing balm. This was a vital counterweight, for usually Erin was not terribly intent on trying to understand herself. In fact, she even took pains to avoid doing so. She was both a practiced liar and a very credulous mark. It had just become second nature to lie to herself if it would spare her from introspection. After all, who knew what discoveries would come of that? She wished not only to avoid the distress, but also their potential destabilizing effect. The present status quo she found herself in could easily be destroyed. Now, this *normal* wasn't exactly nirvana, but it at least kept her from going nuts. And she was, it should be said, wedded to the maxim that anything even slightly conducive to the immediate upkeep of her sanity must be coddled.

However, at the same time, she did sometimes worry about how this habitual resort to self-deception might... change her. What if one day she needed to access some truth about herself and found she no longer could? She'd have become a locked safe to herself. This had disturbing implications. What only she could know, only she could tell. All her pent-up secrets forever being denied salutary release would create immense psychological pressure inside her.

Besides which, if the real landscape of Erin's being became inaccessible to even her, it would go unpoliced. And then that territory would quickly be annexed by something else. All of those convenient falsehoods she had told herself over time would wake from hibernation. And they would invade her mind like toxic spores of *untruth*. As their potency grew, fed by the power she herself had originally lent them, they would seek to contaminate her very essence. Floating hither and thither, they would excrete their corrosive blight onto all that was true about her, the better to unseat it. There was no truce, no treaty which could be brokered with this infection. It longed only to transform her. So that she would gradually mutate into some warped shadow of herself, someone she *wasn't*. A person who did things she wouldn't do, for reasons she would never adduce. And come one distant tomorrow, there would finally be no 'Erin' left. In her place, just a host whose innards were but a tissue of lies.

She couldn't let that happen. It was a very real fear she had, of losing who she was. She did not, even when feeling most grounded, feel very secure in her sense of self. This was why she knew deep down it was necessary to stop going down this dangerous path at all. She had to definitively regain control of her own identity. The smattering of dormant spores in her already had to be plucked out of whatever fetid, miasmic crannies of her psyche they had settled into. So that each one might be bathed in the disinfectant pool of radical self-honesty. Withered and incapacitated, they could then be dissected to learn their origin. The conversations with *A&F* were the laboratory where this could be done. That made them just about the most valuable thing in her life right now.

[20:54] Alabaster&Freckles: Don't sweat it, we all get too caught up in things sometimes. Believe me, I get it!

[20:55] Alabaster&Freckles: And thank you for helping me to comprehend your thought process. I know this type of thing is not easy to articulate.

[20:55] Alabaster&Freckles: Honestly, I find the depth of your self-awareness to be a very reassuring sign.

[20:56] Alabaster&Freckles: Not to mention, there's a certain wariness which, I've come to see, is woven right into your emotional DNA.

[20:56] Alabaster&Freckles: I trust it will keep you from getting blindsided by anything spiralling way out of control.

[20:57] Alabaster&Freckles: I would just advise that you keep monitoring yourself closely, so you can notice if changes for the worse pop up.

[20:58] Alabaster&Freckles: And, look, maybe we'll talk about this again, maybe we won't. As long as you're okay with it, I'm happy to. If not, no biggie.

[20:58] Alabaster&Freckles: But, anyway, we're still totally good, sweetheart! Pinky promise!

It was, Erin had learned, *A&F*'s way to just forge ahead undaunted after moments of friction. She loved this about them. And it worked so well, just bulldozing any weirdness between them before it could even take root.

She found herself re-reading that last message over and over again. It just made her feel so good to see it. And, not one to be wasteful, she sought to wring every last scintilla of reassurance and elation out of it. She happily bit her bottom lip and reflexively went for a little celebratory fist pump in the air. Of course, mid-gesture she caught herself and, feeling kind of silly, aborted it. As if trying to play it off, she bashfully lowered her hand back down. It was funny that she sometimes still retained those self-conscious instincts of someone who had to worry about being seen, about being judged. But, even though she was smiling awkwardly at herself for that, she was still smiling. And wasn't that quite something? A rare occurrence indeed.

[21:00] PluckingPurgatory'sPetals: I'm so glad to hear that!

[21:01] PluckingPurgatory'sPetals: Because, like woah, if you're breaking out the sacred *pinky promise*, I know it must be serious business!

[21:03] Alabaster&Freckles: Oh for sure! I don't bust that bad boy out for just any old thing!

[21:05] Alabaster&Freckles: Now, if you don't mind us moving on, perhaps we might talk about your depression in an overall sense? I mean, while we're warmed up to brave these heavy topics and all...

[21:05] Alabaster&Freckles: So, yeah, how has that been?

Well, it was nice while it lasted, anyhow.

Never a momentary *up* without a long stretch of *down* hot on its heels. Erin was amazed by how this still somehow always managed to catch her by surprise. Despite how forcefully this life lesson should have been instilled in her by now, it just wasn't. Maybe because, in a sense, one can never really get used to a suckerpunch anyway. That was kind of the whole point of it, right?

She eyeballed this latest question with displeasure, the smile a past-tense thing now. She had forgotten that they weren't quite at the end of the checklist yet. It wasn't *A&F*'s fault, naturally, but just as they had pushed

42

through the tension and landed on a happy note, now Erin had to delve right back into some pitch-black shit. No doubt bumming both of them out again. Sometimes even she got so tired of never really having any good news to report. Being a Debbie Downer was awful, but Erin felt like Debbie's *even* more morose, goth, ambiguously-suicidal sister who somehow makes people long for the comparative 'joy' of Debbie's company.

For, to put it plainly, the most notable quality of her depression was its stupendous constancy. It wasn't just a temporary mood or mindstate which came and went. It was an enduring mode of being, colouring every thought, presiding over every day. However bleak it was to have to outrightly admit, the depression had, in some conclusive sense, won. And though this end-state did really suck, when held up beside the terrible conquest preceding it, it was a period of relative calm. Or, at least, she believed so. She could only vaguely recall the time when she had been resisting, instead of abiding. It seemed so very long ago now. And she had, after all, since evolved into a succession of so many distinct persons. So she was but a distant descendant of who she had been way back then. And consequently she retained only a shelf-worn, hand-me-down memory of the war which had been waged for her soul. This was nothing more than some sun-bleached photograph of a photograph of a photograph of a photograph. If she peered real hard into it, there was perhaps some faint suggestion that... what? She had fought the good fight right up until the end? Struggled valiantly against the overwhelming might of her foe? Something comforting like that, at any rate. But probably this was just the same romanticizing revisionism which slipped into every tale of defeat as it was passed down the lineage of the defeated.

Anyway, that was all academic now. She had lost and that was all there was to it. What really mattered were the terms imposed by the victor. As the ever-mocking nature of the depression's triumph was that it only exercised its total domination by enfeebling her. It had won her just so that it might force her to do nothing. That was the point. And it achieved this by making her acutely conscious of the staggering weight of just being alive. Such that she ineluctably felt *existence* bearing down upon her from every angle. Its immense pressure crushing her into her precise shape, and pinning her in place. At her lowest points, she wished that this awareness would prove literally unbearable, that her constitution would prove unequal to the squeeze. Then she would suddenly just get pulverized into a tiny point of mass by the sheer existential force exerted upon her. It would, at least, grant her rest.

It went without saying that this outcome was far too merciful to permit. Her depression was a torturer who took its art very, very seriously. Maximizing efficacy was its one and only ideal. And any mercy would just hinder the perfect execution of its scheme. No, in its all-knowing, all-seeing cruelty, it had exactly granted her *just enough* strength to survive her sentence. But not even the tiniest modicum more.

So Erin spent her days impotently enduring a grievous sense of lassitude. She had learned that there were very many minutes in a day, because she felt them sluggishly tick by one-by-one. That had become a chore in itself. All she could do is find ways to distract herself. Generally, this meant resorting to some trivial preoccupation. Not that she was about to complain, of course. Anything which could clog up her brain's passageways with the mush of thoughtlessness was welcome. To this end, her laptop was indispensable. It was her conduit to an endless supply of expertly crafted engines of timewasting. This strategy worked well enough, but what a hollow success it felt like, to have just whiled away another day. Worse still was the sobering knowledge that she somehow had to replicate this feat again tomorrow.

[21:08] PluckingPurgatory'sPetals: Well, that... depends.

[21:08] PluckingPurgatory'sPetals: Can we imagine there's really *tiny* gradations on the scale used?

[21:08] PluckingPurgatory'sPetals: If that's the case, then I suppose today has been the highlight of this week.

It was always an interesting experiment to prod *A&F* with sarcasm, to see how they would react. Naturally, their conversations weren't always as somber as this one had been. And she had grown fond of *A&F*'s personality, which shone through much more during lighter talk. There was a certain dorky upbeatness and playful streak which rather reminded Erin of that one friend's fun mom who always won you over without even trying. But there was also an unpredictability underneath all that, which is what made trying to pull new levers so enticing.

[21:10] Alabaster&Freckles: So why no hooray then?! Where's the balloons? The confetti?

[21:11] Alabaster&Freckles: Darling, that's a cause to celebrate, if ever I saw one!

[21:11] Alabaster&Freckles: Expect a FedEx package containing a bottle of champagne within the hour!

There it was.

The tiniest possible hint of a smile flickered back into place once more.

Still, then her stomach loudly rumbled, ruining the moment.

And those coagulating traces of amusement slid off her face like a stage-magician ripping away a tablecloth.

Her expression grew dour. She looked over at the half-made meal left abandoned on the countertop and sighed. That sandwich seemed just as disgusting as it had done before. How galling was the recurrent thought that she might have to try and eat it anyway. Even that poor bastard Damocles *only* had a sword suspended above his head to ruin his mood. She had a baguette dangling over her tightly clamped-shut mouth and hated it ten times worse.

CHAPTER TWO

Erin was suddenly yanked from her *infinite* bliss.

The transition had the same impossible abruptness as a falling guillotine blade.

She found herself in the amorphous blackness behind her eyelids, and instantly knew it as such. A profound panic rippled through her as she groggily realized that she was waking up. She kept her eyes tightly shut and held perfectly still, breathing only shallowly. A frantic impulse towards defiance kindled inside of her. She silently screamed at herself to undo what had happened. There must still be, she felt sure, a way to reverse this ejection. Yet the window of opportunity was very slender and growing more so with every passing second. Her only hope was to linger in that murky hypnopompic anteroom one passes through prior to being fully awake. It would take an act of absolute will, but in this crucial moment of limbo, she had to pivot her consciousness back towards where it had departed. And then... she had to return there.

Okay, she could do this. She had to do this.

She told herself she was the master of her own body. If she wanted this badly enough and if she tried hard enough, it *would* obey her command to sink back into slumber. Somehow, the sheer might of her determination would rewire those biological mechanisms which stood as gatekeepers at the threshold of sleep. It would take everything she could muster but it was doable. She just had to forcibly clear her mind, to sear it blank with the fierce heat of her need. Her muscles were tense with purposeful inaction as she lay there. She tried not to even register the feeling of the blanket against her skin. And she tried not to think, and tried not to think about trying not to think. The difficulty of doing this was beyond exasperating. But she forced herself to keep at it. She had only to stay the course until a heavy drowsiness soon re-descended upon her. Then, as she drifted away once more, the deed would be done. And for all these meagre pains, a supreme prize.

Keep going, no matter what.

Just a little bit longer now.

Yes, this would work.

Scratch that. It *was* working.

It *was* definitely working.

It *was* absolutely, for sure working.

She tried desperately to detect even the most preliminary hint of herself dozing off.

Yet the acuity of her single-minded focus made it impossible to pretend she felt something she didn't.

Hot tears crept slowly down her temples from the sides of her closed eyes.

She had given it everything she had to give.

But it was over. She had failed.

Roiling self-hatred stirred up a whirlpool of disgust and regret in the cloudy waters of her psyche. She let its revolutions dizzy her and amplify the irrational force of her rage. Such a simple thing as refusing to wake up, and she was too weak... too inept... too *selfish* to even make that happen. She slowly opened her eyes and the teariness spilled onto them, blurring her vision. She blinked hard a few times to clear it away. Lying on her back, she had to crane her head up off her pillow to blearily look around. With only the faint light emanating from a standing lamp over by the corner, the room was blanketed in near-darkness. It was all just fuzzy shapes and unjudgeable distances. Still, there could be no mistaking where she was. She didn't need to see anything to know that, she felt it; a sensation of absence, akin to being conscious of a missing limb. She was in *the wrong fucking world*. Even worse, it was all her fault that she was still here. She lowered her head back down onto the pillow.

First her features twisted in anger. Then, as if by a downward chain reaction, her body was convulsed by an irrepressible violent energy. It made her flail wildly. She slammed her fists down onto the bed over and over and over again in an animal frenzy. Picking up speed, the muffled thuds rang out with the rhythm of a quickening pulse. She persisted until her shoulders ached and her arms were leaden with exhaustion and her hands hurt from pounding against the mattress.

Falling still, she took a few moments to catch her breath, letting her energy replenish. She was going to need it, to fuel the high-pressure expulsion of all her hate and all her pain. It was bubbling inside the vessel of her heart like burning pitch, and it longed to be set free.

Recharged, she irately kicked the quilt off her legs. But, suddenly not content with this puny gesture, she reached forward to grab it from the end of the bed. After scrunching it into a ball, she threw it far across the room, grunting as she heaved it into the air. That done, she quickly spun over onto her front. She pushed her face deep into the pillow and gripped its sides, squeezing them tight against her ears. The prolonged wail she then unleashed into it was a barbaric song of anguish. And it only grew louder and more intense as the giant unfurling maelstrom of emotion poured out of her ever faster. Even dampened by the thick pillow, this terrible noise still reverberated around the room, its distorted echo a mere silhouette of fury. Eventually it faded into a hoarse roar as her lungs were nearly empty. But she didn't stop, though it pained her throat considerably. She instead fixated upon this, using the hurt as a bullseye to extract every last ounce of effort her body had in it. And so, on and on it went. Only when she truly had no breath left to draw upon was she forced to stop.

She withdrew her face only to suck in more air and then began hysterically sobbing into the pillowcase's clinging embrace. She cried for quite a while, until she felt completely drained in this way too. Flinging the pillow aside, she wiped her wet and reddened cheeks on the sheet. She had no idea what to do now. Her instinctive response was to just curl into a ball. And as she hugged her knees, she dug her nails hard into the firm skin there but couldn't even feel it. She just stared over at the wall. Little sniffles and whimpers continued to jolt her now and then, like diminishing aftershocks which mournfully sound out the epitaph to some catastrophic seismic upheaval.

This was, she sensed, the only respite she was going to get. She had screamed and cried herself into a fleeting numbness. When that went away, she would have to actually process it all somehow. This feat seemed both utterly unthinkable and utterly inescapable. The pain of reflecting, from this world, upon what had happened loomed as a stark unknown. For the few hazy, unbidden flashbacks she had endured already had at least been dulled by the anesthetizing side-effect of shock. But the coming agony would have to be borne with full clarity. And there was simply no way to steel herself for such an ordeal. Yet, deep down, she also felt halfway glad that she couldn't.

She envisioned the gargantuan suffering, splayed out in all its kaleidoscopic hellishness, which was just now breaching the horizon. It was speeding at ravenous full-pelt towards her. And it would be rightful punishment for her failure. So, despite how she quaked with fear, she would make no move to evade it. More than that, even. She knew she must welcome it, as the true penitent must cherish their flagellation. She hoped that when the pain finally immured her within its cruel geometry, she might goad it to ravage her and leave her hollow. It was the only way. Once she emerged as but a husk... perhaps then there could be some measure of proper atonement.

For now though, she had to *remember*.

She unsteadily pulled herself up into a sitting position against the headboard. The cold wooden bars pressed into her back uncomfortably. Her eyes defocused, fading the room from view, as she stared into the middle distance. With a frantic exertion of her still foggy mind, she tried to induce it to sharpen, and recollect the dream with perfect fidelity. Some part of her fretted that to take the memory apart piece-by-piece like this would be akin to performing some gruesome, defiling postmortem. But this was not a time for squeamishness. If she wanted to hold onto anything, she badly needed to do this now. She needed to systematically cement in her long-term memory all that she had experienced. For her brain would soon overwrite this sacred data with the mundane sensory information it was now receiving. And to let even a single instant of it be erased could not be countenanced. This exacting standard was a lot to ask of herself, especially in her present condition. Her entire being would have to be perfectly aligned towards the endeavour. For the remnant vapours of the dream were floating all around her like sparkling airborne gold dust, and *every last speck* must be gathered into the suction of some pristine, impenetrable mental-reliquary. Only then could she be content they were secure. Only then could whatever... connection which remained be saved.

First and foremost, of course, there was *the girl*. What was her name?... Damn, what was it?... Ah, yes, she had asked Erin to christen her with a name.

Tilly. Her name was Tilly.

Now, what about her appearance? Well, she certainly had the burnished gleam of youth, and must be no older than... eighteen or nineteen perhaps. Even with better posture, she stood a little bit shorter than Erin. And she was chubby, her form made up of marvellously curved lines. Then there was her long glossy hair. It was dyed neon-red and wrangled into a messy bun.

As for her face?... Erin strained to recall it, to pluck it out in sharp focus from the distinctive haziness of the dreamworld. Yet she quickly realized that, strangely enough, this wasn't the thing to do. In that realm, as opposed to this simplistically materialist plane, something did not have to be seen to be known. And Erin *knew* Tilly's face. That knowledge was now impregnated in the deepest pathways of her essence. It flowed through her inextricably hitched to the electrical signals prompting the beating of her heart, the drawing of her breath. So, trying to summon an image of that face was an unnecessarily crude recourse. Erin only had to remember how it had made her feel. Then it appeared to her, clear as day. Tilly had a kind, honest, pretty face. Its beauty was derived from the purity which exuded from it. This was an elusive trait sometimes well-captured in oil paintings of serenely dignified women gazing unperturbed into the Eternal, which lurks just beyond the canvas edges.

Finally then, what did Tilly sound like? She had definitely spoken, and in a soft, diffident manner. But Erin now realized that Tilly had no audible voice. Funny, this had seemed totally unremarkable at the time. Perhaps Erin had been able to lipread there? No, that wasn't quite it. She had just intuitively comprehended exactly what Tilly was saying. Somehow she had heard every syllable, and every infinitesimal pause between them, resound inside her head as though via some sort of intimate telepathy. Their conversations had been not only fast-flowing and unreserved, but revelatory too. Tilly had the easy eloquence of someone unafraid to say precisely what they were thinking. And when she got excited, she tried to get it all out so fast that she adorably tripped over her words.

In the dreams, the two of them were *together*. Not just friends, not just lovers, but so very much more besides. There was really no label for what they were. And the wildest hyperbole of the poet was not enough either. For words are small and flawed and sullying receptacles when applied to something so boundless and exquisite. Yet despite the futility, part of her longed to find a way to properly express it. To take it out of her head and give it even that most limited sort of embodiment. Because description, however faulty, may serve as some bolstering keepsake, some crystallised trace of the ephemeral to cling onto here. But it was not to be. She had only the ghostly echoes of all those ineffable feelings she had felt. They would have to tell the story well enough.

What she had had with Tilly was a... melding. Normally the cliché would have made her groan and roll her eyes, but now she genuinely understood how two people could be but halves of the same whole. The truest form of love was transformative, producing the overlapping of souls. And it was this which made the simple life they shared with one another so sublime. Just being in each other's company was all that *could* be wanted. But, hell, it also made everything else better too, bathing that remainder in the hallowed glow of their union. Of course, there was nothing fantastical about what they had actually been doing. It was just the ordinary shared rituals of cohabiting couples, but they had deeply enraptured her with such a potent joy. This only seems so mystifying until one experiences it. Whereas, god, how easy it had been to dive wholeheartedly into that glorious sense of fulfilment. For she had never felt so absolutely sure she was exactly where she needed to be. And that certainty made her feel so safe and happy and content.

Such was the life-affirming euphoria which Erin had been unceremoniously torn away from. One moment she had been *there*... in that transcendental hinterland... with *her*. And in the next, she was dragged back to the hideousness of reality. There could be no deprivation more egregious. Her sense of loss was like the point of a spear pushing with excruciating slowness, millimeter by millimeter, through her chest towards her heart. As she had not only been robbed of a bond more precious than anything she had ever even known existed. But she also mourned for that better version of herself she'd glimpsed too. It was an alternate self which love had repaired, had taught how to be at peace and gracious. That possibility was now wrenched away and cast into the colorless fires of oblivion. She felt her rank deficiency all the more keenly for its death. And it made her feel like an impostor, longing for the love another had warranted.

This multilayered grief lay on top of her like a series of wet blankets, clinging close with every movement. And these heavy shrouds were in fact soaked with the toxin of sorrow, which was seeping into her skin over time. For it was simply too overwhelming to be felt all at once. Her capacity for anguishment was great but, even taxed to its very limit, it could only register so much moment-to-moment. So she would be subjected to it progressively. Each passing hour would bring with it some new realization about what she had lost, some new nuance of distress to torment her with. And when this trial was finally over, she would be able to put the whole jigsaw together. What a vision that would be, that gut-wrenching totality. Perhaps beholding it would even be mercifully Medusan. Stone, at least, felt nothing.

She heaved out a lengthy sigh and switched on the fairy lights strung up above the headboard. They doused the bed with warm, tinted light, making her squint. She rubbed her eyes to dispel the squiggly streaks obscuring her vision. And went on rubbing them, unconsciously stalling. But she eventually made herself scoot over to sit on the edge of the mattress. Then she held her head in her hands for a little while. Now she at least knew she was lingering. It was difficult to explain, but she really did not want to leave the bed. It was the launchpad from whence she had voyaged to meet Tilly. This connection, however tenuous, gave it the feel of a holy site to Erin. And to depart was to take the last symbolic step away from all that had happened, officially consigning it to the past.

But it had to be done.

She impetuously shoved her feet into her slippers and rose. Seething and rueful, she just stood there. Her eyelids fluttered half-closed as she minutely swayed side to side. Then, abruptly, she set off. Padding over to the standing lamp, she turned it up via its dimmer switch. Next she headed to the kitchenette area and jerked the freezer door open. From the depths of one of its drawers, she fished out a large, cylindrical block of cloudy ice. Her breath caught in her throat. With unneeded delicateness, she turned it over and over, swiping the frost from its surface. And afterwards she just held it there in her cupped hands. She licked her lips nervously and stared hard at it for a short while. It was a thing of great power and awful purpose. The chill from the ice was painful but she savoured the stinging, burning sensation in her palms. Blinking a few times, she shook herself out of the reverent stupor. She took it over to the sink and deposited it there. Yet she did not throw it or drop it. She lowered it down and let it slowly slide from her hands onto the basin floor. Turning on the tap, she prodded the ice across until it sat beneath the flowing water. This was always mesmerizing to watch. But she didn't let it grab ahold of her. There was something very important she had to at least try in the meanwhile.

She wiped her wet hands on her t-shirt and bumped the freezer door shut with her knee. Then she passed by the window-seat to snag her laptop before continuing over to the bed. She slumped down and set it in front of herself. Well, here went nothing. Yanking the lid up, she mashed the power button a bunch of times. The boot-up screen appeared. Her fingers drummed an impatient rhythm on the laptop's body, as if she could channel her agitation into it and spur it to load faster. The seconds dragged by. Tension was building inside of her. She progressed to kneading her knuckles hard into the keyboard, pressing random keys. It was an implicit threat to pummel the machine into scrap metal if it didn't comply quicker. She was on borrowed time and that urgency was getting to her. She had to know which it was going to be: salvation or the permission for self-damnation. And it was really out of her hands. Little clues had made her suspect that *A&F* lived in a different timezone, making it possible they would be online, but who knows. She just really, really hoped she'd get lucky here. So much depended on the outcome.

The log-in screen finally came up. She quickly snapped to attention. There was a long string of gibberish her knuckles had inadvertently filled the password box with. So she rapidly flutter-tapped the backspace key with machine-gun tempo. But no delete command registered on-screen. She tried to type something else instead. Now those keystrokes didn't have any effect either. The system had frozen. Perhaps overloaded by the surplus of input. She tilted her head back and grimaced with inarticulable exasperation, baring her gritted teeth like an animal. From past experience, she knew it was useless trying to wait this out. It would just hang here indefinitely until restarted. She cursed herself for sticking with this aging laptop. She cursed herself for having been too lazy to deactivate that silly password-protection feature yet. And then she sucked it up and held down the power button until the screen went dark.

Great, another goddamn wait.

She threw a longing glance over at the sink. It was hard to recall the urge to cut ever being stronger than right now. She needed it like oxygen. The severity of the craving was starting to make her jittery. This was why she sought something to intercede and dissuade her, to haul her back from the brink. Or else there could be no doubt: it was going to be very bad this time. Now, sure, it was *always* scary. Because once that deeply gratifying pain starts to intoxicate you and flood your system with adrenaline, you were no longer really in control anymore. A terrible gluttony descends, a wedge parting you from yourself. It was a disturbing feeling, akin to watching from afar as a stranger wearing your skin indulges their bloodlust at its expense. This meant there was never truly any telling how long it would go. You are but a hostage, at another's mercy. And hostage-takers do not view their prizes as anything more than expendable objects to be used with reckless disregard. Yet, this usual danger was exacerbated tenfold in the present situation. The strength of her deranging emotional turmoil was quite unprecedented. It was something new, something fearsome. She had never so dearly wished to escape herself, whatever the cost. This threatened to entice an extraordinarily fiendish sort of captor tonight.

Tilting backwards, she stretched her legs out and slid her pyjama shorts off. Then she re-crossed her legs and peered down at her bare inner thighs. The sight could never quite lose its effect. Her brow furrowed and she involuntarily clenched her jaw. Her fingertips gently brushed to-and-fro across the erratically crisscrossing lattices of long, thin scars. They were pink and slightly raised and unsightly. Though that was the least of it. For they were also perverse war-poems, composed with a shaky hand during bleak and harrowing battles waged against her own body. Yes, on this most precious canvas was carved a chaotic, indelible record. And it was *all* there. Every occasion when hurting herself was necessary to drown out the stupendous wretchedness of being alive. How desperate she had been, in those grim moments, to transmute pain into the antidote for thought. This alchemy came at a high price, but better to beat the universe to the punch and be the one victimizing herself for once. After all, only she actually had the right to do so. Yet it was such a lonely thing, that private campaign of rebellion. Her chronicle-by-mutilation, the only diary she'd ever kept, was written in a cipher she alone could read. Just like all documents penned in enemy territory during wartime must be encoded. As she looked back over all the entries now, the wave of memories which overcame her elicited a sinking feeling in her stomach. Her mouth became dry. Her breathing grew rapid. She was getting ahead of herself, tiptoeing towards a place she might yet skirt altogether.

She forced herself to rip her magnetised gaze away. Usefully, the half-raised blind allowed the moonlit sky to catch her eye instead. It was striking that no stars dotted the midnight-blue canopy overhead. They had withdrawn from view, happy to desert their posts when the moon was out. And though that glowing, pale yellow disc did have some small charm, it was - perhaps due to its relative youth - *too* bright, *too* eager to please. The stars were not so gauche or obsequious. Like all elders, they had much to offer, and little inclination to advertise it. She lamented their absence; it made her feel her solitude more deeply. How she wished they had been there. On this of all nights, she could really have used with seeing the calm, paternal twinkling of those distant pinpricks of starlight. It was not only their beauty, but also the reminder of her own cosmic insignificance which she tended to find hugely comforting.

Alas, the entire web of constellations being obscured just reminded her of how unreachable, how unknowable the stars were. This, in turn, somehow made them seem depressingly unreal. Sure, computers could hypothetically simulate every minute detail of these fiery spheres soaring with immense, noiseless grace through the lifeless vacuum. But that was just the drab realm of theories. No more than the hubristic guesswork of a race of fallible, planet-bound mammals. The truth was that solving the tantalizing mystery of the stars was like discovering what lay beyond death. Despite humanity's high opinion of its collective genius, such knowledge was simply outside of its ken. And so, as with the afterlife, the stars themselves were best understood as an idea. A mere mirror of the hopes which had imbued them with apocryphal attributes. Yet, relegated to this capacity, they were of no use to her. And given the emergency still unfolding, she knew she had better dwell on immediate reality instead. The bed, the laptop, her scarred flesh, that frozen implement an icy womb was gradually birthing... *these* are what was real. Indeed, they were powerfully, inescapably real. No matter what fanciful star-charts stated, it was this room and her mind which constituted the boundaries of the entire universe right now.

She switched her focus back to the restarted laptop. Very carefully, she entered her password, henpecking each keystroke with her pointer fingers. But when the desktop appeared, she moved with frantic speed. Whipping the cursor over to it, she quadruple-clicked the IM program. As the contact list popped up on screen, her heart fluttered with palpitations and she found herself holding her breath.

Alabaster&Freckles - OFFLINE

She slowly exhaled a single word.
"Fuuuuuuuuuck."
Instinctively, and well aware of the futility, she clicked to manually refresh all contacts' current status.
It was not a surprise when nothing changed.
Roughly slamming the laptop shut, she flipped it away from herself. It landed upside down at the end of the bed.

"Fuck! Fuck! Fuck! Fuck! Fuck! Fuck! Fuck! Fuck! Fuck!" she chanted angrily.

Each time, the short utterance became heavier and blunter. Not unlike if she was bludgeoning the revelation with a club, and her swings were only growing more malicious. She could feel her pulse racing. Alarm was worming its way into her mind, poisoning her ability to think clearly. She hesitantly tried to quell it. Great caution had to be exercised here. She knew only too well that fending it off too vigorously would backfire. It was the same lesson you learned when trying to wriggle and writhe your way out of quicksand: your own eagerness can be your undoing. And, often, the price of that lesson was discovering that sand is a *very* poor substitute for oxygen. However, she had to incur that risk. What else could she do? There was no one at hand to help pull her free from this particular gurgling pit, which was ever-deepening beneath her feet. It was truly now or never.

And so, Erin decided to try one more last-ditch effort before she gave in. She was going to try and vent it all now anyway. Even if *A&F* wasn't there to read it, they *would* as soon as they next came online. Therefore, in a way she'd still be talking to someone, just at a time delay. At least, this is what she tried her best to make herself believe. It was of dubious comfort. But, either way, if she could just articulate the woe consuming her, it may serve to temporarily alleviate it. That would be something, at least. And certainly much, much better than the more... invasive purge she was intent upon. Because trying to slice her feelings out would be a messy process all round.

She begrudgingly pulled the laptop back over to her.

[03:10] PluckingPurgatory'sPetals: Alright, so I know that you're not there.

[03:10] PluckingPurgatory'sPetals: I accept that.

[03:10] PluckingPurgatory'sPetals: I have to just deal with that.

[03:10] PluckingPurgatory'sPetals: But... I gotta get all of this out right now. I just have to.

[03:11] PluckingPurgatory'sPetals: I'm hoping this one-sided conversation might somehow trick my dumb brain into thinking I got to talk to someone in time.

[03:11] PluckingPurgatory'sPetals: I mean, because I *need* to cut. And, shit, I don't know, maybe this will help to avert that.

[03:11] PluckingPurgatory'sPetals: Okay.

[03:12] PluckingPurgatory'sPetals: So, I had this fucking dream.

[03:12] PluckingPurgatory'sPetals: It was beyond incredible. I've never experienced anything remotely like it. It was so vivid and so powerful and so meaningful.

[03:12] PluckingPurgatory'sPetals: There was this girl. I dreamt about this girl.

[03:13] PluckingPurgatory'sPetals: Her name is Tilly.

[03:13] PluckingPurgatory'sPetals: I've always adored that name.

[03:13] PluckingPurgatory'sPetals: In the dreamworld, we were together. Romantically, yes, but best friends too. So close it was almost like being sisters.

[03:14] PluckingPurgatory'sPetals: It felt like... I had always known her, as if we had this fathomless spiritual connection which was outside of time.

[03:15] PluckingPurgatory'sPetals: That sense of oneness permeated everything. It bloomed in every iota of my essence. I was so happy I felt like I was floating. It was just wonderful.

[03:15] PluckingPurgatory'sPetals: There was such a peacefulness in knowing I was exactly where I was supposed to be. In knowing that I would be just fine if eons rolled on by.

[03:17] PluckingPurgatory'sPetals: Yeah, fuck. It was love.

[03:17] PluckingPurgatory'sPetals: *It was fucking love.*

[03:18] PluckingPurgatory'sPetals: God, and it made what I had imagined love to be seem like such bullshit. Like I was just some idiot kid thinking I understood quantum physics because I could scrawl numbers with a crayon.

[03:19] PluckingPurgatory'sPetals: But now... I know. And I won't ever forget what it felt like. I can't. That feeling has soaked into my very being. My declaration of love for her is etched into my fucking bones.

[03:19] PluckingPurgatory'sPetals: I have emerged from a chrysalis, transformed. I am someone new. I am her beloved.

[03:21] PluckingPurgatory'sPetals: I just feel so very lucky, because I'm completely unworthy of her. She's *so* insanely pretty, and just like... I don't know, so nice and so full of life and rosy-cheeked. In the dreams, I could scarcely believe she even wanted anything to do with me.

[03:22] PluckingPurgatory'sPetals: I mean, how could she fall in love with someone like me, you know? She's so... just... elegant and flawless. Whereas I'm all... whatever... scrawny and gross and weird-looking.

[03:22] PluckingPurgatory'sPetals: And, look, I get it.

[03:23] PluckingPurgatory'sPetals: Even as I write this, I can faintly grasp the absurdity of the situation. I dreamt up some perfect paramour. In a way, it's crazy, it's ridiculous.

[03:24] PluckingPurgatory'sPetals: Yet when I try to tell myself that it was just a dream, that I'm not even gay, blah blah blah... it doesn't matter. Not even in the slightest. My time with her was more true than anything I have ever known.

[03:25] PluckingPurgatory'sPetals: Oh, and holy jesus motherfucking christ, when I woke up!! Realizing what had been taken from me, it was like the worst torture imaginable! I wept and wept like she was dead beside me!

[03:27] PluckingPurgatory'sPetals: Since then, I just can't think straight. That infinite loss is always at the forefront of my mind. It's hijacking my every thought and implanting in it a corrosive sliver of my heartbreak. Then the thoughts dissolve before I can string them together. It's infuriating.

[03:28] PluckingPurgatory'sPetals: Okay, I guess that's about the long and the short of it.

[03:30] PluckingPurgatory'sPetals: And I'm sorry, but this... wasn't enough. The compulsion is still there, still so fucking strong.

[03:30] PluckingPurgatory'sPetals: I still need that relief too much, I really do. And, hell, I've never had a better excuse for resorting to it than right now.

[03:31] PluckingPurgatory'sPetals: It's okay. Please don't feel bad. I don't think you could've talked me out of it anyway.

[03:31] PluckingPurgatory'sPetals: I'm going now. Please ping me when you get online.

Her vision had grown blurry from teariness, but she hadn't cried. For now at least, there were no more tears to give. Yet her tear ducts still burned like she had been crying incessantly as she wrote. It was quite fitting really: phantom teardrops shed for a phantom romance.

She set the laptop to low-power hibernation and tucked it beneath her pillow. She felt like she had to hide it away. It was a bizarre, subconscious, symbolic gesture. Because in some weird sense, the laptop kind of *was A&F* to her. And she wouldn't want them to see what was about to happen.

As she walked over to the sink and turned off the tap, there was a newfound calmness to her. The choice had been made and now the process was underway. That's all there was to it. As such, her expression merely bespoke a sort of businesslike determination. It was the look of someone perfectly unoppressed by any fear of whether calamity might possibly descend, for calamity is their destination. And a familiar one at that.

Looking into the basin, she saw it waiting for her. In the middle of a little puddle was the razor blade, gleaming with potential and invitation. She reached in and picked it up with care. It was single-edged, which made handling it a lot easier. She noticed that, despite the lukewarm water it had been sat in, the metal somehow retained a certain essential coldness. This struck her as a byproduct of the spite which sharpened steel bears against as-yet intact flesh. She dried it with some kitchen towel and placed it on her palm. Using the fingers of her other hand, she leisurely flipped it over again and again. She liked to inspect it. There was something reassuring in feeling its weight, in feeling how unyieldingly rigid and strong it was.

This slow-going prelude had become an indispensable part of the ritual. For one thing, it stopped her from rushing into the main event, which was the inevitable impulse. By taking her time, she was able to relish the thrilling anticipation, to imbibe it sip by sip. For another thing, it also impressed upon her the gravity of what she was about to do. This was useful because it being so bad was what made it so good. Thus, she tried to remain cognizant of how dangerous what lay ahead was, simply to intensify the experience. This calculus would be mind-boggling to a normal person. But addicts have endless depraved ingenuity when it comes to devising ways to heighten their fix.

She went over to the cubicle and placed her razor blade down onto the outside rim of the speckled-stone shower tray. This produced a satisfying *clink.* Then she took off her underwear and hung them over a spare rail on the towel rack. From the nearby bathroom cabinet, she grabbed some supplies. She used a lighter's flame to disinfect the blade's edge, holding it out with tweezers. Once she was satisfied, she put it back down to cool, balanced freestanding on its flat spine. Next she thoroughly rubbed all possible cutting sites on her thighs with alcohol wipes. These were imperfect methods of sterilization, but good enough for her. And a far cry from when, as a self-harm neophyte, she had taken no precautions whatsoever. She escaped sepsis during those dark early days sheerly through dumb luck. Which, famously, is fond *only* of beginners.

Opening the cubicle door, she stepped into the enclosure. To force herself to remain present, she took to performing long, controlled breaths: in and out, in and out, in and out. At the same time, she rolled up her baggy t-shirt well above her navel and knotted it there. It would be preferable to not even have to be *half*-naked while doing this, to avoid the mental discomfort. But the dictates of necessity cared not for convenience. She lowered herself down into a sitting position, frowning as she felt the frigid surface press against her skin. Her legs were spread apart and stretched out in front of her. She had orientated herself so that the little square drainage grate was between her knees. This was just one of the many tricks she had learned to help make everything go smoothly. Finally, she reached outside the door and retrieved the razor blade.

Taking her time, she meticulously surveyed the marred swathes of skin which covered her inner thighs. She was searching for an appropriate spot to start at. This had become increasingly difficult as the accumulation built up over time. Still, there was a hierarchy she adhered to, in an attempt to retain control. To cross over ancient scars was no big deal. But she would not reopen those which had been inflicted in recent months. It was simply a

61

matter of pragmatism. Best not to interfere with the healing process if possible. Of course, the workaround to all these considerations seemed obvious. She could just cut somewhere well beyond the scarred patches. But she was very hesitant to concede to the expansion of their already wide territory. If she did not maintain her self-imposed limits on this annexation, it threatened to become boundless. And given she already hated her body enough, transforming it into a full-blown freak show seemed... gratuitous. So she had long since made her peace with the scarring being so densely concentrated in its allotted areas. She did have a preference for the form it took, however. This was meant to minimize the hideousness of how she was defacing herself. Ergo, the straight overlapping lines. They at least created a wound pattern with some semblance of purposefulness and uniformity. A neat facade for the horrifying evidence of an unwell mind.

The best location to make the first incision had been found. She pulled the skin there as taut as possible. Then she secured a firm grip on the blade. Pausing, she closed her eyes and readied herself. As soon as they re-opened, she got to work. She employed the corner of the cutting edge like a scalpel and quickly pushed it down into the meat of her thigh. It pierced the skin and with light pressure she sunk it very, very slightly lower. She threw her head back. Her eyes widened as a gasp flew up out of her throat. A moment later, the bite of the sensation peaked, and she bit her bottom lip hard.

She knew this pain intimately well, and treasured it. But it still hurt. Indeed, this was a sensitive place with a lot of nerve endings, so it *really* hurt. That was the crux of the matter. The pain never stopped being pain. It didn't magically morph into some pleasurable tickle because you were a committed enough masochist. Everything lay in how you taught yourself to receive the feeling. No one likes the taste of wine at first. Yet, down the line, the palate can be attuned to it. Rabid connoisseurs even spring up. Erin was just such a one. And what made this severe pain so delicious to her was simple. When it came on, it became one's whole world. As her consciousness zeroed in on it, probing from all angles, all else faded from view. It was as though examining such white-hot agony dazzled the mind's eye with snow-blindness. And the mindlessness which resulted felt very liberating. Its character was not unlike a meditative trance.

The aftermath of this first sharp influx of pain was diminishing. A thin trickle of blood slowly dribbled from the incision. She watched, with a glassy incurious gaze, as her thigh's gentle twitching made it zig-zag its way down. But now it was time for the main event. With a considerable mental exertion, she flipped her focus back onto the task before her. Her whole arm tensed as she ensured her hand was steady. Then she grimaced and yelped as, with measured pressure, she gradually drove the blade through her flesh. *This* pain was way, way more intense. It radiated outward from the cut in fast staccato pulses, dizzying her. Keeping this slicing motion going, despite the protestations of one's most primal instincts, required a lot of willpower. It took all she had to give. And as she lost herself in the effort, she let out a long guttural groan. Her toes were repeatedly curling and uncurling as though she had touched a livewire.

It took about thirty seconds to shear open a two-and-a-half inch slit. Faintly registering that she had reached the preferred length, she stopped. It took several moments to try and get a handle on the shakes assailing her. Before any hesitation could intrude, she withdrew the razor blade quickly, eliciting a sort of choked-off cry. Then she simply held it there above her handiwork with a swaying hand. It was no longer even present to her. She was just sitting there, panting heavily. Staring as hard as one could stare at nothing at all. Reality had been subordinated to the immaculate, overpowering pain which now enthralled her. And she drank *deeply* of it.

A few tranquil minutes passed as Erin enjoyed her private bubble of stupefaction. When she started to regain her senses, she became mesmerized by the rivulets of blood seeping out from along the cut. It had been pooling beneath her thigh, but was now flowing towards the drain. Somehow, despite this being the umpteenth time, seeing it go remained so deeply affecting. It was no coincidence that so many disparate cultures throughout human history had embraced voluntary bloodletting. It is an incredibly powerful symbolic act. For discarding this strange and crucial fluid is so easily construed as also expelling some other undesirable thing. Erin revered it for this effect too. Even though it's a very costly way of convincing oneself that a psychological disturbance has been shed. Because sometimes it's equally true that desperate straits brook no half measure.

For a little while longer she went on watching the bleeding and luxuriating in her insensibility.

But then she set about making a new incision.

And then another one.

In begrudging acknowledgement of her enervation, she decided she really should stop now.

Yet, then, she made another one.

And then a final smaller one.

Finally she summoned up the dregs of her self-control, forcing herself to throw the razor blade from the cubicle.

She shifted up onto her knees. Then, very slowly and unsteadily, she went about standing up. Not only were her joints stiff, but there was little strength left in her body to draw upon. Even once she was upright, she did not feel stable on her feet. She had to lean against the clammy cubicle wall to support herself. And she just stood there shivering, with her arms wrapped around herself for warmth. To look at her, one would suspect she'd go on standing there for quite a while. Her face was drained of color. And she wore a cadaver's rigidly blank expression, though without any of its peacefulness.

However, the sequence of steps Erin now had to follow, she had long since self-inculcated. Repetition had so deeply instilled them in her that they were unfailingly accessible, like her ability to recite the alphabet. This was necessary because she was so spacey that thinking straight, or at all really, would be very hard. Thankfully then, she could just cede control to the pre-programmed autopilot part of her mind. And it was this caretaker-function which was just now kicking in, bypassing her current impairment.

Grabbing the showerhead, she turned it on and swiped the forceful spray back-and-forth across the shower tray. Most of the blood had already drained away, but some patches were still coated with a sticky red film. She used the bottom of her heel to rub at these stubborn spots, which was effective. It didn't take long to rinse away all traces of the blood spilled there. Afterwards, she adjusted the temperature until it was warm and angled the water to wash her legs. With her fingernails, she picked at where the dried blood had caked onto her skin. This caused flakes, like starched crimson petals, to fall off and plummet down the drain. As soon as that too was done, she switched to drenching the cubicle walls to get any micro-splatter from when she stood up. To return to normal herself, she had to return everything else to its zero-state.

At last, she switched the shower off and stepped out. Feeling the soft fibres of the bathmat beneath her feet, she let out a long slow exhalation to recenter herself. Step one was done, at least. Just a few more to go. She pulled an out-of-sight bath towel from the back of the towel rack. This particular one was only for use in this situation. Its long history in this role was testified to by countless faded blood stains which macabrely discolored it all over. She went about drying herself with it. The cuts were still stinging rather badly, so she employed a very light touch when patting that area dry. Thankfully, clotting had already stemmed much of the residual bleeding, but she now held the towel there with steady pressure to help impede it further.

Shuffling over to her chest of drawers, she retrieved her medical gear. Although inclined to get straight to work, she could feel her lips were gummy and sticking together, so she tucked it under her arm and first passed by the fridge to alleviate her dry mouth with a couple gulps of apple juice straight from the carton. Then she finally laid the towel out upon the bed and sat down on it. With a flick of the wrist, she unrolled the self-care kit beside her. Everything she needed was slotted, in order of sequential use, into this long strip of leather. And she now wasted no time in dispassionately applying the proper aftercare treatment to her cuts. Her expertise here was very narrow, having been sourced from online video tutorials. But it got the job done. These were simple, minor wounds which didn't require very much being done. She was grateful for this. Especially because she knew what she was potentially capable of in the drunkenness of that mind-altering pain. She recalled how, once, she had almost made a very bad decision indeed whilst sat in that cubicle. She had toyed with the idea of trying to pry open one of the slits with her slippery fingers. There had just been this potent, inexplicable need to know what lay *inside* of herself. But, at the last moment, she stayed her hand. Somehow she already knew there were no answers in there. Just blood and tissue and hurt.

When all the cuts had been tended to, she double-checked each one's final dressed and bandaged state. And only when she was fully satisfied did she allow herself a sigh of relief. Now she unhurriedly returned the roll-up kit and dumped the towel atop the laundry basket's towering load. Although she tried to make a mental note that the towel should be washed on its own, she doubted it would stick. It also occurred to her that she had been meaning to buy a dry-erase board to jot down reminders of this sort. Ironically, she figured she was unlikely to recall that intention later on either. She next put her underwear and pyjama shorts back on, gingerly pulling them up over the tender sites. Then she tugged her t-shirt back down and smoothed it out over her stomach.

Equipped with a handful of kitchen towel, she went over to where the razor blade came to rest after its short flight. She crouched down, with difficulty, to pick it up. Upon rising, she was momentarily transfixed by how it glinted with a dull carmine luster as it caught the light. It was beautiful, but not in a way that ought to be admired. She recomposed herself and traced the trajectory it followed when thrown. There were a few tiny specks of blood that had dripped onto the hardwood floor as it flew. She wiped them up and threw the wad away.

She didn't dispose of the razor blade along with it, however. First, she set about thoroughly ruining its edge with a heavy-duty metal file kept for this purpose. And only when completely sure it was no longer fit for use did she consign it to the garbage. She *wanted* to believe that this was overkill. She *wanted* to believe that she'd never stoop to the humiliating indignity of hunting through the trashcan to retrieve a used one. Yet, as was eventually the sorry fate of all addicts, she knew herself too well. In the throes of some frenetic urgency of need, her capacity to stomach self-abasement was not to be underestimated.

The simple truth is that everyone has their limits, their breaking point. When nakedly weathering an assault upon one's self-control, it becomes a war of attrition. And the *craving* is a besieging army of shadows, as well-stocked as it is patient. Perhaps this attack or that attack might be rebuffed. But the conflict is asymmetrical: fortress walls cannot return fire on the ballistae and trebuchets. A long-game is being played. The odds, therefore, are increasingly not in one's favour. This must be remembered. So Erin thought it best to remove certain options from the equation altogether, performing damage control in advance.

Outside of her window, the sky was just starting to shift from its dark repose. Soon there would be light and there would be color. Life would resume. Making it to daybreak was probably, she mused apathetically, some kind of victory. But if that was so, she found it conspicuously easy to stifle any urge to celebrate. She grabbed a can of soda from the fridge and thirstily chugged almost all of it. Maybe that could be her unbelievably lame reward then: replenishing lost fluids.

She plodded over to the bed to retrieve her laptop and awaken it. It was time to check whether *A&F* had come online yet. She tried not to even let herself hope. Once upon a time, even a small personal blood sacrifice was a surefire way to curry divine favour. But those were the *old gods*, who had withered and perished alongside their uncivilised devotees. The universe now went unwatched, unhelmed. No more supernatural egos to stroke with propitiating gestures. There was only *luck*. A primordial force which had outlasted each and every pantheon. And it took no notice of how many gallons of bloodshed wet the dust. Preferential treatment could not be pled or wrest from it. This is why she shunned the folly that hope exerted any effect upon chance. The coin was, right now, spinning in the air. She could only discover which side up it landed.

Alabaster&Freckles - OFFLINE

Damn. It still really fucking stung to see.

She would have to go it alone for a while longer then. Her head hung low and she gnashed her teeth in frustration. Somewhere on the periphery of her mind's stage, a mysterious female figure was pirouetting gracefully through the dusky haze.

The after-effects of cutting would help her keep it together for a few hours, if that. Once that grace period elapsed, things were going to become very... difficult. She would be flung back into the wilderness, easy prey for all her unbearable emotions. They would be like snarling beasts circling closer and closer around a helpless babe. Still, there was nothing to be done about that. Catastrophizing was a pointless self-inflicted blow. No amount of fretting now would serve as a down-payment to lessen her future suffering. All she could do is accept that what would be, would be. Such was the anxiety-soothing mantra of the fatalist. Of course, it was one thing to recognize that truth, and quite another to be stoic enough for it to actually pacify your fears.

Regardless, now there was only the waiting. She would get to briefly linger in this temporary reprieve, which was something. Then... well, *A&F* would surely get online soon. And beyond that? She had to get back to sleep, eventually. That indeterminably distant point was, in a sense, all she really cared about. Every atom of her being yearned to be reunited with Tilly. And she couldn't help but imagine that Tilly felt equally stranded in the dreamworld. Picturing her lover distraughtly awaiting her return was unbearable. The distressing injustice of the whole thing stoked Erin's anger. It felt like noxious fumes were rising from the boiling rage in her belly and choking her.

She had to get back to that place. She had to. This was an animal imperative. Like *eat* or *drink* or *kill*.

But only slumber could re-open the portal. This meant that every breath she took would be in supplication, pleading with it to do so.

She mouthed the promise with slow, deliberate movements of her lips, "I *will* come back."

It was as solemn and as binding an oath as could ever be made.

Whatever it took, she would find a way to be with Tilly.

CHAPTER THREE

9:08 AM. SEPTEMBER 4TH.

(APPROX. FOUR HOURS LATER)

[09:08] Alabaster&Freckles: Okay... please listen to me, honey.

[09:09] Alabaster&Freckles: I know you won't like this, but please remember I'm saying it 'cause I wanna help you.

[09:11] Alabaster&Freckles: I'm worried that maybe something has been triggered in your mind. I can't say I understand exactly what or exactly why.

[09:11] Alabaster&Freckles: But it seems... not good. To say the very least.

[09:12] Alabaster&Freckles: Look, I think you should probably speak to someone. A professional, I mean. And ASAP, ideally.

[09:12] Alabaster&Freckles: You don't even have to leave your apartment, I looked it up and there are therapists who do sessions via videochat.

[09:13] Alabaster&Freckles: They're very nice, well-trained, sympathetic people. There'll be no pressure, no expectations, you'll just be talking, like *we* do.

[09:13] Alabaster&Freckles: And hopefully they'll be able to figure out what has or hasn't happened and help you fix it if necessary.

[09:13] Alabaster&Freckles: So, will you please consider doing that?

[09:14] PluckingPurgatory'sPetals: WHAT?!

[09:14] PluckingPurgatory'sPetals: 'Fix' my connection with Tilly?!

[09:15] PluckingPurgatory'sPetals: It is NOT a thing to be 'fixed'!

[09:15] PluckingPurgatory'sPetals: If you had experienced it, you would never think of saying something as awful as that.

[09:15] PluckingPurgatory'sPetals: I had nothing in my life. Nothing!!

[09:16] PluckingPurgatory'sPetals: Which is why I'm so lucky that I was given this strange gift!

[09:16] PluckingPurgatory'sPetals: And I definitely don't need some dipshit shrink telling me that what occurred didn't occur. I know what I saw and I know what I felt!

[09:17] PluckingPurgatory'sPetals: I get that you're alarmed by the suddenness of all this, and I know you're a good person. So I'll chalk up this insult to you misspeaking out of shock...

[09:17] PluckingPurgatory'sPetals: But *DO NOT* bring that up again.

CHAPTER FOUR

10:13 AM. SEPTEMBER 7TH.

(APPROX. THREE DAYS LATER)

The few days which followed were utterly hellacious.

Looking back, it was so painfully obvious what was going to happen. For there was an exact and terrible mathematics which had ensnared Erin. The worst possible outcome was now guaranteed; such was the pitiless dowry the cosmos bestowed upon her. To commemorate the advent of her great love. And to avenge the puncture in spacetime which had allowed it.

The thing was, she had even had a faint suspicion that something like this might happen. But it was too nebulous a paranoia to articulate as useful self-counsel. And, moreover, she was too fixated upon the chase to heed anything else. It consumed her. There was only longing, there was only pursuit. So that the more energetically she tried to refute her fear of failure, the more it unsurprisingly morphed into a self-fulfilling prophecy.

She often wondered whether that was all actually moot. Perhaps even perfect foreknowledge wouldn't have spared her the deepening of her torment. Yet she could have readied herself for it, or at least tried to. Instead, it got to blindside her with doubled effect.

The sentence imposed was simple: all of her yearning was to be turned against her. Her own body conspired to betray her mission. For her rabid desire to sleep as much as possible had caused a persistent, ironclad *insomnia*. This meant that each day she was lucky to steal even a few fitful hours of sleep in total. The significance of this development was not lost on her. She was already stuck within this apartment, but the confines of her imprisonment had just shrunk even smaller. She was now also trapped in her waking mind. This is a bondage which can never be forgotten, for the arising of every conscious thought serves as an inherent reminder of it.

Even when she did manage to doze off, it took desperately fighting against her own mind first. What exhausting combat this was! As the psychic toll of warring with oneself is immense. But, oh, what bliss awaited her in those occasional triumphs. Because now when she slept, she always dreamt. And in those dreams she resumed her life with Tilly. Indeed, only by dwelling on the memory of these infrequent doses of serene felicity could she endure the waking interim at all. Though even this meagre salve had a catch. Trying to mentally relive these reminiscences just emphasized their hollowness, and deepened her pining for the real thing. This blasted push-and-pull between agony and relief made the trial even more trying. Of course, all that wasn't even the half of it. For she was also suffering greatly from the effects of the sleep deprivation. The constant tiredness made her so numb and so despondent that she felt like she was walking underwater.

Passing the time had never been easy for her, but it now seemed preposterously hard. Yet... it was her object, and she gave it her all. She strove to feed every waking hour to the flames of distraction. But the resulting blaze did not burn evenly, and required continual tending to. This, in turn, coated her with the soot of immolated time. And incurring this residue rather defeated the point of the exercise. Still, she took what she could get. She would gladly resort to anything that could occupy her mind. Even sample the most crass wares of the infinite artisans of opiate triviality who ply their trade across the internet. She already had her favorite go-tos. Playlists, each a few hundred videos long, of stupid people doing or saying mildly amusing stupid things were pools of mind-numbing tar to swan dive into. Effective enough, if one doesn't mind the prospect of accidentally inhaling some specks of it too. But, even still, there were limitations. As her concentration was already impaired from her being dog-tired, it would soon wane. Then it would vanish. Even with frivolous entertainment which asked so little of it. And so, she would once again be left stranded in the barrenness of the *waiting*.

This meant that often she ended up just moping around, which made time crawl by even slower. Sometimes, she zoned out on the window-seat, barely registering what she saw. Sometimes, she crawled under the covers, scratching her arms red-raw as she blubbered. Sometimes, *A&F* was online, which allowed Erin to whine endlessly about her heartsore misery. Sometimes, she forced herself to go through the motions of eating. Sometimes, she sat staring at the freezer, visualizing what the ice blocks withheld and futilely wishing her numbness would turn to frenzy so she might pluck one out. All in all, it was a wretched non-existence. She had become a braindead clone of herself, stuck on a treadmill and just shambling forward in place. That was her whole world now: merely putting one foot in front of the other, over and over. And it was getting her nowhere. Just depleting her energy and fatiguing her muscles. Yet, she knew there was an even worse possibility. The belt could stop turning. She would keep walking, only to find there was nothing beneath her feet. This was not a tumble she would be getting up from. She would just be twitching on the floor, her legs pumping to no avail. And then she wouldn't even have the pointless trudge to preoccupy her.

Now, there was maybe one benefit of the overabundance of idleness she endured. It spurred her to reflect upon things. At least, when she felt up to it and her scattered thinking fleetingly cohered. This contemplation dwelt upon how to make sense of what was happening. It did first have to be granted that her baseline of normality wasn't zeroed particularly well even beforehand. And... she would readily admit that her analytic clarity was hampered by her lack of sleep. Nevertheless, she could still see that her predicament was bizarre and very much incredible. This is why she had to at least make some headway towards understanding it better. And so, to mentally dissect the matter, she had identified a trio of main possibilities.

First, it could be that she was going mad.

Second, it could be that she was *already* completely mad. This would be extremely upsetting, because insanity ought to be so much more cushy.

Third, it could be that she had stumbled onto something very real. A miraculous phenomenon which was merely unprecedented, but wholly genuine. Was it not the case that everything had to happen for the first time once? She could just really be the very first person to ever encounter this. Perhaps one day people would think her discovery as unremarkable and elementary as the first caveman to chance upon another's rotting corpse and uncomprehendingly behold that a skull had somehow lurked beneath the face all along.

Unsurprisingly enough, it was this third explanation which she found most believable.

Yes, she did want it to be true. But she also felt that a solid case could be independently made for it. It's fair to say that the material world is so intrinsically and indubitably 'real' because, in every way, it imposes itself so convincingly upon the mind. The seams of the illusion cannot, should they exist, be discerned. By the same token, the dreamworld she shared with Tilly could also be credited with 'realness'. While she was there - although the texture of the experience itself was very... different - it inspired the same decisive *feeling* of being true and meaningful. For, in either realm, she was simply an observer stranded in a turbid blizzard of thoughts and impressions and sensations. Fundamental blocks of data input which, even transplanted elsewhere, were equivalent.

And thus, to second-guess the conclusions drawn from one realm was to tacitly concede the untrustworthiness of the other. This was a powerful rhetorical anchor. Her earthly existence would have to be false in order to similarly indict her *un*earthly elysium. The neatness and self-reinforcing logic of this syllogism appealed to Erin very much. It seemed to her the only way to square things. Of course, taking refuge in this crucial solipsistic gap between the absolute certainty of 'I' and the imperfect certainty of 'that' had a separate incentive. It served to legitimize her obsession with Tilly. Still, that was just a... happy coincidence.

Unfortunately, as for what the dreamworld itself actually *was*, she had no answer. She had been ruminating upon it, but it was a slippier mystery altogether. In some ways, that place felt like a completely different dimension. Yet, it could also simply seem like a deeper layer of normal reality. She frequently vacillated between which it might be. It was not an unimportant distinction, after all. But she had reached a bottleneck in her ability to parse the complexities here. How was she to expound upon the dreamworld's nature, even to herself, when her scientific and philosophical knowledge was so sorely lacking? The disparity between all she had experienced and how much of it she could actually describe was galling.

She continually found herself grasping for all the formal terminology she needed to unpack the minutiae. Sometimes the five-dollar word really was the indispensable tool one needed.

However, maybe even this hankering was her thinking too small. If she really wanted to get to the heart of the matter, was even that weighty academic language insufficient? Given the character of what she had been exposed to, even more esoteric wisdom could be the needful lens. Probably, there was a secret lexicon to be found in the writings of some cadre of dream-delving mystics from bygone centuries. Probably, these ancient words of great power were the key. They would enable her to properly articulate the dreamworld's facets. But probably, these very scrolls were lost in the musty libraries of this sect's hidden, long-abandoned fortresses. And probably, their lineage of disciples had not reached to the modern day. The arcana they harbored perishing with them.

Erin found the sheer cumulative *probability* of that scenario overwhelming and depressing. But, in either case, the shortcut of scouring the insights of others was not available. It was up to her. She had only her own wits, her own limited understanding, to figure this out with. Still, this quest didn't have to seem so bleak. If her connection with the dreamworld truly was unprecedented, that made her like some sort of... pioneer. Placing this romanticizing overlay of adventure on the whole thing did have a heartening effect. The map of the earth had already been filled in. Yet here she was with a brand new virgin domain to explore. Though it had to be remembered that grave peril can lurk in the as-yet unknown. As heady as the rush of discovery might be, intrepidness needed to be balanced with caution. She couldn't get reckless just because the realm she ventured to was immaterial. This didn't mean it was free of consequences. If she was going to insist it was as meaningful as the physical world, she had to accept it could be as dangerous too.

For example, if she was the first-in spelunker of some vast, unmapped underground cave system, what would she do? Would she fling herself down random tunnels? Delving further and further into the bowels of the earth with no precautions? Or would she carefully clamber through that darkness, crushing and smearing glowworms along the walls to leave a fluorescent trail by which to retrace her steps in a hurry? Recast in this real world context, it was a no-brainer. Even if she had no idea what experiencing a cave-in without an escape route equated to in the dreamworld, it didn't matter. She did not want to find out first hand. Because she would surely lie buried in that rubble a very long time before anyone found her. Or maybe the kindly excavation wouldn't even come. And then that would be her *final* resting place, her accidental tomb.

At the present moment, Erin was on the bed, lying on her stomach. The laptop lay open right in front of her face. An internet browser laden with an obscene number of tabs occupied the screen. She had stumbled upon a promising rabbit hole online and for hours and hours had been plumbing it. Thankfully this had paid off, given what she found at its bottom. That endpoint had been research into how to find and use 'darknet markets'. It was at times slow-going and confusing, but she persisted.

She learned that they were aggressively anonymized online marketplaces. Buyers and sellers conducted their transactions with a near-total degree of privacy. Obviously, this empowered them to ignore certain trivial considerations, like... legality. The cost-of-entry here was just the meagre technical know-how needed to use the software which accessed their special websites. Then, upon making an account, you were in. Perusing the catalogue of items for sale, one found exactly what one expected: the majority of it was illegal recreational drugs. When it came to the most popular ones - marijuana, cocaine, MDMA, et cetera - one was positively spoiled for choice by all the varieties on offer. Yet, this was not all. No matter how rare, every mind-altering substance humanity has ever invented or cultivated was available. At least, if you knew where to look and didn't mind paying a premium.

Of course, as befitted virtual bazaars specialising in black-market goods, there was a cornucopia of other illicit things to purchase. This included counterfeit money, fake versions of high-value clothing and electronics, forged IDs, hacking services, pirated software, stolen passwords, and so on. However, there was also a much deeper, more disturbing level one could delve into. There was a category of darknet markets with heightened secretiveness. They were harder to find and a lot more exclusive about admitting new members. Some did not even have names. Some had URLs which changed very frequently. Some required a large deposit to be paid to allow you access. This added layer of paranoia was understandable. For these sites had an absolutely amoral, hands-off approach: being so unflinchingly permissive that *anything* goes. Predictably then, it was only truly sinister criminal merchants who called them home. This made them cesspools which were not fit viewing material for digital tourists faint of heart. On offer were untraceable guns, explosives, chemical weaponry schematics, assassinations, snuff films and all the types of pornography whose very existence blights the human race. Indeed, simply knowing about these umbral meeting places for the most hardened, despicable evildoers was an unpleasant burden. It made visiting even the tamest darknet markets a pulse-quickening endeavour at first.

In light of this, Erin carefully restricted her search to only the *very most* innocent darknet markets. The ones whose rules made them solely drug orientated. This at least allowed her the comforting fiction of picturing the sellers as essentially being goofy, mild-mannered pot dealers. From the handful of reputable sites she found, she chose the one with both a large userbase and security practices which reassuringly verged on overkill. It was loftily named the 'Psychonautica Mercatus', becoming known as PsyMer for short. Overall, it seemed as non-seedy as could reasonably be hoped for. It was also endearingly undergrad-pretentious: a verbose mission statement outlined the strain of radical libertarianism the site was meant to embody. There was a final quirk which set it apart too. The site was renowned for its many vendors who specialized in painfully obscure, chemically synthesized drugs. These were highly sought after by so-called psychonauts, who made a hobby out of using themselves as test-subjects for these strange compounds.

Erin had taken to keenly scouring the section of PsyMer dedicated to the sale of prescription drugs.

She wanted *sleeping pills*.

The more potent, the better.

Employing Google to do some very, very amateur pharmacological research, she had cobbled together a short-list of the medications known for inducing sleep even in clinical insomniacs. These were so powerful, doctors knew only to issue them as a last-resort. That's why they were her first choice. Next, she looked for domestic sellers who stocked any of them. There were thankfully quite a few who did. She vetted each one to whittle this group down even further. Maybe it was a weird line to draw in the sand, but she only wanted to buy from those who didn't sell harder drugs. If their listings included, say, black-tar heroin or crystal meth, that scared her away. It just gave her a really bad feeling. She wouldn't, if pressed, have been able to produce good reasons for this reaction. And she knew that hypocrisy and cognitive dissonance were probably at work in this high-horse mounting. But she also didn't much care. She figured she was surely entitled to veer away from sellers who made her uneasy, however silly the reasoning.

At last, having applied all her self-imposed criteria, she narrowed the field of candidates down to one: 'yourfavoritepillman!'. The username was a little cringeworthy, yes, but their profile page was set out very professionally. It was surreal to see a drug dealer with an FAQ section and a customer-support email address. What's more, they had evidently been active for quite some time, accruing a mountain of glowing five-star reviews from satisfied buyers. Their wares were mostly the sort of amphetamines prized by desperate students the world over. This seemed innocuous enough to her. Anything that enabled the retention and subsequent regurgitation of exam-answers was clearly a lucrative, reliable business to be in. She was just glad that they also troubled to sell a small assortment of other prescription drugs. This included the brand of sleeping pills which topped the wishlist she had drawn up. Even the asking price being twice their street value couldn't dampen her excitement at finding them for sale here.

She had no hesitation when placing the order. In her mind, as soon as this outcome had become her goal, it already felt like a done deed. So her only focus was on following the proper procedure. This meant paying via cryptocurrency, bought nigh-untraceably, and communicating via encrypted messages. She was painstakingly diligent about doing this part correctly. This purchase did not represent a very serious crime, but getting hauled down to a police station for anything at all could not be stomached by someone like her. Thankfully then, taking these precautions made the likelihood of that happening vanishingly slight. Besides, this method was far safer than trawling a sketchy neighbourhood for a street dealer and taking a chance on whatever mystery-pills they had on hand. And that dicey expedition wasn't exactly an option for her anyway.

The confirmation page popped up on screen.

It pleased her very much to see it. Her plan was officially in motion. The time-frame was established. She went over the details in her head. The order should be dispatched today, and she chose the expensive 'overnight delivery' option. So, if all went well, her package would arrive tomorrow. Of course, this would still be a gallingly long wait in her current condition. But at least she had a *solution* to look forward to now. The prospect of being able to regain control by self-medicating, and thereby sleep eighteen or twenty hours a day, was incredible. It seemed like a fantastic, unattainable superpower. Yet it was now within her grasp in a very real way. The whole thing made her want to squeal with glee.

As for how significantly this enthusiastic overuse might affect her body, she could... honestly say she wasn't exactly sure. And while this was indeed true, it was a fact which dangled by a contingent thread. Hers was a carefully manicured and preserved shortfall in understanding. For she had done only superficial research into a really very complex matter. It also didn't help that much of the information was trapped in the jargon of medical journals, whose pages were in turn trapped behind pay-walls. So she stuck to skimming the occasional news articles which poorly summarised some new finding or another. And from this worthless rockface she mined worthless ore. She subconsciously gravitated to the studies which suggested that heavy usage wasn't *necessarily* damaging. Many of these studies were, if examined closely, financed by shell companies whose actual owners one might find named on the pill boxes themselves. But, to put it bluntly, Erin was already many removes away from this close examination. So too, she would not have been too aggrieved at uncovering the deception. Quite the opposite, actually. That would have jeopardized her present dividend from it.

However, this was all rather moot anyway. It would scarcely have mattered if she *had* discovered some great harm was entailed. For what was more harmful than being kept from her lover? As was the requisite in every good, healthy relationship, she was willing to make sacrifices to be with Tilly. Her body was an expendable resource, after all. And 'organ failure' probably sounded so much scarier than it actually was...

[11:44] Alabaster&Freckles: So, it's definitely ordered then?

[11:44] Alabaster&Freckles: How do you feel now you've gone through with it?

Erin had debated back and forth about whether to tell *A&F* what she planned to buy. On the one hand, she couldn't abide any lectures or attempts to dissuade her. She was doing what she had to, and that was that. Yet, on the other hand, she didn't relish the possibility of having to deal with this next step alone. Luckily, a compromise had presented itself. She decided to present her scheme in as favourable a light as she could. Nothing so sordid as active deceit. Just a little vagueness here, a few strategic omissions there. No big deal. The same effect *could* have happened organically, if some inadvertently clumsy explanation had occurred in the right places. She was just making sure that... it did happen.

A&F's response had been very subdued.

Mostly they had just diplomatically inquired whether Erin had considered an alternative recourse. Something even just a little less severe, perhaps? And they had also asked Erin whether she appreciated the compounded risks of what she was doing. It was all said in a very polite, non-judgemental way. In fact, even worded rather like the stiffly formal questions from a doctor. Now that this particular plan was locked in, *A&F* had evidently switched to simply prodding Erin to expound upon her mindstate.

This cautious approach was understandable. Relations between *A&F* and Erin were still rather strained. Just yesterday, Erin had *yet again* taken offence at the troublesome phrasing of an otherwise innocuous comment *A&F* had ventured about Tilly. She saw red, giving into a volatile fit of pique. And, to put it mildly, she sent some strongly worded rejoinders to convey her displeasure. It had taken half an hour for her to calm down somewhat, and shed her belligerence. But it took even longer for clarity to re-descend. A period of taciturn sulking afterwards also passed before she even dimly sensed the extent of her overreaction. At which point she finally apologized profusely. And sought to try and give some explanation of her behavior. *A&F* registered both with magnanimity. Just as they had been nothing but patient and unruffled whilst absorbing Erin's irrational fury. Even when the barbs had that trademark pettiness of the moody teenager melodramatically lashing out at the world calling their puerile romance a puerile romance. Perhaps because there's usually a sort of forced, over-the-top character to them which makes them hard to take seriously. Now that Erin looked at her messages with regret, she was rather glad this absurdity had inadvertently defanged them.

She had given some thought to these flare-ups. Obviously, she wished that she wouldn't get so incensed so easily, especially given the recipient of her anger. But, in all honesty, it seemed unstoppable. She just felt so very, very protective of Tilly. There was a sort of hair-trigger paranoia she felt about it. As if some grand disaster might at any time befall Tilly, necessitating that Erin compensate by defending her from every conceivable slight. She knew that she needed to get a handle on this, but that was much easier said than done. Because, deep down, she felt a perverse pride about it. Wasn't she demonstrating the intensity of her love by flashing tooth and claw at anything which even remotely threatened or disparaged it? And that was truly what it was: an animalistic guardian-instinct. It would come upon her totally without warning. She would suddenly just feel like some bony, bedraggled mountain cat moving in front of their mate and snarling at perceived aggressors, even if they were just feckless hikers who had roamed too far from the trail.

Even after making amends with *A&F*, things were still a bit tense and a bit awkward. Anytime *A&F* had something to say about Tilly, they would put it as delicately as humanly possible. And they outrightly pussyfooted around any hard questions. This change had not been lost on Erin, and did make her feel a little guilty. Certainly, she wasn't happy that *A&F* might feel apprehensive about tripping some invisible emotional tripwire at any moment. Having to employ that self-censorship in real time must be kind of sucky. But... that being said, this new state of affairs was not without its benefit. She did secretly think it was probably for the best that, however it came about, *A&F* had learned how not to talk about Tilly.

However, Erin didn't know that *A&F*'s newfound timidity was not what it seemed. It actually wasn't akin to those frightened hikers nervously backing away from the mountain cat. Not at all. It was more like the park ranger who, spotting the animal is injured, approaches ever so slowly with their hands held up non-threateningly. All the while speaking soothingly to it, in the hope that it won't flee before it can be helped. The fact that Erin didn't realize this was a testament to *A&F*'s self-control and acting ability. It had been very difficult to pull off. At first, *A&F* had felt such a gut-wrenching powerlessness at witnessing someone, whose identity or location was unknowable, crossing deep into the ruinous no man's land of self-delusion. There was a crushing weight of responsibility in being the only lifeline, however gossamer and fragile, Erin had left. And *A&F* was terrified of being unequal to the task. After all, who the hell had experience dealing with this sort of dire crisis via an IM window? How was one to know what to do? But these concerns were irrelevant. No-one else even knew this poor woman was cooped up all alone as her long-mouldering sanity finally crumbled apart. Finding a way to save her from herself had fallen to *A&F*, and that was that. So, when the direct approach at imploring Erin to get help had failed, *A&F* resolved to figure out another way to achieve that end. Currently, that meant doing whatever was necessary to keep Erin under observation. And guilefully nudging her to describe the nature and symptoms of her derangement. This was very useful information to accumulate and note down. Hopefully it would provide some insight into how to make Erin do what she least wanted to do.

Totally oblivious to these machinations, Erin was just worried that her tantrums might be embittering *A&F*. It didn't seem like it, but perhaps the effect was being concealed? She really hoped not. She ideally wanted their rapport to return to normal, becoming more playful and lighthearted again. But most of all, she wanted to feel like *A&F* accepted her relationship with Tilly. To start over with a clean slate. She certainly wouldn't hold *A&F*'s initial... *confusion* against them. Of course it would be perplexing for someone else to grasp the otherworldly connection she had forged. Erin got that, she really did. In fact, this contributed to why she was trying to better understand it herself. So that she could, in turn, render it more comprehensible for *A&F*. She deeply felt the need to be able to do that.

At times, she fretted that *A&F* might even think she was lying about it all. As though she was merely putting on an elaborate performance. As though this was but some tawdry psychological experiment meant to gauge the reaction to such a strange, fabricated story. This possibility was maddening and insufferable. Erin just prayed that the earnestness of her maniacally voluble accounts of the dreamworld would suffice to convince *A&F* for now. And as she got better and better at articulating it all, that certainty should hopefully harden yet further. Because another person *had to know and believe* that she was going through this. It wasn't a matter of corroborative verification. She didn't require external confirmation of the things she already knew to be true. But, like any rapturously lovestruck fool, she wished for a friend to endlessly prattle about her joy to. Someone receptive to bonding over these talks, someone truly happy for her. She gleefully pictured the day when it would simply be second-nature for *A&F* to speak of Erin and Tilly like any other blossoming romantic relationship. God, that was going to be *so* awesome.

[11:46] PluckingPurgatory'sPetals: I'm super psyched it's done. It's a step which gets me closer to where I want to be.

[11:47] PluckingPurgatory'sPetals: But it *will* suck sitting around waiting for the dispatch notification. I mean, I'm going to wear out my refresh-page key, I'll be mashing it so much.

[11:48] PluckingPurgatory'sPetals: And THEN there'll be the sitting around waiting for the actual delivery itself.

[11:48] PluckingPurgatory'sPetals: It's kind of funny. I've always been supremely impatient for anything I order online to arrive. And that was for trivial little purchases.

[11:49] PluckingPurgatory'sPetals: Whereas, this is fucking *everything*.

[11:49] PluckingPurgatory'sPetals: This is the keys to the kingdom trudging to me via goddamn snail mail.

[11:49] PluckingPurgatory'sPetals: So, well, I think the wait is going to be pretty bad.

She kneaded her closed eyes with the heel of her palms.

They were starting to hurt, due to the long, unbroken stretch of screen time. Usually she would remedy this eyestrain by turning all the lights off and just staring into the restful darkness for a while. The problem was that this would make her drowsy, whose onset would annoyingly be to no avail. Such was the insomniac's paradox she suffered under. The degree of sleepiness she felt no longer had any relation to her ability to fall asleep. She was always yawning, always dopey from tiredness. But sleep simply came when it came.

Oftentimes, she would awake from dozing for an hour, with no recollection whatsoever of even having nodded off. Slumber was a skittish bird who alighted upon her out of the blue, and then quickly flew away at the slightest jostle. There was no good reason why this should be so. And searching for one just dispirited her. Furthermore, the ineffectual brevity of these naps only deepened her sense of being physically and mentally drained. This was a vexatious cycle, to say the least. Erin was downright indignant about being subjected to it. It was her newly-discovered conviction that falling asleep when she liked wasn't merely some pleasant luxury. It ought, in fact, to be respected by the behind-the-curtain designers of mankind as one of her most basic, inalienable rights. She wished she could step into the infinite coordinate, their control room, to mount her soapbox and berate them about this. To scream that their sick little joke was inimical to not just her wellbeing, but her dignity too. Having sleep meted out to her in pittance after pittance was humiliating. It felt like being some feeble beggar ignored by the passing crowds until, rarely, someone deigns to visit insultingly miniscule charity upon the wretch. The being-without was itself an affront, but so too was the receiving.

New-message chirps issued from the laptop. But Erin's palms still lay upon her eyelids. The dull ache behind her eyeballs was presently peaking. She had decided that she had better rest them for at least five minutes straight. Even that should do some good, given how badly they hurt. So she was unwilling to abandon it so soon.

"*Command*: play newest messages," she stated slowly and forcefully.

The laptop beeped loudly to signal it had registered this.

It then started reading them aloud. Once upon a time, this functionality had been neat, but its novelty was... rapidly fading. The artificial voice serving as *A&F*'s proxy hadn't actually changed, but the recent weirdness between the two of them made Erin hear it differently. To her ear, it had taken on more than a smidgen of imagined coldness. That was the insidious power of the robotically neutral tone which parroted the messages. It so easily took on whatever unnerving quality one's mind was predisposed to hear in it. An aural Rorschach's test, favouring negative interpretations. And Erin, longing for a renewed warmness from *A&F* themself, heard only that chilly indifference in every non-inflection. It was hard not to let this affect her, whether or not it was merely illusory.

"**Eleven fifty PM.** I see. Well, hopefully the wait will pass quicker than you think. **Eleven fifty-one PM.** Maybe doing some more research into this particular medication would help keep you occupied? **Eleven fifty-two PM.** On another note, I guess there's one thing I'm still not quite clear on. Do you see these sleeping pills as a short-term thing to kickstart your sleeping again and dissolve the insomnia? **Eleven fifty-two PM.** Or do you plan for it to be implemented as a long-term change? Something to be continually relied upon?"

Erin became pensive.

In truth, she had given almost no thought to the long-term. Because her need was so urgent, her goal *had* to be so immediate. Trying to speculate beyond that seemed ridiculous. Each day, she was just trying to find a way to survive until tomorrow. Speculation about the future was a fairytale she couldn't afford to indulge in. If she started overthinking what far-off ramifications may arise, it could psych her out of doing what needed to be done. All of those tiny, inchoate worries would become a swarm of flies buzzing around her which she would always be trying to bat away and evade. A catastrophic distraction. The difficulty of her quest was substantial enough already; self-created obstacles needed to be vigorously shunned. For there was only Tilly, and devising ways to be with her. What contributed to this end was good, what detracted from it was bad. That was a comforting moral binary to take refuge in. It made everything simple. It allowed her to be single-minded. This focus was going to be crucial if she were to succeed.

Still, there was no call to dismay *A&F* by spelling all this out too explicitly.

"*Command*: begin dictation."

She paused, going through what to say in her head.

"I'm... probably not... g-going to... be, like..."

Halting again for even longer this time, her shifting facial expression betrayed her inner turmoil as she deliberated.

"It's more... like... it's gonna be... dependent on... how... certain..."

At last she sighed and gave up.

It just always felt so dirty to be saying her dodges aloud. Of course the dictation thing didn't exactly transform this into a face-to-face conversation. But it sure made it feel a lot more like it than clacking away on a keyboard ever did. And saying something to someone directly just made it, and whatever equivocation it was laden with, feel all the more weighty. She was keen to preempt this guiltiness if she could.

"*Command*: erase all dictation."

She finally opened her weary eyes and started typing it out instead.

[11:58] PluckingPurgatory'sPetals: Sure, I'll maybe see what other information I can dig up when I get chance.

[11:59] PluckingPurgatory'sPetals: As for the timeframe thing, I haven't really definitely decided upon anything yet.

[12:02] PluckingPurgatory'sPetals: Don't wanna get ahead of myself, you know? First I've got to actually get them, and figure out the proper dosage and whatever. Can't really schedule my usage until I really understand their potency.

[12:03] PluckingPurgatory'sPetals: And, naturally, it would be great if they're just a catalyst which jolts me back into a normal, unassisted sleep pattern.

[12:04] PluckingPurgatory'sPetals: It's just that I can't really pin my hopes on that happening.

[12:04] PluckingPurgatory'sPetals: So I'll just see how things play out, and go from there.

She re-read what she had written.

Yes, that was all alright.

A lie was an ugly thing.

But this, a shaky murmur in her mind asserted, was merely a salad of half-truths.

CHAPTER FIVE

11:20 AM. SEPTEMBER 8TH.

(APPROX. TWENTY-THREE HOURS LATER)

CLANG, CLANG.

Erin started, and then froze.

That harsh sound had caught her completely off guard.

Yet, even with the cogwheels of her mind also momentarily held immobile in shock, she knew exactly what that clamorous double-clang meant.

Without unfreezing the rest of her alerted pose, she solely swiveled her head around to look over at the noise's source. There she spied a small padded envelope lying at the foot of her door. She hadn't expected it to arrive in the morning. The mail carrier usually didn't make their rounds of the apartment building until well after noon. But Erin wasn't exactly complaining. Today of all days, this was a very welcome anomaly indeed.

With an effort, she made herself relax her stiffened limbs and finally exhale her bated breath. And then she pulled her hand free from where it was still buried down the front of her underwear. The video playing on her laptop caught her eye again, and she clumsily bashed the spacebar to pause it. Then she scooted awkwardly across to the edge of the bed and, dangling her legs over, pulled her sweatpants back up from around her knees. She paused and looked back over her shoulder at the door. Her mouth, now slack-jawed, was slightly open. Her eyes were goggling. The weight of anticipation was upon her, and it was difficult to burst through its hold. For there's a peculiar quality to being ambushed by the moment one has been obsessively, impatiently awaiting. One can experience a counterintuitive hesitancy. But, when broken down, it did make a kind of sense. How could one not be even a little trepidatious when wading unprepared towards such an overwhelming micro-second of emotion? And she felt daunted in precisely this way.

But she powered through it and forced herself to stand up. Shoving her feet into her slippers, she shuffled over to the door. She couldn't help but glare at the letterbox as she approached. Its heavy, stiff metal flap clanged when pushed open and then, to achieve maximum obnoxiousness, clanged again as it fell closed. This one-two punch to your eardrums was shockingly loud. And would rudely interrupt whatever you happened to be doing at the time. Thankfully she hardly ever received any mail. Still, if she wasn't a renter, she would have undoubtedly tore it out and replaced it with a quieter version. Having a several hour window each day where, even just subconsciously, she was aware she *might* abruptly be made to jump out of her skin was... unideal. It wasn't particularly conducive to being fully at ease, especially with someone already subject to a superabundance of stressors.

Crouching down, she picked up the plump, unremarkable envelope and just marveled at it for an instant. Her nostrils were flaring wide as she pulled in nervously excited deep breaths through her nose. So too she could feel the goosebumps popping up all over her arms and legs. As she turned it over and read the printed label, there was a certain surrealness to it. Although she had obviously known this would be the case, it was nonetheless disquieting to see her actual name there.

Yet those-in-the-know did emphatically advise you to use your real information. If the package was intercepted before it reached you, having some made-up recipient on it was not the boon it seemed. For that would slot neatly into the later prosecutorial narrative that you predictably addressed it to a fabricated identity as a precaution. Oppositely, using your real name allowed for two distinct strands of plausible deniability. Firstly, you could employ the age-old 'who would be stupid enough to do that?' defense. It may be facile, but juries do not have a reputation as sticklers for nuanced logic. Anything catchy that a lawyer can sloganize *ad nauseum* is a mind-virus more valuable than hard evidence. Secondly, you could suggest that some devious (and unknown) enemy must have sent it hoping that its seizure would embroil you in legal trouble. Thus, all you had to do was pick one, or some hybrid of both, and stick to your story. Like so much of the instruction found in this sphere, she thought this gameplan was an amusing blend of paranoia and ingenuity. That fratboys hoping to order a little weed also troubled themselves to opine upon the intersection between game theory and courtroom chicanery was absurd in the best possible way. What's more, if you really wanted to be *rigorous* in your safeguards, you were supposed to write RETURN TO SENDER on the envelope and leave it unopened a day or two. Just to solidify your excuses in case anyone with a badge and a warrant should come knocking with a battering ram. Alas, Erin knew she didn't have even a fraction of the self-restraint required to do that.

She eagerly tried to rip open the envelope. First with her hands, then with her teeth. But this was made almost impossible by the thick bubble wrap which lined the interior. Pushing down a pang of frustration, she grabbed the crappy kitchen scissors to snip the end off. An effervescent exhilaration was bubbling through her veins and making her giddy. She reached in and pulled out the contents. Nestled between a few folded sheets of card was a heat-sealed plastic pouch. It was transparent, so she could already see it held twenty nondescript white pills. They were oval-shaped and quite large. She just stared at them in amazement and fingered each one through the plastic.

They were actually fucking here.

She was literally holding them, in her hands, *right now*.

That was the character of her thoughts in this moment. Even though she was looking directly at the sleeping pills, the sheer farfetchedness of this outcome taxed her power of belief such that she also had to *tell* herself they were really there. It felt silly to do, but the necessity was undeniable. Only via this conjunction of testimony could her brain be compelled to lower its guard and totally accept the truth of the thing.

Ever since she committed to making the purchase, she was not without misgivings which threatened to sour her high hopes. She had this tiny nagging doubt rattling around like a can being kicked down the alleyways of her mind. It insisted that this was just a foolish, futile gesture of desperation on her part. It insisted that this was the stupidest feat of self-incrimination ever. Ordering something illegal online and having it sent, in plain sight, to where you actually live did have an... almost farcical quality. It seemed like something which would earn a malicious belly-laugh from both the cops as they handcuffed you and the judge as he sentenced you.

Yet, here she was, *not*-arrested, with the package in hand. It had worked. She really had successfully paid some internet stranger to mail her drugs and gotten away with it scot-free.

"Gosh, what a time to be alive," she croaked, smiling weakly at her own joke.

This was the first deep, unequivocal happiness she'd enjoyed in the waking world for such a long time. If only she could bottle this feeling to restoratively siphon from during her usual dispiritedness. Still, what did it matter? That was all behind her now. She had her ticket to get to the dreamworld. She could be with Tilly whenever she wanted. All that was left to do was planning out how to divide each block of twenty-four hours to allow for maximum sleep time. She wondered what limitations upon daily sleep her body, or perhaps her mind, would try to impose upon her. Furthermore, were these *really* hard limits? Or could they be surpassed with dogged perseverance and excessive pharmaceutical aid? Rules were, it was said, meant to be broken.

Ultimately, she would have to discover for herself what her biology truly would and would not allow. And also discover how to train it to continually give unto her the very most it possibly could. This would all come down to trial-and-error experimentation with different doses and how soon she could re-medicate after waking up. Even in this hypothetical stage, she found herself preemptively resenting that she would be forced to allocate a portion of time to nourishing and servicing her body each day. What an inconvenience the fleshy vessel anchoring her to this lesser world was going to be. It was so irksome to consider the extent of its crude, unignorable 'needs': eating, drinking, minimal exercise, bathing, excreting waste, and so on. They were like a raucous choir of hatchlings crammed into the same filthy nest-cavity, *cheep cheep cheeping* incessantly. Always, always mindlessly demanding attention from the ever-wearied mother bird. And Erin didn't even have the benefit of that wellspring of patience which nature imbues alongside the maternal instinct. She felt only annoyance at her obligations. Hopefully she could figure out how to compress these distasteful chores into a short period of daily upkeep.

She went about cutting the envelope and the packaging into shreds to disfigure any evidence, and then threw it all away. As an afterthought, she even poured, of all things, some orange juice onto it for good measure, hoping to make it soggy and fingerprint-free. Next she pulled open the packet and fished out a single pill. Gently tossing it up and down upon her palm, she watched it rise and fall and jiggle and spin. There was, of course, a degree of inherent danger to ingesting something whose make-up and effect were testified to only by an anonymous drug-dealer. And though the threat of bad reviews being submitted *was* an incentive not to sell a laced or phony product, even this had its limitations. For there is, conspicuously enough, no wi-fi in the grave. So, no doubt, all this would have given the average person pause, making them nervously dawdle. But it did not deter Erin from wanting to try them right away regardless. To put it off would just be a pointless charade of caution. Unless the opportunity for a private lab test was likely to present itself sometime soon, the risk was going to remain the same. Besides which, it *had* to be now anyway. She had no more power to hold off on her next reunion with Tilly than to delay her next heartbeat. If she breathed, if she could act, she would be with Tilly or be finding a way to get back to her. Such was the debt of love.

Based on their potency and her virgin tolerance level, she actually only needed half a pill. So she carefully snapped it into two pieces, using its score line. One of the halves went back into the packet. The other she swallowed with a big glug of water from the kitchen tap. Now, if what she had read was correct, she had about fifteen to twenty minutes before the drug's impact would hit her full force. She was glad of this brief time-delay. It meant she could finish masturbating. And the resulting overlap may even prove rather beneficial. Certainly, it depended upon how the biological die landed after being thrown, but she did often find herself in a soporific haze afterwards. That could surely only add to the pill's efficacy. She took off her sweatpants and lobbed them onto the window-seat. Then she lay back down on the bed in the same position as before.

After the first dream, she actually held off from touching herself for a little while. She had fretted that it would henceforth verge upon disrespecting Tilly somehow. The act suddenly seemed burdened with some element of... unfaithfulness. However, after much consideration, she had made her peace with it. This was partly because Erin decided that Tilly's boundless compassion wouldn't begrudge her merely trying to make the stretches of absence pass faster and more bearably. It was also partly because, now more than ever, she couldn't afford to exclude this crucial crutch from her limited toolbox of coping mechanisms anyway. Needless to say, this latter realization had preceded, and precipitated, the former. Necessity is a powerful stimulant to one's ability to reverse-engineer a justification for something.

There was just one rule which had to be obeyed: she didn't masturbate thinking about Tilly. Even the prospect of doing so felt unalterably wrong. To do something so vulgar while Tilly was enshrined on the pedestal of her mind's eye would be akin to the gravest sacrilege.

She tugged the laptop back by her side and roused it from its blank-screen dormancy. The paused video reappeared, showing an unflattering freeze-frame of some orgiastic jumble of glistening, writhing bodies and theatrically contorted faces. This one was from the collection of go-to videos she had amassed. To put it mildly, these were far from the most artful examples of erotica ever made. But, well-made or not, they were still reliably effective catalysts for her. They hit the spot when she simply wanted a quick, untaxing session: it was just cheap fast-food pornography. Each one featured some performer or fetish or position, or whatever, which could get her off without any difficulty. That was all that mattered because that was all she needed from them. And even though she had watched these cherry-picked videos a few dozen times a piece, unwittingly memorizing them beat for beat, they still worked just fine. The mind wasn't very finicky about the novelty of stimuli. It was hardwired to respond accordingly to the same favoured imagery whether it was the fifth time or the fiftieth. Feed the right input into the machine and it will react how you want it to. Always, always, forever, and always.

After she hit play on the video, which was muted out of preference, the motionless figures sprang into life and resumed their mutual flailing and thrusting. She just lay there watching the overacted fucking for a few minutes. Only the incredibly faint sound of her own breaths fended off an absolute silence. Her eyes followed the locus of the action as it moved about on-screen. She pinched each of her nipples in turn, to see if they were hard yet. Then she jammed her hand beneath the waistband of her underwear, sliding it down until it found its wonted resting place. As usual, this was to be a utilitarian affair, without the superfluous self-indulgence of foreplay. The diabetic, readied syringe in hand, doesn't tarry; they just inject the needful insulin.

Her fingertips rubbed hard, tight, fast circles in a familiar and unerring motion. This perfected technique wouldn't take long and it wouldn't fail. She was gawking intently at the screen, laser-focus fixated on the specific little details she liked most. Her breathing soon grew more rapid. And her hips started subtly bucking up and down, trying to push herself even harder against her fingers. Quiet moaning now sporadically flowed through her barely parted lips. She could feel that she was already getting close. Knowing that the video was approaching a certain climactic moment, she upped her rhythm to sync up her finish with it. Her breathing entered its final stage, with each inhalation sharply drawn and each exhalation given fluttery release. She dug her heels into the mattress to counteract the quivering of her legs.

She sensed herself tip over the edge, earlier than intended. But there was no going back now. Her toes were involuntarily curling and uncurling. The circular momentum of her fingers kicked into hyper-overdrive, as she began to slightly convulse all over. She came *hard*. Crackling high-voltage electricity surged from her fingertips into her body. It coagulated into dense ball-lightning at the point of impact, then explosively streaked out long pulsating thunderbolts in every direction. She was battling to keep her eyes partially open to continue watching. But a spray of brilliant sparks danced across her vision, blurring it anyway. She arched her back and grabbed at the quilt with her free hand, clutching at the material and pulling it upward. Her gritted teeth muffled the deep groans of pleasure as they forced their way through.

As soon as the thunderstorm had come, and raged, the thunderstorm had subsided, and passed. Its ravaging had not *at all* been unkind. She slowed her fingers to a halt and let her body fall limp. Her breathing gradually steadied, returning back to normal. Then she just lay still, to better luxuriate in the static-electricity afterglow of the orgasm.

God, that was great. What a fucking great twenty seconds of ecstasy.

But it was over now.

Once even the faintest residue of the endorphin-rush faded away, it was a stark transition. She reemerged into the drabness and harshness of real life as though plunging into frigid waters. The switch was as galling as it was unpleasant. Presently, several tiny rays of daylight were penetrating the blind where its slats were cracked or bent. One of these extended across the room towards her, passing over her head. When she peered up through it, a hidden world of swirling dustmotes was now illuminated and exposed to view along it. So too, the spot where the ray landed, which was a section of the headboard, snatched one's attention. She saw how thickly its spotlighted surface was coated with dust, a sprinkling of hair and unidentifiable fluff caught throughout. Try as she might, she couldn't yank her gaze away from this repellant sight. It held her transfixed, determined to ruin the moment. She could only glare angrily, resenting it for its unsightliness. Even without being a clean-freak, certain things were just universally gross.

Keen to be free of this aggravation, she resolved to just put it behind her. She made herself pull in a very long, slow, controlled breath. Then she lazily freed her hand and wiped her slick fingers on the sheet. However, as she yawned and stretched her arms up in the air, they passed through the sunbeam. And daylight is no less obnoxious a revealer when it comes to flesh. All the things she hated about her arms were highlighted to her. The boniness of her forearms, how her skin hung a little loose at her straightened elbows, the knobbly part at the back of her wrists, and so on. She usually needed little in the way of enticement to get hung up on her perceived bodily flaws, and this was a powerful invitation indeed.

But with a concerted mental effort, she emphatically declined. And brought her arms back down by her sides, skirting the light this time.

"Good fucking try," she murmured with a smile of defiance, addressing the universe itself.

Quite inadvertently, she let out an earnest laugh. She was *so* happy to spite its attempt to sully something so enjoyable, so nice, by inflicting an abrupt dissatisfaction afterwards. It simply would not be allowed to derail things in this way.

And it was, after all, easy enough to just let this nonsense roll off her, given the circumstances. She was too greatly buoyed by having gotten exactly what she wanted. A prize which could not be spoiled or robbed by petty annoyances. For it was now irretrievably swimming through her bloodstream. In fact, she found she could acutely discern a very heavy sleepiness tugging at her. She welcomed it with eagerness and fondness, because she knew what awaited her in it.

She quickly closed the video. It now seemed so bizarre and distasteful that it was laughably intolerable to behold. Exercising care, she lowered the laptop onto the floor. Then she scrambled under the quilt and hugged it around her like a cocoon, relishing its warmth and its softness. During another big yawn and big stretch, she elongated her body with feline relish. And, perfectly content, she rolled over onto her side. Her hand slipped underneath the pillow to cradle her head.

A few minutes elapsed.

Once they did, she was already fast asleep.

She woke up very gradually.

Her consciousness reassembled itself piece-by-piece and sluggishly began functioning once more. The first few attempts at opening her eyes made her head spin. And then making herself slowly sit up in bed proved arduous because her body felt so stiff. As she sat there, back against the headboard, she got a taste of just how groggy she really was. It was reminiscent of the opening notes of a hangover. Squinting, she looked around. But her vision was still incredibly fuzzy. In the soupy mix of blurs she saw, the luminous numerals on her alarm clock stood out like blazing beacons for her to lock onto.

02:31 AM

Woah, that meant...?

It was embarrassingly hard to do the simple calculation in her head right now, but she persisted until a rough answer emerged. Fourteen hours? Fourteen hours?! How had she slept for that long?! It seemed to zip by instantly. As though she had merely blinked and, rocketing time forward, reappeared here. Wow, the medication must have really knocked her out. Maybe that was why she somehow still didn't exactly feel rested. That was probably just the trade-off one had to make for the potency. And this brand certainly lived up to its billing if half a pill could...

Wait...

"No... I didn't...? How could it have...? No! No! It was... No, no, no, no, no," she whispered frantically to herself.

She tugged hard at her hair with both hands and bit her lip painfully hard. Her eyes were wide now. But her gaze had a certain shellshocked vacantness to it, as the juggernaut realization crashed full-force into her.

She had not dreamt.

Not at all.

She had been as fast-asleep as one could be, no doubt about it, but in a mere dreamless repose. It was a bait-and-switch which had trapped her in that useless unconsciousness otherwise acquired from a knock-out blow. Just hours and hours of the most unremittingly smothering black the mind could mimic. Just a bleak preview of the pristine state of non-existence which only the dead truly know.

With savage reproach, she berated herself for being such a damn fool. What had she been thinking? How could she have been so blind? She got so swept up in the exhilaration of executing the plan that she never considered, let alone readied herself for, the prospect of failure. At the time, it just didn't even seem feasible that she might be thwarted. Yet, now here she was, adrift in that 'impossible' future. Her scheme simply hadn't worked. There had been no dreamworld and no Tilly. The pills had indeed been powerful enough to break the tyrannical stranglehold of her insomnia, but the cure was no better than the disease. For that unnaturally heavy type of sleep which was imposed turned out to be, perforce, inhospitable to dreaming.

It was over.

It had to be over.

She couldn't take it.

This was too much to bear.

She rushed from the bed, but her benumbed, unsteady legs gave out almost instantly. She dropped first to her knees. Then, instinctually trying to jump back to her feet before she had even registered what the problem was, she tumbled face forward. Luckily she brought her hands up at the last second to absorb much of the impact, and awkwardly rolled with the fall. But, now lying there on her back, she certainly didn't feel lucky. She just grunted in annoyance. And, sitting up, she methodically bashed her thighs and calves with her fists. Her intention was to try and beat some feeling back into them. It succeeded just enough for her to be able to stand back up. Testing the stability of her legs for a moment, she found them just responsive enough to proceed. So she quickly stumbled, with a drunkard's wobbling gait, over to the kitchenette countertop. There lay the packet of sleeping pills. She snatched them up and held them to the dim lamplight. There were nineteen and a half left, which she counted, and then recounted to stall momentarily. She was no expert in toxicology, but that would surely amount to a lethal dose.

Once upon a time, she had actually toyed with the idea of buying a cheap pistol for home defense. Despite having never shot a gun before, and disliking guns, and rather distrusting those who did. It was just that when this apartment became her sanctum, the possibility of a break-in became especially anxiety-inducing. Not least because, having no surefire way to repel a burglar, she would be easy prey for the invasion. A knife or a bat would be of little help given her slight frame. But a firearm was the force multiplier *par excellence*. Still, after meditating upon all of the implications, she became too afraid to own one. She simply didn't trust herself with the capability to so easily and painlessly kill herself in an instant. Something like that, for someone like her, was just too great a temptation to have close at hand. To always be just a trigger-pull away from total freedom would be a ticking time-bomb. It would ensure that her very next *really* bad day would also be her last.

However, she now had in her possession a simple, infallible way to die anyway. All that she need do was swallow them all and let the chemical reactions do their job. She stared long and hard at the stark truth of that *choice* really existing. And, undaunted, she felt strongly that she could do it. Yet, she struggled to visualize herself performing the action and it being a good thing. Her mind, fearful and petulant, was rebelling against the command to embrace its own destruction. A panic-switch had been hit, dropping emergency shutters over her imagination's portholes. She was not going to be allowed to picture her suicide in a positive light to bolster her resolve. Not now her personal zero-hour was fast approaching. If she couldn't bring herself to do it without leaning on that mental propaganda film prettifying her own death, she couldn't do it. After all, it wasn't for rationality to soberly rubberstamp this decision. She would have to want it badly enough to accept that its motivation originated in a swell of high emotion and unthinking impulsiveness. Levying that cost upon her was the best her mind could do in the way of self-preservation.

Denied any refuge in fantasy, Erin did start to fret about the genuine details of the *how*. The key gaps in her understanding here were troubling. She didn't know, exactly, how dying from a massive overdose of sleeping pills actually played out. This made the tiny voice of curiosity pondering aloud in her thoughtstream nigh-irrepressible. Would she really just drift off and, as it were, sleep peacefully through her death? Or was that just romanticizing nonsense the left-behind employed to retcon the suffering of their loved ones? Would she, instead, be subjected to a zoetrope of all the profoundly disturbing clichés about the death-agony of chemically assisted suicide? The feverish meltdown of her cognitive faculties. And the cascading loss of organ function as her insides begin to quick-rot. And the crippling, burning pain which encircles every sinew and every neuron round and round, squeezing maximum misery from them. And the seizures which shake her to her bones. And the blood-speckled frothing at the mouth. And the paroxysms of delirious terror, as invisible monsters seem to descend upon her from all angles. And, as the concluding indignity, an infantile regression to calling out into the unpeopled emptiness for *mother*. Then, as but a half-conscious wreck, the last few moments spent in distinct awareness that her heart has just stopped. Frozen upon her lips, a final impotent wish to undo what she had done.

These scraps of speculation and half-knowledge and projected fears she melded together to form a dread-inspiring whole. If that vision bore even a slight resemblance to the reality, it did not strike her as a particularly... palatable way to go. Yet, this encroachment of reason into her internal self-dialogue was short-lived. For it was being shouted down by a much more forceful source of counsel. This contrarian voice, this infiltrated salesman for abaddon, had a very different message. It insisted that dying was dying and death was death. Underneath this sophistry lay a seductively simple calculus: no finite degree of unpleasantness could possibly outweigh the reward of becalming her soul upon the placid sea of eternity. And alongside this persuasion, the voice knew to employ some aggressive browbeating too. Don't be a coward, *it told her*. You are finally enraged and distraught enough to go through with this, *it told her*. This is the perfect opportunity, *it told her*. Don't you dare waste this fucking chance, *it screamed at her*.

As if a puppeteer was jerking her strings, Erin now saw herself move but did not feel wholly in control of her actions. She began to feel more like an observer than a participant. This sense of distance was incredibly unnerving, but also helpful. It was like she merely had to go along with what was happening. She emptied all of the pills out into her palm, and then carelessly filled a glass with water until it was brimming. It spilled all over her wrist and arm as she brought it away from the sink. She didn't even seem to register the sensation. She just stood there stiffly raising each hand, in turn, up towards her face and then back down again. This was to practice the motions of dumping the pills in her mouth and then gulping from the glass. She wanted to be able to do it fast. She *had* to be able to do it fast.

Her psyche was in an incredibly fragile state. It was a mighty engine in overdrive, pistons pumping and belts whirring, being precariously held together by duct-tape and fleeting luck. And as best she could, she was trying to ignore the equally intense tumult her body was experiencing. Yet this was becoming no easier as her symptoms rapidly intensified. Adrenaline was coursing through her veins with woozying effect. She was sweating all over and her heart was pounding so hard it seemed like it might explode. The pressure exerting itself upon both sides of her temple felt like a vice tightening on her skull. She was stricken with that distinct queasiness which precedes vomiting. Severe tunnel vision narrowed her sight, such that all she could see were her hands.

This was it.

She was really going to kill herself.

There was a surrealness which hung over the proposition: it felt like she was about to do the impossible. Of course, she had been, unsurprisingly enough, gripped by suicidal ideation in the past. Yet it seemed such tortuous fantasizing back then precisely because she suspected it to be a longing after something unattainable. Those who are starving long for food they cannot procure, and feel the hungrier for it. So too the wretched crave the relief of death, which their timid hands refuse to furnish, and only feel the more miserable for it. It was now just bewildering to recall those past occasions, and how badly she had *thought* she wanted to end it all. Undoubtedly she had had very real grievances against life then, but... actually working up the nerve to relinquish it? In truth, she had only played at that. Put it on like a costume, to see how it felt. And, sure, she was sometimes able to forget that she but wore the garb of the death-aspirant, and relish in the bleak pleasure of her assumed credentials. Nonetheless, with better insight, she could only marvel at the childish falsity of these past moments. And quake in awe at the unmistakable authenticity of what presently animated her. Good god, she was so different now. Everything was so different now.

Another startling dose of newfound clarity became available to her too. She now grasped that an instinct already quietly percolating inside of her was triggered by her first contact with Tilly. She had been thirsting for the answers to questions she did not know. And this aimless yearning manifested itself as a desperate need for... pursuit. Something, anything, to lose herself in wanting. All that time, she had been jogging on the spot, awaiting a worthy target to dart after. Then, someone she could love, someone who might give meaning back to her life, had appeared. And the chase was on. She had set off in a blind sprint, throwing herself at breakneck speed towards some solution obscured in a faraway fog. When she finally barged through it, however, she discovered that only a slick precipice lay beyond. Alas, momentum is a difficult wealth to divest oneself of when it becomes burdensome. So she skidded off the edge and plunged headfirst into the abyss below. That's where she was now: tumbling end over end in an uncontrolled free-fall, about to reach terminal velocity. The ground was fast approaching. It was seconds to impact.

She need only carry out this one last step. So why was she hesitating? Why couldn't she embrace this imminent merciful demise? What would she really be throwing away? The only thing which redeemed her squalid, abject existence was Tilly. And wasn't Tilly mostly kept from her anyway? Wasn't she held hostage in some orbiting domain Erin could scarcely reach? There was surely some callow optimist who would tell her that no matter how bad things seemed now, they *would* get better. She would like very much to throttle that person. Merely to communicate just how emphatically she disagreed. Indeed, that patronising bromide made her blood boil. Because the hard-earned truth was: *things did not get fucking better*. They just morphed into a different shade of bad and tricked you, a pattern-seeking creature prone to conflate change with constructive progress, into thinking otherwise. Then, over time, you simply acclimatized to the new headaches, the new hardships, the new sadnesses.

In the starkest contrast imaginable, death approached with an outstretched hand and a far more enticing offer.

It would take away the bad. In its entirety. Forever.

The catch being that it actually intended to rob you of everything, good and bad alike. That was it. Take it or leave it. For death is not a businessman willing to negotiate; death is a king issuing an ultimatum. But at least the terms of the deal were fair, at least they were laid out honestly. And what difference did it make anyway? However long one manages to spurn the moment's arrival, all must bow before death eventually. The outcome of life *is* dying. The culmination of all that we do is our departure. Therefore, there's really only one decision which matters. Do you want to cause it, or simply let it happen to you? After all, clawing back some final semblance of volition is not without value. And that's all suicide is. Just choosing when and how to bend the knee before the throne of the destroyer, in order to knowingly assent to its bargain.

Although... if the manner of one's death is the coda to the story of one's life, could she really stomach it being *this*? It would come to retroactively colour and define all that she had done, all that she had been. What an awful taint to splash across all of that. Because just look at what she was about to set in motion. On a practical level, once she was dead there would be so much foulness, so much disgrace. How long would it take for her body, in its vile posthumous state of decay, to be discovered? Days? Weeks? For people like her, who had madly sequestered themselves in their homes, it always seemed to come down to the *stench* eventually alerting the neighbours. Yes, their passing wasn't noticed because they were missed. It was merely the alarm bells of disgust which signaled that lifeless flesh lay somewhere nearby. In other words: once you became rotting meat, you became a nuisance. For the putrid stink of her mid-decomposition corpse wafting out underneath the front door and polluting the hallway would be as unbearable as it was unmistakable. A profound physical and mental nausea washed over her as she imagined this smell filling her nostrils.

Additionally, what would they do with her body? Bury it? Cremate it? Would there even be a service? It would be a waste of time if they did have one: who would come? Maybe some pious crones who undertook to mourn the unmourned, if she were lucky. But more likely it would just be an array of empty folding chairs presided over by a clergyman muttering through terse, general-purpose obsequies. That would be her send-off. That would be all which marked her passing before she was promptly lowered into a lonely grave. As just another fractional percentile added to a cautionary statistic. Then the shovellers would start their work, trying to hide her shame with mounds of dirt. And, finally, everything gets packed up and moved over to where the next perfunctory state-ordained burial is to occur that day. It was an appalling image. To be put in the ground, unloved and unremembered. Without any funerary pomp, without any teary onlookers. No better than some sorry carcass on a conveyor belt getting dumped into a ditch. So endeth the sad tale of Erin.

And... of course... there was Tilly to think about.

Unless an afterlife existed, which she doubted, and it encompassed both terrestrial and dreamworld lifeforms, which seemed less than even doubtful, she would be permanently separated from Tilly. Now, Erin would also be dead, sparing her the pain of that unthinkable loss. Yet what would happen to Tilly? What unremitting sorrow would Erin inflict by shackling Tilly to their murdered love. How could she do that to someone she claimed to care for so much? For her to go through with that abandonment, on the basis of a selfish whim, would be the ultimate betrayal. A truly hateful act, wicked beyond measure.

All these various reflections had monopolised her thoughts. Naturally, some were more compelling than others, but they all possessed a certain persuasive heft. The problem was that she had been weighing them against one another for... too long. And it was now a moot point. Having been so caught up in mulling over implications and vacillating between alternatives, she had ended up letting the moment pass. She was no longer sufficiently deranged by the onslaught of harrowing emotion. That crazed drive to do it, to *just fucking do it*, had vanished. Distracted by the grim promise of the horizon, the landscape had radically shifted beneath her feet without her even realizing. She tentatively probed inside her own mind, and sensed the absoluteness of the truth. Her resolve had deserted her. It really was over now. There was no point pretending otherwise.

Letting the pills drop from her hand, she watched them fall to the floor. They bounced and skittered about before coming to rest in a wide circular blast radius around her feet. Her indecision had lit the fuse of the explosion and left her standing in its epicenter. From now on, she would have to exist in that deep, ashy crater which resulted.

She had spared her own life.

She had won the prolongation of her own misery.

She screeched and flung the glass at the wall as hard as she could.

CHAPTER SIX

01:55 PM. SEPTEMBER 11TH.

(APPROX. TWO DAYS AND ELEVEN HOURS LATER)

[13:55] PluckingPurgatory'sPetals: I don't know.

[13:55] PluckingPurgatory'sPetals: I'm just so tired, you know? Always *so tired.*

[13:56] PluckingPurgatory'sPetals: Sometimes... I almost can't remember what it's like to not be out of your mind from sleep deprivation.

[13:57] PluckingPurgatory'sPetals: This feeling is just so ruthlessly all-consuming. Its taint is everywhere, obstructing everything.

[13:58] PluckingPurgatory'sPetals: It sneaks about, and puts a dagger between the shoulderblades of everything you might want to do.

[13:58] PluckingPurgatory'sPetals: You can't think straight. Your body doesn't act right. It's a really creepy experience.

[13:59] PluckingPurgatory'sPetals: I know I could simply take the pills again, and start whittling down my colossal sleep debt.

[14:00] PluckingPurgatory'sPetals: But I won't. I can't.

[14:00] PluckingPurgatory'sPetals: Only real, natural sleep imparts the chance to dream, to be with her.

[14:00] PluckingPurgatory'sPetals: And so I have to wait for it. I have to make that sacrifice for her.

Erin had told *A&F* about how the sleeping pills had failed her.

However, she *hadn't* gone on to relate that she nearly committed suicide because of it.

This was a decision she agonized over for quite some time beforehand. For she could not, try as she might, label this magnitude of omission as merely 'stretching the truth'. It would simply be a naked lie. And she knew it. So the prospect had seemed dauntingly consequential. A tangible turning-point in their relationship. Yet she had concluded that it must be done. Firstly, there was no telling just how badly A&F would react. If they had misguidedly freaked out over Tilly's arrival, this far more dire revelation would surely provoke an absolute firestorm of an argument. And it would be a pointless one at that. Erin didn't need to be castigated for her own good. She *already* wasn't going to try and kill herself again. Especially now she'd discovered she didn't quite have the stomach to do it. So riling up A&F over this would just be inflicting needless panic and worry.

Secondly, she was loath to mentally revisit that moment, even merely during a recounting of it. It was behind her now. And tightly wrapped in the obscuring winding-sheet of the past was where it ought to stay. The only lasting effect Erin would permit it to have was as a lesson. It had shown her that there would be no easy way out of this, no trying to just run away. The comforting possibility of resorting to death as a final, desperate escape had been revoked. And thus, her predicament was recast in an even more severe light. The pit she had long been plummeting down into was now effectively bottomless. This was actually worse than the alternative, because even the grisliest of ends *is* an end. So, what was she to do? Fashioning a parachute in mid-air was no doubt too much to ask for. And trying to grab a hold of the walls would, given her velocity, just part her from her fingers. Therefore she would have to embrace her hurtling descent, to find a way to live as a falling woman. It was mad, but humans are nothing if not adaptable. Besides, even madness has a sort of internal logic which one can rely on.

Recognizing that her options had narrowed to... one... did have a benefit. It granted her a renewed manic focus and drive. She would need that, if she was to discover exactly how to make her new reality workable. And, too, she needed to finally heed what her recent vicissitudes had revealed to her. This was precious knowledge, delineating what the *constants* and *variables* were. No more banging her head against the things she couldn't change; all her energy had to be applied to those scant few she could. The objective was now all about finding some novel existential loophole to exploit. For it was up to her to concoct her own salvation.

[14:01] PluckingPurgatory'sPetals: But the problem is how to survive the waiting itself.

[14:02] PluckingPurgatory'sPetals: So I have to start looking at the whole equation differently.

[14:02] PluckingPurgatory'sPetals: I can't bend the sleep to my will, that has become clear.

[14:03] PluckingPurgatory'sPetals: Yet I am, at least, still the master of my waking hours. Moulding and *remaking* them has to become my priority.

[14:03] PluckingPurgatory'sPetals: If this time can be fruitfully reclaimed, there is still hope.

[14:05] Alabaster&Freckles: Well... first let me say that I agree that putting your quest for sleep aside is wise.

[14:07] Alabaster&Freckles: As we've discussed before, its counterproductive nature was only destined to upset you further. And I do hope that recognising that played into your decision-making. You know, it being the right choice from a *self*-care perspective?

[14:09] Alabaster&Freckles: I'm also glad that you seem to have regained a sense of purpose and optimism. But I do have some questions...

[14:10] Alabaster&Freckles: Hasn't the failure of your sleeping pills plan given you pause about trying to manipulate things?

[14:10] Alabaster&Freckles: Doesn't it suggest that perhaps it's best to just hold off, take care of yourself, and let things resolve themselves naturally?

[14:11] PluckingPurgatory'sPetals: Frankly, not at all. I see the teaching as just being that some delicacy is required.

[14:12] PluckingPurgatory'sPetals: I was trying to interfere in such a simplistic, brute-force way. That's why I didn't succeed. I have to employ a scalpel, not a hammer.

[14:12] PluckingPurgatory'sPetals: Besides which, I understand what you're saying but passivity won't help me anyway. The material world is not looking to do me any favours.

[14:13] PluckingPurgatory'sPetals: What I have with Tilly is *not* natural. So if we are to be together... nature will have to be defied, biology will have to be transcended.

[14:14] PluckingPurgatory'sPetals: And it falls to me to make that happen. Tilly is powerless, outside of time. She is depending upon me.

[14:15] Alabaster&Freckles: Okay. So lay it on me. What is this new plan you've devised?

[14:16] PluckingPurgatory'sPetals: I'm going to recreate the dreams and experience them whilst *awake*.

[14:17] PluckingPurgatory'sPetals: I believe that half-decent facsimiles can be created digitally. And then I just strap on some VR stuff and step into the simulations.

[14:18] PluckingPurgatory'sPetals: Reliving those moments, even if it's just virtual, will be like communing with Tilly. Almost like a form of prayer, paying homage to our time together. And... I'll get to feel close to her again.

[14:20] PluckingPurgatory'sPetals: Plus, of course, it will give me something to do. Helping to get me through the day until I can *actually* be with Tilly in her world. So it's win-win.

Several months back - which already felt like a lifetime ago - Erin had chanced upon an article detailing the current state of high-end virtual reality gear. She wasn't much of a techie and had never even played a video game before, but it was an interesting read nonetheless. And, afterwards, a few kernels of that information had remained lodged in the recesses of her memory bank. These had thankfully re-emerged as she racked her brain about how to ameliorate her waking life. Just as she started contemplating somehow imbuing her waking hours with even a fraction of the nectar of the dream-bliss... it had hit her. Instantly, she knew she was on to something. It was perfect: she would bridge the gap technologically. That would give her control, that would grant her so many *possibilities*.

[14:21] PluckingPurgatory'sPetals: So I researched the very best VR equipment you can buy and a crazy high-spec computer to make full use of it.

[14:21] PluckingPurgatory'sPetals: There's a specialist store in my city which sells both. I made the purchase online early this morning.

[14:22] PluckingPurgatory'sPetals: Impatient as I am, I emailed the store and arranged for a courier service to deliver the items to me same-day.

[14:23] PluckingPurgatory'sPetals: They've already been picked up. I'm actually on the 'delivery status' page right now, watching a little truck icon move about the map.

[14:25] PluckingPurgatory'sPetals: I'm listed as drop-off #31 and this guy's still only on #18. Apparently I'll get my shit sometime in the evening. But if this dumbass keeps dawdling, I'm afraid it'll get pushed to tomorrow.

[14:25] PluckingPurgatory'sPetals: I won't lie, that's giving me some pretty gnarly anxiety.

[14:27] Alabaster&Freckles: Wow... you've really moved fast.

[14:28] Alabaster&Freckles: You definitely get things done when you put your mind to it, I hope you see that. And that it can apply to other things too.

[14:28] Alabaster&Freckles: Anyway, I'm sure your delivery will come today. Please try not to obsess over it, as best you can.

[14:29] Alabaster&Freckles: That will just build it up in your head more and more. And then the disappointment will be all the more crushing if - knock on wood - it doesn't work out the way you want.

[14:29] Alabaster&Freckles: By the by, I'm guessing that buying all this stuff was pretty expensive?

[14:30] PluckingPurgatory'sPetals: Sure, it wasn't cheap. Especially with the stupid retail mark-up.

[14:31] PluckingPurgatory'sPetals: But... I guess the money in my savings account *was* just collecting dust. Might as well start putting some of it to good use.

[14:31] PluckingPurgatory'sPetals: I mean, what could be more worthwhile than investing in Tilly and I's future?

[14:32] Alabaster&Freckles: I appreciate where you're coming from, but will this put you in a precarious position money-wise?

[14:34] PluckingPurgatory'sPetals: Nope. My savings can bear the brunt, believe me.

[14:34] PluckingPurgatory'sPetals: It'll take a lot more than that to put a dent in them.

[14:35] Alabaster&Freckles: I get the sense that you're maybe understating the cost?

[14:35] Alabaster&Freckles: Surely Tilly wouldn't want you to start imperiling yourself financially, even in a minor way?

[14:36] PluckingPurgatory'sPetals: Seriously, I appreciate the concern, but you don't need to worry. It really wasn't... that much... at all.

[14:37] PluckingPurgatory'sPetals: Especially given what it might do for me. Then it'll be money well spent, however you look at it.

[14:39] PluckingPurgatory'sPetals: And as for Tilly... hmm, well, she would make whatever sacrifice was necessary. I mean to do no less.

[14:39] PluckingPurgatory'sPetals: Because she wants what I want. Our wills are aligned. Of that, I am certain.

CHAPTER SEVEN

08:44 PM. SEPTEMBER 11TH.

(APPROX. SIX HOURS LATER)

It had been an hour or so since the concierge had signed for the delivery and directed the courier to leave the boxes outside Erin's apartment. Once she had lugged them inside, it had taken that long just to fully unpack everything. The computer had to be messily carved free from its excessively taped-up styrofoam cocoon. And the different parts of the VR headset had to be unearthed from boxes nestled in boxes nestled in boxes like matryoshka dolls. Now, after nightfall, all of her purchases were neatly laid out on the floor in sections. Yet this arrangement was messily surrounded by a sea of packing-peanuts, cardboard scraps, zip ties and plastic bags. Sweeping up this packaging detritus littering her apartment was just not going to happen. After all, how was she to detach herself from the excitement of setting her new toys up long enough to do it?

Eager though she was to just dive right in and figure out how it all worked on-the-fly, she knew that wasn't smart. So she made herself first scrutinize the many instructional booklets as ardently as a zealot poring over religious texts. Much of their contents was little better than gobbledygook to her, but she made herself drag her eyes across each sentence nonetheless. For she was *very* aware of how much all this stuff had cost. And so she was *very* intent upon trying to do everything exactly as the manuals stated, to avoid accidentally damaging the hardware.

Plus, this extra meticulousness was the necessary counterweight to her well-proven propensity for bad luck. Any missteps she made now could later serve as hindrances when it came to testing out her plan. And she really didn't want to be the one who made it fail; there were already enough external forces liable to ensure that. So any and all avoidable errors were to be avoided. Maybe the ripple effect of her carefulness would even radiate out to the aspects of her plan beyond her control and keep them on track. Or it could make them more inclined to spitefully scupper the whole endeavour. Either way, no use fretting about it now. Just head down, blinders on, and... onwards.

When it came to physical assembly, thankfully both the computer and VR headset were halfway pre-assembled already. The rest was mostly just a case of connecting some wires and slotting some components in. Taking a break once that was done, she found herself just sitting and staring at the computer tower. She had been ambivalent when seeing it in photos online. Yet now it was here before her, she found its appearance very satisfying. It wasn't exactly what she would have, if unprompted, dreamt-up as the most desirable look. But, sitting there in the middle of the room, it did have a certain undeniable *presence.* Perhaps even a slightly intimidating one.

The case itself was an aggressively minimalist design, made almost entirely out of a matte black metal. The only exception was the large see-through panel on one side. And through that glass one glimpsed a miniature cityscape of technological innards. The exposed circuitry and the little whirring fans and the tubing of the water-cooling system were all bathed in ghostly neon-blue light. Truthfully, she couldn't have said what almost any of these assorted parts actually did. But she knew that it was all absolutely cutting-edge tech. To her, that made it seem to exude an aura of omnific power. Yet she was going to harness that immense computational might - a thousandfold of what was once employed to take man to the moon - simply to render new realms for her to intellectually despoil. Now, something about the sheer absurdity and hedonism of that was intoxicatingly cool.

She had opted not to buy a monitor. This saved some money, countering her slight flickers of guilt by making herself feel *relatively* parsimonious. And, anyway, it was easy enough to plug the computer into her laptop and employ it as a substitute screen. Next, she began initializing the OS and then installing all the software needed to use the VR headset. It was a lot of mindlessly, repetitively clicking checkboxes and 'proceed' buttons. But she was just glad that it afforded her little opportunity to screw something up. As she waited for the last few progress bars to sluggishly fill up at a snail's pace, she went searching online. She needed to find a suitable VR experience to use as an introductory test-run.

This was something she had been giving a lot of thought to. Her time with Tilly did not take the form of lucid dreaming: she didn't control what occurred, it simply *happened* to her. Accordingly, she needed to see what passive, on-rails VR experiences were actually like. That would give her some sense of how well trying to reproduce her Tilly dreams would go. With this in mind, she seized upon what in the VR-enthusiast community's parlance were termed 'scenarios'. These were simulated worlds where you were a mere ride-along observer, looking around from your avatar's perspective as it did whatever it was programmed to do. This mirrored the distinctly unalarming lack of agency in her dreams, making them a perfect match for her purposes.

She found the most prominent online repository for scenarios and scanned through its library for one which piqued her interest. As she scrolled down the page listing them all, worlds and worlds and worlds passed before her discriminating gaze and were judged unworthy. There were just so many samey, unremarkable ones, taking place in really lame contexts. But, at last, the intriguing screenshots for a scenario caught her eye and made her pause. It was simply named 'Come Hither, Ye Weary - v.1.4.4'. And it was catalogued under the user-specified genre of 'Visual Poem'. She had to repress a shudder at the pretentiousness. Then she clicked through and read the no less cryptic one-line description from its creator: "Only animals roam in the wilderness; do not pity or revere them; perhaps you too are just an animal."

Without intending to, she passed a few minutes just contemplating this tagline as though it were a zen koan. And once she gave up on puzzling over its meaning, she quickly downloaded the scenario and got it ready to play. Standing in the middle of the room, where the computer was set up on the floor, she put on the VR headset. She settled the boxy display-unit in front of her eyes and pressed the integrated headphones snugly over her ears. It was a tight fit. She couldn't help, as her mind began to wander, but feel like it was actually the contraption which had *her* in its clutches, like a parasite clinging onto its intended host.

An invigorating mix of curiosity and nervousness passed through her as she prepared to dive in. She tried to tell herself to relax, that this was only to see what it was like, that it was super low-stakes. Yet, having no frame of reference for the coming experience still elicited a little of that familiar thrill of stepping into the unknown. She faintly worried that she might start getting addicted to that feeling if things kept up this way. When she had double-checked everything was on right, she blindly reached her foot forward and found the keyboard with it. Then she slapped the spacebar with her toes. This keystroke streamed the ones and zeros of a new reality to the strange interdimensional periscope attached to her head.

Timidly peering around, Erin saw that she was standing in the midst of a lush, dense forest.

Its appearance had a sort of stylized simplicity in both shapes and colours. This lack of detail combined with a thin mist hovering in the air to create a pleasant, visually undemanding aesthetic. She looked down at her virtual body, which was extremely surreal, and noticed that it was dressed in hiking apparel. Moreover, as if on cue, her avatar went to re-pocket some things in its hand. Although this seemed to intentionally happen so quickly that seeing what was held was impossible, the distinctive crinkle of paper could be heard.

As she was still stationary, she decided to simply take in her surroundings. It was incredibly tranquil here. Watching the branches gently sway whilst listening to the rustling leaves and wistful birdsong produced an almost hypnotically calming effect. It was hard not to let it lull her into spacing out. Eventually her stare did drift up toward the tops of the thick trees looming all around her. High above, they formed an intermeshing canopy which allowed only small, patchy glimpses of the cloudy sky beyond. Despite it seeming like the forest had swallowed her, she did not feel caged or claustrophobic. She just felt safely enclosed.

She was actually still craning her neck back when her avatar suddenly set off walking. This very much caught her by surprise and disorientated her for a few seconds. But she was fine once she was looking ahead again. She was now sauntering along, hands leisurely brushing against each tree trunk she passed. Occasionally, they had vines entwined around them, which had some kind of exotic flowers dotted along their length. These flowers were larger, more ostentatious and delicate than nature would ever dare adorn an invasive squatter with. But in this place, it seemed to make sense. It was an offering of beautiful enhancement from a weed, to plead forgiveness for its trespass. And also one made - or rather, paid, like a tax - in recognition of the sacrosanct loveliness of *this* forest.

Little birds flew from their hidden perches high above at the sound of her approach. She barely noticed though, too focused on the novelty of being carried along like this. It was, at first, very weird being but a spectating passenger in a body that wasn't her own. Yet her mind soon acclimatized and the disconnect faded away.

At one point, some quadrupedal critter, vaguely resembling a big squirrel, darted up a tree as she drew near. But it stopped mid-way to gawk and sniff inquisitively at her. So too her avatar paused to stare back at it. Then the moment abruptly burst and the animal rushed upwards again, disappearing into the labyrinthine tangle of boughs overhead. She felt a surprising pang of sadness at its exit. For this suddenly attuned her to the loneliness of wandering in a place full of life which shunned her. After walking on for a while, she found she was coming to a stream which cut across the forest floor. Her avatar knelt down by it and raised cupped handfuls of water up to her face. Now she was closer to its surface, she saw that peculiar little fish were swimming along with the current. They seemed completely oblivious, or perhaps indifferent, to this other creature using the stream too.

Having finished supping, the journey continued. Her avatar followed alongside the meandering route of the flowing water. It was oddly rather affecting to hear the fallen twigs snap beneath her feet. She was leaving a trail, an inadvertent record of her passing. But this proof that she existed would be seen by no-one, would disappear with just a brisk wind. There was thankfully no time to dwell on the frustration of this. For the stream had led her to a little clearing in the heart of the forest. Here there were a cluster of large, irregularly shaped boulders strewn about, covered with thick curtains of moss and ivy. Her avatar clambered up one of them and sat down on top of it. When it became clear that she wasn't going to be decamping from this position immediately, Erin took to just looking around again. She was soon distracted by the falling leaves, absentmindedly tracking each one as it airily spiralled down to earth.

Something else finally caught her eye, however. In the distance, shifting in and out of view as they traversed through the obscuring veil of mist, were what looked like a pair of deer. They both had oddly patterned coats and the male had very big antlers which knotted together into such a long, narrowing protrusion that it almost resembled a horn. Beautiful and somehow disquieting. They were unhurriedly moving from one area to another, grazing upon the foliage which dotted the forest floor. In time they drifted over closer to her, but still always gave her boulder a wide berth. And eventually they even paused their feeding to inspect her warily with wide eyes and twitching ears. Her avatar kept perfectly still, did nothing to spook them. But they skittishly pranced away anyway, bolting through the forest in the opposite direction. She watched them slaloming through the trees with lithe grace, right up until they passed out of sight. Her avatar then rose and slid off the boulder top. Leaving the clearing behind, it ventured in a new direction, marching onwards with a quickened pace as though seeking out something.

It didn't take long to reach the apparent destination. Although... Erin was initially confused to find that it was simply a tree, near enough identical to its brethren. But there was, at eye-level, a patch of bark defaced by some kind of extremely faint lettering. She couldn't make out quite what it was though. The scarring was almost completely healed over now, which must have taken years and years. She saw her avatar retrieve something out of a pocket. Using the end of a little metallic item, which looked like a really old-fashioned house-key, it reached out and began laboriously scraping into the tree's bark. Re-opening all the exact same lines that, though faded, were already etched there. This was a slow-going and methodical process, and kind of fascinating to observe.

Once finished, the crudely-written epigraph now clearly read: *LO, I AM HERE.*

She re-read it several times, feeling as though she must be missing something. She had just started to toy with embryonic inklings about the futility of self-expression and the impermanence of all things. But then her avatar abruptly began walking once more, cutting off her rumination.

It seemed as though she was just aimlessly striding through the forest again, until she came to another standstill. At first, she tried to espy whatever it was she was meant to see here, but found nothing noteworthy. Yet, when she finally stopped looking for some specific thing, she realized she was back at the exact same spot she had *originally* set off from.

All of a sudden, the whole world changed before her eyes. Seasons began to pass at fast-forward speed. The leaves on the trees changed colour, and were soon shed. Then the trees stood bare as they were pelted with unrelenting snow. Then the canopy gradually re-grew, becoming as lush as ever. Then the sun blazed in the sky, lighting up the forest floor with its bright, irrepressible reach.

This repeated itself over and over and over, the forest always dying and always being reborn. She watched in awe. And she felt acutely, as never before, how bizarre it was that this nature-ordained euthanasia and resurrection should happen on such a grand scale and happen so repetitively, and yet be so blithely ignored by most people.

The sped-up flight of seasons finally came to a gradual halt. It was now autumn again, as it evidently had been to begin with.

She looked down and noticed that the clothes were different. Before she could even wonder why, her avatar pulled out a small velvet drawstring-pouch from their pocket. Inside, there were two things. One was a folded note which, in handwritten text, read:

"I'm so sorry you've been having such a hard time recently, my little sweetpea. Inside this pouch is an heirloom, passed down in our family for a *long* time. It is a help in times like these. Take a trip to the woods and find what it unlocks. I once did, I know you can too. Love, Mom. XOXO."

The other object was a familiar house-key, all beat up and scratched.

She quickly understood what was going on. And, despite herself, she actually gasped.

This was the end of the scenario. But clearly if she waited long enough, she'd start the same journey through the forest once more. And after that, it would restart all over again and the next descendent would find themselves here. On and on it would go.

Of course...

It was a cycle. It was, all of it, a never-ending cycle.

She found that she was crying, though she didn't really know why. Yet the tears came and came nevertheless. They dampened the foam which formed a light-tight seal around her eyes. She pulled off the VR headset and threw it on the bed. Then she sank down to the floor, clutching her knees and softly rocking back and forth. The weeping burst forth in earnest. She had to bite her fist hard to stifle the violent sobs. An overwhelming, amorphous, undefinable wave of emotion had crashed into her with tidal fury. There was surely no reason this should be happening, and that made it all the more intense. It did, in fact, take quite a while before she had finally cried herself out. At which point, she simply let her body slump backwards, and lay upon the floor. She stared blankly up at the ceiling whilst she wiped the wetness from her cheeks and chin with her sleeves.

When at long last she picked herself up and rose to stand, there was no sadness upon her face. Those had been tears of relief, of catharsis, of renewal. And only a newfound sense of purpose was now animating her. The worth of the undertaking before her was suddenly so very clear. A resplendent figure at its far-off endpoint beckoned her. It was an invitation which promised to infuse her with the ingenuity and dedication needed to answer it. And answer it she would.

Her alarm clock said that it was **1:59 AM**, which meant that somehow three hours had passed. The time had just flown by, in the best way. She would have smiled, but both her facial muscles and her emotional reserves were so fatigued that no smile was forthcoming. All she could think about was what a godsend this technology was; it was just perfect for what she wanted. From the get-go, she had been completely swept up by the VR illusion. Her mind had solely been occupied by what she saw and heard. That entrancing forest had become her whole world during her stay in it. And it wasn't even that she had actively believed it *was* real. She had merely been coaxed into forgetting to constantly remember that it *wasn't* real. Usefully enough, this achieved near enough the same effect.

She had been hoping that whatever unique mental receptiveness and plasticity it was which enabled her to visit Tilly would also give her a heightened susceptibility to VR. And it sure seemed like that was the case. She was ecstatic that this initial expedition into the VR space had so definitely proved, at least in theory, that this medium could realize her vision. But she knew that she had a lot of work ahead of her. Figuring out just how to wield this nascent technology to meet her very singular and exacting needs was to be the true challenge. As she was becoming accustomed to, there was no precedent to guide her. She would have to be a trailblazer in what was already a state-of-the-art sphere of possibilities. And whatever breakthroughs she made, the world would never know of them. They were to profit her, and her alone. Yet this was not greed, nor spite. It was merely a single-mindedness which permitted no thought but of one's objective.

She took her laptop over to the window-seat and got set up in a comfortable position. Straining to reach the hanging cord, she finally snagged it and raised the blind all the way. She hoped that at least the night sky would keep her company. The stars were visible tonight but, disappointingly, only some of them. This produced an unimpressive, uneven distribution of little twinkles up above. And that imperfection displeased her. She thought to herself that if she were the omnipotent shaper of this world, she'd easily rectify that. She would dip her paintbrush into primordial liquid-light and flick it toward the heavens, bespattering the gaps with newborn stars. And this is why she now haughtily turned her face from the sky she usually revered and adored. For she had her own micro-worlds she intended to create. And these stood to be far better, for they *would* be to her specification.

She wasted no time getting the next stage of her research underway.

Erin knew she needed to find a way to have VR scenarios made for her. But she *didn't* know how to do that, or what it would entail. Or, really, even where to start. Her lone certainty was that bungling novices would

119

not suffice. It was vital that she procured the services of those with solid expertise in this craft. So she tracked down the hub where the most hardcore enthusiasts discussed both making and enjoying scenarios. It was called 'Something in Nothing', or SiN to the regulars. She thought this was... quaint, a throwback to the gauche-but-lovable early years of the internet when pseudo-edgy forum names were all the rage. After registering an account on there, she considered how to proceed. This was not a tribe which reacted kindly to ignorant newcomers demanding to have answers spoonfed to them, so she held off on making any posts. Instead, she studiously read through the various subsections of the bustling messageboard, trying to get a sense of how the community was structured.

Evidently, the actual content creators were known as 'architects'. And, as in all things, there was a hierarchy here. Some were mere hobbyists who collaborated to produce mediocre scenarios and release them for free, simply to garner distinction amongst their fellow community members. Whereas, the especially talented architects often banded together into larger teams, forming a well-rounded mix of sound designers and visual artists and programmers. They made their own detailed, high-quality scenarios and sold them online. But there were also freelance teams who could be privately commissioned to make custom scenarios, if one was willing to pay rather handsomely for the privilege. This was the niche she needed to delve into.

She trawled through all the architect team websites she could find, looking for those who advertised themselves as presently available. This slashed the pool of potential choices quite dramatically. Waiting-lists abounded in this particular marketplace. And although waiting six months for work on one's commission to begin was, in normal circumstances, not unreasonable, in her case it was a no-go. Then, upon scrutinizing the remainder this left her with, narrowing them down to a single choice was easy. For she applied the dual criteria of *can produce good work* and, much more crucially, *are not prohibitively expensive.* Only one team fulfilled both. They went by the name 'The Skylarks'. That did make them sound more like some hipster indie band than anything else, yes, but Erin was not about to hold it against them.

Nevertheless, this wasn't to say she didn't have her qualms. As if their rinky-dink website hadn't given it away, her research revealed that they were a relatively small-time, inexperienced operation, still trying to make a name for themselves. So it would be risky taking a chance on them. But there were obviously a good few weighty counterpoints to recommend them. For one thing, they specialized in character animation, making the people in their scenarios seem believably lifelike. For another thing, samples of their previous work displayed, to Erin's eye, great promise. Their painstaking craftsmanship could not be doubted. They were evidently keen to overdeliver on their commissions' quality to show what they could do.

Yet another thing was that they had a surprisingly large number of people in their team, which was unusual for a young outfit. But they went by the principle that they'd endeavour to give a shot to talented would-be architects who other teams were wary of recruiting due to their nascent skills and empty resumes. She also liked that, looking at their listed roster, the team's composition was majority-female, which she saw as a benefit given what she wanted. And finally, what really sealed the deal was that their prices were remarkably affordable. This was likely done in an attempt to attract more work and, by quantity as well as quality, begin remedying their present lack of renown. If nothing else, she definitely admired their hustle.

It was with great nervousness that Erin contacted The Skylarks. For if they declined, she would be at a loss about what to do next. So she fretted over how best to explain to them her request without coming across as... unhinged. She revised the phrasing of her email so many times that the sentences began to lose all meaning to her. And it was at this point, when the diminishing returns of obsessive rewording were beyond maxed out, that she made herself finally just do it. Timidly peering through her fingers, she hit 'send'.

Re-reading the email more clear-eyed now that she couldn't change it, she was glad to find that it had ticked all the right boxes. First off, outlining her relationship with Tilly had, of course, been out of the question entirely. As outsiders trapped in the intellectual fetters of the mundane, they just wouldn't be able to understand it. And their stark

121

miscomprehension would likely act as a dealbreaker. Although that was all true, she had also decided that she must, at the very least, state plainly that she wanted to recreate a dream. Or else how was she to properly convey the distinctly dreamlike features the scenario needed to have? But outside of that, she knew not to give any other background context. It would just muddle things.

As for the proposal itself, she eeny-meeny-miny-moe chose one of her favorite Tilly dreams and outlined the scene to them. In it, her and Tilly were sitting together on a couch, 'watching' a favorite movie in that trademark way that playful lovers do. They'd go from raptly watching whilst holding hands, to play-wrestling over who held the television remote, to spooning together under a blanket, to Tilly massaging Erin's feet, to sword fighting faux-dramatically with long dinner candles, to Tilly resting her head in Erin's lap to have her hair played with, to a giggly foot-war, to Tilly trying to balance a precarious tower of scatter cushions atop Erin's head.

Erin was grateful to receive a prompt response from The Skylarks. Their email was friendly and receptive. It stated that they would happily agree to take on the project. Rather than be deterred by the strangeness of her request, they seemed pleased to have an unorthodox scenario to hone their skills by making. She was overjoyed to hear it, and corresponded with them over the next few hours to articulate the specific details of her vision better. She provided them with some sketches, employing the residual drawing ability from a youthful artistic period, to illustrate how the room had to look. Then she did her best to describe Tilly's mannerisms, muteness, and... physical appearance. Since the very first dream, she had progressively developed a much better picture of what Tilly actually looked like. Such that now she could even hazard a detailed drawing of Tilly for them to use as source material. Finally, she explained the need for some slightly fuzzy visual filter to approximate a dreamlike semi-abstraction and haziness. Her hope was that if her (exceedingly hospitable) mind was given four-fifths of the picture, it would step in and impose the final fifth itself, adding the finishing touches of verisimilitude to it all. For their part, The Skylarks seemed glad of this last request, for it gave them welcome leeway to soften the impact of any graphical shortcomings.

Once all the needful instruction had been relayed to The Skylarks, she told them she was willing to pay *considerably* extra for speedy completion. They were very amenable to this offer. It wasn't like they currently had any other commissions to distract them. Additionally, the simple nature of her proposed scenario meant it could largely be constructed with scavenged open-source assets and pre-made assets they kept around for general-purpose use. It was animating the physical interactions between her and Tilly which would be the time-consuming element. Yet even that could be expedited given that the blurry first-person perspective meant these only had to be functional, not perfect. Plus, a lot of it could be quickly produced using motion-capture technology.

The Skylarks stated that due to all these useful shortcuts, and the team working overtime on the project, a timeframe of delivering the finished product in about three weeks was possible. Just a few days ago, this would have seemed like an insuperable eternity. Now it was perfectly agreeable to Erin. After all, she could occupy herself by playing around with VR until then. Its supreme effectiveness as an engrossing, time-wasting tool was clear. This made it a lot easier to be sanguine about having to while away the exactly five hundred and four hours - not that she was counting, of course - in the meantime.

She sent the payment to them, and left her virtual dreamweavers to their work.

Although Erin was trying to bask in the satisfaction of initiating her plan, that sadly just wasn't how she worked. A new concern soon arose in her thoughts. It started as... just an inkling of doubt. Politely tapping on the door to the most vulnerable innermost chamber of her mind. Tap, tap, tap, tap, tap. A gentle, persistent solicitation of entry. She ignored the doubt, but it still refused to depart. Then she tried to pretend she couldn't even hear its taps. But the childish indignity of the pretending started to irritate her in itself. Then she started to feel the ceaseless, monotonous rhythm of the tapping spreading through her like a shiver. Her very essence vibrated along with every muffled impact, her bones resounded like taut violin strings. It got to the point where she couldn't bear it. And so finally, all worked up, she confronted the little doubt-bearer, meaning to quickly vanquish it. Yet it had grown bigger and stronger while it was rebuffed. What had been a faint misgiving had now snowballed into a massive worry, looming grave before her. This newly brawny doomsayer told her how her well-laid plan would implode spectacularly.

All of this happened in the course of about ninety minutes. The mind is a devious, pitiless thing.

She was now forced to consider the alleged fatal flaw in greater detail. It seemed to check out, much to her chagrin. The logic was straightforward. This scenario she had commissioned would, of course, be somewhat simplistic and have various rough edges. Taken by itself, this wasn't really an issue. But her fear was that if experiencing it didn't match the depth of immersion and believability of the actual dreams, she might tarnish or even *damage* her connection to Tilly. Because spending, say, twelve hours a day seeing Tilly before her as merely an animated VR mannequin must have psychological consequences. That awareness could inadvertently condition her mind to perceive Tilly, in an overall sense, as an unreal made-up thing. Then maybe she'd lose her ability to be with Tilly at all, becoming locked out of the dreamworld.

The more she considered all this, the more it made perfect sense to her. Given what she stood to lose if this breakdown occurred, even a one-percent chance of it happening was intolerable. She *needed* to take strenuous precautions to remove the risk entirely. Or, else, the plan could not proceed. She had already recently veered far too close to being unforgivably derelict in her duty to Tilly. She wouldn't let that happen again.

So began a new line of research. From the outset, it was tinged with what was fast becoming an all-too-familiar difficulty: she didn't know what she was looking for, only vaguely what it needed to do. Still, she was determined to overcome this hurdle just like those before it. That repetition gave almost a sort of predestined quality to her next success, bolstering her. She had only to go through the motions, to put in the online legwork, and the answer would present itself. It was just a matter of time.

Her first instinct was to search for leads somewhere in the VR community or its periphery. These were, after all, people who took great pains to make the simulated seem real. She just had to find the utmost extremists therein, and look to follow in their footsteps. That meant bypassing the top level, public-facing world of VR enthusiasts altogether. It had been a useful stepping stone beforehand, but now she saw it was too conventional, too myopic. More interested in squabbling over screen resolutions and overclocking CPUs, than wondering how VR might be used as a scalpel-less surgery to rewire the brain. More interested in salivating over a future where VR becomes fully mainstream and corporate-owned, than exploring what can be done in the fertile, lawless shadows. In short, they had been given the philosopher's stone, and were obsessing over how best to employ it as a paperweight. She would leave them to it.

No, she had to tap into the vein of perverse innovation which could only be fostered by the weirdos, the deviants, the crazies. This meant rooting around in the burrows of some very peculiar subcultures. Down, down, deep as they went. And there could be no dainty reluctance to get her hands dirty here. She was going to have to sift through the many-hued effluvia of disordered minds to find something of value. Unpleasant and potentially hazardous, sure. But also quite unavoidable.

Accordingly, it was hours and hours of dead ends before she stumbled upon something promising. The 'cyberkin'. They were an eccentric, secretive group of VR fanatics who saw strapping on a headset to visit virtual worlds as partaking in a... transcendental religious experience. Or, at least, that's what their website claimed. At first Erin couldn't quite decide what their deal was. It did all seem a bit far-fetched. And their old-school website featured enough technobabble and gaudy microchip iconography that it could almost pass for the preserved guerrilla-marketing campaign of some 90s sci-fi movie.

Yet it was also clear that the website was actively maintained and updated, with a very active community too. So, what were they then? A band of committed pranksters trying to troll the reader? Or nostalgic posers merely drunk on cyberpunk pretensions? Or was it just some kind of cynical money-making cult, probably hawking 'special' proprietary VR gear? This latter possibility certainly seemed to *feel* right. But it just didn't add up. The cyberkin weren't proselytizers. They displayed their main doctrines proudly, but did not seek to disseminate them. And they weren't exactly recruiting either. They didn't hound people to join them, or even make it easy for those who sought to.

So... perhaps... they were actually genuine?

It took quite a bit of further reading for Erin to overcome her own incredulity and accept that was the case.

Eventually she just encountered so much meticulous documentation of the group's history and internal structure and beliefs that her doubt fell away. Their sincerity was undeniable, at the very least. But madmen were often plenty sincere, that didn't mean their ravings amounted to anything. She had to closely examine what these cyberkin were actually *saying*.

Their creed was both very expansive and very nebulous. And unlike the revered immutability of holy books, it was rather slippery to piece together, being subject to ongoing collaborative revision on their private wiki. Still, it was at least possible to point to the crux of what they believed. The idea being that the advent of VR was a gift from some deity to humanity in recognition of it having breached a crucial threshold of development. This endowment would allow man to, at long last, interact with all the sublime and precious things which the profaning earth was not fit to directly bear. Thus, the virtual plane was a sort of buffer middleground between *heaven* and *here*. A hermetically sealed nowhere-place where sacred experiences could be vouchsafed to us, safe from the taint attached to flesh and the ground trodden by it.

Now, much as Erin thought the idea of a deity intervening via consumer electronics was amusing enough, she did have a bunch of questions which she found to be starkly answerless. Who was this deity, anyway? Why did it even care to enlighten mankind? Which civilizational attainment in particular had spurred its holy largesse? (Driverless cars? Apocalyptic nuclear weapons? Hi-def porn?) These were not inconsequential sticking points, to be fair. Yet, the cyberkin's priest-like figures, heeding the example of most spiritual traditions, spoke of these deeper truths only in grand esoteric riddles. These were of course inscrutable to an outsider layperson like herself. Oppositely, the specific practices expected of the cyberkin flock were, by necessity, laid out plainly. The dullards inevitably attracted as followers must be accounted for, after all. And dullards fare best with step-by-step instructions.

Lowly initiates were tasked with grunt work. They had to try out all the new VR experiences made available anywhere online. Then they had to write detailed reports, for internal circulation only, about whether or not each one showed any potential for granting mystical insight. This dragnet scouting approach made for a repetitive grind, but it therefore proved one's dedication. Do it for long enough and you graduated to the worship itself. This took several very different forms. But one in particular really stood out.

It required subjecting oneself to an *extremely* emotionally intense VR scenario, which was enigmatically referred to only as 'beholding the vista'. According to cyberkin lore, this file had originally been discovered floating on a very dark corner of the web. There, it was being passed around as but a strange and perturbing digital curio by those who seek to sample such things. Its actual creator and the story of its provenance were unknown, and no amount of exhaustive investigation had been able to rectify that. Needless to say, this endeared it to the cyberkin immensely. They speculated that it was the handiwork of some reluctant prophet. Someone seized by an overwhelming sense of divine inspiration, who felt compelled to channel it into art and then thrust that out into the world just to retain their sanity. And naturally the end result had then found its way to the true believers, albeit by a circuitous route.

Erin was at least passingly intrigued by what the hell this scenario could be. She would obviously have liked to see for herself what all the fuss was about. But it was a password-protected torrent which made this sacrament available to cyberkin adherents of sufficient rank. And there was seemingly no way to find a pirated copy of it elsewhere, which was a very rare thing indeed on the internet. Still, it *was* possible to find firsthand accounts, from the faithful themselves, of what the experience was like. Piercing through the gibberish, she ascertained that there was a wide spectrum of responses.

Some saw God.

Some knew God.

Some spoke with God.

Some felt they became God.

And some simply took the opportunity to spurn God face-to-face at last.

However, although that was all very interesting, Erin soon became far more fascinated by a secondary detail. When she got good enough at deciphering the cyberkin's guarded manner of referencing such things in publicly viewable forums, she inferred something eye-opening. The highest echelon of cyberkin did not use this scenario by itself. The consumption of some hallucinogenic substance, to enhance the numinous effect of the rite, was mandated of that priesthood class.

It was this which really set the gears in Erin's mind turning. She wondered. And she pondered.

For if she could chemically employ a very precisely altered state of consciousness to make the Tilly scenario seem absolutely real, it would preempt the issue she foresaw. Alas, that did seem rather like a pipedream. She had never even heard of a drug which could do something as unorthodox and sophisticated as that. So she started scrolling through tables listing the purported effects of a huge variety of psychoactive drugs, both recreational and medical. It was astounding how many there were. A pill for *almost* every problem. But not hers.

Then, simply not knowing where else to turn, she half-heartedly delved into the world of conspiracy theories. In particular, the ones regarding shadowy government agencies experimenting with compounds which brainwashed people into believing whatever implanted falsehood was desired. There was a massive whirlwind of rumor and guesswork and fanciful anonymous testimony which surrounded this. And at its very heart was just a tiny fragment of real evidence. These were declassified documents whose every unredacted word, and every interpretation of those words, had been scrutinized ten thousand times over. They told of the bumbling, ruthless attempts during Cold War hysteria to create some sort of psychological superweapon. But none of these initiatives had truly been successful. Or, at least, none whose existence *was* admitted to.

Maybe there was one which had been kept secret because it worked. The abrasive dorks whose tiny kingdoms were conspiracy theory messageboards certainly had a plethora of ideas about that. But she was not psyched about having to venture into their domain. This was a species of loser who smugly pretended to be the discoverers and custodians of humanity's *most* important secrets. Yet, in truth, their only 'accomplishment' was having deposited so much lonely semen into their favourite washrags that, over years and years, the accumulation had actually solidified and hardened. And one could, if one was so inclined, trace the history of this damn near mineralized substance by looking at its gradient of aged discolouration. Somewhat like how excavated rock can be dated by looking at its layers. A modern anthropological marvel, in other words. But, fascinating as it perhaps was, that didn't make reading the messageboards any less annoying. These dweebs put forth and defended their beloved pet conspiracy theories with the rabidness of die-hard sports team fans rooting for their side.

She browsed them wearily. Maybe artificial sweeteners really were as progressively corrosive to independent thought as the sugar they replaced was to teeth. Maybe that distinctive modem dial-up sound, heard in just about every home at one time, really was the perfected acoustic signal which unlocked the brain's defenses. *Maybe. Maybe. Endless maybes.* But not a jot of this what-if bullshit helped Erin. If only the mad scientists on the illuminati's payroll had carelessly included the recipe for some credulity-toxin in the memos which, decades down the line, would trickle out into public view. Of course, they didn't. No one in that situation ever did. That's why the whole thing was just a wild goose chase. And she knew that well enough. She was really just looking to gather inspiration and kill time until she came up with something better to look into.

It was imperative to take a step back and try to re-examine the problem in its most basic terms. So, she decided to give some real thought to *exactly* what she wanted the drug she was hypothesizing to do. As she mapped out just how complexly multi-layered the desired effect needed to be, it finally dawned on her that no such drug could currently exist. Trying to imagine a context besides her own which would necessitate that ultra-specific solution was impossible. Given all this, she was forced to accept that she would have to somehow bring it into existence herself then. Contemplating how this could possibly be done, or what it would entail, made her head spin. She was way, way, way out of her depth now: molecular chemistry seemed just about as arcane as witchcraft to her. Although... hadn't she recently come into brief, tangential contact with people who used themselves as guinea pigs for mind-altering experimentation? Perhaps they could point her in the right direction...

She logged back onto the darknet market PsyMer. This time, however, she went straight to its forum section. As she was growing well-accustomed to doing, she first spent a while just skimming through post after post after post, to figure out the jargon and how their community worked. Evidently, the psychonauts were a distinctly cagey and tight-knit group. Everyone claimed to have been doing this for twenty years. Everyone seemed to know everyone else. And they had deep bonds of comradeship forged over mutual tales of chemical misadventure. In light of that fact, it became clear that it would take far too long for her to approach this directly. That would require her to start posting frequently enough to embed herself amongst them, building trust and contacts over time. She'd have to fabricate a whole new identity to fit in, making up entertaining stories about 'her' mental battle scars from trying out the effects of mysterious powders. In other words, it was a sucker's bet. It could work, it could not. But it would be weeks or months before she even found out which was more likely.

Instead, she aimed to bypass all that, with a little more machiavellian subterfuge. She began by shooting off private-messages to a selection of the most well-respected elder-like figures. Posing as an eager neophyte, and faux-inadvertently revealing herself to be a young woman, she stroked their egos by fawning over their contributions to the psychonaut knowledge base. Only a handful were foolish enough to take the bait, but she knew she had these ones well and truly on the hook. They were plenty talkative, that was for sure. After a long enough exchange had cemented their image of her as a mere flirtatious groupie, she got to work.

She dispensed with the smalltalk and went about deftly plying each of them for information. The plan was to inundate them with enough easy, filler questions that when she ventured the only one she actually cared about, it would slip in camouflaged amongst this chaff. And when the time came, she dropped it in so casually. Just out of curiosity, what *would* someone do if they wanted to explore a very specific mindstate, but no known compound was suitable? Only a single interrogatee seemed willing to volunteer a real way to tackle this conundrum; the others feigned ignorance or simply bluffed with tall tales. This last-man-standing went by the handle 'MindhackinCityslicka74' and had been the most welcoming of her advances all along. However, she was initially... nonplussed... by his answer.

He had just wryly commented, "intrepid psychonauts who want to undertake a unique voyage requiring a unique craft should probably retain the services of a shipwright."

What the fuck this actually *meant*, she hadn't the foggiest idea.

After the exasperation of trying to fathom the secrets-nestled-in-gibberish of the cyberkin, she wasn't pleased to encounter yet more pompously cryptic doublespeak. These stupid subcultures and their stupid argots were becoming a real pain in the ass. But, of course, she had to temper her annoyance. She wasn't in a position to refuse assistance just because she had to jump through a few hoops first. So, playing along, she pretended to be overawed by the inscrutable profundity of his response. And she begged only that it might be rendered more plainly, by such a wise teacher as he, so that she could better understand it. Unsurprisingly, he expounded only slightly. He said that 'shipwrights' were essentially the modern day witch-doctors to this clan of reckless ingesters, whipping up new potions to induce new trips. She was now running dangerously low on patience. She took some deep breaths and visualised throwing bricks at this dude's face, which helped. And then she applied even more cajoling. It was some time before it was finally, begrudgingly given over candidly: they were mercenary chemists, known only to the psychonaut elite, who operated on the black market. For a price, they'd concoct a custom-made drug which would produce just about any effect you specified. But doing business with them was strictly invite-only: you had to be vouched for by a longstanding trusted customer. Now that he had divulged all this, he even boasted that his particular go-to shipwright was the finest artisan of them all.

Unfortunately, when she made the obvious follow-up request, she hit a brick wall.

He evinced great hesitation to make an introduction for her, protesting that it was too dicey a proposition. After all, didn't she realize that if things went badly his treasured reputation would be dynamited? Naturally, this hypothetical tragedy was very moving, a real tearjerker. More importantly though, she sensed that it was also an invitation to barter. And that she could actually do something with.

She first reiterated what an exciting privilege it was to converse with such a revered higher-up in the psychonaut sphere. Then, as coquettishly as could be, she stated that she was *really* looking forward to talking to him on an ongoing basis, to get to know him better. All the while hinting that he was exactly the kind of man she had always seen herself falling for. Now, she was definitely piling it on thick, and he would have to be stupendously dumb to believe she intended to follow through in this way. But... then again, horny guys did tend to abdicate all wariness, all rationality. Hopefully that would hold true in this case too.

Her luck held, somewhat. He really seemed to be taken in by her gambit, believing her attraction to be genuine. But though it went some way to gaining his acquiescence, it still fell a little short. This was very frustrating. He was clearly so close to giving in. Yet his preoccupation with the potential downside of granting the favour meant he was surely going to need something significant to push him over the edge. At this point, she was starting to feel that she had wrung all that she could from this particular ruse. She was now more than willing to just change gears and test his venality instead. As tactfully as she could, she began typing out a message implying that she'd happily pay him a hefty 'finder's fee' for being so gracious as to connect her. As tactlessly as he could, he preempted her by saying it would be great if she could send 'nudez' to prove she really was 'interested' in him.

"You... gross... motherfucker," she whispered aloud as she scrunched her face up in disgust.

Still, at least it laid bare what he was actually after, obviating all the pretence. Besides, she could work with this transaction. Not only did it spare her an expensive bribe, but it would likely be easy enough to fake her side of the bargain. She told him that she would love to share some pics with him. But shouldn't they take things slow, given the long road of courtship which lay ahead of them in the coming months? Wouldn't it be so much *hotter* if things unfolded in the manner of a striptease, preserving some mystery at each step? So, as a compromise, she offered to start with a topless pic. For his part, he seemed taken with this logic - undoubtedly already dick-in-hand - and the prolonged string of future rewards it implied. This was exactly what she wanted to hear. She started to find a suitable stand-in image to yank from Google and send him. But then he piped up again to say his only condition was that she write his username on her chest and give a thumbs up, to prove it was really her. Reading this, she actually guffawed in surprise. She had to give it to him: obviously he wasn't quite as dense as he seemed. After agreeing, she asked for fifteen minutes to get a little more dolled up for him and then send the photo over.

The clock was now ticking.

She had sort of boxed herself in here. She would have to think on her feet if this opportunity was to be salvaged. Of course she had no intention of sending this sleazy jerk a photo of her breasts. And, besides, she highly doubted that her A-cups would get the job done here. So she needed to outsource the acting-out of the role of compliant bimbo. Working fast, she searched for camgirl sites and clicked through to the topmost result. She scrolled down the preview windows of active streams looking for someone who was buxom but, for believability's sake, not bleach-blonde or thickly spackled with make-up. Also, by the same token, it couldn't be a professional camgirl filming with an expensive camera in front of a lighting rig. Erin needed an amateur with a laptop webcam in a messy bedroom. Perhaps someone vaguely alternative-looking; that felt right somehow.

Luckily, she quickly came across someone who fit the bill. Cute face, jet-black pixie-cut, sleeve tattoo, back-problems busty. She entered the public chatroom on their channel and instantly offered to buy a private show. A moment later, a prompt came up to pay for it, and she did. Then a new window opened and it was just the two of them. Her hired camgirl stared expectantly into the camera lens with a bad fake smile. Erin typed out a quick, blunt explanation of what she wanted and asked for a price. The woman seemed completely unfazed by the bizarre request. She just thought it over for a second and named a pitiably small amount of money.

This made Erin feel weirdly sad; she responded that she would pay double. And then in the time it took for the removal of some clothing and some haphazard scrawling with lipstick to occur, Erin had her 'nudez'. She sent the payment and closed the window with a sigh. Next, she cropped the screenshot she had taken so that it looked like a selfie. And she sent this finished product to the lustful psychonaut with her regards.

Some more enthusiastic playfulness on her part in the ensuing back-and-forth sealed the deal. He was too blinded by the now seemingly very real prospect of acquiring a sexy, slutty penpal to exercise his previous caution. It had taken a lot of effort, but she finally got what she wanted. He handed over the information she needed, spelling it all out plainly. And once the trade-off was complete, she blocked the creep with great relish. The whole thing had made her feel a little dirty and she was very glad to wash her hands of him. It was impulsive, yes. But not at all as foolishly rash as it seemed. Given his fear of losing his standing in the community, he couldn't very well shout from the rooftops that some wily seductress had so easily conned him into the disclosure, could he? His best bet was to keep his mouth shut and hope nothing disastrous happened. Or, at least, nothing that could be traced back to him.

Erin now knew the current way - given that it cycled regularly - to hail the master-level shipwright called 'Ka-Sumedy' over an encrypted chat app. She started their conversation with the (unsurprisingly grandiose) passcode phrase which testified to her vouched-for status: "pray, the sea is wide and deep and full of wrecks, and I've an odyssey to make." It worked. She was in. Once she started talking to Ka-Sumedy, she found it to be an... odd experience. Not bad, just unmistakably odd. They were definitely a man or woman of few words. And it wasn't that she had been expecting to be wooed with pleasantries or anything like that. There was just something so robotic, so cold about the way Ka-Sumedy reeled off brusque questions about what she wanted to order.

She did not let this deter her. In fact, she would certainly prefer this businesslike demeanour, with its implications of focus and seriousness, than the opposite. So she just mirrored their directness, and began specifying her requirements in great detail. She explained that what the drug needed to do, for a relatively precise duration, was threefold. Firstly, it had to induce an absolute suspension of disbelief, in order to make her mind pliantly accept whatever she saw as being real. Secondly, it had to soften the acuity of her senses and perception, to help mimic the dreamstate's haziness. Thirdly, it had to have a very, very mild hallucinogenic quality. Thereby encouraging her mind to superimpose its own, more accurate, open-eye hallucinatory imagery onto the scene it beheld. Taken as a whole, she knew that this request was somewhat of a tall order. But, then again, she *was* talking to an expert in the field of illicitly messing with brain-chemistry.

Ka-Sumedy was thankfully game, conceding that it would be challenging but probably doable. Then they gave Erin a boilerplate warning about what she was getting herself into, to ensure she appreciated the risks. Principally, she had to realize that the chemical makeup of her proposed drug could not, by dint of practicality, be formulated from scratch. It would, instead, be a knowledgeably assembled hodgepodge of pre-existing compounds whose effects were well understood. These would hopefully combine to produce a novel overall effect. How this final mixture would interact with the human body could be theoretically determined with considerable accuracy, but hypotheses were called hypotheses and not certainties for good reason. Even with software which played out every permutation of the outcome before rendering a verdict, a margin of error had to be allowed for. There was no way around this. Given that Erin was going to be her drug's first and only test subject, she had to accept that it was still inherently a gamble with her very life at stake. She might not overly fear dying. But when it came to messing with one's own brain, there were fates... *much* worse than death. There existed wards full of bedridden dribblers, having chemically lobotomized themselves, who would warn her of this, if they still could.

Although it was, on *some* level, rather funny that a black-market drug maker issued the same kind of responsibility-shirking disclaimer that billion dollar pharmaceutical companies did, it was also deeply disconcerting. Of course, nothing would have allayed Erin's anxiety about trusting the shady mystery substance she was buying, but this definitely did not help. Still, sufficiently undaunted, she said that she understood and wanted to proceed anyway. She provided info like her weight and age and sex to facilitate the tailoring of a dosage to her body. And once that was all settled, she added that she'd pay a premium to expedite the process to three weeks. Ka-Sumedy agreed, and stated the total fee for designing and synthesizing and delivering the drug.

Erin's eyebrows shot up when she saw this price.

Look, she wasn't naive. She had expected that the miraculous feat she was asking for wouldn't come cheap. But this was a *lot* of money. 'Normal' people spent this much buying a car, and not a crappy one either. So, between this and her other recent expenditures, her savings were going to take an absolute beating. Once upon a time, plundering her inheritance this freely would have been unimaginable. Now it seemed like... nothing. For she was driven by a goal worth every penny she had. And hoarding for the future suddenly just seemed so goddamn silly. There was only here, only now, *only Tilly*. Money spent in service of their relationship was, indubitably, money well spent. With this in mind, she agreed to the price, without even trying to haggle it down. She transferred the payment via cryptocurrency. This was a little more complicated than before given the amount, but she managed to do it.

And then the deal was done.

Somewhere, in an amateur laboratory set up in someone's grotty basement, her elixir to remedy a Tilly-less world was about to be made.

CHAPTER EIGHT

2:35 PM. OCTOBER 15TH.

(APPROX. TWENTY-TWO DAYS LATER)

The delivery had come about half an hour ago. She had carried the large parcel onto the middle of the bed with her. Using scissors, she slit the tape sealing the flaps with exaggerated slowness and care. Then she opened it up, but did not lean forward to peer inside. A sense of foreboding stayed her hand. Several minutes passed as she just sat there, collecting herself. Though the room temperature did not change, she felt a stark chill come over her from nervousness. Her fingertips actually felt a little numb. Once she had summoned the resolve, she pulled the box closer and started scooping out the packing peanuts it was densely stuffed with. Nestled within was a smaller, unsealed box. She placed it in her lap and flipped open its top.

It was full of little vials that contained a clear liquid. Each one was labelled 'Ikelos'.

They were all neatly arrayed in a grid, separated by cardboard dividers. At the sight of them, she involuntarily pulled back and began anxiously chewing her bottom lip. She really would have preferred if it could have come in pill form. But Ka-Sumedy had been unequivocal. The delicate, patchwork molecular structure of her frankenstein drug meant that stomach acid would be too inhospitable a vestibule before the bloodstream could be reached. Hence, the direct method was required: intravenous injection. This was not ideal, to say the least. But she could deal with the inconvenience. She had bought all of the necessary items online, and read tutorials on how to inject safely. The process was simple enough. She felt... fairly confident she could do it properly.

Her attention was drawn to the inside surface of the box's lid, where a single word was written in thick black marker: "godspeed." She grimaced, and hung her head. Given Ka-Sumedy's inscrutable personality, there were so many ways to interpret this message. And she was no doubt going to torture herself by considering them all. Let's see... perhaps it really was *just* a gesture of well-wishing. Or was it actually a knowing joke at her expense? Or was it apprehensive hand-wringing, an ominous sign of how dangerous the drug's own creator feared it was? Finally she made herself give up the game. With no way to ascertain the true intended meaning, obsessing over the matter was a fool's errand. Still, it sure as hell served to disquiet her yet further.

She swallowed hard as she reached in to pluck one of the vials out. Holding it up to the light, she shook it gently to watch the contents slosh around. Her aim here was quite ridiculous. She was obeying some unconscious instinct which demanded she check it over to see if it looked right, looked safe. But what the hell was it *supposed* to look like? She had no idea. It could simply be water inside that vial, or it could be liquid cyanide, or it could really be Ikelos. Of course, even if this transparent fluid was what it purported to be, that was sobering enough to behold anyway. And as she went on staring at it, she realized why. Clear, concerted thought was shapes and colors and substance. But the unsettling compound in her grasp was its nemesis. A poison made to insidiously smother and incapacitate it. That was why it just *had* to be so amorphous, so colorless.

Erin gently placed the vial down onto the quilt. Then she cleared the boxes and packaging away. Whilst awaiting the delivery this morning, she had gotten everything prepared for her maiden voyage. She moved it all over to the bed now. The first Tilly scenario was already loaded up onto the computer. It was ready to launch at her command. As she sat back down, the VR headset was close at hand. But laid out right in front of her was the injection kit she had assembled. She looked it over one last time, recalling each step she was to follow. It was hard to stay calm. Having to inject herself made her extremely uneasy. On a surface level, the act itself was definitely pretty unpleasant. She had always disliked needles, even if this aversion didn't rise to the level of a phobia. And how could she not? She was going to be jabbing a sharp, hollow metal tube through her skin, to dump some strange liquid into her system. It was all just so very... crude.

Yet, it was also something else, something more. There was, conceptually, a deeply troubling quality to the whole affair. Whether self-inflicted or not, it felt like a violation to have the citadel of one's body forcibly breached and occupied by a foreign presence. And it was an unshakeable feeling, at that. Savage eons of tribalism, practiced from lowly huts and ornate palaces alike, had encoded a very specific wariness into our subconscious. It was implanted into some overlooked nook amongst our tangle of neurons: an ineradicable fear of *invasion* in all of its forms. Whereas, here she was, about to deposit a hostile chemical battalion inside the passageways of herself. Knowing full well that it would quick-march to that fortified keep in her head, and ruthlessly convert the inhabitants huddled there to its outlander creed of mindlessness. Yet she would play the willing victim to its pillaging, its brainwashing. She yearned to be but a thrall, if that was how true power was come by.

Still, before she could go through with it, she first had to overcome the anachronistic protestations of her brain.

Do not hamstring me with your vile concoction, you know not what you do, it begged.

You are my possession, to modify however I like, she retorted with haughty disregard.

Fool, you do not own me, I am you, it muttered, and henceforth sulkily held its silence.

She shook herself free from her self-engrossed thoughts, and took the syringe in hand. As she drew the specified dosage from the vial, she watched closely for any air bubbles appearing but was satisfied none had. Then she looped a thin leather belt around her bicep and tightened it. Bucking against her attempt to ignore it, her low-level fear was making her faint-headed and slightly jittery. The deep breaths she began sucking in helped. So did focusing only on rhythmically opening and squeezing closed a fist with the hand on her tourniqueted arm. Soon enough, she had regained some crucial fraction of composure and felt okay to continue. She cleaned the injection site near the crook of her elbow with an alcohol wipe, zeroing in on one of the raised veins there.

When she picked up the syringe once more, she inspected her fingers' hold on it, ensuring that no residual shakiness was present. This was not a time where even the smallest of errant movements could be afforded. Thankfully, her grip was as still and sure as a surgeon's. She did, after all, have *some* experience with keeping a steady hand in high-stress moments. Now she squirted out the tiniest drop from the needletip, to double-check no air was trapped, and then lined it up with the vein. The tension had become so unbearable that she actually involuntarily let out a short convulsive laugh, though her expression stayed as serious as ever. Absurd though it was, she barely even noticed it happened. All of her intense focus was lasered onto the syringe. She mustered her determination and held her breath. Then she pierced the needle through without hesitation. It hurt, but only a bit. And she did not allow herself to break concentration by stopping to wince or yelp. She just minutely pulled the plunger back, muddying the pristinely clear Ikelos in the syringe chamber with tiny streaks of blood. She had indeed hit the vein.

Here she was. Everything ready, everything perfect. It was go time.

"Alright. Oooookay. Okay. This is good. This is... I can do this. Just do it. Do it," she whispered to herself whilst blinking excessively and licking her dry lips.

There was an oppressive duality she was now caught betwixt. She felt like both the poor wretch standing atop the gallows trap-door, scared witless it might fall open at any moment, and the executioner resting a tentative hand upon the lever, appalled at the terrible power within his grasp. Yet, the crowd is baying with crushing psychic might for the completion of the drama. So that each of the men are similarly forced to play out their roles. To hang someone, to be hung: the difference somehow fell away. Just moving parts in the totality of the event. And though she had only the universe as her audience, she could feel that it too was already growing impatient.

She closed her eyes tightly, told herself once more to "do it" and then just *felt* her thumb depressing the plunger.

Opening her eyes, she saw that the chamber's payload had been emptied into her vein. There was absolutely no turning back now. Nothing in the world could pluck out each individual molecule as it was whipped away by her coursing blood. It... wasn't quite relief which greeted this realisation. But whatever remained of her fear *was* abruptly drowned by a tidal wave of emotional numbness. There was simply no time for fretting, no time for lollygagging. She had things to do and precious little time to get them done. Ka-Sumedy had said that the potency of her dose would result in a 'fuse' of about ten minutes, and *she had better* be wherever she wanted to ride out Ikelos's effect by then. Though she didn't much care for the unseemly bomb metaphor, Erin was inclined to take this warning seriously.

She wasted no time pulling the needle out and taking off the improvised tourniquet. Leaning over, she placed the used syringe and the vial atop the bedside table. Next she wiped up the pinprick of blood on her forearm, before slapping a bandaid over it. There was an indescribably *weird* quality beginning to infect and distort her thoughts, racing across every facet of their surface like a rapidly spreading fungus. They were starting to seem like unfamiliar things she was merely encountering, rather than authoring. Also, the objects around her were taking on a certain disconcerting *lightness*, as though they were just hovering in their spatial position. Even the slightest bump seemed capable of sending them floating away.

It was really, really hard, but she tried to suppress the urge to freak out. Obviously, the spark had almost eaten through the length of the fuse. She couldn't believe time was moving so fast and she was moving so slow. It was bizarre. There was no time for delicacy anymore; she had to catch up. Swiping her arm across the quilt, she just brushed all of the injection-related detritus onto the floor. Then she roughly pulled the VR headset into place on her head. Her heartrate was soaring. She reached out with her hand to tap the spacebar on the keyboard in front of her and then threw it down towards the end of the bed. Just as she resettled herself in place, it happened.

Suddenly, she was on the couch with Tilly.

Suddenly, she wasn't on the couch with Tilly anymore.

141

She was only staring at the blackness inside the goggles now. It was such a stark, abrupt transition that it confused and frightened and disorientated her. She didn't know where she was or why she was blind. Just as she was about to cry out in panic, she was preempted. From somewhere, the sound of something vibrating and emitting a loud chiming alarm reached her. It gave her a sensory anchor to focus upon. Even though, initially, she couldn't remotely place *what* the noise was. It took considerable mental effort before she brought the image of her phone before her mind's eye. Remembering this started a crucial domino effect where she became more and more cognizant that she was back in the material world again. Finally, she clumsily wrenched the VR headset off and set it down in her lap. Confronted with a room not projected on a screen an inch away, her eyes had a lot of trouble readjusting. Though despite how poor her vision was, the flashing phone screen nearby still managed to snag her attention.

She scooped it up and squinted at the large text of the displayed message: "YOU WERE IN A VR SCENARIO, UNDER THE EFFECT OF IKELOS. EVERYTHING IS OKAY. LIE DOWN AND RELAX. WAIT FOR IKELOS TO WEAR OFF *COMPLETELY* BEFORE YOU TRY TO STAND. THERE'S WATER ON BEDSIDE TABLE IF YOU'RE THIRSTY."

She re-read it several times, letting the words penetrate her muddled mind and coalesce into meaning. When she was able to grasp that she had set this alarm for herself, it somehow put her at ease. Everything was going to be okay. That past version of herself had sympathetically planned all this out; present-Erin was content to now be in her care. She did exactly what the prompt said. She lay down, resting her head on the pillow, and waited. The Tilly scenario had lasted two hours and her Ikelos dose was calculated, at her request, to last as close to that as possible. However, the departure of the drug's effect was not like flipping a switch. Its remnants had to gradually fade away. Thankfully, it didn't take all that long. She soon regained full control of her senses and felt like herself again.

She sat back up and considered the incredible experience she had undergone.

It was a fine testament to the efficacy of Ikelos that recalling it seemed just like half-remembering a recent dream. This signified that she had achieved exactly the result she was hoping for: something which felt like wide-awake, open-eye dreaming. Her mind had just readily accepted what it was shown. And it wasn't merely that Ikelos had bulldozed the usual mental safeguards against embracing illusion. It had induced her subconscious to employ whatever tricks were necessary to fill in the blanks and make it all seem profoundly real to her. Such that it was very difficult, especially in hindsight, to distinguish what was actually part of the scenario and what she had just unwittingly inserted herself. But it didn't matter. It had all added up to sublimity. She had simply *been* there with Tilly. God, she had even *felt* Tilly's touch. Really felt it. Such rich, vivid phantom sensations which somehow her brain had interceded to manufacture too. That was beyond anything she had ever dared to hope for.

Unfortunately, now she was on the other side, she was hit by the familiar blast of deep sadness at being parted from Tilly. But it wasn't anywhere near as gut-wrenching as it had once been. This was partially because just as the body builds up a resistance to certain illnesses the more it's exposed to them, she had grown progressively inured to the post-Tilly sorrow, allowing her to at least function during it. Yet, it was also because another, very different emotion was seeking to overpower and quash the sadness. It was the feeling of being downright exultant. However much she had sought to suppress the lurking doubt, her plan had always seemed like something of a long shot. There were just so many factors outside of her control and so much had to align in her favour for it all to come together perfectly. But it had! And here she was, bestowed with the newfound ability to be with Tilly at will. By sheer ingenuity and tenacity, she had clawed back some power over her situation. This achievement filled her with an elating sense of pride. She hadn't felt anything like it in a very long time.

Mentally surveying this new chapter of her life she was about to enter was... rather vertiginous. Everything was slotting into place, and a staggering surfeit of opportunity now confronted her. There was so much to do, because there was so much which *could* now be done. But first she had to cement the fundamental scaffolding which enabled it all. She would need to commission more Tilly scenarios and order another, larger batch of Ikelos for when she exhausted her current supply.

How freeing it was to see the exact right path unfurl before her, and know she had only to walk it.

CHAPTER NINE

7:03 PM. OCTOBER 26TH.

(APPROX. ELEVEN DAYS LATER)

[19:03] PluckingPurgatory'sPetals: It's almost funny how this shit goes.

[19:03] PluckingPurgatory'sPetals: Now that I'm not just sitting around desperately waiting for sleep, the insomnia seems to have lifted.

[19:04] PluckingPurgatory'sPetals: Like, for example, I slept for almost eleven hours yesterday. I'm talking about real sleep, replete with *dreams*.

[19:04] PluckingPurgatory'sPetals: It was fucking glorious.

[19:06] Alabaster&Freckles: Woah, I'm so glad to hear that, that's really great!

[19:07] Alabaster&Freckles: I think not having to deal with the tiredness is really, really going to help you. You'll be able to think more clearly about things.

[19:07] PluckingPurgatory'sPetals: Yep, I sure hope so!

[19:08] Alabaster&Freckles: Umm... so, there's no good segue for this, but can I ask you something?

[19:08] PluckingPurgatory'sPetals: Shoot.

[19:10] Alabaster&Freckles: I hope you'll forgive my confusion, it's just that there's something I think I don't fully understand.

[19:11] Alabaster&Freckles: I'm not sure quite how to put this... but is the Tilly you see in the VR goggles really her?

[19:12] Alabaster&Freckles: I mean, is that the *real* her, from the dreams? Or is it just lit-up pixels on a screen which look like her?

[19:13] Alabaster&Freckles: Obviously, I haven't been lucky enough to enjoy the unorthodox sort of relationship you have with Tilly. It's all so new to me, I'm just trying to keep up.

[19:14] PluckingPurgatory'sPetals: Hmm, okay, so I've been thinking about that a lot myself lately.

[19:15] PluckingPurgatory'sPetals: Originally, I believed that Tilly existed solely in the dreamworld. That intuitively made sense, because it's her home, it's where we first made contact.

[19:15] PluckingPurgatory'sPetals: And like we talked about at the time, I first intended the VR stuff to be a sort of reenactment of my time with Tilly.

[19:16] PluckingPurgatory'sPetals: Yet, more and more I'm starting to see that it's... more than that.

[19:17] PluckingPurgatory'sPetals: Jesus, I can barely contain my excitement as I write this: I think Tilly can *transfer* herself!!

[19:20] PluckingPurgatory'sPetals: All she wants is to be with me, and vice versa. There's something very powerful about that. It means that if I can create a suitable venue (i.e. the VR scenarios), she can find a way to incarnate herself there.

[19:21] Alabaster&Freckles: But... aren't you just re-experiencing the couch scenario over and over right now?

[19:22] PluckingPurgatory'sPetals: Sure, until I finally get sent the new ones I'm having made.

[19:24] Alabaster&Freckles: Then how can it really be Tilly if you're simply doing the exact same thing with her each time?

[19:25] PluckingPurgatory'sPetals: Well, I have the same Tilly dreams many times over. It's no different to that repetition.

[19:27] PluckingPurgatory'sPetals: Look at it this way. You spend the next five minutes eating a peach, and then I rewind those five minutes. Once they restart, you now eat the exact same peach again, in the exact same way. Don't you think you still *really* ate the peach both times?

[19:28] PluckingPurgatory'sPetals: It's all just slices of time.

[19:29] PluckingPurgatory'sPetals: And given the weird nature of my connection to the dreamworld, it doesn't seem too far-fetched to me that non-linear time might somehow be tied up in it all as well.

[19:29] PluckingPurgatory'sPetals: The rules are simply different. Everything is becoming fluid, commingling. That's the ripple effect of my bond with Tilly. Our love must function like... an existential mutagen.

[19:30] PluckingPurgatory'sPetals: I'm really starting to believe anything is possible now. That scares me, but it also makes me feel so alive!

CHAPTER TEN

10:50 PM. DECEMBER 9TH.

(APPROX. FORTY-FOUR DAYS LATER)

The blender was very, very loud.

Even with a folded dishtowel beneath its base to absorb the vibrations, its screeching, rumbly din was nonetheless grating. But Erin barely even heard it anymore. She just stood there absentmindedly resting her hand on the blender's lid and staring off into space.

It always took a little while to mix this brand of meal replacement shake to the thin-ish consistency she wanted. So she had gotten into the habit of using this time to just zone out and think. At first, this hadn't seemed like an opportune context in which to do so, for obvious reasons. Yet she soon saw the whirry racket filling the room as but a mind-focusing background of aggressive white noise. Besides, she definitely had a good enough incentive to *make* it work. Getting lost in thought was hugely preferable to just staring at the utilitarian nutrient-sludge as it sloppily spun around and around. That would just be gradually psyching herself out of drinking it when it was done, and it was a hard enough feat already.

Although these shakes were almost all she consumed now, it obviously wasn't because she enjoyed them so very much. The way that this gloop looked and smelled and tasted was *anything* but appetizing. She had found only one workable method of drinking them: brace yourself and then take big, fast gulps in order to taste it as little as possible. Unpleasant though this trial was, it was also over quickly. That's what made the whole thing so worthwhile. She only had to down them twice daily and then she gratefully needn't think about sustenance again until the next day. To her, food was just fuel, and this approach made refueling as convenient as possible. With minimal time and effort, her body simply got what it needed, tastebuds be damned. All in all, a very good deal for someone like her.

She learned about how to implement this liquid food program, and many other things besides, at an online hub for VR addicts called 'Elsewhere'. She had unintentionally become aware of it during her research into the cyberkin, because of the substantial participation overlap between the two unaffiliated groups. It was a small, intensely passionate community. Its members were united by a preference for the infinite possibilities of virtual worlds over the constraints and vexations of what they derogatorily referred to as meatspace. They were, in other words, her kind of people! This was her tribe, and she had come *home!* How satisfying and reassuring it was to find others who truly grasped why sojourning in VR was more meaningful than one's captivity in material reality.

First she had omnivorously absorbed all the available teachings. Then she began posting, frequently and with great enthusiasm. Naturally, she opted not to articulate her Tilly situation specifically. (It was not a thing to blab about like some trollop boasting of a past lay.) But she *was* able to talk, in general, about how much VR had helped her and become a central part of her life. And she unburdened herself of these thoughts rather... volubly. The group, seeing this ample proof she was undoubtedly one of them, had welcomed her with open arms. Her new brethren, partaking in the age-old self-denigrating humour common to fringe subcultures, had adopted the name 'triple-zeds' for themselves. It was a wry allusion to how they endeavoured to spend their lives dreaming whilst asleep *and* awake, as though 'zzz...' was cartoonishly ever-floating above their heads. And now Erin was one of them.

What made Elsewhere such a lovely safe haven, and why she had gravitated to it so strongly, was its accepting attitude. It wasn't seeking to rehabilitate triple-zeds towards resuming a so-called 'normal' life. Quite the opposite in fact. The group's most cherished credo was that VR addiction was not to be viewed as an illness, or as any detriment at all really. It was, instead, but a rational reaction to the emergence of a better way to spend one's time than plodding through the mundane monotony of physical existence. Whether outsiders considered heavy VR use unhealthy was irrelevant. It ought to be considered the same as any other unusual lifestyle choice someone might adopt.

The key philosophical conviction which justified this stance was called 'freedom of reality', which asserted an inherent human right to form one's own belief about what reality is. Sure, the regnant consensus of society was that the earthly plane was the sole, indubitable bedrock of the objectively real. That was fine. It was their choice to make for themselves, however poorly they decided. Still, no matter how great the peer pressure from the rest of mankind, the triple-zeds were steadfast. They fiercely claimed that their outlier conceptions of meaningful reality were just as valid, just as worthwhile. Now, when Erin first heard this ethic being espoused, it had a peculiar effect upon her. It felt so right. It felt like words which had silently been welling up inside of her for so long. She had never really had any patience for the uncomfortable rigidity, both intellectually and physically, of taking one's seat at the pew. But the distinctly secular church of Elsewhere was a different matter entirely. *Its* gospel she could stand to hear preached all the livelong day.

However, for all their advocacy efforts, the triple-zeds were not a bunch of pushy evangelists at all. This made sense given the notion they fundamentally adhered to: live as you will. Yet, if you *did* feel the same affinity as them and you made the pilgrimage to Elsewhere, they were only too happy to help you. It was a very positive, friendly community. They provided encouragement and guidance on how to best remould one's waking life so that it revolved around VR. Erin had found this support invaluable. She had employed many of their techniques to try and maximise her daily VR use. Still, in doing so, she grasped what a novice she was in this art. How much there was to learn! How much greater dedication there was to achieve! The most hardcore triple-zeds had complex, precisely devised arrangements involving urethral catheters and sponge baths and feeding/hydration tubes and various other things which still scared the hell out of her. Nonetheless, though she couldn't stomach these extreme measures just yet, she was glad to know how they worked. A very distant goal to aspire to, perhaps.

Now that the comfort of her Tilly scenarios had thankfully dissipated the insomnia, she was sleeping normally again. The sense of relief she felt because of this was marvelous. She had even briefly debated whether to experiment with new, less powerful sleeping pills to extend her sleep-time even further. But she became terrified that this greediness would only wreck the balance she'd finally regained, and inflict an infernal sleeplessness once more. That was not a risk to incur lightly. So, she focused on the portion of her life she could still safely tinker with. Based on how long she usually slept, she ended up with about fourteen to sixteen daily waking hours. If time was currency, this was the wealth she had to play around with. But, given she only wanted to buy one thing, she needed to figure out how to spend it most wisely. After the long stretch of powerlessness she had endured, this newfound control over her life was intoxicatingly gratifying. There was such an exactness in how she could divvy up her hours in service of VR. She had taken to the practice with great zeal.

In the notation system of the triple-zeds, she was currently at 60/VR. That meant she had reached the point where she could consistently spend sixty percent of her waking time in VR. This was more difficult to achieve than it seemed. Not least because it was necessary to gradually acclimatize oneself to copious VR use. Both the body and the mind had to be eased into the transition: like any other servants, they had to be trained to kowtow to a new master. Fortunately, the physical problems which had to be overcome were relatively minor niggles. An example was the eye strain which staring into VR goggles for so long caused. It could be combated with eye drops and special contact lenses which lessened the fatiguing of one's eyes. Another such example was the muscle cramping and soreness which accompanied prolonged periods of sitting or standing still. This, in turn, could be remedied by stretching and self-massage between sessions. Always, there was a workaround. The body is just a dumb beast-of-burden; it could be made to bear whatever yoke one chooses with only minimal grumbling.

Instead, it was the psychological difficulties which were truly formidable. For the brain is *not* like a mere brute one employs to till the field, and cannot be broken as easily as one. Its servitude is valuable precisely because it is capable of finer exertions, of complex and delicate toil; yet this imparts a much more fearsome power to rebel. That was not an idle threat either. If one tried to place excessive strain upon one's own psyche, it was sure to mightily resist. And this represented the bottleneck for achieving the highest percentages of waking VR use. Because even if you were willing to forsake patience and finesse, and try to ram past the limits, you risked irreparable damage. A bruise spreading through the tissue of the mind. It would produce a sort of numbness, a sort of distancing.

At the moment, she experienced only faint, but ominous, symptoms of this. In particular she had noticed a very subtle *alteration* to her perception whilst in the material world. It was hard to pin down and even harder to articulate, but she could definitely feel it. It was as though she was a little more disconnected from the reports of her senses than normal, like they had a fraction less impact upon her. She wondered whether this was indicative of a certain... misalignment she was cultivating by immersing her mind in an illusory world and re-calibrating it to the falsity therein. It was easy not to fret too much right now, given how mild the phenomenon was. But she knew that, even if only slightly, a *wedge* had been driven between her mind and physical reality.

What really worried her was a wider fissure arising from that wedge taking too many more heavy hammer-blows. She even had some sense of what that would look like. For she had often seen the other triple-zeds discuss their ultimate fear: *depersonalization* and *derealization*. Whenever they spoke of these things, it was tinged with great superstitious apprehension. As if these strange polysyllabic words were part of the incantation for some ancient curse, and even uttering them risked bringing about one's doom. Yet, they were in truth just psychiatric terms. They referred, respectively, to the emergence of an unshakable belief that one's physical body is no longer one's own or that one's physical surroundings are no longer real. As if it even needs to be said: to lose one's grasp on these crucial anchors is to lose everything. The resulting existential alienation and homesickness are crippling. They can cause raving, hysterical panic attacks which prove to be intensely traumatic. And eventually the affliction, escalating to its severest form, rots away one's sanity completely and brings about a catatonic state. As the triple-zeds are usually hermits, this fate would lead to a slow death via dehydration.

Thus, however much they may want to conclusively migrate from this material realm to the malleable wonderland yonder, the triple-zeds were forced to respect the necessity of dual-residence. Withhold meatspace from the mind for too long and it would someday become permanently, ruinously decoupled from it. This was the simple, stark truth. There was no getting around it. Of course, the triple-zeds wouldn't acknowledge that this proved that meatspace was the one true reality. They conceded only that once the mind got so accustomed to something, weaning it off of that would inevitably be fraught with... difficulties. Yet, begrudgingly or not, they employed the requisite caution. After all, they had to seek a *sustainable* way to overindulge in VR, given that they saw it as not a short-term whim but a lifelong realigning of their very existence.

Erin's shake had finally reached the right consistency. Or, well, close enough. She turned off the blender. The switch back to silence was almost jarring. Then she detached the jug and removed its lid. It would be pointless to decant the contents into a glass. That would simply be dragging it out. She raised the jug's rim to her lips and paused to ready herself. It was always a mistake to peer inside, especially this close up, and it was one she repeated again now. She saw air pockets popping on the tilted surface of the viscous slop, leaving behind slowly-refilling craters.

"God fucking damn it, that is nasty," she murmured to herself.

Huffing through her nose as she mentally chided herself for having foolishly inspected it for the umpteenth time, she closed her eyes. No point in putting the plunge off any longer; the damage had already been done. She tipped the jug upward and the shake thickly slid into her mouth. Only stopping to suck in a quick breath after every few mouthfuls, she hurriedly gulped it down. The competition between which was the worst part was too close to call. There was the way that the gross cocktail of artificial flavourings tasted. And there was the unsettlingly chemical-y way that it smelt, which was redolent of anything besides food. And there was the fact that, somehow, it slimily coated every millimetre inside her mouth. When she chanced a peek, she saw that she'd so far managed to drink three-quarters. Although she wanted very badly to just quit, she marshalled the scattering troops of her willpower for the mad dash to the finish. She guzzled the rest and, at last, it was over.

She slammed the jug down onto the counter. Her fist was held against her closed mouth as she did her utmost to stifle the reflexive dry heaves which usually assaulted her afterwards. To have to vomit all of that back up and *then* clean it off the floor and *then* try to consume another shake would be spirit-breaking. Once she was reasonably sure that she would be able to keep it down, she rinsed out the blender jug and also rinsed out her mouth. She was still shaking. It always seemed kind of unbelievable to her that she had actually managed to do it. Given her problems just eating regular food, a torturer trying to extract information from her could have done no better than force-feeding her some disgusting liquid. Yet, here she was, doing it to herself. It thoroughly amazed her that she was even capable of it. The reason why she was happened to be both simple and predictable. She was able to draw from a hitherto unknown reservoir of power when it came to doing things to be with Tilly. It was eerie. But it was emboldening too.

To lessen the sloshing in her uncomfortably full stomach, she waddled over towards the door as slowly and steadily as she could. She made sure the temperature control dial was up high; she wanted it nice and toasty in here. Then she headed over to the bed and, sitting down there, checked the time on her phone. Usefully, her dilly-dallying at the blender had eaten up the remainder of her self-imposed VR break. She scooted up the bed until her back was against the headboard, which now had a pillow firmly taped to it. The VR headset lay beside her and she stared at it whilst trying to decide which Tilly scenario to go with this time. She had a total of three now. The Skylarks had been her dream-crafters of choice each time.

After the initial success, it had been tempting to commission a few other architect teams simultaneously, in order to receive scenarios faster. But there had just been too many good reasons to stick with The Skylarks. The main one was that they were really very good at what they did. Such that Erin had no doubt they were destined to go onto great things soon enough. Still, the fact that they were *presently* languishing in early obscurity meant that the cost-to-quality ratio they provided was truly astonishing. It was the type of insane bargain one only rarely stumbled upon. On top of all that, there was such a compatibility in how they seemed to intuitively understand the nuances of what she asked them for. This made the whole process a lot easier and a lot less error-prone.

Additionally, the working relationship she'd developed with them as their current de facto patron had given her a glimpse into what kind of people they were. Based on what she had gleaned, she felt quite sure that she could trust them to honor the confidentiality they had sworn to uphold. Whereas the danger of adding more architect teams into the mix was the accompanying uncertainty. It only took one gossip for word of a spendthrift client seeking to reproduce their dreams about some woman to spread throughout the community. And if she entrusted her secret to a multi-team arrangement, it would just give each of them better cover to disperse it at will. After all, how could she track back the disclosure when there were so many possible culprits? This was a danger she had mulled over at length.

Limiting who knew about Tilly, in even the most controlled way, was only ever seeming more and more important to Erin. As her access to Tilly seemed dependent upon a mental connection, it surely could be sullied or diluted if knowledge of Tilly was disseminated too promiscuously. It was an idea which was childish in both its jealous and absurd qualities. But it was also one she found quite impossible to dispel. Right now, Erin was the only person who *really knew* about Tilly. Who was to say that Tilly might not effectively be kidnapped by some stranger if they somehow came to really know about her too? That may well strike the... uninitiated as preposterous, as self-obsessed. Yet Erin had learned that the true hubris was assuming one knew the limits of the universe's inventive skulduggery. That was not a trap she would fall into twice. Given all the profound weirdness she had already experienced, she had to at least be open to every possibility.

She idly fiddled with the straps on the VR headset and ran through the choices in her mind. The scenario she had just undergone was the original couch-based one, so that was out. She preferred not to repeat them back-to-back, now that she didn't have to. So that left the two new ones to choose from.

The first scenario featured her and Tilly at a supermarket getting their weekly shopping done. She was pushing the shopping cart down the aisles as Tilly walked alongside and held her hand. Sometimes Tilly would suddenly veer off to pluck something from a shelf and toss it into the cart with a playful smirk. Thereby flaunting her power, as she wasn't the designated cart-pusher, to unilaterally amend the usual grocery list. Sometimes Tilly would sit on the front end of the cart and ride it as Erin pushed, like a lookout affixed to the prow of a ship. Sometimes they would toss canned goods back and forth like inept jugglers, and giggle. Sometimes they would brainstorm exotic new meals to try and then ferret out the guessed-at ingredients. Sometimes Erin would chase Tilly with the cart. She would pretend it was a charging bull, but always allow Tilly enough time to gracefully leap out of the way like a matador.

The second scenario featured her and Tilly painting their bedroom together. There was much patient demonstration from Erin on how to use the tools. And there was much eschewing of proper coverage to paint amusing shapes and figures on the walls for each other's appraisal. And there was much slo-mo jousting with the extended paint-roller poles. And there was much sneakily splattering each other's backs with flicked paintbrush bristles. And there was much energetic, carefree dancing to the radio's music during the many breaks they took. And there was much taking turns holding the paintcan for one another and pointing out spots which had been missed. And there was much cooing over the haphazard mixing together of the assembled paints to try and produce some peculiar new colour the world had never seen before. A secret colour just for them, which they'd each bear a swatch of on their wrists as a clandestine symbol of their *sui generis* union.

In point of fact, there was also an eagerly-anticipated third scenario currently being built. It featured her and Tilly cleaning out their walk-in wardrobe. Inbetween working together to empty out drawers and move boxes and decide what should be thrown away, there was naturally plenty of horsing around. This could take the form of throwing musty rolled up clothes-missiles at each other. Or it could take the form of holding up individual items of clothing to stage mock auctions for their salvation. Or it could take the form of trying on ridiculous outfit combinations to make the other person laugh.

Interestingly, when she had outlined this next-to-be-built scene to The Skylarks, an issue had arose. Although no actual nudity was required, it did involve a woman repeatedly undressing for the observer. And The Skylarks had initially questioned whether this was intended to be somewhat erotic. For obvious reasons, sexual scenarios of varying quality, but mostly crude, were an enormously popular and well-populated genre online. Yet, however lucrative this specific market may be, many architect teams stridently refused to create that type of content. Perhaps out of a desire to cultivate respectability. Or perhaps simply to avoid artistically cheapening themselves. So when The Skylarks half-suspected that Erin might be seeking the virtual fulfilment of an odd fetish - like some middle-aged sleazeball who wanted to insert himself into his favorite softcore, pseudo-artsy girl-on-girl film - they had tactfully pointed out they were among this class of abstainers. This was certainly fair enough. But she also knew that it was just a misunderstanding. She vehemently assured The Skylarks how decidedly *non*-sexual her envisioned scene was, which alleviated their concerns. The truth, moreover, was that she could never have any interest in commissioning some kind of sordid VR lapdance. Even the very prospect of skewering Tilly's flayed likeness upon some hyper-sexualised, lewdly gyrating cyber-mannequin made Erin feel furious and nauseous in equal measure. It would be an unconscionable act, a desecration of their love.

She made her choice of scenario and used the nearby keyboard to select it from her burgeoning library.

Obviously, she had experienced each of the Tilly scenarios she had amassed many times over at this point. It was just immensely fortunate that the expected dampening effect of this repetition had been prevented by how Ikelos clouded the mind. There was this blank openness that Ikelos induced which forced one to really *be* in the moment. So that there was only what was presently before one's eyes and ears; previous memories simply did not intrude to ruin the novelty. Thus, in a sense it still felt like a new experience each time. For all the miraculous things she had originally hoped the drug would do, the unexpected range of its utility was perhaps even more incredible. In effect, it was a skeleton key attuned to unlock the every winding passageway of one's mind.

She was rather in awe of the dextrous, wondrous mastery which Ka-Sumedy evidently possessed. What a bizarre set of talents to choose to foster in oneself. All in service of becoming a latter-day alchemist who can, with precision, tinker with wayward whirlpools of molecules in pristine glassware. Each time seeking to snatch yet another perfected high from its tragic imprisonment in mere theory. Yet she was so glad to have encountered just such a savant. And so indescribably thankful for the tool which had been created for her. How dearly her fellow triple-zeds would have longed after Ikelos if they learned it now existed. They would surely have given just about anything to have such a versatile drug as this at their disposal.

In fact, if she pried the exact formula from Ka-Sumedy and deigned to covertly sell it to her more well-off triple-zed peers, she stood to profit rather handsomely. Those sales would probably even recoup her very substantial recent expenditures. The problem, of course, was that she didn't *want* to share it. Not at all. It was part of the apparatus she used to be with Tilly, and even that tangential relation gave it some residual sacredness. It was therefore to be jealously protected. So, her close-fisted grip upon Ikelos was destined to endure. And what a stockpile she now owned. It had been a lot cheaper to have Ka-Sumedy simply produce a new batch of the already-created drug. Accordingly, she had bought a large amount in case anything should ever happen to cut off her supply.

With the scenario loaded and ready to launch, she rested the VR headset in her lap and reached over to the bedside table. She grabbed a pre-prepared syringe, filled with Ikelos, as well as the fraying leather belt.

It was time to go back in.

A wide, manic smile rearranged her face.

CHAPTER ELEVEN

4:11 AM. DECEMBER 21ST.

(APPROX. TWELVE DAYS LATER)

Although Erin would have liked to get it off her chest, she had not told *A&F* about Ikelos. How could she?

Everything else she had been doing, she related freely, but Ikelos was in a... very different category. It had been a drastic, perilous gambit. And no-one else, not even *A&F*, would be able to fully appreciate why no measures were too extreme if they brought Erin closer to Tilly. That was just the nature of things. That was just Erin's personal burden. Still, she had to begrudgingly admit that it was not without an element of fairness. Love *is* selfishly enjoyed as a private boon, therefore one *cannot* ask that its reclamation be a communal effort. And so, the lover's quest is always going to be littered with a thousand tiny lonelinesses. They had to be borne with abiding grace. For if one spurns the trial, one belittles the prize at its end. And she was not about to insult the worth of Tilly's affections, was she?

It had, at least, been easier than she'd expected to keep this aspect of her new routine from *A&F*. For one thing, she simply didn't talk to *A&F* as much anymore, having something rather more compelling which monopolised her time now. That helpfully reduced the frequency of her even having to service this ongoing omission. But there was more to it, too. Lying about the aborted suicide attempt a while back had broken a mental barrier. Now, she didn't even bother torturing herself by trying to justify this new lie. She just did it, and then it had been done, and then she didn't even give it a second thought. The unspoken thing merely blended into a background of other absences, and was forgotten. A shadow deposited into a dark room.

The plain reality was that *A&F* could handle a lot of the truth, but not all of it. Erin merely adhered to this exact demarcation. No more, no less. She never lied gratuitously, just to make her life easier, she lied only when she *had* to. She'd decided that telling things to *A&F* which they had no hope of understanding, which would just upset them, was actually not the moral choice at all. Causing pointless strife was simply being cruel to *A&F*, and indulging her own emotional masochism. As soon as this seemed self-evident to her, the lies to hide her Ikelos use had spilled from her with ease. They were, after all, for everyone's benefit. A merciful kindness, really.

Yet, a little mistake had brought her deception before a blazing spotlight. It had been a mix of bad timing and her own carelessness, but she'd accidentally hinted at what was really going on. During an otherwise trivial conversation about how she was salivating over some just-announced VR equipment, she had sent *A&F* a screenshot of the pre-order website to show how a deluge of customers had crashed the order page. It had taken thirty seconds, maybe. She had done it automatically, without even thinking.

Alas, visible at the top of her browser window were the *other* tabs she had open. And unfortunately, she wasn't lucky enough for these to have merely been some really weird porn videos instead. That would have just caused a momentary stab of vaguely-funny embarrassment and regret. No big deal. Whereas they actually included several medical supply websites, where she was comparing prices on boxes of disposable, pre-sterilized syringes/needles. She was going to run out soon. This should have been just a minor annoyance. Yet, with her life being so much better, so much happier now, these little hassles irked her more than usual. That led her to toy with the idea of buying in bulk so she needn't worry about this again. And, as luck would have it, the page titles on the tabs clearly gave away that this was what she was shopping for.

A&F did not feign obliviousness, nor beat around the bush. They seized upon it immediately, asking Erin why she would need to buy such things. Stunned at what her foolish blunder had brought about, Erin just sat there for ten minutes, scrambling to devise an alternate, innocuous explanation. In her mind, she ran through possible medications or supplements she could be taking intravenously, but nothing seemed even remotely believable. And eventually enough time had passed that even if she tried to offer up some contrived story, it would be painfully obvious that she'd just been stalling to think it up. Otherwise, why would it have taken her so long to respond to a simple question? Besides, it wasn't worth blatantly insulting *A&F*'s intelligence just to try and pass off some babyish falsehood. Especially when it had such a miniscule chance of success. No, Erin knew there was no way out but forward. Because *A&F*, when they wanted to be, was very persistent. And that meant this particular cat was *not* going to go quietly back into the bag. So her best option now was simply crossed-fingers and damage control. She would even try her best to be patient with *A&F*, and their scolding, whilst doing it.

[04:11] Alabaster&Freckles: Hello?...

[04:14] Alabaster&Freckles: Are you still there?...

[04:18] Alabaster&Freckles: Please, just tell me what's going on!

[04:20] PluckingPurgatory'sPetals: Okay, look, this is just a little thing really. For real. It's, like, really not that serious.

[04:21] PluckingPurgatory'sPetals: And I only kept it from you because I didn't want you to overreact.

[04:21] PluckingPurgatory'sPetals: I know how you worry sometimes... and it didn't feel right to stoke that unnecessarily.

[04:21] Alabaster&Freckles: This preamble is not helping. Just tell me.

[04:23] PluckingPurgatory'sPetals: It's kind of a long story, but the short version is this: when I'm using the Tilly scenarios, I take a drug which helps make me more... receptive to them.

[04:24] PluckingPurgatory'sPetals: It's nothing crazy. It just softens your perception and encourages the mind to believe whatever's presented to it. That's all.

[04:25] PluckingPurgatory'sPetals: I didn't want to have to inject anything, but that's the form it comes in, so I just deal with it.

[04:25] PluckingPurgatory'sPetals: I mean, I know my stuff, I do it safely.

[04:26] Alabaster&Freckles: Jesus, this drug sounds really dangerous! It basically turns off your brain?!

[04:26] Alabaster&Freckles: Wait...

[04:26] Alabaster&Freckles: You use it *every* time you do the VR stuff?

[04:26] Alabaster&Freckles: That's like most of your day! What the hell?!

[04:27] PluckingPurgatory'sPetals: Hey! Relax! It's my choice!

[04:27] PluckingPurgatory'sPetals: And I know what I'm doing, I'm not a fucking child.

[04:28] PluckingPurgatory'sPetals: I *need* to take it, to make contact with Tilly in VR. I have to believe it's real in the moment. That's what makes the connection work in the first place!

[04:29] Alabaster&Freckles: I just...

[04:30] Alabaster&Freckles: I'm speechless.

[04:30] Alabaster&Freckles: I truly don't even know how to respond to this.

[04:31] Alabaster&Freckles: How long have you been using this wacko drug?! Since you got the very first Tilly scenario?!

[04:31] PluckingPurgatory'sPetals: Yes.

[04:32] PluckingPurgatory'sPetals: Like. I. Said. There was no other way to do it.

[04:32] PluckingPurgatory'sPetals: And, hell, I was damn lucky to figure out this solution in the first place!

[04:33] Alabaster&Freckles: Lucky?!

[04:34] Alabaster&Freckles: Wow, I can't do this anymore. This is just too much. I cannot stand idly by any longer. I don't know what else to do.

[04:34] Alabaster&Freckles: Listen to me: *you need to get help*! Today! Right now!

[04:35] Alabaster&Freckles: I know it will be hard to leave your apartment, but you have to!

[04:36] Alabaster&Freckles: You are *SERIOUSLY* unwell, mentally. You obviously had some kind of catalyst episode that first night. And now something is broken in your mind. You need to seek professional help, before it's too late.

[04:36] Alabaster&Freckles: Tilly is not real!

[04:37] Alabaster&Freckles: I repeat, Tilly is not real!

[04:37] Alabaster&Freckles: She isn't now, and she never was. She's just a figment of your imagination! A symptom of whatever mental illness it is that you're suffering from.

[04:38] Alabaster&Freckles: I know *you* can't see things clearly right now, so please trust *me*. You're injecting some messed-up drug all day, so you can pretend you're spending time with a virtual version of an imaginary friend. That's absurd! That's not something a mentally sound person would do!

[04:38] Alabaster&Freckles: This isn't your fault! None of this is your fault! You're just unwell!

[04:39] Alabaster&Freckles: But you have to really take in what I'm saying to you! You have to let it get through to you! I'm saying all this because I care about you!

[04:39] Alabaster&Freckles: It's crucial that you go to a doctor or a therapist or a psychiatrist or whatever, and get the help you need! Please, if you won't do it for me, do it for *yourself*! Before this gets even worse!

[04:41] PluckingPurgatory'sPetals: Are you quite finished?

[04:41] Alabaster&Freckles: Um... yes...

[04:42] PluckingPurgatory'sPetals: Fuck you.

[04:42] PluckingPurgatory'sPetals: And how fucking dare you. You have no right to lecture me!

[04:43] PluckingPurgatory'sPetals: And you definitely have no right to diagnose me with made-up maladies so you can disparage my love!

[04:43] PluckingPurgatory'sPetals: You know nothing about Tilly, evidently. And you know ab-so-fucking-lutely nothing about me.

[04:43] PluckingPurgatory'sPetals: You have NO goddamn idea just how broken I really was before I met her.

[04:44] PluckingPurgatory'sPetals: How every day I heaped all the newly crumbling pieces of myself to my chest, fucking terrified they'd slip through my fingers forever.

[04:45] PluckingPurgatory'sPetals: How her love turned out to be the only thing which could help me glue myself back together and face tomorrow.

[04:46] PluckingPurgatory'sPetals: God, you're just like the rest of these closed-minded sheep! Anything new, anything they don't understand, they call 'insane'. I thought you were different! I thought you were better than that!

[04:47] PluckingPurgatory'sPetals: Now, I can't believe I ever trusted you. But I won't make that idiotic mistake again.

[04:47] PluckingPurgatory'sPetals: I never want to talk to you ever again.

[04:47] PluckingPurgatory'sPetals: Do not try to contact me.

[PluckingPurgatory'sPetals - is now offline]

Although Erin was scowling, her eyes were brimming with tears.

She blocked *A&F*, uninstalled the IM app altogether, and shoved the laptop far beneath the bed. She wanted it as far away from her as possible. Then she just sat there trying to affect a fake nonchalance by inspecting her fingernails with exaggerated interest. Even as little teardrops periodically splashed onto her knees and she struggled to bring her quivering lower lip under control. She suddenly felt very childlike, and resented the feeling with a burning intensity.

"I. Don't. Fucking. Need. Them... I. Don't. Need. Anyone. But. Tilly."

She slowly spat each word of this declaration through clenched teeth. It was hard to tell which hurt more, all the ways in which this was true or all the ways in which it was untrue.

The tears finally began to flow freely. Yet, still she refused to acknowledge them, still she fought them.

She *wasn't* crying. She *wasn't* crying. She *wasn't* crying.

Because there was *nothing* to cry about.

CHAPTER TWELVE

It wasn't enough. It just wasn't enough.

Erin had been resisting this admission for some time now, but it could be ignored no longer.

The Tilly scenarios were just *not* enough anymore.

Strangely, there hadn't even been a period of incrementally building dissatisfaction which preceded this change of heart. It kind of just... happened, like a fuse had been yanked out of her mind. No warning, no instigating event. This annoyed her perhaps even more than the alteration itself. It would somehow have been less galling if, despite how strongly Ikelos tried to mask this effect, the incredibly excessive repetition of her VR use had made her grow tired of the scenarios. That at least would have been understandable in some basic sense. It would merely reaffirm that human psychology is fickle and, no matter how well coerced, will demand novelty eventually. The solution would have therefore been clear: introduce newly-made scenarios faster than her mind became numb to them. Now, this may or may not even have been possible to achieve. But either way she'd know the nature of the predicament. And that was crucial if she was to retain a placating sense of understanding.

However, instead she had just all of a sudden started to find the VR stuff so unbearably, woefully deficient. In an unflinchingly critical side-by-side comparison of the scenarios with the dreamworld itself, there was actually something newly *offensive* about just how pale the imitation really was. This gulf of fidelity had become so unignorable. She could now *only* see all of the profound flaws. And that was the kind of thing you couldn't unsee. There was simply no going back to the blissful ignorance of how things had been before. That had only been weeks ago, but what a glorious past it now seemed. Back then, her halcyon life had seemed so fixed, so permanent. And that had been true, in a certain sense, for a certain time. But the hardened cement keeping everything in its perfect place had somehow been wetted, becoming malleable again, whilst she was too happy to notice. Then, in a flash, it had shifted into some new malign formation and set once more, solid as rock. So that now it held her trapped, enclosing her in a terrible new present. There was no use whining about this. She was just going to have to reshape it from the inside, reshape it with a sledgehammer. Contouring a new reality for herself with every blow. It wasn't going to be pretty and debris was sure to fly everywhere, littering the floor with jagged chips of how things had been, but she'd rather be a sloppy impromptu self-sculptor than let the situation be decided for her.

The question, then, was where exactly to go from here. First of all, in point of fact, merely going back to how things *were* no longer seemed remotely desirable anymore. For she'd begun to dwell upon the ethical dimension: had the VR rendezvous been fair to Tilly? The more she thought about this, the more she was inclined to answer... no. She could now appreciate how the artificial and unchanging nature of the scenarios had placed Tilly into a sort of existential bondage. It had made her be just a wretched marionette puppet forced to play out the same movements with the same painted-on emotions *ad nauseum*. Was this not a tortuous captivity? Was this not a twisted charade for Erin's amusement and solace? Whatever it was, it wasn't okay. And it was never going to seem fucking okay again. Erin had wept at realizing how she might have been selfishly hurting Tilly, and silently begged her for forgiveness. Yet that was only the very beginning of the reparations she intended to make. How dearly she wished she had seen the truth earlier, but now that she finally had, she was going to make up for lost time. She was going to do what she ought to have done from the get-go. She would use everything in her power to grant unto her love the greatest gift possible: liberation.

Tilly must be freed.

Those four words echoed in her mind on a loop, like a forever-chiming bell calling her to action. The goal, she now realized, should always have been to bring Tilly into the waking, physical world. And not Tilly as some diminished virtual ghost either, but as herself, as the complete person she really was. This, and only this, would allow the two of them to truly be together. It was all or nothing. Erin wanted this unity more than anything; she was determined to make it so. That was her new mission, her new reason for moving and breathing. She was going to be with Tilly, *really be* with her. It would be incredible, not being bound by the unchangeable nature of the dreams or scenarios, but interacting with Tilly in a freeform, spontaneous, unpredictable fashion. Exactly like any other two normal, real people might. There would be a sort of validation in that.

Moreover, everything they did together would be gloriously enhanced by the clear lens of waking lucidity. The haziness of the dreamworld had its charm, sure, but it also strained the mind and obscured so much. She wanted to admire Tilly's beautiful totality in the light of day, seeing its every minute nuance with utmost clarity. She wanted to submerge into it, to become one with it. Lying in it as though in the waters of a tidepool, where a million tiny forms of life - all colourful, eccentric, marvelous, benign - would explore her body like a reef, infusing her with their strangeness. So too, she'd surrender herself to Tilly's beauty, let it take over her like a second home. And, as but a host for its permeations, be remade into something better.

Of course, she knew that what she was trying to do, transferring Tilly into real life, would be fantastically, colossally difficult. If some divine umpire *was* bemusedly maintaining a leaderboard of all human feats, this would get her ranked near the top. Of that there could be no doubt. Yet, the prodigiousness of this undertaking did not daunt her. It would have, once upon a time. But now she could look back upon what she had already managed to do, and remind herself that she was clever and she was tenacious. With just these two qualities alone... cities had been built, stars had been mapped, thrones had been taken. She knew she was cut from the same cloth as these rare figures who had defied 'impossible'. And, like them, she was bolstered by a perfect, serene certainty that her objective was attainable. What else did she even need? The rest was just details, was just legwork. She would sniff out the answer like a frenzied bloodhound trailing its quarry. It was just a case of finding the right scent and following it all the way.

The right domain of inquiry was, at least, obvious. Once again, everything hinged upon how well she could manipulate her mind. This was good. It meant that success or failure was going to be up to her. A lot of responsibility, yes, but a sort of empowerment too. That sense of control would be key, because the task before her was going to demand absolutely surgical precision. She had to find a way to radically self-rewire her own grey matter and attune it to the frequency of the dreamworld; her brainwaves lengthening, stretching forth like a bridge, to allow Tilly to step between the dimensions. There was a caveat though. For this alteration to be suitably meaningful - as there was functional importance in it being a *gesture* too - she had to do the work herself. Relying upon the aid of chemical expedients to do most of the heavy-lifting for her might well be easiest, but it would also be cheating. How could her mission really be a heartfelt expression of love to Tilly, if she cheapened it by shirking the sacrifices which gave that expression value? No, she was going to do this the right way, the hard way, and be damn proud of it too.

She put on some ethereal, minimalist ambient music for concentration. It filled the room like a thin, swirling sonic mist. And then she made herself some coffee. It... wasn't mild like the music. Quite the opposite. She'd never had any patience for all that fancy mocha-caramel-vegan-frappuccino-with-rainbow-sprinkles bullshit. She liked the type of coffee which didn't *let* you forget you were, in fact, slurping down a drug. The benefit of this was that it was so easy to make. It was just strong filter coffee: thick and black as molten tire-rubber, brewed bitter as battery acid. It woke one up not so much via caffeine, but by the startling experience of drinking it. She made a pot of it and poured herself some, leaving the rest on the heating plate. She had a feeling she was going to need more than a few cups of it before this night was over.

She took a sip from her steaming mug, grimaced, and then got down to researching.

This was, of course, very familiar territory now. Given she'd become more capable at this process, it wasn't as intimidating as it had once been. Yet, that didn't actually make it any quicker or simpler. Because that first step of leaping the chasm between cluelessness and an initial good lead always felt the most inexplicable, the most arduous. Although, despite this part being such a big timesink, she had even started to find it slightly enjoyable. The repetitive visual monotony of preceding through the simplistic pages of a google search, slowly scrolling through the links on each one, produced something not unlike white-line fever. She was harvesting possible-leads, throwing them into new tabs to be examined more closely later, with robotic automaticity. The whole thing was a bit meditatively hypnotic, serving to focus and quiet the mind in a pleasant way.

However, the actual challenge of scouring the internet was, in an abstract sense, rather maddening. As it was an open repository for just about every single piece of information ever recorded, hunting for one particular thing sometimes felt like trying to find a needle in a... nebula. Still, having become well acquainted with this roadblock had at least taught her what bypassing it required. It was just a diligent grind, through and through. She had to venture in every direction which was conceivably related to what she needed, and scan through whatever she encountered.

The trick was to not let this mere scanning become actual *absorption*. She would only get slowed down and overwhelmed if she let her brain get clogged by the ninety-nine percent of useless data she came across. That was why she had to make her attention sieve-like. It was the most efficient way of sifting through it all. Her eyes just drifted down the hundreds and hundreds of webpages, speed-reading through any relevant sections. The key was that all this input simply fell *through* the filter of her short-term memory, like so many worthless grains of sand. And eventually, something of some considerable size and weight would fail to pass through the sieve's little holes; it would therefore warrant deeper scrutiny. That was all there was to it. But slowly, slowly, went the search. She needed patience, and the discipline which upholds it. Many seemingly promising finds were going to be examined only to get tossed aside as but glimmering junk. She couldn't let this dispirit her. Even a laborious process of elimination was a form of progression towards the endpoint.

Accordingly, six hours passed before she finally stumbled upon something very, very, very intriguing. It was lurking more than forty pages deep - that shunned, occluded wasteland few care to trawl - on her latest google search. Hosted on an indiscriminate online archive was a fascinating time-capsule: an almost twenty-five year old blog, preserved in its entirety. This antiquated website's design was, being distinctly old-old-web, somewhat of an eyesore. Its layout was almost comically blocky. And she would never have guessed that there even *were* so many shades of beige and grey. Judging by the pageview counter hardcoded into its homepage, the blog had enjoyed relatively few visitors at the time. Then, after being scooped up into the archive's dragnet, it seemed to have received no digital footfall whatsoever. She couldn't help but get tingly-excited about that. It was almost like this dormant chronicle had just been waiting for her to chance upon its undignified final resting place.

The website's author was a man named David Faustman, who self-identified as a scholar of ancient mysticism. When Erin googled the strange name of the 'university' he had received his doctorate from, she immediately saw that procuring it must have involved great effort. After all, there would have been the writing of a cheque, the placing of it in an envelope, *and* then the transporting it to a mailbox... Still, the fact that he had resorted to a diploma mill in order to append some fancy letters after his name did not disturb Erin very much. She was far more interested in what he knew than which pieces of paper he could present as credentials. And as she read his work, it became apparent that he was not just some crackpot or dilettante. Indeed, nothing of the sort. Why he'd opted for that disreputable shortcut to a PhD was baffling, because he was obviously smart and committed, with a real knack for this sort of academic study.

He had started his blog when the internet was still largely just a curiosity, using it as a novel medium for his diarist impulse. The first year of his posts were fairly unremarkable. Most of them were just commentary on news in his field or gushing over the quaint little bookstores he visited in the course of his work. But... then... he seized upon a new research project. Though he didn't yet know it, it was going to become an obsession. Truly, it was going to take over his whole life. Erin saw this unmistakable descent unfold, post-by-post. She felt an acute pity for him because she could so easily relate. As she read through the entries in chronological order, she sometimes forgot that she was really peering back more than two decades. Such that, mid-way through, she had to stifle an absurd desire to intervene and save him from himself. Because, of course, it was all already long over.

The whole thing began with a centuries-old tome which a friendly colleague had just discovered, and asked David to consult on. Between those crumbling covers, all that could be discerned was that the contents were written in the ornate script of the Tibetan language. But it was thoroughly garbled by some kind of cipher. That was highly unusual for what was ostensibly a simple Tibetan buddhist annal, because it would have already been physically guarded from prying eyes by its keepers. Why, then, had whatever was recorded upon those fragile, yellowed pages been deemed worthy of an extra layer of protection? That was the all-important question which so ensnared the two of them.

They worked hard for a year and a half, unceasingly trying to unearth whatever tantalizing secrets lay trapped behind the book's obfuscation. Although approaching it from every angle they could think of, they still could not figure out how to decode the writing. There were many posts during this time which were just David bemoaning their lack of progress, simply to vent his exasperation. He wrote with great vehemence about his growing hatred for the impasses which were thwarting them. He wrote of the seething anger and crushing sense of failure which kept him awake at night. To an ignorant onlooker, this would have seemed to testify that he was becoming unhinged. But Erin knew the truth. She knew that it was just the emotional cost of surrendering himself so wholly to the endeavour. He wasn't mad, just absolutely dedicated. Though the strain of that *could* be just as mind-ravaging and life-deranging as madness.

The duo's breakthrough finally occurred during an amusingly inauspicious brainstorming session: they had been idly chatting whilst waiting for a pizza delivery to arrive. But, nevertheless, the solution had presented itself to them. And they immediately began the painstaking process of, bit by bit, rendering the book's contents into plain text. They were flabbergasted by what they found therein.

Before relaying this discovery, David provided a helpful preface. He explained the highly arcane concept of summoning a 'tulpa' in Tibetan buddhism. It was a self-improvement exercise where, during deep meditation, one utilized every iota of one's sheer spiritual will to manifest some sort of entity. This could either be an inanimate object or a sentient creature. But, whatever it was, the tulpa was *solely* intended as a tool for one's own betterment. It helped the summoner work through their hang-ups and shortcomings, advancing them as a spiritual being. Once that was done, the tulpa itself was allowed to dissipate.

At the time the tome was penned, the knowledge of how to perform tulpamancy was only transferred orally, and vigorously safeguarded from outsiders. Contained in its pages was an account of how this secrecy had once very nearly been betrayed. A wayward monk-in-training had transcribed the teachings and sought to sell them, in pursuit of paying off family debts, to wealthy travellers who had solicited the theft. This plot was evidently foiled before the hand-over could be made. Still, David conjectured that even the little which that monk had already told his buyers may be the idea germ which first crossed the ocean and caught the attention of western occultists, who would later come to re-name tulpas as 'thoughtforms'. Regardless, the account ended by saying that the monk was caught and subjected to an ominously euphemistically-named punishment before being banished. Erin did not imagine that it was in fact merely a light scolding.

The reason why this tale had been recorded in such detail was simple. Like most religious orders, the Tibetan mystics sanctified their own history. They were thus scrupulous about self-importantly jotting down not just every happening, but the minutiae of each one too. That meant a record of the exile's transgression and his 'trial' needed to be made. And his illicitly created tulpa-summoning manual, presented as evidence against him, would have to be reproduced in the book. The monks had *not* wanted to do this. But their religious graphomania forbade any exception. So they found a compromise instead. That was why the entire thing was encoded.

And it had succeeded in its secret-keeping for hundreds of years. Right up until a certain pair of fringe academics had gotten their hands on it, that is.

Jubilant in his success, and keen to show off, David wrote at great length about their discovery. He even reprinted much of the book itself on his blog, with accompanying translations. Serendipitously enough, this included the only part Erin cared about. She scrutinized these pages with wide-eyed, pulse-quickened fascination.

Unfortunately, his last few posts just conveyed his outrage at how the other peers he'd confided his discovery to had said he must be falling for some kind of elaborate hoax or forgery. And his final, sign-off post before the blog fell silent forever more was no cheerier. It confirmed just how dejected and embittered he felt. For he railed against the closed-mindedness of his field, burning bridges with his former contacts left and right. This was really *quite* the tirade; no venomous invective was spared use. The tome itself, he intimated, had now passed into a private collector's hands for a pittance. Erin was bummed out by this anti-climatic, ignoble end to such a worthy endeavour. She hoped the poor guy had found happiness doing something else.

Still, she had what she needed. And now it was full steam ahead.

Her next step was looking at everything she could find online which dealt with tulpas and thoughtforms or anything related to them. Something became apparent to her right away. No matter where the practice sprung up in history, either in eastern or western mystical traditions, once one chopped away the facade of magical mumbo-jumbo, the core act was the same. It was hacking your brain with just the toolbag of your own thoughts, to create and sustain self-induced hallucinations. Naturally, this was infinitely easier said than done. The difficulty was overriding the mind's safety mechanisms in the first place. It took a stupendous exertion of willpower and mental focus to forcibly delude oneself about the genuine, physical existence of some imagined object. Then, maintaining this effect beyond even a few seconds required unblinking determination.

Irritatingly, all of the texts, penned by figures from all corners of the globe, she consulted had the same purposely built-in limitation to their tulpamancy instruction. They only taught one how to summon something for a fairly short time. Just long enough to achieve whatever spiritually enriching result was sought. That was all that mattered. Indeed, it was even feared that allowing the tulpa to persist for too long would inadvertently enable it to forge an independent permanence for itself. A dangerous outcome, for it could turn on you or escape to wreak havoc elsewhere. But, obviously, this was not a measure of caution Erin cared to honor. It was fortunate, then, that she would not need to. She didn't have to make do with these weak, hobbled forms of tutelage. She had something better. She had something special. She had David's superannuated blog and what it housed.

For the period in which the tome was written was the fabled golden age of Tibetan buddhism's tulpamancing masters. Their sublime virtuosity in the art and the incredible feats which came of it were supposedly never again repeated. It was said that they were so confident in their control that they would even sustain daylong tulpas, just to hone their abilities. Naturally this could merely be the myth-making hyperbole of past centuries, but she didn't think it was. Her research led her to suspect that the perfected tulpamancy skills extant then were gradually corroded into mediocrity because of their faulty transference, generation to generation, via word of mouth. So, David's text might very well be one of a kind, the only surviving description of how to perform these original, prodigiously powerful tricks. A backdoor into that fount of lost wisdom. And Erin was going to reverse-engineer these methods, and their radically heightened potency, to bring Tilly into reality permanently.

It would take an extremely concentrated stint of hard work and perseverance, but Erin believed that she could pull it off. And in a short timespan too. The monks of old talked about years and years of practice being required to gain even a novice's skill at tulpamancy. Yet Erin had something they didn't. She had Tilly. And she had a mind and soul which were inflamed with yearning, which were crying out with ferocious longing. Everything she did, every action and every thought, was a paean to their love. Erin's very existence was calling to Tilly, drawing her here. It was like a gigantic celestial body exerting the faint whispers of its gravitational pull far across the cosmos, attracting some distant object towards it ever so slowly but surely. It might take millennia but then, finally, there would be a magnificent consummation when they collide. An event which seems so improbable, yet which was also always predestined. If that held true even for dead moons and boiling suns - mere floating space-crap - she thought it had *better* hold true for two lovers of perfect affinity.

First, there were many things she must learn, many abilities she must develop, before she could ever hope to actually bring forth any tulpa. In acknowledgement of this, she printed out all the relevant pages of David's blog, binding the pile of printouts together into a little makeshift book. This was to be her bible. And she began intricately annotating it throughout, to determine which order her self-education should take. So too, she went about buying or pirating e-book versions of the most highly regarded literature - which varied from religious texts to philosophical treatises to self-help manuals - on tulpamancy. This would just be secondary material, to skim through and consult as necessary. But it would be good to have on hand. Just in case any useful modern innovations could be patchworked into the old ways. She rather doubted it, but who knows?

When she had amassed all the information she might possibly require, she breathed a sigh of relief. She once more had a way forward, and a wholehearted commitment to it. That was awesome. Now there was just the work before her, simply waiting to be done, and she was eager to get started. She could lose herself in the doing and, blessedly, not have to feel. The pursuit and the sense of purpose would combine to help anesthetize her emotionally. This would only make her more capable.

What's more, she was truly doing *all* that she could to be with Tilly. And it was so profoundly bolstering to know that Tilly would realize that, would see just how much Erin was willing to do for their love. That was all she needed. That was all she could ask for.

CHAPTER THIRTEEN

1:00 PM. FEBRUARY 11TH.

(APPROX. 33 DAYS LATER)

The last few weeks had been a raging furnace.

But it was one which Erin had knowingly built for herself, and willingly stepped inside.

She *had* to just sit in it, serene and blackened, as the flames nimbly licked at every inch of her like the thousand flickering tongues of a thousand vipers. Needless to say, she hadn't expected this would be a... pleasant experience. Yet for all that she had steeled herself for, even worse had come. What pain - what terrible pain - had become her bedfellow amongst the cruel, glowing coals. How little she had even been capable of anticipating the true character of what she was to endure. But she tried her best to bear it all unshrinkingly anyway. Because the furnace-fire was an indispensable expedient. She was buoyed by the hope that the fierce heat of its blaze would temper her and make her stronger. If she emerged from this existential crucible intact, as a victor who could not be reduced to ash, she felt sure she'd be capable of achieving anything. How could it be otherwise, with the fire having cauterized her many pre-existing wounds? She'd be not just healed, but hardened too. Still, this belief didn't make her dwelling-place feel any less hot or her singed flesh any less painful.

As for what specifically had been plaguing her, the explanation must be severalfold. It was, after all, a varied cohort of tribulations which had united in conspiracy against her. Firstly, she had abandoned her VR use altogether. The Tilly scenarios had radically improved her quality of life, in so many ways. Now, that was all gone. Her waking time was devoid of Tilly once again. Having to continually just swallow down the thick bile of sorrow, so she could focus on her work, was spirit-strangling. And could this not have more permanent effects too? By so forcibly ignoring these pangs, she feared she might be deadening the tender part of herself which felt love in the first place. To be deprived of even that one redemptive feeling would be... well, it would rather obviate the need for a tomorrow.

Secondly, by forgoing VR, she was also forgoing Ikelos. The cost of abruptly discontinuing her habitual use of the drug was predictable: she was now suffering both physical and mental withdrawal effects. The toll on her body was mostly confined to being visited by migraines and an overall achiness. Whereas, the psychological aftermath was much more subtle. The sheer blandness and hard edges of reality seemed so overwhelming, so eye-wearying, so galling to her now. She often had to retreat behind her closed eyes for a little while to avoid becoming paralyzed with hysterical loathing for it. And there was also an unfamiliar *strain* upon the very act of cognition as well. It was like she could feel the energy being sapped from her each time her mind automatically registered and evaluated every individual thing in sight. Similarly, the sheer effort required to fuel each new thought seemed so oppressively palpable now. If the mind was a muscle, it had atrophied all the while Ikelos had been reducing its workload so considerably. Now that she was constantly trying to flex it herself again, she found it sorely wanting of strength. This was especially infuriating because the feat which lay undone before her would definitely not succumb to a mental weakling. So she had to pursue a sort of preparatory mind-rehabilitation too.

Thirdly, without the Tilly scenarios to sustain and cheer her, the insomnia was beginning to creep back in. It was very gradually diminishing the duration of her daily sleep. She watched this theft progress with a wordless, deep-clutching fear. It was the countdown timer always hanging over her head. Getting to be with Tilly in the dreamworld was her only respite, the only thing which replenished her soul after it had been subjected to each day's subtracting ravages. Yet, all signs pointed to near-total sleeplessness once again becoming her lot sometime soon. At which point, how would she cope? She'd be unable to do anything, let alone complete the strenuous mental endeavour she had embarked upon. This meant it was a race against time. And she didn't even know exactly how *much* time she had. Thus, her anxieties here were compounded.

Fourthly, there was the... loneliness. Of course, physical solitude didn't faze her, but she was *really* alone now. She no longer got to commune with the VR-incarnated Tilly during her waking hours. Plus, she hadn't spoken to *A&F* since the blow-out argument and nor was she posting on the triple-zed messageboards anymore. The sense of isolation which now descended upon her was almost always on her mind. She tried to tell herself that being undistracted by other people was good, for it would foster greater focus and dedication. But the way she actually felt belied this feeble bravado. The lack of any form of contact with others weighed upon her, saddened her. It just did. Somehow, hurting so badly and having no-one know about it made everything hurt even more. She might as well have been thrashing about in a coffin, buried alive, for all the rest of the world knew. Her struggles were absolutely private, and intensified for it. They were not diffused - even a little, even only seemingly - by being related to a sympathetic ear.

And all of this was the background to her tulpamancy efforts. It gratuitously added a few extra obstacles to what was already destined to be spectacularly difficult. Of course, she just soldiered on and on and on. Always trying to push her suffering to one side. Always madly fixated upon her goal.

The program of education and training she had laid out for herself was at least straightforward. Naturally, the crucial first step was to learn how to meditate. She had expected that this wouldn't take very long. But that was because she had been gulled by the deceptive simplicity of meditation's objective. In truth, it turned out to be quite a complex and subtle art. And the process of getting better was intensely tedious. None of these were exactly auspicious things to discover. Yet her resolve did not waver. She just responded by dumping even more hours into practicing, applying herself even harder. There was a strange ostentatiousness to this redoubled commitment. As if she meant to show the meditation how ironclad her determination to master it was, like a beast rearing up on its hind legs to intimidate a foe.

Still the skill went on eluding her. Merely trying to really, really concentrate on her breath going in and out each time - and only that - was maddening. There's a sort of humiliating infantilization in finding that one cannot do something which seems so basic. She was exerting every ounce of willpower to try and channel her attention, and failing within five or ten minutes each time. Her consciousness was simply too abuzz with distraction. It was a jumble of inner-monologue commentary *and* memories flashing before her *and* a reflexive, starved hyper-focus on the irrelevant sensory data she was trying to ignore. If she could not tame this chaos and quiet her mind, she would get nowhere.

She eventually realized that she was, in fact, trying *too* hard. Maximum effort and maximum desperation. And a drowning person flailing erratically with all their might but neglecting the rhythmic, precise movements of actual swimming is doomed. You cannot bash or claw your way through the water, no matter how strong you are. Yet you *can* lithely carve through it with ease. She refused to go on clutched tightly by her failure, like how the strands of kelp reach up and entangle the sinking, lifeless wretch in their embrace. She had to employ some finesse. Her approach couldn't be to fight against her own thoughts, hoping to overpower them. Instead, she had to coax and gently prod them towards receding. An acquiescence, not a domination. That was the only way.

With this smarter strategy in hand, she actually began to make progress. Now spending all day, every day, practicing could finally pay commensurate dividends. She soon graduated to other, more and more trying, meditative exercises. And she stuck at each one until she got it right. Although her relentless determination enabled her to advance at a steady rate, she was, alas, still only human. Doing nothing but trying to train one's mind is draining in a way which can scarcely be described. One starts to hate the tiresome act of concentration itself. For it is a disciplined middleground which only makes the extremes seem all the more enticing. One cannot help but lust after either the bliss of being engrossed by frivolous daydreaming or of sinking into an absolute mental quiescence. In Erin's case, it also made her crave Ikelos even more, and that craving was plenty bad enough already.

Nevertheless, however psychologically fatiguing it had been, she did achieve her aim at last. She had honed her powers of attention and could meditate adequately well. This meant it was time to move on to the main event. She now applied herself to trying to summon a Tilly tulpa. In doing so, she would be skipping past the most fundamental instruction which *all* of the relevant literature - no matter which school of tulpamancy - exhorted beginners to observe. One was supposed to start off by manifesting a very small, very simple inanimate object. A pebble, perhaps. Then, with glacial slowness, advance in tiny increments of complexity as one's competency grows. Only after many years was creating even the *most* primitive sentient tulpa to be attempted. And only under the vigilant supervision of one's teachers.

The reasoning behind advocating this slow-going approach was sound enough. A metaphor Erin had encountered in one particular book illustrated it well. The mind's inherent resistance to the goal of tulpamancy was like a great wall blocking one's path. Recklessly trying to topple the wall would likely be counterproductive. Not only because throwing oneself at it will only leave one bruised and bloody. But also because the more one slams against the wall, the sturdier it becomes. For the mind sees this blatant attack, and the danger of being rendered helpless, and seeks to strengthen its defenses. Whereas, one could exercise some patience and self-control, and every day go about wiggling a new stone free from its mortar. After much time, a small hole will be created, which one can squirm through unscathed. The mind is therefore tricked. It's oblivious to the intrusion because the wall itself is left standing.

Erin was... *not* going to heed this time-honoured, universally-subscribed guidance. She was going to strike hard and fast, before any defensive response could be mustered. First of all, she would line up a row of cannons and put some fucking daylight through that towering wall. Just because she could. Then she was going to bulldoze it utterly, even grinding its stones to a fine dust with which to treat the wind. Her mind could rage and fume all it wanted; she cared not. It wasn't just that she didn't want to be patient - though she certainly didn't - it was more so that she simply couldn't afford to wait. She needed to bring Tilly over as quickly as possible. Otherwise she was soon going to become a wreck again, and then she would *never* get Tilly here.

So, her only recourse was attempting the feat which had taxed even the greatest tulpamancers in history. Her *very first* act as a student would be summoning the absolute most difficult type of tulpa: a human-level creature. She even meant to do it in the space of weeks, not decades. And just to round things out, because she was obviously a glutton for challenge, she also aspired to give that tulpa a permanent, independent existence. That last wrinkle was not only unprecedented, but even the ancient masters had been terrified of *accidentally* letting it happen with their creations. Always, caution had been their watchword. Haste and unrestraint would be her own.

Erin was sitting in the lotus position on the window-seat. Her back was against the glass, her back was to the world. She had been staring hard at the empty space at eye-level in front of her for the last few hours, her second stint today. With utmost concentration, she was visualizing the image of Tilly standing there. Now that she had a fair bit of practice under her belt, she'd reached the point where she could maintain this vivid mental projection in an unflickering form for quite some time. But, unfortunately, that alone wasn't enough. She had to look at it and make herself *know* that Tilly was really, truly there. Just as she looked at the hardwood floorboards and *knew* they were there. Just as she looked at her clothes and *knew* they were there. Just as she looked at her own body, and *knew* she was there.

This current session had been particularly trying. She was dealing with a migraine from the Ikelos withdrawals which felt like a cinderblock roughly teetering atop the crown of her head. Trying to completely ignore this terrible discomfort so that it didn't impede her focus even in the slightest was exceptionally difficult. Still, that was exactly what she had to do, unfailingly, for hours on end. There was just no way around it. If she threw in the towel every time she got a withdrawals-related headache, she would be severely handicapping herself. Thankfully, the deep meditative state she put herself into went some way to helping her block out the pain. The rest was all grit and resolve.

As Erin went on 'seeing' Tilly before her, she sought to mould her own thoughts so that they endorsed, to her brain, the reality of this vision. This really was mentally gruelling to keep up with sufficient vigor. And she only ever got back a continuous string of *no*'s from whatever truth-adjudicator function presided over her inaccessible substratum of cognition. It would be nice to, just once, even get a *maybe*. That wavering response would signal the mounting success of her campaign. But it was not to be.

She found that very dispiriting. She longed for a way to discern the improvements in her ability here, to let her know she was on the right track. At least with learning to meditate, her progress had been readily apparent. For all the frustration and setbacks she had encountered as a would-be meditation autodidact, going from total ineptitude to acquiring each particular skill always felt so good. As each milestone was a vindication of her efforts. Yet this was a different animal altogether. The progression was invisible because there were only two clear-cut outcomes: the tulpa was either manifested or it wasn't. No matter how long it took you to build up to being able to do it, in the end it would feel like the flipping of a switch. The tulpa would suddenly just seem to have a stable, convincing existence.

That was the glorious far-off endpoint, anyway. Until then, how unbelievably hard it was to wrench a something from out of the frozen sea of nothing. Not merely a genesis moment, but an actual self-willed transubstantiation of the very materials of one's imagination too. It seemed so miraculous, to breathe life into her own literal brainchild, that she could hardly envisage what having that ability would feel like. In a single instant, everything was going to change for her. She would become something new. She'd go from being abject, worthless, powerless to... arguably... a member of the most powerful class of beings who have ever lived. And this wasn't like some raving, drunken homeless madman with delusions of not just grandeur, but godhood as well. It was more like a demigoddess (or thereabouts) who had hitherto suffered under constraining delusions of patheticness.

Or all that might well never happen, of course. Because first she had to get the damn thing done. That is, somehow make the binary switchover from not being able to do it to... being able to do it. A proposition which only seems simple to the uninitiated. For the distance between that *zero* and *one* feels dauntingly infinite when you're actually trying to traverse it yourself. And how many of those who applied themselves to tulpamancy were simply not even capable of the stupendous feat? How many had obliviously and fruitlessly whiled away their lives trying anyway, despite being doomed to languish in the withouthood of zerospace?

The personal relevance of these questions was not lost on Erin. Indeed, it had been eating away at her for the last few days. She knew that though the glories of success here were so great, the anguishes of failure would be profound and lasting. They could barely be countenanced, in fact. Such that what had sustained her thus far was an uninterrogated certainty that she would *necessarily* triumph. How could she not, when it was her destiny to be with Tilly?... But she had now started to let herself wonder about the fallibility of this verdict. Surely the smart money had to be on the universe not caring about her, or her love, even one jot. What if she was putting herself through this hell, and would persist in doing so indefinitely, to no avail? How much more time was she willing to waste? Rationally, shouldn't she disregard the sunk cost and just stop now?

"No!" she shouted suddenly, jolting out of her stillness.

These heretical, insidious doubts had risen to their boiling point. They had to be confronted. This was going to be a turning point, for good or for ill. Though her joints were stiff and her muscles sore from maintaining strict posture for so long, she leapt to her feet. She began shaking her head and erratically opening and closing her fists. Her expression was a melding of intense anger and intense fear.

"You can do this! You are fucking *meant* to do this!"

These statements seemed to be blurted out involuntarily. She looked around in frantic exasperation. Her eyes darted across everything in the apartment, searching for an implement of correction. The thin leather belt, which had until recently served as a tourniquet, caught her attention. It was perfect. She sprinted over to grab it.

"You're not trying hard enough! You're so goddamn lazy and selfish! You should have done it by now!"

She ripped open her shirt, with some difficulty, and threw it in tatters to the ground. Clutching the cold metal of the buckle, she wrapped some of the belt tightly around that hand to ensure she couldn't lose her grasp on it. She was going to see this through to the bitter end. However long it took, whatever the cost. This had to be done. Broken oaths *must* extract a high penalty, or else they are merely glib boasts to be forgotten whenever convenient.

Gritting her teeth, she whipped the other end of the long belt over her shoulder.

When she felt it strike her back, she couldn't help but let out a loud cry at the stinging pain.

"You are failing her!"

She lashed herself again. Another yelp was brought forth.

"You are fucking failing her!"

She lashed herself again, harder. Tears were welling in her eyes as she screamed in pain.

"She is counting on you. On you! Keep your promise, you worthless sack of shit!"

She lashed herself again, *even* harder still. This one finally cut her. She screeched like a wounded animal.

Altogether, she managed seventeen lashes, and accompanying self-beratement, before she fell to the floor. She would have willed herself to deliver even more punishment, but her body simply gave out. Nor was there a coherent thought in her mind as she lay there sobbing in the foetal position, as though a flashbang grenade of misery had exploded in it. Yet, somehow jumbled echoes of accusatory abuse kept playing on a loop beneath the sizzling static noise.

Her back was raw and bloody; even the very air passing over it smarted.

She cried and writhed in agony for a long time.

CHAPTER FOURTEEN

5:34 PM. FEBRUARY 21ST.

(APPROX. TEN DAYS LATER)

Erin was going to give her mind no choice. She had to force the issue. This seemed to be the *only* option remaining. For there had been an unmistakable clarity imparted alongside the whip's bite. The words spilling unbidden from her lips during that self-flagellation were precious revelations. Confessions under duress have, after all, a wondrous ability to unearth sins one didn't even know one harboured. And she had been contemplating this hard-won intel on her own failings as though evaluating an opponent. It had opened her eyes to how she had cowardly been taking refuge in half-measures, in the mere pretence of extreme commitment. In other words, making a mockery of the very devotion she claimed to be serving.

What little time she had left was running out with alarming rapidity. The insomnia was almost back in full force. So she needed to do something as drastic as possible to shunt the tulpamancing along. This meant being so genuinely all-in that it revoked even the option of failure. Accordingly, and as she was wont to do in crises, she came up with a plan. She crafted and re-worked its every detail until it seemed surefire. Because it had to be. This was the big one. If this last-ditch rally fell short too, what would come afterwards was uncertain. In the way that the *most* terrible things often come hither cloaked in a dread-inspiring mist of unpredictability.

The first thing she had to do was the remedial bolstering of her and Tilly's bond. This was not a sentimental indulgence, it had crucial practical importance. She'd deduced a hindrance which was working against her tulpamancy attempts: having quit VR, it had been so long since she had communed with Tilly whilst awake. This had clearly caused their spiritual link, as experienced in the material realm, to gradually wane. And at this point it was weakened to a significant degree. Consequently, Erin encountered much more difficulty in drawing Tilly's soul here to occupy the hollow-shell tulpa created as its worldly vehicle.

The way to fix this was painfully obvious. She had to take Ikelos, and put on the VR headset once more. A final unavoidable, preparatory visit to Tilly in her cell before the coming... *jailbreak*. She truly hated to have to revive this distasteful form of bondage for Tilly, but if it would help with the liberation, it was an evil which had to be borne. She further quieted the complaints of her conscience by resolving that, whilst in VR, she would even try to convey to Tilly, via their telepathic connection, that a rescue mission was underway. Hopefully this message would be received. Hopefully it would help Tilly bear the unpleasantness of being sucked back into the VR straitjacket better.

Of course, the catch to all this was that she had just one chance to strengthen their waking connection. On compassionate grounds, there could be no second try, no repeat infliction of discomfort upon Tilly. That was a slippery slope she did not intend to try and inch her way partially down. This meant Erin had to make the absolute most of this sole opportunity, had to do whatever it took to ensure that it worked.

She thought long and hard about how to amplify her own ability to re-establish a direct, potent tether to Tilly. It occurred to her that this was essentially a form of transcendental love-magick. Therefore, she ought to at least peruse the tricks used by historical practitioners of bygone sorcery and witchcraft. Even if what she did and what they did weren't exactly a perfect match, they must surely be cousins. Or, at the *very* least, tapping into vaguely the same sort of immaterial energy. Happily, her search didn't end up taking very long. One of the most basic staples seemed to suit her needs. This technique has many names, but is generically referred to as creating 'magic circles'. These are - unsurprisingly, usually circular - spaces delineated by some special variety of physical markings, often replete with geometric patterns or mystical inscriptions. The aim being to imbue the interior zone, and anyone who occupies it, with useful magical properties.

These magic circles, whichever tradition they appeared in, were almost always intended for protection. Such that they were designed to erect an impassable, invisible, supernatural barrier around the circumference. For example, this would serve to keep out any entity or force being conjured outside of it, securing the safety of the conjurer themself. Naturally, Erin had no need of this craven tactic. If anything, she sought its inverse: a means of making herself *more* accessible, *more* inviting. A signal boost for her beckoning, not a refuge meant to exclude. Hence, she required a magic circle which concentrated the spiritual energy of its user, adding extra force and accuracy to any connection they sought to strike. To go from haphazardly throwing a lasso to firing a laser-guided, rocket-propelled grappling hook. An upgrade which could very well make all the difference.

The only problem was that this exact type of magic circle was exceptionally rare. Only the most recklessly power-hungry magick wielders would dare to trade protection for heightened ability. That would result in them having only their wits and skill to guard them when confronted by, say, any malevolent demon they summoned. Yet, thankfully, men of such foolhardy ambition *had* indeed existed. And a few thereof had even troubled to jot down their methodology. Still, she had to pore over the online databases of countless libraries, and their scanned versions of countless medieval grimoires, to find an instance of this. But find it, she did.

This particular book was principally authored by a figure named Sebastian von Tecklenburg, though he also had many fanciful *noms de plumes*... by necessity. Out of curiosity, she did some light reading on his background. And soon wished she hadn't. She discovered him to be an unsavoury character, to put it mildly. Between publishing treatises, primarily on demonology, he was a keen experimenter with the spells and summonings of so-called black magic. Such that several times he had to depart towns in a hurry, fleeing an accumulation of awful rumours. These suspicions ranged all the way from tormenting hexes being placed on those he disliked to grave-robbing and attempts at necromancy. This earned him a scandalous notoriety which preceded him everywhere he went like the wafting of a vile odor. And eventually that just proved too much of a hassle.

So he retreated to a rural village with a band of like-minded occultists and formed a sort of private commune. One of the works produced during this time was the grimoire Erin now consulted, a nominal collaboration between von Tecklenburg and some underlings, but clearly almost entirely authored by him. It contained the description and multiple illustrations of a magic circle whose purpose very closely matched what she sought.

She was not exactly pleased to be taking posthumous tutelage from a man of such ill repute. However, she couldn't afford to be picky or snobbish about *whose* magical know-how she used. After all, were not the alleged misdeeds of obscure long-dead men but grist for the dusty, pointless debates of historians? Her interest was solely in achieving her goal. And if that meant cribbing tricks from a goddamn evil warlock, so be it! This von Tecklenburg was, if nothing else, a very credible authority here. Contemporary accounts of his power were plentiful, *even* from his enemies. Regardless of whether he was seduced by the dark arts, he certainly knew his stuff. And proved it only too often. That was the one and only box he had to tick in Erin's estimation.

She studied the detailed illustrations with mild dismay and premonitions of her coming frustrations: this magic circle was painfully, painfully elaborate. Figuring out how to reproduce it herself, and with exactitude, was going to suuuuck. Yet, the accompanying claims of its tremendous potency made this seem like a more palatable trade-off.

Her first step was to find the highest resolution version of the scanned pages and zoom in to the most helpful illustration of the magic circle. Next she blew up this magnified image until it was huge. And began printing it off - section by section, A4 sheet by A4 sheet - until the whole thing was in hand. Lastly, she taped the printouts onto one of her apartment walls, systematically reassembling the image. When she was done, it was, in scale, almost as tall as herself. This would be her guide. Squinting at her laptop screen was fine, but she also wanted to be able to stand before the illustration and get a nice, close look at all the intricate details. It would be an invaluably intuitive means of reference as she went about drawing it.

She got down to work.

The specified width of the magic circle was such that she actually had to turn her bed sideways against the wall to free up extra floor space for it. And, following the grimoire's instructions, she'd use thick sticks of white chalk to draw everything, which would thankfully stand out well on the dark hardwood floor. She had even bought an excess of it to account for all the many times she expected to mess up and have to start over again. Yet, the first part, at least, proved to be so simple as to be foolproof. She used the same method which people had employed for thousands of years to draw a perfect circle: a length of string attached to a pivoting central point. And then she used a long ruler to draw the perfectly straight lines of the shapes which were overlaid upon it. The only wrinkle was that the whole thing had to be orientated northward. But she kept her phone in her hand, with the compass app open, and that made it fairly easy.

Now she sharpened each chalk to a point and moved on to the delicate inscription work. It was this next stage of the drawing which proved to be the really maddening part. There were peculiar, unsettling letters from an occult alphabet. Then there were an assortment of strange and complex symbols. Then there were what vaguely resembled ancient runic markings. Trying to *precisely* replicate each of these individual adornments, and also their *precise* size and positioning, was quite a challenge. It required so much trial and error. All while she dealt with the added worry of where to place her feet as she worked, to avoid accidental smudging. This awareness that one false move could obliterate all her progress made her extremely tense, especially as she held herself in certain necessary contortions. Not exactly conducive to the focus her work demanded.

But, at long last, she finished it all to her satisfaction. She had created an exact mirror image of the one upon her wall.

Frustratingly, as she looked upon her handiwork, she almost began to have second thoughts about its worth, *almost* began to feel a little silly. There was simply no telling whether this thing would even do much good here. But then she reminded herself that sometimes even a single grain of sand can decisively tip the scales in one's favour. The scoffer who scruples against the indignity of throwing it on there makes himself, therefore, a fool.

And so, her faith that this aid may indeed be the all-important difference-maker was reinvigorated.

There was no time like the present to put it to good use.

She had just dutifully injected herself with a dose of Ikelos. Now she carefully tiptoed to the magic circle's very center, VR headset in hand. There wasn't all that much empty space allotted there, because it had originally been designed with the assumption of a standing occupant. However, Erin couldn't very well stand in place for two hours, not whilst drugged. And there wasn't even enough space to sit down normally. So, having placed a folded blanket there for comfort, she slowly settled into a relaxed kneeling position. Holding the VR headset aloft while she did this made things rather dicey. For she had had to prop up its trailing wire with an old camera tripod so that it didn't touch the floor and disturb the chalk. This created a precarious balancing act. She only dared make small, slow movements, her eyes fixed on the hoisted wire the whole time. If it swept across the floor and wiped away all of this painstakingly intricate drawing, she didn't even know what she would do with herself. Probably scream. And break stuff. Then perhaps go from there.

As it happened, she managed to kneel down without causing the feared calamity. She would now have to draw upon some of that extraordinary physical discipline she'd cultivated with her meditation training, and hold perfectly still in this position for the whole duration. Nothing worth having comes easy, as they say.

All that was left to do was put on the VR headset, which she did with a similar degree of trepidation. Everything was ready to go now. With the keyboard perforce out of reach, she had set up a voice-activation function for launching the scenario. The words simply had to pass her lips.

She took a moment to ready herself, ignoring the comfortably familiar feeling of Ikelos taking over her mind.

Then she called out the custom phrase she had keyed in. Her loud voice wavering under the weight of its own emotion.

"Take me there!"

And thither, with a heavy heart, she was indeed betook.

It was a terrible thing that what was normally such a joyous communion should be so solemn this time.

There was, in fact, only one redeeming feature.

At the moment of her return, she'd be saying what she hoped would be her very *last* goodbye to Tilly.

Now came the second stage of her grand plan. She had already bought the items she needed to carry it out online. They had all been delivered and readied. After all, time was of the essence. It was crucial that this subsequent act be performed as soon as possible after her heightened reconnection with Tilly, to capitalize upon the bond being at its very strongest.

She checked one last time that the venous catheter, whose needle was inserted into her forearm, was still taped in place securely. Then she traced her finger along the tiny plastic tubing which connected it to the large capacity syringe on the bedside table. The syringe itself was, in turn, installed within a rectangular device called a syringe driver. The function of this small machine was straightforward: it depressed the plunger by a user-specified amount at user-specified intervals. The capacious chamber of this particular syringe was filled with a metric *fuckton* of Ikelos, which she was going to receive in four parts. Each of these doses was 1.5x her usual amount. She had programmed the machine to give her the first dose five minutes after she turned it on, and then administer a new dose every two hours. This meant she'd spend eight hours under the constant effect of Ikelos. That was a dauntingly long time to be relegated to the passenger seat of her own mind. But long enough, she hoped, to do what needed to be done, to tear down the barriers which remained. And if she had somehow even allotted herself too much time... well, that was a small price to pay to avoid the alternative.

Although she had previously scrupled against using the drug during her tulpamancing efforts, she no longer cared to make such a persnickety moral distinction. She simply didn't have the luxury of staying perched atop that high horse. Ikelos or no Ikelos, she just wanted to summon the Tilly tulpa. This was the only thing which mattered. Besides, she had already laid all the mental groundwork without Ikelos. With just her own willpower, she had gotten so close. *That* had sufficiently proved her devotion to Tilly. Now she just needed something to... push her over the edge. Those last few inches were evidently the very hardest, so there was no dishonor in resorting to artificial aid. If anything, pigheadedly sticking to a futile approach because of some silly abstract reservation would be the shameful path. It was actually a self-centred indulgence. Because with her ends being what they were, the means were not merely justified, but irrelevant.

Now that she intended to introduce Ikelos as a catalyst, she was going to do it right. She had to make sure it gave her the greatest advantage possible. Thus, the increased dosage size and the extremely prolonged duration of being under its influence. That was basically guaranteed to make *something* happen. And hopefully that 'something' wasn't a brain aneurysm. To that point, she had reached out to Ka-Sumedy and asked whether her planned Ikelos use could be lethal. This was the response she received: "I don't think it'd kill you, no... but it would be a really bad idea." She barely even registered the latter part of this reply. The green light was all she was after.

She reached over and pressed the start-program button on the syringe driver.

Sitting there on the bed, she leaned forward to look at her legs. They were stretched straight out, and bound together at the ankles and knees with wide, strong leather belts. She quickly checked them over, confirming they were fastened properly. Yet not so tight as to cut off circulation. Next she lay down, as gingerly as possible due to her still tender back. Reaching up towards the headboard, she found the loops of soft rope on either side of it. She slipped each hand into its respective loop and paused. This was her last chance to back out. She took a big, deep breath and nodded to herself almost imperceptibly for a few seconds, psyching herself up. Then she pulled down hard on the loops and they tightened firmly around each wrist. The knots required for this set-up had been easy enough to learn. More importantly, they could not be escaped by the person tied up.

However, Erin had incorporated a clever way to ensure that once the time was up, she would be freed. The other ends of the two ropes involved met behind the headboard, where they were each attached to the same ice-lock. This mechanism was as simple as could be. It was just a long metal cylinder into which a metal rod was fully inserted. One rope was tied to the former, one was tied to the latter. And the cylinder had already been filled with water and left in the freezer until that became solid ice. So she had to wait for the ice to fully melt in order to separate the two parts again. When she did that, her rope bindings would no longer be anchored by anything immovable, thus freeing her arms.

This particular model of ice-lock she had bought even had fill-lines inscribed on the cylinder too. Based on a specific room temperature, which her thermostat now maintained, these lines showed how much water to pour in to produce certain wait-times. Accordingly, she had filled it up to over the eight-hour mark when she froze it. And it would now keep her hostage for that amount of time. Because, perfectly, it couldn't be reasoned with or bribed or cajoled into releasing her early. It was just going to hold her there until the ice was gone. That was exactly what she wanted. To be trapped in this very spot, and thereby be downright forced to do what was necessary. This self-bondage would remove *all* distractions, *all* ability to run away from her task. It was her best bet of engendering the needed state of meditative hyper-concentration. From there, it was up to her.

Presently, she just lay still and waited. Her mettle was not deserting her, but a sense of acute claustrophobia *was* beginning to set in. This was very much unexpected. She had not at all had a propensity for it before; to the contrary really. Still, it now took a very concerted act of self-control to quell the animal urge to freak out and thrash against her ties. But she managed to do it. And she desperately prayed that this feeling would not reoccur. Hopefully it was just her mind throwing a brief, perfunctory tantrum to protest this predicament she had placed herself in. In which case, it had better quit its childishness and accept the situation. She would crush any further, more feeble attempts at mutiny... just to send a message. It was time to get on board. For better or for worse, she was not leaving this bed before eight fateful hours had elapsed.

In light of that, she had made some practical arrangements to help things go smoothly. One such example was that playing quietly in the background right now was a lengthy playlist of soft ambient music. This could easily be zoned out when she was meditating. And it would prevent the absolute silence from becoming too oppressive and distracting. Another example was the thick tube taped on the bed just by the side of her head. It was connected to the kind of backpack-style hydration pack which runners favour. And she had filled the internal reservoir therein with half a dozen bottles of so-called 'sports drink'. So that she need only turn her head to suck the sugary blue liquid through the drinking tube. She suspected this was going to very much come in handy. What she was about to undergo would probably be not unlike a night marked by taxing fever dreams. If that were true, there was going to be a lot of sweating involved, which meant that rehydration would be key. A third example was how she had purposely tapered down her food intake for the last day or so. This semi-fasting was in recognition of the fact that there would be no bathroom breaks and to try and make this a moot point. Of course, there was also the adult diaper she was wearing as a backup, just in case. As with everything else, her dignity had to be subordinated to the mission too.

She suddenly realized that the song had changed without her even noticing. The compulsion to catastrophize had been occupying her mind so fully. Wouldn't it be a godawful time to randomly start choking? Or what if the building caught on fire and everyone evacuated besides her? Or what if some would-be burglar-slash-rapist chanced to slip into the apartment right now? Or what if a gas leak...? Or what if the ice-lock somehow got stuck...? Or what if a swarm of insects...? She yanked herself out of this cascading stream of fears. And, forcefully as she could, told herself to stop it! Nothing like any of that was going to happen! So there was no point getting worked up! Allowing herself to become hysterical over some imagined disasters would put her in the worst possible mindstate for what was coming. She had to pull herself together. She had a job to do.

Time to get her head back in the game. She sought to focus on the music, to listen to it and lose herself in the listening. She wanted the soothing sounds to intrude like putty into the cracks in her concentration, giving it some semblance of being unbroken. She tried and she tried. Yet the music just seemed to pass right through her, making no contact with her mind. Perhaps because her mind was so inhospitably abuzz with a chaotic hubbub of competing, contradictory thoughts. She couldn't even get a read on her emotional state whilst it was being buffeted this way and that by the pandemonium. All she knew for sure was that her growing alarm was not going away. Underpinning it was that same indescribable feeling which she'd last known when looking down at a handful of pills. It was hard not to interpret that correlation as a sinister foreshadowing.

That also served to remind her that she didn't know what was going to happen here, not really. For all her familiarity with using Ikelos during VR, she had never tried it outside of the safe confines of the virtual. Whatever comfort level she had built up might not translate over. Adding on to that, she'd never taken as high a dose as those she had lined up for herself. This was new territory too. And the fear of the unknown was unavoidable. How *would* the Ikelos affect her with both these aforementioned variables changed? Perhaps it would feel totally different. The problem was that the positive and negative outcomes here were not equivalent. If things went well, the Ikelos would merely be a more useful tool. That would be neato, sure. Whereas if they went badly, it might well be a profoundly horrific experience.

Those were the stakes here. There was no pretending otherwise. Whenever you took to radically, chemically messing with your own perception, the difference between heaven and hell becomes a razor thin line. Daring to dance on that fearsome knife edge was part of the thrill, of course. But that was easy to say flippantly when you hadn't yet fallen down the wrong side. If ever she had been in danger of learning this the hard way, today was the day. Given how suggestible she was about to become, whilst having no control over the situation, the *tiniest* negative notion sneaking into her mind could be the trigger for a downward spiral. And an eight-hour bad trip was a very, very long bad trip. It would be the type of nightmarish odyssey into the darklands where you *didn't* emerge on the other side with your sanity still among your belongings.

The music was abruptly pierced by the whirring of the syringe driver's gears turning, as it depressed the plunger. She whipped her head around to look at it. With wide-eyed apprehension, she watched as the first portion of Ikelos was pushed through the tubing and disappeared into her vein. Given the altered dosage, she wasn't sure how long it would take for the drug to hit her full force. She lay there digging her fingernails into her palms and biting her top lip. The seconds ticked by and ticked by and ticked by. She had been wise to remove her alarm clock from the bedside table. Otherwise, she would have been anxiously transfixed by it like a dumbstruck rustic waiting for an inexplicable eclipse to pass.

Little beads of cold sweat had appeared on her forehead. Tickling her in the most annoying way, they ran down through her hair to the bed. Her breathing was fast and shallow, and solely through her nose. It made her chest rapidly rise and fall with the hysterical rhythm of someone desperately trying to suck in breaths whilst drowning. She realized that this could very well be what the start of an *actual* full-blown panic attack felt like, for all she knew. Incredibly, because she was such a prime candidate for them, she had never had one before. They were just one of those weird scary things which you heard about other people getting, like sleep paralysis or stomach ulcers.

Yet, if her suspicion was correct, she would have voluntarily tied herself up *and* drugged herself during her very first experience of one. An... interesting move. In the way that sacrificing one's queen and sending one's king, alone and unguarded, sallying towards the opponent's pieces as an *opening* chess gambit is definitely, at the very least, bold. And not much else. Put one way, her blunder was the very height of foolishness. Put another way, she was now truly fucked. Maybe it was a silly response, but she began to frantically wonder if there were any mental exercises she could do to limit the traumatizing effect of this thing. Perhaps if she acted quickly enough, she could make sure it wouldn't open the floodgates. She really didn't want to start suffering from them regularly in the future. That's why it was imperative that she-

It was then that the Ikelos finally kicked in and saved her from herself.

There were twin benefits of this submersion into strangeness. It made her forget all about her bondage. And it was so stunning as to leave her mentally speechless.

At first she simply spent some time acclimatizing to being under Ikelos's spell whilst in the real world. All in all, it turned out to be actually quite pleasant. The bleary-eyed softening of her perception was a fascinating novelty. As her surroundings took on a slight floatiness and fuzziness, her position at the centre of it all felt like a cosy, insulated nook. And she watched the minute existential shimmering of the objects around her with the gawping amusement of a newborn babe cooing at a mobile. This was very relaxing indeed. Soon enough, every last trace of her unease just faded away. It drifted from her unnoticed, as though it were an invisible vapour drawn out of her pores by the suction of the room's sheer calmness.

But there were also some bizarre aspects to the experience. Her mind started to tire of the unchanging pittance of visual stimulation provided by the small amount of her apartment she could see. It rebelled by preoccupying her with richly vivid daydreams. These were really something to behold. Complex and unpredictable. They chased her attention with equal presence whether her eyes were open or closed. She would even get so lost in this tumbling collage of mental scenes that she'd truly begin to forget they weren't real. It was always quite the startling jolt when something in the room would catch her notice, and rip her from her imaginings. This cycle repeated itself more than a few times before she realized what was happening. Boosted by Ikelos's hallucinatory effect, her mind was now an unchained, supercharged creative powerhouse. And it was petulantly trying to find *anything* to concoct, to flex its new capabilities.

She finally remembered what she was here to do. Her *purpose*. As a result, all the new mental doors Ikelos had opened for her became noticeable at last. This new power, this new potential she had been imbued with felt wonderful. And it was time to try it out. She now applied herself to the most intense session of attempted tulpamancing of her life. It was beyond anything she could have ever envisioned. Her newfound ability to mould reality with even the faintest exertion of her imagination was just... astounding. Beforehand, she had been trying to sculpt Tilly into existence by chipping away at a stubborn block of stone with some puny chisel. An imprecise subtractive process where every tiny step was intensely hardfought. Whereas Ikelos gave her an endless supply of pristine wet clay and a flaming kiln. The difference was night and day. More even, because those still happen on the *same* planet. She couldn't believe she had been wasting her time with the idiotic previous method. Now she knew how much simpler and easier things could be. This new way would let her start from the ground up, and retain absolute control throughout.

Invigorated by this eye-opening revelation, she just dove right in. New materials and a new form of artistry did not faze her. She picked it all up as she went, even gaining a quick mastery. That wasn't because she was a genius, but because the work itself was so intuitive. And the time just flew by as she lost herself in it. It was a deeply enjoyable labour. With painstaking care and devotion, she piled the clay up and worked it and moulded its every inch. She cut no corners whatsoever. She double-checked the fidelity of each alteration a dozen times. She poured utmost love into her creation. Only when she was satisfied that this was an unimpeachably, comprehensively exact copy did she allow the clay to finally harden.

From nothing, she had *built* a perfect simulacrum of Tilly. The only thing left to do was to make this truly *be* Tilly.

Five hours had elapsed. She felt like she was getting so very close. The breakthrough was imminent. For the proper form had been created and prepared as a vessel. It was now just a matter of what the mystics called ensoulment. To exhale vitality into the inanimate matter. Thereby giving the clay the crucial spark of life and inviting a recipient to assume its form as their own. The problem was that she was exhausted. Her mind was just so tremendously overworked and worn out. Though she wanted nothing more than to carry on, she couldn't help but let herself rest her eyes for just a minute. And for her tired brain, of course, this was too tantalizing an opportunity. She dozed off into a dreamless sleep before she knew it.

When Erin opened her eyes, a face greeted her. A face she was not *trying* to see there.

Someone was floating several feet above her, aligned with her like a mirror image. She blinked in quick succession a few times and saw that the apparition did not dissipate. She couldn't choose *not* to see it. A momentary chill penetrated right down to her bone marrow. The color drained from her face and she began hyperventilating. Her body did not seem to be responding to commands. All she could do was just stare upward in bewilderment, with her mouth agape.

"I'm here," Tilly stated without any particular inflection. Her face was completely at rest; no emotion could yet be discerned from it.

Judging from the unchanged audibility of the music still playing in the background, no physical voice had spoken over it. But Erin saw the lips moving and *heard* the words clearly nonetheless.

She just kept staring into Tilly's eyes. Responding was quite impossible right now.

After all, she was too busy trying to get her erratic, laboured breathing under control. Tears were streaming down onto the sheet. Her whole body was quivering. And there was the strangest sensation of her insides having been replaced with a boundless incandescent light which was desperately trying to escape. She had never experienced anything even remotely like it before.

It was perhaps vaguely akin to an unbelievably intense adrenaline rush, but where the stimulant was just pure, potent joy instead. Whatever the hell it was, it felt so good that searching for an explanation seemed pointless. As far as Erin was concerned, it made sense in a basic way. Beholding Tilly's beauty in person was bound to cause an ecstatic seizure of the mind. How could it have ever been otherwise?

Yet she was not only overawed and jubilant. She was triumphant too. Lurking at the back of her mind, there had of course been a chorus of merciless hecklers. They had never tired of reminding her what a pathetic fool she was for trying to do something so plainly, laughably impossible. But, now, here Tilly was. Undeniably perfect and perfectly undeniable. Not just a refutation of the self-doubts that had been plaguing Erin, but somehow also a retroactive vindication of all the seemingly stupid things she had *ever* done. She greedily drank in this influx of validation. And she unreservedly gave herself over to being consumed by this redemptive, life-affirming moment.

"I'm, uh, still here, Erin."

Tilly had been watching Erin carefully, and with great curiosity. This time she spoke with a tone which suggested she wanted a response in order to ascertain whether Erin was okay. Her eyebrows were raised in concern.

Without thinking, Erin spat out the word "yes" between heaving deep, shaky breaths. This was the best, and only, reply she could manage right now. She felt like she might pass out due to the intensity of the phenomenon overwhelming her. Fending this off was not easy. But she was giving the struggle maximum effort. There was no goddamn way she was going to let herself be taken away from this situation. Not now she was poised to get exactly what she desired most in the world. That could not be jeopardised. And it wouldn't be, as long as she had any say in the matter. If the universe wanted her unconscious again, it was going to have to come beat her head in with a shovel. Anything short of that, she was staying right here in this blessed product of all her besotted toil.

Neither of them spoke again for several minutes, during which Erin tried to ride out whatever was happening to her. Once she had recovered some bodily control, she lifted her head off the pillow to peer forward. She saw Tilly's body hovering parallel to her own, wearing precisely what she wore in the dreamworld. It still seemed almost too good to be true. Although anything beyond her nearsighted vision was blurry because of Ikelos, she looked up at the headboard and across at the bedside table. She wanted to thoroughly confirm that she was in her own apartment, that she was in the real world. And so she was.

"You brought me here?"

Erin's head snapped back around to look at her.

"Y-yes."

Tilly seemed about to go on, but then stopped herself.

With just the faintest hint of a mischievous smirk resting upon her lips, she asked, "is that all you can say, 'yes'?"

The jolting surprise of this playfulness shook Erin free from the remnants of her stupor.

"I just... c-can't... believe you're here. *Actually* here."

"Why?" Tilly adopted an expression of mock puzzlement. "Isn't that what you've been trying to do all this time?"

Taken off guard again, Erin actually gave a little involuntary smile. Tilly's strategic levity was working. Erin was starting to feel like herself again. Now, if only she could get her limbs rid of the shakes. Her mind may have recovered from the discombobulation of her intense emotional tumult. But her nervous system was evidently a bit slower to return to normal.

Something seemed to occur to Tilly and her countenance became newly serious. She glanced away in hesitation.

"It's amazing that you were able to do this. To bring me here," she said slowly, peeking back at Erin to see her reaction.

Erin almost reflexively said "yes" again, but caught herself and decided to just nod instead.

Tilly licked her lips nervously and seemed to be steeling herself to say something else. There was an uncomfortably long pause. Every shred of lightheartedness had been torn from the room. Erin was confused by the abrupt solemnity and began to feel uneasy. She had absolutely no idea what could possibly be the cause of it. But it must be important if Tilly was willing to let the mood be dampened so severely.

"I'm... just..." Tilly started to say, only to trail off uncertainly.

She broke eye contact with Erin yet again and stared at the pillow instead for a few moments. What the hell was going on? Erin was becoming really quite concerned. She was looking at Tilly intently, almost willing her to speak. Anything would be better than this anxiety-ridden waiting.

"I really don't want to seem... ungrateful. I know this isn't the reaction you were hoping for. But there's something... I can feel. Something... disturbing I can't just ignore. *I... I think I'm not supposed to be here, Erin.*"

Erin had been following along with profound concentration on every word. And when the final point hit home, it struck her like a blow between the eyes. Not only because it was so unexpected, but also because it really hurt to hear. It had completely staggered her. She didn't know what to say to something like that. What could even be said? She stared deeply into Tilly's eyes, searching for the intent behind her statement. For her part, Tilly grew bashful from the sternness and intensity of Erin's probing gaze. She even blushed very slightly.

At last, Erin guardedly began, "don't... you want..."

Tilly's eyes widened in dismay.

"But I do! I do want to be here! Of course I do!" she interrupted with a frantic energy. So eager was she to issue her defense, she adorably stumbled over her words. Her face lit up with an earnest remorse. She was animated by the realization that she might have wounded Erin with her point. And that wrong could not possibly be allowed to persist. It tore gravely at her heart. "You are mine and I am yours! And our love is what matters most! I know that, of course I know that!"

Erin tried to take all of this in, tried to focus on the reassuring quality of Tilly's declaration. But her head was spinning, and doubt was seeping in fast. She was still so flabbergasted by how Tilly was acting. It wasn't what she expected. All of the countless times she had feverishly imagined their first meeting in the real world, it had never been anything remotely like this. She didn't like it, or what it implied.

A lengthy wordlessness persisted between them. They occasionally met each other's glances, but more often nervously looked away. Notes of fierce concern and self-reproach were splashed upon Tilly's face. And Erin didn't even try to hide that she was deep in contemplation, trying to make sense of things.

Eventually, though still at a loss, Erin ventured the obvious to reopen the dialogue.

"I just don't understand..."

"I'm sorry. I was... in my own way... in a state of shock too. I probably should have waited until... Or maybe phrased it differently. It's just..." Tilly cut herself off, her cheeks reddened with shame. She thought hard for a second and then continued. "I *know* you, Erin. I would never question that whatever you've done, you did for us. Never. But I do not know this place, or your life here. And looking at you, my mind is running wild with worry and speculation. Y-you're... you're tied to the bed. There's a tube going into your arm. And I'm guessing that big empty syringe used to have something in it."

Erin instinctively glanced over and saw that the Ikelos was indeed all gone, emptied out into her system. Two things now dawned upon her. She firstly imagined how she must look from Tilly's vantage point. What a weird and disturbing scene it must present. A wave of acute embarrassment washed over her. She had never even thought about that aspect when planning this whole thing. Secondly, she wondered how much longer the final Ikelos dose was going to last. She had no way whatsoever of knowing how long it had been since she received it. Even worse, there was no telling what might happen when its effect departed. Ikelos undoubtedly giveth - and in spades, at that - but would it be so cruel as to taketh also?

"I may not know exactly what all this stuff is for, but I can make some educated guesses. And I'm *afraid*. Seriously afraid of what you might have done to yourself" - she sighed, with downcast eyes - "for me."

She was growing teary and her voice was quavering with emotion.

"It just doesn't... seem right. *I* didn't have to... go through anything like this for you to come to my world. You just did. As if it was natural. As if it was just supposed to happen. That's why I can't help but fear what it means for us meeting here to have taken... *all this*. I hate that you might have had to suffer for it. I'm just thinking of you Erin, always of you. Always." Her bottom lip was trembling and tears were clinging perilously to her eyelashes.

Choked up from watching this unfold, Erin could only dumbly sputter, "I... thought... you'd be happy."

"Erin... please... of course I'm happy to be with you. But what heavy price have you paid? I... don't want that for you."

The teardrops were finally loosed and they fell upon Erin's face. Impalpable splash after impalpable splash.

A reversal suddenly took place inside Erin's mind. She became incensed, and huffed through her nose. Although she tried to tamp her anger down, it bled through into her raised voice nonetheless. Having to *sell* Tilly on all this was completely ridiculous, and insulting to boot. She either wanted to be with Erin or she didn't.

"None of that matters! None of it! I'm here and you're here! Whatever I had to do, it was worth it. If it had been ten times worse, I'd still have done it. And it *still* would have been worth it! And, anyway, all that's in the past now. The sacrifices have already been made. And they worked! They. Brought. You. Here! Screw everything else! Don't you get that?!"

Closing her eyes, she told herself to calm down. She knew that getting hot-headed was not going to help anything. It took a minute or two, but her annoyance did start to quickly drain away. And when she finally re-opened her eyes, her expression had altogether softened. The gentleness and affection had returned.

In a low voice, she plaintively explained, "I couldn't *live* without you, Tilly. It was killing me. So I did what I had to do. Though... obviously... I hate that the form it took upsets you. I wish there had been an easier way but, believe me... there wasn't. I just want to put all that crap behind us and move on. We can be together now. That's all that truly matters."

"You're right. I'm really sorry," Tilly said quietly, nodding. She sniffled and wiped her wet eyes with the back of her hand.

"I'm sorry too."

Erin felt bad about having directed her anger at Tilly. Whether or not the instigating pang of resentment was justified, she shouldn't have spoken to Tilly the way she did. Of course, she hadn't *made* Tilly cry, but she also didn't exactly help the situation either. Now she wanted nothing more than to reach out and touch Tilly's face, to comfort her. She began to pull weakly at her wrist bindings, which still held her fast. That visceral impulse to fight against her bondage came upon her anew. And this time it was even stronger, because now the restraints were stopping her from drying her lover's tears. It really did take a great degree of self-control not to start tugging and squirming to try and tear her hands free. But she knew that, even ignoring her enervated state, it would only result in rope burns and frustration. The last part of that damn ice had to finish melting first. She couldn't help but picture it as it shrunk one drip at a time with insouciant slowness. In desperation, she willed the ice to melt faster. A waste of effort, to be sure, but she had to discharge her violent impatience somehow.

Between sniffles, Tilly sheepishly put forth a question, "so... where... do we go... from here?"

"Just... talk to me. Talk to me about everything." Unconsciously, Erin smiled in fondness and relief as the next thought occurred to her. "In a way, we've never really spoken to each other without rules, without constraints. I've wanted that freedom for us so badly. And now we have it."

"I've wanted that too! So very much. Naturally, I was glad of the worlds which served as our meeting places. But it was impossible not to wish they didn't place such limitations on our time together."

"I know exactly what you mean. We played out scenes I would have happily done anyway. But what a difference it is between choosing or being forced. I couldn't help but feel that... rigidity... was a sort of invisible barrier between us. But we made do, because of... our love."

Here they smiled warmly at each other, their eyes sparkling.

Erin went on by saying, "that made it worth it, could easily make anything worth it. But I couldn't have gone on without the hope that we'd find a better way. Or without striving to make that hope real. And now we're here. Now we're free to truly be together, however we want."

Tilly looked like she might begin shedding tears again... albeit, of a very different kind. They beamed at each other. Their faces were illuminated with radiant happiness. Nothing needed to be said. They just shared a perfect moment together, elongating it to savour their mutual joy.

Buoyed by her elation, Erin finally renewed the conversation. Her voice was light with giddiness.

"There's a lot I'm dying to ask you. So many burning questions. So much I want to know about you and your home and our link and... and... just..."

After a good-natured chuckle, Tilly jumped in with a cheerful tone to say, "I'm not sure I'll have all the answers you want. There's a lot of mystery on my end too. But how about this: I'll try my best... and then *I* get to grill you, deal?"

She had an impish grin as she nodded insistently to playfully compel Erin to agree.

"Ha, deal!"

"Okay, fire away then."

Erin thought it over. There was so much to consider. Where to even start? How to phrase her query?

"Alright, so... the dreamworld, is that, like, a..."

"The 'dreamworld'?" Tilly batted back, puzzled.

"Oh, yeah, *your*... world, where you're from..." She paused to try and think of how else to explain. "Where we first met."

"Ahhh, sure, got you. And so, wait... you... get there by dreaming?"

"Yes, of course! That's how everything started. And I had no idea how... Hold on a second, no, I'm the one who's supposed to be questioning you! No more of that mental judo!"

They both giggled. Tilly shrugged with tongue-in-cheek nonchalance, and mimed zipping her lips shut and padlocking them. She daintily gestured for Erin to continue.

"Like, I don't even know how to put this. I guess what I'm trying to get at is... is that its own dimension or, uh, maybe... some kind of alternate reality? Or is it... kind of... just some other... location in *this* universe? Or..."

"You do know I'm inclined to ask you the exact same thing, right? I doubt I understand this aspect of things any better than you. To me, where I'm from is just *the* world. Much like - I'd hazard a guess - to you this is just *the* world. And best I can tell, the two seem pretty much the same type of place. Apart from the fact that they're... distinct from one another. Separated in time and space somehow."

"Separate... but the same?" Erin slowly mumbled as she pondered this suggestion.

Tilly tilted her head slightly and raised her eyebrows, to convey that this was simply her best guess.

But Erin was already too enraptured by the sprawling implications. She had a whole new set of questions, which she breathlessly posed.

"Okay, but then why are they separate? What separates them? Is one of the worlds, like, nestled in the other? And why did a... bridge... pop up between them, seemingly just for us?"

Tilly seemed confounded by this line of inquiry. She smilingly scrunched up her face in mock pain.

"Arrrghh, you're hurting my brain, Erin! I have no idea. I mean, possibly it happened... just by accident, I guess?"

Erin snorted, and remarked, "some kind of transdimensional gateway randomly opened between two people who just luckily happened to be soulmates? I'm thinking.... no. There has to be something behind it, some kind of... reason why it occurred."

Tilly genuinely considered this point for a few moments. Then she threw up her hands in surrender.

"Beats me. Anyway, what does it matter? Maybe there *is* some shadowy cabal of pan-dimensional alien matchmakers who... intercede every so often to put two lovebirds together. Just because they get a kick out of it. But who cares? No use in looking for something we... might not want to find. Sometimes you just gotta ignore that loose thread you really want to tug, or the whole thing could come apart." Tilly's eyes lit up here as the perfect punchline occurred to her, which endearingly gave away that it was coming. "And that's especially true... if you happen, like us, to be soaring on a flying carpet!"

Erin groaned at the bad joke and they both laughed. She also couldn't help but notice that this was the most she had smiled for a very, very long time.

"Reeeeaaal funny, you. Hardy har har, and such. Still, I take your point. I guess I am getting ahead of myself. I should just be here in the moment with you, I know."

"Couldn't hurt."

"No, I suppose not. Though..." Here Erin lapsed into contemplation before soberly finishing her thought. "Just... one last question?"

The sudden seriousness of Erin's demeanour did somewhat disconcert Tilly. The resulting trepidation was present on her face as, with more than a hint of uncertainty, she replied, "sure..."

Erin craned her neck to slowly look Tilly's body up and down a few times over.

At last, she asked, "you... do realize you're, like, levitating?"

Tilly emphatically exhaled her held breath and her face relaxed, awash with relief. Then she realized she had to get Erin back. So she caught herself and put on an expression of astonished incredulity.

"No way!" she exclaimed, looking down at her body hovering in mid-air with a dramatic gasp. "Gosh... look at that... So I am."

Erin sniggered and rolled her eyes.

"You are hi-larious."

"Yep, pretty much."

"So, it's seriously not weird to you that you're floating?..."

"I don't know, is it weird to you that you're not?"

"Hmm, touché."

"Just so I know, how many more questions can I expect about how *weird* it is that I'm here or how *weird* whatever I'm doing is?..."

"Uh, like, a... lot?"

"Then... I fear I'll only be a source of disappointment in my capacity as answer-giver. Much of what I think you're hoping I know, I'm pretty sure I don't."

"You could never disappoint me, Tilly."

"Oh you," Tilly replied with a bashful smile and a theatrical wave of her hand. But her blushing and averted gaze betrayed just how much it had really affected her.

"There's just... I... I've been trying to decipher a whirlwind of mysteries and impossible things all by myself, for a good while now. And... so... I guess it doesn't even matter if you don't have the answers from the get-go. I'm just glad to have someone by my side helping... to figure things out."

Tilly nodded understandingly.

"Right... yes... I didn't think of it like that.... I can do that. I *want* to be that for you."

Erin started to say thank you, but Tilly resumed without even realizing she was interrupting.

"But... what if it's an enigma we can't unravel, even together? Can... you... uh, live without the answers?"

Here, Erin's jaw clenched almost imperceptibly. It was clear that she was very carefully mulling over how to articulate her response. Tilly watched this pensiveness with vague disquiet.

"I... don't know. I'm not sure. I... I... it's, like... hmm... I don't *need* to know the answers. But without them, or even some of them, I'm just... more susceptible to these... stupid doubts. I mean, like, the rest of the world would call this," she used a finger on one of her bound hands to point at herself and then Tilly, "crazy, and they would label you... a... mere hallucination. And I would just-"

Tilly murmured poutily, "do you care a lot about that kind of thing? What... others would say?"

"No, no! Of course not! Absolutely not! That's not it at all!"

Erin was quick to issue this loud, insistent denial. How the tables had turned.

Once some awkward silence has passed, Tilly grew impatient and, barely above a whisper, prompted Erin by saying, "but 'you just' what?"

"It would... just help me if I understood certain things better. Really help me." After heaving out a huge sigh, she finished by saying, in a manner which suggested she was mad at herself, "I don't want to feel like that. I just do."

"Alright, Erin. Alright. I'll do what I can, obviously. Maybe I'll even surprise myself with how much we're able to figure out. I suppose there is no way to tell until we actually try. I just... don't want you to get your hopes up for..."

As Tilly was speaking, Erin noticed that her vision had actually been getting clearer and clearer in recent minutes, and her thinking was getting more and more lucid too. At first, this development baffled her. But then the terrible realization came. The Ikelos had been rapidly wearing off. Its effect was now very nearly gone. She couldn't believe it: the end had snuck up on her.

"Tilly!" she cried out, yanking hard at her wrist restraints.

The last tiny sliver of ice snapped and the two parts of the ice-lock came free of each other.

She reached upwards to embrace Tilly. But as she did so, Tilly fell straight down into her and vanished.

CHAPTER FIFTEEN

12:20 PM. MARCH 13TH.

(APPROX. TWENTY DAYS LATER)

Erin kicked the brake lever on the wheeled base, and stood up from the window-seat. She got a firm grip of the metal pole and carefully dragged the whole thing over to the kitchenette.

"Gotta wash a bowl, no?"

"Who says I'm having cereal?" Erin replied, with a raised eyebrow.

"Well, you know I can't stand how that liquid food looks. And you wouldn't want to expose me to that sight if you don't have to... would you?" Tilly affected a teasingly demure pose, tilting her head down and looking up at Erin questioningly. Her big puppy-dog eyes were doing all the work here. "Besides, you've been doing so good with eating, these last few days... might as well keep the streak going, right? Build on that progress?"

"I... don't want you to start thinking that... I'm on a certain track, Tilly. Because I might not be able to keep it up, and then I'd be letting you down somehow... and just about the worst thing in the world is how you look when you're crestfallen."

"I'm sure I don't know what you mean." Batting her eyelashes playfully, she blew a kiss. "And I don't *expect* anything. I just think that you should maybe, you know, take advantage of being able to stomach regular food for however long it lasts."

Erin blew a kiss back and inclined her head in concession to this worthy point.

"You're right. Okay. But just half a bowl."

She reached up to the cabinet, right by where Tilly was sitting on the countertop, to grab the bowl and cereal box.

"A *full* bowl."

Erin paused as she was putting the items down and looked into Tilly's face.

"Oh yeah? Says who?"

Although she tried to ask this in a faux-serious tone, even knitting her brow too, a quiet underlying chortle accompanied it.

"Says me! That's who!" Tilly answered, confidently jabbing her thumb towards her chest. Her adorable little smile was too winsome to deny.

"Hmm. In that case... three-quarters then. Final offer! And you're only getting even that because I've got such a weakness for cuties!"

"No deal! Full bowl! Full bowl! Full bowl! Full bowl!" Tilly began to chant, happily jigging around in her seat.

"Jeez-louise. What are you, on commission here? You're in the pocket of Big Cereal, admit it!"

"And break my non-disclosure agreement?! Forget it! They say if I meet my yearly bowls-eaten numbers I'll make it to exec yet!"

"Best of luck with, uh, that, but in the meanwhile, let's meet in the middle! Three-quarters!"

Tilly jumped to her feet with haughty swagger.

"Look, do you think I got to be a covert operative for the world's second largest cornflake conglomerate by being a pushover?" Then, switching tacts, she added sweetly, "those bowls you have are pretty small; a full bowl isn't that much at all. You'll barely even notice the difference."

"I won't even notice it, huh?" Trying and failing to stifle her smile, Erin heaved a big melodramatic sigh and said, "when did you become the boss of me, that's what I want to know!"

"As long as you're in my house, you'll obey *my* rules, missy!" Tilly put her balled fists onto her hips and nodded assertively.

"Ha, your house. You *are* impossible, Tilly." Tittering the whole time, she began pouring the cereal. She watched to ensure her judicious tilting of the box wasn't filling the bowl overmuch.

"Yes, quite," Tilly proudly declared with a smirk.

When Erin put the box down, Tilly tutted and said, "hey, up to the rim!"

Glancing back at the bowl, Erin had a pouty hand-caught-in-the-cookie-jar expression. She was just about to protest and offer a defense of her bowl-filling metric, but Tilly spoke up first.

"Don't think I don't see your little tricks: making a heap where only the tip comes close to the top of the bowl." She wagged her finger and adopted a tone of parental disapproval. "All the way to the rim, now, or else! You're a growing girl and I know what's best for you!"

Erin doubled over in hysterics. Tears were forming at the sides of her eyes as she positively howled with laughter and struggled to breathe. Tilly was beaming with satisfaction as she watched this unfold. She adored being able to do this to Erin. It was like a little achievement each time.

The laughter had become a regular occurrence now. For, in idle moments, they would exchange the giddy, elaborate nonsense that lovers bat back-and-forth perfectly unabashed. And in no time at all, they had developed a substantial lexicon of bizarre, self-referential inside jokes. And unexplainable songs. And incredibly specific weird little noises. All this was their private cipher. It was a means not only of making each other laugh but also of implicitly reminding themselves of their bond. Erin cherished this more than she could possibly express. It made her so incredibly happy, made every mundane task into a pleasure. One time she'd laughed so hard and for so long that she had hiccups - a real pet peeve of hers - for about the next forty-five minutes, and *couldn't* have cared less.

When Erin was finally able to control herself, she dragged her sleeve across her eyes to dry them. Still fighting off the occasional residual giggle, she said, "it was the tone that got me! I swear... to... god... that was *so* funny!"

"Looks that way alright. Man, I love making you laugh, it's like my favorite thing in the world!"

"I'm glad! I love it too! Though my jaw might disagree. It's legit sore from all the goddamn laughing recently. Believe me, there was none of that before you came along. My jaw's probably strained from the surprise of it alone!"

"Could be, could be. But enough gabbing, you! Eat your cereal!"

"Affirmative."

Erin stood up straight and saluted. Then she poured a bit more cereal into the bowl, along with some milk. Dunking a spoon in too, she picked up the bowl and turned to go.

"Window?"

"Window," Erin confirmed as she switched to precariously clutching the bowl from underneath with one hand.

With the other hand, she pulled the IV stand with her again. Conveniently, it wheeled along easily on the hardwood floor. The only tricky part was not getting tangled in the long thin tube connecting the IV infusion pump clamped on the pole to the venous catheter in her arm. Still, though she often thought of herself as clumsy, she hadn't made this mistake yet. And she hoped to keep it that way. Too much was at stake. That device enabled her to continually microdose herself with Ikelos throughout her waking hours.

The logic behind this set-up was simple. That first successful tulpamancy session had shown her the way. Once freed from the bed and suddenly without Tilly, she instantly grasped the crucial role that Ikelos had played. Being under its influence was not only required for creating Tilly's tulpa, but for maintaining its manifestation as well. However, repeating that heightened Ikelos dosage scheme would be overkill. Erin now already knew how to bring Tilly into this world. Besides which, it just wasn't viable, either healthwise or financially, to consume the drug in that prodigious daily quantity. All that was needed, really, was the minimum intake of Ikelos which would enable her to keep Tilly around. This had the benefit of being a sustainably efficient practice. Not to mention the fact that it would also allow her to retain the maximum degree of lucidity when interacting with Tilly.

Of course, Erin did *consider* consulting Ka-Sumedy about how best to divvy up Ikelos doses in this way. But she ultimately thought better of it. Her last request for advice had evidently perturbed them; she did not wish, or dare, to spook them any further. Even though she paid them a generous stipend to be her personal drug manufacturer, they could only be pushed so far. She still had to tread lightly. Ka-Sumedy's concern over her erratic and excessive Ikelos use was one thing. But if it escalated to a full blown panic that they were abetting her crypto-suicidal ambitions? It was very conceivable they would cut ties. Someone in Ka-Sumedy's line of work does not need a dead body with a vial full of their work helpfully framed in the rigor mortis death-clutch. That leads to investigations being pursued and newspaper articles being published. A very risky level of scrutiny to draw upon oneself indeed. No matter how good of a customer she might be, she wasn't worth *that*. Not by a long shot. And if Erin lost Ka-Sumedy's services, she had no replacement.

So, she undertook to figure the matter out for herself. She read up on both the idea of intensive microdosing and the dosage calculations which undergirded its efficacy. Then she tried to apply this hastily acquired knowledge to Ikelos. This was obviously destined to be... imperfect. The math here was not exactly child's play. But she felt that she only needed a functional starting point. She could refine things as she went. Relatively confident in the numbers she'd settled upon, she bought the IV equipment and set everything up to her specifications. Once she hit start on the machine, she never looked back. The ongoing trickle-infusion of Ikelos worked just as she hoped. She was able to bring Tilly back on even this light a dose. And keeping the manifestation stable was a breeze. Mission accomplished.

Erin stood before the window, slowly moving spoonfuls of cereal into her mouth. She was staring out at the cityscape. It was hard not to stand in awe of the gleaming, orderly masterpiece it constituted. But this was not why she stared. It was what lay embedded deep within this sight which kept her transfixed. Something in the city's very magnificence and enormity seemed to brazenly offer up the premonition of its destruction. This was a tantalizing invitation which the annals of war showed rarely went unaccepted for very long. That was just the way it went. She often felt it must be near enough a universal law. Things that were *too* grand were merely displaying the schematic of their own annihilation. This applied to metropolises just the same as to, say, happy lives. Sudden misfortune could strip away all one's joys, much as winter spitefully denudes the trees of all their beauty. It was a sobering truth which echoed in her mind, making her skittish and paranoid. She was just glad that her and Tilly were hidden away here in this apartment. Their love, that most conspicuous of treasures, had to be kept safe from prying eyes.

Still, their love was *so* perfect that she couldn't help but feel nervous. If she tiptoed even an inch out of this hallowed, occluded cubbyhole apart from the outside world, the danger could not be overstated. She would be attracting the notice of fearsome cosmic forces, too old to have a name. They were laws whose influence was exerted through the murky, impossible empty space *between* the fibres of the universe's tapestry. An extradimensional substrate where the very character, be it good or ill, of imminent events was bred. And when these forces detected Tilly? They would see her as an aberration, upsetting the... equilibrium they sought to maintain. Setting upon the lovebirds, they would use her fellow man as not only the murder weapon but the carrion-eaters to dispose of the evidence afterwards too. The fact that these people would be but unwitting puppets should, perhaps, have nullified her anger towards them. But it didn't. For she could not forgive the pre-existing prejudice and hatred which made them such fit tools of assassination in the first place.

She tried to banish this fretting from her thoughts. Not least because it was pointless and crazy-making. As she went on gawking at the city, she decided to instead occupy herself by accepting *its* particular invitation. With just the artillery of her mind's eye, she idly envisioned all the ways in which it might be brought down to smouldering ashes. This was no half-measure demolition either. Down from the sky screeched a biblical rain of sulphurous hellfire. So that no man-made shape was left unmangled. So that not one brick lay mortared atop another. A radical undoing, in other words. She overlaid these hallucinatory scenarios upon the sight of the city itself, watching each of them play out with a detached half-interest. Even the resulting scenes of utter destruction stirred her but little. In truth, she didn't want to obliterate their world, not really. She just wanted to preserve her own tiny sphere from that fate.

"Not sitting?" Tilly asked, snapping Erin out of her barbarous daydreams.

"Nope."

"How come?"

Erin just shrugged and said noncommittally, "feel like standing."

She kept eating and Tilly began staring down at the city too.

"What do you see when you look at it?"

"Some days... *good* days... it seems like it's a hundred million miles away. And I find myself really just marvelling at the distance."

"But given your... animus towards it... why do you feel so drawn to stare at it at all?"

Erin carefully put her half-eaten breakfast down on the window-seat.

"I can't not, I suppose. I find it too... fascinating, in the worst possible way. It's like... when I was little..."

She paused and glanced at Tilly as if to take strength from the sight of her.

"Well, it reminds me of... we had this mangy tomcat, Glitch. He was fickle and irritable and seemingly always dirty. And I loved that little fuck. Doted on him endlessly. I was the only one he ever really trusted. He'd climb into my lap and curl up and go to sleep for so long that I'd eventually forget he was even on me. But one day... he just... *disappeared*. He was an outdoor cat, and finally he just didn't come home. I was distraught. I put flyers up, scoured the streets, the whole nine yards. Once weeks had gone by, everyone just told me to stop looking, that he was dead. I figured he was probably dead, the fucking idiots, but that wasn't the point. I had to *know*. And so, I was pulled by some inexorable force to the... discovery... itself."

She stopped speaking again and looked down at her hands for a little while. By the time she continued, her gaze still hadn't raised.

"I finally came across his body accidentally. It was in this tiny, tiny gap between the toolshed and the backyard fence. Even for a cat, it would've been super hard to access, but there he was. Cats... uh, go off to die in weird, isolated places apparently. And it had been, well, months and months since he had gone missing. So he was... just... just... a little skeleton with a layer of gristle attached at this point. Everything else had rotted away or been eaten by, like, whatever..."

"I'm sorry Erin, that's awful," Tilly offered quietly.

In response, Erin simply chuckled in a dry, mirthless way. It didn't sound very much like laughter at all.

"Ha, you haven't even heard the worst part yet. Obviously, coming across the remains was... traumatic in its own way, but I'd already accepted that might be the cost of finding out his fate. What I hadn't thought about, and what would've stopped me searching, was how seeing it would affect things. Because I just stood there, still as a statue. Stared at it for like... I don't know... twenty minutes. Tears were streaming down my face and, still, I couldn't look away. And couldn't help inspecting every part of it over and over. From then on, that sight was stored in here" - still without looking up, she tapped her forehead - "with perfect clarity. When I'm in a nursing home, scarcely able to feed myself or remember my own name anymore, I bet I'll still be able to recall exactly how it looked. And I mean *exactly*."

"God... I... I..." Tilly began, overwhelmed. But then she remembered her role here. This wasn't about her. She just needed to get out of the way. "H-how did that... affect you?"

"It robbed me of all those good memories of Glitch, invalidated them. I couldn't think of him without that... sight flashing before my eyes. That was all he was to me now: flecks of viscera on bone. It made my pet not a pet but just a carcass. Like, what I saw retroactively tainted all that I had already seen and felt. And that's fucking scary... and fucking horrible and..."

"Erin, breathe."

She did just that, taking several long deep breaths. As her heart rate began to fall back to normal, she wiped the burgeoning moisture from her eyes.

"I... uh... didn't let anyone know I found the body, felt like it was *my* private shame somehow. So no-one else ever came across it. By the time the toolshed got moved, years down the line, even the bones were gone. Dust on the wind. And I've never told anyone this story. Never thought I would, either."

"Thank you for sharing it with me then, that really means a lot." Tilly moved closer. "I love you."

"I love you too."

"Now, how is *that* like *that*?" Tilly asked gently, pointing to the outside world.

"Oh yeah. Well, I also know the revolting ugliness which lies underneath the surface of *that*. And... revolting things have a way of keeping you transfixed." Here, Erin gestured to the window too. "That's all I can see when I look at it. Or even when I think of it. I'm serious, I'm so sick of this decrepit, small-minded world, and this little rot-box I have to occupy in it. I can't help but wonder why we don't just abandon it *completely*. Just up and fucking leave it."

"Erin..."

"No, for real, Tilly. Why the hell not? I brought you *here*, didn't I? I don't see why, in principle, we can't find a way to shoot our asses back the other way together. Whatever opening has been torn open, it can't just be one-way. So why not betake ourselves to the dreamworld, permanently? Why not have our happily-ever-after *there*? There's nothing good for us here. But there we could explore an infinite, spectacular wonderland. Or just... spend a couple millennia having fun remaking it every which way. Do whatever we want, basically."

Tilly had been nodding along sympathetically enough.

"I understand what you're saying. But that's not what you really want, Erin. I think you have some faint sense of the... cost of what you're proposing. And it's not a price you *truly* want to pay. Listen, can't we just forge our happiness here? Surely this world is not irredeemable?"

There is something I think it's time I explained to you." Erin heaved a heavy sigh of responsibility. And cast a stern gaze upon Tilly. "That world out there won't ever welcome people like us. To put it very fucking mildly."

"What do you mean?"

"We know - really know - that reality is *more* than they think. And at first they may feel sorry for you, thinking you a poor broken-minded thing. But then, when they see your clear-eyed conviction, that pity will... mutate... into something much worse. Not *even* anger. That's fleeting. That can be defused. No, it'll be the stark, dispassionate abhorrence they usually feel towards disaster or... disease."

Tilly was increasingly wide-eyed with apprehension as she listened.

"Oh that's right, they'll view us like a pestilence come to wring the life from them." She beckoned Tilly closer to her and went on in a lower, conspiratorial tone. "I don't say this to upset you. But you need to know what the stakes are. What awaits us beyond that glass." With a sweeping gesture, she indicated the cityscape outside, and pretended to spit on the floor in disgust.

Tilly could only whisper, "I-I... don't understand. Why?... Why despise us if we're just... like, keeping to ourselves, loving each other?"

"Because!" Erin exclaimed, straightening up again and getting fired up. "Because you *cannot* disagree with them on the fundamental nature of reality. That's a... sacrosanct... and immutable... fact. Disputing it can't be stomached. To do so is not just wrong, but evil too. It feels like an attack. As though you're shoving them from hallowed philosophical terra firma... to drown in a sea of the unknown."

She slapped the glass disdainfully and went on.

"That's why even keeping it in your head is not enough: the belief itself is transgression enough. They'll sniff it out in no time. And then... at best... they will... forcibly *disabuse* you of your 'delusion'. You'll be deemed a psychotic 'patient', meaning they can do whatever they want to you! Insidious extraction techniques which centuries of grisly insane asylums have perfected! Pills and brainwashing in lieu of the lobotomy ice-pick!"

"But... w-why do they see it as... s-so very dangerous?"

"It's simple why they abominate people like us more than, say, a murderer. The murderer is just a rabid dog. Lock him up or put him down, and be done with it. A crude threat, easily contained. Because he can't sell you on randomly killing people, can't convince you why dismemberment is fun. But us? If we could show... *really* show others what we've seen... well, we could corrupt" - she put the word in air quotes - "how they perceive reality. See, it's not just the infliction of a depraved idea, but an acid-bath for all their pre-existing ideas too."

Tilly was unblinkingly rapt and silent like a frightened child listening to a scary story. She had never seen this side of Erin. It was... eye-opening.

Oblivious to this, Erin continued. She had picked up a fearsome head of steam. The words poured from her like gospel.

"And from that reset, there would be unmanageable chaos. Can't keep people fretting about mortgages and promotions or... obsessing over vapid celebrities and new smartphones if they know there's another fucking dimension! I mean, good luck with that! But without that crap, the shackles of society fall open. And who knows what the freed will do?..."

She was raving fanatically, saliva flying from her mouth. Her eyes had defocused. They had a terrifying glint.

"That's why I doubt they'll even suffer a witch like me to live. The saintliest of them would burn me at the stake with maniacal relish. They'll say that such savagery was needed to stop the advent of some... Typhoid Mary of otherthink, the one who'd spread the contagion far and wide. And then they'll salt the earth at my unmarked grave!"

"Fuck..."

The word sounded strange and unpracticed coming from Tilly.

Erin's breathing was heavy and rapid.

"Yes! Fuck! And that's why I'm the prisoner of my own... goddamn... *hate...*" She spat the word with revulsion, as though it were some dire curse. "This... boundless and indiscriminate hate. It's circulating *inside of* me, like some thick... black... septic slush which has curdled within my veins. Which sluggishly crawls a few inches forward with every laboured pump of my heart. And I can feel that energy all *around* me too. It envelops me, brushing my skin like searing static! Blooming a phantom prickly heat across my body! I... I just... like... Fuck..."

She hung her head and shut her eyes, sighing deeply. A pained expression squirmed across her face.

Though wearied, she wasn't spent. Not quite yet.

She opened and closed her fists a few times, cracking her knuckles.

When her eyes opened again, they had a martial calm.

"Look, Tilly... in a sense, none of this is important. All you really need to know is that *I will protect you*. I will protect you from them. I will protect you from everything."

CHAPTER SIXTEEN

3:59 PM. MARCH 25TH.

(APPROX. TWELVE DAYS LATER)

Erin was leisurely walking back and forth in her apartment, to get some exercise. Just like all prisoners have to learn to make do with pacing the length of their cell. At first she had made a game of it, taking turns with Tilly to count each lap she made. But because it was such a short distance to travel, the number quickly got into the triple-digits. The game didn't seem that fun anymore when it became a constant reminder of the smallness of her confines. So, next she had progressed through a series of other ways to keep her idle hands busy as she made her laps. It had been shadow-boxing, then it had been bouncing a ball, then it had been twirling a drumstick in her fingers. Anything to help keep herself distracted. And her hands were free to do this because they didn't have to be wrapped around the IV stand now.

She had made an improvement. It was somewhat of a pressing necessity in fact. She had started to find having to push the IV stand around all the time very annoying. And constraining. And burdensome. And, not to mention, a tad demeaning. She didn't want to feel like some pitiful old lady stuck traipsing across a hospital ward. The fix had been pretty easy, as she was *not* usually accustomed to finding was the case. All that had been required was, first, to put the IV stand braked in the centre of the room. Then she extended the tubing from the top-of-the-line, powerful infusion pump and left it loose-hanging on the floor. So that now there was enough slack that she could basically walk around the cramped apartment freely, the excess tubing following her wherever she went. A nice compromise between function and pride.

Erin had finally started to break a sweat, meaning that the drumstick got tossed onto the bed. Carrying on the tiresome walking required all the physical effort she had to give now. Still, she was happy enough to resume her repartee with Tilly to preoccupy herself.

"You know... given you're, like, a magical being or whatever, what kind of cool shit do you think you can do?"

"You mean... like, uh, tricks?..."

"Yeah!"

Tilly, leaning against the wall, jokingly scoffed.

"I don't *do* 'tricks'. I'm not like some performing seal, Erin."

"Oh, but you'd be the cutest little sealie-wealie if you were!"

Tilly laughed and said, "thanks?... I guess?..."

"And I'd throw you yummy fishes to eat! And I'd stroke your weird slippery fur! And polish your tusks! And tug on your adorable seal-whiskers!" Erin gushed in an exaggeratedly mushy, high-pitched tone. And she skipped along to the rhythm of each declaration of intent.

"Oh no! Don't you even try to out-lovey-dovey me! You never beat me at this game!"

"Ah, but I can't help it! You're just ever so... *dreamy*, Tilly!"

"I *will* throw something at you, you know."

"You can try, but you'll miss. I'm too agile. I've got catlike reflexes, see," she boasted as she halted and theatrically juked side to side as though dodging a missile of comic reprisal. "Which is perfect, because cats and seals are well known to bond in the wild."

"I... don't think that's true..."

"Yeah, well, there's a first time for everything!"

"Sure, and it'll certainly be a first if I ever start doing magic tricks for your amusement!"

"I'm just saying... maybe we should toy around with it. See what you can do. See what the limits are. Might be a fun way to pass the time. I mean, like... you can float around and all that, but do you think you can pass through walls?"

"Well... I dare say... I probably could..."

"I'd almost suggest you should go spy on the neighbours, maybe find something funny to report. But I assiduously try to pretend they don't exist, so... like, nix that. Plus, I'd fear for your dainty sensibilities. You might well end up stumbling upon, say, someone getting... pounded."

Erin was intentionally trying to provoke a reaction with this vulgarness. Weaponizing her own dirty sense of humour was always an enjoyable way to mess with Tilly. And, as such, she was doing very little to hide her sly smirk of anticipation.

"Gross..." Tilly whined, scrunching up her face in distaste.

Erin burst out laughing, clutching her sides. Tilly just looked on bemusedly. She was trying and failing to mask her own smile with a faux-disapproving expression.

When Erin managed to pull herself together, she said, "hell, I don't really disagree! It's a good thing the walls in this apartment building seriously seem to be presidential-nuclear-bunker thick. Never heard the slightest peep from whatever... weirdos might reside on either side. Really lucked out there."

"I should have known that your mind would go straight to shenanigans. How about, instead of causing mischief, trying stuff out for... oh I don't know, science?"

"Oh gosh... soberly documenting things like some egghead staring into a microscope. Where's the fun in that?"

Shrugging, Tilly half-heartedly countered, "someone's got to do it."

"Suuuuure, I suppose I'll just stick some electrodes to your butt then. And I'll surely get an article entitled... 'The Bio-Electrical Fluctuations of Tulpa Lifeforms' in a peer-reviewed journal in no time. Book deals and Nobel Prizes will, no doubt, be close behind."

"Stranger things have happened."

Erin shot back her riposte with a significant glance.

"Oh, I'm *well* aware."

Tilly gave a nod of acknowledgement as if to say 'touché'.

While she stopped to take a drink from her water bottle, Erin excitedly snapped her fingers as something occurred to her.

"Ooooh... I guess there are some cool tests we could do. I wonder... do you think you'd appear in a mirror? Or in a photograph?"

Squinting with mock puzzlement, Tilly asked, "are you, like, trying to figure out if I'm a... vampire?"

They both giggled.

Tilly went on, "hey, I could be! You did have to *invite* me into your home, right?"

"Yeah... yeah... my word, you're onto something! It's all adding up now! Woah, you *did* start burning when I threw that holy water on you..."

"That was soooo rude of you by the way..."

"You're quite right. Let me make it up to you by cooking you a delicious meal. Heavy on the garlic."

"As long as it's not a stake!"

"Man, we're dorks," Erin said with a chuckle, getting back to her walking.

"Damn straight!"

"Anyway, wily vampiric seductress though you obviously are, you picked the wrong girl to prey on. My faith in the good lord will keep me safe," she announced, looking skyward reverently. Her hand was hovering over her heart.

The delivery was impeccably deadpan.

Tilly looked at her askance.

"I know, right? Can you imagine?..." Erin began with a sardonic laugh. "Shit, now that I think about it, it *is* such a hilarious image for someone being attacked by, like, some 'dark creature of the night'", she made an oscillating 'woooooooooo' noise and waggled her fingers in the air, "to hold up a crucifix for protection. What an unlucky time to find out god doesn't really exist: just as some crazy monster starts eating your fucking face."

"Only you would find that funny!"

"Guilty as charged."

Tilly perked up a bit. An opportunity had arisen.

"So you're not a believer, huh?"

Swivelling round as she walked, Erin curtsied.

"Depraved godless heathen, through and through. Pleased to meet you." And then she quietly mumbled the afterthought, "hmm, really didn't intend for that to rhyme."

"If I know you, I can expect a speech about how, like, dangerous the churchgoer's mentality is for society in five, four, three..." Tilly quipped with impish snark.

Erin just chuckled at a ribbing well landed.

"Ha, maybe once upon a time. But... nah, modernity is a motherfucker. You've got to give 'the people' credit for resourcefulness at least, they don't even *need* religion anymore." Here she started absentmindedly picking food out of her teeth in between every few words. "They can... you know... find a way... to make... an opiate out... of most anything... nowadays."

"Well, how about you in particular then. I'm curious, did you ever believe in a god?" Tilly asked carefully, trying not to give away that this segue had been her true goal.

Erin decided she had had enough exercise for one day. She gave a laboured huff of relief at finally being done. Coming over to the bed, she flopped down and pulled off her sweaty socks and slippers. Then she gave Tilly's question some real consideration. Her head tilted side to side metronomically as she thought it over.

"Back when I was a little kid... sure, I'd have said yeah. Listen, my grandparents... okay, fine, they weren't exactly *pious*. They were more... Jesus-ornaments, Mass-on-special-occasions kind of people. But they did teach me prayers to say and I said them. I literally never even thought about what the words truly meant. I was just reciting memorised lines in a memorised cadence, because they wanted me to. And I assumed god existed because I was *told* that and I didn't think to question it."

"Doesn't that mean that-"

But Erin was on a roll now, and she wasn't about to be interrupted.

"Basically, I 'believed' in god like I believed my sister's claim that if I snuck into her room when she was out, there was... a spider she'd trained to pounce on my head and lay eggs in my scalp. I really fucking thought that must be true when I was seven or eight. Uhhh, held a dinner-plate over my head when I'd tiptoe in there and everything. A few years later, no-one had to tell me it wasn't possible, I just... knew it. Same with the story of ol' whitebeard. As soon as I got old enough to have a little extra brainpower at my disposal, it was over. Because once *I* could properly ask *myself* the question, I instantly knew I didn't think it was true and never really had. I wasn't even abandoning anything. It was just a... first-time realization."

"Fair enough, I get it. But... how would you feel if a god *did* exist? Like, if tomorrow something was discovered. I don't know... some fantastical deep-space scan found an... unmistakable astronomical maker's mark. And that proved it definitively. What then?" Tilly ventured.

"Hmm... well... that's a good question..."

Erin trailed off, staring into space as she weighed it up.

"I... think..." she began again, choosing her words very carefully. "We'd need to find a way to *kill* it."

Tilly's eyes widened slightly.

"Okay..." she said uncertainly. "Care to, like, elaborate?"

"What's unclear?"

"Uh, well... I guess 'why'?"

"Alright, picture this scenario. Let's say that... ummm... you're locked in a room. A really, really big room. All the way on the other side of it is... a full-grown gorilla."

Tilly chortled and remarked teasingly, "*again* with the animals. What's with this freaking metaphor menagerie you keep on hand, Erin?"

"*Any-way,*" Erin said emphatically, to slide right past this quip. "It's giant, insanely strong, could snap you like a twig. The whole deal. And as far as you can tell, this gorilla must be aware of you. How could it not be? But it hasn't yet shown any interest in you, isn't displaying any aggression."

"Sure..."

"Now, you have a gun. Do you use it?"

Tilly rubbed her forehead, puzzled and hesitant.

"Damn, I-I... well, how long am I going to be locked in there?"

"Indefinitely."

"Is it possible to ever find a way out of the locked room?"

Erin was getting a bit crabby and impatient. She slumped forward theatrically, as if folding from exasperation. And she let slip a petulant groan.

"No!"

"What if the gorilla never... uh, attacks or whatever?"

"It might, it might not. But what matters is that it *can*. At any time. And it would overpower you with ease. You'd be mauled and ripped limb from limb."

"Is the gun... I don't know, like, high-calibre enough to take down a gorilla?"

"Sure."

"Then... then... I suppose I'd... just... wait and see if it attacked me. If it did, at that point... fine, I might be okay shooting at it in self-defense. But only as a last resort."

Erin's whole mien now bespoke just how rapidly her annoyance was growing.

"What about when you fall asleep?! You'd be defenseless!"

"I guess... hopefully... I'd wake up in time if anything happened."

Erin snorted.

"Alright, Sally fucking PETA Pacifist, we get it! You're compassionate as a motherfucker! But do you really think you'll be able to trust your aim when a gorilla is charging at you? Those scant few seconds are going to whizz by, real quick!"

With a shrug, Tilly nonchalantly said, "maybe so."

With a scowl, Erin forcefully retorted, "then shouldn't you riddle the fucker with bullets before it even knows what's happening?! No other option is worth the risk."

"So... that's your big idea? *Preemptive deicide?*"

Erin oh-so-humbly inclined her head to assent.

It was tempting to explain herself in greater detail here, but she held her tongue. After all, it might be... a little too much to say plainly that she believed humans *had* to be the most dangerous beings in the universe. That just had a certain egomaniacal, dreams-of-cosmic-domination ring to it. Like she spent her free time sketching fancy spaceships with pew-pew lasers for herself to pilot and annex other galaxies with. Or was it that it seemed to be laden with more than a trace of homosapien-chauvinism? Hard to say. And maybe neither of these misconceptions would even be sufficiently dispelled by offering her actual reasoning for it.

Her feeling was that true freedom means being able to vanquish anyone or anything who'd deprive you of it. Otherwise, you're only 'free' due to the largess or indifference of a potential master. It's nothing more than contingent, temporary good fortune. Likely just the misidentified intermission - of uncertain length - between periods of serfdom. Not exactly very appealing when put like that. And to whatever degree she *could* be counted a part of humanity, she didn't want the species to allow itself to be debased by the hypothetical specter of future bondage. Because some of that collective shame would trickle-down to her. Like gunk oozing down from cracks in the ceiling while you sleep. And that was some unfair bullshit. So she had better be spared it! For all its other sins, the rest of mankind surely owed her at least that much...

But, yes, she kept this part to herself. One outlandish thing at a time. Best to... give each one room to breathe. Even with your soulmate. Maybe *especially* with your soulmate. At any rate, there was plenty of time ahead of them to expound on that other stuff. Another day perhaps.

Erin had momentarily zoned out while she was thinking about all this. Tilly pulled her back into the room by saying, "isn't this a moot point anyway? I suppose you *can* shoot down a gorilla. But, like - damn this is a weird thing to say out loud - there's obviously no... whatever.... *gun*... big enough to kill a god."

There was a pause as Erin picked up this previous train-of-thought again.

"Uh-huh, well... that's just details. We'd... figure it out."

"Ha, and who's 'we', exactly?"

"Jeez, I don't know. Just, like, whoever those... guys... are in all those movies where there's an asteroid on a collision course with Earth. The ones who figure out how to blow it up or... knock it off course... or shoot it into the sun or whatever the fuck. Get those lab-coat brainiacs to invent some shit that can turn an asteroid the other way and blast it at a target. Make it into a big ol' space-cannonball. And then put a couple of those in god's noggin. See how omnipotent he really is."

Tilly was marvelling at her in amused disbelief.

"You really are something, my love."

"Yes ma'am," Erin replied with a goofy smile and a wink. "Plus, it'd also be a... shit, what's that word?... ah, *humane*... way to do it. Don't they bash cows in the head at the slaughterhouse to stun them before they get offed? Well, if it's good enough for Bessie, it's good enough for god. Better deal too, because we're not *even* going to eat him afterwards. I mean, come on, can't say fairer than that! Talk about courtesy!"

"That's definitely a... novel way of looking at it," Tilly said distractedly, trying to blow her fringe away from her eyes. "So what *are* we gonna do with the remains then? I mean, given that we're kind enough not to tuck into them medium-rare and all."

"Wow, you really do get hung up on the strangest details..." This remark was coupled with an arched eyebrow. Yet Erin was also smirking, enjoying letting her imagination run wild. "Look, I'm just the idea-man here. I'm not trying to micromanage all the boring practical crap as well. So... I don't know... maybe... hollow out a whole huge-ass planet, and have that be a makeshift crypt? Or, actually yeah," she nodded to herself, "might be better to just leave the remains floating *in situ*. As, like, a warning. To scare off any other would-be gods who may want to... uh... coalesce out of the nothingness... now there's a power vacuum."

"And as for the devout who can't stomach your murderous plan in the first place? You don't mind overruling them?"

"Fuck it, I'm not a miracle worker. The desire for servility is just an incurable disease for some people." She shrugged and idly gnawed at a rough piece of skin beside her thumbnail. "What're you gonna do?"

"But seriously..."

"Meh, let 'em pick through the... unspooling celestial entrails... of their god. Try to finally reverse-engineer some meaning from the dissection. That's a far better deal than organised religion ever gave them. Like, for real, am I wrong? No horseshit parables to endlessly puzzle over. Just face-to-face with the exact anatomy of their lord, even... splayed out by blunt-force trauma for their convenience. I mean, they'd ought to thank me, if you think about it."

"Uhhh... I wouldn't set aside too much shelf-space for thank-you cards, if I were you. Either way, I gotta tell you, I don't really agree with the whole premise of your analogy to begin with. I see what you're trying to say, but a god is not really like a gorilla."

"Yep, we're smart enough to keep *those* in cages, or in a crosshair..." Erin muttered, with a drawn-out eye-roll.

Tilly just gave her an unimpressed look. As if to say 'half-assed jokes that weak don't even get credited with a courtesy-laugh'.

"That's not what I meant. My point is that god is... something else. Something very different. It's not a mindless beast. If anything, it's more like... a... parent."

"That's a matter of perspective..."

Tilly let about ten seconds go by expectantly, before snickering and making an encouraging circular-motion gesture with her hand.

"Okay... Anything a little more substantive to add?"

Erin laughed too and lazily threw the stinky balled-up socks in Tilly's general direction to retaliate.

She considered it for a moment or two and said, "can't say I'm terribly psyched to have been sired by some fatherly deity who then just wanted to disappear into the backdrop. Like, I know they say the universe is a giant fucking place, but what happened? Did he lose our address or something? That's an... absentee dad... deadbeat shithead in any other context. Right? So glorifying the whole thing in spite of that is... just... grotesque. Hell, as far as I'm concerned, even the concept of the *terrestrial* paternal bond is already overrated enough as it is."

"'Course, maybe you'd feel differently if you got to hear god's side of the story," Tilly shot back simperingly, with a subtle smile, just looking to push some buttons.

"Well then, I'll be sure to read his trashy tell-all memoir when it hi-"
KNOCK, KNOCK, KNOCK.

The hard bangs of this rapping made Erin stop mid-word. Her head span whip-quick around towards the door. Her open mouth was still frozen in the shape of the syllable it had been pronouncing. Her eyes were startled-animal wide and searching.

In the very next instant, she exploded into motion. Her speed was truly a remarkable thing to behold. Acting entirely on instinct, she clambered across the bed and dived behind it, hiding herself from the doorway's line-of-sight. Unfortunately, during her frantic movements, she had knocked the drumstick towards the corner of the mattress. And as there *are* no lucky breaks in a situation like this, it duly rolled right off the edge, unseen. Upon hitting the floor it made a series of those distinctive wood-on-wood thunks until it came to rest. This nearly made Erin just about leap out of her skin. Yet she managed to hold her position and just glare with unbelievable furiousness at the drumstick now lying several feet away. If it was possible to stare daggers into an inanimate object, this one would be completely covered with a hedgehog-esque profusion of hilts.

As she was crouched there on the floor, her back pressed to the bedframe, she was gripped by desperate fear. Fittingly, she rather resembled a soldier who had thrown themselves behind cover at espying an enemy scouting party approaching in the distance. Every part of her was tensed, somehow both stiffening her *and* making her tremble. She didn't dare breathe. Her heart seemed to be ricocheting around her ribs, about to burst. And she could almost actually *feel* the blood flooding to her limbs. In short, her body was preparing her for a mortal struggle. As though a swarm of mighty inhuman assailants were about to stream in, bearing impolite intentions.

Tilly drifted down beside her.

"Who is it?" she whispered softly. A question she didn't expect to be answerable. It was just a probing instrument. She was, unnoticed, looking at her stricken lover intently.

But Erin was not about to chance even a single spoken word. Not now. Not in this moment of impossible peril.

She simply shook her head firmly. Her eyes were glazy, filmed with the ommatokoita of intense fright. They stood to be of little use to her here anyway. She was just listening as hard as she could.

CLANG, CLANG.

She jerked around and, kneeling, peeked up over the bed.

Gliding down from the letterbox was a single sheet of glossy paper.

She snapped back down into her defensive position.

And waited.

More than a few minutes of tense silence passed before she could summon the courage to venture out of her hiding place.

Still not totally convinced the coast was clear, she crept in a low crouch over towards the door as noiselessly as she could. Then, with utmost caution, she slowly lifted up the piece of paper.

Tilly delicately asked, "what is it?"

Erin did not respond right away. She was speed-reading the leaflet. She flipped it over and did the same to its other side.

"I... fucking... shit you not: they're collecting for a... charity. Some kind of dog shelter..."

She clenched her jaw and exhaled through her nose with indignant ire. The feeling was building and building. She couldn't stop it, nor could she have explained it if she tried. A thousand hard little pellets of nitroglycerin were trapped just beneath the topmost layer of skin all over her body. They were racing towards her head, to string together and form rings, *interior* halos erratically twirling around her skull. Primed. Volatile.

And then came the silent detonation.

"These f-fucking... fucks and their fucking door-to-door bucket shaking! If you've gotta corner people in their homes and pester them into donating to a good cause, doesn't it kind of invalidate the whole 'charity' thing?! Jesus, how the fuck did they even get in here?! I'd like to find the sap who let them sweet talk him into buzzing them into the building, and punch him right in the fucking throat!"

Her face was taking on a distinctly reddish hue. She was nearly hyperventilating, almost coughing with rage.

"Just breeeeeathe, Erin. You're alright, eveeeeerything is okay. It's over now."

She was not, just now, terribly amenable to this advice. And she did not even acknowledge it. Rather, she took to tearing up the leaflet over and over again, shredding it into needlessly small pieces. Then she ferried the resulting pile in her cupped hands over to the trashcan and scornfully dumped it in.

"Who... did you *think* it might be?"

Erin flashed her an irritated glance. It wordlessly conveyed a... very strong recommendation that this line of questioning be dropped. Yet, in truth, she was just bitterly mad at *herself* for having, when tested, shrunk from her role as protector. This may have turned out to be a false alarm but, still, she had failed Tilly. Her own body had betrayed her. The fear had bested her. And that was that. There was nothing more to be said. Having cowered as she did was just abjectly humiliating. *Had* all her tough talk about defending Tilly really just been bullshit? *Was* it no better than some creep's braggadocious bluster to impress a girl at a dive bar? No, she couldn't abide that, couldn't abide the self-suspicion now brewing in her mind. It would not go unremedied. This disastrous trial run had opened her eyes. Caught off guard or not, it didn't matter. She would be better next time! She would never disgrace herself like this again!

"I had no fucking idea who it was!"

Tilly blinked in surprise, taken aback.

"O-okay..."

"I just..." Erin trailed off briefly. "Whatever. It's... nothing. I'm fine, I'm fine! Let's just... move on, get back to whatever the hell we were doing, okay?!"

But she was still faintly quivering with anger.

The lukewarm spray fell evenly down Erin's body. She had zoned out, and ceased to really notice the water at all. She was just standing there, staring blankly at the tiled wall where the showerhead was mounted. Her torso was still partially slick with a soapy lather because she'd paused in the middle of washing herself.

This dillydallying was not usual for her. She had never exactly been a fan of long showers to begin with, but they especially had to be ultra-quick affairs now. There could only be a short interruption to the Ikelos microdosing if one wanted little to no diminishment of its effect. Therefore, she had gotten accustomed to haste. She would jump in the shower, perform a condensed set of ablutions, and jump back out. Then, the second she was dry, she'd re-attach the IV line. Easy enough. That is, after a bit of practice. But at this point she'd definitely gotten the whole thing down to a well-oiled sequence.

Yet, here she was, lost in thought and letting precious minutes slip by. This was no accident. Snapping back to reality, she nudged the cubicle door open just a crack and slyly peeked outside. She was checking that Tilly was still curled up on the window-seat, looking up at the yellow sliver of moon as she waited for Erin to finish. This was indeed so. Now Erin stared hard at the shower unit. She roughly sawed her lower lip side-to-side between her teeth as she mulled something over. Then she reached out to the temperature dial. But as soon as her fingertips touched it, she paused. A little time passed without a decision being made, though periodically her fingers did flex as if about to move, only to stiffen again. Her mask of vacillating expressions showed just how conflicted she was. Or, at least, it did. Right up until it fell away. When, all of a sudden, she finally just... *did it.*

Moving rapidly, her hand shot up and tilted the showerhead so that its spray was aimed at her chest, just above her breasts. And then returned to spin the dial all the way around. It took about ten seconds for the water to change temperature. The suspense was incredibly nerve-wracking. And she couldn't help but get excited by it. Preparing herself, she gritted her teeth and threw her head back out of the way.

When the hot water first hit her, she scrunched her eyes closed and emitted a choking bark of shock. And as she settled into the feeling, a low, pained whine - dampened by her now clamped-closed lips - continually rose from her throat. She tried her best to revel in the burning pain, to savour it. But she couldn't, not really. It was all she could do to simply *endure* it. This agony was nothing as delicate and enjoyable as with cutting. It was just a huge wall of crude hurt, whose shape or edges could not even be made out, smashing into her over and over again. Subjected to such an onslaught, her mind could barely function. The more it tried to feebly grapple with that monolithic sensation, the more it wilted and was overpowered. A positive-feedback loop of defeat.

She refused to give up, however. There must surely be a way to make it work. And if so, this rare treat ought not be squandered for lack of fortitude or perseverance. So she gave it one last shot, with everything she had. Focusing intently on the pain, she tried to mentally separate it into its constituent parts. One stuck out immediately. She zeroed in on this sharp, stabbing quality of the searing heat, and felt for its complexities. The problem was it stung so badly that she had to tense her muscles as hard as possible to fight her body's desperate urge to jerk away. And without being able to even somewhat relax into the pain, she would have little hope of probing it.

Tilly casually slid off the window-seat and sauntered over.

"Erin, what's with all the steam? Is the fan not-" she abruptly cut off as she came to a standstill a few paces away from the shower cubicle.

Hearing the voice, Erin's eyes briefly flickered open. Then it was instantly forgotten.

From the outside, obscured by the white-ish veil of the frosted glass, she was just a ghostly silhouette. But Tilly did not need to be able to see in, to be able to *see* what was going on. Her wide-eyed, slack-jawed look of shocked dismay testified to that. And so did her loud gasp. But Erin was in her own world right now. A tiny private domain where she, wreathed in swirling steam, partook of dark, inhumane pleasures. Competing with this, Tilly could hardly be expected to command her notice.

The thing was that... as it happened, Tilly wasn't very inclined to heed her assigned place in this current hierarchy. She bolted forward, rushing towards the cubicle. Erin only dimly registered this. Acting reflexively, she lifted up her foot and, bending at the knee, pressed it hard against the cubicle door behind her. This, of course, made *no* sense to do. Yet, unintentionally and unwittingly, the symbolic power of this act created a sort of... forcefield of refusal.

A split-second later, Tilly reached the door and fruitlessly sought to pass through it to get to Erin. She was stunned by the inexplicable barrier which prevented her. Looking around for the source of the obstruction, she saw Erin's foot blocking the door from moving. She quickly pieced together what was going on.

"Erin! Erin! What are you doing?! M-move... Erin, move your foot! Let me... please let me in!" Tilly shouted pleadingly.

With no means of entry, Tilly resorted to slapping against the glass. Erin didn't even look around. She just kept her eyes shut and concentrated on the pain itself. She didn't think her willpower could withstand the additional brunt of seeing what she was doing to Tilly. And that would be plainly and abundantly written all over Tilly's face. Moreover, now that the cleansing ritual of self-harm was begun, it had to be seen through to the end. Much like murder or an orgasm, it was not the sort of thing one could just abandon midway through.

"Tilly! Go! Go away, Tilly! Just go!"

This was as much as she was able to gruffly yell back, though the words were barely intelligible.

"Erin, stop! Turn it off! Turn it off, Erin! Stop! You have to stop!" Tilly screamed at the top of her lungs. She was absolutely hysterical, and now flat-out hammering her fists against the glass door.

The pain helped Erin easily tune these pleas out. She'd stopped her futile attempts to map it, and now simply surrendered herself to it. It was like staring at the sun. One is not actually *supposed* to... see... anything in it. The blindness *is* the sight. And there is something rapturous about overwhelming one's pupils with such cruel, super-massive effulgence. Because nothing else can possibly exist in that moment. She longed to step further into this light, to more fully bathe in it.

Alas, it was not to be.

She noticed that a growing numbness was starting to dull the pain. The nerve endings in her chest were so overloaded that they were failing to register new stimuli. Quite irreversibly, the point of diminishing returns had been reached. This was the tradeoff one made when resorting to such simplistic, makeshift, amateurish methods. Were they easy? Yes. Were they convenient? Yes. That's why they were so often the self-harm novice's gateway drugs. But although they could provide a quick-and-dirty fix, that was it. They were not suited to any elaborate prolongation. A razor blade could, at length, be employed in several different ways to achieve several different effects. Whereas scalding-hot water was really as short term and one-dimensional as it got.

"Let me in! Erin! Erin, open the door right now! Stop!"

Her fingers still clenched tightly around the temperature dial, Erin spun it all the way back round. And, sinking into the hazy afterglow headspace, it took three tries before she finally succeeded in bashing the on/off button with her knuckle. The flowing water ceased. She unsteadily stumbled backwards until she hit the cubicle door. Her legs gave out and she dropped roughly onto her butt. She sat there against the door, soaking in a glorious new rush of pain. Now exposed to the open air, and with pain receptors reset, there was an excruciating tingling from the raw skin on her chest. She really seized onto this unexpected grace note. It would help sustain and lengthen the post-self-harm high.

On the other side of the door, Tilly fell to her knees in physical and emotional exhaustion. Her palms and forehead were pressed to the glass.

She no longer shouted. She couldn't summon the energy. Her voice was now, perforce, quiet and defeated and puling. But still suffused deep within her tone were the barbs of resentful disbelief. She almost couldn't even accept that this was really happening.

"Goddamn you, Erin, you let me in. Let me in. Why won't you let me in?... Erin, please. Just let me in..."

As the next five minutes passed, Tilly cried softly and sometimes half-heartedly renewed her imploring. Naturally, Erin hardly registered either sound. She just went on shamelessly swimming in her own depraved buzz. But eventually even the unexpected dregs of pain faded away. When they did, she slowly and clumsily picked herself up. Her back was still soaped-up because she hadn't yet washed it off. This rather escaped her notice. Right now, her whole focus had to be on not falling down again. She shakily opened the cubicle door and stumbled out. Tilly sprang to her feet and helped lead her safely over to the bed. Slightly more mentally present now, Erin noted that Tilly was glowering at her the entire time. And as if that wasn't enough, Tilly pressed the issue in a forcefully terse, low-voiced way.

"What. The. Hell. Erin? What were you doing?!"

With her mind still somewhat beclouded and slow, Erin struggled to respond. She could do little more than try not to unintelligibly slur her words as she muttered, "I... don't know... Hand... slipped on... dial."

At this, Tilly glared away and scrunched up her face in affronted anger. When she shot back her reply, as she carefully guided Erin down onto the towel laid out on the bed, the gloves came off. Her tone had been upped a good few notches in its furiousness.

"What?! Slipped! *That's* what you're going to say?! That's *seriously* what you're going to say to me?! Jesus, Erin, really?!"

Erin was clearly affected by the brunt of this chastisement. But she said nothing. She just wriggled her back against the towel and awkwardly tried to pull its edges around to dry herself elsewhere. She looked feeble and pitiful.

The fire in Tilly's eyes began to extinguish.

"Didn't... didn't you hear me yelling at you? I was yelling, Erin. You blocked the door."

Erin seemed on the verge of tears.

"I'm... I'm s-sorry."

Tilly sighed. She just sounded disappointed now.

"We talked about your... scars, the cutting. You said... 'no more'. That you didn't need it anymore. You said that."

"I-I... know... I'm sorry, Tilly... I'm sorry."

"Is that all you're gonna say? You owe me a real explanation here. What happened?"

Erin wrapped herself in the towel and pulled it up to hide her face in a very childlike way. She couldn't meet Tilly's gaze anymore. As her ability to think clearly returned, she was becoming painfully aware of the full extent of what she had actually done. What it would seem to signify, and imply, from Tilly's perspective.

"I don't know!" She spat the words with an odd mix of defensiveness and self-pity. "I don't fucking know. I... I... I just... had to. It was... out of my control."

Tilly was unmoved, unconvinced by this evasive non-answer. She was still dead set on pulling the truth out of Erin. And she decided she couldn't afford to be above exploiting Erin's present defenselessness to get it. After all, the cause was just. So there could be no let up.

"But why? Seriously, tell me why! I don't understand it. That was your old life. That was your crutch, *then*! Why do it now? It doesn't make any sense. Damn it, Erin, you hurt yourself to feel good and you hurt yourself as punishment for having messed up! Don't you see the world you're creating for yourself? The existential Iron Maiden you're stepping into? Just... why?!"

Uncovering her face, Erin sat up and started roughly, hurriedly toweling herself off all over. Her emotional state had been heading in one direction. But now her burgeoning defiant scowl showed it had spun around on a dime and rocketed the other way instead. The guiltiness she felt had been suppressed by something else arising in her. She deeply resented being berated and quizzed like this. And giving into that was a lot easier.

"I get it! I get it! I just *don't* have a good explanation for you. I can't fully understand it myself. It... just happened. Things just happen!" she said irately, as she took the folded clothes from off her pillow and got dressed.

"That's not good enough. This is *not* okay! You can't just skip past all of this!"

"Yeah, I know."

Her covert little dismissive eye-roll rather negated this concession.

She reached over to the venous catheter, pre-prepped with a new needle, and got ready to reinsert it and tape it to her arm.

"I have to get this done now, Tilly."

In response, Tilly just sternly huffed and threw her hands up. She went over and sat back down on the window-seat.

It took several minutes for Erin to go through the motions of returning Ikelos to her system.

"I'm just trying to *help* you," Tilly muttered unhappily once it was done.

Erin was presently double-checking her IV set-up, making sure the kink-resistant tubing was living up to its name. She knew Tilly was trying to draw her back into the same conversation. As such, she was almost tempted to make a show of letting Tilly's point stand as an unanswered comment. But she thought better of it. That would be a tad too far. Still, she wasn't exactly thrilled to be diving back into this aggravation. She spoke slowly and distractedly, without stopping to look up.

"I appreciate that. But why are you always so frantic and insistent about it, anyway? I know I... fuck up sometimes, but I'm... like, *trying*, you know? I'm trying to be better, I really am, but it's not an overnight thing. In the meanwhile, it's not like I'm in some great peril, am I? So... just... ratchet it down a bit from maximum *save-you* mode, alright?..."

Tilly became pensive, her expression troubled and unsure. She looked down at her feet and seemed to be willing herself to say something. When she gave voice to it, several moments later, the retort was delivered with a quiet intensity.

"I... don't agree with you... that there's... no... peril."

This made Erin pause and look over at Tilly.

"Really? 'Cause I'm pretty sure I'm doing just fine."

She stressed the words emphatically, as if it were an undeniable conclusion.

"It's... not upon you yet, Erin. But I fear it may be... imminent."

"Is that so? And what *evidence* is there for that?"

Tilly rose and approached Erin. Her demeanour had become grave.

"You remember... a week or two ago... you showed me that video of the recent dam disaster? The slow-mo, close-up footage of the seconds just before it breaks?"

Taken aback by the strange question, which seemed apropos of nothing, Erin raised a quizzical eyebrow.

"Uh... no... can't say I do."

Tilly nodded sadly, more so just to herself really, and said, "well... okay. Will you indulge me then? I'd like to remind you what it looked like."

"Sure..." Erin murmured, stretching out the word skeptically.

"The concrete freaking ripples, Erin. Like a wave. Needless to say, concrete isn't supposed to do that. But at their absolute breaking point, things have a tendency to act *really* weird. Anyway, a millisecond later... an intricate spiderweb of cracks races across the dam with blinding speed. It's really something to behold. Millions upon millions of gallons just *insisting* upon being free. And finally, of course, the whole structure buckles and lets forth the... flood."

Erin narrowed her eyes and said, "okay?..."

"You have an incredible strength to you. It's truly... remarkable. And it's why I'm wondering - always wondering - how all that mighty concrete *you've* erected between your heart and your brain can be... *rippling* before my very eyes. I can't help but fret about what something so heavily-fortified could be holding in. What profound secrets could possibly be exerting such colossal pressure upon it. I don't want to find out what happens to you when it shatters, Erin. I really don't. And neither should you."

Visibly perturbed, and more than a little annoyed, Erin pointedly went back to finishing her task.

As patronizingly as she could, she remarked distantly, "hmm, yes, that's all *very* interesting, Tilly."

Stunned for a few seconds, Tilly couldn't think how to reply.

All she could summon up to say at last was "interesting?..."

"Yep, real interesting. Hell, you know what else is interesting? What if I said that I think you might just have the type of personality where you *need* to be saving someone from themselves? And that if you can't find a reason to appoint yourself savior, you may well be liable to invent one."

Tilly's eyes shot open wide and she took a sharp intake of breath. Her face flushed pale crimson from sheer indignation.

"I am not a liar!" she barked heatedly, folding her arms. "You can't see what I can see!"

Erin merely started to clear away the stuff on the bed. She did her best to appear nonchalant after her insulting accusation, to rub it in. How dare Tilly pretend to know her better than she knew herself? What ridiculous, arrogant nonsense. It could not be allowed to stand. It had to be repudiated and banished, once and for all. Even if that required a little rudeness to do. Or even a *lot*.

"Yeah, well, maybe that's for the best, huh? I mean, shit, I've definitely got enough *real* problems to try and fix. So I guess thanks for deputizing yourself to worry about all the phantom catastrophes. I suppose that takes them off my plate, at least," she stated mockingly.

Now Tilly just seethed silently for a while, watching Erin go about her business with a bitter stare.

But, in time, she remembered herself. She remembered the true nature of this situation. And then her gaze shifted to pity, and study.

Inside her burned a scathing self-castigation for having allowed herself to be goaded into fruitless combat with the *denial* that was but a mere symptom.

She had to be subtler, smarter, more careful. She owed it to Erin.

There was vital work to be done.

CHAPTER SEVENTEEN

6:06 AM. MARCH 28TH.

(APPROX. TWO DAYS LATER)

[06:06] PluckingPurgatory'sPetals: Hello?

[06:07] Alabaster&Freckles: Hi there.
[06:07] Alabaster&Freckles: So you finally unblocked me, huh?

[06:08] PluckingPurgatory'sPetals: I didn't block you.

[06:08] Alabaster&Freckles: Oh yeah? That's weird then, 'cause the app itself said I was.
[06:09] Alabaster&Freckles: And I couldn't send any messages to you, just like I was on your 'blocked' list.
[06:09] Alabaster&Freckles: Look, though I'm *definitely* glad you've decided to talk to me again, maybe we shouldn't restart things with an untruth...
[06:10] Alabaster&Freckles: Better to start as we mean to go on, don't you think?

[06:10] PluckingPurgatory'sPetals: Sorry for the misunderstanding.
[06:10] PluckingPurgatory'sPetals: You *were* blocked, yes. I know, because I just unblocked you.
[06:10] PluckingPurgatory'sPetals: But it wasn't me who blocked you in the first place.

[06:11] PluckingPurgatory'sPetals: That was Erin.

[06:11] Alabaster&Freckles: Okay?...
[06:11] Alabaster&Freckles: And who is Erin?

[06:11] PluckingPurgatory'sPetals: Ah, right, I forgot you just know her by this username.
[06:12] PluckingPurgatory'sPetals: Erin is who you've been talking to all this time.

[06:12] Alabaster&Freckles: I... see.
[06:12] Alabaster&Freckles: Who might you be then?
[06:12] Alabaster&Freckles: And why are you on her account?

[06:12] PluckingPurgatory'sPetals: I'm Tilly.
[06:13] PluckingPurgatory'sPetals: Erin is here with me on the bed. But she's asleep right now, totally dead to the world.
[06:13] PluckingPurgatory'sPetals: Trust me, having heard her snoring up a storm many times before, I can assure you she's not exactly a light sleeper.
[06:13] PluckingPurgatory'sPetals: Which makes this a precious opportunity.
[06:14] PluckingPurgatory'sPetals: I'm using her laptop because I need to talk to you.

[06:14] Alabaster&Freckles: You're... Tilly?
[06:14] Alabaster&Freckles: As in, chick-from-the-dream Tilly?...

[06:14] PluckingPurgatory'sPetals: Ha, yeah, sure, if you wanna put it like that.

[06:14] Alabaster&Freckles: Uh, I'm... confused. What's going on?

[06:15] Alabaster&Freckles: How is it that *you're* able to talk to me?

[06:15] PluckingPurgatory'sPetals: Yeah, I bet.

[06:16] PluckingPurgatory'sPetals: Well, it's... complicated. But long story short, Erin found a way to bring me here, into your world.

[06:16] PluckingPurgatory'sPetals: She made a form for me to occupy, at great cost. Perhaps even greater than she realizes.

[06:16] PluckingPurgatory'sPetals: Still, what's done is done. And now we are together.

[06:17] Alabaster&Freckles: Alright...

[06:17] Alabaster&Freckles: And... you know about *me*?

[06:18] PluckingPurgatory'sPetals: Oh my, yes. Erin has talked about you... more than a few times.

[06:19] PluckingPurgatory'sPetals: Of course, it's all tinged with the bitter frustration she feels towards herself for how she left things with you.

[06:19] PluckingPurgatory'sPetals: But, still, I can read between the lines enough to know that you've been good to her, and good for her.

[06:20] PluckingPurgatory'sPetals: That's why I'm messaging you. I think you're the only other person out there who cares about Erin.

[06:20] PluckingPurgatory'sPetals: She needs help. Badly.

[06:21] PluckingPurgatory'sPetals: And so I need to figure out what to do. Thought you could be a useful sounding board for that.

[06:22] Alabaster&Freckles: I *do* care about her, absolutely! And I *do* want to help her, I really do! I hope she knows that...

[06:23] PluckingPurgatory'sPetals: Okay, great.

[06:23] PluckingPurgatory'sPetals: There is one small problem though...

[06:23] Alabaster&Freckles: What is it?...

[06:24] PluckingPurgatory'sPetals: I'm kind of... torn about whether I should even be doing this.

[06:25] PluckingPurgatory'sPetals: First of all, she'd probably hate me if she knew I was going behind her back. Even if it *is* for her own good.

[06:25] PluckingPurgatory'sPetals: And secondly, I don't know you.

[06:26] PluckingPurgatory'sPetals: Erin knows you - well, to a certain degree - and she trusted you. That definitely counts for something.

[06:26] PluckingPurgatory'sPetals: But, ultimately, you're still just an anonymous stranger on the internet. No offence.

[06:27] PluckingPurgatory'sPetals: And I'm not sure if it's right to be partnering up with a relative stranger when it comes to something as important as this. To entrust someone I don't know with Erin's darkest secrets.

[06:27] PluckingPurgatory'sPetals: I've been wrestling with it. And I... just... don't know if it's right...

[06:28] Alabaster&Freckles: Please, I don't *have* to be a stranger! I never wanted to be a stranger!

[06:28] Alabaster&Freckles: I'm Grace, forty-eight, divorcée. I have three beautiful daughters.

[06:29] Alabaster&Freckles: I live here in the midwest, in a big empty house now my girls have all moved out or gone off to college.

[06:29] Alabaster&Freckles: I worked in publishing, until I got laid off a while back.

[06:30] Alabaster&Freckles: I've got a bad knee, so I don't get out all that much. Mostly I just sit around, reading or drawing or going online.

[06:30] Alabaster&Freckles: Listen, I'll tell you whatever you want to know. I just want to help Erin.

[06:31] PluckingPurgatory'sPetals: Okay, well, thank you, that's a start at least.

[06:31] PluckingPurgatory'sPetals: But that's all just facts, right?

[06:31] PluckingPurgatory'sPetals: I need to know who you *really* are.

[06:32] PluckingPurgatory'sPetals: Tell me, are you a good person Grace?

[06:32] Alabaster&Freckles: I... don't know.

[06:32] Alabaster&Freckles: I hope so. I want to be. But... I don't know.

[06:33] PluckingPurgatory'sPetals: Glad to hear it.

[06:33] PluckingPurgatory'sPetals: I fear that anyone who 'knows' they're a good person would be of little use here.

[06:34] PluckingPurgatory'sPetals: If we are to do what must be done to save someone like Erin, some righteous ethical flexibility is no doubt going to be required.

[06:34] PluckingPurgatory'sPetals: Difficult, unsavoury things await us before the light at the end of the tunnel is to be glimpsed. We will need to be unshrinking, for her sake.

[06:34] PluckingPurgatory'sPetals: Moving on.

[06:35] PluckingPurgatory'sPetals: Why do you want to help Erin? And I mean *deep down* why.

[06:35] PluckingPurgatory'sPetals: I need to know this, and I need to know the full truth of it.

[06:35] Alabaster&Freckles: Alright, I'll try to be as honest as possible then. I want to show you that's who I am. As a token of good faith.

[06:36] Alabaster&Freckles: You know how Erin and I started talking. I signed up as a 'listener' on that site because... I like how it makes me feel when I try to help people. It's that feeling which drives me to do it.

[06:36] Alabaster&Freckles: I wish the nobler motives - which are *also* there of course - trumped that self-gratification, but I can't pretend they do.

[06:37] Alabaster&Freckles: Anyway, when I came across Erin, I knew she was what I was looking for all along. I had subconsciously been trying to find the right person to zero in on and put time into and really try to fix.

[06:37] Alabaster&Freckles: Good lord, that sounds messed up...

[06:37] Alabaster&Freckles: I'm not going to lie though. That's what it was at first: a project.

[06:38] Alabaster&Freckles: Something to pour my energy into. And not have to worry about my own problems.

[06:38] Alabaster&Freckles: Yet then I really got to know Erin, and it became way more than just a weird feel-good project. I came to truly care for her.

[06:39] Alabaster&Freckles: She... reminds me *so much* of my daughters.

[06:41] Alabaster&Freckles: I'm sorry, just give me a minute.

[06:41] PluckingPurgatory'sPetals: It's okay, take your time.

[06:44] Alabaster&Freckles: Look, I... made a few missteps when raising my kids. Always prioritized my work way, way more than I should have.

[06:44] Alabaster&Freckles: You think you have forever with them. You don't. You think you can always just make things up to them at a later date. And then one day you're co-signing their first lease for them, and they're moving to another city.

[06:45] Alabaster&Freckles: This is not the type of thing you realize until it's too late to change, of course, but there you go.

[06:45] Alabaster&Freckles: And so... in Erin I think I saw a chance to try to... what? God, I don't know. Even out the karmic scales a little, I guess?

[06:46] Alabaster&Freckles: I know that's ridiculous. But you kind of just fall into doing these things, without ever really spelling them out to yourself.

[06:46] PluckingPurgatory'sPetals: It's not ridiculous. In fact, it gives us something important in common.

[06:47] PluckingPurgatory'sPetals: I'm also trying to help Erin in order to atone.

[06:47] PluckingPurgatory'sPetals: In a way, I'm responsible for the way she is. I have my own misstep to try and make up for.

[06:48] Alabaster&Freckles: Okay, so we both care a lot about her and we both want to help her. We're on the same team, in other words.

[06:48] Alabaster&Freckles: So... can you tell me what you think is going on with her?

[06:49] PluckingPurgatory'sPetals: Well, to avoid dancing around it: she is deeply, deeply broken.

[06:50] PluckingPurgatory'sPetals: I'm guessing that this has been obvious to you all along, but I couldn't see it until Erin brought me here and I'd been around her for a while.

[06:51] PluckingPurgatory'sPetals: That revelation was... quite the surprise. In the *other* place where we first met, all of this was obscured from me.

[06:51] PluckingPurgatory'sPetals: However, now I know the glaring truth. She's a wreck.

[06:52] PluckingPurgatory'sPetals: There are *cracks* in her mind. Some are small, but some are gaping fissures with terrible artifacts of sorrow nestled in their craggy nooks. And she is wildly unready for any serious self-archeology here.

[06:53] PluckingPurgatory'sPetals: That's why she doesn't realize the true extent of her brokenness, Grace. She is a mystery to herself most of all.

[06:53] PluckingPurgatory'sPetals: Truly, I love Erin more than I ever thought it possible to love anything. I want to fix her, to make her whole.

[06:54] Alabaster&Freckles: We have to face the reality here. As well-meaning as we both are, there's only so much either of us can do.

[06:55] Alabaster&Freckles: I think she desperately needs outside help. I'm talking about professionals, who really know what they're doing.

[06:55] Alabaster&Freckles: You want her to get the treatment she needs, right? Please, tell me where you are, and I'll walk you through bringing that about.

[06:56] PluckingPurgatory'sPetals: If only it were that easy...

[06:56] PluckingPurgatory'sPetals: Believe me, I don't disagree with you. But you have to understand... the way Erin feels about the outside world means that is currently not an option. It's just not.

[06:58] PluckingPurgatory'sPetals: After hearing her raging antipathy towards it, I know it's futile to try and convince her to venture out there for help. Right now, she would just feel like a POW stuck in enemy territory. And how can she be helped, if she'd then greet any doctor's attempt to get through to her with refusal and hostility?

[06:58] PluckingPurgatory'sPetals: As for the other way... my god, if we *did* get some people sent over here to take her to the hospital, there's no doubt that she'd go down fighting.

[06:59] PluckingPurgatory'sPetals: She is thin and she is fragile, but she'd fend off the straightjacket like a rabid dog fighting for its life. I mean, seriously, she might well perish in the attempt and then... all would be lost.

[07:00] Alabaster&Freckles: Are you sure of this? *Absolutely* sure that it can't safely be done at the moment?

[07:01] PluckingPurgatory'sPetals: I could not be more certain.

[07:01] PluckingPurgatory'sPetals: I don't like it any more than you do, but for the time being it's up to us, Grace. You and I are all she has.

[07:02] PluckingPurgatory'sPetals: I know it's not fair that you won the reverse-lottery with your new IM buddy, that you got saddled with this responsibility. It's truly not.

[07:03] PluckingPurgatory'sPetals: But we're here now. She needs us. And we have to do this right.

[07:03] Alabaster&Freckles: Yes, we do.
[07:03] Alabaster&Freckles: So, do you have a plan?

[07:04] PluckingPurgatory'sPetals: Perhaps. Or... the beginning of one anyway.

[07:04] PluckingPurgatory'sPetals: I've found myself hemming and hawing over it a bunch, because... it's got to be perfect.

[07:05] PluckingPurgatory'sPetals: When we eventually make our play, I think we're only going to get one shot at this, if you see what I mean. So all the covert groundwork has to be laid to make sure it works.

[07:06] Alabaster&Freckles: Hey, something is better than nothing when you're brainstorming, trying to get the ball rolling. And then it can be refined over time.

[07:06] Alabaster&Freckles: You wanted to bounce things off me, didn't you? So go ahead. Loop me in on what you're thinking.

[07:08] PluckingPurgatory'sPetals: I think the best way forward is to get her to open up. Because even around me, she has this... protective shell up. It's subtle enough that it can sometimes be hard to pick up on, but it's most certainly there.

[07:09] PluckingPurgatory'sPetals: There are thoughts and feelings she won't express, not even to me. And there are strange things she is keeping close to her chest.

[07:10] PluckingPurgatory'sPetals: I have to push her to do away with this reticence, this secrecy. Then I can start to really figure things out. The better I understand her, the closer I'll be to knowing how to change her mind about leaving.

[07:11] PluckingPurgatory'sPetals: My main worry, though, is that I just don't know how much time I have. Presently, she's spiralling, but it's relatively slow, and stabilized by my influence. That's why I even have a chance in the first place.

[07:11] PluckingPurgatory'sPetals: But who knows when it'll ramp up to an accelerated, out-of-control tailspin? Because once we reach that inevitable final stage... it may be too late.

[07:12] Alabaster&Freckles: Alright, your idea sounds like it would be a solid place to start if you can pull it off. Hopefully it will make her recognize her own precarious state and become more receptive to seeking outside help.

[07:12] Alabaster&Freckles: You *are* definitely correct about the time-sensitive aspect, though. That's a real danger.

[07:13] Alabaster&Freckles: Do you think you'll be able to get her to open up quickly enough? She has to want to, after all.

[07:15] PluckingPurgatory'sPetals: She does want to. That has become clear to me.

[07:16] PluckingPurgatory'sPetals: I think she hoped that when she brought me into her life, things would change. That she'd no longer be controlled by those deeply-buried parts of herself which she hates or fears or feels ashamed of.

[07:17] PluckingPurgatory'sPetals: Mostly, that turned out to be the case: she *has* shared a lot with me. But there's still that final layer of self, right at the very bottom, which she cannot bring herself to truly face.

[07:17] PluckingPurgatory'sPetals: I'm telling you, Grace, she wants nothing more than to fully unburden herself. She's just terrified of standing truly naked before me, before herself.

[07:18] PluckingPurgatory'sPetals: Damn.

[07:18] PluckingPurgatory'sPetals: I don't believe it.

[07:18] PluckingPurgatory'sPetals: She's starting to stir. She might be awakening. I'd better go.

[07:18] Alabaster&Freckles: Wait!!!

[07:19] PluckingPurgatory'sPetals: I'll have to re-block you, but I will try to contact you again when I can.

[07:19] Alabaster&Freckles: Please! I have more questions!

[PluckingPurgatory'sPetals - is now offline]

CHAPTER EIGHTEEN

11:22 PM. APRIL 2ND.

(APPROX. FIVE DAYS LATER)

Erin picked up the apple again and took another small bite out of it. This produced a wet *crunch* which pierced the awkward silence. As she began to chew, she set the apple back down onto a single square of kitchen towel placed on the kitchenette countertop.

"You know, if you just kept the side clean in the first place, you wouldn't need a buffer," Tilly pointed out peevishly. She was lounging on the bed, looking on.

In response to this unsolicited advice, Erin just scoffed. It didn't *even* warrant anything more.

She returned her full attention to what she was doing. In one hand she had open the dogeared instruction manual for the IV infusion pump. Her other hand was hovering above the tiny buttons dotted all over the front of the device. Periodically, one of her fingers would drift towards a button. Her fingertip would even come to lightly rest upon it, as her brow furrowed with uncertainty and trepidation. Yet, only after intently re-consulting the page for a while longer would she finally actually press the button. Then she'd pause and observe the effect this had on the figures shown on the little embedded lit-up screen. If she was content with the change, she took a leisurely bite of the apple as a reward. If she wasn't, she'd frantically flip through pages in the manual until she figured out how to reverse it. Either way, afterwards the slow-going cycle would begin again.

Unfortunately, she now found she couldn't properly focus on this task. Tilly's bitchy jibe had really stuck in her craw. It just wouldn't stop bugging her. Even though almost ten minutes had passed since the offending remark, she snapped as if it had just happened.

"I swear to god, Tilly, you're like a little fucking egg-timer of irritation sometimes! You're always just *there* and every so often, like clockwork... *bzzzzt...* you pipe up to say something that'll aggravate me. Just cut it out already!"

"Hey, don't get snippy with me just 'cause you know what I said is true," Tilly murmured tauntingly.

"Ha! As if! Firstly, why would I waste my time cleaning? The apartment is hardly a dirty hovel. Besides, to squander even a single second scrubbing a countertop when I have... well, what I have, is tantamount to a crime of ungratefulness, if you ask me."

She fixed a pointed stare upon Tilly.

"And, secondly, that's not really what you're mad at me for... so, just, don't even."

Tilly was quick on the draw in replying.

"Maybe I wouldn't... if you'd just freaking *talk* to me, Erin!"

Momentarily, Erin just closed her eyes and took a deep breath. She was trying to decide whether or not to allow herself to get baited into a full-blown argument here. It wasn't really what she wanted. Yet Tilly had doggedly been trying to instigate it for a day or two now. And even though Erin took umbrage at this, she could do little to actually stop it. So, as with all things, if a squabble was coming, it was best to meet it head-on. She would *not* be ambushed unawares and made flustered. Thereby being put on the back foot from the get-go. To cede this advantage was foolish. She'd rather plant her shield upright in the sod, brace herself behind it, and call the challenge on. Telegraphing her immovable will across the field of battle. And though her sword was held aloft, it would clearly seem just as ready to be re-sheathed. Thus, hopefully by readying for the fight, it might perhaps be avoided altogether.

The course was therefore clear. When that deliberative moment suddenly elapsed, with all the startling fugacity of a popped soapbubble, she made her move. She threw the manual down and shoved the IV stand back towards the centre of the room. Then she stormed over to the bed. Her face was now the very picture of pushed-too-far annoyance. She stood before Tilly, towering over her.

Eyes fierce, nostrils flaring, she loudly announced, "alright, you know what? Enough. *E-fucking-nough.* Let's have it out. No more biting your tongue. Say your piece, right now."

A little stunned by the forcefulness of Erin's tone, but trying hard not to show it, Tilly sat up on the bed.

"Fine. Why won't you *really* talk to me? Outside of a couple random little stories from when you were a kid, you've barely shared anything about your life before me. I ask and I ask, and you just avoid or divert like it's nothing. It's as though you want me to pretend that you've only existed since we first met..."

Erin waved her hand dismissively.

"Look, I just... don't think about that stuff."

"What, ever?" Tilly asked, unconvinced.

"Pretty much, yes. And a small goddamn mercy that is, too. The past, right? It's just a repository where good memories and shitty memories are dumped in. But they all get jumbled and mixed together, like... in a garbage can. So, even to try and pick out something good, I've gotta rummage through that other disgusting junk too. And then finding that happy memory is pointless. Because after sifting through the rotting detritus of a misspent life, I'm now sad-as-fuck anyway. That's why I don't mind *at all* if my memory bank's becoming like a trash compactor for all that shit. Just squishing it down into a smaller and smaller cube until it's scarcely even noticeable anymore. That's the fucking dream, Tilly!"

"But that stuff, all of it, makes you.. *you*. The good *and* the bad."

"Oh, it sure made me, alright, but *that's it*. I don't owe any of it anything more. Once upon a time, I thought you had to dwell on the horrible stuff. As though to... honour... having survived it by remembering each individual ordeal. So every day I'd let myself feel a hundred dead pains all over again. Every day I'd meticulously resurrect them. But then? Then I finally realized that I didn't need any more sorrow in my life. That I didn't need to prove to myself that I could endure lugging that extra load of grief around on my back. It's just... *useless* hurt, okay? You get that? And I no longer hate myself enough to keep subjecting myself to it. That's something, at least."

"I understand that it's hard to reflect on the... unhappy times. But... you seriously just try to pretend your past doesn't exist?"

"Like I said, the funny thing is... I don't have to 'try'. I don't know or... care... why, but my brain just doesn't go to those places anymore. For better or worse, I'm a creature of the present moment. I take things day by day, that's how I've survived."

"But it's not right. It's... not healthy."

"Healthy? What the fuck is 'healthy'? I do what I need to do to get by, and *no-one* should begrudge me that."

"Erin, please, I can't stand being shut out from this! You *are* your past. And I want to... help you. But there are things I need to know first. I need you to open up to me!"

"I... I just... jesus, why the hell do you care so much about this, Tilly?!"

Tilly realized she was losing her composure, showing her hand too much. Time to pull it together. She was finally getting somewhere; she couldn't blow this now. She just had to... change her approach, that's all. First, her fired-up demeanour abruptly departed. Then her voice dropped to a hushed, plaintive register. And she looked up at Erin with big sad eyes.

"How do you think it makes me feel? You say you love me... but you won't share these things with me? You won't share your whole self with me? I mean, what is that? How am I supposed to square those opposing signals? It seems like you refuse to be truly vulnerable around me, and that freaking hurts, okay?"

Looking around the room exasperatedly, Erin clenched her jaw and *pretended* to think it over. Because as soon as Tilly had put it this way, Erin knew she was boxed into a corner. And the option of concession had started to seem so very easy. After all, there was no way she could disparage their love by keeping her lips sealed any longer. Regardless of however unpleasant the disclosures may be. Yet, given she was still in a hot-headed place, having been shown the error of her ways so instantly and decisively also served to stoke her irritation. That's why she had to make a show of debating it. She felt that dragging things out under the pretence of tortured

257

consideration was the only way to retain some dignity, some control over the matter.

Eventually she said, through a weary sigh, "okay... I can... see what you mean."

Tilly flashed her a pleased smile of relief, for positive reinforcement.

"Good! Thank you!"

"So... what... do you want to know?"

"Hmm... have you ever talked to anyone about your family? Like, really talked about them?"

Erin just shrugged and looked away, visibly uncomfortable. Her silence was answer enough.

"Well then, don't you see that this is the perfect opportunity? You don't have to confide in some stranger. It's *me*, Erin. You know you can trust me with anything. So you can finally just put it all into words and let it out. And then you'll get to feel that awesome sense of release at sharing it. Win-win, right?"

Erin still didn't reply for a few moments. She was steeling herself.

Once she felt ready, she plodded over to grab her apple. And then she went to the window-seat, saying under her breath, "naturally we have to start at the goddamn deep end."

She sat down on the ledge, putting the apple there too. And, staring over at Tilly, crossed her arms. She looked ornery as hell.

"Okay. You want me to tell you about my family? Let me tell you about my fucking family."

There was a long pause.

Taking in a long, deep breath, she declared bluntly, "my mom died the day I was born. 'Complications arising from childbirth', whatever the hell that really means. Never did have the stomach to find out the specifics. I already knew enough: I was... quite literally... born from death. That's some seriously messed-up shit to have to carry. And carry it, you do."

"Oh... I'm so sorry, Erin," Tilly offered feebly, taken aback. Her expression was contorted by a deep vicarious sorrowfulness.

Quite surprisingly, this seemed to instantly rile Erin up.

"Let's get this straight right off the bat: cut that shit out. Cut it right the fuck out! I didn't know the woman. I mean, are you also sorry that my great-grandfather died before I could meet him? No? Then let's not play the polite condolences game. Besides, if you're gonna make those knee-jerk sympathy bleats as we go along, you're... like, going to wear out your fucking tongue. Because this is not at all a happy, schmaltzy daytime-movie type of family history I'm going to be relating, got it?!"

Tilly, thoroughly dressed down, just nodded. She could sense that this brief flash of anger wasn't really directed at her. It was just the excess heat venting off of the violent processes going on inside Erin's mind right now. Erin was, after all, wrestling with difficult memories, striving to bring them to heel. That was bound to be incredibly trying. So a little emotional volatility was only to be expected. In fact, Tilly would think it very lucky if this turned out to be the *worst* byproduct.

"Like, for fuck's sake, that kind of thing is exactly why as a kid you learn not to even tell people about it. Because then you get an invisible 'dead mom!' label pinned to your chest. Which is a bit like being a three-legged puppy: everyone wants to coo over you in pity, but no one truly wants you and your sad shit around long-term, bumming them out every time they look at you. So, do you really want to be reminding me of having to deal with that?"

Tilly just shook her head, all doe-eyed and apologetic.

"Alright, whatever, forget it. Anyway... where was I? Oh yeah. I was told that she got to see me before she died. But who knows if that's even true? And what difference would it really even make? We were ships passing in the night. That's... just the way it is. No amount of clinging to bullshit stories can change anything now."

She paused, collecting herself. This was already affecting her more than she had anticipated. She took a faux-nonchalant bite of the apple to cover the intermission.

"Frankly, I know little of substance about her. I remember poring over photos of her and trying really, really hard to intuit what kind of person she was. When you're young and dumb, you believe all that vague mystical horseshit about there being some kind of... I don't know... transcendental fucking bond between mother and child. So I figured I surely *must* have access to some special insight about her. But it doesn't work like that, does it? We share genes and a last name, and that's it. I might as well have been scrutinising the image of a total stranger in a history book."

"Did you take *anything* away from the photos?"

"Hmm, not much. People would sometimes say I had her eyes. Maybe so. But I always felt it was an unremarkable similarity at best. Like, you and I have brown eyes too, what the fuck does that amount to, you know? Anyway, in all honesty, what I remember most vividly was trying not to admit to myself that she... wasn't pretty. But, of course, I knew it was true. I mean, she wasn't exactly ugly. She just kind of had a... hard... face."

Erin's gaze drifted into the middle distance. Without beckoning it, that plain face appeared before her once more. There was certainly no mistaking its hardness, its weariness. The type of face which emerges over countless generations of ancestors enduring bleak, arduous lives. A tough mask for tough times. In its inherited creases and sharp angles, a record of countless stories lurked. One felt almost able to perceive the cycles of poverty and repression and tragedy whose combined pressure had sculpted these physiognomic traces of suffering. Indeed, what she had learned of her family's history bore this notion out to be true. She wasn't sure how to feel about knowing this was the milieu of the stock she came from. Or if she *should* even feel anything at all. Perhaps it was... just one of those things. Whatever that strange platitude meant.

"I guess the interesting thing is that those severe features were... well, I suppose you could say... an ill-fitting hand-me-down. She apparently didn't have the harsh personality to match them. From all I ever heard about her, she was... very timid and soft-spoken and kind. Still, who's going to share the faults of your dead mom with you? So I always grasped that I was probably only getting half the story, if even that. And eventually I just came to accept that I'll never know who she truly was. It sort of lifts a certain weight off you, accepting that."

Another lengthy pause stretched out between them. Tilly couldn't think of anything to say besides "I see."

"My dad, however.... *him* I got to see only too well. He was... what they call a functioning alcoholic. You know, people are usually exaggerating for effect when they talk about someone being 'always drunk'. But that's *not* what I'm doing when I say that my dad was *always* drunk. He'd start during breakfast and keep it going until he went to sleep. Don't get me wrong, he wasn't a sloppy drunk. Quite the opposite really. He'd stay just lucid enough to work his job. It was all very measured, very low profile. Vodka in this beat-up old hip-flask. Covert little top-ups throughout the day. So dispassionate and systematic, like taking a medication to manage a disease. I didn't get it at the time, but the symptom he wanted to subdue was... reality."

"Wow... And he was like this the whole time he raised you?"

Erin gave a bitter little laugh.

"'Raised me'," she repeated derisively. "He didn't raise me. From the get-go, he didn't know what the hell to do with my sister and me. He travelled a shit-ton for his job, so we continually got dumped on anyone who'd take us for a while. That was a lot of my childhood, just bouncing around other family members. And even when we were staying at his house, he'd be at work most of the day. Not that my sister was really old enough to be left looking after me, but who cares about that, right?!"

She... wasn't looking at Tilly as she angrily issued this question. Its true recipient was elsewhere.

"And, shit, whenever he *was* around, he might as well have been a goddamn robot. You'd talk to him and he'd just be so out of it and unpresent. He'd look at you as if from twenty miles away. And you just *knew* that, inside, he was simply waiting impatiently for the conversation to be over and for you to go away. That was the thing of it really. Sensing you weren't wanted, feeling like a tolerated burden. But never understanding why. It... gnaws at you, at your sense of self-worth. Makes you always feel like you ought to apologize for just being there."

"Jesus. And I'm guessing there are probably two ways to react to that. Hating him or trying even harder for his affection?"

Erin nodded, furrowing her brow in concentration.

"That's not too far from the truth. In my case, I knew that trying to compete with the almighty booze for his attention was futile. Which leaves hate, right? Well, believe me, I *wanted* to hate him. And I think for a while I pretended that I did. But it just didn't really stick. He wasn't an evil asshole.

He was never mean, never violent. Hell, I can barely even remember him raising his voice. That's not who he was. He was just infinitely checked-out. So I found that I could really only summon up a sort of contempt for his distantness and his neglect. At the time... I thought he was so fucking selfish. I resented that he got to erect this haze of intoxication between him and the world, to keep at a comfortably numb remove from it. And we got... nothing. We had to bare all the undiluted shittiness of the world, alone."

"'At the time'? So you think differently about it now?"

Erin cinched her folded arms more tightly and shrugged.

"I don't know. Whatever."

"You can tell me, Erin."

"It's... stupid."

"*I* won't think so. I promise."

Snorting air through her nose, Erin just reluctantly offered, "look, this would all just be after-the-fact speculation, right? Probably just me idiotically trying to find a way to redeem the fucking guy."

"That's okay. I want to know. Please."

Erin heaved a deep sigh.

"It was only natural that I'd suspect he was just a selfish fuckhead. But now... I know more than I did then. I know that there are things which may not kill you, but which still cannot *really* be survived. I think my mom's death broke him. And after that" - she halted for a few seconds, struggling to bring herself to say it - "he probably... would have preferred... not to live. To just follow my mom into the serenity of the grave. Yet, here's these two little girls he has a duty to. And who also only remind him of what he lost. So he had to find a way to trudge on like a zombie and keep putting food on the table. The alcohol... let him deaden his pain. A devil's bargain. He took on a sickness and became a husk, rather than die. But, hey, like I said, maybe this *is* just me trying to foist some rose-coloured revisionist crap on all this now that he's gone. Because if love is out of the question, who wouldn't prefer to look back with pity rather than disdain?"

"And by... 'gone'... do you mean...?"

"Yeah, worm-food. Died a week before my fourteenth birthday. Had a heart attack on the train. By the time the paramedics got to him, not even a direct fucking lightning strike was going to restart his ticker. His borrowed time was well and truly up."

"Man, that's heavy..."

"Oh, sure. And one of the things which really eats at you is that... you weren't there. It just *happens*... somewhere else. Then you get the news and in your mind that person's entry just automatically gets flung from the box labelled 'alive' to the one labelled 'dead'. It makes you feel so... hmm... how can I describe it? Excluded? Distanced? Whatever it is, it's truly a godawful feeling. Because you become an outsider to their ending. Relegated to no better than all the strangers reading the obituary in our small-town paper."

Tilly was once again lost for words. She was a hopeless empath at the best of times, but it was especially hard not to get paralyzed by the runoff dolefulness of *this* whole tale. Still, she knew she had to come up with something to say. Getting Erin to open up this deeply was a bit like plate-spinning: it all came down to keeping things going, maintaining momentum. Any question which moved the conversation forward, no matter how banal or corny, was much safer than the silences which threatened to perhaps derail it altogether. Strategy was everything here. Erin couldn't be given any time to reflect - no doubt with increasing sourness - on just how candid she was being persuaded to be.

At last, forced to pick the best of a very bad bunch, Tilly burst out with, "was there, like, something you wanted to say to him before he died?"

"Ha, no, I'm not talking about that crass hollywood shit. And, fuck me, what *would* I even say? The relationship we had was already cemented. Its nature was glaringly obvious. No deathbed heart-to-heart was going to change that. You know, that reminds me... it's funny, I didn't cry at his funeral. I just sat there reading the psalms in those grubby books slotted in the pew-backs. And why? Well, I looked around at all these people venting their grief with that typical theatrical weeping and I realized something. Their sadness was completely unlike my sadness. *I* was sad that my dad had never really been my dad, had been just about a non-entity in my life. *They* were sad because they'd known him before my mom died, when he was a different man, a man worth mourning. And that made my blood fucking boil. I resented them all so much. If anyone deserved to meet that *other* guy, it would be his fucking daughter. But... of course not..."

Tilly seemed about to speak, but something else occurred to Erin and she just had to get it out.

"Holy fuck... how could I almost forget? After the funeral, most of the mourners went for a sit-down meal together. And at one point, his idiot brother - who we'd hardly ever seen before - joked to some dipshit next to him: 'I reckon his heart was just trying to spare him the liver disease he's been paying into all these years like a bloody pension'. Still remember that line verbatim. Doubt I'll ever forget it. Anyway, after I heard him say it... I threw my drink in his face and stormed off."

"Woah, you did that in front of everyone?"

Erin had taken to absentmindedly tossing the apple from hand to hand. She stopped to look up and exaggeratedly scoff for effect.

"You think *that's* a big deal?... Dude got off easy. He's lucky I wasn't who I am now, then. That girl was barely more than a child. She was a hell of a lot more meek, more gentle. I think you know that I'd have put a salad fork into his fucking bicep. And, whilst being pulled off him, would've made a sporting effort to relieve him of his sight with my fingernails. But, well... alright, fine... for teenage me, drink-throwing *was* pretty extreme, yes."

"I can imagine. What did people say about it?"

Now the apple was set down again. Her expression became very serious indeed. She pondered her answer for a little while, rubbing her eyebrow.

"Once the dust settled... meh, they just put it down to the derangements of grief. But, of course, that wasn't it at all. The callous wisecrack I overheard just reminded me that all these strangers, this invisible 'extended family', were complicit. They knew that he'd become this profoundly broken person. I mean, they fucking *knew*. And yet... what the hell had they done? They'd turned a blind eye and let it ride. Because it was easy. The guy was at least ostensibly taking care of his business. He never made a scene, never embroiled himself in fucked-up shit. But, still, there he was: the walking-dead, shambling around pretending to be a man. And only the booze circulating like embalming fluid through him was keeping him from disintegrating. Meanwhile, they were just nudging each other at family get-togethers and smirking about how he 'likes a drink'..."

Erin's fists were balled and her face was flushed with deep-simmering rage.

Scowling, she looked down and, in a low voice, growled, "cunts."

There was a tense, uncomfortable silence. It was more powerful than usual, as if densely concentrated like a gas. And it was fraught with the faint hint of lunatic emotions which are mercifully rare enough to not have names.

Tilly gave this as long to dissipate as she thought prudent. And then as soon as an opportune moment appeared, she made herself jump in.

To draw Erin out of her angry reverie, she said, "I really appreciate you sharing all that with me, Erin. I feel so privileged that you trust me like this. Though I am sorry if these memories have upset you. Perhaps we should move on?..."

"Yes, let's," Erin replied, tilting her head back and sucking in a shaky breath.

"Tell me about your sister?"

This seemed to jolt Erin back to normalcy. She rolled her eyes.

"Eurgh, what's there to tell?"

"Well, indulge me. What was your relationship with her like?"

"Okay, fine," she said begrudgingly. "Even though she was way older, I suppose we *were* close as kids. Had to be, really. You just end up spending so much time together."

"Go on... What was she like?"

"She was... very headstrong. A bit of a hellion. And it was the typical thing: I looked up to her, always wanted to impress her. But when she went to college, we might as well have been different species. Suddenly I was just the embarrassing, dorky little sister. And then, after graduation, she fell for this total dirtbag. Yet... that story doesn't go where you think it's gonna." She tutted, and casually rubbed the sleep out of the corner of her eyes as she went on speaking. "I'm not fucking with you: she ended up following him to Africa to do missionary work. For, like, uh, some culty offshoot of Christianity, I don't know. Aaaand... yeah, she'd call me once in a blue moon to keep up the pretense of us still being in contact. But I could hear in her voice how forced it all was. So eventually I just... stopped answering the phone... to let her off the hook. Our lives had completely diverged, and that was that."

"That's fascinating. Erin... at this point... I kind of *have* to ask: given all this stuff you've been through with your family, doesn't it seem a little weird that you don't even think about it anymore?"

"Listen, I don't really think of myself as having had a tragic childhood or whatever. Because, sure, it was dysfunctional and had some really sucky elements. But it wasn't like some... Dickens novel where crazy, terrible things were always happening to little ol' orphan Erin. It was actually pretty stable, and... basically... you can get used to anything over time. You focus on what you do have. We were never poor. I did well at school. And, I mean, no-one *wants* to have to have some jumbled rotation of surrogate parents, but, look, I had my grandparents. And my kick-ass aunt, who actually tried to understand my strangenesses. All super nice people. Very warm and giving. They were really good to me. So, how am I going to focus on the complaints? I still had that close family, still had some positive stuff to cling onto at least. A lot of kids didn't even have that."

"But it's *okay* to look back on the sad parts too. And even to still be mad you had to go through them. You don't have to put it all away, out of sight."

Erin's eyebrows raised. She seemed irked by this suggestion. Her tone now became strident.

"Let me tell you something. Some people constantly dwell on the ways that fate really fucked them over during their upbringing. They love, love, loooove nothing more than just sitting around and whining about it all. Their shitty childhood becomes this... like... fucking... giant, ravenous black hole. And they *willingly* never reach escape velocity from it. It's just always there, looming over everything they do. Their whole lives are spent whirling around and around it." She held up a fist. Then she violently whipped the upside-down middle finger of her other hand in circles around it, making little *whoosh-whoosh-whoosh* noises with her mouth to imply the extreme speed. "A decaying orbit of reverence and loathing. Anything which conflicts with their sick worship of it? They jettison... to be devoured. Because they soooo badly need that ever-present excuse for all their flaws. So that they can luxuriate in being a fucked-up person, safe in the knowledge that it was made *inevitable* by their childhood. And, of course, one day their drain-circling reaches its climax: the darkness finally swallows them up too. I... flat-out... refuse to go down that path."

"But isn't it possible to-"

Erin, having grown increasingly aggravated, slammed her hand down to cut Tilly off. The apple rolled along the window-seat, away from the impact.

"Nope, you know what? No more. I'm not talking about this shit anymore, I'm fucking done."

"Erin... let's not ruin the nice thing we just had. You really opened up to me, it was very special. It was amazing."

Snorting and glancing away, Erin ranted breathlessly, "oh, I'm sure it was special as unicorn droppings, for *you*! Jesus, pumping me for information like you're some... some... fucking spy! I mean, what the fuck is that?! You knew that I don't like to talk about all this depressing shit, that it just bums me out and takes me to a dark place. But you just... keeeeeep... on *pushing*, wearing me down until I give in just to end the goddamn badgering! Get this into your head: you're not here to transcribe my fucking autobiography for me, Tilly! This is not what I want! Do you hear me?! You're supposed to love me, and make me happy, and just... eurgh, I don't know, be with me! Not subject me to endless prying!"

Tilly had now become very used to weathering these rapid, drastic mood swings. They were petulant and caustic, sure, but generally also harmless and relatively fleeting. However, she sensed something suspicious underlying this one. It was not the impulsive flare-up it pretended to be. It had a tactical purpose. And she wasn't going to just let that go unchallenged, not this time.

She sat perfectly unruffled and silent for a moment, which rather unnerved Erin. And then she said, calmly but firmly, "you know what I think?... I think that this hollow, put-on outrage is just total bullcrap. I think it's a weak ploy. Transparent as could be. This is simply you trying to divert, yet again."

"I don't know what the fuck you're talking about!" Erin hollered, jumping to her feet. Her hands rested on her hips like, forebodingly enough, a twitchy gunslinger.

"I think you do! We both know that you don't want me asking questions because eventually I might start asking them about all the *current* stuff you're keeping from me!"

Erin tried to hide her reaction, but her poker face kicked in a millisecond too late. The slight pulling back of her head and widening of her eyes which preceded it had already betrayed her surprise and panic well enough.

"What?! That's... c-crazy, that's fucking stupid! What are you even fucking talking about?!" she called back, growing more belligerent to cover her slip-up.

"Hmm, gee, let me think," Tilly said sarcastically. She held her chin and looked off into the distance as if racking her brain. "Oh yeah, that's right, you wouldn't even tell me what you were doing to the IV machine! 'Nothing important' is not a real answer, and you know it! This is the third time I've seen you fiddling with it like this, and you seriously still expect me to believe that nonsense?! Stop treating me like an idiot, Erin!"

That hit home hard. And this time Erin thought better of trusting her caught-off-guard acting ability. She just turned away, as though in disgust, to hide her involuntary facial reaction. This also provided a very welcome opportunity. Whilst in this temporary argument time-out, she did her best to mentally regroup. Her heart was racing and her mouth was dry. She realized she was fast losing control over the situation. If Tilly kept the upper hand in this exchange, and went on digging, things could get bad for Erin. Really bad. That could not be allowed to happen. It was time to play a little dirty.

"I'm getting... pretty fucking tired of this, Tilly," Erin retorted icily as she turned back around. Her face was shadowed with carefully maintained solemnity. There was a pregnant pause. Then she followed up by asking in a wearied, disappointed voice, "don't we have an awesome time together? Aren't you happy being with me?"

Now it was Tilly's turn to be taken aback. Put on the spot, she instinctively just stammered out, "y-yes. Yes, of course."

"Yep, we *do* have an awesome time together, except when you try to pry, when you try to mother me. Then... it's just friction and hurt feelings and butting heads. And for what? What the hell do you think I'm trying to pull, huh? Some bizarre nefarious plot? You know better than that. I'm only ever doing what it takes to keep us together. That's my job."

Tilly very, very nearly fell for this apparently heartfelt scolding. But, at the last second, she snapped to and saw how Erin was trying to play her.

"Hey, stop that! Stop with the mind-games! Stop with the diverting! Just... tell me, Erin! *Tell me!*" she demanded resolutely.

Overwhelmed by frustration, Erin suddenly let her mask drop and blurted out, "I'm... I'm upping the dosage amount of the microdosing, okay?! It's... just... I... I... can't..." She pointed frantically at the IV stand. "The... the effect! The effect is s-starting to... fade! I can't let that happen!"

Stunned, Tilly could only stare in dumbfounded bewilderment at the infusion pump.

Eventually she numbly asked, "you're... building a.... tolerance to the Ikelos?..."

Erin knew she had already said too much. Yet she still couldn't stop another incriminating answer just springing from her mouth. Breaking eye contact guiltily, she exclaimed, "yes! Okay?! Yes!"

"Erin... God, Erin... and t-this.... this means it's the third time you've had to up it, doesn't it?"

For her part, Erin just went on staring seethingly down at her feet, her jaw moving side-to-side.

"Erin! Look at me! How much are you upping it each time?! How *much*, Erin?!"

When she did finally glance back up, her eyes were hard with resentment. Both at having been found out and at having to explain herself.

"To... overcome... a tolerance build-up, you *have to* up the doses you're working with significantly!" she stated slowly, with viperish condescension. She was even gesticulating exasperatedly as she spoke, as if she were a learned scientist forced to outline some painfully obvious fact.

Tilly's eyes went wide and she cupped her mouth with her hands in shock as she tried to process this revelation.

Seeing this, Erin pushed down her actual emotional response by going on even more animatedly, even louder.

"That's just how it works, Tilly! I didn't make it that way, okay?! That's just how it is!"

Now Tilly just covered her whole face with her hands and began to quietly cry. Erin bit down on her bottom lip in anger and stared hard out of the window. She knew she should put this spat aside and comfort Tilly, but was held in place by petty pride.

A long, heavy wordless state persisted between them.

At last, Tilly wiped her eyes and broke the silence. She had a mournful, hopeless, rueful air about her. Like when someone talks to a gravestone.

"Erin, *my beloved*, this... escalation... is going to hit a disastrous ceiling. You only have so much of yourself to give. And what are you going to do when you're... *depleted*? What then?"

Erin said nothing. She just kept her face turned away and huffed in disdain.

Then Tilly asked the most important question of all, despite half fearing that in the answer lay her own obliteration. Her voice was so timid and faltering it barely made a sound.

It was a whisper sent sailing into a void she did not understand.

"Why... do... you feel you have to... *sacrifice*... yourself for me?..."

This, Erin could not ignore. She reflexively shot Tilly a look which hadn't even the faintest trace of warmth in it.

"This conversation is over."

She was disquietingly even-toned as she uttered this haughty declaration and began to walk away towards the kitchenette.

Completely staggered, Tilly could only dumbly gesture towards the window-seat and say, "the... apple..."

Erin looked back, and then kept walking as she said, "I'm not eating the core. That's something I guess I'm learning now: be careful what seeds you sow inside yourself."

Tilly knew Erin did not *truly* mean this. That Erin was *just* saying this in the heat of the moment to spite her.

But it still hurt really bad nonetheless.

CHAPTER NINETEEN

1:01 PM. APRIL 14TH.

(APPROX. TWELVE DAYS LATER)

Erin was wrapped in a thick blanket. She was sitting on the floor, with her back leaning against the fridge. It did not look like a comfortable position *at all*. A plate covered with sandwich-crumbs and cut-off crusts lay in her lap. There were also a couple of potato chips caught in the folds of the blanket. The IV stand stood nearby and the excess tubing was needlessly coiled around her arm like a tame snake.

Although the laptop was open right beside her, it had been left idle so long the screen had gone to sleep. And plugged into one of its ports were the headphones she was wearing. Loud, fast-paced music could be heard blaring from those little speakers resting on her ears. But it seemed to have no effect on her. Her eyes were totally glazed over as she went on staring blankly into space. Additionally, her mouth hung open very slightly and a thin, glistening rivulet of drool ran from one side of her lips down to her chin and then down her neck.

On the other side of the room was Tilly. She had her eyes scrunched closed and was rapidly tapping her forehead as if trying to induce herself to focus. She had to pull it together. She *had* to pull it together. That was proving so much easier said than done, however. Finally, she gave it up and started to get up off the bed. Her movement was very jittery, a little like a glitched-out character stutter-stepping around in a laggy video game. She was really trying to fight against this, to keep it under control. The problem being that this was like trying to stop a muscle spasming by flexing it hard... but when your whole body is the muscle in question. The stupendous effort required to do that was made plain on her face.

She shakily sidled over to Erin, and was aghast to find there was no visible change. Somehow, Erin was *still* in the exact same position, in the exact same stupefied trance. It was unbelievable. Now, if only that wasn't merely the half of it. As she drifted in front of Erin's sightline, it disturbed her to discover that she didn't attract any kind of notice. A look of barely held back horror dawned upon her face. This might be so much worse than she had even feared.

Erin had been indolently doing her own thing, procrastinating online mostly, for much of today. And, trying not to be overbearing, Tilly gave her her space. But when a blanket-mummy Erin had gotten up and very sluggishly trudged over to the kitchenette, *dragging* the laptop behind her across the floor with the headphone wire, Tilly realized she ought to start paying closer attention. Whilst observing Erin make her snack from afar, there had been little warning signs that something may be amiss. A lack of bodily coordination, fleeting moments of disorientation, and so on. And then when she had just kind of slumped down by the fridge, and stayed there, it definitely seemed worrisome. But, at first, Tilly hoped it was no more than 'just' a minor drugged-out languor - not all that uncommon recently - which would soon be shaken off. So she had watched and waited and prayed. Trying to battle her own strange symptoms all the while. Now, as the passage of time had thoroughly calcified Erin in place, whatever was happening to her seemed like... something else, something more, something very dire indeed.

"Uh, hey?... Hey there?... Erin?..." Tilly ventured nervously, waving her hand before Erin's gaze.

When this failed to break the spell, she drew in a sharp intake of breath and involuntarily stepped backwards in shock.

She clapped her hands repeatedly, just an inch or two from Erin's eyes, and shouted, "Erin?! Erin?!"

It took almost twenty seconds of repetition for this forceful wake-up call to work. But, at last, Erin seemed to come to. She blinked excessively for a few moments as her eyes refocused upon the world. Then she saw Tilly, and her freaked-out expression. Frowning with confusion, she clumsily pulled her headphones off and threw them down. She also noticed her chin was wet and embarrassedly wiped it with the blanket edge.

As she went to speak, however, the true extent of her humiliation was revealed.

She almost choked. And then, panicking, let a big soggy chunk of sandwich fall out of her mouth and onto the plate, where it rolled around in the crumbs and became thickly coated with them. It had been in her mouth, half-chewed and forgotten, all this time. Sending this last bite down the chute had simply... slipped her mind it seemed.

Staring at it dumbly, she mouthed the words, "what the fuck?"

Looking back up at Tilly, she winced with half-cognizant shame and blew out a long exhalation. She was deeply mortified by the grossness of what had just occurred. The plate was duly slid far, far away, banished out of eyeshot. But the sense of her own utter disgustingness remained. A giant video billboard mockingly replaying imagined-footage of the incident on a loop. Unerasable, unignorable evidence.

"Tilly?... What's... going... on?" she just about managed to slur out.

Tilly swallowed hard. She leaned in close and, with doctorly scrutiny, peered into Erin's eyes to make sure she was *fully* back. If not, she would be rather at a loss about what to do. She didn't exactly have a magical knapsack containing a bullhorn or smelling salts on hand.

Thankfully, as it happened, Erin did indeed seem at least lucid enough for a simple conversation. Of course, that wasn't really saying very much.

Speaking as slowly and clearly as possible, Tilly asked, "are you okay?"

As Tilly straightened back up, something caught Erin's attention.

"Whoa... are... *you* okay?... You're... all, ummm... uhhhh... herky-jerky..."

Tilly glanced away anxiously.

"I'm... It's nothing. Please, tell me how you're feeling."

"Of course I'm... fine, why... wouldn't I... be?"

"You were completely zoned-out and unaware just now..."

For a moment, Erin strained to remember. Only to then shake her head.

"What?... No... way, just... got lost... in... thought... for a sec. That's... all."

"Erin, you're, like, speaking weird..."

"No I'm... not. I'm... speaking... totally normally."

Even as she offered this denial, the syllables were slow and blurred into one another. She didn't even realize how seconds seemed to be unduly stretching out or contracting for her. Or how this time-dilation effect in her mind was plaguing her speech.

Tilly's expression bespoke her incredulity. And then something struck her. Suddenly her eyes closed and she hung her head and sighed.

"Oh god. You... you upped the dosage yet again, didn't you?..."

"Does... it... matter?..." Erin muttered querulously, turning her face away.

"Yes Erin! It does freaking matter! What is this, the fifth time now? The sixth?!"

Erin just skipped right past this.

"Come on... let's just... watch something... together... on the... bed."

She began unravelling the blanket from around her and, with a groan of exertion, unsteadily went to stand up. This was not... entirely successful. She slipped awkwardly and dropped heavily onto one knee to avoid a much nastier fall. Tilly gasped and hopped over by her side, counseling slow movements and caution. Erin stayed in her fallen position for a little bit, inadvertently swaying back and forth. She was trying to regain her equilibrium and prepare herself for another attempt at rising.

"Alright, you need to sleep this off, and we'll... talk about this dosage thing when you wake up."

"What?... No, I'm fine... I'm... fine," Erin weakly protested once she rose to her feet.

She was trying to make insistent eye contact with Tilly to show just how *perfectly* 'fine' she *obviously* was. Rather undermining this deception, alas, was the fact that her pupils kept uncontrollably drifting away from Tilly. And her upper body was still swaying a little. And her knees weren't quite locked straight and seemed like they might buckle at any moment. As she kept up this failing effort, she nervously licked her dry, cracked lips. She began to feel a tad foolish and self-conscious. Even in the cognitive impairment of her present state, she realized her act couldn't possibly be working. It was too paradoxical. Anyone stupid enough to believe it wouldn't even need to be fooled in the first place.

Tilly watched all this with unconcealed skepticism and took a deep breath through her nose. Like oil and water refusing to commingle, there was the simultaneous but divided presence of frustration and pity upon her face. She was trying to decide which competing emotion to indulge and allow to steer her. Eventually it seemed that love, impossibly skilled diplomat that it is, must have waded in to cast the tie-breaker vote. Because the compassion just spread and spread, displacing the irritation altogether.

She now looked on Erin with soft, sad eyes and said, "let's go, I'm going to put you to bed, you need to sleep for a little while." After a little pause, she offered, much quieter than before, the concluding word, "please."

Erin began weighing her options. The fact that she had lapsed into deliberation showed plainly on her face. She couldn't understand why Tilly appeared so concerned and saddened. But she fervently wanted to remedy that, if possible. And she *was* feeling more than a little drowsy anyway... So didn't the two-birds-one-stone aspect make this a no-brainer? It certainly seemed that way to her. Her mind was made up.

Nodding, Erin mumbled, "okay... but... just... a short... nap."

She squinted at the infusion pump and took a stab at pressing one of the buttons. Her finger missed the machine entirely. By almost a foot. This seemed inexplicable to her. She shuffled much closer, squinting even harder to keep her target in focus, and tried again. This time she did manage to jab the 'STOP' button.

"Goooood job, babydoll," Tilly cooed as supportively as she could. She made an exaggerated beckoning hand motion to catch Erin's attention. "Now, come onnnnn, over here, follow me over to the bed."

As Erin precariously waddled behind Tilly's lead, she pulled the tubing out of her venous catheter and threw it on the floor. Because she was looking elsewhere, she didn't notice how close the bed was, and hence whacked the very bottom of her shin on the bedframe. This earned a yelp and a brief little hopping-dance of pain. It took a minute or two to fully pass. Then she crawled beneath the quilt - obliviously, with her slippers still on - and snuggled her pillow.

Tilly came and sat by her. She lay her hand upon Erin's head and gently stroked her hair. And she wished, more than *anything*, that Erin could have actually felt her touch.

"Thaaaat's it... you get some sleep, I'll watch over you, don't worry. It's oooookay, everything's oooookay, you just get some sleep now."

Tilly went on issuing these soothing, reassuring words of comfort right up until Erin was fast asleep.

[Alabaster&Freckles - is now online]

[14:10] PluckingPurgatory'sPetals: Heello Grac.e..

[14:11] Alabaster&Freckles: Hello! I've been waiting and waiting for you to get in contact again! It's been driving me crazy!

[14:11] Alabaster&Freckles: There's so much I never got to ask you!

[14:11] Alabaster&Freckles: Uh, wait, am I talking to...?

[14:12] PluckingPurgatory'sPetals: yes,its me, tilly, dont' worry. I've been waiting for you to come onlien for likean hour now, so I guess that makes us Even..

[14:13] PluckingPurgatory'sPetals: I' am sorry aboutt the radio-silence though. ive just been tryin to deal with things onmy end, trying to help Erin.,

[14:13] PluckingPurgatory'sPetals: I didn't want to take the risk of gettingbackto you untill I had some real progress to, report,so we could plan plan the next steppp.

[14:14] PluckingPurgatory'sPetals: BUt nothing i've tried has really worked, she just

[14:16] PluckingPurgatory'sPetals: shuts me ouut and now...shes spiralllllling and I'm afraid and i i i i don't know what to do and i need someone!! to talk to and I didn't know whoelse to turn to and i dont knoow what T odo .

[14:17] Alabaster&Freckles: It's okay, just calm down. Everything will be okay. We can fix this, together. Just focus on talking to me, okay?

[14:17] Alabaster&Freckles: What's going on? *How* is Erin spiralling? Tell me everything I need to know, and I can help you Tilly.

[14:18] PluckingPurgatory'sPetals: she takes her drug all dayylong and she has been taking higher andhigher doses to stave off the tolerance Build -up. But THe dosage she's using now is jutst insane .

[14:19] PluckingPurgatory'sPetals: IT"s... bad ; She's,, like, reallydrunk? slurring her sepeech and just kinda stumbling about. she wont admit how much it' s affecting her., maybe can't adMit it..

[14:21] PluckingPurgatory'sPetals: This isnt her fault . she Did not know this would happen . she; did NOt intend for the drug' thing to get sooo outofhand. but she is so scared of losing me .

[14:21] PluckingPurgatory'sPetals: So Scared. so scared.. soscared.!..!

[14:22] Alabaster&Freckles: ERIN, NO MORE GAMES, GET HELP! CALL AN AMBULANCE! YOU NEED HELP! THIS IS GOING TO KILL YOU! YOU DON'T WANT THIS! PLEASE, CALL FOR HELP!

[14:22] Alabaster&Freckles: PLEASE GET HELP BEFORE IT'S TOO LATE!

[14:23] Alabaster&Freckles: YOU DON'T HAVE TO GO THROUGH THIS ALONE! TELL ME WHERE YOU ARE AND I WILL FIND A WAY TO COME TO YOU! I WILL COME TO WHATEVER HOSPITAL YOU GO TO! I WILL BE THERE FOR YOU!

[PluckingPurgatory'sPetals - is now offline]

CHAPTER TWENTY

Erin awoke screaming.

It was so full-throated and so hoarse that it actually sounded more like an oscillating roar, though her enervated body greatly constrained its loudness. Still, it had a certain quality which would have undoubtedly frozen the blood of any listener. Perhaps that was because she did not *mean* to scream, and wasn't even particularly *aware* she was doing so. Her face was perfectly at rest; the noise was just streaming from her open mouth. That made it seem very, very strange. For it was not like the normal scream of horror at a phantom intruder glimpsed half-asleep at the foot of one's bed. Nor was it like someone screaming in pain at accidentally injuring themself. It was more akin to the type of frenzied, guttural sounds an animal instinctively makes when intuiting that they are being led to the slaughter. A scream not really summoned from the lungs, but from the mind.

Indeed, this scream was the involuntary reflex of a psyche which had finally *snapped* under colossal tension. Her mind was presently broken, presently inactive. Any aspiration towards cogent thought was thwarted by the cacophony of impossibly loud white noise blaring inside her head and drowning everything else out. So that she was not now a thinking creature. She was, in fact, no more than that beast deranged by vague, unfathomed premonitions of the cattle gun. And as a result, her body was not in her control either. It would henceforth merely be carrying out crude failsafe orders. This was the most dire automaticity. A state where its every movement was to become decoupled from the direction of the mind. As though her body was simply compelled to somehow expend the residual energy stored in its pre-wound clockwork innards.

Diminishing her screaming not one decibel, she scrambled out of the bed and leapt to her feet. And as soon as she was upright, she sprinted across the room. In doing so, she inadvertently knocked over the IV stand, which crashed to the floor. But she did not even notice this had happened. She got to the wall and pressed her back to it, removing the possibility of her being snuck up on from behind. Then she frantically looked around the darkened apartment with wide, deathly-frightened eyes. Despite repeating this reconnoitring sweep several times, her gaze was blank and unseeing. It didn't seem to actually be taking in the apartment at all. What she was actually looking *for* was unclear. Tears had, by now, begun to stream freely down her cheeks. Yet she wasn't sobbing in any way. It was more like her tear ducts were simply leaking. And so the only effect of this was to make her blink more rapidly to clear her sight.

She went to dart forward again. But then abruptly froze mid-movement and ceased her screaming. She cocked her head like startled prey listening for sounds of pursuit, and glanced to-and-fro even more intently. Next she slowly dropped down onto her haunches to crouch very low. Squatting there and straining to hear non-existent attackers, certain facial muscles began to randomly twitch now and then. This erratically contorted her features in a disquieting manner, making it seem like she was receiving tiny electric shocks. And, as incredible as it was unsurprising, there was no sign that she even realized this was happening. Perhaps because more pressing things were afoot. Or so one inferred. As she gave full concentration to her vigilance, she nervously rubbed the back of her clenched fists together.

It was then that she began to... speak.

This took the form of a sort of loud burbling. She was quickly spilling out long strings of incomprehensible, slurred non-words. Awful to hear, even more awful to *see* pronounced. Each one an arrhythmic jumble of horribly mangled syllables. An observer could *almost* have mistaken it for a real, though wildly unsuccessful, attempt to actually say something. Yet because this manic chattering hadn't even the cadence of real speech, it truly was no more than chaotic gibberish. Besides, she didn't seem to be directing it at anyone or anything. But simply issuing it into the room. Rather like the sounds which bats make to view their surroundings by echolocation.

This continued for some time. It only faded away as Erin tensed her whole body, like a big cat getting ready to pounce. She was staring at an otherwise insignificant spot on the floor about ten feet away. Before she could ambush whatever transfixed her there, she let out a high-pitched squeal and bolted upright. And then she jumped away from where she'd been crouching. As she landed, she was already desperately trying to brush away something on her stomach. She swiped and batted endlessly there but without any apparent success at dislodging anything. It was fortunate that her t-shirt was covering the skin there. Or instead of merely the faint scratch-lines which her nails inflicted through the cloth, there would have been long, bloody streaks.

Abandoning this effort as abruptly and inexplicably as it had been started, she made her next move. She rushed across the apartment, towards the tall chest of drawers, with a warcry-esque holler. However, a rather serious problem arose. It was only a short distance and she had near enough flung herself across it. This meant that when trying to come to a sudden halt at her destination, she couldn't possibly shed her momentum fast enough. She instead skidded forward and crashed into the front of the drawers. One in particular had been left open. Given the height of where it was situated, its protruding handles jabbed very hard into her hips. She snorted in pain and doubled over. She was clutching at where the bones there were radiating agony.

A lot of what had been left stood up atop the chest of drawers - mostly books and knick-knacks - fell off now, due to it being heavily rocked by the impact. Some of these items missed her. Some of them didn't. Those in this latter category glanced off her without issue. That is, until a big, weighty hardback book fell right onto her back as she was bent over, and knocked the wind out of her.

She dropped to her knees and began hacking up a lung. Coughing and coughing as if her insides were imploding and liquefying and desperate to come out. She violently convulsed for a second, and then *saw* herself projectile-vomiting out a high-powered stream of dead ladybugs, seemingly without end. They were shooting out of her nose and mouth. She could feel them tickling every millimetre of her esophagus as they came up en masse. Their hard little shiny red and black bodies quickly began to pile up into heaps. Some of them had their weird transparent wings limply hanging out. Her eyes shot open so wide in shock and horror that her eyeballs seemed like they might pop out. She clamped a hand over her mouth and used the other to squeeze her nostrils closed. As she scrambled backwards, her flailing legs kicked the large mounds of regurgitated bug-corpses all over the place.

She awkwardly rolled away sideways until, now facing it, she dragged herself over to the kitchenette. She just lay there on the floor before the sink. After a few minutes of wheezing and whining, the pain in her hips and back had settled to a stomachable level. She gingerly returned upright with a wince. And then leaned over the sink and turned both taps on to full blast. Cupping her hands, she began repeatedly splashing copious amounts of water onto her face and rubbing it into the back of her neck. But soon the hot tap heated up and she barked in frustration as the water became warm. She irritatedly reached over to quickly turn it off before continuing her drenching with the cold tap alone. On and on she went, throwing handfuls of water at herself. She even made little satisfied noises as each one hit her. Her t-shirt was damp and clinging to her. A wide puddle was growing at her feet.

Yet again she froze statue-still upon seeming to hear something in the apartment with her. Her cupped hands, just refilled with another payload of tapwater, were held immobile halfway between the sink and her face as she listened. Then they spilled it out onto her feet as she finally reacted. Spinning around to confront the source of the perceived noise, she had her fists raised in front of her, ready to punch out at the darkness. She actually gulped - like a frightened cartoon character - and her eyes darted around the apartment, searching for the threat. It was obviously *very* stealthy and elusive. She maintained her posture of combat readiness for a little while, anxiously surveying her immediate surroundings. Eventually her alertness was rewarded. Something caught her attention near the bed.

Gasping and exclaiming something unintelligible, she sprang into action to defend herself. She turned slightly and grabbed a little plate left on the drying rack beside the sink. Without any wind-up, she threw it like a frisbee at the spot which had startled her. It flew across the room without much force and skimmed the side of the mattress before impacting the wall beyond. Although it clattered against the wall, it amazingly did not break. It just fell to the floor and noisily spun a few times before coming to rest.

She shrieked in frustration and looked around in dismay for another, better projectile. With limited options close at hand, she seized upon the metal, pot-shaped cutlery holder which was on the draining board too. It was filled with a bunch of stuff that had been left to dry, ranging from spoons to spatulas to a long serrated bread knife. She grabbed the whole thing and lobbed it, with a clumsy double underhand thrust, as hard as she could at the target for bombardment. Much of the heavier contents fell out mid-flight, littering the floor beneath its trajectory with jetsam. The now half-empty container hit the wall hard, spilling the rest of the cutlery, and then ricocheted off to somewhere else in the room.

Erin whooped triumphantly and shouted some aggressive babble. She now had a taunting, confident swagger to her. Not content with just the one ostensibly-successful blow, she prepared to follow up on it. Evidently, she'd decided that victory against the spectre was not quite secured yet. She looked back around to appraise what improvised weaponry was left to her. Alas, there was very little to choose from. Undaunted by her scanty arsenal, she was going to resort to a massive escalation which would serve as a savage *coup de grâce* and conclude the battle. She picked up the heavy plastic draining rack itself, upon which still rested a bowl and two mugs. She struggled to even hold it aloft. With many grunts of exertion, she shifted her grip around to find a decently secure manner of clutching it. But quickly gave up when none could be found. She focused, instead, on how to loose it as forcefully as possible.

Her deliberation took only an instant. She started to spin around on the spot. Like a graceless hammer-thrower, she twirled around with all her might to impart momentum into her throw. Already dizzied by the third revolution, she unintentionally let go of the draining rack prematurely. It soared through the air in the wrong direction. Then it plunged heavily onto the hardwood floor and skidded along for several feet, stopping well short of the wall. The bowl, somehow, had managed to stay firmly jammed between the stiff separating prongs atop the draining rack itself, but a long crack split it into two. She gave voice to her anger and misery at the failure with inarticulate shouts as well as frantic gestures. Even stamping her foot with utmost petulance.

Before long, she noticed the mess on the floor not far from where she stood. She abruptly ended her tantrum and stared in dumbstruck awe at it, like a child might. As it happened, during her spinning both mugs had traitorously jumped ship from the draining rack. One simply fell onto the floor and rolled away intact. But the other had glided across the counter before cracking into several pieces upon hitting the microwave. As it travelled, however, it also knocked a jar of mustard off the countertop, which had smashed upon the floor. It had gotten everywhere, splattering the cabinets too.

She sat down before the mess and cooed appreciatively at the potential she saw in it. Yet, safety first. Or thereabouts. Extending a wary hand, she tentatively prodded it and then drew back. Only when a minute had passed without it attacking her in reprisal did she feel confident she could proceed. She started smearing the yellow paste, littered with shards of thick glass, with her palm. She spread it across a wide surface area, to create a better canvas. It was an absolute miracle that her hand was not horrifically cut up in the process. But luck has something of a soft spot for braindead fools and madmen.

Now her tongue peeked out ever so slightly as she thought hard about the next step. In this bizarre moment, she seemed to regain some small fraction of lucidity. And what did she use it for? Well, she began to slowly drag a fingertip through the mustard, *writing* in nigh-illegible chicken scratch cursive. It being dark should have made this very hard. Yet, to her eye, her finger left a ghostly, glowing comet-tail in its wake. And by fixating on that, she was able to keep track of the spacing. There was something rather astounding about this. In her present state, articulate speech obviously eluded her. But she was still somehow able to scrape together enough diminished shadows of muscle memory to draw squiggles which at least halfway mirrored the written word.

Once her message was committed to the unconventional medium of spilled food, she got up and stepped back over to the sink. She returned to deliriously throwing cupped-handfuls of water at her face and neck. And, huffing in annoyance, she picked up the pace and splashed herself faster and faster. Still, her growing scowl suggested that she just couldn't make herself do it as rapidly as she wanted or perhaps needed. She slammed her fist down onto the countertop. Glancing around, she spied the shower cubicle on the other side of the apartment and her brow furrowed as she seemed to contemplate its applicability. Then she ran over to it, once more at full-pelt.

Coming to a stop before it, she quickly bent over at the waist to reach down and pull her socks off. Unfortunately, she had misjudged how close she was to the shower cubicle itself. So as she leaned forward, she hit her forehead against the edge of the flat metal frame enclosing the corners of the glass structure. It was quite a hard impact. And it sure felt like it too. For about fifteen seconds, her vision deserted her as she saw stars. Once she stumbled backwards and slowly returned upright, a thick wooziness settled upon her. She uttered some gibberish in a plaintive tone over to the left, as though pleading against the scolding of some invisible persecutor. And then, vaguely remembering her goal, she clumsily opened the cubicle door and lumbered inside.

She turned the shower on with some difficulty. The dial was presently set to just a tad above cold. It immediately drenched the pyjamas she was wearing and they hung heavy and wet against her skin. As she stood there and allowed the shower spray to soak her, she began to laugh. It was drawn-out, hysterical laughter which seemed to involuntarily emanate from deep inside of her. She laughed and laughed though her face showed no traces of mirth whatsoever. It died down as she started to shiver at the frigid water. It wasn't easy to fight off the urge to back away.

She went about catching the water in her cupped hands and emphatically throwing it at her face again until she was interrupted by a light-headedness. The woozy feeling had suddenly grown so much more intense. She now became unsteady and very, very nauseous. She guessed what was about to happen and dropped down onto her hands and knees. Her body was insisting that *actual* vomiting was both imminent and unavoidable, and she had no power to dissuade it. The shower was still spraying hard upon her lower back as she began to retch. But all the dry-heaving produced was a little pool of thick saliva she spit up.

Her dazed condition pressed its advantage. She felt incredibly faint and an ever-narrowing black frame had imposed itself at the edges of her sight. Dimly recognizing what this in turn presaged, she acted fast. For to stay beneath this apathetic, artificial waterfall would be a death sentence. She summoned what minuscule strength was still available to her and strained to reach up her hand. She took aim at the slider on the shower unit which dictated water flow, trying to push it back to the other end with ill-aimed slaps. She clipped it once or twice, but just couldn't seem to really hit it.

Sensing that her time was up, she was forced to abandon her effort to turn off the shower, having only managed to diminish it down to a weak, sputtering spray. Crawling forward, she used her shoulder to push open the shower door enough for her to get through. It was unbelievably hard to keep her balance, even moving slowly along on all fours, disorientated as she now was. As she more or less dragged herself away from the cubicle, her field-of-vision shrunk to a pinprick. She collapsed onto her belly and finally just gave in to the urge to pass out.

The darkness cradled her aloft and took her away.

She woke up many hours later.

Before she could even *think* about opening her eyes, she had to reckon with the breathtaking pain smashing about in her skull. It felt like a sadistically heightened version of the worst possible throbbing migraine. So, for quite a long while, she just lay there with her eyes tightly shut. Trying to find some way to deal with the pain and its immobilizing effect. Yet, to tamp something like this down to a manageable state was a big ask. It was akin to struggling to stifle a forest fire with the squirts from a water pistol. But she persisted and persisted.

She was doing all she could to try and reframe the suffering as something felt merely in the background. And therefore *not* a brutal sieve which all experience had to squeeze itself through in a perforated form. This mental exercise did end up helping; not enormously, but just barely enough. Though this might seem like a meagre triumph, most people would have purely floundered upon attempting it. Whereas she had not only done it, but done it fairly swiftly too. For the product of all her travails in the craft meant that Erin *understood* pain, could to some extent work it like putty between her fingers.

Lifting her fluttering eyelids, she saw the dirty surface of the floor up close and realized she was lying upon it. That was... not a good sign. She slowly lifted her shoulder up and rolled over onto her back. As she did so, several different things she felt each gave her some insight into her current predicament. There was, firstly, the fact that her muscles were sore and her joints were achy from sleeping on the hardwood floor. Next, there was the residual dampness to her pyjamas which revealed that she had slept in wet clothes. She really hoped there would be no health repercussions for this. Because anything worse than catching a cold would be uniquely disastrous for someone, like her, with no access to doctors or their medicine. Although it's often true that one *can* get by without that help, the abrupt discovery that one *cannot* is lurking just around the corner. Old-wives-tale home remedies and herbal nostrums sold on kooky websites right alongside healing crystals would be of little help with, say, pneumonia. And lastly, she noticed something which really put the cherry atop this whole unpleasant sundae. The combination of the small puddle around her butt and the acrid odour of urine let her know that she'd wet herself at some point. Her cheeks burned with shame at this humiliating realization.

Still caught in the post-waking brain-fog, her thoughts were rather scrambled. And she certainly couldn't remember how she had ended up passed out on the floor. All that presently occurred to her was that she really, really didn't want to get up and deal with this situation. Let alone deal with whatever had caused it. The little that she had already discerned was enough to make her want to just go back to sleep and selfishly burden future-Erin with having to sort everything out. Because she suspected that her limited discoveries were likely to just be the opening tranche of bad shit. If she actually got up and looked around, what else was she going to find? And once she saw that stuff, there would be no going back or putting it off. She would have to go about fixing it. This made for, when one felt as crappy as she did right now, a very tricky dilemma. She considered the opposing options for some time. However, she eventually decided that tempting as it was to just retreat back into the obliviousness of sleep, she could not. She had to know the full details of what had transpired. Her curiosity was just too strong.

She gradually pushed herself up to a sitting position. There would be no stalling. It was time to just do the damn thing. She slowly rotated her head to take in the full aftermath of last night's carnage. One did not have to be a detective to piece together the disturbing story told by the debris of deranged rage littered across the floor. As she took it all in and shook the cobwebs loose from her mind, she recalled what had happened: the *epiphany* she had underwent during a long, unbearable dream. Plus, she even got a very dim, patchy picture of what it then instigated. The severe psychotic episode when she woke up. And the frightful things which had taken place during the accompanying freak-out. This trio of pent-up remembrances hit her all at once. And she physically recoiled as if absorbing a kick to the ribs.

Her face blanched and her breathing became rapid and shallow. This was the all-too-familiar road to hyperventilating. She was desperately trying to suck in a long, deep breath, but there was this crippling tightness in her chest which made it futile. All of a sudden, she let out an anguished howl. It was the uncontrollable eruption of the profound pain exploding within her soul. She let herself fall backwards into a supine position once more. All she could do to vent the unendurable emotion welling up inside her was frantically slap her feet and palms against the floor over and over. She tried to howl again but scarcely had the air in her lungs to spare. So that it emerged only as a truncated shriek. She felt like she was suffocating, like she was sure to die from asphyxiation if this crushing invisible weight on her sternum didn't depart. Her breathing was so fast and laboured that it resembled an animal panting, but it was the best she could do.

After several fraught minutes of fighting to get her breathing under control, she managed to bring it back to an elevated baseline. She could now feel the tears coming. This made her absolutely spitting mad. She was sick to death of fucking crying over everything. Especially in this moment, it would not be permitted to spill forth. For she didn't dare to commit the self-indulgence of giving in to the weeping. She did not *deserve* to be consoled by the catharsis of having cried out all the pain. Yes, that was right. This misery was as well-earned and righteous as anything which had ever happened to her. To try and alleviate it was to spurn the very prospect of remorse. But even penitent acceptance was not enough. Passivity was still, in its way, cowardly evasion here. There had to be an embracing, an active participation in her own punishment. That was the only true gesture of apology for wrongs which could not be righted.

Oh god, this was going to hurt.

Shifting over onto her stomach, she steadied herself with her hands and bit down on her t-shirt collar. What she was about to do was even worse than she suspected. Quite unbeknownst to her, her forehead *already* bore a dark bruise, at whose center was a small cut. She now began banging it against the floor with moderate force. Each impact elicited a shrill wail of wretchedness and suffering. After three of them, the hitherto dampened pain flooded thickly back into her head, coating every crevice of her consciousness with its burning residue. She wanted to continue but could not. She clutched her head and rolled side-to-side at the pounding torment inside her skull. Her legs were erratically kicking out into the air. This went on for... some time. The part of her dearly wishing she hadn't done it was warring with the part which was proud that she did. But the *whole* of her was dealing with the after-effect regardless.

Once it subsided just a little, she groggily rolled onto her back again. And she stared dead-eyed up at the ceiling, shaking her head softly and moving her lips without a sound. When this did finally raise to the volume of a murmur, it became clear that she was pleading.

"Tilly... Oh Tilly... Tilly... Tilly... Oh Tilly..."

And then she heard a response.

"Hello, Erin."

Her blood ran cold as the current passing beneath an arctic floe.

Ignoring how it sloshed around the pain in her head, she shot upright to a sitting position and looked all around. It did not take long to find the source. Sitting on the window-seat, right up against the closed blind, was Tilly. She had previously been half-obscured from Erin because of the room's dimness and her low vantage point. Looking on with a deep melancholic pity brimming in her eyes, Tilly just observed the effect of her greeting.

Time seemed to slow down to a crawl. Erin already knew what she was going to find, but she instinctively glanced down at her forearm anyway, where of course no needle or tubing was present. Ikelos was not being infused into her system. That meant this *shouldn't* be happening. This *couldn't* be happening. There was no conceivable way for Tilly to be right there, talking to her. It just wasn't possible.

She felt very much like she might faint. Eyes wide in shock and disbelief, she scuttled backwards with her hands. And, in the process, just kind of flung herself up to her feet.

"T-T-Tilly! T-Tilly!"

That was all that Erin could manage to stutteringly offer up.

"Yes." A small, sad smile twitched Tilly's lips. "I suppose we have a lot to discuss, don't we?"

"I-I'm so sorry! So sorry! So, so, so sorry!"

Erin could scarcely get the words out fast enough.

Tilly just nodded and said, "I know, Erin. I know."

After quite a lot of patient persistence, Tilly managed to calm Erin down.

She was still reeling and had a million questions, but Tilly said they would have to wait. She then instructed Erin to bathe and tend to her wounds and clear up the apartment. That had to come first. Erin wanted to protest, but sensed she needed some time to process things anyway. At least, if she wanted to be able to put together any cogent sentences. So she stripped off and took a long, hot shower. Allowing herself to get lost in the repetitive motions of thoroughly scrubbing herself all over did help clear her mind a bit. If only this new clarity of thinking didn't simply equate to wishing she could scrub hard enough to purge the stain of guilt and shame too.

After drying herself, she threw her towel and a bunch of other bath-towels from the rack onto the floor. Tilly silently watched from the window-seat as Erin, still naked, pushed the towel-heap around with her feet to soak up all the wet patches throughout the apartment. Then Erin dumped the dirtied towels into the laundry basket and retrieved her roll-up medical kit from the chest of drawers. She tended to her various cuts and scrapes as best as she could. She could faintly recall how some of them had been inflicted; the ones she couldn't made her deeply uneasy. As she worked, she risked a couple furtive glances over at Tilly, who just went on staring with disquietingly statuesque stillness and impassiveness. If Erin wanted to cheat by preemptively trying to read Tilly, she'd meet with no success. Once she was done with her task, she put everything back and threw on some clean clothes.

Rolling up her sleeves, she grabbed a big garbage bag and got to work. She first tossed in everything she had been wearing when she woke up. These clothes were soiled both physically and symbolically; she could not bear to keep them. Next she went around picking up and resituating the thrown things which hadn't broken, and used a little dustpan and brush to sweep up the pieces of those which had.

She very intentionally kept the patch of dried mustard and broken glass for last. Some strange intuition told her that it had some special significance, that it was a thing to be dreaded. She approached it slowly and peered at it with great anxiety. When she saw the message scrawled in the mess, she comprehended its contents instantly. Her brain did not give her any choice in the matter. No matter how sloppy and deformed one's handwriting may be during times of extreme duress, it is a cipher which can always be cracked by oneself later. She now found herself rather ungrateful that this was the case.

The message read: 'please, please forgive me'. And, underneath that, 'I want to die'.

Eight words. Two wishes. An interlocked symmetry.

A samurai's lofty, flowery, abstruse death-poem, it... was not. For there was *no* ambiguity here.

Much as she longed to look away, she could not. She just went on staring in horror. These strewn fragments had been all that could be chipped away from the monolithic hunk of inarticulable anguish inside her. She knew this. Oh, she knew this deeply now. For as she scrutinised this lone missive which escaped the black hole of her recent episode, she tapped into the resonance of its creation. And it stirred in her the mercifully faint memory of what she'd felt when writing it. This was a self-hatred so pure that its only true and full expression would be utter self-annihilation.

Snapping herself out of it, she swallowed hard and backed away. She needed this horrible... memento gone *right now*. She speedily unfurled half a roll of kitchen towel and used it to mop up the whole thing. Thankfully, the thick jar-glass seemed to have just shattered into a bunch of large shards, which made clean-up easier.

After tying the top of the garbage bag in a knot, she dumped it by the apartment door. It would be snuck to the garbage chute in the hallway during the middle of the night like usual. But that felt like such a long time away. She couldn't wait to be rid of it, and all that its contents represented. In fact, she found that she actually couldn't even bear to see it. So, doubling back, she instead took it over to the kitchenette and crammed it into the cabinet beneath the sink. Hidden but not forgotten.

In a soft voice, Tilly called across the room, "you can come over to me now, Erin."

Erin traipsed over to the window-seat and awkwardly stood before it, unsure whether to actually join Tilly on it. It simply didn't feel right to do so. She instead sat down cross-legged on the floor, looking up at Tilly.

She had no idea what to say. So she just settled on offering up a sheepish, faltering, "h-hello."

And instantaneously felt very foolish for it.

She couldn't sit still: her burning need to know what Tilly was thinking made her fidgety. She watched Tilly closely, hyper-vigilant for any sign, any minute twitch, which might indicate something. She felt like a child sitting in a vigil of awaited-judgment before an angry parent, longing that she might incur only simple, fleeting wrath instead of some silent, inner reaction which was tenfold more worrying.

"What do you know?"

With a maddeningly neutral tone, Tilly deployed this question like a baited hook cast out between them.

"Everything," Erin answered simply. "I remember *everything*."

The terrible truth had been inflicted upon her and there was no going back. She now knew *who* Tilly really was. Because Tilly was not a mysterious outlander sojourning, for love, in a foreign dimension. Nor was she merely a dreamt-up figment of the imagination. She was a real person. And Erin had mentally projected an imaginary friend based upon her. But the actual flesh-and-blood Tilly existed out there in the physical world.

She had been Erin's girlfriend for two years.

They lived together in this apartment and were madly in love.

But then, *the accident* happened.

Tilly had snuck out early one wintry morning, whilst Erin was still sleeping, to run a quick errand. And halfway to her destination, she slipped on an icy stretch of pavement. It was the simplest thing in the world: a stumble and a fall. But she hit the back of her head on the curbside, and impacting the frozen concrete was not kind to her brain. Due to the very early hour and her having ventured down a sidestreet, it was ten minutes before anyone found her limp form crumpled upon the ground. An ambulance was called and she was rushed to hospital. All this time, Erin was fast asleep, enjoying a lie-in in the warm bed. Her weakly vibrating phone didn't succeed in waking her up until the fourth call from the hospital nurse.

Bleary-eyed and still half-asleep, Erin was told that her girlfriend had fallen and was currently in the intensive care unit. Struggling to comprehend what was being said, she only registered that the call was from the hospital and was regarding Tilly. This alone was enough to jolt her bolt-upright and fully awake. She asked the nurse to repeat herself. This time she listened closely and, as the point hit home, she felt her stomach drop and her pulse begin to race. Darting around like a whirlwind, she was dressed and out of the apartment in less than two minutes flat. She flagged down a cab and promised the driver quadruple-fare if she could be raced to the hospital. Unlike in the movies, there was no red-light running, but the speed limit *was* now taken only as a suggestion. On the way, her mind tortured her by picturing all manner of horrible, mangled states she might find Tilly in. These images really did a number on her. She felt like she was going to explode, and tried to channel that volatile energy into the car to make it go faster.

She arrived at the hospital and ran to the front desk, quickly extracting Tilly's floor number from the startled receptionist. She got to the main elevator just as it was being filled by a group of hospital staff with a gurney-bound patient. Scowling and swearing at this obstruction, and loathe to wait, she sprinted to the staircase and went up six flights of stairs, taking the steps two-at-at-time. When she eventually crashed through the doors on the right floor and checked in with the nursing staff there, she was huffing and puffing, with a face that was bright red and sweaty. Of course, all this theatrical haste-making was for nought. It was merely her trying to assuage her own sense of guiltiness by proving her dedication. Whether she'd gotten there ten minutes sooner, or had even somehow managed to teleport there the second Tilly was brought in, it would have made no difference. This bell was not going to be unrung.

With expert politeness and poise, a nurse led Erin over to a waiting area to take a seat and even quelled her protestations at not getting to see Tilly immediately. Erin was assured that Tilly's doctor would be over shortly and would explain the whole situation. So she just sat there quietly fuming. And she'd insistently lock eyes with any doctor who passed by, as if by sheer force of will she could both draw one over and transmogrify them into who she was waiting for. At long last, Tilly's actual doctor did finally come over and introduce himself. Despite how many times she had mentally rehearsed this conversation, now that it was upon her, she found herself dumbstruck with fear and utterly tongue-tied. The doctor seemed to pick up on this, and took the lead. He cut straight to the chase and said that Tilly appeared to have suffered a rather serious Traumatic Brain Injury, or TBI.

As he paused to let Erin take this in, she suddenly felt like she was having an out-of-body experience, watching the conversation from afar. She rolled the three words around in her head. She'd look at each one individually and then string them together again - trying to make sense of the term, trying to make it seem real - but with little success. Her mind would just not play ball. As the doctor went on, she tried really hard to absorb what he was saying. Inbetween all the impenetrable jargon and mealy-mouthed, non-committal platitudes, she garnered a few salient facts. The next twenty-four hours were supposedly the most critical. Tilly was unconscious, in a medically induced coma. There was significant brain swelling and they were going to do all they could to reduce it. Depending upon how Tilly reacted to the emergency treatment being given to her, it was possible that a risky surgery would need to be performed.

This was all a *lot* to take in.

Throughout the explanation, Erin had just been staring at the doctor's mouth and involuntarily nodding along like an empty-headed fool. And when he had finished, a hundred useful, pertinent follow-up questions swam about before her mind's eye. But they all darted away whenever she tried to seize upon one, like a school of fish scattering as a net draws close. Awkward seconds ticked by as the doctor waited for her to say something, *anything*. This pressure got to her. Before she could pull it back into her mouth, she just blurted out an idiotic question: 'is she going to be okay?' The doctor simply inclined his head sympathetically and intensified his well-practiced grave demeanour. He replied that it was far too early to tell what *damage* may have been caused. He let this point hang for a moment. And then went on to emphasize that Erin needed to understand that given the apparent severity of the injury, there would likely be some long-term ramifications no matter what.

Vouchsafed an assurance that she'd get to see Tilly as soon as possible, she was then left alone with her thoughts in the drab seating area once again. As the hours passed, she felt like she was in a daze. But her mind was still plenty able to make her suffer. She kept running through all the ways in which she could have - nay, *should* have - prevented this from happening. None of them made much sense. Of course, they didn't have to. Their mere conceivability was enough for her to tell herself that she was selfish, worthless human garbage.

And then she recalled all the arguments and falling-outs they'd ever had, and with great malice castigated herself for each and every one. Why had she not been the prideless creature of infinite kindness that Tilly deserved?! The answer brought with it an ineluctable judgement of guilt.

And then she thought about all the inventively horrific ordeals she would gladly call down upon herself if it would just turn back the clock and prevent Tilly's fall. She saw herself being stretched on the rack, or dunked in a cauldron of boiling oil, or being vivisected alive. In each scene, a smile of unbelievable gratitude and relief was seen upon her face, at what was being bought.

And then she hated the world, and everyone and everything in it, with a burning passion. Especially herself. Especially the laws of physics. But *most* especially, she cursed the imbeciles who bleated that mankind was somehow intelligently designed. Our entire self contained within a delicate spongy mass inside our skulls. And yet we happen to be on a planet with hard ground and unforgiving gravity. What a fucking stupid, stupid combination. What a fine recipe for happy outcomes.

The urge to cry came over her many times. But she fended it off mightily, and allowed herself nothing more than the occasional bout of dewy-eyed sniffling. Because she hadn't even seen Tilly yet. The truly horrible bit hadn't even begun yet. This was just the prelude. Yet, here she was, in danger of falling apart in every moment. So she resolved to stave that off with everything she had. The most important thing of all was that she be there for Tilly. That meant keeping it together and trying to stay clear-headed. Unthinkable decisions may have to be made and she was the only one around to make them. Her love entailed a crucial duty, and she meant to uphold it.

After what felt like a miniature eternity, a nurse came over to take her to Tilly. She tingled all over with a nauseating dread. It felt like jagged icicles were darting through her arteries and her stomach was inching its way upward to squeeze itself out of her mouth. Led to a small room on the other side of the floor, the nurse unceremoniously opened the door and... there Tilly was. Erin just stood in the doorway, staring at the appalling fate of the woman she loved. Tilly was deathly pale, and clad in a weird, ill-fitting hospital gown. The back of her head had been shaved. And there was a tube stuck down her throat, which stirred in Erin a heavy rage she'd never known before. She wanted nothing more than to rip out that tube and fight all comers who sought to stop her tooth and nail. It was a childish, nonsensical urge and she pushed it down, but its embers lingered in the background. She felt the nurse place a guiding hand on the small of her back and, with a compassionate expression, gesture into the room. At this, like a fireplace suddenly stoked with a billows, the flames of anger roared up inside her, building to a ferocious blaze. The primordial part of her mind, which millennia of evolution has tried to dull, spoke up in a commanding voice. It told her to seize upon the offending arm like a feral creature, snap it using the doorframe as a fulcrum, and bury the resulting bone shard into the woman's jugular.

But she didn't.

She just walked slowly to Tilly and extended a trembling hand to brush the hair from her face. Then she collapsed into tears, sobbing at a howling volume, bent over the side of the bed.

Hours later, they did take Tilly into the operating theatre after all, to relieve the pressure upon her brain. And when they brought her back, the worsening of her ghastly pallor made her look closer to death than ever.

Erin did not want to leave Tilly's side. But no matter how she begged or threatened or cajoled, the hospital staff would not grant her a bed to use. So in the days to come, she simply made do. She sometimes slept upright in the chair in Tilly's room and sometimes slept splayed out on empty rows of seating in the waiting areas. At one point, she went home briefly to grab a duffel bag full of clothes and other essentials, but that was it. Her whole life was relocated to the hospital. She ate in the canteen and 'bathed' using the sinks in the restrooms.

A week passed. At which point, Tilly's doctor took Erin aside and informed her of the latest test results. Before even a word was spoken, his expression rather telegraphed their unfavourable import. He said that they suggested that Tilly would *not* regain consciousness even if the medically-induced coma was ended. Therefore, further attempts at repairing the damage to her brain were necessary if any hope of her waking up was to be achieved. This meant more courses of treatment and more surgeries. Could she please sign this stack of forms densely filled with baffling legalese? She didn't even read them, there was no need. She just scribbled her signature on all of their dotted lines and told the doctor to save her beloved.

And so began Erin's tireless, stubborn bedside vigil.

She continued living in the hospital, occasionally having to bribe or sob-story the nursing staff and security guards to ignore this fact. Her days were very simple. For they had only one object. She lovingly watched over Tilly, tending to her however possible. For hours on end, she would just talk *at* Tilly as though she could hear. Mostly she read newspapers or magazines aloud, interjecting snarky commentary here and there. Or she would just prattle on unendingly, disgorging a vapid stream-of-consciousness monologue. And sometimes, in moments of ultimate weakness, she would lean in very close to Tilly's ear and whisper frantic encouragement, willing her to rejoin the waking world. Beyond this, she often sought to flag down Tilly's doctor and beseech him to focus more of his time and energy on trying to revive Tilly's brain. So too, she spent any idle moment on her phone, googling where the best specialists in the field were located and what cutting-edge, experimental medical trials were going on.

By the time that a month and a half had gone by, things started to feel very different. Erin was infinitely exhausted in mind and body and soul. The doctor took her aside once more and gave her his final verdict. All the conceivably effective options had now been tried. Short of a prodigious string of miracles, Tilly was going to be in a machine-assisted, vegetative comatose state for the rest of her life. She would likely be consigned to a long-term care facility, where all the other burdensome living dead were stored until... they were a burden no more. If there are words to truly describe what it feels like to receive this news, none in humanity's long, long lineage of poets has yet coined them.

Deep down, she had of course feared that this would be the outcome. But she never allowed herself to genuinely acknowledge the possibility. This meant that the revelation hit her even harder than it would've anyway, because it was smashing through layers of denial too. Up until she heard it from the doctor himself, Erin had just been telling herself, over and over again, that this *couldn't* be the end of Tilly's story. It just couldn't. It wasn't right. It made no sense. Tilly had merely... fallen. Just a simple, stupid little stumble. It should have resulted in some brief embarrassment and perhaps a pair of scraped elbows. Not... *this*. It should never have caused... *this*. Erin could not accept it, wouldn't ever be able to accept it.

She saw the impossibly bleak decades to come stretch out before her, where she would be stuck orbiting an artificially sustained corpse. Every day trekking to some depressingly sterile and silent windowless building, to perform a perfunctory demonstration of devotion. And with *nothing* to bolster her. For it had been the lingering hope, as fervent as it was irrational, that Tilly might yet recover which had enabled Erin to persist even this long. That's what gave her the superhuman emotional strength needed to treat a quasi-lifeless husk as if it were still her girlfriend. Now that hope had been extinguished. Now cometh the endgame. Wherein, there is only the soul-crushing waiting and waiting and waiting for the perversely euphoric relief when the one you love the most finally dies. Or, at least, the one you *did* love. Because as time passes, the latent resentment would build inside Erin like a cancer, necrotically eating away whatever affection she had left. Yet, the cruel irony being that the longer she is able to stick it out, the more the obligation itself will solidify and become unshirkable. To cease the daily visits after a few months is one thing: lamentable but somehow... understandable. But to do so after, say, five years of unbroken fidelity will seem an unimaginably egregious betrayal.

Sitting there, contemplating the manacles imminently closing around her wrists, she felt chilled to the bone. And then, she calmly stood up and strode down the hallway towards the elevator. It was like she didn't actively choose to leave, she just left. Some other things just happened too. Her feet *just* carried her out of the hospital, her arm *just* flagged down a taxi, her hand *just* opened her apartment door.

When she got home though, she was hellaciously consumed by shame and grief. More than that, the tragedy's pitchblack hopelessness had a mentally destabilizing effect upon her. It made her feel like her brain was on fire. It made her feel like her mind didn't work. She longed for anything which could alleviate this. The two easiest choices were obvious. Despite a deep-seated antipathy towards alcohol, she took to glugging cheap liquor with reckless abandon, relishing how plainly it tasted like poison. And despite a queasiness at the sight of blood, she found herself applying sharp things to her skin with bad intentions for the first time. Yet even these desperate recourses were not quite enough. She *had* adored this hitherto shared apartment and its nimbus of jumbled happy memories. But now it seemed like just some twisted cenotaph. So, she purged every trace of Tilly's existence and the accumulated residue of their love, to spare her fragile psyche from the sight.

Several weeks were spent in this limbo, this speedy unravelling of her sanity. Then her mind finally snapped. A catastrophic mental breakdown descended upon her. Triggered by this cataclysm, some kindly failsafe embedded in the motherboard of her subconscious activated to try and save her. It quarantined *all* memories of Tilly into a remote and consciously-inaccessible place. So that she emerged on the other side without any recollection of Tilly, or any ability to notice this gap in her memory. This was certainly a drastic, costly last-ditch measure. But even a bad short-term fix was better than her brain's circuits being totally fried.

Afterwards she just began to live her life as if nothing had happened. But eventually she stopped leaving her apartment, as an 'inexplicable' depression started to plague her. The whole underlying framework of her mind was unbelievably frail now, but somehow the sloppy buttressing held up. For about ten months, at any rate. Then Erin had her first dream about the seemingly mysterious figure of Tilly. This was her lost memories fighting against their imprisonment, seeping out through cracks in the vault they were secreted away into. And her dreamworld went on playing host to this fractured, incomprehensible recollection. Alas, with this gradual return of Tilly into Erin's life, so too did the soundness of her mind begin to deteriorate anew. That was why her behavior had been so irrational, so erratic in the months which followed. It was all leading her, inexorably, to this moment right now. Where she was re-burdened with the knowledge she had tried so badly to escape forever.

Tilly stared down into her lap and nodded pensively as she absorbed Erin's answer.

"Everything, huh?..." she murmured, as if just to herself.

But then she gradually looked up and, with a sombre countenance, locked eyes with Erin.

"Okay, first things first." Her gaze became hard and sure. "You need to *say it.*"

Erin glanced away, pouting like an unruly toddler. She rather resented, after what she'd gone through, being made to do *this* too. Or even being asked to. It faintly seemed like kicking someone while they're down, though she couldn't have said quite how that was true. It just felt like it. At any rate, how quickly her longing to prostrate herself and grovel for absolution was forgotten.

"No I don't. I... know it."

Each drawn-out syllable was tinged with snippiness.

"This is important. Very important. You *have* to say it, you *have* to acknowledge it out loud. That means something."

Almost a minute of tense silence followed, with Erin shifting around agitatedly on the spot. As if trying to summon the courage to accede or refuse. At last, she met Erin's gaze with wet, defiant eyes.

"*You're... not... real.*"

The words hung in the air like a horrible reverse-incantation.

Changing nothing. Changing everything

A little smile of compassion and triumph flickered upon Tilly's face. This was a very promising start. She looked warmly on Erin and said, "yes. Good, thank you."

The traces of annoyance in Erin's expression did not dissipate. She decided this damn well ought to be a give-and-take. And that meant it was her turn now.

"H-how am I seeing you *without* Ikelos?! Why... why are you still here?!"

The questions spilled out quickly, forcefully, sounding much more like demands.

Tilly just laughed genially.

"That's a good question..."

And a mischievous twinkle glinted in her eyes as she conspicuously declined to elaborate.

Several moments passed, where Erin muleheadedly just stewed and waited. She was giving Tilly the opportunity to reconsider and decide *not* to be a total dick. And, all the while, staring coldly at her. She was very much in no mood for games.

But the dirty look, tickling her, only widened Tilly's smile.

This, in turn, rankled Erin yet further. She inflated her cheeks and blew out an ill-tempered puff. Then she finally gave in. Which meant beckoning Tilly to continue with all the indignation she could muster.

She even added, "come on!"

"Dear me, if you insist. Ah, well, who knows, right? Perhaps I'm not done with you yet. Perhaps you'll need me beside you as you see this thing through. Or... perhaps..." - she gave a little wry half-smirk - "you were just dumb enough to flip a switch in your brain and it's stuck like that now."

Erin bit down on her tongue to keep from lashing out in response.

Bringing herself under control, she bitterly remarked, through barely parted lips, "I'm so glad you find all of this a joke."

Tilly made a show of looking mock-wounded by this, but her levity clearly did not diminish.

Yet there was also a sincerity in her eyes as she said, "Erin, let me spell it out for you. If you're going to survive this tragic ordeal, you'll need to find a way to step outside of it sometimes. And, yes, that means seeing the funny side of things. Because if you make yourself an open vessel for the immense seriousness, the unbearable gravity, of it all, it will eat you alive."

Despite the spirit in which it was given, Erin did not take this advice well.

"Gosh, thanks Confucius. I'll be *sure* to keep that in mind," she said sarcastically, rolling her eyes hard.

"Hey, just my two cents."

"No," Erin interjected sharply, suddenly rising to her knees and becoming animated. "It's *my* two cents! You *are* me! And I..." She paused as the thought irrepressibly unfolded before her. "I... am... *alone*."

As the emotional impact of her own words abruptly hit her, she quickly glanced away, glowering and clenching her jaw as she rode out this galling self-ambush.

The stark truth occurred to her. A weakness she had always tried to avoid, but could no longer. In this very instant, she felt it too acutely. And as she was so existentially exhausted, she hadn't even the energy for pretence anymore. Her face relaxed into a sort of self-pitying sadness.

"Fuck... I-I... just wish... I had... some-"

But she cut herself off. Like veering to a skidding halt at the very last second as one drives towards the cliff edge and its promise of release. Even after all that had happened, all she'd suffered, she still couldn't say it, couldn't grant it that power over her. When all else was deprived of fuel, her pride apparently had an extra emergency reserve secreted away. She was not glad to learn this, but not exactly displeased either. It just neatly meshed with the person she thought she *had* to be.

"It's okay, Erin," Tilly offered softly. She had been looking on with concern as Erin's melancholy almost-admission came out. Now she tentatively stretched out a hand as if to call Erin up to the window-seat.

Erin didn't need the invitation. She jumped to her feet anyway. There had been a precipitous switchback in her emotions.

"No! No, it isn't!" she snarled as she came close and glared at Tilly. Her voice was raised and her face was flush with anger.

"Well... perhaps not." Inclining her head in concession, Tilly finished her point in a whisper, "but... in time..."

"Ha! Time?! What has time ever done for me?! Time has stolen her from me! And time is the fucking knife at my back, pushing me towards the big pit where they dump all the corpses to rot into mulch. Time is the *enemy.*"

"I... see."

That was all Tilly could weakly say in return, failing to hide the worry in her voice.

"God, why am I even talking to you? You're just... You're not... I mean, what the fuck even *are* you?"

"I'm the part of you which still loves yourself, which thinks you're still worth saving. And most of all, the part which wants you to forgive yourself."

"Bullshit! How can a part of my own mind be my... what's even the way to say it? Some kind of sappy guardian angel?"

"You 'contain multitudes', Erin."

"What the hell does that mean?! And fuck 'multitudes', one Siamese brain-twin is already too many!"

Tilly just shrugged.

Erin scoffed and shook her head in frustration.

"This is moronic. I should... just be ignoring you. Or, better still, hating you. Because you're not really... *her*! You're me! And I'm a piece of shit!"

Tilly had been trying to remain unflappable. But she lost her patience here.

She retorted sternly, "so... what? Huh? What? You'll just... like, *hate* yourself to death? That it? And what does that achieve? It doesn't help Tilly, doesn't make anything up to her."

"Given I can't draw-and-quarter myself, nothing I could do would properly atone for my abandonment! Nothing! But a good fucking start is to treat myself exactly how I deserve. A thing worthy only of disgust and contempt. Recognising that is something, at least!"

The last thing Tilly was going to do now was pile on. It was time to de-escalate this, steer it in a better direction.

She explained in an understanding, kindly tone, "look, yes, you messed up. You did something stupid. But you were... scared... and traumatized... and alone. That's it, Erin. That's all it is. Just a mistake. You didn't do it out of malice or cold-heartedness. You just... did it. So stop hoping to manufacture a way to think of yourself as a monster. You're not. And you never were."

Erin just looked around in exasperation, as she tried to find a way to refute Tilly's point. She tried to stay fired up, to hold onto her aimless rage, but that anger inside her was rapidly simmering down to nought at the genuine compassion in Tilly's voice. The best she could do was keep the facade of being mad plastered upon her face.

"I... can't... accept that!"

"I get that. I do." A great, knowing pity flashed in her gaze. "You wanted to allocate blame for Tilly's accident, so you could make sense of it. But there was no-one and nothing, just the impartially cruel caprice of chance. And so you found the... whole world guilty of inflicting her misfortune, and withdrew from it. Yet all that accumulated... venom... was still swirling around inside you, with no target close at hand. So, like a corrosive acid, it ate through its casks and spilled onto you. Because there was only you left. And despite the fact that you didn't deserve it, it was better than always having no outlet for your hatred."

"I... *did* deserve it. Or... some... of it, at the very least."

"No. What happened to Tilly was a tragedy, but in a very real sense that tragedy happened to you too. Making a poor decision in the wake of a horrible event which scrambles your thinking and upends your life is totally understandable. Totally forgivable. You say that you know time as a thief and a murderer? Well, eventually it will rob you of your sense of blame and kill your self-hatred. And... then... you will be able to heal."

"It's... it's not about me! It's about her! She needed me!"

"Erin, she was *unconscious*. She had no awareness of whether you were there. You wanted to be by her side, and that's fine. It made sense because she might have woken up and you being there would've been important then. But she didn't and she wasn't going to."

"But-"

Tilly cut her off. No more digressions. The most consequential test had to be issued. Tilly didn't know if Erin was ready for it. But it was nevertheless time to see if she could make herself be.

"Now you need to ask *the* question. You know which one I mean. It's the one you'll scarcely even let yourself utter in your own head. The one weighing on your heart with impossible heaviness, like a skyscraper squeezing the granite it's atop. It has to come out."

"W-what..." Erin started off unsteadily. But then she clamped her mouth shut as her lower lip began to quiver and the teariness appeared in her eyes. She quickly stared upwards, willing the tears not to fall. All she could do was firmly shake her head in overwhelmed muteness.

"You can, Erin. You have to."

She stamped her foot repeatedly to try and spur herself to say the *hideous* thing. It seemed impossible that she could ever build up to something like this, but she was trying. And trying and trying. And then, finally, she hit herself in the leg with the back of her fist and convulsively just made herself do it.

"What if she's now... d-dead?!"

The words spilled from her lips rapidly, inarticulately. The first tears ran down her cheeks.

"Then... she's dead."

Tilly took a long pause to let that sink in.

"And she would have died whether you were there or not."

CHAPTER TWENTY-ONE

5:55 AM. APRIL 17TH.

(APPROX. THREE DAYS LATER)

It was incredibly windy outside. The gusts could be heard rushing fiercely against the window, as they smothered the sides of the apartment building. It was like a predator tentatively probing the defenses of prospective prey, trying to find any vulnerable openings to exploit. And in light of that, nothing reminds someone that they're in a tall building better than hearing nature surreptitiously testing whether it can be knocked over. Yet, it's also true that nothing makes one feel cozier in one's dwelling than hearing these attempts and knowing they're doomed to fail. A safe vantage point to observe the impotent fury of the elements as though any other minor amusement. Or even to simply ignore it, as whim dictates. Such is mankind's supreme domination of the natural forces which once exercised totalitarian rule over his ancestors.

"You're going to make yourself feel sick to your stomach, young lady," Tilly scolded in a semi-ironic mothering tone.

"Yeah, maybe," Erin mumbled back, self-consciously covering her still half-full mouth with her hand. That was all she was willing to concede. And she definitely didn't hold off from again digging her spoon into the big rectangular tub of ice-cream.

They were both sat upon the bed, facing each other. Erin was up by the pillows with the laptop open before her, and Tilly was down by the end of the bed. Erin was disinterestedly scanning through a news article on the screen. Whereas Tilly was just blatantly staring at her eating, wearing an expression which somehow mixed mild concern and judgemental scrutiny and curiosity.

"Do you even like ice-cream? I've literally never seen you have it before."

"Meh."

"Meh? Then why are you eating it?"

"What does it matter?" she replied casually, shrugging. "I remembered it was at the back of the freezer, and... yeah, I don't know, it just felt right in some weird way. For this situation, I mean. Plus... it doesn't really seem like 'food', you know? It's just, like... frozen... flavoured... sugar."

"Alright..."

Erin kept eating, but the growing irritation on her face made it clear that the needling had succeeded. She was thinking more about Tilly's comments than about trying to enjoy the ice-cream she was shovelling into her mouth. She lay the spoon down for a moment, resting the handle on the edge of the tub, and looked up from the screen peevishly.

"It's not poison, you know. I mean, jeez, I can't treat myself to a little ice-cream?"

"I know it's not *poison*, Erin. But, two things." She held up a finger. "You obviously don't even really like ice-cream. You're just anxiety-eating." Then she flipped up a second finger. "That's a big tub of ice-cream to finish in one sitting. And it seems like you're just going to keep eating and eating while we wait, unless someone helps you stop."

"Golly gosh, you're so right. Thanks so much for saving me from myself, *mom*. Go ahead and take it from me." She picked up the whole tub and, poorly suppressing an arch smirk, offered it to Tilly to take. "Here you go."

Tilly did not reach out to grab it.

She just raised an eyebrow and looked both irked and unimpressed.

"No?... You're sure?... Damn, I guess I'll just have to keep on eating it then."

Erin put the tub back down and picked up the spoon to scoop out another unsatisfying mouthful of the bland vanilla ice-cream. Who she was really spiting by doing this was... debatable.

"You... are... a... hoot," Tilly said slowly, stressing each word.

"I know, right?" Erin batted back smugly. With a big toothy smile, she theatrically raised the spoon high in the air in triumph. As if she were a

307

knight cheering and waving the enemy's standard after a great battle.

"Hey, just don't come crying to me when you're running to the toilet to throw up two liters of yellow goop..."

This disgusting visual served its purpose. And then some.

Erin's merry cockiness was rudely punctured. And her expression soured with startling immediacy. Maybe she had been having fun at Tilly's expense, but... there was still no call to do *that*. She twitched her mouth to one side in annoyance and emphatically dumped the spoon into the tub, even though it had been half-way towards delivering the next mouthful.

"Nice. Real fucking nice."

"Yeah, well... it can be a thankless job, trying to help you."

They now spent a while without saying another word. Just intently avoiding each other's eyes, as the ice-cream lay there gradually melting.

Eventually, Tilly took the plunge and broke the tense silence.

"How long are we going to wait for?"

"As long as it takes."

"And if she doesn't come online for another, say, four hours?"

"Then we'll just have to keep each other comp-" Erin stopped mid-word as her brain re-parsed what Tilly just said. "Wait, 'she'?"

"Ah, yes..." Tilly said through an exhalation. The pained look on her face betrayed her frustration at having been caught out. "She."

"I... never mentioned a gender... I don't even know it."

"Yes. Hmm. About that..."

"Just spit it out, would you?"

"I... like, kinda... sorta... talked to her."

"*You*... talked to her? What... the fuck... does that even mean? You're... just... me."

"Uh... *yeah*..."

As Tilly let this hang, she jutted her chin out and narrowed her eyes, encouraging Erin to see the obvious and catch on.

"Ahhhh..." Erin stretched out the syllable as she tipped her head back and the realization dawned upon her. "Oh, that's just great. Another feat of fucked-up-ness from my brain, clearly going for the goddamn gold in the schizophrenic olympics."

"Yeah, uh, sorry about that..." Tilly offered, abashedly looking down and rubbing her elbow.

"Well, fuck, can I expect many more fun little revelations about how broken my fucking mind is?"

Tilly met Erin's gaze, with the tiniest hint of sadness coalescing in her eyes.

"Not many, no."

Erin was too busy being sulky to pick up on the subtle doleful tone of that answer.

"So, awesome, now that I know that... uhhh, *myself* and my friend were conspiring together against me, I suppose I ought to ask what *I* learned behind my own back..."

"Hmm, there wasn't that much you'd really care about. We were just, like... uh... talking shop."

"You've gotta give me something, at least!"

"Oh, well, her... name is Grace."

"Grace..." Erin pronounced the name slowly, rolling it around in her mind and seeing how well it fit. "Okay. Grace. What else?"

"Umm... she's in her forties... three daughters... a homebody, and lonely, like us-"

"Not *quite* like us, of course," Erin interjected, expecting herself to smile as she said it, but finding she could not.

"Yes, not... quite." Tilly became bashful, glancing away and nervously drumming her fingers on her legs. Then, as her eyes drifted back to Erin, there was a striking soberness displayed upon her face. "Listen to me. She has... a good heart, I can tell. And she really does want to help you."

Erin gave a terse nod in acknowledgement.

"I know it," she muttered guiltily. "Uh, is there, like, anything else about her I ought to be apprised of?"

Tilly thought it over for a moment and then answered simply, "no, not really. Your talks with her should be insight enough. I suspect she has already given you all you need to judge her character for yourself."

Although the actual emotional content of annoyance didn't materialize inside her mind, Erin felt like she *should* be vexed by this answer. So she just decided that she was.

"Hey, no more secrets, you!"

Tilly was getting pretty tired of hearing this kind of thing. It was high time that she laid down the law.

"*Erin...*" She stressed the name as she began, as if explaining something impossibly simple to a child. "I am the eidolon *you* fashioned from the raw material of your hoard of secrets. So *I* decide what you need to know and when you're able to hear it."

"You... know more than me?" Erin asked, furrowing her brow skeptically.

Tilly just gave her a bemused, condescending look.

"Given all that's happened, don't you think you should proceed on the assumption that I do?..."

"How... can you know something I don't? I don't get it... you're just a part of *my* mind."

"More than, uh, most people... your mind is... well, made up of intermeshing labyrinths of... *compartmentalization*. I can navigate and manipulate them, because I'm operating from the inside. Whereas, you?... Ummm, not so much..."

"I... don't know what... to do with that fact..."

"There is nothing *to do* with it. Which is why I didn't feel the need to expound on it to you before now. Generally, I try to just give you... useable truths."

"And I'm supposed to just.... have faith... that you can make that distinction for me? That you should get to decide which crumbs to mete out?"

"*I am your mind, Erin, trying to fix your mind.* Don't you think that warrants a certain level of.... solidarity? Of... trust? I mean, damn, don't you trust me?"

Erin briefly considered this and then said tartly, "no more than I have to."

"Ha, now we're getting somewhere. Maybe you're not as dumb as I thought," Tilly responded airily, with a chuckle.

"This isn't fair! I want to know absolutely, positively everything!"

"Of course you do. But, look, even if there was a button I could just press, you would be struck utterly snowblind by a... jumbled and incomprehensible... blizzard of raw information. The crucial bottleneck of that wetware in your head is that you can only think *one* thought at a time. A long, unbroken monologue... but rendered sentence by sentence. So, if someone tried to cram the lost novella of your life into the very next sentence-sized slot? You'd have to attempt to process it all at once. Computers *hard-crash* when they're overloaded with input... Let's not find out what the brain does, hmm?"

"Bleh, where the hell is the glitzy future that sci-fi has been promising me? In between, whatever, banging androids and jacking hover-cars, I could fix this problem lickety-fucking-split. I'd just go get a back-alley cybernetic implant and my upgraded grey matter would have no problem crunching this shit!"

Tilly couldn't help but chortle at this. Still, she had the sense that Erin was rather missing the point.

"Maybe so. But you'll have to make do with the old-fashioned way for now. Besides, you are in an incredibly rare position of opportunity, of insight. Here you sit as searcher, and here I sit as sage. But we are one and the same. Not many are lucky enough for a fruitful conversation with themselves to be possible. It just requires a little patience, you know?"

Erin rolled her eyes and folded her arms petulantly.

"Some fucking opportunity if there are questions you won't answer."

"Hey now, just like the world you live in, my playground has certain immutable laws I must abide. You can't defy gravity and I can't tell you the things you're not ready to hear yet. But just because you can't fly doesn't mean you can't get to places worth going. Even if it does take a bit more effort to walk there. So just set about thinking of the *right* questions, and you'll learn a lot more than you did before, at the very least."

Another eye-roll, even more exaggerated this time. And a scoff for good measure.

"Goodness gracious, how exciting! I mean, seriously. *Hold. Me. Back.*"

Tilly was now starting to get a little miffed. Erin wasn't just looking a gift horse in the mouth, she was 3D-printing an exact replica of its teeth for closer inspection *and* demanding to see its last ten years of detailed equine dental records... only to, at long last, emphatically *still* turn her nose up at it. There was ordinary, everyday ungratefulness and then there was making an art form out of it. And Tilly wasn't particularly inclined to credit Erin for this achievement. Not one bit.

"I'm soooo sorry that getting to interrogate your own psyche face-to-face is a trifling affair to you, just because there's a couple limitations. I suppose I should also apologize because I couldn't make it a three-way call with freaking... Yahweh... himself as well, right? Like, for real Erin, you're getting hung up on the silliest thing. Hasn't it occurred to you that if there *is* stuff you don't know you know, you probably wouldn't even be able to formulate a specific enough question to get at it?"

"Oh, I bet I could!" Erin fired back with self-assured quickness.

Just the faintest hint of a furtive smile passed over Tilly's face. A teachable moment, perhaps?

"Oh yeah? Let's see then. You can ask one totally free, unconstrained question. Just one. Maybe we'll run into some of those invisible walls, but I'll do my very best to answer it truthfully. Scout's honor. So, go for it, *hotshot.*"

At this invitation, Erin clapped her hands together excitedly. Then she bit her lip in concentration and set about devising the perfect loophole question. She wasn't going to waste this chance. No way, no how. She was going fishing for bombshells.

Tilly just sat there impatiently rolling her head around on her shoulders in slow revolutions.

Soon enough, Erin slapped her knee happily and locked eyes with Tilly.

"Okay, tell me: how does all of *this* end?"

Tilly tutted and retorted, "how the hell am I supposed to know that? I'm not some fortune-teller in a carnival booth."

"No shit. Look, I'm not asking you for the damn lottery numbers. I'm just perceptive enough to realize that I'm not fully in control of what's going to happen. Now, maybe you aren't either, but I figure you've got a better vantage to issue a, let's say, educated guess from."

"I should have guessed that you were going to pull some smart-ass crap, huh? You know, you're usually not one for spoilers..."

"Yeah, well, whatevs. When it's your life that's the movie, you make exceptions. Now, quit your bellyaching and tell me."

Tilly was very hesitant to speak. She ran her fingers through her long flowing red hair as she deliberated. This was not at all the way she had seen this going. She had inadvertently backed herself into a corner.

"I... truly believe... that you'll end up in a good place," she said softly, with a voice made fluttery by a heavy heart. "And hopefully... that's enough."

Galvanised by a sudden spasm of exasperation, Erin threw up her hands and huffed.

She muttered in a surly tone, "eurgh, be more vague. Like, if you could."

Tilly instantly smiled as the most appropriate response came to mind, and struggled to keep from laughing to herself before she delivered the punchline.

"Play stupid games, win stupid prizes."

Despite herself, Erin smiled at this too. Jousting with Tilly was always fun at least.

She picked up the spoon and started eating the ice-cream again, which was now half-melted.

Between idly shoving spoonfuls into her mouth, she said, "this is medicinal ice-cream, don't you know?" And, after gesturing at her throat with the spoon, she explained, "sore throat. Struggling to speak as it is."

"Uh, for the umpteenth time, let me reiterate: you don't actually have to speak out loud. You can, like, just think the words and-"

"Yeah, yeah, I know all that. I... just like real talking. And this gives me a reason to. Otherwise it's just... the silence, and the silence reminds me that I'm actually-"

"Okay," Tilly interrupted quickly. "That's fair enough."

They both awkwardly looked away. Tilly's face twitched with self-reproach. She was kicking herself for having walked straight into that one. Preserving the wellness and stability of Erin's mindstate right now was her first priority. And that had been an avoidable fumble.

The only noises which punctuated the uncomfortable quiet were from Erin eating. There was the wet thud each time she stabbed the spoon edge into the bed of ice-cream, and there was the faint clinking whenever her teeth touched the spoon.

Keen to rectify her mistake, and get things back on track, Tilly threw out a question.

"How are you feeling about reconnecting with Grace?"

"Anxious. Very anxious. And..." - she paused her devouring of the ice-cream to glance up at the ceiling and sigh - "ashamed. Just, like, really fucking ashamed of how I treated her. I couldn't really blame her if she wanted nothing more to do with me."

"You were... *unwell*, Erin..."

"Ha, 'were,'" she shot back with a dry chuckle.

"Yes, yes, very good," Tilly granted, with raised eyebrows and a poorly concealed smile of her own. This burgeoning newfound ability to poke fun at the situation was a reassuring development.

"Sure, okay, yes, I was... well, yeah... but still, it wasn't right, it doesn't excuse..."

Erin trailed off as something popped up on her laptop's screen, catching her eye.

"Shit! Your timing was fucking impeccable!" Panicked, she tossed the spoon into the tub and dumped it down beside the bed. Then she locked eyes with Tilly for emotional support. "She's online! Fuck, fuck, motherfucker, fuckity fuck fuck. It says she's online now. Like, right this second!"

"Relax... Just breathe. Stay calm and just breathe. It's going to go just fine."

"What do I say?!... What can-"

"Erin! Just say hello..."

[Alabaster&Freckles - is now online]

[06:42] PluckingPurgatory'sPetals: Hi Grace, it's Erin.

[06:42] Alabaster&Freckles: Hello there, Erin.

"She said hello back!" Erin exclaimed with exuberant happiness, punching the air. It was like seeing someone surprised to get the big-ticket birthday gift they hadn't dared to even hope for.

Tilly smiled good-naturedly and said, "imagine that..."

[06:43] Alabaster&Freckles: I can't even tell you how glad and relieved I was to see your username pop-up on my screen just now.

As Erin was just staring at this follow-up message in pleased astonishment, Tilly broke her reverie by prompting, "sorry to cut short your rejoicing and all, but don't leave the woman hanging now."

"Yes. Yes! You're right!"

[06:45] PluckingPurgatory'sPetals: I know the feeling, believe me! I've... really missed you.

[06:45] PluckingPurgatory'sPetals: And I would really like to talk.

[06:46] PluckingPurgatory'sPetals: There's... so much to discuss. So much I need to say.

[06:46] PluckingPurgatory'sPetals: Uh, I mean, if that's okay with you?...

[06:46] Alabaster&Freckles: Darling, if you want to tell it, I want to hear it.

Erin first apologized *at length*, sparing no elaborate expression of contrition. In return, Grace was kind enough to say that she was not the grudge-holding type, that all was forgiven. It was possible that this was even true. After all, Erin had heard it said that mothers were creatures of endless clemency.

Moving on to the business at hand, Erin went about giving a full overview of what had happened and what she had learned. She forced herself to omit absolutely nothing. That made it a very, very emotionally onerous undertaking. There was so much which made her face redden with shame to admit, so much which made her cringe at how crazy it sounded when typed out plainly. But she swallowed her embarrassment and self-pity. This comprehensive disclosure had to be done. Someone else besides

Erin had to know this absurd tale in its entirety. That, at least, would go some way to unburdening her soul.

"Hey there, babycat, you're still, like, actually breathing, right? You're so still when you're watching that screen that it's sometimes hard to tell."

Tilly spoke softly, asking a question she didn't need the answer to, just to get Erin's attention.

It took Erin more than a few seconds to register what Tilly had said. At which point, she jerked her head away from the screen and looked at Tilly curiously.

"Of course I'm still breathing! You see me hooked up to a ventilator machine or something? I mean, what kind of question is that?..."

She was about to return to obsessively staring at the chat window but then stopped and looked at Tilly again.

"Alright, I... admit that I *have* sometimes been holding my breath when I'm waiting for her response. I mean, this bizarre, batshit crazy story I'm telling her... like, just, fuck. I'm all light-headed and panicky as I'm typing this out. Fucking fight-or-flight is kicking in, man."

"This feeling is gonna pass, I promise. You just need to keep breathing nice and slowly, Erin: in and out, in and out. It will help keep you grounded."

"I'm trying! I'm just so nervous each time I send the next serialised installment of this grade-A fucking insanity to her. It's like pins and needles in the base of my skull. I'm talking the *bad* type of tingle, the type that makes you feel like you might, uh, pass out."

"That's exactly why you should try to control your breathing, deep breaths will-"

"Enough with the incessant 'breathing' shit! Okay?! You're starting to sound like some weird fucking infomercial for fresh air!"

"I was just trying to offer some advice..." Tilly said reproachfully. She looked away, a little injured by the put-down.

"Hey…" Erin cooed quietly at seeing the effect her brusqueness had had. Tilly looked back around questioningly and Erin went on, in a conciliatory tone. "I'm just… look, I'm sorry, I'm just… like, trying to… like, I *have* to finish writing this up for Grace. I'm very nearly at the end of recounting it all. And I have to get this out of me. It's like fucking word vomit. I just… want it out of me."

"Okay. I get that. Do your thing."

With her face impassive and her tone flat, a shrug was all that accompanied this answer. This lack of any emotional clues was maddening. As was the intention. For it was, in its way, a subtle little punishment.

Erin continued staring at Tilly, trying to figure out whether or not this was a mess which still needed to be fixed. Soon, she decided that either way it would have to wait and went back to attending to the IM conversation.

[07:29] Alabaster&Freckles: And what was your reaction to 'Tilly' still being there without the drug? Beyond just the surprise of it. I'm talking about how it made you feel, on a deeper level.

[07:31] PluckingPurgatory'sPetals: Hmm, I don't know, first of all it kinda made me feel sick to my stomach. Because it proved, beyond any doubt, that something had snapped in my mind, something is definitely on the fritz.

[07:32] PluckingPurgatory'sPetals: They say that reality is whatever persists regardless of whether you believe in it, right?

[07:32] PluckingPurgatory'sPetals: Well, I've made 'Tilly' *my* reality now. I'm stuck with it. She's with me all my waking hours. I can't just blink and make her go away. And that's pretty alarming.

[07:33] Alabaster&Freckles: Woah, wait, so she's there *all* the time? Every single second?

[07:33] Alabaster&Freckles: Like, she's with you *right now*?

Erin looked up at Tilly and just took her in for a long moment. Tilly met her gaze and held it unblinkingly. Chafing at the thick tension resulting from their staring at each other, which was like the stifling gas given off as the byproduct of some chemical reaction, Erin decided to explain herself.

"Grace, uh, asked-" she began, uncertainly, but was abruptly cut off.

Uttering the words with slow, firm emphasis, Tilly interjected, "I know what she said."

The tenseness resumed. Erin nodded very slightly and her face advertised her irritation at her own stupidity, as if to serve as an apology.

"Yes..." she said quietly. "Yes, of course."

"'*Stuck* with it', huh?"

Resentment flashed in Tilly's eyes as she issued this question sternly.

"I... well, uh, I-I didn't... I, like, wasn't trying to... It's just a kind of, uh, figure of speech... And I didn't think that... it would... h-have..."

That was all Erin was able to stammer out, her voice thin and wavering. She stopped herself, recognizing that she was just stumbling over her words and making things worse. It's generally best to stop trying to dig yourself out of the hole when you *start* to feel the blistering heat of the Earth's molten core. Because through that, you will not burrow. So do not try. However tantalising the imagined-escape of emerging at the other side of the planet, or the shitty situation, may be.

There is no refuge for you at the glorious antipole of things. It cannot solve your problems. It cannot shield you from your errors. It is but a chimerical place, a false and malicious lodestar whose pursual only serves to hasten the end of the easily-duped.

Striving to regroup and figure out what she *should* say, Erin just looked down into her lap to buy some time.

But Tilly continued staring pointedly at her and seized upon this apparent retreat.

"I'm here to freaking help you, Erin." She narrowed her eyes and repeated harshly, "*you.*"

The weight of this fractious response was bearing down upon Erin oppressively. She nervously twiddled her fingers around in the material of her pyjama shorts. Most of all though, she was just confused. She was questioning whether she should even feel bad about hurting her imaginary friend's feelings. But the fact is... she did.

Nevertheless, now that she knew *this* Tilly wasn't real, oughtn't there to be certain benefits? A certain lessening of responsibility? It surely stood to reason that she didn't have the same social obligations to an apparition as she would with a flesh-and-blood person. In fact, she could ultimately just ignore what it was doing or disregard what it had to say, as she saw fit. And yet... she knew she could never bring herself to do that. 'Tilly' was not a real person, but, still, she sure felt like one. And, crucially, she kept Erin company. Erin did not want to jeopardize this, by constantly reminding her brain that the hallucination was just that, and end up entirely alone. This delusory companionship was better than nothing, at least. And it was therefore worth expending some effort to preserve.

"I... didn't mean it like that, okay? I was talking about the... like... umm... phenomenon itself. Not you," she said apologetically, without looking up or ceasing her anxious fidgeting.

"Okay."

This was an unconvincing reply, to put it mildly. But it was also evidently the best she was going to get.

Erin slowly looked up, searching Tilly's face. The animosity had definitely faded, but the fact that her arms were crossed suggested that some residual defensiveness remained.

"So... alright... uh, what now?..." she carefully ventured.

Tilly just jutted her chin towards the laptop and said, "we both know the IM window is flashing again. So, go check it."

"I... meant... like, are we actually okay?"

"It's not..." Tilly started to say, before sighing heavily in displeasure. There was quite a lengthy pause. Then she concluded, flatly, by simply restating, "just check the chat, Erin."

Erin had no choice but to acquiesce. The alternative was to keep on poking the bear to ask whether it's definitely *sure* you're not appetizing. She pulled the laptop a bit closer and looked at the newest messages.

[07:36] Alabaster&Freckles: You still with me, chica?
[07:39] Alabaster&Freckles: ...Erin?

She began typing very slowly and deliberatively, newly wary of the fact that Tilly was also reading all of it.

[07:40] PluckingPurgatory'sPetals: Yeah, sorry, I'm still here.

[07:40] PluckingPurgatory'sPetals: And, yes, Tilly is here opposite me, on the bed.

[07:41] Alabaster&Freckles: Wow, okay. So, were you just talking with her?

Erin hesitated before responding, slightly raising her fingertips up off the keyboard. She took a deep breath and glanced at Tilly.

"What are you looking at me for?" Tilly asked, with a faint sharpness infused in her tone. "Tell her the truth. That's the whole point, isn't it?"

[07:42] PluckingPurgatory'sPetals: Kind of. Something I just said to you upset her.

[07:43] Alabaster&Freckles: I see. And you were dealing with the fallout, I take it?

[07:43] PluckingPurgatory'sPetals: Something like that, yeah.

[07:43] Alabaster&Freckles: Well, I'm sorry that happened. That sucks.

[07:44] Alabaster&Freckles: (By the way, hello Tilly! Long time, no speak...)

Quickly looking up to check in with Tilly once more, Erin saw that she was now sporting a little smirk.

"Okay... that *was* cute," she said bashfully, failing to keep her smile from growing.

Erin smiled back, very glad that something had finally cut through the tension.

"Tell her I say hi back."

"Sure thing."

[07:45] PluckingPurgatory'sPetals: Ha, she liked that!

[07:45] PluckingPurgatory'sPetals: And she asked me to say hello back.

[07:46] Alabaster&Freckles: I'm glad to hear it.

[07:46] Alabaster&Freckles: Hopefully she understands that you're not trying to hurt her feelings, you're just being honest.

[07:47] PluckingPurgatory'sPetals: I think she does. Don't worry, I can speak freely.

[07:47] Alabaster&Freckles: Alright, good. Well then, is there anything else you need to tell me to bring me up to date?

[07:48] PluckingPurgatory'sPetals: Hmm, if memory serves... I don't think so. I think you're basically all caught up now.

[07:48] Alabaster&Freckles: Great, then I hope you don't mind if I ask some more questions?

[07:48] PluckingPurgatory'sPetals: Nope, go for it.

[07:49] Alabaster&Freckles: Given you've had some time to get used to it, how does having Tilly around make you feel *now*?

[07:50] PluckingPurgatory'sPetals: Frankly, it can be a source of... sadness, because it constantly reminds me of what I've lost.

[07:51] PluckingPurgatory'sPetals: And, on top of that, it's also a painful reminder of what's really going on with me. I mean, like, what's wrong with my head.

[07:51] PluckingPurgatory'sPetals: I wanted sooooo badly to believe in tuplas, to make myself think they were truly real.

[07:52] PluckingPurgatory'sPetals: Deep down, I *needed* that to be true. I *needed* to be able to pretend I was... special, that there was some kind of forgotten magic at work, not just... well, mental illness I guess.

[07:53] PluckingPurgatory'sPetals: I couldn't bear for the explanation to be something as commonplace and mundane as that. I didn't want to be broken in a... *boring* way.

[07:54] Alabaster&Freckles: I completely get that. It's natural to try and find a way to exceptionalize our problems.

[07:54] Alabaster&Freckles: We build up stories around them to try and make them seem more interesting, more complex. Because a potent desire to be unique is always at work inside our psyches.

[07:55] Alabaster&Freckles: So, just to confirm, you *do* now accept that it's mental illness?

[07:55] PluckingPurgatory'sPetals: I suppose... I... kinda have to.

[07:55] PluckingPurgatory'sPetals: I just know too much at this point. It's impossible to stop my brain putting two and two together.

[07:56] Alabaster&Freckles: Erin, sweetie, please don't try to minimize the significance of that realization or pull back from fully owning it.

[07:56] Alabaster&Freckles: This is a big deal, it's a giant positive step forward! You should be really proud!

[07:57] Alabaster&Freckles: And what of the epiphany about your girlfriend and the hospital? How do you feel about that whole situation?

[07:58] PluckingPurgatory'sPetals: It was strangely freeing, in a sense. To finally know the truth. It made me feel... I'm not sure what the right word is...

[07:58] PluckingPurgatory'sPetals: *Complete*? If that makes any sense?

[07:59] PluckingPurgatory'sPetals: Like, you're not really *you* without your real history trailing behind you, showing you how you were made the way you are.

[07:59] PluckingPurgatory'sPetals: But that reunification has come at a heavy cost, obviously. It has reacquainted me with my sins and it has reopened old wounds.

[08:00] PluckingPurgatory'sPetals: Oddly, if I'm being totally honest, the resulting sorrow isn't quite as strong as I would've expected it to be. But I suppose that's because I already had to mentally deal with this whole thing once before.

[08:00] PluckingPurgatory'sPetals: The main thing is just... having to live with myself now I know what I did. And that self-disgust is seriously getting to me.

[08:02] PluckingPurgatory'sPetals: Learning who you *really* are is great and all, right up until you realize that you *really* are just a fuck-up and a coward. Selfishly, having that black mark once again stamped in my psyche's recordkeeping somehow feels so much worse than remembering the abandonment which caused it.

[08:03] Alabaster&Freckles: Honey, here's the rub: we are all trying to make up for something or other we once did. That's essentially what life *is*.

[08:04] Alabaster&Freckles: We don't want to be the people who did those things. We hate those people, like mortal enemies. But, in an escapable sense, they *are* us. So we have to make peace with these unpleasant bedfellows, maybe even come to forgive them.

[08:05] Alabaster&Freckles: In the end, we can either seek to actually make amends or try to run away from ourselves.

[08:05] Alabaster&Freckles: And if there is absolution to be had, only one of those options offers the path to it.

[08:06] PluckingPurgatory'sPetals: There is a part of me which still longs to be redeemed. But I... know that simply cannot happen.

[08:06] PluckingPurgatory'sPetals: The story has been written, the ink is dry, the book is now closed. Willing those words already indelibly trapped on the page to change is not going to help me. It's just self-indulgent fantasizing.

[08:07] Alabaster&Freckles: No, that was just one chapter of your life, Erin... it will not define you. There are many more to come before your particular volume is complete.

[08:08] Alabaster&Freckles: And you will now be a more-cognizant author of that remainder. Because I know you'll want to pen an ending which reflects who you truly want to be.

[08:08] PluckingPurgatory'sPetals: Perhaps. I'd *like* to think that's true, anyway.

[08:09] Alabaster&Freckles: Now... I suspect you know what I'm going to ask you next, right?

[08:09] PluckingPurgatory'sPetals: I could field an educated guess, yes.

[08:10] PluckingPurgatory'sPetals: You want to get your hands on my super-secret brownie recipe, no doubt? Haven't made them in a long time, but they *do* have the perfect blend of gooeyness and cakeyness...

[08:10] Alabaster&Freckles: Well then, I can't wait to taste them one day.

[08:11] Alabaster&Freckles: But... just to give us something to do in the meantime...

[08:11] Alabaster&Freckles: Will you go to the hospital? You could visit Tilly AND get help.

[08:11] Alabaster&Freckles: That's a hell of a twofer. It's very rare that everything you need can be found in the same place. Can't say fairer than that, no?

Erin didn't look up from the laptop, but she could feel Tilly staring insistently at her.

"Now's the time to tell her about your... *plan*, don't you think?"

Tilly let the question hang in the air.

Erin just groaned and glumly declared, "I told you, I don't think she's going to take it well. Like, not at all."

"Maybe. Maybe not." A knowing slyness had spread across Tilly's face. She was enjoying this moment tremendously. "But it's what you decided, so... there you go."

Tapping the screen for emphasis, Erin finally glanced up and asked in a whiny tone, "if it's not going to go over well, what's the use in even saying it?"

"I guess... it's... just another thing you *have* to do to get where you're going."

Tilly's grin at Erin's expense was now brazenly obvious. It was reminiscent of the one which big sisters wear because they know they're bugging you with impunity.

As Erin took this answer in, her expression showed she was unimpressed. And nor was she particularly happy about not being in on the joke.

She just offered up the mocking rejoinder, "oooohhhh, another cryptic answer from sensei." And as she returned her attention to the screen, she tacked on the sarcasm-laced addendum, "what *wooould* I do without your wisdom?..."

[08:14] PluckingPurgatory'sPetals: I have to be straight with you... I still can't stomach the idea of going to the hospital. Like, not at all.

[08:15] PluckingPurgatory'sPetals: If I go, they will see how fucking insane I am in a heartbeat. And then they'll, like, keep me there. Do things to me.

[08:16] PluckingPurgatory'sPetals: I'd have NO say about what happens. And that's the only thing I have left: the ability to choose my own fate. Things are bad now, yes, but to be bereft of even that minimum degree of self-ownership, I would have... *absolutely* nothing.

[08:17] Alabaster&Freckles: I don't think that's the way to look at it. Not least because I really, really, really don't think your fears will come true.

[08:17] Alabaster&Freckles: Please trust me: this is your way out of all of this. The people at the hospital will just want to offer their help...

[08:18] PluckingPurgatory'sPetals: That is what they'll say, sure. But, when push comes to shove, they won't hesitate to inflict their 'help' upon me. And that I cannot abide.

[08:19] PluckingPurgatory'sPetals: Look, I'm not naive, I know what they do to crazies. *Especially* crazies with no family to speak of.

[08:19] PluckingPurgatory'sPetals: I'll be thrown into a padded room and put on a diet of tranquilizers to render me a compliant, drooling invalid.

[08:20] PluckingPurgatory'sPetals: And they'll only remember to take me out of my cell for fucking shock therapy, where they try to zap away the last of your personality.

[08:20] Alabaster&Freckles: This is me you're talking to, Erin. So, *knock it off* with the paranoia theatrics.

[08:21] Alabaster&Freckles: I'm dead serious, from now on, no more of this 'aw shucks, woe is me, the whole world is out to get me' baloney.

[08:21] Alabaster&Freckles: You may want to play the wised-up cynic, but I know you don't actually think that way. You're way too smart to really believe in that silliness. I mean it.

[08:22] PluckingPurgatory'sPetals: Okay... fine... maybe I am being a *wee* bit hyperbolic for effect.

[08:23] PluckingPurgatory'sPetals: But it is true that they'll be able to do whatever they want to me. I've read all about 'psychiatric holds'. And I'll appear to rate pretty highly on the potential-danger-to-themselves chart, don't you think?...

[08:23] PluckingPurgatory'sPetals: So I will most likely be kept there "for my own good" and subjected to whatever treatment they deem necessary. There's no way in hell those things will be pleasant.

[08:24] PluckingPurgatory'sPetals: Yet even if they *were* simply gonna prescribe back rubs and cotton-candy... I don't give a shit. It's the loss of control alone which makes me feel sick to my stomach.

[08:25] Alabaster&Freckles: I understand why you're afraid, I really do. I know it would be really difficult for you to give up control and put yourself in the hands of doctors who want to treat your mental illness.

[08:26] Alabaster&Freckles: However, that is the price of getting the help you so sorely need. And once you're there, being tended to by good people who just want to help you get better, you'll see that there was nothing to worry about.

[08:27] PluckingPurgatory'sPetals: It's... possible that you're right.

[08:28] PluckingPurgatory'sPetals: But it's also very possible that you're mistaken. And if so, I will be trapping myself in a situation I'll detest so much that it will gradually kill my soul.

[08:28] PluckingPurgatory'sPetals: So, the potential upside is... fine; the potential downside is unbearable hell.

[08:28] PluckingPurgatory'sPetals: That's why, in my judgment, I'm just better off not risking it at all.

[08:29] Alabaster&Freckles: Oh darling, you have to rip off this band-aid. It's not helping to heal your wounds, it's just hiding them from the world.

[08:29] Alabaster&Freckles: You can't go on kidding yourself that as long as you keep them out of sight, everything can just stay the same.

[08:30] Alabaster&Freckles: The wounds will start to fester, Erin. *That's what open wounds do.*

[08:30] Alabaster&Freckles: Letting that psychological-gangrene just spread and spread is a really bad idea.

[08:31] Alabaster&Freckles: Because if things do get to that point, losing the parts of yourself you'll have to amputate to survive will be ten times worse than the hardship of seeking help now.

[08:33] PluckingPurgatory'sPetals: Hmm, I suppose this would be the time to explain something to you...

[08:33] PluckingPurgatory'sPetals: (Gah, this is not easy. I feel like I'm always disappointing you.)

[08:34] PluckingPurgatory'sPetals: First of all... look, you know I appreciate your advice, like soooo much. I know it comes from a place of concern, of friendship, of kindness, and that means a lot to me.

[08:35] PluckingPurgatory'sPetals: But I just don't agree with your assessment here. I mean, sure, on a long enough timescale, my condition *may* start to worsen.

[08:35] PluckingPurgatory'sPetals: However, I believe things with me are at least... *stable* for the time being. I've sort of arrived at a strange kind of equilibrium point. It's a chance to finally just breathe.

[08:36] PluckingPurgatory'sPetals: I suspect that I can eke out an okay existence right now. Because I'm no longer the captive plaything of my own ignorance. And I'm not just constantly tripping from one derangement to the next. And I have Tilly as a companion.

[08:36] PluckingPurgatory'sPetals: So... I think I just want to sit in this comfortable stasis for a while.

[08:36] PluckingPurgatory'sPetals: That's, like, what I've decided on.

[08:37] Alabaster&Freckles: Jesus, Erin, you *want* to just try and coast along in limbo? I'm not even sure what to say to that.

[08:37] Alabaster&Freckles: Besides to ask this, I guess... did 'Tilly' convince you that this was what you should do?!

Tilly had been passing the time by absentmindedly picking at her cuticles. When this last message appeared on-screen, she suddenly stopped and snorted air through her nose in amusement.

"That. Is. Awesome." Her face lit up with merriment. "She really doesn't get it yet, does she?"

"Just relax, you," Erin dispiritedly muttered. She was visibly unhappy at having to state what now *needed* to be stated.

She began typing slowly, hesitantly. And she winced miserably at the difficulty of trying to word things correctly. Her henpecking fingertips bashed out heavy keystrokes, as though hoping to hurt the keyboard in retaliation for what it was enabling her to say.

[08:39] PluckingPurgatory'sPetals: No, Grace, it's not like that. It's not like that at all.

[08:39] PluckingPurgatory'sPetals: In point of fact, Tilly really tried to *dissuade* me from choosing this path. She was actually advocating for exactly the same thing as you.

[08:40] PluckingPurgatory'sPetals: So, like, you needn't fret about Tilly being a bad influence on me. The truth is that you two have made common cause together. You're both paid-up, card-carrying members of the 'Save Erin' club, don't worry.

[08:40] Alabaster&Freckles: Well, I suppose I should be heartened to learn that you do have another voice of reason counseling you, but given the particular source, I find it rather hard to be.

[08:41] Alabaster&Freckles: I just don't get it. Everything seems to finally be aligned to help you end this nightmare you've been trying so desperately to wake up from. And yet, somehow, still you demur...

[08:41] Alabaster&Freckles: It just... doesn't make any sense to me. Not at all.

[08:41] Alabaster&Freckles: The fact that you're still so hellbent on this self-destructive path really saddens me. Do you really dislike yourself that much?

"Ha, 'dislike,'" Erin repeated aloud, mocking the euphemism contemptuously. She had a hair-trigger aversion to even the slightest trace of an attempted guilt-trip.

Tilly didn't even look up from braiding her hair.

[08:42] PluckingPurgatory'sPetals: Of course I do. And as far as I'm concerned, there's nothing irrational about it.

[08:42] PluckingPurgatory'sPetals: Listen, I basically live in my own head, alright? I know what it looks like in there. All the flaws, all the neuroses, all the ugliness.

[08:43] PluckingPurgatory'sPetals: And if what I see there was transposed onto somebody else, I would despise them. Like, straight up.

[08:43] PluckingPurgatory'sPetals: So why should I grant myself some special dispensation? What makes me *so* great, *so* worthy that I deserve the wholesale forgiveness I wouldn't give to others?

[08:44] Alabaster&Freckles: I think it's about looking at those things in a different way. Viewing them as temporary barriers to becoming the person you want to be, rather than permanent, disfiguring marks of shame.

[08:46] Alabaster&Freckles: I'm not gonna sit here and pretend that I've managed to fully achieve that enlightened perspective-shift myself. But there *are* people who have truly found a way to love themselves unconditionally. So it must be doable, wouldn't you say?

[08:46] PluckingPurgatory'sPetals: Bleh. I'm infinitely suspicious of those people and their supposed accomplishments...

[08:47] PluckingPurgatory'sPetals: I mean, what kind of twisted motherfucker looks inside their mind and actually *likes* what they see? That's some dark shit right there.

[08:47] PluckingPurgatory'sPetals: Although, hey, I'm sure that if you allow yourself to be brainwashed by the gospels of the 'self-help' hucksters, you can probably make yourself believe anything.

[08:48] PluckingPurgatory'sPetals: But I've heard their spiel, and it's not for me. It's all make-believe, feel-good bullshit. Absolving you of accountability for your sins by saying *awww, poor baby, it's not your fault, you didn't know any better.*

[08:49] PluckingPurgatory'sPetals: If that's the price of the pardon, fuck that. I'd rather live honestly, even if it means consciously being on the run from perdition. That's just how it is.

[08:50] Alabaster&Freckles: But if you want to retain that sense of personal responsibility at all costs, doesn't that entail trying to improve yourself and your situation?

[08:50] Alabaster&Freckles: I won't deny it will be difficult. Yet, if you can summon the strength to do it, it will have been *earned*, you know? No-one will have just given you anything, you'll have fought for it yourself.

[08:51] Alabaster&Freckles: And whatever you may think about past mistakes weighing you down, you would be making some real headway in proving that they don't define you anymore.

[08:52] PluckingPurgatory'sPetals: What you suggest sounds real swell and all, but let me tell you something I've come to realize. Something I've thought about... a lot. Hopefully it will help you to understand the impossibility of my predicament.

[08:52] PluckingPurgatory'sPetals: Grace, I'm *weak*.

[08:53] PluckingPurgatory'sPetals: Weak in the soul, weak as a person. It's not easy to admit that - to yourself, or especially to someone you like and respect - but there it is. A cold, hard fact, as unmalleable as coal.

[08:53] PluckingPurgatory'sPetals: It's why I didn't stay at the hospital and do the right thing. It's why I can't leave my apartment now. Don't you see? It's why I only ever choose the easy way out.

[08:54] PluckingPurgatory'sPetals: Of course, we all fear that we might be weak, don't we? That gnawing suspicion lurks at the back of your mind. It's always passionately arguing its case, always making you question your every past deed.

[08:54] PluckingPurgatory'sPetals: And how badly you hope, with every ounce of your flimsy being, that it's not so. *No, please, not me,* you beg no-one in particular.

[08:55] PluckingPurgatory'sPetals: But I no longer have even that comforting uncertainty. The accumulated proof is just too undeniable.

[08:56] PluckingPurgatory'sPetals: I mean, when a very specific set of symptoms line up, nobody denies that person has the associated disease, right? It's just that weakness happens to be *my* hideous cancer.

[08:57] Alabaster&Freckles: Okay, honey, you know I'm not going to sign off on that self-description. I couldn't, even if I wanted to. Because sooo much of what I've learned about you completely contradicts it.

[08:57] Alabaster&Freckles: I know you to be almost-preternaturally tough, determined, and gifted at getting things done. A tenacious survivor, through and through.

[08:58] Alabaster&Freckles: Please remember that your view of yourself is *warped* because of the mental illness. You think you're beholding a true reflection of who you are, when it's actually like staring into some malevolent funhouse mirror.

[08:58] Alabaster&Freckles: Besides, even under the terms of your own analogy, a person isn't to blame when they get sick.

[08:58] Alabaster&Freckles: They deserve sympathy. They deserve to be helped, to be treated so that they can get better.

[08:59] PluckingPurgatory'sPetals: You're right, of course. But that's the thing: the analogy *is not* quite precise. When it comes to finding that you're weak, there's an added sting in the tail.

[09:00] PluckingPurgatory'sPetals: To be stricken with some dire illness is indeed the gratuitous malice of fate. You are, as you say, blameless.

[09:00] PluckingPurgatory'sPetals: But to let *weakness* infest, like termites, the scaffolding which props up your soul?

[09:01] PluckingPurgatory'sPetals: That is not an affliction, that is a failing. And this is what really gets to you. The shame of it burns like a rash across the entire surface of your mind.

[09:02] PluckingPurgatory'sPetals: All else falls away: here I am, weak and naked and alone and afraid. The only way I could possibly be more wretched would be to childishly deny any of that. And if my only solace is to wallow in the pig-shit of the truth, so be it.

Tilly was wide-eyed with surprise and dismay.

"Woah. I didn't think you were going to lay it out... so... I don't know... *like that*." The weight of the shock dragged her voice down to a slow, pensive whisper.

"Yeah, well... it had to be said." Erin's face was very serious. She ground her teeth together as she reflected on her confession. "To myself as well."

The minutes passed sluggishly while Grace conspicuously hadn't responded yet. Erin soon realized she felt a little sick. She was telling herself that she was glad she had said it, and even managed to get halfway to believing that sometimes.

At long last, Grace began messaging back again. And meditating upon how to reply had evidently convinced her not to hold back.

[09:08] Alabaster&Freckles: Erin, I'm not gonna pretend that I'm okay with the 'wallowing' you propose.

[09:08] Alabaster&Freckles: I'll always be here as your friend, always be here to talk to. But I can't help you normalize this state of affairs for yourself. I can't be your enabler. I just won't.

[09:09] Alabaster&Freckles: You seem to think that the worst of it is over, that the storm has passed and you now have the luxury of just serenely sitting around in the wreckage.

[09:09] Alabaster&Freckles: *It hasn't.* This only feels like a respite because you're presently encloistered by the eye of the hurricane as it passes over you. But soon enough, that zone of deceptive calmness will move on, and the tempest-winds will batter you anew.

[09:10] Alabaster&Freckles: This is a crucial tipping point. Because you are, in a sense, both the storm *and* its victim. Which fortunately means that you get to choose how this plays out, what the moral of the story will be. It can either be a tragedy from start to finish, or it can be an arduous journey to salvation.

[09:11] Alabaster&Freckles: Now, you say that what you value most is your personal agency, but frankly I'm starting to doubt that.

[09:11] Alabaster&Freckles: I think that, deep down, you're hoping that if you just wait around long enough, you can eventually pretend you're past the point of no return. And then you'll get to tell yourself that you're officially a lost cause and you simply *have* to go along with the ride.

[09:12] Alabaster&Freckles: Yet your fate is anything but sealed. It rests, even now, in your hands. You can't just abstain, sweetheart: doing nothing is still a choice. And, in fact, the worst one you could make.

When she finished reading these messages, Erin was positively seething. If she had to rationally justify this anger, she would have been hard pressed to do so. But, still, there it was, flowing through her like a dark current. The truth was that, subconsciously, she resented that Grace implicitly claimed to understand what was going on better than her.

She started typing, without thinking.

[09:12] PluckingPurgatory'sPetals: And what if I'm too fucking spineless and too fucking stupid to make any other 'choice' besides that?!

[09:12] PluckingPurgatory'sPetals: What if I'm just a selfish little bitch, and that condemns me to this path?!

She sat back, scowling. Her hands were shaking. Without shifting her position, she reached back and dragged one of the pillows in front of her. Then she elbowed it as hard as she could a dozen or so times, grimacing at the exertion and the venting of rage.

Tilly came close and spoke calmingly into Erin's ear.

"Easy now, Erin, just... take a sec. Just... breathe. Try to stay present, try to stay here with me. Just let this feeling roll off you."

But Erin seemed to take no notice of this. She just went on pounding the point of her elbow down into the now severely misshapen pillow. Brutalizing it as one only ever can bring oneself to do with a voiceless victim. But she soon started to tire, and lose interest in the violence. It was well-timed, then, that she now saw new messages popping up on screen. And so, she threw the pillow back up the bed. There was something disquieting about how that wrath-sponge was promptly discarded once its usefulness was exhausted. For this seemed... revealing, in some uncertain way.

Returning her focus to the laptop, she scrutinized each response as it appeared.

[09:15] Alabaster&Freckles: Erin, I know what you want. I have daughters, remember. You want me to snap at you and haughtily bulldoze your little pity party, so that you can bitterly retreat even further into your position.

At this, Erin's scowl deepened and she muttered under her breath, "that's great, but I'm *not* your fucking daughter."

Just as soon as the words had left her mouth, she huffed and momentarily glanced away as a twinge of intense shame stung her.

[09:15] Alabaster&Freckles: But luckily for you, I know better. I've already made that mistake enough times before.

[09:16] Alabaster&Freckles: So, instead, I'll just point something out. It seems to me that you've become addicted to the torment. And, astonishingly, you have still yet to truly 'bottom out'. In some weird, messed-up way, that fact also serves as a testament to just how *strong* you really are.

[09:17] Alabaster&Freckles: The vast majority of people simply could not have gone through what you've already endured and yet... somehow kept going.

[09:17] Alabaster&Freckles: But this incredible resilience is working against you. There *is* such a thing as sometimes being too tough for your own good.

[09:18] Alabaster&Freckles: Let me put it like this. My brother was a kickboxer for a while, so I ended up seeing a lot of fights. And the saddest thing was when you could just tell that one guy had no chance of beating his opponent. Because the tougher he was, the more unnecessary punishment he'd soak up before inevitably going down.

[09:19] Alabaster&Freckles: My fear is that you may be *so* able to endlessly absorb the beating that there won't be a *no more, no more, I'm done* moment for you, Erin.

[09:20] Alabaster&Freckles: And, at long last, you'll just keel over and die in the ring.

[09:21] PluckingPurgatory'sPetals: We're ultimately on the same page then! Don't you get it?! I'm trying to leave the fight behind, Grace. I want nothing to do with it anymore.

[09:22] PluckingPurgatory'sPetals: Life *has* slugged me in the head too many times recently. I'm bruised and dizzy and the fighting spirit is rapidly deserting me. My skull feels brittle and I suspect that the next good punch may... shatter it.

[09:22] PluckingPurgatory'sPetals: The difference is that I view throwing myself into the maw of an uncaring medical bureaucracy as walking straight into that final knockout blow.

[09:23] Alabaster&Freckles: So your plan is really just to slip away mid-fight and hide under the ring?

[09:23] Alabaster&Freckles: That might buy you a little time. But when you're fighting against yourself, there is no hiding for long. Eventually what you're up against *will* drag you out from underneath there and finish you off.

[09:23] Alabaster&Freckles: Please, I'm begging you, don't let that happen.

CHAPTER TWENTY-TWO

9:28 PM. APRIL 24TH.

(APPROX. SEVEN DAYS LATER)

Erin had one foot in the shower tray and was bending over to reach it. Using little silver nail scissors, she was slowly, carefully trimming her toenails.

"What does it say now?" Tilly called from across the room.

Pausing, Erin looked over at the laptop sitting a few feet away on the floor. She squinted hard, trying to make out the tiny ever-changing numbers and zero in on the right one.

"I... think... it says fifty-four minutes."

Tilly groaned and then exclaimed, "it's gone up?!"

"Yep," Erin replied uninterestedly and returned to her task. "That happens. It's just the download speed fluctuating."

"Did you *have* to torrent this movie? Couldn't you just buy it? From a legit site, it probably would have downloaded by now."

"Hey, I spent a lot of money in recent months, as you may recall." Upon saying this, she threw a significant glance over her shoulder at Tilly. "I'm scared to even add everything up, it will just depress the everloving fuck out of me. But I do know it put a serious, serious dent in my finances. Now, believe me, I'd happily sell all the VR crap to recoup some of that, if there was a way to do it without leaving the apartment. But there's not. So I'm-"

She cut herself off mid-sentence to lend all of her focus to snipping the trickier toenail on her little toe. Her tongue was peeking out between her lips as she concentrated. When the nail fragment pinged into the shower tray, she made a little noise of satisfaction and switched feet.

"As I was saying... I'm just gonna keep a tight grip on every penny from now on. And hope for the best."

"I mean, okay, fair enough," Tilly began gingerly. "But you do realize that we're going to have spent longer waiting for this thing to download than it's going to take to actually watch it?"

As the question hung in the air, all that could be heard was the metallic swish of scissor blades quickly closing and opening. Eventually, Erin just offered a casual "meh," alongside a little shrug of her shoulders.

Rolling her eyes hard, Tilly sighed as loudly as possible and then grumbled, "well... that's just dandy. I guess I'll just carry on counting the knots in the floorboards then."

"Important work, that. Gotta catalogue that info for future generations, after all," Erin returned in a neutral tone, disinclined to engage further.

"Oh yes, when the historians come to recreating everything that happened here via hologram, because you'll be such a well-known icon by then, they'll want to get all the little details right. I can just imagine it now... 'Teacher, teacher, did Erin really have *two* dents in her fridge door?', the fascinated students will demand to know."

Erin looked back again, with a cocked eyebrow at all the effort Tilly was putting into trying to distract her. She retorted dryly, "you know, your boundless ingenuity when it comes to mocking me is not my favorite thing in the world."

"Yeah, well, I guess I'm just the yin to your yang, painful as that is to bear. And, hey, when the people whisper about the rumours surrounding your *legend*" - she made a monastic, reverent 'ahhhhhhhhh' sound - "they'll say it's believed that you too once had whimsy in your heart."

Snorting with derision, Erin said, "whimsy is for the half-formed brains of children... and the half-wit dipshits who write books for them."

After a beat had passed, Tilly shot her a bemused, unconvinced look.

"What in the actual *fuck* are you talking about?" she asked slowly, squinting skeptically.

The very strategic use of a word she almost never said hit its mark. Taken aback, Erin burst into earnest laughter, and nearly fell flat on her face into the shower cubicle in the process.

Tilly looked on her handiwork happily, laughing too.

"Yeah, okay, that's probably fair," Erin offered good-humoredly when she recovered, wiping her eyes.

"Ha, there's no *probably* about it! That was one of those jibes I know you're just saying because it sounds kinda, sorta clever and incisive, but you don't actually believe a word of it. It's just us girls here, you don't have to play at being 'too cool for school' all the time!"

"Me? Do that? No...." Erin protested playfully, blushing and smiling wide as she rubbed moisturizing cream into the cracked skin at the back of her heels.

With a cute little snort as she chuckled, Tilly went on by saying, "tell it to the history books, missy. I'm sure they'll mention that tendency in the 'personality' section of your five-volume biography. Hell, *I* may even allude to it in the foreword they'll no doubt ask me to pen..."

As Erin straightened up and began to trim her fingernails over the shower tray, she seemed plunged into contemplation for a moment.

Then she said, "shit, you're joking about this stuff, but you know what really gets me?"

"What?"

"It's like... all the crazy shit I've gone through... who the fuck is ever going to know about it? People like me - and I'm guessing there's been at least a few - how often do our strange tales die with us? We're so trapped in our own heads, so distrustful, that we keep it all to ourselves. Yet, I'm betting you could fill a couple of dry lakes with the... meticulously detailed diaries... that all the boring people are writing *right now*. Every mundane moment of their mundane lives immortalized for posterity. There they are, just blithely clogging up the record with their ten-a-penny stories..."

"Well, *they* don't know that they're unremarkable, Erin. Or, you know, they don't want to believe it. To them, what they're going through is the most interesting thing ever. So they jot it down. I mean, what else can you really expect of them?"

Erin stopped what she was doing and turned around. She could feel a full-effort rant coming on. It deserved to be done right. She gestured loftily with the scissors as she pontificated.

"Maybe you're right. Maybe it is too much to expect they'd have the good sense, the fucking self-awareness, to voluntarily keep the channels clear for the stuff truly worth reading. But... it's not like that unselfish instinct doesn't exist, right? Look at Kafka. He spent his life as the high-priest of a one man cult of... meaninglessness and futility. Then he ordered all his own writings burned when he died.

"Firstly, I mean, fuck, we should all be so lucky to live such internally-consistent lives. Where even your last wish is the perfect embodiment of your beliefs. Like, holy shit. And secondly, think about the nature of his request. I figure that it must have stemmed from a... righteous fear that what he'd written might just be dross... taking up precious space on the bookshelf of humanity. Now, okay, yes, that suspicion wasn't exactly correct. But you *gotta* credit the weird bastard for his heart being in the right place. So I just think that all the boring fucks might at least be considerate enough to go out with a Kafka-like bonfire, you know?"

Then she abruptly went back to the nail-cutting, as if to emphatically punctuate what she'd said. It was the slightly tongue-in-cheek version of a maestro ostentatiously leaving the stage before the cries of 'bravo' and the thrown-roses can come.

Tilly licked her lips uncertainly. It was hard to know what to say to something like that.

"Sure..." she offered with barely concealed skepticism. "But if you're so worried about all this, why don't you just go ahead and share *your* story then?" Here she slipped seamlessly into a parody of southern drawl to finish her ribbing. "They do have this new-fangled contraption called *the internet*, if you can believe it... Why not slap one of those bloggity thingamajigs up on that big ol' cyberternized corkboard in the cloud or what have you?"

Yet Erin skipped right over this joke, sandbagging the obvious invitation to mindmeld and build on it with some comedic rejoinder of her own. After all, her next point was *clearly* too serious, too important to be cheapened by clothing it in humor. Or... so she now feigned.

"And entrust my tale to the mouth-breathing hordes? The ones falling over themselves to tell you how pop songs penned-by-committee in marketing firms are just as good as Shakespeare? Yeah, fuck that shit. The cretins would never know it for what it was, anyway."

"Ah... of course, of course," Tilly replied knowingly, and snickered to herself. "You know, I dare say that exact sentiment might be rather common amongst the 'people like you'. I'd even really go out on a limb and say it could explain that conspicuous absence of their chronicles you're lamenting."

"Maybe. Maybe not. I guess we'll never know..."

"You always say that when you know I'm right and it's always-" Tilly began to argue, but she cut herself off upon seeing the playful smirk creeping onto Erin's face.

They both giggled and Erin happily explained, "oh man, it was so hard keeping a straight face during that, you have no idea! But, hey, it sure is nice to be getting *you* for once!"

"Yeah, yeah, I'm slowly growing wise to your little tricks though! And make no mistake, I will be paying you back when you least expect it!"

"Ooooh, I'm shaking in my boots, Red!"

Erin was still smiling as she surveyed her work to check that nothing more was left to do, before putting the scissors away. Then she plucked the showerhead from its cradle and turned on the spray to its weakest setting. She patiently sloshed water around the shower tray, washing all the nail clippings down the drain.

When she was done, she scooped up the laptop and took it over to the kitchen with her. She placed it down on the countertop and pulled the screen forward so it could be seen better.

Without needing to be beckoned, Tilly drifted over from the window-seat to join her there. She watched, wordlessly, as Erin stood before the kitchenette and slowly passed her gaze to-and-fro between the cabinets and the fridge. It was possible that if she couldn't decide what to have as a snack, she would flee from the weight of her indecision and simply opt to not eat anything. Hopefully this could be avoided with a little push in the right direction.

"Toast, perhaps?" Tilly suggested. "You haven't had that in a while."

"Hmm, toast?..." Erin repeated absentmindedly. She pulled a slice of bread from the bread-bin and looked hard at it. This was a common ritual: she was visualising what the experience of eating it would be like, and trying to decide whether she could manage that in this moment.

At last, she dropped it into the toaster slot and pulled down the lever.

Then she nodded very slightly to herself, to acknowledge the small victory, and turned to face Tilly.

"What does it say now?" Tilly asked sweetly.

Mildly irritated at having to answer this question yet again, Erin just pointed to the laptop and said wryly, "check it yourself, it's literally right beside you."

Tilly closed her eyes and pressed her fist to her forehead in mock-frustration.

"I'm so looking forward to the day that you get tired of doing that."

With a smug look, Erin declared, "yes, what a glorious day *that* will be."

"How is it still so funny to you? I mean, like, seriously."

"Oh, I don't know..." Erin hit a button on the toaster and the slice of bread sprang up into reach. Hesitantly using her fingertips, she very quickly flipped it upside down. Then she depressed the lever again. "I suppose maybe I just like reminding myself that we're both powerless in our own ways," she finished her thought by saying.

She made little noises of relief as she ran her singed fingertips under the cold tap, savouring the soothing chill.

"Yes, well, isn't that just... lovely," Tilly said sarcastically. "Anyway, given that you *are* my eyes, can you please - like, pretty please with rainbow sprinkles on top - tell me what the download says?"

"Sure. But only because you asked me so nicely." Erin checked the torrent as she daintily patted her fingers dry with some kitchen towel. "Damn. I'm guessing my internet connection must have dropped. Because the thing now says, uh, like '2y' something. And... I think 'y'... means *years*..."

"Tell me you're kidding?! This is one of those times where I'm actually hoping you're messing with me!"

"No such luck, I'm afraid. It's now downloading at zero-point-one... um... kay-be's. I forget what those are again..."

"It doesn't matter what they are. What matters is we don't want - uh, whatever they're called - the... kaybies. We want the embies! They're how you actually get a movie downloaded well before you have to start worrying about the... the... friggin' heat death of the universe!"

"Oh you're pushing at an open door, believe me. I hate when this crap happens too. My router's just kind of a little shit sometimes. I keep meaning... Wait, hold on, the download speed is shooting back up. Just a sec... keep going... keep going... ah... okay... so, it's back to... forty-two minutes now."

"Eurgh! That's not much better than two years!"

Huffing dispiritedly, Tilly let her head loll around on her neck.

"Why so glum?"

"We've just been sitting around doing nothing. I'm bored."

Erin's eyebrows raised in astonishment. Her confused expression showed she was trying to make sense of this idea. And then the way that her eyebrows knitted together in consternation showed how futile this effort had proven.

Finally, as she poked the button again and retrieved the mildly burnt toast, she just asked outright, "you're... bored? Like, you genuinely... *feel*... boredom in this moment?"

"Well, I'm not really a distinct entity, so I don't *actually* feel anything... but, in my very real capacity as a fragment of your subconscious, yes, I am colossally freaking bored right now."

Erin took the piece of toast over to the sink and, with a butter knife, briefly scraped off as much of the burnt blackness as possible. Looking down, she couldn't decide whether the pile of dark dust which collected in the basin reminded her more of gunpowder or human ashes. And, moreover, wished that her imagination would go to more... innocent reference points first. So she tried to just put it out of her mind altogether.

She placed the toast atop her abandoned half-empty coffee mug on the countertop, to wait for it to cool. Then she held up her palms in concession and said, "alright, alright, fair enough."

But as she went on thinking it over, she couldn't help but ask a follow-up question.

"Hold on... I just don't get it... given the complexity of where you reside" - she tapped the back of her head - "how the hell can you be bored?..."

Tilly seemed to be a little incensed that this line of questioning was still being pursued. That indignation carried into her tone as she retorted, "believe it or not, your brain is not some... infinite theme park where I can just entertain myself in every idle moment."

"Uh, that's... just great." Erin scrunched up her face in displeasure. "I mean, I'm so sorry that traipsing around every inch of my mind like a prowling cat-burglar isn't sufficiently stimulating for you anymore."

"Look, don't take it personally. I'm sure no human mind can sustain an endless fascination when you get to peek at the inner workings up close."

Erin made a dismissive hand gesture and reached for the toast.

"So the sightseeing tour of my brain is just as tedium-inducing as it would be with Einstein's or Mozart's? That... is... really comforting, thanks. You sure know how to compliment a girl..."

"It's not like I'm-"

As an additional point struck her, Erin pulled back her hand and abruptly interrupted Tilly.

"And don't even get me started on the irony of claiming that *I* should be entertaining *you*. Jesus, just about the only upside of having an involuntary imaginary friend is that *they* keep you from getting bored!"

Tilly seemed to sense that the time to defuse this silly mounting argument had come. She smirked mischievously, and put on a dorky voice to respond, "*hey maaaaan...* that's just, like, what society has conditioned you to think! Shouldn't we be totally upending those... societal norms about how crazies should interact with the voices in their heads? Isn't it time to invert those oppressive hierarchies which, like, privilege the imaginer over the imagined?!"

Erin tried to hold on to being annoyed, tried not to find this funny. But the attempt to suppress her delight at this bit only made her find it even funnier. It started off with a little titter but then, as she gave in to it, she broke out into hysterical giggles. She looked over at Tilly with happy 'oh you' eyes, thoroughly charmed.

She finally picked up the toast and, after swiping a thin smear of raspberry jam on it, began nibbling at it. It wasn't delicious - not unless your tastebuds were imbeciles - but it *was* inoffensively palatable. And that would do.

In between bites, she adopted a pompous air and volleyed back, "ah, so you're saying the prescribed relationships need to be, you know, more *intersectional?*"

"Damn right they do," Tilly proclaimed with a smile. She theatrically raised a defiant fist in the air.

"Seems to me that you imagined-folk really should unionize one of these days. Collectively present your demands to your owners and-"

"'Owners'?! 'Owners'?!" Tilly playfully roared, causing Erin to chortle mid-swallow and very nearly choke on her toast. "How daaaare you trot out that dehumanizing term!" Moving even closer, Tilly grinned as she gained gusto with her faux-impassioned rant. "We are not objects to be 'owned'! We are a proud, free people, who just want the same rights as you damn flesh-and-blood-ers! Down with the bourgeoisie bigotry of the physical!"

"Of course, my mistake; please accept my sincerest apologies."

Erin straightened and, pressing her palm to her chest, humbly bowed in contrition.

"Quite right! Quite right I say!"

Tilly made this haughty announcement as she pretended to strike a cane against the ground. And, then, returning to her normal voice, she added, "now hurry up and finish your toast before it's completely stone-cold."

Erin took a few larger bites in quick succession to appease Tilly, but then said, "bit late for that, I gotta tell you. But, no matter, I kinda like cold toast."

"Oh yeah, I forgot, you're weird like that," Tilly said, and they both beamed warmly at each other.

Erin was lying down on the bed, with her fingers interlaced behind her head. She was staring up at the ceiling spacily, lost in thought.

"I hate to interrupt your reverie, but shouldn't the thing be done now?" Tilly inquired gently, laying beside her.

Focusing her eyes back on the room, Erin rolled onto her side to look at the laptop, which was perched precariously atop the alarm clock on the bedside table.

"Nine minutes," she answered, rolling back.

"Oh man, how is that possible?..." Tilly said, flabbergasted. She let out a long, whistling exhalation. "I swear, you must be unknowingly downloading some... devious new anti-piracy deterrent. Like, some government-uploaded honeypot torrent which looks just like all the real ones, but it's.. uh, rigged so that no matter how close it seems to get, it'll never actually finish downloading. Thus, driving you freaking mad. And making you swear off ever torrenting again. Ingenious, really."

"Yeah, umm, maybe," Erin said flatly, without even bothering to feign interest. She was too preoccupied with trying to kickstart her previous train of thought.

"I mean, what's the betting that in nine minutes, it'll say... 'fifteen' minutes? And so on and so on. You know? Like, that's how they try to infuriate you into just buying the damn thing."

"Could be."

Finally picking up on the fact that Erin was simply not going to bite this particular conversation-bait, Tilly switched tack.

"Oh my god," she declared loudly and gasped, startling Erin. "I just realized! What if I'm the real life girl and you're the imaginary friend? And we've somehow just gotten so... confused... that it's ended up getting flipped in our minds?!"

Caught completely off guard, Erin's eyes widened and her jaw dropped. Her mind was slowed by her flummoxed state as she scrambled to process this proposition and its implications.

It was very difficult but Tilly managed to maintain her grave and astonished expression for another fifteen seconds. And then she burst into ferocious laughter, clutching at her sides.

"Your face..." she managed to squeak out through the guffawing.

"Bitch!" Erin exclaimed with a wide embarrassed smile, red-faced at having been had.

Now wiping away the tears that the laughter had squeezed out, Tilly remarked giddily, "the lengths I have to go to, to elicit some kind of reaction! But it was so worth it! And consider that payback for earlier!"

"I should never have let you get a taste for mischief, you little trickster!"

"Hey, I just wanted to get you talking, missy! For real, what the hell is the point of having me here if you're not going to take advantage of it? Isn't it better to think out loud and spitball ideas with me than just getting lost in your own head?"

"You may have a point," Erin conceded, the bemused grin still lingering upon her face.

"You bet your cute little butt I do! So now will you tell me what you were thinking about?"

"Well, I don't know... it was just... just... kinda... abstract wool-gathering..."

"Erin!"

Put on the spot, Erin suddenly felt rather self-conscious. She swallowed and wet her lips with her tongue.

"It's... like... well, it's... shit, look, it's stuff where I'm... uh... like, really out of my depth..."

Tilly laughed softly and light-heartedly retorted, "maybe! But who's to know? I'll hardly be able to gainsay you, will I?"

Erin pursed her lips and slightly inclined her head in acknowledgement of this point. She began, still unconfidently, "okay, fine, I was just thinking, like, you know how there's this idea that the whole universe is just a... simulation?"

"Sure," Tilly answered, eagerly rolling onto her front and resting her chin on her hand in order to look at Erin as she spoke.

"Well, it occurred to me that if you had just some unbelievably great life - like if you're some beautiful, super-rich, super-famous hollywood actor - it makes perfect sense to ponder whether you're actually just... the centerpiece of a simulation. I mean, you'd rightly think to yourself 'what are the chances that I could simply be this lucky?' It's just so much more probable that you'd be born as a... shoeless orphan... in a village without clean water, than that you'd be born into a wealthy family, destined to be groomed to become a movie star, right? So, like, you'd just *have* to wonder."

"True enough, it is insanely good fortune to find oneself in those shoes. But someone has to win that lottery, no matter how long the odds are, no?"

"Of course, but, like, well, it's just, you know, the type of thing where..." she began, speaking rapidly. Then she stopped herself and, taking a breath, tried to formulate her response in a coherent way. "There's no actual reason why it was you. No explanation, no justification; it just... *was* you. And that would surely bother you, on some level. Because we need everything, even our very existence, to fit into a comprehensible narrative... even if it's a really fucking bizarre one. Which is precisely why you'd wonder if it somehow makes more sense that you're just a pawn in some... inconceivably elaborate experiment... to see how the human psyche, uh, deals with such a strange life. You know, make a lab-rat feel like it's king-of-the-world type of thing."

"Yeah, I can see that. I guess those questions would have to enter your mind sooner or later and-"

"And then I thought-" Realizing she was blithely speaking over Tilly, she quickly said, "sorry, I'm just kinda on a roll here."

"Hey, absolutely, do your thing."

Tilly smilingly gestured for Erin to continue. She'd certainly got her wish now.

"Okay, so then I thought: why don't the extraordinarily miserable also sit around wondering the same thing? I mean, it's just as odd and just as unlikely that you ended up in the top one-percent of hardship and misery as it is that you ended up in the top one-percent of comfort and opportunity."

"Yeah..."

"And that's when I realized that we just can't stomach the hypothetical the other way around. We *could* accept that we might have been set up as a pampered dupe for the purposes of a weird psychological experiment. But we'd fight so hard against accepting the idea that there might be some omnipotent being who, with infinite maleficence, crafted a... what? A grotesque torture-chamber universe... meant solely to house the mundane suffering of one upright, talking ape. That's just too much to let ourselves believe."

A small, sad smile upturned the corners of Tilly's mouth as she sat up.

Then she grandiosely recited, projecting her voice as if performing a public reading, "'mine brethren, hear me now/ enlighten thee of just exactly how/ though his instinct is to kowtow/ Man should rather labour under heavens blind and heedless/ than, as heathens or devout, bear divine cruelty preordained and needless/ for it's that very notion which, from holy masochism, freed us'... right?"

As she listened, Erin's gaze drifted around aimlessly as she tried to process how sharply and how strangely hearing those lines had affected her. She parted her lips to say something and then closed them again, biting with slight pressure upon the inside of her lower lip. When she went to speak again, her eyes still searching the middle distance for something unseeable, she only silently mouthed a single question. And it was really just to herself.

"What... *is*... that?..."

Tilly waited a minute or so, giving Erin as much chance as possible. Then, when it became clear that no recollection was forthcoming, she gently pointed out, "it's from... a poem... you were fond of once."

Still engrossed in rumination, Erin again spoke without sound, "that *I*...?"

"Once upon a time, yes."

She distantly murmured back, "really? It's a bit... overwrought... isn't it?"

"Well... you had a bit of a soft spot for that kind of thing... when you were younger."

Erin now looked over at Tilly, studying her face. Her voice was troubled and uncertain as she said, "you know, I... don't recall reading it... but it does feel... weirdly familiar, like... I don't know... something I saw someone in, like, a movie remembering." She paused and scoffed as she made a half-hearted eyeroll. "As if that makes any sense at all."

"It does make sense, Erin. There are sometimes memories we kind of... *bury*. Not to lose forever, but so that they're hidden and protected during moments which have... destructive force. So that we can dig them up in the future when we need them again. It's just a, uh, temporary relinquishing."

"Well... whatever... maybe I did once know it. But..." Erin sat up against the headboard and managed to muster a weak, self-deprecating smile. "Fuck, are the only profound thoughts we ever have just us... plagiarizing something we've forgotten having read?"

"Ha, not always." Tilly's warm smile in response faded a little as she continued. "But... sometimes, yeah. Pure originality is a false idol anyway. There's nothing wrong with being intellectual hermit crabs, every so often putting on the shell of some new idea we come across. Well, new to us, at any rate. Because, most likely, it has given... shelter and solace... to countless others beforehand. Still, we wear it and make it ours for a time, adding to it or strengthening it in some small way perhaps... before switching it out again. I mean, that's, like, the product of all human contemplation: a beach strewn with a million shells, ever-accumulating more. Pick one up, put one down. On and on it goes."

"I suppose. But... sometimes I just want to speak in *my* voice. Not inadvertently paraphrase somebody else's thesis."

"Look, did you mean what you said?"

"Well, yes-"

"Then what does it matter? You expressed what you truly thought, in the way that came most easily. That's the most important thing."

"I'm not sure I completely buy that. But... I also have an inkling that... ultimately... it doesn't really matter either way." Having said this with an air of conclusion, Erin went to grab the laptop from beside the bed. But then she halted in her tracks to look back and say, "wait, hold on a sec missy, you didn't tell me what you thought of the actual point I was making."

"No, I guess I didn't. Okay, hmm, let me think..."

Tilly conspicuously fell into deliberation, idly rapping her fingers on the mattress and looking off into the distance.

Erin chortled and, slapping her hand down right next to Tilly, laughingly exclaimed, "fuck off with that shit! You *don't* need to think it over. You already know. Hell, you probably came up with your response before I even started explaining myself. You're like an... A.I. that can crunch a gazillion-digit equation in a nanosecond but... throws up some lengthy, fake-ass loading screen anyway. Just to ensure that the idiot humans won't find its abilities too threatening."

"Well..." Tilly began, stroking her chin as she theatrically pretended to mull over this objection. "I *am* a supercomputer level intelligence, so that does check out..."

"Ha, yeah right, you're precisely as dumb as me, in fact."

"God, you're right!" Tilly clutched the sides of her face in mock-distress and let her jaw fall open in shock. "Why, god, why?!" she croaked skyward, now distraughtly clawing at the air above her head.

"Yeah, yeah, a fate worse than death, blahdy blah blah." Failing to suppress a grin, Erin waved away this 'much-too-immature' digression and said, "anyway, get on with it, you: spit it out, at long last!"

Like a drop of ink blooming outward in crystal clear water, there was an abrupt seriousness which spread across Tilly's expression.

"If there were some all-knowing, all-powerful deity up there... who was responsible for all the ills that plague us down here... we'd at least have someone to blame."

"A paltry consolation for the victims, don't you think? They'd merely get to hate a being who's beyond all redress."

Tilly nodded somberly as she replied, "can't argue with that. It isn't much. But surely it's better than nothing at all?"

Erin thought hard about the underlying suggestion here. She didn't want to be flippant in her response to it. She had no idea why, but this question had affected her rather intensely. And she felt very strongly that she needed to answer it *truly* - whatever that meant - as though she were not merely offering an opinion but deciding the matter altogether. The runoff anxiety from the debate raging in her mind manifested itself in her absentmindedly twirling and pulling at her eyebrows, eliciting tiny sparks of pain as she occasionally yanked a stray hair out.

Eventually she had her answer fletched and nocked. She took a deep breath, steeling herself, and let it fly.

"I think that... the *nothingness* is still way more palatable, strange as that is to say. At least it's... well... neutral, I suppose. In the way that, say, russian roulette is... like... you know... 'no respecter of personage'. Whereas, I mean, just think about what the holy books' horseshit actually gets you. It's basically stipulating that..." She rubbed her eyes hard and sighed. "You're just one of countless marionettes being forced to act out some fucked-up god's eons long fucked-up stageplay. And why? Uh, I guess choose whichever dumb... non-sequitur... excuse takes your fancy. But the better question is: what satisfactory reason could there possibly be?"

Scrunching her face up in disgust, she answered her own rhetorical question with another one.

"We were made because we're *loved* by that god? Loved so very much that we were then promptly abandoned on this rock to just... fight and fuck each other... forever and ever? You know, suspiciously like all the other lowly beasts apparently created just so we could eat their flesh? That's really fucking... something. Or maybe it *is* true that the motherfucker did finally get antsy... and intervened at a random stage in human history. Ummm, to remind some ancient primitives that they had better worship him. And, oh yeah, lecture them on the sanctioned ways to conduct their barbarism. I mean, of all the idiot-bait that unimaginative charlatans have ever concocted to-"

Tilly tapped an imaginary watch and interrupted.

"Alright, alright, I get it, that does suck. Now keep it moving, sister. What's so great about the other option on the god-or-no-god prize wheel?"

"Yes, well... um... so... hmm..." Erin murmured, resting her chin upon both fists as she considered it herself. "Look, the upside is doing away with that bumbling supervision from the heavenly fucktard. That's good enough by itself, if you ask me. But... what you're then left with is.... well, you could argue it's not exactly much of a bonanza. Because all the other existential suckiness remains just about unscathed. No doubt there are people who'd say that part's actually made *even* worse, in a sense."

"Care to make their case? You know, play devil's advocate," Tilly prodded wryly. "I mean, with the big guy upstairs gone, you gotta find a new liege to curry favour with, right? No time like the present to start accruing billable hours."

Erin scoffed good-humouredly at this bad joke. Then she tilted her head back and pursed her lips thoughtfully, signalling that she accepted the challenge. She pondered what this hypothetical rebuttal might entail. Her head was almost imperceptibly rocking back and forth as she began lining it all up in her mind. Strikingly, her expression gradually morphed into a more and more serious, dour form. The conclusions she was producing *were* for a thought-experiment, but the laboratory of the mind is ill-equipped for quarantining abstraction. Just as mixing chemicals in open test-tubes risks them splashing out onto you, the mind has no hermetically-sealed chambers in which to cultivate foreign arguments. One's thoughts are simply one's thoughts. Regardless of the nature of their provenance, they exert their effect on the thinker. And in this case, they had darkened her mood. But the price hadn't been for nought. She came away with her surrogate diatribe polished and ready to go.

"Cause then you're just... *there*. Creatures with no maker, doing shit really just to keep ourselves occupied, like monkeys making faces at each other. None of it mattering in the slightest, because there's no higher force to see or care about any of it. So, you're just, like, a simplistic meatsack who... randomly ended up with the illusion of consciousness, carrying out a lifetime's worth of pointless bullshit. We live, we die, more of us are born. A cycle that just... happens because it happens. Just an inscrutable brute-fact coincidence. And... perhaps... we will wipe ourselves out someday, but the universe will take no notice whatsoever. It will just put our atoms to use in something else... recycling us like cardboard pulp. Maybe that's what hell really is, you know? For us to truly be no more than *matter*, precisely as unspecial as rocks or dung. But doomed to think, to think itself into misery. All the while, adrift in a sea of uncaring void..."

"Okay, damn... yeah, that is super dark. So, basically, every possibility sucks?"

Erin shrugged.

"Arguably," she just offered gnomically.

"And I can totally tell that you've not spent too much time thinking about all this before now, right?..." Tilly tried to break Erin's somberness by cracking a knowing smirk as she said this.

Erin now had her eyes tightly closed, visualizing her target as she jammed a hand up the back of her shirt to scratch an itch. But she was still able to pick up on the lightheartedness of Tilly's quip. And she was very happy to grab onto anything that could pull her out of her own stuffy seriousness right now.

She forced herself to make her tone light - meaning to fake it until she felt it - as she replied, "gloomy existential musings are the shut-in's fine wine, what can I say? I've got my favorite vintages. And, hey, I like to get wine-drunk before noon *most* days."

"Uh-huh, 'existential musings', masturbatory navel-gazing; toe-may-toe, toe-mart-oh." Tilly had a childish ear-to-ear grin as she made this point. "Like, where did you even learn about all this stuff?"

Opening her eyes, Erin couldn't help but reflexively smile back at the happy face greeting her. And she sheepishly joked, "oh, I don't know. I've never really read philosophy textbooks or anything like that. But I have kind of absorbed what's in them third-hand, by reading what philosophy-majors badly summarize in forum posts."

"Ding, ding, ding! Give our girl an award for self-awareness!" Tilly hollered through laughter.

"And I've seen, like, a whole *bunch* of space documentaries on YouTube. I mean, if you want me to switch to talking about astronomy stuff with the same passing semblance of knowledge," Erin added in a cheerfully self-deprecating way, pleased to be making Tilly smile and laugh.

"Oh I can't wait to hear that, beee-lieve me! But for now, I'm still too interested in all the totally delightful ways that life can make no sense. So, let's say that we know the game is rigged and both prizes are awful. When we slink away dejected, what's behind the sparkly mystery door off-stage? There's gotta be something good... uh, somewhere. Surely?"

"Not much, alas. I guess... theoretically... you can make either scenario better if you insert, like, the consolation-prize of free will or whatever. But I gotta tell you before you get your hopes up: even as a proposition, it's bare and bleak and fucking rickety. Because, to put it mildly, there are more than a few parts that are hard to swallow."

"Jeez, some saleswoman you are! You gotta at least try to sell me on it a little first. What makes it so desirable?"

At this, Erin fluttered her eyelids and shook her head condescendingly, as though the answer to this question was so painfully obvious that to have to state it aloud was an inflicted indignity.

"Self-authorship. *I* want to be the reason why I am how I am, however shitty that may happen to be. That's why."

"Please forgive my impossible stupidity..." Erin issued the sarcastic disclaimer through a grin which suggested that she was enjoying the role of irritant. "But why exactly is that so awesome?"

Seeing that Tilly was taking pleasure in needling her, Erin tried to extinguish her own annoyance so as not to provide any further entertainment value.

Instead she merely explained, with exaggerated politeness, "if you do not get to make your own choices, get to decide who you become, you're not really your own person, are you? And so I'd quite like it if *this*" - she made a sweeping circular gesture around herself - "is an ongoing project I'm actually in control of. Do you see what I mean now?"

"Gosh, yes, I do see, I do! But pray tell, oh learned one, what of the aforementioned niggles?" Affecting a prim-and-proper accent and tearoom-debate manner, Tilly had found another way to have fun at this conversation's expense.

"Well," Erin began, ignoring the mockery, "the sad truth is it's hard to see how free will could exist. For real, think about the subatomic, uh, *stuff* which makes the universe... go. It isn't just drifting around or smashing together randomly. There are physical laws which govern all of that, which decide each outcome. People can argue all they want about whether the very first domino simply fell or was pushed. But, like, what the fuck does it matter? From that genesis-moment sprang forth an... inconceivably complex string of cause and effect. A runaway chain reaction stretching on... and on... and on. Every single thing that happens inescapably predetermined by - you guessed it - every single thing which preceded it."

"Sure... that's not ideal," Tilly conceded, nodding along in feigned solemnity.

"Not really, no. Because our brains aren't somehow unique, somehow exempt. They're not magic control rooms helmed by some... like, ghostly soul or whatever the fuck. They're just meat-computers. And every process which plays out in that mushy circuitry is subject to the same old causal certainties. A straight-jacket and leash on all of humanity. I mean, right there, that's the universe whispering 'game, set, and fuck-you.'"

"Buuuut teeeeeacher," Tilly smirkingly whined like an insufferable schoolchild, "*if* we were to just, like, put all that aside for a hot second? Is there any way we can finagle it then?"

Erin tutted.

"Oh, you mean if we somehow just 'put aside' the fundamental nature of the motherfucking universe? Just sweep that under the carpet?"

"Exactly!"

This chipper exclamation earned an eye-roll, but Erin obliged nonetheless.

"Even if you ignore all of that, your prospects for true agency don't get any rosier. Not by a long shot. Firstly, no-one gets to choose their brain. Meaning.... your parents already imparted whatever genetics they imparted. Your ability to mould things from there barely amounts to table scraps. Secondly, we opt for one choice over the other based on... what? I mean, seriously, what? Subconscious biases we don't know about... and neurochemicals we can't control. The feeling of 'deciding' is just an illusion to cover that hidden ballet - or, depending on your perspective, clusterfuck - of brain activity. So, unsurprisingly, it's turtles all the way back *up* too."

Tilly finally gave up her little act with a sigh.

She muttered, disheartened, "well, if turtles were... punches in the face."

Erin just nodded.

"Quite."

A little patch of awkward silence passed before Tilly perked up and sought to revive the game.

"So now I'm suitably depressed, isn't this where you give me the long-awaited silver lining? That little 'but wait...' which makes it all work out okay somehow?"

Crossing her arms, Erin said, "nope."

"Nope?" Tilly asked with an arched eyebrow.

"Yep. Nope."

Tilly shot back her sassy riposte with a smirk.

"*Explain* the nope, dummy!"

"Best I can tell, there's just no way to quash all the objections to anything resembling free will. Well, unless tomorrow a rogue super-genius scientist discovers some crazy new revolutionary shit. I'm talking, like, some ridiculous fucking deus ex machina particle. The type of thing which somehow just injects an aspect of... slippery randomness... into the whole machinery. And at that point you might as well just ask for an old-fashioned miracle. Because they really would be indistinguishable. The holes you're trying to fill? You'd basically be *remaking* the universe."

"Eurgh. And so that's that, then?"

"Pretty much, yeah. I promise you it gives me no joy to say it, but the whole idea is bogus from the ground up. Fool's gold, through and through."

Tilly opened her mouth to respond, but Erin rudely held up a hand to stop her in her tracks. She wasn't finished. She just wanted her last point to hang in the air for a beat, for effect. Then she pulled her hand back and resumed expounding.

"Yet, there's the thing, fool's gold supposedly glitters *just like* real gold, right? Maybe that's what's important. Because what the fuck is real gold? A shiny metal some... rich assholes... arbitrarily decided was worth a lot. If all their hoarded gold bullion vanished tomorrow - *poof* - they'd probably just swap in its look-alike cousin and carry on as normal. Now, yes, they are just being greedy dipshits, but there's something else at play too. That... inherent capacity... for substitution. That... unsinkability of the system. It keeps economies from dissolving and people from then having to eat their pets."

"Hmm, what a pleasant image."

"Exactly. The, uh... whatever... fucking mouthfeel... of fur is probably not a foodie's wet dream. Anyway, to complete the analogy I'm making here, I think we pretty much have to act as if free will exists. It's the, like, lynchpin fiction... at the very heart of civilisation, keeping it all together. Versatile and durable. Contradictions arise and it just morphs to absorb and defang them. And... in a sense... why not? If nothing matters anyway, fuck it. Pick your lie. I think you can do a lot worse than this one, right? It at least preserves that crucial sense of self-determination and personal responsibility. And they're the goddamn anchor points keeping the... whole edifice of personhood hanging upright at all."

"On the face of it, that sounds all fine and dandy. But what if people just *can't* act as if free will is real, once they see the evidence saying it isn't? Did you ever think about that, huh brainiac?"

Erin laughed darkly.

"You know, *somehow* I don't think that'll be much of a problem. Look at it like this. In the, uh, days of yore... it took the wisest scholars a lifetime of study and contemplation to even faintly grope towards an anti-free-will conclusion. Now? It takes a google search and twenty minutes of half-hearted attention... and you get it definitively spoonfed to you. You could do it whilst waiting for a fucking bus. But... as always... prizes which are easily gotten are poorly valued. Like, it's one thing to learn a truth and quite another to really believe it. And, frankly, I doubt you even could convince most people that free will doesn't exist. It's just too fundamental to how they mentally engage with the world itself. I'm talking, like, whatever the hell's *below* bedrock, that's what you'd be trying to tear up in their minds. You might as well try to tell them that... that... well, that the fucking sun doesn't exist."

"Umm, isn't that kind of a big problem then? This intentional cognitive-dissonance you're proposing is one thing. But if people don't believe that it's a lie they're just employing for its utility... aren't they simply labouring under a delusion like usual? Nothing noble in that, right?..."

Erin smiled widely all of a sudden, as the benevolent game-inside-a-game Tilly was pulling off dawned on her. She nodded happily at the realization of having been played so well. After all, it would be downright unsporting not to credit this worthy effort.

She intoned sonorously, with the exaggerated seriousness of a stage-actor, "you and your damn endless questions. I now regret ever skimming that wikipedia page about the Socratic method. I mean, is there anything you can't weaponize against me, impudent chit?!"

"Ah, see, there's where I get my flair for the dramatic from!" Tilly replied playfully. "And, at any rate, I'm sure I don't know what you mean..."

"Yeah, yeah, sure thing. Maybe you just know I like the sound of my own voice too much then."

"Or maybe... talking is good for the soul, and it's nice to provide opportunities for it. Or maybe I just wanna try to establish certain... things.

Who knows?" Tilly batted back slyly. "Now, don't be trying to duck my well-reasoned objections. Hop to, missy."

"Look, I can't really disagree with what you said. As has been true at, uhhh, literally every point in human history, the current generation is a lost cause. So... we'll just have to teach kids about it, chisel the truth straight into the *tabula rasa* from the get-go. Then you can get some shit going. It'll just take time."

"And you'll get this past the, like, philosophical-luddite parents... how exactly? The same people who won't let their kids get vaccines in case it secretly implants a tracker chip or smallpox or... I don't know... homosexuality, might possibly take umbrage at you teaching little Timmy that up is actually down."

"Yeah... shit... there's that." Erin interlocked her fingers atop her head and blew out a long exhalation in frustration at this challenge. She was quiet for a little while and then she just deflatedly said, "alright, that is a pretty big problem, I'll admit."

"Well, look, it's surely not, umm, insurmountable or anything. Where there's a will there's-"

Erin jumped in here with comically overacted enthusiasm, "yeah, you're right! Brainwashing camps it is!"

They locked eyes and burst into hysterical laughter together. Erin was holding her sides, she was laughing so hard.

As it finally subsided, Tilly wiped the tears from her eyes and gigglingly exclaimed, "jeez, talk about zero to a hundred, you freaking lunatic!"

Also trying to talk through giggles, Erin replied, "of course, of course, point taken. Subtlety is king, after all. I suppose we'll go for slipping old-fashioned subliminal indoctrination into the cartoons instead."

"Ha, look at you! 'We'? Damn Erin, you already allocated yourself a seat on the illuminati?"

"Hey, look, if I don't tell them how to get this shit done right, those crusty old fuckers *will* royally fuck it up. So... I'm willing to bear this onerous burden, for the good of all mankind." Erin gave a little bow, which was made awkward by the fact that she had slid back down into a half-sitting, half-reclining position. "Well, now that's settled... I mean, jesus, what the hell were we even talking about originally?"

"More importantly, I know we sometimes unwittingly slip into a... subordinate realm where time... doesn't exactly seem to have the same purchase on things as it normally does. But, still, the movie *has* to be done by now, right?!"

Erin checked and said, "yep, a good twenty-five minutes back."

Tilly just groaned and rolled her eyes.

"Go, go, go, go," she urged with a smile, pointing insistently at the spot in front of them where the laptop needed to be.

The screen cut to black and the credits began to roll.

Tilly squinted at the screen, like she was trying to figure something out.

Shifting her mouth side-to-side whilst making faint little kissy-type noises, Erin just frowned and rubbed her arm.

A maudlin orchestral score started to play through the speakers as names continued to scroll slowly by.

"So..." Tilly began tentatively.

Erin switched her gaze over to Tilly and returned, just as noncommittally, "yeah..."

They just looked at each other searchingly, waiting to see who'd be confident enough to go first.

"That... kinda... sucked?" Tacking on a question-like rising intonation at the end, Tilly hedged her bets.

Breathing a sigh of relief, Erin excitedly gestured at the screen and declared, "hell yeah, that movie fucking blew! Buh-leeeeeeeeeew!"

"Yep... it... wasn't the best." Chortling softly, Tilly went on to point out, "and weren't you Ms. 'I've-heard-good-things'?"

"Well, I-I had! Reviewers were falling over themselves to heap praise on it!" Erin spluttered, earnestly seeking to defend herself.

"Guess they steered you wrong on this one then."

"Oh, don't you worry. Next time I'll make sure to avoid any critics who get bowled over by an... all-you-can-eat buffet... of artsy, pseudo-deep ambiguity. I mean, hell, the whole thing was basically 'thanks for your money suckers, here's a dozen vague, unresolved strands of plot... and some inscrutable visual metaphors'. Like, totally just grist for the ramblings of film studies PhDs."

Tilly weakly offered the hypothetical counterpoint, "well, it's... like, *experimental*... I guess?"

"When you force your audience to think up some cockamamie explanation to try and make sense of your garbled, scattershot storytelling, that's not 'experimental'... that's *lay-zee bool-sheet*. Or, at least, the only experiment is to see how much money you can bilk from people who believe that the more incoherent a movie seems, the more artistic it is."

"Ha, tell me what you *really* think, why don't you?"

"Whatever." Erin scoffed as she patted her ruffled hair down flat. "They borderline robbed two hours from me. I have a right to be pissed."

"Oh yeah, because I'm sure you totally had that time earmarked for something else, right? Some relaxing needlepoint perhaps?"

"I *would* rather set about embroidering a full size replica of the fucking Magna Carta than watch that crap!"

"Look, I don't know what to tell you. I mean, although I didn't hate it quite as... passionately... as you do, I definitely didn't enjoy it. But you did say that a lot of people really liked it, so," raising her hands in the air, Tilly just shrugged, "maybe we're, like, just missing something?..."

Erin quickly crawled over in front of Tilly and reproachfully jabbed a finger at her.

"Noooooo! Fuck. That. Noise. They know that-"

Rolling her eyes, Tilly waved Erin's finger away and interjected to counter in a sarcastic manner, "let me guess: that's exactly what these underhanded filmmakers want you to think?"

"Exactly." Erin pointedly ignored Tilly's skepticism, repeating the word as if it actually did represent agreement between the two of them. "That's what these garbage-artists do. They slap together some shoddy, vacuous potboiler and preempt the usual criticism by labelling it as 'avant-garde'."

"But at some point they do have to actually start showing it to people, right? So the jig is going to be up quite quickly."

"Not necessarily. They just herd a gaggle of impressionable critics into a private screening, confident that every shortcoming will be forgiven as, like, trying to 'push the boundaries of cinema'. Then... the glowing reviews predictably start rolling in. Cut to its release, and people start to judge the film through the lens of its reputation. It's basically bulletproof at that point. Because they're already granting it the, you know, presumption of fucking profundity."

Pressing a fist to her forehead, Tilly closed her eyes and quietly said, "that is pretty much the weirdest conspiracy theory I've ever heard."

"It's not a 'conspiracy theory'" - Erin made air quotes here - "it's an age-old moneymaking ploy: 'why is this thing good?', 'because I've heard it's good'. That's just Marketing 101 right there. I mean, I bet even the neanderthal who invented the wheel probably paid a couple tribe-members in... uh, berries... to spread the word that his circular roll-y thing was hot shit."

Tilly did not even try to hide the disinterest on her face.

"I could not be more *over* this conversation," she announced, as if just informing the room itself.

"Okay, okay, I get it. What do you wanna talk about then?"

"How about the actual plot of the movie?"

"Oh come on! Don't even get me-"

"Woah now," Tilly made a slicing motion with each hand, in opposite directions, to stop Erin in her tracks before she gained steam again. "Not the whole thing. Because I don't need you to launch into the second act of your diatribe." She mock-shuddered, heaving a deep sigh, and continued. "I *definitely* don't need that. A girl can only take so much, after all. I was actually thinking we could... like, talk about a... specific scene."

Almost imperceptibly, Erin pulled her head back and narrowed her eyes. She rubbed the back of her neck uncomfortably.

"Alright..." she began cautiously, "which... um... scene?"

"The car accident."

"Oh," Erin said at a volume resembling a whisper. Clearing her throat, she nervously pulled at her earlobe and muttered, "yeah, okay... that one."

Catching herself, and her blatant tells, she took a moment to summon up a sturdy facade of indifference. Her face shifted into an expressionless mask. She relaxed her posture and lay her fidget-prone hands awkwardly in her lap. The impression she was now trying to give was of almost being bored by this turn in the conversation.

Her performance was not... convincing. Not only because the acting was such that a thespian would have fruitlessly tried to commit seppuku with a spring-loaded prop dagger, rather than bear this insult to their craft. But also because, of course, Tilly had watched the entire unmistakably artificial transition between before-and-after. To say that this kind of gave the game away would be understating it.

However, Erin's effortful insouciance did at least smooth out her faltering voice as she said, "what... about it? I mean, the whole set-up was pretty lame. Like, it was really, really obvious what was coming. When someone's about to drive through an intersection and the camera is looking at them side-on, so you can see out their passenger window, you just... well, *know* that they're about to get t-boned. Sooo many films have-"

"Erin." Tilly merely said her name with a calm, emphatic tone. Yet it cut through Erin's rambling like a falling stalactite. She stopped speaking immediately, subtly wringing her hands and biting her lips closed as her anxiety surged. Tilly continued, surveying Erin carefully, "the women in the car. Talk to me about them."

Feeling Tilly's stare boring into her, Erin spent more than a few seconds looking down at her lap. Her little act was rapidly falling away. She had now taken to roughly scraping her knuckles together. She was so painfully aware of being scrutinised that she momentarily felt a powerful urge to physically turn away from Tilly's gaze, before realizing how silly that would be.

"I... They didn't... I mean, uh, that whole thing was really... bleh. Like, you know, with the policeman and shit. When he races over to the crashed car and they've both disappeared into black mist or... whatever it's supposed to be. And... and then the blonde shows up later, all tatted up, as the mute bartender and no-one even mentions-"

"Erin," Tilly interjected again, patiently employing the same measured intonation. "I noticed you clench your fists very tightly during the crash scene. And the sound that caught in your throat. And... the tears you wouldn't let fall."

The vaguest hint of a scowl drifted down onto Erin's face, and she grit her teeth.

"Well, so what? That was... a fucked-up scene. Jesus, I'm not a goddamn robot. Aren't you supposed to cry during sad parts?"

"They were tears of *anger*, Erin."

And with that, Erin's expression escalated in the blink of an eye to the one a moody teenager wears when called out for something undeniably obvious. Pouty, defensive, and mad.

"Why... why w-would... I be angry?..."

"I don't know, why would you be?"

Erin licked her lips and swallowed hard. She squeezed her thighs, so that feeling the sensation would anchor her.

"What am..."

She stopped upon finding how dry her mouth was, and how it made her voice croaky and faint. She tilted her head back, ostensibly to look up at the ceiling in frustration. But it was actually in the vain hope that gravity would compel the growing teariness back into her eyes. At this point, she wanted to take a soldering iron to her tear ducts, to seal them up with drops of molten lead. Because their betrayals were just never-ending.

With a single fingertip, she slowly tapped up and down the midline of her throat. And blew out a very long exhalation.

When she finally looked back down at Tilly, she shook her head at herself and murmured, "what am I supposed to say? It doesn't make any sense..."

"It doesn't need to make sense. You just need to verbalise it."

"I don't know... I don't know... It was a car crash. And neither of the characters even looked anything like... well, you. Or *her*. Or... fuck, whatever." Erin stopped and grimaced with irritation. "This is fucking stupid," she concluded sourly.

Completely ignoring Erin's attempt to retreat into sullen indignation, Tilly prompted her by saying, "and they were, what? Twenty,

364

thirty years older?"

"Yes! That's what I'm saying! It's so fucking stupid!" Erin's voice was raised and she was gesticulating animatedly with her hands. "There's... just.... no similarities, nothing to connect them!"

"Apart from the one huge, all-important, unignorable thing?"

Remarkably, there was something so sincere and calm about Tilly's demeanour that this rhetorical question managed to come across without being mocking at all. And one can be absolutely sure of that, because Erin tried her damndest to find *any* trace of mockery there. She wanted a reason to be pissed off at Tilly. That would give her an excuse to abandon this conversation. Still, it was not to be. Tilly was smart enough to ensure she didn't accidentally make this easy way out available.

So Erin just begrudgingly held her tongue, with some difficulty. She knew that, having been so well outplayed, her compulsion to respond would prove to be a sort of self-inflicted zugzwang trap. Anything she might say to try and avoid the inevitable would just backfire and worsen her entanglement. The only move here was to halt, and hope for impossible deliverance.

Tilly waited a beat and then softly volunteered, "*they* didn't deserve it either."

At this, Erin was undone.

There was simply no defense against it. Her body reacted before her mind could even attempt to stop it. She instantly seemed to lose herself in staring unblinkingly into the middle distance. The tears welled up and began trickling down her cheeks at irregular intervals. Her nose started to run and she sniffed hard to stem the flow down her top lip.

Some time passed with her like this. When she finally spoke, it was in a slow, detached way, as though she was gradually coming out of the depths of a trance.

"She was a *good* person... like, truly, in her heart, you know? I know that sounds corny as fuck, but... there you have it. We were kinda similar in that life had put her through the ringer too, had done its best to make her hate it. But she found a way to... refuse. She still knew how to find joy in things. I mean, not like those smiley dimwits inanely delighted by anything and everything. It was more like... she just retained some pristine, uh, hope... deep down. Like, this weird optimism, that maybe people weren't all shitheads... that maybe living was worthwhile... that maybe she was ultimately destined for happiness. I suppose I'd consider that naivete now. But, hell... maybe it's no more wrong than *my* nihilism, *my* misanthropy. And probably a far better kind of wrong, if you see what I mean."

There was a prolonged, weighty pause.

Then, with anguish in her voice, she declared, "god... she had her whole life ahead of her. So much she could have been. So much she could have done."

"She deserved so much better than what happened to her," Tilly concurred sympathetically, nodding.

With startling quickness, Erin plucked her gaze from the middle-distance and fixed it on Tilly. It had transformed into a bitter glare during the switchover.

"Better than having her skull cracked open for no fucking reason?!... Better than lying there, crumpled in the filthy, freezing gutter, for ten minutes before anyone came across her?!... Yes, she *did* deserve better than that!" Erin coldly exclaimed, as if having somehow been offended.

After letting it pointedly linger for a few moments longer, she lifted her stare from Tilly to dry her eyes with her sleeve and wipe her nose with the collar of her pyjama top.

"In a split-second... she was obliterated from this world. Because she *slipped*. Because she stepped an inch or two too close to the icy curbside. And that's enough? That's enough to steal a girl's life like some scumbag cutthroat?!" she growled.

Hearing this animal rage which had infiltrated her voice, she took a very slow, very deep breath. During the exhale, she lay her palm over her brow and massaged her temples with outstretched thumb and forefinger. She rubbed the taut skin there forcefully, as though she was trying to push the knots out of a sore muscle which would not yield them. Then she just sat there very still, with clenched jaw and the occasional unacknowledged tear still snaking its way down her face. Her anger started to dissipate bit by bit.

Eventually she just reflected quietly, "a death worse than death: buried in the halfway-grave of her own body, held hostage by a heart too dumb to stop beating. And where? Oh yeah, grotesquely stored away in some dingy corner. On a... a... bier they politely deign to still call a hospital bed."

Now the pendulum swung back the other way without warning.

Erin convulsively struck a blow at the empty air in front of her and shouted, "and what's left?!... *Me.*" It was incredible how she managed to load a single syllable with such deep disgust. "Just some wretched shadow. Just some fucking worthless amalgam of ugliness and brokenness of every stripe."

She hung her head and scowled.

"*I should have died and she should have lived,*" she concluded bitterly.

Tilly sat there, looking on in patient silence. For a short while, it seemed as if Erin might not speak again. But Tilly knew better. There was more Erin had to get out. When she did finally resume talking, her voice was very different: it was faint and carried a defeated, mournful tone.

"It's just so... senseless, you know? It's the very definition of senseless. Truly, a perfect encapsulation of what a fucking hateful universe we occupy. And if you think about that too hard or for too long, it'll... shit, it will just, like, make you absolutely fucking nuts. And so, your whole life becomes that constant *trying not to...*"

Suddenly noticing the laptop again, she unhurriedly pulled it over and started closing the windows and shutting it down. As she did so, she matter-of-factly explained, "yet, you have to hold that truth inside yourself nonetheless. Like... a thousand tiny pieces of shrapnel which... materialise in place... throughout the spongy meat of your brain." Here she pulled a hand away from the laptop and raised it to her head. She drummed her fingers across the top of her skull, pretending to deposit the fragments therein with every touch, like a seed-drill dragged across a field to sow the seeds.

She had casually acted out that illustration but, afterwards, it gave her pause. She stopped what she was doing on the laptop for a moment or two. Her stomach turned as she really thought about a flotilla of sharp little shards blinking into existence inside her brainpan, imagining how it would feel. No worse than this pain, perhaps.

Shaking it off, she went on.

"And then they're just... *nestled* there. With all the quiet, knowing menace of unexploded bombs lurking beneath a cityscape." She gave a dry, mirthless laugh and shook her head. "All the silly platitudes say that time will heal your pain, will help you move on. But do you wanna know what actually occurs as time passes? Occasionally, your shudders of anguish are so forceful that you... jostle... the shrapnel. And they shred a little bit more of the gray matter around them. After this gets repeated enough, fine, maybe you'll be so addled that you'll have forgotten what once happened. But at that point... having paid that price... it's all pretty fucking moot, don't you think?"

"Erin, is it possible that... maybe... you just... kind of... *want to believe* that's how it works? That your self-loathing inclines you to think that you're sentenced to this misery forever? I'm saying, couldn't embracing that belief just be your way of punishing yourself?"

Erin could scarcely contain herself after listening to these insulting insinuations. Becoming visibly flustered in her impatience to give voice to her anger, she slammed the laptop lid closed and slid it away from her.

She sucked in a deep, lung-ballooning breath to fuel her rant and squawked, "you think I want this hurt for the rest of my life?!"

Startled by the violence of the emotion spilling forth, Tilly could only begin to splutter, "look, I w-was just-"

But Erin just steamrolled this attempt at placation, speaking over Tilly to cut her off.

"You've got it completely backwards: this is pain which cannot be borne sanely! Do you get that? Do you fucking get that?! It's only the blithe idiots who *haven't* yet experienced any lasting, profound agony who readily... just... puff themselves up with bravado and say" - she mockingly assumed a proud, boasting tone - "'oh gosh, yes, of course, if this worthy thing or that worthy thing demands it, I'll gladly endure some great suffering.' How easy it is to say! And how romantic they imagine martyring themselves to be..."

As she pictured the self-important smugness of those imbeciles, the burning enmity she felt abruptly derailed her train of thought. It was a visceral reaction and it completely seized hold of her. She was forced to turn her head to one side and grind her clenched teeth together as she tried to ride it out. There was no other choice, for under its influence she could not think or speak properly. It had passed before her mind's eye like an occluding cloud of superheated volcanic ash and was stubbornly disinclined to disperse.

"Look, I understand that you-" Tilly ventured diplomatically, sensing an opportunity to insert herself and defuse things while Erin was immobilized.

"Shut. Up."

Erin only managed to push these two blunt words through gritted teeth, as it was the most she could presently muster. Still, it succeeded in instantly shutting Tilly down again. Tilly frowned, but did not argue. The silence went on.

A few minutes later, Erin looked back round at Tilly. Now that her anger had simmered down somewhat, her tone had also downgraded to a mere note of irate resentment. She picked up exactly where she left off.

"But people who *have*... who *know*... they don't give a single solitary fuck about bravery, or honour, or any other dumb shit like that. They just want the pain to... stop. They'd cut their own fucking eyes out if that was what it took to escape it."

Tilly did not want to incur another cutting rebuff. So she held off replying for a few moments longer to ensure that Erin was definitely finished.

When she felt sure it was now safe to insert herself again, she said guardedly, "I believe you, Erin. But then isn't it better to take your chances with the doctors? I know you view turning yourself over to them as risky, but at least it's possible that you will simply be helped, right? Whereas if you stay here... and do nothing... *you will not get better*. This is not like some toothache which you can just wait out. The problem is fundamental. You are a broken machine, trying to fix yourself without the schematics of how you fit together. Or even the, like, tools needed to disassemble and reassemble everything! Because of that, there is only one life awaiting you in here. I fear it will not be... very enjoyable. But don't you see that, once you get help, there are a million potential lives for you out there?"

And for a moment, Erin did see them, couldn't help but see them. They were like a firmament crowded with distant stars, each one twinkling with invitation. As with their real-life counterparts, she was merely staring at them with idle fondness, with no intention of setting off to reach them. But as time drags on, they're going to extinguish themselves in silent implosions, one after another after another. So that Erin's sky was gradually going to darken. If she waited long enough, hidden away within these walls, only a lone victor would remain. *A black sun.* It would magnetically drift closer and closer to her until, quite unnoticed, it replaced the neutral darkness of the unlit heavens with a possessive inky radiance. She'd be wreathed in it. She'd dance in it. And trapped in that clinging embrace, she would eventually forget that the sky was *ever* speckled with possibilities. So that on one far-off morrow, in a final degradation, she'd swear that it was never even so.

Annoyed, she shook her head to dispel this bleak reverie from where it was hoisted before her gaze.

And, on cue, the petulant urge to argue reasserted itself.

"Well, fucking enlighten me, what are these wondrous futures which await me out there, huh? I'm not exactly overburdened with 'marketable' skills, am I? Meaning I'll be lucky... eurgh... if I can elbow my way ahead of all the other would-be wage-slaves and get a job... waitressing or pushing papers or something just as crappy and low-paid. And that's just practical shit. Can you imagine *me* befriending people?"

"Hey, come on now, don't put yourself down, you're very-"

"Yeah, yeah, *you* may think I'm a sparkling conversationalist, and that's... uh, nice. But given that you're, like, whatever, a personified symptom of my insanity... and you're..." - she rolled her eyes and sighed - "wearing the pelt of my nearly-dead lover, no less.... I hope you can see why the stakes are kind of low with you. It's a bit different with real people, believe me. And like all goddamn hermits, whatever social skills I once had have *radically* atrophied from disuse. They're basically akin to... some useless, shrunken vestigial limb now."

"But, even if that's true... you could surely just re-learn how to be around others..."

"No! That's the part you somehow still don't understand! There are things I can't shed, things I can't get away from! Why can't I get that through to you?!" Erin jumped in, with irascible impatience, to say. She rubbed her brow wearily. "Okay, you know what? Storytime. And I sure as hell don't need you to say anything, just fucking listen, got it?"

Taken aback, Tilly just nodded complaisantly.

"I *was* planning to take this bad boy to the grave, but shit, I guess I am on the... unlovely escalator... down to it. And besides," she paused and scoffed in annoyance, "technically you already know everything..."

She was halfway hoping that Tilly might reflexively say something pithy in response here, just so she could jump down her throat and put off telling this painful anecdote. But no such luck.

"Alright. We moved house when I was a kid and I finally got my own room, with a lock on the door. I'd never had that feeling of privacy before. It was pretty intoxicating. And I started doing some... bizarre... things just because I could. Okay, so... I would... take this blunted knitting needle I found... and, uh... push it into my vagina. Like, all the way. And... kind of... just poke... the *back wall* or whatever. It didn't hurt. Or feel good. It just felt sorta weird and interesting. And, yeah, I'd do this occasionally, like, just while watching TV. I mean..." - she shuddered - "what the fuck, right?...

"God, you know what else? I vaguely knew that I should, like, sterilize it after each time. But I wasn't about to steal the cleaning supplies from under the sink and hoard them in my room, in case that gave the game away. So, dumb little shit that I was, guess what sprang to mind? We'd done this thing in science class where you clean a really, really grubby penny with different liquids to see which works best. And which is the winner? Oh yeah, that's right... Coke. Works like a fucking charm. So once I was done I'd take this metal knitting needle and dunk it in Coke. I figured that counted as cleaning it. And then I'd dry it with my hair-dryer and hide it away again for next time.

"Anyway, I stopped doing it after like six months or so. It was just sort of one of those inexplicable, infinitely embarrassing things you do as a kid. The problem is though... It's odd, later on the memory would randomly spring to mind during, you know, just like normal, happy moments. And totally... well... ruin and deflate them for me. Because I'd remember that I had done this really humiliating shit years ago, which I could never ever tell anyone about, unless I wanted to disgust them or get laughed at. And there

371

was this sense of loneliness and paranoia attached to that which really fucking sucked."

Tilly was following along raptly. She was stunned, and more than a little pleased, that Erin was choosing to share something so personal with her. Even if she couldn't fathom what its relevance here might be.

"Yet, if I go back into the outside world, I'll have a secret which is somehow... amazingly.... a hundred times more fucked up than that one. How could I carry on a conversation with someone when I'm just always thinking 'if they knew that I was once so batshit crazy that I had a long-term relationship with a fucking imaginary friend, they'd run away screaming'? Can't you finally wrap your head around that?! Out there, their aggressive normality would just make me feel like the world's biggest hidden freak, every moment of every day..."

At this point, Tilly waited a few moments to make sure Erin was finished. And then timidly raised a hand like she was in a classroom.

"Can I, uh, speak now?"

"Sure... Knock yourself out."

"Erin, firstly, thank you for sharing that with me. I know it can't have been... easy... to. Now, I suppose the big question I have in response is: is it possible that you're thinking only about what would be... umm, unpleasant... out there... because you'd rather not think about all the drawbacks and difficulties of your life in this apartment? I mean, seriously, consider that inverse calculus. What can you possibly have for yourself in here?..."

Erin's eyes glazed over as she fell into contemplation. And she absentmindedly zig-zag scraped her nails along her forearms while she thought something troublesome over. When she emerged, she gave her explanation slowly, very carefully meting out the words like she was afraid of over-sharing.

"I'm trying to be a *realist*. And okay, perhaps it's... like, too much to hope that I can actually make myself better. For now, at any rate. But, in the meantime, I just need things around me to get better. I just need to get to a new normal, where I'm... well, whatever passes for 'okay' with someone like me... and where I'm not constantly tormented by... what's going on with me and... what I know..."

To Tilly, this all just seemed like babbling.

"So... what? Do you have an actual plan for how to achieve this... this..." She hesitated, her expression contorting as she tried to think of a word which wouldn't somehow tick Erin off. But she soon gave up. There was simply no way to win at that rigged game. Better to not even play. "Uh, *whatever* this would be?"

Erin just micro-shrugged and crossed her arms.

"Not as such. An inkling or two, perhaps."

"Seems like something I'd be aware of..." Tilly said slowly, narrowing her eyes suspiciously. She inspected Erin's face for answers, or even the clues which precede them, but came up empty-handed.

"Yeah, maybe." A dark smile curved Erin's lips very slightly and her eyes glinted with slyness and mystery. "Or maybe... *compartmentalizing* is a two-way street after all."

CHAPTER TWENTY-THREE

1:10 PM. MAY 4TH.

(APPROX. TEN DAYS LATER)

"Why... do you keep... visualizing... yourself falling?" Tilly hazarded gently.

Startled by the broken silence, Erin pulled her forehead off of the windowpane, her face beet-red. She convulsively exhaled her held-breath and, rapidly and jerkily, sucked in a few shallow breaths after it.

She was standing atop the window-seat, and had been staring straight down. Having gotten so used to the view, she had to resort to holding her breath for a while and *really* focusing in order to artificially re-summon the feeling of vertigo. But it was worth it. It made what she was imagining seem so much more real.

"Good fucking lord, Tilly! Could you have picked a worse time to pipe up?" she barked. Her oxygen-starved redness seemed not to dissipate, because it was seamlessly replaced by a deep flush of irritation.

"Please answer the question," Tilly said with calm insistence, sitting at the other end of the window-seat.

She was facing away from Erin, keeping her gaze directed towards the room itself. And she was idly plaiting her long red hair, as if to occupy herself. These choices were not just incidental. She could tell that Erin was in a weird mood, the sort which could easily swing very hard either way.

Yet, by now, Tilly had figured out some cheat codes for how to deal with Erin's anger issues. She'd especially gotten good at judging when to use her body language to preemptively defuse potential blow-ups. For example, if she were to stare up at Erin right now, it might subconsciously antagonize her. Because, as with all other untamed animals, eye contact can sometimes be perceived as confrontational. So instead Tilly made sure she just seemed passive and even a little distracted. That was often, ironically enough, the best way to get Erin talking. It made her feel in control. It made her feel as though she was somehow actually the initiator here. This wasn't trickery *per se*, just a little well-intentioned reverse-psychology.

"Jesus, doesn't it answer itself? For real, aren't you a perpetual witness to how my life is? Don't you think maybe someone like me might occasionally just... want... to try and actually *feel* something?"

"But... I still don't understand it... Hell, I know you. I know that you don't actually want to die."

Erin crouched down, gingerly lowering herself into a sitting position. She was sat sideways with her legs splayed out along the window-seat, taking up all of the free space. This was both a comfortably lazy way to sit and, in some strange sense, a means of asserting her dominance. As if to double down on that, she didn't even respond right away. Rather, she stretched her arms up into the air and scrunched her eyes shut as a big yawn seized her. She seemed to really milk it, extending its duration.

At last, she just muttered mordantly, "yeah, well, a girl can dream, can't she?"

"That's not funny, Erin. Would you just explain it to me properly?"

"Eurgh, fine, have it your way. You're right, maybe I don't truly want death. *Maybe*. But fuck, how much do I really want... all this? I'm just floating through life without purpose or meaning, touching nobody, affecting nothing. Like some damn wind-up toy aimlessly bumping against the walls for however long its little winding-charge lasts. I mean, isn't that... pathetic? Isn't that a fucking squalid imitation of a real life?"

Tilly finally swivelled around fully and seemed to be taking a moment to weigh up the right answer. Unfortunately, Erin got impatient very quickly. So she just made a dismissive hand gesture and went on.

"Ah, forget it, you don't see it, Tilly. You can't. But the all-consuming *greyness*... the *numbness*... of my existence is becoming unbearable. The... the... aggressive tedium of that nothing-world starts to feel like it's gradually suffocating you. It really does. You get frantic to fend it off before it finally crushes your ribs like a boa constrictor. And so every day becomes a... hmm... how to put this? Well... an excruciatingly slow-motion panic attack. I mean, try dealing with that for a few months and see what mindset it puts you in."

"Even if that's all true, why picture" - Tilly flicked a significant glance towards the window - "*that*, then? I'm no expert, but plummeting to one's death can't be much fun either..."

"You really wanna know?" Erin asked as she pulled the open laptop up from the floor and toyed with the order of a music playlist.

Tilly responded firmly, "I really, really do."

Having set some soft electronic music playing through the laptop speakers, Erin abruptly got up and took it over to the bed.

Tilly re-appeared there, but Erin had already deposited the laptop and was now heading over to the kitchenette.

She reached into the freezer and grabbed one of the rectangular *EZ-MEAL* brand frozen meals. She pulled back the cardboard sleeve, which bore a laughably too-perfect picture of plated and garnished lasagne, and peered through the clear plastic. Even accounting for its dusting of frost, the contents did not look anything like the picture. Or, for that matter, all that much like food at all.

Swallowing hard, she grabbed a fork and stabbed the taut plastic a few times. Then she tossed it in the microwave and, her face tense with apprehension, slammed the door shut behind it. She clicked the dial around to the 'defrost/cook' symbol, span the timer all the way around, and jabbed the start button.

Through the transparent section of the microwave door, she saw the interior light up and the tub of alleged 'lasagne' slowly revolve.

When Erin turned, she saw Tilly had been standing behind her, looking on.

In explanation, Erin inclined her head towards the microwave and, with a deep sigh, simply said, "maybe if it's hot and in front of me it'll magically jump into my stomach..."

"Fingers crossed."

Now Erin leaned against the countertop and picked up the previous conversation thread.

"I saw this blog post once. It really stuck with me. It's this surfer guy and he's giving a first-hand account of... drowning. So, initially, he relates all the stuff you expect. The, uh, agony and terror of thrashing about, trying desperately to resurface. I mean, it's real harrowing stuff, no doubt about it. And... then... the water finally invades his lungs... and his body, sapped of all strength, falls still. But he claims that... in those last seconds... he felt this sublime, euphoric sense of... *relief*. His mind had made peace with the fact that the fight was over: not just this one, all of them. Life was just a fading memory and death was an approaching embrace, no scarier than any other dreamless slumber."

She paused to crane her neck over and look into the microwave again. Nothing much seemed to have happened yet, which elicited another sigh from her. Having to spend her time just waiting around for something as crappy as this was somehow an added insult, and uniquely exasperating.

Turning back to face Tilly, she concluded the story in a deadpan tone.

"Of course, then some plucky lifeguard pulls his ass up onto the beach and brings him back from the light. So it goes. But... that relief, you know? That sense of being done with all the hardships and indignities of the great farce? Yeah, I... think about that a lot."

Tilly's eyes lit up with newfound understanding. She nodded to herself and said, "that does make a weird sort of sense. So that's why you never imagine yourself hitting the pavement? You're really just lusting after that abstract... moment of freedom... right at the end?"

"Oh shit, wait, I haven't even told you the 'best' part yet," Erin, who hadn't really been listening, jumped in animatedly to say as she slapped the countertop. "I remember looking it up after I read the post, all scared and tingly with anticipation. And part of me was hoping I'd be wrong, but somehow I just knew what I was going to find. And... of course... he had committed suicide two years later. The people who knew him say he'd just fallen in with a bad crowd and become a real troubled dude. Hard drugs or whatever. Still... you can't help but wonder... what if the drugs were just to... like, try and forget? What if he had simply learned something you can't unlearn? An argument too profound, too persuasive to ignore. Because he had already glimpsed just how... *easy*... it was to be dead, you know? I mean... yeah... fuck."

Erin let this hang in the air for a moment and then walked along the kitchenette to the stovetop. She switched one of the electric hobs on to a low heat.

Stifling a quizzical look, Tilly said, "isn't that a... *tragedy*, Erin? All the incredible feats he could've gone on to do, all the wonderful things he had left to see and feel. But his demons overcame him and forced him to throw away something of immense worth... His life."

"Oh yeah? He squandered something of 'immense worth', huh? Well, isn't that convenient. Because the only people around to pronounce on that also happen to be alive. And, hell, who doesn't want to glorify their own circumstance if it can't be changed anyway? But I think there's another way to see it. You.... I'm talking, your consciousness, your whole *being*... are just plucked out of the soup of nothingness and crammed into a body, to be ceaselessly bombarded with experience. No-one asks you if you want to be alive. The 'gift of life'" - here she put two fingers in her open mouth and made a mock puking face - "is just foisted on you. What kind of shit is that? Seriously? 'Cause I can think of some much better fucking words for a gift, of very dubious value, which you *cannot* refuse."

Tilly did little to hide her aghast reaction.

"But however it comes to us, life is the only thing which gives anything meaning. I guess I kinda can't believe I'm having to ask this... but... you know that ultimately life *is* better than death, right?"

Erin gave a short, sharp laugh as she watched the hob slowly start glowing as it warmed up.

"Says fucking who? People who are terrified of dying? Well, shit, real convincing that. Like, what else would you expect them to say? But what good, objective reasons can they produce? Anything at all? Nope, they just spend their days playing around with every possible permutation of sophistry which will let them worship life and hate death. It's just the same old nonsense. Frightened by the stark unknown, they straight up regress to... children afraid of the dark. Cling to fairytales about some rosy afterlife. That's how desperate they are that the party never end. I mean, what is this invisible fucking cult of life? And I'm supposed to listen to its foot-soldiers?

You've got to be kidding me. Even if I'm still more or less agnostic about the question, I at least know that *that* camp is full of shit."

Impassioned though this diatribe was, it also seemed to be delivered in a weirdly detached way, like firing a gun at a target without even caring to look at it. Indeed, Erin was much more absorbed by what she had been doing with her hands. She was holding her palms up towards the hob, theatrically rubbing them together and warming them as though at a campfire.

Tilly was champing at the bit to pose her counter-argument, but this startling disconnect caught her attention. She seemed far too puzzled by what Erin was doing to not pause and inquire about it first.

"You're... cold?"

Without missing a beat, and now blowing into her hands like some frostbitten arctic explorer, Erin replied, "not particularly."

"Then...?"

Erin took a melodramatic sharp intake of breath. Then she condescendingly explained, "it's just something to do, okay?"

"Okay."

As if the fun of this game had somehow now been spoiled, Erin ceased her hand-warming and turned to scan the apartment, looking for something else to do.

Tilly realised she had better return to the point, before it submerged irretrievably beneath the passing moments.

"Out of curiosity... don't you think there's something to be said for not... obsessing unhealthily... about death? Doesn't that keep someone from becoming paralysed by the gravity of it all? And allow them to focus on actually making the most out of their life?..."

Already walking across the apartment to fetch something, Erin simply looked back over her shoulder with a peeved expression. This was to serve in lieu of an actual response for now. Upon reaching the shelf, she held the bottom of her t-shirt out like a canopy and dragged off a bunch of dusty, unused candles so that they fell into it.

Once she was done, she archly inquired, "you wouldn't be thinking about any morbid *obsessive* in particular, would you?... I mean, jeez, that's some spectacular, world-class subtlety on display right there, kiddo."

"I was just saying-"

"And I'm *just* saying: relax, alright? The last thing I need is you fretting over me like a paranoid helicopter-parent. Just because I have... fantasies... and I dwell on certain things a lot..." She briefly trailed off as she returned to the countertop and dumped out her cargo on it. "Look, I *am* deeply fascinated with death, yes. And, uh, I dare say you've some sense of the very good reasons why. But, well, I'm fascinated by a lot of kooky shit. Like, check my fucking bookmarks, it's esoterica on top of esoterica, and you can scroll down until your eyes bleed. So... just give me a break, will you? There's nothing wrong with, you know, being interested in weird stuff."

"Erin... I get what you're saying. But... 'fantasies'? That's a whole different thing, and you know it. I mean, come on, that's not normal..."

As she was inspecting each of the candles, Erin scoffed and sharply retorted, "is that right? Well, maybe fucking so. But I'd much rather be a freak than conform to the head-in-the-sand bullshit which passes for normal out there!"

Hearing her own hostile tone, she realized how disproportionately aggravated she was getting. And thankfully she was still in that goldilocks-zone where she wasn't yet *so* mad that she'd think this irrelevant. As it was, this development just didn't sit right with her. So she lay her palms on the countertop and leaned against it, closing her eyes. It took considerable effort but she forced herself to breathe deeply and slowly count backwards from twenty. *A&F* had recently recommended that she learn new ways to deal with these moments. Erin had taken this on board, somewhat. Her cursory Google search into methods of dissipating irrational rage had equipped her with only this basic technique. And it did not always work.

Tilly looked on, waiting patiently. Her mouth was slightly pursed with concern. These sudden anger flashpoints had been appearing more and more frequently. They were becoming a real problem. Especially because it really seemed like the bar for what could set Erin off was reset a bit lower with each passing day. The logical endpoint of this worsening temper was scary to think about.

When Erin re-emerged on the other side of her breathing exercise and opened her eyes, she didn't acknowledge what had happened or even resume talking to Tilly. That whole thing was just... put behind her now.

She just stood there holding her chin and appraising the possibilities presented by the line of candles.

Eventually she picked up the trio of tall dinner candles and carefully stood them up on the hob. Next to them, she placed a small, ornamental elephant-shaped candle. And then she swept the rest of the candles into a drawer, before stepping back to admire her work.

Tilly drifted over right beside her. For a little while they both just watched, shoulder to shoulder, as the heat began to slowly melt the wax. Only the whiny hum of the microwave could be heard.

"What am I looking at exactly?" Tilly finally asked, in a soft voice.

Pointing, Erin murmured, "well, those are skyscrapers."

"Sure."

"And all together it's a sort of... ephemeral tableau... entitled..." She tapped the tip of her nose as she spent a few moments coining a name. "'Lone ungulate witness of armageddon.'"

"Hmm, I must say, it's quite a privilege to have gotten to see its brief exhibition then."

Erin just gave a sober nod of acknowledgement.

The dinner candles had half-disappeared, each one tilting at odd angles as they were pulled down into the pooling wax at their base. Whereas, the elephant, due to the disparity in size, had already all but vanished into its respective puddle. Just the upper part of its head remained, seeming like an otherworldly sightseer tentatively poking its head up through a portal to look around.

Abruptly reaching out, Erin took hold of one of the dinner candle halves and jerked it free.

She nervously bit her lip and slowly brought it close. Holding it high above the open palm of her other hand, she tapped it to make it shed some hot wax droplets. More rained down upon her skin than she intended. She winced and gasped and nearly dropped the candle. But at the last second she tightened her grip on it and regained her composure.

Smiling spacily to herself, she moved her palm back beneath the candle and prepared to do it again.

"You're freaking kidding me, right?" Tilly asked irately.

Erin glanced over and mockingly answered, "hey, it's not self-harm... It's, like, fun and kinky or whatever."

Then she returned her focus and let another shower of molten wax pelt her palm, wincing again.

"Yeah, not in this context it's not. Cease and desist, please."

Huffing, Erin petulantly lay the candle back down on the hob, like a toppled tower. It quickly started liquefying again.

"I just wanted to see what it felt like, chill out. You don't have to be in full on fun-police mode all the time, you know. Besides, it wasn't even really pain. It is a little intense, sure, but mostly it's just the shock of the thing. And once you get over that, it's actually kind of a nice sensation."

"Okay, whatever you say. But you're not the type of person who can have *just* a teeny-tiny taste of heroin, Erin. So let's just move past this, why don't we?"

Erin folded her arms in annoyance at having been thwarted. And they both went on watching the hob again.

As the minutes passed, the tension gradually faded away.

Once all the candles had melted completely, their different coloured waxes began thoroughly intermingling.

"Sort of pretty in its own way. Is this stage part of the piece too?" Tilly inquired, to break the ice.

Despite herself, Erin chuckled dryly.

"Oh, yeah, sure. Let me think. What new-agey spiel would pass muster at some hipster art gallery?..."

She rubbed her jawline as she pondered.

"Well, shit, let's try this on for size."

Pretending to pompously push a pair of glasses further up her nose, she cleared her throat and put on a professorial tone.

"'Yes, yes, come closer chums. *See* how we think ourselves voyagers, distinct from our little stomping grounds. Yet in truth, we are but mere fragments of the cosmos, a means it has devised of observing itself. And, in the end, we all become one. A grand reunification with a universe that is mother of everything we love and everything we despise.'"

The amusement in her voice somewhat disappeared as she inclined her head in concession and added, "now... if only there was some way that

didn't sound so horribly true. To be just the latest cycle of the churn?...
Eurgh."

She reached over and turned the hob off. The accumulated wax
started hardening into the new shape it had formed. It now resembled some
flattened blob-like marine creature whose impossible ugliness is usually
hidden away in a pitch-black ocean trench. And the wicks snaked in and
out of its chaotically multi-coloured body like ropey half-exposed organs.
She looked upon her ungodly miscreation with no small degree of
gratification. To have taken objects with actual utility and then mutilated
them for the sake of art - even the mocking imitation of it - did elicit a
certain ironic delight. It recast creation as just the foreplay to the climax of
destruction. Finally, this was a form of order she could approve of.

She peeled her little monstrosity off the hob and broke it apart,
sprinkling the pieces into the trash. An ignoble burial, to be sure. But if she
was going to play god, she would at least be a merciful one. She had given
this poor, malformed thing a wretched existence. So she would make sure it
wasn't a long one. Fair is fair.

Going over to the microwave, she looked inside again.

Something was definitely happening, at any rate. To what degree this
visible change could be called 'cooking' was another matter entirely. The
pale yellow cheese sauce slathered on top was bubbling in a way that was
rather unpleasant to behold. Erin almost gagged at the sight, but the urge
thankfully departed just as quickly as it arose.

"Oh joy, we're well under way now."

Tilly glided over and offered weakly, "umm, good things come to
those who wait, they say."

With a little smirking eye-roll, Erin just sardonically retorted, "that
has *not* been my experience."

Tilly saw this moment of levity as an opportune moment to segue
back. The proverbial spoonful of sugar to help the medicine go down.

"You know, I'd like to go back to what we were talking about
earlier..."

Now Erin's mirth dissolved and her expression soured. An
involuntary growl of displeasure arose in her throat.

"This again?"

"I'm sorry that it upset you before. I didn't mean it to. I just think it's... really important that we talk this out."

"Forget it. I'm, like, beyond done with that conversation."

"Respectfully... no, you're not. You've been thinking of all the things you wish you'd said, all this time."

Wrinkling her nose in disdain, Erin shot back exasperatedly, "for fuck's sake, there should be some sort of self-imposed rule against you pulling that shit! Where's your goddamn sense of sportingness? If you're always just going to resort to... *that*, it's like playing tennis without the fucking net!"

Tilly made sure to remain even-keeled. She sensed that, despite this show of flailing against it, she had Erin right where she wanted her.

"Be that as it may, what I said is no less true. You've got more to say about this, I know it. So why don't we just jump back into it? You'll feel better for having gotten it all out."

"Oh it's for my own good, is it? That's really something! I mean, jesus, fuck me twice on tuesdays, sometimes I think you try to rile me up like this on purpose!"

"That's not what I'm trying to do at all. I suspect it's actually the subject which makes you angry, Erin, not me. And that's what I'd like to try and understand better. Why *does* other people's approach towards death aggravate you so much?"

Erin was perfectly primed for this little push to work. She was already so heated that it was easy for her to switch tracks without even realizing it.

"How the fuck could it not?! The hypocrisy of these motherfuckers is enough to make you wanna scream. Like, on the one hand, their whole society is set up to keep the reality of death obscured from view. People go to sterile hospitals to die. Shit, having been born there too, that symmetry is probably pleasing to the simple-minded sheep. And hidden away in some drab room, they play out their neat little... prosaic... anesthetized deaths. But even that's not enough! Because then the corpse is taken away, preserved and prettified, and used for some, you know, ritualized outpouring of grief at the funeral. So that *everything* is kept nice and clean and self-contained."

Looking for something new to occupy herself with, she pulled open a little kitchen cabinet containing odds-and-ends. And she noisily rifled through it as she talked.

"Mean-fucking-while, just look at all these weird torture-porn movies being pumped out like clockwork. Why are they so popular? Is it because they're just so... wildly fantastical? No, it's because they're *realistic*. In a scene where some poor bastard strapped to a chair gets his throat slit, the audience *wants* to see it go down like it would in real life. We're talking... the arcing spray of bright arterial blood... the thrashing... the gurgling... all that shit. That's what makes it so thrilling, so affecting. And that's why people will pay good money for the privilege of seeing it. Hell, more than that. They'll go and see it with their friends, completely unabashed. Even though this is, uh, a really fucking dark impulse they're seeking to satisfy, right? And it's all about that satisfaction, right? 'Cause, I mean, when it comes down to it, they're mentally masturbating to a depiction of murder..."

She finally pulled out a meat-tenderiser mallet from near the back, and slammed the cabinet door shut with her hip. She held it up to the light and inspected it. It was wooden, but it still had a substantial weightiness to it. So too, the pyramidal points on either side of the mallethead were nice and sharp to the touch. Whilst thinking over what she could do with it, she twirled it around in her hand and tossed it up and caught it a few times.

"Yet, what if you were magically able to put *exactly* the same scene - like, I'm talking frame for frame - before them, but with footage from a real snuff film? The question answers itself, no? They'd vomit into their fucking laps and call you a monster. Because not only do they want the cathartic emotional rush of seeing the thing... but they greedily also want the ethical get-out-of-jail-free card of it being labelled fiction. I mean, wow. Straight up, the cognitive dissonance needed to enshroud that... sublimated death-fetish... is some perverse shit. But who the fuck can really be surprised that's going on? If the reality of violence and dying is frantically hidden behind the curtain, people will instinctively seek out some way to... simulate contact with it."

Slotting the mallet into her waistband like a holstered weapon, she walked over to the center of the room. She sat down on the thick oval rug there. It was day-glo orange, the type of visually-indigestible colour which even the psychedelic '60s would have vomited back up for being *too* garish. It had been in her bedroom as a young teen, an ambiguously 'ironic' thrift store purchase. And, not too long ago, it was rescued from collecting dust beneath the bed at Tilly's behest, to try and brighten up the place. This had been... reluctantly, begrudgingly agreed to. Erin now made herself comfortable on it, with her legs stretched straight out and slightly parted.

"And isn't it just so perfect that that vicarious contact be as an observer? Because that's what it has all become about: partake without partaking. Like, woah now, don't get too close to the actual experience... or you'll be tainted by some of the splashback. No, no, stay at a safe distance, put up a few layers of abstraction to keep your conscience clean. 'Sure, it looks just like someone's really getting their throat slit, and I'm *enjoying* watching it, but, hey... it's just a movie being projected onto a screen... and it's just actors being paid to play pretend.' Yeah, okay buddy, whatever helps you sleep at night, I guess."

She lightly tapped the mallet on each knee a few times to feel some slight semblance of what the harder version might be like. It would not, she gathered, be terribly pleasurable. Nor would the joint itself escape unscathed.

Putting the mallethead between her knees, she shifted her legs apart so that there was just enough space for it to fit there.

Then she took a deep breath and hit the mallet down hard beside her left knee. Bringing it back up, she slammed it down again between her knees. And, readying it once more, she hit the empty space on the other side of her right knee.

Slowly and carefully, she took to repeating this sequence over and over.

"So... what's the alternative?" Tilly asked, eyeing Erin's motions with suspicion. She did not like this dicey 'game' - not one bit - but if letting it continue was the cost of keeping Erin talking, this was a compromise that had to be stomached. For the time being, at least.

"Shit, don't try and saddle me with that," Erin replied, as the rug-muffled *whack* of each impact went on. "Seems to me that 'how to fix everything' is just a... parlour game... for tyrants and utopianists... to play over brandy at their fucking clubhouse. I just know how *I* went about it. I wanted to see what death really was. So I'd... well, look... I was basically raised by the internet, right? Where you're never really more than four or five errant clicks away from stumbling upon some girl getting gangbanged or... some guy getting beheaded. Now, once you've gotten over the initial shock of seeing that fucked-up shit... I don't know, you get more and more curious. And the videos are, like, all right there at your fingertips. Autopsies, traffic accidents, war footage, et cetera. I mean, why the hell not? I refuse to be ashamed of such an... an... inevitable fascination. But then you're some weirdo freak? Some danger to the community?"

As her anger stirred once more, she increased the pace and the strength of her blows.

"And why?! Well... that one's fucking easy, isn't it? They don't want you thinking about dying, thinking about what it *means*. They want to make sure you just see it as a word, as a sort of abstract concept. Otherwise how the fuck can society hope to appease and mollify you with all its trivial bullshit anymore? And if you're beyond that, if the understanding is already in you so deep that... like... even trepanning couldn't siphon it out, you'll pay a steeeep fucking price. Oh believe me, you will. Because people are conditioned to sense that there's something... *wrong* with you. Something askew with your programming. They'll look at you like you're some, ummm, mad animal bashing its head against the floor, willing to eat its own... f-fucking... offspring or faeces. And you'll look back at them with... profound envy and profound disgust... for the vapid life their naivete allows for."

Whack. Whack. Whack. Whack. Whack.

Faster and faster and faster.

Harder and harder and harder.

"Because *you* know what the... slippery tangle of viscera... inside their bellies actually looks like. And *you* know that people can turn into terrified children at the end... hysterically begging loved ones to save them, to trade places with them. And *you* know what it is to... just... watch the human machine simply turn off, as the eyes go dark, as the lungs deflate one final time. 'Cause, like, the first couple times you see it? Yep, you bet your ass it really shakes you to your core. You think: Jesus fucking Christ,

387

the spark leaves a person and then they're suddenly just... *meat*. Is that right? How can that be right? But then you see it enough times to realize the truth is somehow even worse, even more disturbing. There was no transformation! Sure, for a little while, it roamed around... and thought itself special... and kept secrets and made plans... and loved and hated... and maybe begat more little versions of itself. But it was always - *always*, you hear me?! - just... just... moving-meat with delusions of grandeur!"

She reached the peak of her crescendo, and left the words behind. Her whole being had become attuned to the rhythm of the pointless violence. She closed her eyes, trusting that the spacing was now sufficiently instilled in her muscle memory.

Whack. Whack. Whack. Whack. Whack.

Somehow, the mallethead did still find only the rug each time.

"Erin, what the hell are you doing?!" Tilly shouted as she glided over at great speed. This idiotic multiplication of the danger could simply not be abided.

With an angry sigh and a shudder of annoyance, Erin abruptly halted. The meat-tenderiser was held motionless where it had been passing back over her right knee.

Scowling, she hissed, "just as I was immersed in the fucking flow!"

"Well, I'm tremendously sorry about that," Tilly batted back with fierce sarcasm. "But I can't just stand idly by while you try to hurt yourself!"

Erin was slowly pushing herself up to her feet and, upon hearing this, threw Tilly a haughty glance.

"It only *becomes* self-harm if I fuck up. And I was not going to fuck up."

"That's ridiculous! You know that's ridiculous! Nobody is that lucky!"

Kicking the meat-tenderiser underneath the bedside table out of frustration, Erin ranted, "god, you still don't get it, do you?! 'Nobody is that *unlucky!*' is what you would have said if you did! Because I *can't* miss. Don't you see? That would be too easy."

"Call me crazy, but I have the strangest feeling that you were really playing this... 'game'... and risking hobbling yourself... just to spite me."

"Yeah, well, not everything is about you, you goddamn narcissist."

"Why *were* you doing it then?" Tilly demanded to know, tapping her foot in growing agitation.

"Obviously you weren't listening at all earlier," Erin commented under her breath. She then recited with condescending slowness, "The. Need. To. Fucking. Feel."

"You can call it whatever you want. I just think it's a shame that whenever I try to get you to talk about difficult stuff, you have to come up with some way to derail or escape the conversation."

"Oh gosh, that is weird. But, personally, *I* just think it's a shame that it so often feels like I'm trapped in a shitty therapy session I never fucking asked for."

With that, she turned her back on Tilly and strode over to the microwave.

Jamming her hand in a tattered oven glove dangling from a hook, she pulled out the lasagne. Then she placed it down on the countertop and shook off the glove. As she ripped off the clear film covering the container, a blast of rising steam billowed out, forcing her to jerk her face out of the way.

"Damn... Nuked the fuck out of it," she remarked to herself. "Doubt you can really 'undercook' something like this, but there's definitely no danger of that now."

Unsurprisingly enough, she decided she had better leave it to cool for a little while.

She went over to the toilet to pee. Afterwards, she put some socks on, for the cold floor had once again progressively bested her desire to stay barefoot. She also rummaged through her wardrobe until she found a thin hoodie to throw on.

Tilly just kept out of the way and went on holding her tongue.

Finally Erin traipsed over to the bed and, pulling the laptop close, skipped the song that was playing.

"Oh fuck off with your self-indulgent fourteen minute track," she murmured.

Tilly came over and, as a peace-offering, softly quipped back, "it's like, just because your musical instrument is your computer, it doesn't mean you can just copy and paste the same part six times. We know what you're doing, dude."

A smile fleetingly passed across Erin's lips at this lame joke.

Tilly took this as a sign of success. She sat down beside Erin.

They were both just staring over at the container on the countertop, from which was still issuing a very thin form of steam.

Several moments went by and then Tilly said, "I know it sucks, but you *will* feel better with some food inside you."

Erin deliberately chewed her nails for a bit before responding.

"In one sense, perhaps. In another, it's actually just the opposite. It feels like another tiny little part of me is chipped away every time I manage to choke something like this down."

To that, Tilly had no ready answer. Or no good one, at any rate.

So Erin filled the silence instead.

"But, anyway, don't you see how the act itself is... so... inherently loathsome... already? I mean, you're just mashing up some dead animals or plants, and with... well... what?"

Her hands shot up to her mouth and she tapped the pad of each thumb against the sharp points of her fangs.

"*These* ridiculous fucking things! Repurposed bone-nubs jutting up out of your gums. Jab, jab, jab, they go. And then you're sliding the mush down your gullet into... an honest-to-god sack of acid. Like, what the actual fuck?"

There was a pause as she mulled it all over. She was also absentmindedly inspecting the faint indentations left on her thumbpads as they faded away.

"And the thing of it is: *you can't fucking not.* Hell... if only I could *just* see the absurdity of it, and not all the grotesqueness too. Seriously, can't you see the knowing smirk lurking right there in the fucking design? It's... just... absolutely infuriating. I don't know how anyone functions, knowing this shit."

Now Erin stood up, still staring intently over at the lasagne. She slowly shifted her neck from one shoulder to another and back again, and cracked her knuckles both ways, like a streetfighter preparing to go blow-for-blow with their opponent.

"I mean, Mother Nature knows that we're so dumb that we have to actually be goaded and incentivized towards doing the things needed to keep ourselves alive. So the little trickster bitch gives us the ability to 'taste', right? Imbuing the matter we need to ingest with some... umm... phantom quality which makes it seem pleasant. And that's why no-one gives even one half of one half of one fuck. Because we are only too happy to be willing dupes. You never stop being a child, you know. Because... the true custodian... of your most profound state of childhood never changes. God, what a raw fucking deal it is to be human..."

Taking a deep breath, she started walking back over to the kitchenette.

"Okay, come on you fucking fuck," she said to the container. "Let's do this."

As riled up and newly determined as Erin certainly was for those few seconds it took to approach the countertop again, it was to just as quickly become a passing memory.

Once she looked upon the lasagne again, her nerve was already deserting her.

The cheese, having cooled and kind of set in place, had a dull plasticky sheen. It was mottled with unsightly gradients of colour all over. And it was flecked with the beads of grease it had sweated whilst cooking.

Forging ahead nonetheless, she grabbed a fork and held it poised above the lasagne. Her eyes briefly fluttered closed and she took a deep breath to prepare herself. Then she dug the fork in and levered it up and across, like turning over a spade.

With the lower layers unearthed, she inspected each one individually as if she were a geologist looking over the various strata exposed at a dig-site. The separating sheets of pasta themselves were so flimsy that they shredded like wet tissue paper when moved. And there was a thin tomato sauce throughout which seemed to serve as the lifeblood of the dish. She sniffed at it suspiciously, and it smelled very little like actual tomato... which was, no doubt, not its primary constituent. Next, there was some unidentifiable mix of ground meat which, when examined closely, had a disquietingly anemic colour. It wasn't *quite* grey, but even being in the same ballpark as grey was surely cause for concern. And finally there seemed to be some liquid run-off from the thick cheese topping which had wormed its way downward, suffusing everything else.

She ended up staring at it for so long that she zoned out and began idly rearranging the contents with her fork.

Eventually Tilly came over to check on her.

And Erin, without pulling her gaze from the safe remove of the middle-distance, said distantly, "you know, I really, truly, despise this fucking thing. Like, I genuinely feel a sort of deep, unremitting hatred towards it. How crazy is that? No point denying it though."

Tilly didn't know quite what to say to something like that.

She resorted to just feebly trying to comfort her by saying, "please don't let it get to you so much, Erin, it's just an... unappetizing... lasagne..."

Without moving her head a millimeter, Erin snapped her gaze onto Tilly with arresting speed.

"No," she uttered firmly. "It's not *just* that. And you know why?"

A little flustered by Erin's intensity, Tilly shook her head meekly.

In a deeply weary voice, Erin explained.

"Because that thing" - she stabbed a finger towards the lasagne - "is just a microcosm of *all this.*" Here she derisively made a swirling hand gesture to indicate the whole apartment. "Neatly contained fucking misery."

She paused, collecting her thoughts and sighing.

"And, shit... you wanna hear what I resent most about it? This cheap, nasty congealed crud they have enough... unveiled contempt for humanity... to call 'food'? They *know* it's fucking horrible. I mean, they assembled this unholy hodgepodge of low-grade ingredients, didn't they? And they chose all the unnameable preservatives to keep the thing from... putrefying... right there in its little plastic coffin before it can even reach you. So, trust me, they know only too well every nuance of its... just... utter repulsiveness."

Going over to the sink, she started washing the fork beneath the tap, aggressively scouring it clean with a scrubber-sponge. She did not want any trace of the lasagne slop remaining on it.

"But then... what does that say about all the motherfuckers who buy it? Because, in a sense, they know too. Whether they'd admit that to themselves before the final forkful gets deposited in their stupid snouts or not. Deep down, they know it's bad and they won't enjoy it... yet they still eat it anyway. And *will* go on eating it."

She was getting very worked up. Her breathing was fast and shallow. Grabbing some kitchen towel, she roughly dried the fork and threw it back into the drawer, where it clattered against the other cutlery.

Facing Tilly again, she concluded in a voice that got progressively louder and more vehement, "because that's just the way it is, right?! It's there... right there in front of you... a hot meal, technically edible. The lasagne *must* be eaten and you *must* do the eating. Who cares if you don't want to? Who fucking cares? 'Fuck your preferences, it's inescapable.' I mean, no, really, that's life, isn't it?! Because every time I wake up, a new day is thrust into my fucking face like that disgusting, steaming tub of lasagne. I know that I'm being presented with something truly awful. Still, there it is patiently waiting before me, mocking the high irrelevance of that fact. And then before I know it, it's the end of the day already and I'm putting the fork down and I'm wiping the grease from my lips and I simply *cannot fucking believe* that I've eaten it yet again. It doesn't seem possible. But it happened and it'll keep happening. The day after and the day after and the day after. And... I... I just... Jesus, 'I just' what? What? There is nothing. There *is* nothing! Here comes tomorrow again! Open wide! Oh god!"

Weak as she was from her daylong empty-stomach, the effort of expelling all of that seemed to exhaust her. She all but collapsed against the counter, awkwardly holding onto it for support. And though she was equally on the verge of either weeping or screaming, either one would have been preferable to what actually happened. For they would have provided a *release*, at least. Whereas she ended up just biting the insides of her cheeks in anger and exhaling a growl through gritted teeth. The surging emotion itself stayed trapped inside her, contained but still ominously visible, like a giant pocket of air seen beneath the surface of a frozen lake. And tiptoeing across that ice was henceforth to be her lot.

Tilly did her best to stay beside Erin and, striking a difficult balance, to speak both reassuringly and consolingly to her.

And when Erin had taken a good number of deep breaths and calmed herself a little, in the midst of a thousand-yard stare she announced somberly, "I... want it gone."

Picking up the lasagne, she held it with stiff, outstretched arms to avoid contaminating herself. And kept her face turned away to spare herself even the sight of it. She carried it over to the trashcan and stepped on the pedal to lift up the lid.

As she stood holding the container over the open garbage bag, the hot smell of the lasagne was nauseatingly wafting up towards her. She found it so viscerally revolting that for a split-second she feared she might just throw up then and there.

The thought of simply leaving this here, to stink up the apartment and serve as a malodorous reminder of another failed attempt at getting a meal down was incredibly galling. She just couldn't bring herself to do it. That would be giving *it* the last laugh.

Paying close attention to Erin's thought-process from afar, Tilly gently suggested, "you could take it to the garbage chute in the hallway..."

"Hmm, that's a fucking negative, Houston," Erin batted back brusquely. "Maybe you've forgotten, but I only ever take the trash out in the middle of the night for good reason."

She strode over to the window. At the very top of the window pane was a small horizontal section that could be opened inward, meant to allow additional airflow if so desired. Erin had to stand atop the window-seat, rising up onto the balls of her feet, to even reach it.

And straining up with her fingertips, she did just that. She tugged its handle to one side and pulled it open.

The aperture seemed just slightly not tall enough to fit the lasagne container through - even sideways - but she managed to cram it in there anyway. And with the judicious application of a good few hammerfist blows, she bashed it through all the way.

Like a spring contracting, she quickly dropped down into a crouch in order to watch.

She glimpsed it through the window for just a fleeting second as it fell. Then it was gone.

"Return to sender," she whispered bitterly. "With my regards."

"Erin..." Tilly began, her voice tinged with disbelief. "What... if that hits someone?..."

Nonchalantly, Erin reached up and slapped the window flap closed again. And with just a hint of sadistic enjoyment moulding her inflection, she said, "well, maybe it'll give the oblivious groundlings some sense of what life is really like. 'Cause some days you just get hit by a falling lasagne. Plow!"

She mimed something landing on her head out of the blue.

"But we're so high up... It's *not* a joke if-"

"Hey, hey, relax!" Erin interrupted, frowning at this killjoy deflation of her schadenfreude. "Firstly, I'm not exactly dropping an orbital bombardment from a space station, am I? It's just a plastic tub that weighs next to nothing and some fucking lasagne. And secondly, directly below us on this side is the entrance down to the underground carpark. So, at the very most, someone is just gonna have to hit the carwash later, okay?"

She flounced away and went over to the bed. She hadn't been particularly inclined to notice it at the time, but the music had inexplicably stopped a little while ago.

Looking at the laptop's screen, she saw that the music-streaming program had crashed for some unknown reason. She went about launching it again and signing into her account.

Tilly appeared on the bed too.

"Feel better now it's done?"

Erin just snorted air through her nose.

"Oh yeah, now that I've pushed a lasagne out of a window, all my problems are behind me."

Trying to be funny and lighten the mood, Tilly quipped, "hey, you've still got me, don't you?"

Stoney-faced, Erin slowly looked up at Tilly. She was clearly not amused by this.

"Yes, I still have you," she snapped, pausing her activity on the laptop.

And as she went on staring at Tilly, her countenance betrayed a sudden lapse into contemplation.

She mumbled faintly, "god... at least when you were... *her*... I had... something..."

Coming out of her nostalgic reverie, she returned her attention to the screen.

"And now... Jesus, Tilly, I still don't rightly know what the fuck to think about you. Or how to feel about you. I loved you once, because you were so pure, so outside of all this. You were a beautiful reminder that it's possible to be beyond the filth of this life, to be untouched by its taint. But... shit, now your presence sometimes just seems like a joke at my expense. So maybe you really *are* just another part of it, right? Another drawn-out ordeal thrown my way."

Erin didn't even deign to look at Tilly as she said all this, which made it even more hurtful.

Knowing this was done intentionally, Tilly tried not to let its crushing effect show on her face.

She just held her ground and asserted forcefully, *"that's not true, Erin."*

"Whatever."

Erin noticed that the tiny icon in the corner of the screen had changed to indicate that the laptop's battery level was very low.

Shifting about on the spot, she looked around the apartment to see where the charging cable was. She spotted it plugged into a socket near the window-seat. So she pushed the laptop aside, and quickly clambered to her knees. Then, in her haste, she pushed hard off the mattress to jump up to her feet.

However, as her feet landed heavily back down on the bed, the impact sent a rippling shockwave across the mattress. And the open laptop, which was already teeter-tottering precariously upon the bed's edge after being shoved away, was bounced off.

It did not travel far, rising and falling in a short parabolic arc through the air. Erin looked on, helplessly frozen in place, as it was coming back down. Trapped in that infinitesimal moment of watching, it truly seemed like she could feel each individual heartbeat as they very *slowly* thumped inside her chest.

The laptop hit the floor hard. It then rolled end-over-end for a few more feet and came to rest with the lid having been forced shut.

Naturally, as soon as it was over, Erin was freed from her paralysis. She leapt into action, scrambling off the bed and darting to the crash site. She delicately scooped up the laptop and, bracing herself, pulled the lid open.

It was no longer turned on, unsurprisingly. And the uppermost area of the screen itself, which bore the brunt of the fall, had become slightly warped and now stuck out of the bevel. There was also a dark streak, almost like a bruise beneath the glass, which extended in a curve from the impact zone down to the bottom left corner of the screen.

Erin couldn't help but be relieved that the screen was at least intact, because the alternative - a nice big crack - would have unmistakably spelled doom. Whereas *this* damage could perhaps be merely superficial. Still, a bleak panic was definitely creeping in as she mashed the power button, holding her breath.

The sound of the laptop turning on could be heard: a soft beep and the noise of a little interior fan whirring into action. But Erin tried hard not to allow herself to hope.

Five seconds passed. Then ten. Then twenty. Then forty-five.

The operating system's boot-screen should have appeared almost immediately. Yet, more than a minute had now elapsed and the screen wasn't even lit up, let alone displaying anything.

Erin just stood there, still cradling the laptop and dumbly staring at the dead screen. It was a goner, no doubt about it. And with it, went her ability to contact Grace. That was a real kick in the teeth. She knew she *should* be incredibly upset, but she already felt so spent that there was only a numbed echo of that emotion. It was, in a way, a much worse feeling.

Her expression was unsettlingly blank as she swivelled around to Tilly. In a calm manner which required great effort to erect and sustain, she simply said, "that's... just... fucking... great."

Then she emphatically dropped the laptop back onto the floor with spiteful disregard.

CHAPTER TWENTY-FOUR

7:50 PM. MAY 12TH.

(APPROX. EIGHT DAYS LATER)

All that could be heard was the sound of heavy breathing.

Erin's pyjama bottoms were bunched around her knees and she was vigorously masturbating.

Her other hand was clamped upon her breast and she massaged it roughly, over and over in the same mechanical way. She was sat on the toilet, on top of the closed seat with her back against the tank. There was not even the *slightest* trace of enjoyment upon her face. Her eyes were tightly scrunched shut and the tip of her tongue was just barely poking out from her intense concentration. The sharp chill of the cold plastic against her bare butt was distracting, and she was struggling to think of anything other than how much she resented it.

Suddenly she abruptly ceased. Her eyes shot open and she glowered in irritation. Wiping the sweat from her brow, she watched Tilly go by. Tilly was hovering supine just a couple feet above the floor, silently backstroking her way along the room's edge, gliding through invisible waters. Completing circuit after circuit after circuit. She was trying to somehow keep herself occupied as she waited for Erin to be done. The goal being to just stay out of the way as best as possible.

However, as she now swam past the toilet again, she inadvertently caught Erin's eye. An easy enough thing to do, especially when someone else is *trying* to make it happen.

Erin glared at her and muttered, nearly under her breath, "could you stop fucking glancing at me like that? It's, like.... eurgh, whatever, breaking my rhythm or something."

Tilly stopped dead in her tracks. Swivelling her body in mid-air, like an astronaut in zero-gravity, she re-orientated herself so that she was floating upright a short distance away from Erin. The weary expression that she now wore conveyed a perfect synthesis of disbelief and reprimand.

She sighed and said, "are you being serious right now, Erin? Quit your bullshit. I wasn't looking at *you* in particular. I was just looking around the room. There isn't really anything else for me to do presently, okay? *This isn't exactly happening very quickly.*" She rolled her eyes. "I mean, jeez, don't you think a vibrator would help speed this up a bit?"

"Fuck yeah it would. And so would wrapping a scarf a little-too-tightly around my neck. How about it, you wanna hold hands and jump down that whole rabbit hole with me? No? I didn't think so. So what's your fucking point?"

Tilly scoffed.

"Just a *bit* apples-to-oranges there, champ. I can think of thirty gazillion reasons not to do one, and none at all not to do the other."

"Listen, I already use machines for just about everything. So I guess I would like there to be one or two things I still do by hand. Just a tiny gesture of rebellion. An analogue act of self-pleasure... in an age of shitty digital gratification. I mean, if that's all okay with you, your highness. Or do I need to get your written permission to touch myself however the fuck I want? Like, which am I allowed to do, clockwise or anticlockwise circles? Are little spanks allowed? Pleeeease, I *really need* your sign off here..."

"Whatever. Just cool it, alright? All I'm saying is that this is taking so long that I'm guessing you're probably not getting your payoff this time. And I'd rather not have to wait around for *nothing*. Don't you realize that if-"

Provoked by this passive-aggressive barb, Erin angrily interjected, "hey! Yes, it's taking me... uh, longer than usual! But watching porn on my phone's little screen makes me feel gross, it's skeevy as hell. Can't do it. And having to now use my imagination fucking sucks! It sucks a... giant, swirling cauldron full of dead dicks! So, like, just give me a goddamn break already!"

Tilly jutted her chin up in defiance, and observed with dry condescension, "that's odd. I would've thought that you, of all people, would have no problem relying upon your mind to conjure up some... stimulating phantasm."

This comment seemed to deeply nettle Erin, causing her to sullenly purse her lips in resentment. She just glanced away and huffed, in childish non-acknowledgement of the point.

Undaunted, Tilly went on by saying, "here's how it is: firstly, unless you creepily want me to sit in the corner facing the wall while you... do your thing, you're just gonna have to put up with my wandering eyes as I try to alleviate my boredom."

Erin had not been expecting the sheer causticness of this put-down. It caught her so off guard that she looked back at Tilly with shock plainly plastered upon her face. Discombobulated, her mind drew a blank as she sought to compose a suitably scathing riposte to fire back. In this battle of wits, she had been disarmed. While she just floundered there in wordless consternation, she opened and closed her mouth a few times without ever actually speaking.

Tilly was not about to just wait around for Erin to come up with something. She seized the opportunity to hammer home her other criticism.

"And, secondly..." she began emphatically, with a sort of schoolmarmish lecturing tone. "Perhaps - just perhaps, *mind you* - you're struggling to orgasm because this will be... hmm, let me see... the fifth time today. So it's not all that surprising that at this point you're not getting much more than friction burns and finger cramps for your effort."

This cheap jibe hit Erin just as hard as the previous one, but as a follow-up impact it did at least serve to jolt her to her senses. It became instantly obvious that this was to be a zero-to-sixty moment. Her expression hardened into a war-mask of pure bestial hostility. In her impatience to fire off her first return salvo of wrath, she yanked up her pyjama bottoms and pulled the drawstring way too tight around her waist.

Then she jerked her hips forward to hop off the toilet, and strode over to Tilly, getting in her face.

With her fists balled at her sides and her face flush with fury, she launched into a rant.

"Screw you! How dare you fucking judge me! I don't need your permission or your approval! Every day is a thousand hours long and every hour creaks under the weight of a shitload of mood-crashing moments! So if I decide I need a pick-me-up, I'll do just that! Got it?! This shit is just about my only medicine and I don't need someone trying to make me feel ashamed for taking it!"

Erin's voice rose to a yell towards the end and she had barely noticed the spittle flecking her chin. She was fuming so hard, she was almost hyperventilating. And there was more than a hint of frenzy in the urgency of her wide-eyed stare. Her knuckles were now strikingly white, looking like snow-capped mountain peaks.

Tilly was very taken aback by the ferocity of Erin's reaction. Seeing Erin fly off the handle like this never stopped being distressing. She did not want to become similarly enraged and risk things escalating yet further. Still, she was not about to just back down and slink away with her tail between her legs. To concede this argument would only serve to encourage Erin's unhealthy mentality. So she had a responsibility to stand firm.

She turned her cheek to Erin and said in a low voice, "what-the-hell-ever, Erin. You said you were going to cut down, yet here we are: if anything, it's been increasing again."

Looking back around, she fixed a fierce gaze upon Erin.

"And, on that note, don't think I haven't noticed the 'surreptitious' self-harm," she added with an air of challenge.

Erin just about exploded at this goading.

"Self-harm?!... Fucking self-harm?!..." she practically screamed as her hands shot up towards the ceiling in frustration. "What the fuck are you talking about?! I said I wouldn't do it anymore and I haven't! Have you seen any *blocks of ice* get thawed recently?!"

In turn, this indignant denial seemed to push Tilly over the edge in her own way.

She replied with a standoffish energy, "oh don't play dumb. You know precisely what I'm talking about."

Tilly's posture became more assertive and she leaned in towards Erin as she spoke. This spurred Erin to reflexively take a step backwards, rather than be put nose-to-nose. She quickly dropped her hands down in front of her chest and kept them half-curled into fists, as though this were a physical confrontation where she might need to either shove someone back or strike them.

"You've just decided to be sneaky about it! All those times you 'accidentally' hit your knee on the bedframe as you go past it... or when you 'accidentally' nick yourself when you're shaving in the shower... or when you pull your hair hard as you're running your fingers through it... or the myriad other ways you do it! I see it Erin, I see it all. I see you savouring the pain each and every time! Hell, I see your actual thoughts as you decide to do it! Or did you forget that I'm cohabitating inside that freaking *ice-block* you call a head?!"

Erin's expression shifted into surprise and defensiveness. Her hands opened and slowly descended back down to her waist. More than the fact that her artifice had been uncovered, it was the reminder that she had foolishly attempted it at all which stung most. She had just been studiously preventing herself from thinking about how easily Tilly would suss it out. That had been the only way to make herself do it. A child who knocks over a vase doesn't think the broken pieces *won't* be found, they just put that completely out of their mind because they really want to knock over the vase. The tantalizing impulse trumps all, if you let it. So it was with Erin. Her ears and cheeks were now burning hot from embarrassment. Fittingly, it felt just like when she was a little girl being scolded for some recently discovered misdeed.

Noticing the change in Erin's demeanour, Tilly knew she had to take advantage of this opening. She dropped her voice a few more decibels, but made it even sharper in tone, even thicker with embittered disappointment. Her eyes were piercingly aflame. They held Erin petrified on the spot.

"And I kept quiet about it until now, because I figured this was probably just you working through some kind of emotional withdrawal effects from giving up cutting. But perhaps that was simply me being naive. Perhaps I gave you the benefit of the doubt when you didn't actually deserve it. Is that how it is? I mean, really, tell me. Do I have to freaking nanny you every step of the way to make sure you don't do anything stupid and self-destructive?!"

Erin was speechless and visibly shaken by this dressing-down, which had erupted forth like the spray from a newly unblocked geyser.

She turned and walked over to the bed. Sitting down on its edge, she put her head in her hands, with her palms covering her eyes. It seemed like she might be about to cry. Tilly averted her gaze. She was conflicted. If she had indeed pushed Erin to tears, she of course felt badly about it and wanted to go over to comfort her. But she also thought that this lesson had to be allowed to really sink in. That was the only way any good was going to come of this dust-up. So, if that meant letting Erin shed a few tears by herself before Tilly swooped in to offer some consoling tenderness, so be it. Such was the difficult choice one had to make when trying to help someone like Erin.

Completely oblivious to these well-meaning machinations, Erin was not playing her expected role in them. She was, in fact, not crying. Quite the opposite really. She was *seething*. After about a minute had passed, she suddenly ripped her hands away from her face. Her countenance bespoke how she had been re-energised by allowing her soreness over getting found out to recuperate her anger. She had taken a few unanswered shots, yes. But now she'd got her second-wind and was keen to rejoin the fight.

"God... thanks *sooooo much* for trying to mother me, imaginary friend my fucking craziness keeps around! How *wouuuuld* I survive without that in my life?!" she announced derisively.

Tilly briefly closed her eyes and took a deep breath which was shaky from profound annoyance. She couldn't believe her own foolishness. Here she was complaining that Erin never learned and yet evidently she was no better.

She was now so livid that she forgot about everything else. Erin had really, really gotten under her skin. As soon as the whites of her eyes reappeared, she drifted speedily towards the bed with the bearing of someone charging headlong into the fray. Doing this the hard way was A-okay with her. Bring it on.

So, once again they were alike. Even any inclination towards making peace had flown from both their hearts. And now the possible outcomes here had narrowed considerably.

"Oh yeah, you're so right Erin: fuck me for trying to help you make better choices, huh?! I forgot you'd much rather be left alone in a pit of despair, free to... to... pull the security-blanket of all your mistakes around you for comfort! This stupid self-fabricated mythology that your flaws have doomed you to always mess up! Wouldn't it be easier to just admit the twisted joy you get from screwing yourself over at every turn?!"

Leaping to her feet to confront Tilly as she came closer, Erin jabbed towards her with an accusatory finger and bellowed, "holy shit, can you do anything other than put me down and bitch at me! You're *soooo* wise, and you're *soooo* good! What a bunch of fucking horseshit! You're a fucking nagging shrew! No different from any other self-righteous know-it-all!"

These insults really hit their mark. Tilly's head involuntarily pulled back and her eyes widened a little. Her nostrils flared and Erin saw her swallow hard. Things just got ugly. Meaning that the state of play had shifted to a very dangerous place.

"And *you're* a selfish brat who pinballs between manic or depressive with the regularity of a freaking metronome! You will destroy anything good in your life if it means you'll get the *pathetic*... sulky... pleasure of feeling all aggrieved and misunderstood! Why don't you just grow up!" Tilly hurled back maliciously. She had issued her retribution in a quiet, measured voice, nonetheless dripping with acrimony, which had made the invective seem all the more sincere.

They just stared daggers at each other as the tense silence hung thick in the air.

Soon enough, having had time to precisely formulate the declaration, Erin spoke. She made sure to do so without breaking the insistent eye contact which tethered them, just as a snake-charmer does lest they inadvertently cede control of their subject. A mistake just as costly to make with fanged serpents as with unruly interlopers in one's own mind.

"To think I once saw you as my friend, as my... *protector*. I was a real fool's fool, wasn't I? How could I have ever trusted you, ever believed you had my best interests at heart? Well, no more. Because I see now that you are, and... really, only ever were... my *tormentor*," she said slowly, deliberately.

Tilly's face fell. It was an abrupt, total transformation. She didn't even seem angry anymore, just aghast, and hurt. Her taste for battle was draining away. Everything had been eclipsed by how this had wounded her deep inside. For it wasn't merely a slip of the tongue in the heat of the moment. It was an earnest repudiation. The type of thing you can't *really* take back, can't *really* unsay. No, it will linger as an invincible shard of alloyed suspicion and disquiet in the recipient's mind forever more.

Erin, however, didn't even care to notice any of this. She was too busy crawling across the bed and settling down into a cross-legged sitting position at its centre.

"I'm so fucking sick of this, of all of this. All I want is to be with *her*. Fuck everything else," she stated with cold-hearted determination. Her eyelids slowly drifted down and she gently rested her hands upon her knees.

But she suddenly scrunched her mouth up as though a troublingly unsaid point had just occurred to her. Her eyes shot open again.

"Just so you know, I *had* planned on something a little more, like... subtle and... voluntary." She looked away with an uncertain, sad stare - just for a moment - and then her gaze returned to Tilly. In a quiet voice, she quickly mumbled, "sorry... goodbye."

Her eyes closed once more.

"Erin?... Erin?! What... what are you doing?..." Tilly demanded to know, sounding confused and worried.

Yet Erin didn't even seem to register this, let alone respond. Her breathing had fallen into a purposeful, steady rhythm and everything about her read of extreme concentration.

Tilly had no idea what was going on or what to do. She was so seized with apprehension that she could do nothing but watch and wait.

Almost five minutes passed with Erin having retreated into herself in this way. When she opened her eyes again at last, she looked upon Tilly with an anxious expression.

She tilted her head inquisitively and ventured unsurely, "hello?..."

Tilly put a hand on her hip. The fact that this bewildering quasi-question was the first thing Erin said really set her off. What in the world was Erin doing? Was she *seriously* just trying to toy with Tilly at a time like this? The whole thing seemed either inexplicable or maddening. That was an easy choice to make. Tilly's look of concern morphed into one of vexed impatience.

"'Hello'? 'Hello'?! What are you playing at, you damn maniac?"

A deep scowl overtook Erin's face, and she let out a pained, guttural noise of pure frustration.

"Fuck!" she then exclaimed. She slapped her palms against her knees hard. Shaking her head, she hissed under her breath, as if just to herself, "I can't believe it didn't fucking work."

Tilly studied Erin's face very intently, as her perplexment began to admit the comingling of suspicion too.

"What the hell are you talking about? Jesus, princess, who else did you expect to greet you when you op-"

She stopped herself as the realisation made the question unnecessary.

Scoffing in incensed disbelief, she said, "you are just... unbelievable, Erin.... just unbelievable... You were trying to make me go back to just being *her* again?!"

Even emboldened by her anger, Erin couldn't meet the betrayal in Tilly's eyes. So she just sourly looked down at her feet, muttering, "that's all I *ever* wanted."

"How the hell did you think you were going to pull this one off despite me being inside your head?!"

"I-I thought... I'd found a way to circumvent your oversight and change how..."

Erin paused.

She had started to speak without really thinking. But as she noticed what was happening, how this was all turning against her, she caught herself. Now she felt the indignant rancor flare up inside her once more, and became awash with outrage. What was she doing? She didn't have to explain herself!

"Listen, you," she shouted, shifting up onto her knees to regain eye level with Tilly. "Let's get one thing fucking straight. You have all these delusions of control, but you are *not* the master of this vessel! You are just a... goddamn uppity stowaway. And you get to stay around simply because *I* opt not to fucking throw you overboard!"

None of this seemed to sting Tilly at all. She just laughed bitterly, and mockingly retorted, "if only that were true, you silly girl. How grand that would be. After all, if you *were* your own master, I wouldn't need to be here. Because... as in all facets of life... those who will not rule themselves, will be ruled over instead."

As she went on, she sobered and crossed her arms. So too, her voice regained its harsh edge of seriousness.

"I came about because your existence was utterly rudderless. You would not take ownership of who you've become, of what made you like this. You just begrudgingly occupied this 'sorry' body, this 'sorry' life... like they were decrepit hand-me-downs from some unknown wretch. But they are in fact precious, Erin, beyond measure. And yet you considered them as fit only to be despised and spurned. There isn't even a word for that kind of... profound... self-inflicted destitution."

She came over and sat down by Erin. Her voice softened. She was trying to strike a real connection here, to cut through the haze of anger that was clouding everything.

"We both know this is true. And what all that leads to is simple. Unsurprisingly, when you truly disown *yourself*... either you're just going to fade away like a freaking vanquished ghost... or something else is going to spring up to help fill that vacancy. I mean, how can you not see that?"

The way that Erin instantly got up and, without even looking at Tilly, dismissively waved her hand made it clear that she hadn't let any of this penetrate at all.

"Fuck you," she said as she walked away, like a hand-grenade nonchalantly thrown back over her shoulder.

Tilly exasperatedly watched her go. She was downright incredulous at Erin's immaturity in skulking away like this.

"Yes, of course. A devastating rebuttal to all my points, Erin!" she yelled after her.

"Go fuck yourself!" Erin yelled back without hesitation, still not stopping.

There was something about the sheer gratuitousness of this additional shot which seemed to compound its effect. It had much better success in irking Tilly. She jumped up and crossly stalked Erin over to the kitchenette area.

She approached Erin, who was hunched over the countertop kneading her closed eyes, and called out, "you can't just walk away from this!"

With taunting pettiness, Erin made Tilly wait as she took her sweet time finishing up rubbing her tired eyes. This had become one of her favourite ways to piss Tilly off, because she knew Tilly could see exactly what she was about to say. And there was a delicious absurdity in making Tilly wait for it to pass her lips anyway. It was a power move, plain and simple. But flexing that dominance, even in a small way, was key right now.

Eventually she lifted her elbows off the countertop and turned to say, "no? Because that's *exactly* what I'm going to do. I'm going to wash my hands of all of this. Reset it all. You will be *her* again!" Seeing Tilly shake her head defiantly, Erin raised her voice and redoubled her stridentness. "Oh yes you fucking will be! And then I'll find some way to re-bury this awful fucking knowledge I have! I don't want to know any of this shit! I'll figure out how to forget all about the fall and the hospital, and you'll just be the perfect girl from the perfect dreams again!"

This declaration seemed to hit Tilly with the force of an oncoming truck. Shock and panic were running wild all over her face.

In her dumbfounded state, she looked around frantically and whispered to herself, "how in the... Oh man, how have you managed to keep so much from me?..."

Snapping out of it, she sternly locked eyes with Erin once more.

She began gesturing insistently as she said, "Jesus Christ, you've got to be freaking kidding me, Erin. You've come so far. You don't get to just *unknow* all that you've learned!" Snorting out air like a bull conveying its willingness to charge, she slammed her fist down into her palm as she proclaimed, "I won't let you return to the shackles of your ignorance!"

"But you'd have me *shackle* myself to that hospital bed again?! I won't go back to the misery and hopelessness of that bleak non-life! I can't stomach it for even a single second!" Erin returned resolutely, ramping up to outmatch Tilly's fierce tone. "Besides, you don't get a fucking say in what happens! You're just a stubborn goddamn thought in my head. So you will do whatever the hell I tell you to do! And I demand that you be *her* again!"

"I will not! I am not your puppet or your plaything!" Tilly cried with gusto.

"That's *all* you are," Erin growled back.

Tilly became dead serious. Placing great emphasis on each word, she slowly and definitively uttered, "I refuse. It's not going to happen. I won't do it."

In mockery, Erin spoke in the same way as she retorted icily, "watch my fucking lips, bitch: you *will*."

Tilly didn't even deign to answer. She just crossed her arms tightly and set her face with stark defiance, making it clear she was immovable, indomitable.

Erin long-blinked hard as if she had been slapped. She stared at Tilly in disbelief. And then, quite involuntarily, she actually *snarled* as her rage surged anew.

"Alright. Okay. Okay. Oooookay. Oh you wanna push me? You wanna go ahead and push me?!" Erin babbled angrily, more or less just to herself, as she turned around to the kitchenette. She yanked open one of the drawers as hard as she could, nearly pulling it completely out of its frame. "Fine. That's just great. We'll settle this once and for all! Let's go, big shot! Let's fucking play for keeps!"

She rifled noisily through the jumble of assorted cutlery. As she roughly swiped sections of the pile aside, forks and spoons were pushed out over the side of the drawer and fell beside her feet. Then she froze as she finally spied the object of her search. Grunting in triumph, she snatched up the lone steak knife eagerly. She spun back around to Tilly, brandishing the knife with menacing poise. There was a wildness in the alarm that appeared on Tilly's face. And Erin made no effort to hide the relish she took in seeing Tilly's terror-stricken expression.

The knife was not very long, and the metal of its blade was thin and poor quality. So too, the cutting edge was almost dull, having seen much use but nary a re-sharpening yet. All in all then, it was an undeniably shoddy tool. But that did not matter. Not even slightly. For they both knew there were only two salient truths in this room in this moment: the knife was still perfectly capable of doing what knives do best, and it was clearly being held with purpose.

Tilly blurted out, "w-what the f-fuck are you doing?!"

"Well, gosh, you'll have to be more specific," Erin responded, sarcastically feigning confusion. With faux-casualness, she tried to find the midpoint of the knife's weighting by balancing it on her fingertip. "I'm such a multi-tasker that I'm always doing several things at once, don't you know?"

There was now a crazed glint in Erin's eyes, as well as a subtle twitchiness to her demeanour. It gave her the look of someone who was longing for a reason to go too far. It also suggested to Tilly that presently Erin was not entirely herself, not entirely in control of her actions. This was going to make de-escalating the standoff a great deal more difficult.

Obviously, Tilly understood Erin very well, and was usually confident in being able to find a way to reach her, no matter how fraught with chaotic energy any given argument was. But now she was confronted with someone who *wasn't* Erin, not really. In point of fact, this was not exactly a new phenomenon. There had been strange instances in the past where Tilly had glimpsed what it was like when the real Erin took a backseat to some maniacal, hostile doppelganger. These had been just fleeting, partial takeovers but they had been enough to fill Tilly with dread, for negotiating with someone she couldn't read was always very, very dicey. Still, how trivial those past predicaments tangling with that dangerous and unpredictable stranger now seemed. Because the ante had just been upped a thousandfold. What a new level of hate and fear she felt now that the stranger had not only fully kidnapped the Erin she loved, but also put a knife in her hand and bad intentions at the forefront of her mind.

Tilly spoke very cautiously, straining to keep her voice calm and even. After all, this had just progressed to a hostage situation. And a very complicated one, at that. So she had to play along for the moment.

"Erin... *why* have you picked up that knife?"

"Oh, this?" Erin held the knife up and turned it back and forth, making a show of inspecting each side of the blade as it caught the light. "You mean this little ol' thing that... hmm, damn, yeah..." She paused and theatrically peered closer at it. "I suppose it does kinda look like a knife, huh?" Wagging a finger in the air, she went on. "Deceiving, that. Because to my discerning eye... this thing here... is the magic wand that will finally get you to do as I fucking wish."

Tilly just stared at her, petrified with horror. Things were even worse than she had feared. What to do next was unclear. For there was a precariousness here which could not be overstated. It was as though Erin was sat in the middle of a minefield, as oblivious and vulnerable as a newborn. If Tilly sprinted across that hidden constellation of dirt-strewn pressure plates to save her, it would succeed only in relieving them both of the burden of having so many limbs. *Boom.* Yet, if Tilly's hesitation entangled her in inaction for long enough, Erin would likely crawl across one herself anyway. *Boom.* A quintessential damned-if-you-do, damned-if-you-don't dilemma.

On top of all that, Erin was sure as hell not even going to give Tilly time to think, to plan.

"Ah. You don't follow." Erin pretended to nod understandingly as she continued. "It *is* complex, I'll grant you. But, hey, let me give you a demonstration that will make it so much easier to comprehend."

Without warning, she jerked the knife up to her chin and motioned with it like she was going to cut her own throat.

Tilly's eyes shot wide in panic. She gasped and leapt forward, desperately hollering, "Erin, stop! Stop!"

Just as Tilly got close, Erin halted her in her tracks by abruptly lowering the knife again and smiling deviously.

Bewildered, Tilly was frozen in place mid-stride. She repeatedly looked back and forth between the knife and Erin's throat as if she couldn't make sure it definitely *hadn't* happened enough.

"See? See?! *Magic*," Erin exclaimed excitedly, her face contorting with deranged energy as she spat the words. The cruel glee she felt at having all the control in this situation, and exercising it so freely and so callously, was invigorating her in a terrible way. Whether a colossal army hangs in the balance or just one's own beating heart, none are ever so intensely drunk with power as they who take life and death into their own hands. And it is a form of hysteria which, generally speaking, does not spur those afflicted by it to make... admirable choices.

Taking a step back to where she had been beforehand, Tilly held up her open hands like a captive at gunpoint to try and keep Erin calm.

All she could think to say, in a quiet shaky voice, was "Erin, please don't..."

The smile slid off Erin's face. There was something so ridiculous and pitiful, in equal measure, about this response that it threatened to sap the fun from the whole thing. She scrunched her face up in displeasure.

"Number one, put your fucking hands down. I'm not a fucking bank-robber. And I'm not exactly worried that you're gonna come wrestle this away from me, am I?" she said contemptuously.

Tilly complied, slowly lowering her hands back down. She was careful to make no sudden movements.

"And number two. Given that we understand each other now, I'm sure I won't need to use this, will I? But you know I fucking will if you make me."

That this threat was stated so calmly, so resolutely, made it all the more bone-chillingly authoritative.

Tilly just blinked several times and stammered, "please... this... w-won't fix anything, it will only-"

"No, zip it, zip it, zip it," Erin snapped, barking the words like machine-gun bursts, which made them seem almost convulsive. This succeeded in getting Tilly to instantly stop speaking.

Holding the knife beside her hip, its tip pointing downwards, Erin came closer to Tilly.

"All this time, you've been trying so badly to convince me to sacrifice the present moment, to give it over to the effort to win some mythical better future. But fuck that! I'm fucking done with that bullshit!

There is only here and there is only now! And I deserve to fashion some kind of solace from my misery, whatever the cost! Not later! Now!" she truculently rattled off.

"I... can't be *her* again. I'm not her, Erin... I never was."

"You can be anything I want you to be! Jesus Christ, isn't that the point?! Isn't that the whole goddamn point?!"

Erin was getting herself worked up into furiousness again. As hard as it was to resist the temptation to back off and try to soothe Erin's temper once more, Tilly knew that time was running out. Erin's jitteriness was only intensifying. She was so tremendously on edge, so ready to bring this showdown to its climax. That meant taking the timid path would just be letting the timer tick down to zero.

It was high-risk, yet with her options dwindling Tilly had no choice but to act boldly. She had to reason with Erin, however possible. Perhaps find a way to make her stop and think. If Tilly could jam a splinter of doubt deep enough, it would puncture the adamantine armour of thought-shunning delirium Erin had sealed herself inside like the weaponized zenness of a kamikaze pilot.

"You can't go back." As Erin rolled her eyes, Tilly restated it with greater forcefulness. "You simply *can't* go back. There's no way it can be done."

Erin just turned away in disdain, and went back over to lean against the countertop.

Raising her voice, Tilly went on pleadingly.

"She's gone and you're here. I know you hate that. I know you wish you could switch places with her. But you can't! So you have to accept who you are now, what all of this has made you! She would want you to accept it!"

Erin had just been grinding her teeth angrily during this impassioned plea, but that last point caused her to absolutely erupt.

"Shut your stupid fucking whore mouth!" she screamed, gesticulating wildly with the knife for emphasis, so that it swung forth in reckless arcs before her. Tilly watched the knife like a hawk, flinching every time the path of the dancing blade came close to Erin's body. "You're not her, right?! Right?! So how the fuck could you know what she would want?!"

Tilly seemed about to respond, but Erin was not willing to hear it. She preempted it by wailing, "I don't fucking care! I don't fucking care! I'm done talking to you! I'm done with you and all your conniving shit!"

Conspicuously tightening her grip around the knife's handle, Erin held it up in front of her at the end of an outstretched arm as though representing the object and its significance for consideration.

"Let's fucking get to it: make your choice! Make your choice for the both of us! I *command* you to be her!"

Tilly was distraught and completely overwhelmed. She couldn't even bring herself to speak. She just looked at Erin with sad, desperate eyes, like someone impotently watching a tragedy unfold through a telescope.

Erin shrieked at this apparent refusal and brought the blade level with her chest. With a quivering hand, she pointed the tip towards her heart.

"Obey! Obey!" she ordered at the top of her lungs. "Obey, or all you've done to 'save'" - she made scare quotes with her free hand - "me will be for nought! I will perish here, right here, with this knife in my heart and her name on my fucking lips!"

"I... can't..." Tilly whispered, a tear quickly trickling down the side of her nose and falling off her chin.

Erin had never seen Tilly cry before. But it was easy to force herself not to register this and simply persist undaunted, because her brain felt like it was on fire. And *that* was a hell of a distraction.

Her stare was frantic and crazed. She ripped open a hole in her t-shirt and emphatically pressed the knife-tip right up against her chest to show she wasn't bluffing.

Spittle leapt from her mouth as she unintelligibly roared, in a rabid voice which had scarcely any resemblance to her own, "do it! do it! I command you!"

Tilly couldn't take the sight any longer. She bowed her head to avert her gaze as the tears continued to flow.

Seeing this, Erin actually gave a little choke of enraged surprise.

It was as though someone had just spat in her face.

And something inside her snapped.

With blinding speed, she pulled the knife away from herself and lifted it high in the air. Then, with all her might, she brought it down towards the top of Tilly's head in a cleaving motion.

As the blade was falling, Erin saw Tilly look up in shock and then close her eyes tightly as if in anticipation of the impact.

When the cutting-edge swung down through where Tilly had been standing, she had *vanished*.

For about ten seconds, Erin seemed to be short-circuited as she tried to process what had just happened. She just stood there motionless, gawking in blank awe at her hand and the knife.

Then the momentary escape provided by this dumbfounded bewitchment went away. She hopped backwards like a startled animal. Noticing the knife again, she instinctively opened her hand to let it drop, so urgent was her need to get it away from her. The handle bounced off her toes before the knife clattered upon the floor. She stared in frenzied confusion at the spot where Tilly *had* once been, scrutinising it as if it could yield any answers. Quickly giving up, she frantically scanned the rest of the apartment several times. Tilly was nowhere to be seen there either.

"No, no, no," she breathed out, looking again at the murder weapon lying right there on the floor. She felt she could almost make out how it was soaked in the invisible lifeblood of its victim.

But, of course, that knife was not the sole culprit here. Far from it.

Switching her attention to her guilty hands, she goggled at the front and back of them with a sort of... amazement. She felt such repudiating hatred for them that they now seemed as though foreign objects stuck to her body, like vile barnacles. These fingers were *not* hers; these knuckles were *not* hers; these palms were *not* hers. How could they be anymore? This flesh was fit only to be cut off and immolated, so stained was it with disgrace that was monstrous beyond any reckoning. Yea, whoever's it may once have been, it was owed to the flames now. Nothing less would suffice.

She pressed those loathsome former-hands together tightly, holding them up before her and shaking them imploringly.

"I didn't mean... I didn't know that you'd... No, no, please, come back! Come back! Please! Anything! I'll give anything! Please!" she yelled into the emptiness, her grief-stricken words incoherently blending together.

She was begging nothing and nobody. And nothing and nobody answered with great condemnatory silence. The verdict was unequivocal, unmistakable.

The walls of the apartment seemed to close in on her, inflicting an intense claustrophobic dizziness. And the suddenness of this disorientating feeling hit her like a rabbit-punch. It totally robbed her of her equilibrium. She kept changing her footing and stance as she tried to follow what seemed to be an errantly drifting center of balance and stay upright. While she did so, her upper body was swaying to-and-fro like an unbending reed buffeted by merciless phantom gusts. These erratic movements she was having to perform were making her feel even more sick to her stomach.

She was fighting against it mightily, but the universe evidently wanted her felled. And the universe always, always gets to win.

As was inevitable, she soon tripped over her own feet as she tried to shift them to a new position. She staggered unstably for a step or two. Then she crashed forward onto the floor, desperately windmilling her arms all the way down. Her chin was jutting out as she fell and she hit it hard on the hardwood, which sent reverberations through her skull. A split-second before the impact, she had automatically pulled her tongue back from between her teeth, which was very fortunate because if it had been there when the collision forcibly clamped her jaw shut, she would have bitten cleanly through it. This, however, was the only lucky aspect of the fall, and Erin was not even aware that it had happened. What she *was* acutely aware of was the ringing in her ears and the throbbing pain exploding outwards from her chin.

It was an instinctual reaction to instantly try to push herself up from the floor in order to get back to her feet. But once she managed to awkwardly clamber up to her knees, she felt the severe unsteadiness which was still present in her legs and realized the futility. As the fight deserted her body, she just kind of melted. She sunk back down and let herself fall onto her butt.

Sitting there, still wildly distraught and newly defeated by gravity, she felt what was coming and scooted over a few feet so she could lean her back against the cabinet doors. As soon as she got situated there, she could hold it back no longer and burst into hysterical sobbing. Her whole body was shaking. She wrapped her arms around her chest, hugging herself tightly. Letting out a tortured wail of agony like a dying animal, she bawled even harder. She tried really biting down on her bottom lip to try and contain the heaving out of sobs but it did nothing save splitting open her lip. And in a matter of seconds, the little fissure began oozing warm, metallic-tasting blood onto her tongue.

She was blubbering out, over and over, in a childlike whine, "I didn't mean to... I didn't mean to..."

Tiny droplets of blood flicked down her chin as she spoke.

Eventually she swiped the blurrying tears from her eyes, and the glint of the knife caught her attention. She abruptly froze, as if petrified by a lightning strike. Although the crying had spontaneously abated too, the sobs themselves, being a runaway feedback loop, continued to silently convulse her like hiccups.

She fixated upon the knife, marvelling dumbly at its terrible invitation.

Everything happened *very* quickly from there.

Without a second thought, she sprang over to it, literally launching herself towards it with reckless abandon. Her momentum caused her to slide across the floor on her side, and as she passed by the knife she snatched it up. Then once she came to a stop, she wasted no time in draining the very last dregs of her strength to clumsily stand up, albeit in a bent-over form. Wobbling and unstable, she just kind of stagger-ran back over to where she had come from. And as she reached the kitchenette again, she pirouetted around without stopping and threw herself backwards into a sitting position. Her back slammed heavily into the wooden cabinet doors but she barely felt it. Slumped there, she brought the blade close before her eyes, looking it over with a crazed intensity. She was checking whether it would definitely be long enough to score the crucial puncture. Seemingly satisfied, she spat out the blood and heavy saliva clogging her mouth onto the floor and resolutely wiped her eyes again.

She clutched the knife's handle with shaky hands in a reverse grip and aimed its tip at her chest once more.

Blinking rapidly, she struggled to take a deep breath between the diminished sobs still forcing their way out.

She pulled the knife back, holding it there ready.

A total calmness came over her, awesome and inexplicable. Her hands stopped trembling altogether, gaining the perfect steadiness endowed to implements of a foregone act. The final tears squeezed out the corner of her eyes unnoticed. She was inadvertently holding her breath as she summoned up absolute command over her body, banishing the sobs once and for all. Her gaze became distant, her eyes became glassy; she no longer saw the apartment, it had completely fallen away. There was only the seconds ticking by, and the sacred aura of her intention. But this was not sangfroid born of bravery. She was merely buoyed by a profound acceptance of her own death, as if it had already happened.

Slowly and very deliberately, her tongue tapped the roof of her mouth twice as she mouthed a word through lips shiny with blood.

Then she exhaled and plunged the knife towards her heart.

In that ultrabrief liminal moment, as her demise hurtled gleefully on a collision course with her, the universe watched impassively and placed her life in an uncertainty-escrow.

Erin didn't even have time to fully register that through bleary eyes she saw Tilly blink into existence before her and gently lay a hand upon her forehead.

In the very next instant, her eyelids fell shut and her body went limp. It was as though she had been knocked out by the implosion shockwaves produced when every possible outcome but one collapsed in upon themselves.

Her hands, still reflexively gripping the knife's handle, just plummeted heavily into her lap mid-flight.

The blade itself sliced through the thin cloth of her shorts and down into her thigh.

CHAPTER TWENTY-FIVE

At last, Erin came to.

But the state she was emerging *from* definitely did not feel like sleep. And *how* she was coming around definitely did not feel like waking up. Not least because her eyes were already open and her body was already upright and responsive.

Instead, the whole thing felt a bit like rousing her mind from dormancy and reassuming control over her body.

Bewildered by the deep weirdness of this transition and still trying to shake the heavy cobwebs from her perception, she only dimly registered that she was in the middle of her apartment. She was sitting on the rickety folding chair which had previously just been left leaning against the side of her chest of drawers.

She slowly rolled her head around, trying to lessen the uncomfortable crick in her neck. At the point in the revolution where her head was tipped forward and she was looking down into her lap, she pulled back bolt-upright in the chair as a surprise jolted her.

What she saw was the very large bandage wrapped around her thigh, because the lower half of it was peeking out from the *different* pair of pyjama shorts she now wore. A certain area of the bandage was stained with a streak of red. Now, even whilst discombobulated, Erin was obviously not the type to be freaked out by the sight of her own blood. Indeed, her reaction would normally be... quite the opposite. But to see her own blood and not know who or what spilled it? That was another thing entirely. It shook her to her core.

Watching carefully from a few paces behind Erin, Tilly took this as her cue to jump in. She came over and stood in front of Erin, and broke the silence by offering contritely, "hmm, yeah, sorry about that..."

Erin's eyes shot up from scrutinising the bandage.

Upon seeing Tilly again, a mixture of shock and disbelief overtook Erin's face. But somewhere in there was a little burgeoning elation too, shiningly threaded throughout the mask of her confusion.

"I know there are things you want to say - probably a hell of a lot of things actually - but I'm guessing cat's got your tongue, right?"

Erin didn't respond in any way, or really even seem to notice the question. She continued to just stare at Tilly in astonishment.

Observing this, Tilly smiled nervously. She murmured, "well, yes, see, there you go. So why don't I just do the talking for a little while?..."

Her smile faded as she nodded towards the bandaged thigh and, speaking up, went on to say, "first of all, again, I *am* truly sorry about your wound. I can't tell you how much seeing it tore me up inside." She cocked her head to one side, and pensiveness colored her features as she reflected. "The knife falling... I honestly didn't even think about that. It all... happened... so fast, there just wasn't time to. I'm not sure how much you'll be able to remember, especially presently, but..."

She trailed off, briefly closing her eyes and taking a deep breath.

Looking earnestly at Erin once more, she said, "just... please know that I would've prevented it if I could have."

After a few moments had respectfully been allowed to go by, Tilly wasn't about to let the stultifying silence persist any longer than necessary. She wanted to break the tension.

Perking up, she cheerily declared with no small measure of pride, "I patched you up properly though, don't worry. I'm a regular Florence Nightingale, don't you know?"

She smirked and did a little old-fashioned curtsy.

"Well," she began again, squinting mock-skeptically in concession, "without the treating gangrene or war raging all around or, like, uh, the historical significance." A pause for effect. "But besides all that trivial stuff... she and I are virtually identical."

Erin vaguely sensed that Tilly was trying to make a joke here. But she was having to focus so hard to merely follow the actual words being said, that her brain couldn't spare the extra processing power to register humor or irony on top of that.

However, this disconnect was to become moot as the levity present in Tilly's demeanour shifted and she was suddenly smiling sadly.

She sighed and said, "it's almost kind of funny, isn't it? How much energy did I put into trying to stop you from cutting yourself" - she lazily waved towards Erin's thighs - "and then look at what I go and let happen." The smile faded altogether, but the sadness remained. She struggled to meet Erin's gaze. "I... don't think you'll... like *this* scar much though. It's deeper than you prefer... and... well, it, umm, kinda cuts diagonally across all your neat little crosshatched lines. I fear it has rather sullied your careful self-harm aesthetic. So, uh, sorry about that too."

Though it was curiously difficult to work her mouth, Erin managed to ask, "w-wait, how... b-bad... was... it?..."

Tilly's face fell at this question. And she was long in answering. As she decided how to phrase her reply, she rubbed her shoulder anxiously and scrunched up her mouth.

Eventually she said in a timid, ashamed voice, "hmm, okay, so... it was, like, eight stitches."

Erin became wide-eyed, hugely distressed by this revelation. She whispered the word 'eight' in stunned disbelief, as if she needed to hear it again to force it to seem real.

Tilly quickly launched into an explanation, to distract Erin from her worrying.

"It's lucky that you had already watched tutorials online just in case. Otherwise I would have been quite at a loss as to how to do it. And, hey, it is a small mercy that you weren't around to feel what caused the wound, let alone what closed it. Well... not really anyway. So, uh, there's that at least. And I rooted around in your cupboards until I found some painkillers, to dampen any residual pain you might feel upon waking up."

It was evident that this attempted distraction had not worked. Erin was already so lost in thought as to be oblivious to all Tilly had just said. Amplified by the fact that her thinking was rather muddled right now, her mind was ablaze with catastrophizing as she imagined what the laceration must look like. And there was something about learning post-facto that she had had to be sewn-up which was also *deeply* disturbing.

Tilly was painfully aware that time was passing and there were things which still needed to be said.

She ventured, to break Erin's rumination, "Erin? You still with me, my darling girl?"

Abruptly called back to the conversation, Erin's eyes refocused on Tilly. A newfound intensity appeared in her searching gaze that was not entirely unlike anger and not entirely unlike sorrow. Her voice strained beneath its heavy load of jumbled emotion as she put forth the all-important question - the one which had conspicuously remained unanswered so far - as forcefully as her faltering speech would allow.

"T-Tilly... how... are y-you... h-h-here?!"

This earned a dry chuckle.

"Ah, yes, I am *quite* the resurrectionist." Then she paused and scratched her head. "No, wait, I think that refers to, uh, people who steal the dead... That's not what I meant to... Although, hell, I know you'd probably argue that I'm..."

Erin grew impatient with this meandering digression and cut it off. "Tilly!"

Tilly nodded embarrassedly, to acknowledge that this objection was fair. Part of her even knew that she had just been beating around the bush out of avoidance. She licked her lips apprehensively as she now steeled herself to tackle the answer seriously.

"You didn't kill me, Erin. You... well, you *can't* kill me. I'm not yours to kill. I think that would be like, um, 'double jeopardy' or something. It-"

"Then... w-where-" Erin began to interject animatedly.

Holding up her hands, Tilly interrupted in return.

"Easy now. Easy. Just give me a chance, alright? I'm getting to that."

Erin settled down and Tilly went on as promised.

"Okay, look, I... went away. It was a reflex. To... like... dodge, well, you know..." Here, obviously uncomfortable, she gave an evasive shrug. "And... I guess you could say," she heaved a heavy sigh, "I... *stayed gone*... because I was mad at you for... doing it."

Seeing Erin's eyes moving side-to-side as she frowned and tried to comprehend this information, Tilly spoke hurriedly in her own defense.

"But as soon as I saw that you needed me, I came back as fast as I could!" She stopped and unhappily put her hands on her head. Now she spoke softly, evincing her piercing regret. "Still... it's not right for me to be making excuses. What matters is... I should never have kept away out of spite, to try and punish you. I should have... been there. And so... I... apologize for that as well."

Tilly noticed that the very first traces of accusatory bitterness were taking root in Erin's hard stare.

They were quickly banished when Tilly stated in a parental tone, "and, of course, I know you're sorry about what *you* did too."

Pulling back in the chair slightly, Erin's gaze softened and shied away from Tilly. Her cheeks burned with shame and remorse at this reminder.

Tilly just let the statement hang in the air, like some talisman imbued with cleansing power dangling there between them.

When she did speak again, it was slowly and in a hushed voice.

"I know you didn't really mean it, that you weren't really yourself. And I know that you regret it." She tapped her temple. "I *know* these things to be true. And they, alone, are important to me."

Erin was heartened by this enough that she managed to make herself meet Tilly's gaze once more.

"Well, anyway, I suppose what I'm getting at is... I've had some time to think it over... and I truly forgive you Erin. I do."

The corners of Erin's lips and her cheeks began to twitch almost imperceptibly as she fought back the earliest sensations of the urge to cry. She was indescribably grateful that Tilly had offered her forgiveness. Knowing she didn't deserve it, she hadn't even let herself hope it might happen... yet, there it was. A beautiful, gracious gesture. A second chance.

Tilly couldn't bring herself to share in this tender moment. It wouldn't be right, given what she had to say now.

She looked away uncertainly and murmured, "you know, it's sometimes said that love is just two people having endless patience to forgive each other."

The inexplicable nervousness in Tilly's inflection caught Erin's attention and startled her. The coming teariness was immediately forgotten. Something... strange... seemed to be going down and she needed to be alert.

Tilly's heavy heart splashed her angst plainly upon her face.

Her eyelids fluttered as she made herself say, with a cracking voice, "so I hope you will continue our streak by... forgiving *me* for... what I'm about to do."

Erin felt her fight-or-flight instinct kick in. Exactly what that cryptic intimation could be referring to, she did not know, but it was ominous enough that fear began to tug at her. She was quite sure she didn't want to be here to find out what would need forgiving or *why*.

Way before Erin could try to make her move, Tilly looked back around at her, freezing her in place. Tilly's countenance now only displayed grim determination.

"I wonder how we're doing for time. Be a doll and take a look at what the alarm clock says, would you?" Tilly asked with an air of authority, speedily pointing over to the bed. Before Erin could even think about what she was doing, she found she was glancing over her shoulder at the bedside table.

"Ah, okay." Tilly nodded to herself thoughtfully. "Well, good, there we are. Tell me, how are you feeling?"

When Erin paused to consider how she felt, she finally realized the true extent of the peril she was in.

She now saw just how thick a stupor she was trapped in. With marvellous stealth, it had snuck up on her unaware. Like a blind-spot in one's vision, it wasn't even noticeable until one learned how to zone in on it, but then it became powerfully difficult to ignore. And it was a *myriad* of blind-spots in her mind which she now noticed only too well as she made herself focus on the full force of their cumulative effect. It felt like her cognitive abilities were struggling to bridge gaps and make connections, struggling to perceive the world with usual clarity. Her brain was running at *maybe* half capacity, with its security perimeter of skepticism flung wide open.

The low-level fear which had been bubbling away inside of her now escalated to considerable alarm.

But, still, she had been asked a direct question. And she discovered, as she began to speak without really meaning to, that she *had* to answer it.

She managed to slowly sputter out, "I'm... feeling really weird... and, uh, woozy, like... I don't know... kinda spacey... Can't think... properly... Everything is, uh, like... just... God, it's all-"

"It's okay, just breathe. You're okay. Everything is okay," Tilly broke in soothingly.

Erin was not soothed. She was peering at Tilly with saucer-wide scared eyes, like captured prey waiting expectantly to see what the hunter will do with them.

Exhaling dolefully, Tilly let a few long moments whip by before she added quietly, "look down at your arm."

Erin spacily tilted her head to glance down at her arms. In the crook of her left arm was a little circular plaster.

"You're not having some weird medical emergency or anything like that, don't worry. Just before you came to, I... gave you a dose of Ikelos." Tilly crossed her arms and her voice regained its stern, businesslike quality. "Quite... a... *large* dose, in point of fact. It will have fully kicked in now."

"Y-y-you.... *you*... g-gave... me?..." was all a flabbergasted Erin could stammer out.

A black terror seized her, and she felt a cold sweat coming on.

She had never before even considered that Tilly could turn on her, could seek to hurt her. She cursed herself for this infantile naivete. For now that the betrayal was in progress, she had no way to stop it or escape it. She was at the mercy of an antagonist who knew everything about her, who could see her every thought as it spawned and unfolded and then receded. Her most precious fortress had already been infiltrated and occupied. The enemy flag had been hoisted in her mind, and it flew there without any fear of reprisal. Because if this did turn nasty, she was completely unarmed; she had no ability to fire back.

She gulped and licked her bone-dry lips to little effect.

In a frightened whisper, she began to ask, "h-how d-did you-"

Striding over even closer to Erin, Tilly held up a commanding hand and brusquely said, "yes, yes, I know what you're asking. And I suppose you are owed some semblance of an explanation now that we're... here. But listen, Erin, you basically already know the answer. Because you already know that in the past I've taken... *control*... of you for a little while. I'd do it when you fell asleep, so you'd never notice anything was amiss. Obviously this time was a little... different... in that I had to forcibly bump you out of the driver's seat while you were wide awake. But nothing changed when it comes to me being incredibly careful about keeping you and your psyche safe when I'm the one behind the wheel. The stitches, the Ikelos? They both needed to be administered. So *I* took care of it. It's as simple as that."

Then, almost just as an aside to herself, she muttered sorely, "not that I can just do absolutely anything I want to when I'm in control. There are limits. Otherwise, I would've brought this nightmare to a close a long time ago, believe me..."

Erin was so horrified, so awestruck, that she felt like she was floating above her body. There was simply no way to process this new explanation. Merely sending clandestine IM messages was one thing... but that Tilly could keep Erin submerged inside herself whilst making her stitch up her own flesh without anesthetic or jab herself with a needle was unbelievable. It was an impossibility whose sudden absolute reality made the cistern of her mind runneth over. Her pupils were like pinpricks. Her breathing was as slow and herky-jerky laboured as someone knocked senseless by an oncoming car.

"But please don't worry too much about all that right now. There will... hopefully... be plenty of time for you to puzzle over the, uh, implications later. I know this revelation must be rather unnerving, but all that matters at the moment is that you're going to be fine. Just as you know what dosage is too much and how to inject safely, so do I."

There was a significant pause.

Then, with a grimace, Tilly slapped her leg and exclaimed, "Jesus, I'm stalling, aren't I?!... I... don't want to have to do this. I really, truly don't. I wish there *was* another way."

Little of this penetrated Erin's daze of total shock. Her brain was struggling to reboot. And while it did so, it had regressed to animalistic autopilot. In this state, its reading of the situation was binary: danger or no danger. And, of course, the colossal extent of the danger here was as palpable as could be. So the primitive instincts which were presently all that were at her disposal spurred her to react accordingly.

'Fight' was obviously not even an option. That meant its fleet-footed, battle-shy counterpart was her best bet.

Given her opponent, she knew it would take one *seriously* explosive dash to get away from here. She would need to move quicker, react faster than she ever had. Everything inside her primed itself, transformed itself to meet this superhuman challenge. Her dendrites were coated with gunpowder, the strands of her fast-twitch muscle were saturated with rocket-fuel. What would remain of her once the spark of GO! lit this blazing chain-reaction was... immaterial. The only imperative was escape.

Her whole body visibly tensed with potential energy and she went to leap away from the chair.

A millisecond later, in a perfect anticlimax, Tilly merely raised a barring hand and stated authoritatively, "you *cannot* leave that chair, Erin."

Upon hearing this, Erin found that it was true. The declaration had had the effect of a binding spell, making it so. She had only succeeded in raising herself a few inches up off the chair before Tilly intervened, and she now fell back onto it. Instantly, she sought to retry her escape, but strangely her body could not even be compelled to make the attempt. The pleas she sent to her legs to stand up were met with only the impotent flexing of the muscles there, as though they were but limp appendages which had not bones to support her weight with. Her brain was coming back online now and her ability to think, albeit under the narcotic haze, resumed. As it truly dawned on her that even fleeing was impossible, she felt very cold and very small. She shrank into the chair, withering under Tilly's gaze. She was stuck. She was helpless.

Tilly exhaled irritably, her nostrils flaring with tempered wrath. She could brook no challenge to her absolute power in this moment. That could have disastrous effects upon her ability to do what had to be done. And too much was at stake here.

Yet there were also flickers of pity in her eyes.

"I... understand... why we had to get that out of the way, but let's make it a one-time thing please. This *is* going to happen. I mean, I'm talking like death-and-taxes inevitable here. You cannot stop me. It's too late. I *am* your cellmate silverback. I *am* your angry god. So... I know this sounds terrible, and I hate to have to say it so crassly, but the more you fight against this, the worse it's going to be. I need you to be brave, to weather it as best you can."

There was just one simple question on Erin's lips, though she couldn't even bring herself to speak.

But Tilly saw the 'why?' nonetheless.

"All this... may seem like a thing of... wanton cruelty. Right now, at least. And, well... maybe for a good long while afterwards too. But please remember that what I do, I do out of compassion, out of... *love*." She was nodding slightly as she spoke, as if taking the final steps of cementing her justification to herself. "And love sometimes means you must act... ruthlessly. I am going to have to *hurt* you very badly, Erin. I am going to have to break you to fix you. And you're going to..."

She choked up a little and had to stop. Looking up at the ceiling, she gently rubbed her forehead as she tried to recompose herself. It wasn't easy, but she did it.

Then, bringing a steely stare down upon Erin, she whispered distantly, "you're... going to... *hate* me so much for doing it. And... I... accept that."

Erin was barely listening. She was alternating between widening and squinting her eyes as she futilely struggled to focus on Tilly's face. Even when she switched to looking at something else in the apartment, it was just so difficult to really see it and sense its realness. Everything, words and objects alike, just seemed so slippery and elusive when she tried to mentally grasp any of it.

With a tongue that felt heavy and clumsy, she whimpered nigh-unintelligibly, "w-what.... what are you g-g-going to... to do... t-to me?"

Tilly's expression became grave. Her voice became resolute.

"I'm going to try to free you from the sarcophagus of this person you think you are."

Erin had little luck in even vaguely comprehending what this meant, and gave up quickly.

"Look, for so long now I've been trying to figure out how to help you. And the way that that Ikelos overdose seemed to shunt some things loose in your memory and... the way that that crash scene affected you..." Tilly trailed off wistfully.

"I don't know, they just seemed to provide some insight into a possible... uh, methodology. Because I have something I need you to see. And I mean *really* see. Hopefully the Ikelos will make you sufficiently receptive to it. This whole thing is a hail mary, but, well, I don't really have the luxury of waiting for a better, less dangerous option to present itself anymore. You've entered the final phase of your death-spiral. So it's either this or I give up and just read you your goddamn last rites, and... *I'm not fucking giving up on you, Erin*, even if you want to give up on yourself," she declared with feeling, the passion swelling within her spilling over into her voice.

Suitably fired-up now, she stood up straighter and held her hands behind her back.

"Okay, no more preamble, let's get to it. I'll state the situation plainly: your mind is *mine* right now. It is completely and inescapably suggestible. A blank page longing - longing *so very* dearly - for my first penstroke. And it will be just as gratefully receptive when the hundredth glides across it. Hold tightly these things I write upon you, and you will make it through this."

She took a deep breath. And went on.

"Now, I don't have the benefit of fancy technology like VR goggles, so we'll have to do this the old-fashioned way. I want you to listen closely to me, Erin. I want you listening very, very closely to everything which passes my lips. My commands are unrefusable. My words are vivid, absolute truth. The world is precisely as I say it is."

Erin faintly intuited that she was being put into a state of utter vulnerability, and that she had to resist. But as Tilly spoke, she just couldn't stop herself from involuntarily absorbing and retaining what was being stated as true, like liquid flowing through a one-way valve. Once these new synthetic 'facts' lodged in her mind, she could do nothing to dislodge or

429

expel them, and a few seconds later would forget all about their insertion anyway. They became as convincing a part of the fabric of reality as the reports of her actual bodily senses.

Tilly was watching Erin with close, expectant scrutiny, as though an experimenter observing whether the substances swirled around in a beaker were mixing together as they should.

"Do you know where we are?" she inquired flatly.

This bizarre question took Erin by surprise. And it required quite a lot of effort for her to stifle an urge to shake her head no. She also found this urge itself disquietingly mysterious, but there was no time to dwell on that. Her main priority was trying to firmly reassure herself that she *did* know exactly where they were. They were in her apartment. They were in her apartment. Of course they were in her apartment. It felt so very important to hold onto that, even if she couldn't say why.

But Tilly was the sole fount of truth now. And by merely putting forth the question, she had implicitly cast doubt on Erin *actually* knowing where she was. Moreover, this was no ordinary doubtfulness, given that it had the backing of such an incontestable source. So Erin felt her surroundings flicker with uncertainty, flicker with possibility, like a thrown die when in mid-air its outcome is imminent but also presently infinite.

"We're in Gardwell Street."

And as soon as it was said, so it was.

Erin *saw* it.

She looked around the apartment frenziedly but it had wholly disappeared from view. Instead, she was greeted on both sides by the drab brickwork of the building fronts along the narrow side-street. She instinctively gazed down at her feet, but saw only the pockmarked black asphalt of the road, and on either side of it a slender stretch of pavement.

Her eyes were fully bug-wide and unblinking. Her mouth was clamped shut as though she had plunged underwater. She wasn't breathing, and she would have swore that her heart had genuinely stopped beating.

"And look" - with a graceful sweeping gesture, Tilly indicated to her body - "I'm wearing that outfit. The one I *was* wearing. You know, the one you liked so much. The black jeans. The faded BBDC tee. And that little raggedy jacket with the cool patches. You remember the jacket, right? You hunted through that vintage market and picked it out for me, didn't you?"

Erin saw the outfit on Tilly, and it filled her with a profound, fathomless dread which made her want to vomit out any part of her that could think or feel. To spare her from this, and especially what it was preceding. Her insides hurt like they were being stamped upon.

"The early morning chill was so much more severe than the weather app portrayed it as. It's that type of cold you can really feel in your bones, wouldn't you agree?"

Now Erin found herself beset by frigid air, which made her teeth chatter. She flung her arms around her torso in a futile attempt to conserve her body heat and, clutching herself tight, to try and smother the onset of shivering. Traces of numbness were just beginning to alight upon her extremities.

Tilly took keen notice of how this declaration had affected Erin. It also seemed to spark a reminiscence in her though.

She stared off into the distance and expounded in wistful tones, "but I wouldn't admit to myself how cold I really was, would I? It was so important to me that I try to 'toughen up', even if that just meant pretending that being underdressed when it was chilly didn't bother me. Who was I trying to convince, besides myself? But... youth's funny like that I suppose."

Snapping back to the present moment and the task at hand, she returned her focus on Erin.

"Anyway, I've got a quick errand to run, haven't I? For whatever reason, something really appealed to me about getting things done before most people had even woken up. And so, here we are. Gardwell Street. Just an unremarkable little shortcut really. And there's no-one around yet, still a little too early for that. I have it all to myself."

Tilly turned and went to the sidewalk, upon which a dusting of pale frost lay. She strode along it quickly.

Erin managed to just barely part her lips to whisper in fearful abhorrence, "no, don't, please, don't!"

Without stopping, Tilly swivelled around and, walking backwards, responded gently, "it has already happened, Erin. There *is* no preventing it."

She finally came to a halt as she took her position at the beginning of the sidewalk, far off towards the opposite entrance to the street itself. Impossibly enough, this spot seemed no less than about seventy or eighty feet away.

Reverting to her commanding voice, she shouted over with great authority, "don't look away. Don't you *ever* look away."

It now suddenly felt very much like a steel vice forcibly held Erin's head still, keeping her eyes directed towards Tilly. She tried to turn against this invisible grip, but failed. And it felt as though her skull might rupture if she tried to press any harder.

So too, it was incredibly distressing, but not surprising, to discover that she couldn't keep her eyes closed either. If she tried to extend a blink beyond its usual millisecond duration, her eyelids rebounded open like they were spring-loaded.

Tilly grabbed the headphones perched around her neck and pulled them up onto her ears.

She tapped play on the in-line button and set off walking towards Erin. She went at an unhurried pace, with her hands shoved deep in her jacket pockets. Her head was vaguely bobbing along to the beat of the music playing in her ears.

It didn't take long for her to get about two-thirds of the way down the street. At which point, yet another bracing gust of wind picked up. She tucked her chin to her chest and bared her crown to the headwind she was struggling through. Although she had formerly been walking along the middle of the sidewalk, with her head lowered and the stinging wind causing her to squint, she was now drifting left and right as she battled onwards.

A few seconds later, she snaked too close to the curbside. With her vision still limited, she unwittingly tried to step forward with her boot diagonally across the edge of the icy curb. Her boot tread found no purchase and slid off. As it landed on the road beneath at an awkward angle, she rolled her ankle. She let out a short cry of surprise and pain, and reflexively tried to hop back onto the sidewalk. But as she put weight on the newly injured ankle to push off the ground, it buckled.

Off-balance and with her boots finding little traction on the frosty sidewalk, she tripped and, still upright, skidded forward. She flailed her arms and tried to set her feet to end the skid, but the abrupt halt to her momentum jerked her upper body backwards and took her feet out from under her. She shrieked and fell onto her back.

Erin shot forward in her seat, squeezing the arm-rests and letting out a guttural noise of anguish.

As Tilly landed heavily onto the road, the back of her head clipped the curb-edge hard. It produced only a quiet *thud*.

And there she lay, unconscious and splayed out in the dirty gutter.

There wasn't even any blood.

Erin stared at Tilly's limp form unblinkingly. As she descended into herself, to languish in her own personal hell, a catatonic stillness sealed her in there. Her facial expression was frozen in utter mind-bleaching horror and her body, still leaning forward, was completely rigid.

Almost ten minutes then passed, and each one was an inhumane eon.

She registered the barely audible scuffling of footfall far away, but could not bring herself to turn around and look.

They got louder and louder, resolving into the distinct rhythms of two people walking together. She heard the footsteps stop just a short distance behind her.

And a deep voice, with a heavy accent she couldn't place, stammered out, "is that...? Is she...?"

It sounded like the man then cursed sharply in another language, and she heard the two of them break into a sprint. She felt their ghostly presence pass through her as they ran down the middle of the road at full-pelt.

The two men quickly reached Tilly. One of them dropped the duffel bag he was holding and knelt down beside her. It seemed like maybe he was trying to speak to her, but Erin couldn't make out the words. Then he ineptly felt around Tilly's neck trying to find her pulse. Giving up, he hastily switched to her wrist and found it there, weakly fighting on. He yelled at his companion, who was just uselessly standing there stunned.

This other man snapped out of it and swiftly fished a phone from his coat pocket to call an ambulance.

The scene abruptly froze.

Tilly just unceremoniously pushed herself up to her feet and dusted herself off.

She tapped each of the men, and they disappeared.

She speedily marched over to the chair.

She circled around Erin, scrutinising her carefully.

Once she came back around in front of Erin, she paused and mulled it over for a little while.

Then came the verdict.

"Again," she pronounced simply.

And with that she started to walk back to the other end of the street to start over.

By the end of the seventh repetition, Erin's brain felt like scrambled mush. She couldn't think, at all. She was just a vacant receptacle for torture and sorrow. And the anguish was constantly passing through her from head to toe and back again, like whirling thresher blades shredding and re-shredding her soul into ever finer dust.

At times, she had been gripping her legs hard enough that deep purple handprint bruises were beginning to sprout there. Whereas she currently had her arms folded tightly as she rocked back and forth. She hadn't even noticed it, but she had dug her nails into where she was holding her elbows. And the continuous rocking motion meant that she was clawing bloody scratches there. So strong was her frustrated desire to leave the chair, that the run-off energy *had* to be channeled elsewhere.

Tilly approached Erin once more and leaned forward at the waist to inspect her.

She let out a heavy sigh.

"We're done," she announced in a melancholic tone. "I rescind all my commands."

The invisible shackles opened. Erin limply slid forward off the chair, which closed itself back up and fell over. As she lay on the floor with one of her arms awkwardly trapped underneath her midsection, she did not even have the modicum of strength required to free it.

"I... just want... all this... to be over," she breathed out, quickly fading into unconsciousness.

Tilly came over and crouched down.

"It will be soon, Erin. I love you."

But Erin didn't hear it. She was already gone.

CHAPTER TWENTY-SIX

Erin awoke and heard the ringing.

Or was it the ringing which had woken her, had drawn her out of the black like a siren song?

It was hard to say.

Her body was so unbelievably stiff and achy. She blinked groggily and pulled her arm out from where it had been pinned beneath her stomach. As the feeling flooded back into it, the painful buzzing sensation of pins-and-needles followed close behind. Rapidly opening and closing her fist helped alleviate it a little. With a grunt of effort, she rolled over onto her back. Immediately she could feel that the side of her face which had been pressed to the floor was wet. She roughly wiped away the coating of dusty drool there with the back of her hand.

An unsettling sense of *deja vu* was quietly mocking her from the back of her mind. Waking up on the floor seemed so oddly familiar, but in her scrambled mental state she couldn't quite remember why.

That loud, insistent ringing went on. It was so terribly grating. The noise seemed to pass through her body in invasive waves, like bursts of radiation.

Cupping her hands tightly over her ears, she tried to block it out. But still she heard it. And, exasperatingly enough, just as loudly as before.

She groaned in deep frustration.

She tried to sit up, but found her body uncooperatively weak. So she gradually dragged herself across the floor to the towel-rack, and used its bars like ladder rungs to pull herself up with.

The very first thing which had to be done now that she'd regained the vertical was obvious.

Leaning against the wall for support, she looked around and strained to listen for where the noise was actually originating from. It seemed like perhaps it was coming from... the messy corner of the room? She traipsed blearily over there and knelt down.

The clutter in this corner was what happens when you need a cupboard in your apartment but don't have one. It had become a forsaken dumping ground for assorted never-used junk. Some of it was old stuff crammed into shoeboxes stacked atop one another, some of it was just dusty bric-a-brac haphazardly deposited wherever there was free space. There was truly no semblance of order to what found itself here: a few pieces of clothing and various broken household objects were even scattered in the mix too.

She started dismantling the large pile, pulling things out and tossing them behind her with reckless abandon. The time-capsule shoeboxes came open as they were thrown. They spilled across the floor tattered sketchbooks, once-precious trinkets, old letters, envelopes filled with photographs, et cetera.

Still the ringing emanated from somewhere in there. So she kept going, increasing her speed and often sneezing at the dust being kicked up into the air.

Naturally, it wasn't until she had moved almost everything and dug down to the pile's bottom that she made her discovery.

Right in the very corner of the floor, nestled in the crook of the skirting board, she spied the dull sheen of matte black plastic.

She yanked away the handful of things which were still atop it, unearthing it completely.

And there it was: the old-school rotary phone she had been fond of as a teenager.

It was definitely worse for wear. Even through its thick layer of dust, one could see that the plastic was marred with scratches and slightly dented from having been buried beneath a heavy mass of junk. So too, the Roman numerals on the rotary dial had faded to the point of being scarcely discernible.

In its neglected state, time was, at a glacial pace, trying to destroy it. But had not yet succeeded.

And although most of its fraying wire was wrapped around the cradle, the very end was plugged into a phone socket just there on the wall.

She stared at it dumbstruck. It was a simple object made terrible by her sense of it being an inexplicable doppelganger performing some taunting imposture. She had thought that this phone had not only stopped working several years ago, but also that it had been lost or thrown out shortly thereafter. Yet, evidently, neither was true. For here it was before her again: its return a precisely foreordained turning of a key in the penultimate lock.

She sat down before it.

Now that she had found the phone, she *should* have felt an urgency to pick up the receiver before the ringing stopped. But she did not. In fact, curiosity was the furthest thing from her mind. She felt only a profound disquietude, like upon encountering some uncanny object in a nightmare and dreading how, as is necessitated by the rules of that setting, it will prove to be bizarrely horrific in some way.

With the tenseness and bated breath of a bomb-disposal technician working without a blast suit, she pulled the phone over to herself. She slowly unwrapped the wire from around the base. Handling it was a sense trigger which caused a faint memory-artefact to resurface in her mind. She now vaguely recalled that she had plugged it in down here upon moving into the apartment, just out of habit. It seemed ridiculous to even set up a landline phone in this day and age, but because of her grandfathered-in fondness for this particular one, she had ignored that. And subsequently, of course, the phone had been hidden by the accumulating mound of equally useless stuff, and promptly forgotten about.

She used a folded-up pair of hole-ridden overalls found nearby to wipe away most of the dust from the phone. Then she laid her hands down in her lap.

And as soon as her hands rested there, one of them convulsively sprang back out and took up the receiver.

It had been instantly obvious to her that the only way she was going to summon up the courage to do it, to answer, was to seize upon any split-second where her trepidation waxed low. Or lower, at least. It was in just such a fleeting window of opportunity that she had forced herself to blindly give in to her impulse.

She slapped the receiver to her ear and meekly croaked, "h-hello?"

Her body stiffened as she heard a reply. A little yelp of shock escaped her as the caller identified themselves.

She blinked repeatedly and swallowed hard as she listened for a few moments.

"Uh, y-yes, yes, that's, uh, yes that's m-me," she answered as quickly as she could.

The caller continued. Erin's entire body was tingling like crazy. She felt kind of like she was having an out-of-body experience, and at the same time she was trying desperately to focus and keep herself present. The sheer gravity of what was being said to her was nearly unbearable. She wanted to seize upon and dissect every sentence with the meticulous fervor of a scriptural exegesis, but they each slipped out of her grasp as the explanation went on and she was forced to keep up.

"W-wait, I... I'm not sure I... like, I d-don't understand... What is that, uh, specifically concerning?..."

The answer that came made Erin's breath catch in her throat. She pressed the top of the receiver even harder against her ear, to make doubly sure she heard every word over the crackly line. She was so wide-eyed that her eyelids had disappeared, and her mouth had literally fallen open.

Eventually she interjected to say, with a voice that was shaky and distant, "uh, j-just... just one moment please... ummm, just let me, umm, grab something to write that down..."

She lay the receiver down on the floor and frantically looked around where she was sitting. There was a lot of things she could feasibly scribble on, but nothing to write with. She pulled a couple of half-emptied shoeboxes closer to check their contents and then shoved them away again in irritation.

"Motherfucker!" she hissed angrily.

She scrunched her eyes shut and lay her index fingers on her temples. Racking her memory, she tried to think where there was a pen in the apartment.

But it was just not something she had found herself needing anytime recently. So even if there was one stashed away someplace, unless *it* started ringing too, ferreting out its location simply wasn't going to happen fast.

Huffing as she admitted defeat, she snatched the receiver back up and murmured, "go ahead."

A few seconds later, she repeated back, "alright, so... sixth floor... ward B.... Dr. Vance. Got it."

She thought for a moment and then, before the caller resumed, asked, "uh, is there, like, a time... I mean, like, when should I... come in?"

She nodded eagerly as she listened.

"Okay, great, I'll... be there... as soon as possible, thank you."

After returning a goodbye, she very cautiously replaced the receiver onto its cradle as if it were incredibly fragile, and breaking it would nullify the equally fragile hope the call had filled her with.

Galvanised by what she had learned, she essentially just jumped straight up to her feet. But then, keen as she was to get going, the resulting headrush forced her to pause. She stood there, eyes closed, waiting for the pounding dizziness to pass. And under her breath she kept reciting to herself "sixth floor, ward B, Doctor Vance" in a sing-songy cadence, hoping to make it stick.

She opened her eyes again and started carefully stepping through the debris of her search, which was spread in a wide semi-circle behind her. Much as she would have liked to just trample over it all in a hurry, there were quite a lot of more or less pointy objects scattered across the floor now. She eyed these would-be caltrops warily as she picked her way through, very aware of how it would feel to have any one of them jabbing into the naked soles of her feet.

Emerging unscathed, she brought her gaze up again and saw Tilly perched all the way atop the fridge. Tilly was crouched, holding her knees, all compact and still with owl-like poise. An impassive sentinel, she had been discreetly studying the situation with watchful eyes.

Now she had finally been noticed, she glided down to the kitchenette countertop, to sit there instead.

"Howdy," she said, as she gave a short, sharp wave of greeting.

With her other hand, she was gesturing towards Erin's cellphone.

She inquired neutrally, "shall we call a taxi?"

There was something strangely off about Tilly. Erin couldn't help but squint skeptically at her, looking her over as if trying to ascertain whether it was truly her. Because as soon as she had laid eyes on her, Erin had this inexplicable but very potent feeling that she wasn't seeing 'her' imaginary Tilly, but a mere mirage resembling it. Just a copy of *the* copy, a phantom's simulacrum. And there was something unmistakably sinister about that. For you to create an imitation of someone, fine, it's *your* creature. But if it should then organically spawn, at the third remove, a counterfeit clone, there is a vaguely demoniacal quality to that. The resulting progeny would be self-substantiated, would have no ties, no obligations to any maker. Solely empowered by its own aseity. A fearsomely free agent with unknowable motives. All in all, not something you wanted to tangle with, for any reason, at any time. That's for sure.

Of course, there was also some kind of deep irony nestled in the fact that this sort of doubt was only *now* vexing her. Erin did not pick up on this, however. Her suspicion was that this odd reaction may perhaps be due to how the phone call had changed things.

Trying her best to just shake this uneasiness off, Erin ambled over to Tilly.

"So... you heard... all that?" she asked.

Tilly conspicuously waited a beat before answering, like a computer hiccuping as it processes how to respond. She was staring at Erin's pupils curiously.

At last, she dropped her scrutinising and said, "no, it seemed... rude... to eavesdrop. I just roughly got the gist of it from your side of the conversation."

Unsure what to say to that, Erin simply replied, in a flat tone, "okay then."

Tilly wasn't about to let an awkward silence take root. Forward momentum was key here.

"Do you want to tell me what the call was specifically about?"

"There's a, uh, doctor... who needs to consult with me. They... t-they...."

Erin trailed off. She could hardly bring herself to say it.

"The nurse was... umm... pretty cagey about giving too much detail over the phone, but" - she took a deep breath - "basically, she said that Tilly had shown some sort of really significant... *uptick* in brain activity. So she's been moved back to the hospital for analysis. They still have my details down as her... partner, and they need to talk to me before they can do anything else."

"So... there's a chance she might... be coming out of her coma?" Tilly asked, as delicately as she could.

This wondrous prospect actually being said out loud seemed to act as a trigger to free Erin's just barely pent-up excitement.

"I don't know, I don't know, maybe, maybe, I don't know," she sputtered out quickly. Her voice was high pitched with bubbling-over frisson at the possibilities unfolding before her eyes.

There was a skittish joy burgeoning on her face, held back only by her fear of really allowing herself to hope. But still the little smile of happy disbelief gradually grew wider and bolder. It was a sign of how desperately she wanted to abandon that sense of caution.

Deep down, she couldn't help but picture the most miraculous eventuality happening. And she was on the verge of giving herself over to a whole-hearted longing for it. It would be an attempt to lasso that desired outcome with the very fibers of her being, stretched and knotted, risking their unrecoverable loss in the process. Because she suspected there was a subtle power in *wanting* it to happen as only a child can truly *want* something to happen. Wherein, it is the strength and the purity of that desire which is seemingly all that invites the next minute to transpire, and the next, and the next. The unsatisfied wish, therefore, does not just threaten personal disappointment, it seems to imperil the continuance of the universe itself.

A profoundly melodramatic, narcissistic way of looking at it, to be sure. But if the outcome *is* somehow dictated, even in the faintest degree, by the intensity of one's wishing for it, there is no more potent or sincere an offering one may make than this. And if one already has no other means to affect the course of events, such a thing suddenly seems well worth a try.

Unsurprisingly, she was downright jittery as she picked up the cellphone from the countertop.

She looked up local taxi companies and downloaded one of their apps to arrange a pick-up.

There was a long period of hesitation as her thumb hovered over the 'confirm' button which appeared.

Occupying this anticipatory moment of pre-decision was unbearable. She just couldn't make herself do it. Not like this.

So she decided to pretend to launch herself into the moment *after* the decision was made, hoping to trick her brain into a measure of 'retroactive' courage. If she feigned that she had already made the choice, there was - in some weird way - no great willpower needed to merely make reality catch up with that state of affairs. Of course, the average person would find this notion absurd. But, naturally, Erin was no stranger to the practical value of these convoluted gambits of self-deception. For better or worse, she just had more of a... non-Euclidean mind than most people, making it particularly susceptible to such things. And over time she'd developed a whole book of tricks to use against herself for her own benefit.

She glanced away from the cellphone and went to return it to the countertop as if the deed was already done.

"It's booked to come in forty-five minutes," she said.

And as she let go of the cellphone, with faux-mindlessness she just let her thumb gently drift down to tap the screen.

Tilly nodded, a knowing glint flashing in her eyes, and replied, "good. You did well, Erin."

Erin just bowed her head, riding out the powerful feelings of surprise and pride at having actually done it which shook her insides.

Coming out the other side of it, she looked back up at Tilly and gave a quick nod of acknowledgement back.

Then, all business, she abruptly turned and headed towards the wardrobe.

Tilly's face scrunched up with discomfort as it occurred to her what she had to bring up.

There was no tactful way to phrase this, so she just said it.

"A... quick shower first, perhaps?"

Erin stopped in her tracks. She thought it over hastily. It was true, she realized, that she wasn't one-hundred-percent sure when her last shower had been. A few days ago... maybe. Surely no more than a week... she hoped. It definitely wasn't out of the realm of possibility though.

With a huff of annoyance, she reached up to feel her hair between her fingertips and then tucked her nose down into her underarms to sniff there. She looked back at Tilly over her shoulder with an expression which communicated that, at the very least, she did begrudgingly recognise that the point being made was not unfounded.

But nonetheless she brusquely declared, "there's no time."

Continuing to the wardrobe again, she added as an afterthought, "besides, I'm... changing my clothes... It'll be fine."

"Alright," Tilly returned unconvincingly, not keen to argue the point.

Throwing open the wardrobe's doors, Erin shoved the hung-up clothing back and forth, scowling at her dearth of options. All she wanted was something half-decent to meet what she was increasingly aware might be the most important moment of her life in. Alas, it was rather hard to know what the hell *that* outfit looked like. And even harder to make it appear out of thin air.

Five minutes of fruitless rummaging then passed. Until, finally, she lost patience with the search altogether. So she just pulled out a pair of almost-unworn mom jeans, an old band tour t-shirt and a heavy sweater. At minimum, she would at least make sure she was comfortable. That was better than nothing. She threw the clothes onto the bed in order to fish out some socks from the wardrobe's drawers.

Just after she had yanked her pyjama top off, she suddenly paused as an idea struck her. She dashed over to the sink and impatiently turned the tap on to full blast. Wetting one of her hands beneath the streaming water, she used it to speedily wash her armpits. In the process she noticed some scratch marks and a little dried blood near her elbows. There was simply no time to puzzle over these trivial wounds - which were probably the result of some mundane accident anyway - so she just cleaned them too. Then she grabbed a whole bunch of kitchen towel to dry her arms and along her sides where the wetness had dripped. Rubbing the rough paper against her bare skin did not feel good, but she forced herself to ignore the unpleasant sensation.

She hurried over to the bed, put on the t-shirt and sweater, and started stripping off her pyjama shorts. As she glimpsed her bandaged thigh, she paused for just a second before continuing to wrestle the still-too-stiff jeans up her legs and wishing they were so much more worn-in.

"I cut recently?..." she distractedly called over to Tilly. "God... my mind *is* all jumbly from this news."

Tilly's eyebrows instinctively raised, and she pretended to scratch her forehead to cover it.

"Yes... you... cut yourself pretty recently."

This was, after all, not really untrue.

With a little dry chuckle, Erin just remarked, "good thing I didn't pull out a skirt for today then."

Then Erin was pulling on her hi-top sneakers, and seemed to have easily put the matter behind her.

But Tilly spoke up again to carefully ask, "Erin... do you remember... what happened *before*? In... the chair?"

Erin didn't halt her rapid lacing up of her shoes or even look over, she just uninterestedly threw back, "what?... No.... What are you talking about?"

Tilly's face was grave. She was glad that Erin was now facing away and couldn't see it.

"F-forget it, it's not important," she weakly replied.

She bit down on her fist to vent her anxiety.

As it turned out, there were things even she could not foresee.

She was tinkering with unbelievably complex circuitry. It was impossible to monitor all the variables, let alone predict how they were going to tangle together in elaborate strings of interaction as this thing played out.

A newfound fear of dire miscalculation pestered her.

Was Erin truly ready for what was to come?

Tilly gracefully slid off the countertop and drifted over.

As she came close, she cleared her throat and then delicately prompted, "so.... uh... you're going outside..."

Erin flashed her an annoyed glare before returning her attention to trying to brush her messy hair down flat.

"Yes, that had rather occurred to me," she answered quite sharply.

"I just thought it might help to talk it out a little."

"Look, discussing it is just going to psych me out even more. You can see inside my head, so you know exactly how I'm already feeling about this shit and how utterly... just... undoable it seems. But here I fucking am. And there *it* fucking is, a feat that's as impossible as it is inescapable. So I *will* do it, somehow. That's all that's left now, just the doing. And I'm hoping that if I just fling myself into it, I'll be halfway there before my brain even catches up and, well, tries to... smite me... with whatever the mental equivalent of spontaneous combustion is."

She smiled darkly, but her gallows humour did little to actually comfort her.

Of course, there wasn't time for luxuries like comforting herself anyway. There was only the coming trial and the desperate steeling herself for it.

Tilly said slowly, softly, "for what it's worth, I'm sure of two things: you *can* do it, and it *will* be worth it."

She nodded to herself in affirmation as she spoke, her second-guessing dispelled. Something a lot like maternal pride and something else a lot like sadness swelled within her. So... this really was going to happen after all.

Tossing aside the hairbrush, Erin rose and looked at Tilly. But then she paused, as if unsure what to say. Her lips were tightly pressed shut and slightly quivering as she tried to keep a lid on the saccharine emotion struggling to break free.

"Thank you," she managed to get out at last.

Tilly inclined her head in acknowledgement and gratitude.

They stood staring into each others' eyes for a little while longer, sharing a moment together. The sense of approaching conclusion was palpable. These were the last few steps of an insane journey only the two of them had witnessed firsthand. It was a reminder of not only what they had gone through, but also the bond it had forged.

Erin pulled herself away first, heading towards the chest of drawers to retrieve something.

But halfway there, she stopped and seemed to space out, losing herself in peering into the middle distance as she contemplated.

When she snapped out of it, she turned back to Tilly and exclaimed in excited astonishment, "Jesus Christ, I mean... this is all just so crazy... Do you know what this means?!"

"Tell me," Tilly urged gently, drifting closer again.

Erin's voice dropped to a hushed and reflective version of itself. Her eyes were darting around searchingly.

"I wasn't there... you know... like... I-I left..." she began. Then she interlaced her fingers atop her head and sighed happily. "But this?... This is a... chance to *be* there... to start making things right."

"I'm so glad that this is happening, Erin. That this opportunity has presented itself. I hope you'll remember that honest-to-god second chances are even rarer than they say. Especially self-made ones. And I hope that you'll really seize it with both hands."

With a nervous smile, Erin shakily replied, "that's the plan."

Continuing over to the drawers, she opened the second one and dug through its assorted contents until she found a little silver coin-purse. It had been a long time since she had used it for anything, so she checked if there was still some money in it, which thankfully there was.

Tilly called over, "what about a hat? Looks like it's pretty windy outside."

"Hmm, yeah," Erin murmured in agreement and hurried back over to the wardrobe. She grabbed a beanie from one of the internal shelves and pulled it on.

Then she stood there just looking around the apartment, trying to review if she had done everything.

"You should... probably grab your passport, for ID. They might need some proof of who you are... to, like, give you access."

"Shit, yeah... Good call. I totally wouldn't have even thought of that."

She grabbed a backpack hanging off the side of the wardrobe and dumped all the stuff in it out onto the bed. She quickly rifled through the pile, but to no avail.

Tilly chimed in to suggest, with well-practiced faux-uncertainty, "zip-pockets maybe?"

Immediately, Erin snatched the backpack up off the ground and started opening its many zippered sections and jamming her hand into them. She soon made a little noise of triumph as she fished out the passport between two fingers. It slid into her back pocket nicely.

Tilly came alongside and asked, "how we doing for time?"

Going over to the kitchenette, Erin scooped up her phone and checked the screen.

Only to emphatically slam it back down a couple of times in vexed frustration.

"Oh absolutely fuck you, time! *Fuuuuuck you*! How did it go so-"

She cut herself off abruptly and, looking down at the floor, took a series of deep breaths. She had to stay calm, had to keep her head in the game. This was only the first in a long list of things she couldn't control. Given that she was leaving her domain, where everything revolved around her and adhered to her whims, she needed to rapidly acclimatize herself to being powerless again. And that meant remembering it would help nothing to lose her cool when things weren't going her way. She just didn't make good decisions when rattled.

"Okay... whatever. It is what it is. Basically, we should really start heading down now."

Grabbing the phone again, she pocketed it and the coin-purse. But then her nose wrinkled in concern as something occurred to her.

She said, piecing it all together as she explained it, "wait... 'we'? I hadn't even thought about that. Like, I mean, you coming with me. And... well... putting *you and her* together in the same room. It somehow doesn't seem... right? Isn't the two of you coming into close proximity gonna, uh... I don't know... shatter the space-time continuum or some shit?"

Tilly smiled in amusement.

"First of all, I think that rule is for clones. Or time-travellers maybe."

Erin opened her mouth to speak but Tilly held up a hand and wiggled her fingers to forestall it, and went on.

"And secondly, it's not real. As in, it's from sci-fi. Emphasis on the 'fi.'"

"Yeah, yeah, yuk it up, chuckles. You know what I mean. Maybe the fabric of the cosmos will make it through unharmed, but isn't it kind of... god, I really can't articulate this very well... like, umm, disrespectful or something like that?"

"Ah, I think I see what you're getting at," Tilly replied seriously, her expression showing she recognised the worry as valid. "Well, hey, it's up to you, of course. If you don't want me to come, I won't."

With a little apprehension, she watched Erin's face very closely as she made this bluff.

Certainly, having Erin mentally reaffirm the choice to have Tilly there with her was worthwhile. But as relatively confident as Tilly felt that she'd secure that useful result, this was ultimately still a gamble. And even loaded dice have been known to betray their owners from time to time.

Erin scrunched her eyes closed as she rushedly tried to think it over and make a decision.

"No, no, fuck, I need you. I need you there with me," she declared at last.

Tilly kept her relief well hidden.

She just nodded sympathetically and said, "then I'm happy to tag along and help you however I can. And if you decide you don't want me to come into the actual room with you, I'll hang back, you have my word."

Seemingly satisfied by this offer, Erin simply made a grunt of agreement.

Still, things now felt a little awkward.

So Tilly quickly piped up to redirect Erin's attention to the task at hand.

"We, uh, had better get going, no?"

Upon being reminded of the time constraint, Erin strode over to the door. She plucked the keys from the hook on the wall and lay her fingers on the deadbolt.

Then she just kept still. Her mouth hung open a little bit and she was breathing rapidly. She was staring hard at the deadbolt, willing herself to slide it open.

Tilly came behind her and, into her ear, cooed, "you can do this." She put her hand atop Erin's shoulder in a gesture of support. "I'm going to be right beside you the whole time."

"Okay," Erin whispered distantly. "Yes. Okay. Let's go."

Her gaze remained fixed intently on the deadbolt, but her hand didn't move.

"*Let's go*, Erin," Tilly instructed in a firmer tone.

"Okay."

Sucking in a deep breath, Erin jerked the deadbolt open. It made the grating noise of metal scraping against metal.

Then she gradually lowered her hand to the door handle and turned the latch there, unlocking it too.

Yet, once again she became paralysed, just standing there staring at her hand.

"Come on, you can do this. You know you can do this," Tilly stated authoritatively. "Take things step by step. All you have to do is open it and meet me on the other side."

She drifted through Erin and, blowing a kiss as she went, passed through the door.

Surprise and panic jolted Erin free from her immobility. She suddenly felt terrifyingly alone.

She could feel her pulse racing as she slowly depressed the handle and pulled the door open even slower.

As the hallway came into view, there was Tilly, beaming and holding her hands up as if to say 'see, I told you you could do it.'

Erin was just gawking wide-eyed at the open doorway and chewing on her bottom lip. The challenge of venturing into the hallway to take out the trash and of venturing into the hallway to actually leave her home was, it had become clear, worlds apart.

Motioning to the space before her, Tilly purred, "come to me, cutie-pie. Come on, just a couple steps."

Almost convulsively, Erin spurred her legs into action, making them carry her forward. She stepped out of the doorway towards Tilly.

"Don't think about anything else right now. Just lock the door behind you and let's go."

Turning back around towards the door, she carefully pulled it closed, as if afraid to make too much noise and attract attention. She locked it, and then, without giving hesitation any time to set in, set off down the hallway.

Tilly floated in front of her as she walked, facing her and offering a continuous stream of encouragement.

"You're doing great. You've got this. Oh you've got this. You've got momentum on your side now, just keep going. You can do this."

Erin was keeping her eyes solely on the shiny elevator doors at the far end of the hallway, and just focusing single-mindedly on getting to them. She didn't even let herself feel thankful that the hallway was empty, because in her peripheral vision she was, despite her best efforts, faintly registering all the apartment doors she was passing. And tempting fate seemed wildly inadvisable right now.

Once she had walked halfway down the long, narrow hallway, she passed the garbage chute, which was an important milestone. She literally hadn't been any further away from her apartment than this since she had made it her permanent refuge. Yet, she was actually a little shocked by how well she was handling this. Undoubtedly she was on edge, but she wasn't freaking out as much as she had expected to. She almost started to wonder if maybe she had overblown just how much of an impact venturing outside would have on her. After all, given all she'd gone through, what was *this*, really?

It would certainly be easy to seize upon this with both hands and use it to buoy herself. But she also had an inkling that this premature confidence was not to be trusted. The typical chronological arrangement of pride and, say, 'the fall' being what it is and all. Plus, she knew there was a massive difference between the comfortably confined space of this hallway and the dizzying expanse of the outside world. So she couldn't get ahead of herself. For example, by patting herself on the back sixty seconds in as if everything was already done and dusted. No, Tilly was right: one thing at a time. And right now that meant concentrating only on foot-up, foot-down, other-foot-up, other-foot-down. She made that her entire world, and every successive step became a small victory which helped propel her onwards.

451

This crucial concentration was rudely snapped, however, when she was just a few meters away from reaching the elevator.

She heard the distinctive *creak* of a door being opened somewhere behind her.

Her breath caught in her throat. She stopped in her tracks and held perfectly still, like a startled animal.

Tilly drew close and began to offer some words of reassurance.

"Okay, stay calm. You've got this. You can handle this. Just-"

But before the comfort of these sentiments could penetrate, Erin's panic got the better of her and spurred her into action.

From a dead stop, she leapt forward to the elevator doors. Then she hugged close to the wall and repeatedly mashed the call-button. Her jaw was clenched so forcefully that she was pressing her teeth together painfully.

In the seconds which followed, she was frantically issuing prayers to any deity who might happen to be attuned to her particular frequency of pleading. She gave no thought to the indignity of it, or the futility. Considerations of that sort were intellectual opulences which could only be afforded in much more secure moments. Now was the time for desperation and the seeking of impossible aid.

Please make it come! Oh please, please, pleeeease make it come now! Please! Never asked any of you for anything before! Please just this one thing! Just this one thing! Right now, right now!

When the *ding* finally came, signalling that rescue was imminent, it was nigh-euphoric.

Erin slipped in sideways as soon as the doors started opening. She quickly swivelled around to face the control panel and saw, about two-thirds of the way up the corridor, a middle-aged couple with a young boy in tow. The man was putting away his keys after locking the door and now they all started walking unhurriedly down to the elevator.

Tilly positioned herself between the elevator's open doors and waved her arms in the air before Erin's gaze.

"Hey. Hey now. Look at me, focus on me. You're going to be fine. Just breathe and focus on me," she urged.

But Erin couldn't really do either. Her throat felt like it was closing up, which was making breathing difficult. And she definitely couldn't help

452

but stare past Tilly at the approaching trio of strangers who would crowd into the small elevator with her. She was laser-focused on them, watching in helpless terror as with every passing second they moved ever nearer.

Her hand shot up to the rows of buttons and she jabbed hard at the 'ground floor' button over and over.

She was totally wide-eyed with panic. In that moment of horrified self-consciousness, she felt so certain that to merely behold her was to discern *everything*. With just one look at her, they would surely see the insanity she was lugging around with her like a luminescent bindle slung over her shoulder. Every permutation of the outcome she feared most played out in her mind. One stood out most prominently for its apparent plausibility: perhaps the man would seize her while the woman phoned the authorities and the boy laughed maliciously.

Her chest rose and fell rapidly as she sucked in short, shallow breaths through her nose. She knew exactly what the onset of hyperventilating felt like and she also knew how unwise it was to try and fight it off with panicky counter-exertion. Even at the best of times, it was just a case of riding it out and gradually seeking to elongate each breath. Only by careful, subtle resistance could its suffocating bear-hug be pried loose.

How she wished she could just lie down flat on the floor, cocooned in the sedative influence of perfect silence, and do just that. Because the prospect of trying to do it in this already frenetic, high-stress situation seemed preposterous. But if she gave in to the hysteria and maybe let a full-blown panic attack come on, she *was* going to make a scene. By drawing attention to herself like that, she would be making her most dreaded scenario into a self-fulfilling prophecy and all would be lost.

So she told herself that failure wasn't an option and went on inhaling little sips of air, daring for slightly more each time. Still, she was too afraid of telegraphing her breathing troubles to even open her mouth fully.

Although oblivious to this dramatic internal battle that was unfolding not fifty feet away, the woman finally noticed Erin's outstretched arm and instantly knew what it was doing. Her brows knit together in a mild scowl at not just the act itself, but also the aggravating rudeness of doing it so blatantly.

Erin absolutely could not believe the doors had not closed yet. Even though what felt like several unendurable minutes to her had, in truth, been only about twenty-five seconds. At any rate, the indisputable existential conspiracy to *totally fuck her over* in this moment seemed dauntingly vast and elaborate. It was very possible that her pleas had somehow rankled some divine intelligence who, in unbelievably petty retribution, reordered the universe itself to trap her in this predicament. Needless to say, she figured she'd better not issue any more requests for help to it, lest she be punished even more severely. Just about the *only* way this could be worse is if a stampede of diabolical clowns, each carrying a gift-basket full of spiders and smallpox, was thrown into the mix. And, given how things were going so far, she wouldn't be all that surprised if just such a finishing touch did suddenly materialise out of thin air right there in the hallway. But she sure as hell wasn't going to court its infliction any further.

So she could now only resort to addressing the elevator itself.

"Close, you piece of fucking shit! Close! Why won't you fucking close?!" She subvocally subjected the obdurate machinery to this barrage, never moving her lips.

With an inconspicuous jab of her elbow, the woman got the man's attention away from his phone. And by jutting her chin towards the elevator, she directed his gaze at Erin's infraction of common courtesy. The couple then united in shooting her a look of annoyed disbelief. The little boy trailing behind them was entirely unaware of the tension that had just erupted in the hallway. He was holding a tablet in an oversized protective case, with handles on either side, which seemed thick enough to withstand an armageddon or two. Whatever was playing on-screen was clearly very amusing, because his eyes were glued to it and he was chattering happily to himself.

At this point, Erin *really* wanted to stop pressing the button. And she *really, really* wanted to break eye contact with the couple. Unfortunately, she couldn't find any way to make herself do these things. So she just went on poking her now-numb fingertip into the button and helplessly absorbing the couple's projected resentment.

Becoming vaguely aware that Tilly, hitherto tuned out, was actually still speaking to her, Erin tried to listen again.

"-doesn't matter. You're going to be fine. Everything is okay. Just keep breathing. If you can, Erin, move your finger away from the button. I think pressing it so much is just confusing the system."

Erin's body seemed to react to this advice without her even prompting it to do so.

Her hand jerked away from the control panel.

The couple were just about to reach the elevator, and went on glaring at her. Given that Erin's arm was still raised, they couldn't tell she had stopped hammering the button.

On top of everything else, Erin felt like she might explode from the sheer awkwardness of this close-up stare-down alone.

And it was, naturally, just then that the doors began to close. Tilly hopped into the elevator by Erin's side.

Unwilling to even field the pretense of calling out for her to hold the elevator, the man simply quickened his pace to try and shove a barring arm between the doors.

But, infuriatingly slow-moving though they were, the doors still slid together before he got there.

Suddenly Erin was descending.

She finally lowered her arm back down to her side. And, as if to stop herself from collapsing, she stepped backwards and shoved her back against the elevator wall, leaning up against it for support.

Still staring unblinkingly straight ahead, with eyes glassy from fright, she whispered, "oh god, what have I 'escaped' to? I'm heading down to even more of them!"

Tilly quickly drifted back in front of Erin, coming face to face with her. Her voice was compassionate but stern as she laid out the game plan.

"Alright, look, we... we knew the initial shock of being around other people was going to be the worst, right? But you made it through it. So you know you can do this now. Just focus on continuing to slow your breathing down. And when we get to the lobby, we're not going to worry about what's going on around us, are we? We're just going to take a minute to regroup and recenter ourselves, and then we're going to forge ahead. Remember that you've got this, that you can do this. Remember how strong you really are. This is nothing, you're going to get through it totally fine."

Erin did hear all this, but she had received so much concentrated reassuring and comforting in the last five minutes that it was now going through one ear and out the other. She just nodded distantly in response. Presently, she simply had no spare brainpower for wringing what little bolstering effect could be had from well-meaning platitudes.

Her attention was entirely absorbed by practical concerns of a more pressing nature. She was fixated on the floor numbers slowly lighting up one after another. Grateful as she was that the elevator wasn't descending more rapidly, two fears were still dueling for supremacy in her mind. The first was that the elevator was going to stop at one of these floors and let somebody else on. The second was the elevator reaching the ground floor and dumping her out into the lobby. In the aforementioned contest, this latter fear did also have the rather unfair exacerbating factor of inevitability going for it. She couldn't help but visualise the ordeal of having to traverse the lobby, to make her way through whoever happened to be milling around down there. And so, as each little number lit up, it seemed like a mocking countdown to her impending doom.

With just a few floors left to go, Tilly snapped her fingers to attract Erin's notice.

Then she issued some instructions.

"Okay, we're gonna be there in a second. So... just go find somewhere to sit. That's all you have to do, Erin. You can do that. Just go and sit down. Don't worry about anything else."

And just as she finished speaking, the elevator *dinged* and the doors started to open.

But Erin didn't move.

She just fearfully peered out at the large lobby area.

Her eyes instantly jumped from person to person, cataloguing the occupants. Expectedly, the concierge was sat behind his desk, though she could only just spy the top of his head from this vantage. Then there was a small group of teenagers all the way over by the big windows looking out onto the street. They were huddled around a few suitcases pushed together and chatting animatedly. Lastly, there was a man in a fancy suit standing facing the wall, leaning against it wearily with an outstretched hand, and talking in hushed tones into his cellphone.

After about ten seconds, the elevator doors closed again.

"Okay, Erin, honeybun..." Tilly began gently. "We've seen what's out there now. Nothing crazy, right? So just go ahead and hit the button for the doors. Then we're going to head out and do just as we planned, alright?"

With a trembling hand, Erin reached out and tapped the 'open doors' button.

And as the doors opened once more, Erin stayed frozen.

Tilly, seeing this, drifted into the lobby and enthusiastically beckoned Erin in.

"Come on, just a few steps. Just a few steps. You can do that. I know you can."

With slow, stiff movements, Erin trudged out of the elevator. She stopped after about five paces. The sound of the doors closing again behind her sent a chill down her spine.

"Good job, you did great! Now, let's find a seat real quick and head over to it."

Erin scanned the lobby. There were a handful of different places she could feasibly sit, but the best option jumped out to her immediately. In the corner, there was a pair of armchairs facing each other with a little circular table in between.

"Okay, go, go, go!" Tilly ordered.

Putting her head down, Erin quickly strode over to the nearer armchair and slumped down into it.

Tilly sat in the opposite one. She began lifting and lowering her hands in a slow rhythm to encourage Erin to steady her breathing.

"Gooood.... gooood... keep going."

Within a minute or two, Erin managed to get her breathing back to normal and felt her quickened pulse fall back to baseline.

"Awesome," Tilly declared supportively to mark the small but significant triumph of getting here. "Okay, this is going to be our temporary base camp for a few more minutes. We're going to pull ourselves together and then we're going to head out. For the time being, just go ahead and grab a magazine."

There was a small pile of dog-eared magazines that had been left on the table between them. Erin reached forward and grabbed the topmost one. As she splayed it open across her lap, she saw that it had something to do with motorcycles. This was not exactly ideal, but no-one was even remotely close enough to see, so it didn't matter. She just stared down at the glossy pages, her eyes defocusing. The bland coffee-shop jazz which was playing at a low volume in the background did little to soothe her.

"Are they all looking at-" Erin began to whisper, shaking her head worriedly.

Tilly quickly glanced around the lobby reactively and cut her off to say, "speak to me in your mind please."

Resuming, Erin downright screamed mentally, "they're all looking at me, aren't they?! They see everything!"

The onslaught of paranoia and painfully acute anxiety was overwhelming. She couldn't take it. Her trigger-happy fight-or-flight response flooded an invigorating invitation to motion into her legs, urging her to flee.

"Please just try and stay calm. *Nobody* is paying any attention to you. You're just a woman skimming through a magazine, probably killing time while you wait for your ride to show up. You don't warrant a second glance, I promise."

Seeming to ignore this attempt at mollifying her fears, Erin went on at the same fever pitch inside her head.

"It's too much! It's all too much already! And it's only going to get worse, get more intense! I have to get out of here! I was an idiot to even try! Home! I need to get home!"

"Erin, forget the world, just focus on what I'm saying to you. You're seriously doing great. You've already come *soooo* far. You just have to be brave for a little bit longer, okay? I know you have it in you. Just get to the taxi and you're done, you can relax. You don't have to talk to anyone, you don't have to do anything, you get to just sit there and zone out."

Tilly was pushing hard, and with good reason. She sensed that if Erin got bogged down in self-pity and catastrophizing for too long, it was going to make spurring her onward incredibly difficult. And if she ran back to the apartment, the game was over altogether. Successfully fomenting in

Erin the impetus for a second attempt, considering how much of a role luck had played first time around, would be near enough impossible.

It was now or never.

But a new strategy for keeping Erin from losing it was needed. If just getting her down to the lobby had already proven so challenging, the upcoming taxi ride now loomed like a colossal trial, and one that an unaided Erin was totally unequal to besting. Being out-of-doors would mean triggering the added stressor of agoraphobia, which might well be the anvil that tips the scales beyond the point of no return.

Tilly thought it over rapidly, struggling to formulate a plan given the incredibly limited resources at her disposal. There was no time for finesse, she had to keep it simple. And it came down to triage, to dealing with the biggest obstacles first. So, most importantly, she had to find a way to keep Erin distracted, and to give her the ability to retreat into the sanctum of her mind when things got too much. This would just be a temporary band-aid, yet if Erin's forward momentum could be maintained, it might still be enough to get her to her destination.

Recalling what they had seen when surveying the lobby, Tilly had a eureka moment, but kept it concealed beneath a sterling poker face.

It was time to make something happen. She figured she would only be able to take advantage of this trick once... so, readying her best drill-sergeant impression, she resolved to make it count.

Jumping to her feet, she clapped her hands together hard and yelled, "alright, here's the deal! I will get you out of this, I will make it better, I promise you that! But you can't think, you have to just *do* exactly what I say!"

Erin glanced up in surprise. The shock of being shouted at in this domineering way seemed to shake her free from her little self-contained bubble of dismay.

"Get up!"

And with that, Erin found herself automatically standing up. She hadn't quite *meant* to, but she was allowing herself to be dragged along by this new current. Shutting off her brain and just surrendering to someone else making the decisions felt very welcome right now.

"We're going to the taxi! And on the way... we're going to grab those earphones over there! No-one is looking that way, it will be a total cakewalk!"

Tilly pointed over to the man on the phonecall. Nearby, there was a lone chair in between two large potted plants. His coat was draped over its back and nestled in the seat itself was a backpack with a lit-up tablet and some earphones atop it.

The man was still facing the wall, wholly absorbed by his private conversation. But this opening could elapse at any second.

Tilly could tell that while Erin wanted to go on giving herself over to these orders, hesitation had arose. This was an extraordinary ask, which made it much harder to blindly comply with. The cautious instinct within Erin's mind was pleading with her to take a few minutes and really consider this decision. Glimpsing this mental response alarmed Tilly, because once Erin started overthinking it, she would definitely lose her nerve.

"This is no big deal, Erin! They look like really cheap ones and, besides, people lose earphones all the time! We're just going to scoop them up as we go by, nice and smooth! You can do this! Now go, go, go!"

Again, Erin just let her body be directed and she found herself starting to slowly walk away from the armchairs.

She took stock of everyone in the lobby, checking that they were indeed still too preoccupied to notice her imminent thievery. And as it turned out, Tilly was correct: no-one was looking towards the chair in question. Also, fortuitously enough, Erin had everyone in her field of view, and would instantly detect if they were to glance her way.

The chair itself was not precisely located on the straight line she was walking towards the door, so she let herself veer a little right in order to pass close by it. As she came alongside, she merely let her dangling hand inconspicuously drift over the contents piled in the seat, and snagged the earphones' knotted ball of wiring with a hooked finger. Without missing a beat, she pulled them up into a half-closed fist and scanned the lobby once more to ensure no-one had seen.

Unfortunately, as she then began to move her hand towards her pocket to deposit the prize, one of the earbuds slipped from her grasp. And as it fell, it jerked the rest of the tangle with it.

It all happened in a split-second, way faster than she could react. As soon as she saw the earphones on the floor, she stopped mid-step and held dead still. The jig was surely up.

"You're fine! It's nothing! Just pick them up and keep going!" Tilly hollered insistently.

She knew that Erin would just self-defeatingly draw attention to herself if she stayed frozen here in the middle of the lobby. Thankfully, no-one had looked round yet. This plan could still be saved. But Erin had to move, and she had to move now. Admonitions against lingering at the scene of the crime - no matter how small it may be - exist for a reason.

"None of them have noticed! You're still good! Just pick them up! Go! Now!"

Erin crouched down and plucked the earphones off the carpet. As she rose back up, she quickly mashed them into her pocket.

She resumed walking and looked back at the man, who still had not turned around.

When she drew close to the gaggle of teenagers happily chit-chatting away, she instinctively held her breath and forced herself not to look their way. In the corner of her eye, she noticed two of them briefly look up from the huddle as she went by, taking her in with uninterested gazes, but then return to the conversation.

Their momentary glances had quite the outsize effect on Erin however.

Adrenaline was having its way with Erin's body as though she was making her getaway from a bank heist. Her hands were shaking and clammy, and she could feel perspiration beginning to trickle down her back. Oppositely, her mouth was totally bone-dry. So much so that her tongue was sticking to the roof of her mouth. And as for her heartrate, it felt like her heart was clumsily trying to bash its way out of her ribcage however possible.

"It's over, it's done, you did it Erin! Now, out the door, go, go, go!"

Erin was just a few paces away when a delivery guy appeared at the door. He had several boxes stacked in his hands and a clipboard balanced precariously atop them, so he pushed open the door with his back. Once inside, he saw Erin coming towards him and stepped backwards to keep the door open for her with his shoulder. As they made eye contact, he nodded at her and gave her a friendly little smile.

"It's fine, he's just trying to be nice... Just nod back and keep going!"

But she could not bring herself to do it. The surprise of this random guy suddenly appearing before her had very nearly caused her to swivel around and walk the other way. It was really all she could do to simply keep moving and to make herself pass through the doorway in such close proximity to him. So she just quickly darted through the opening with downcast eyes.

Hearing the door swing shut behind her, she actually shuddered involuntarily from the sheer awkwardness of that moment. Perhaps fortunately, there was no time to dwell on what had just happened or even to take in the outside world. She saw the taxi parked by the curb straight away. And the driver, seeing her too, gave her a curt little wave of acknowledgement. As if pulled to it by a tractor beam, she speed-walked over to the car and got into the back seat.

The driver eyed her in the rear-view mirror and gruffly remarked, "it isn't nice to keep people waiting, you know. I was just about to pull off."

Erin struggled to hear him over the pounding of her own heartbeat in her ears, but his frown and surly tone carried his point well enough.

Forced to think on her feet, Erin just mumbled out a one-sentence apology, offering a vague excuse about a delayed notification on the app. As she spoke, she was really only half-cognizant of the actual words she was saying. They were just tumbling out of her mouth because it was taking maximum effort to keep her voice even remotely normal.

In turn, the driver was probably only able to make out every other word in Erin's quiet babble. Yet her distinctly apologetic demeanour seemed to suffice in appeasing him. He just grunted in reply and the car jerked forward, taking them onto the road.

Tilly blinked into existence next to her and instantly said, "seatbelt, Erin."

Erin had to consciously restrain herself from looking around at Tilly. She just nodded very slightly and buckled herself in.

"Okay, good, good. Now, like I told you, I've got you covered. Go ahead and plug the earphones into your phone, and put them in."

Having fished the earphones from her pocket, Erin shakily did as she was told and awaited her next instruction.

"Now go onto that rain-noise website you like."

Erin quickly brought up the website on her phone and the sound of heavy rainfall began autoplaying immediately.

Tilly gave her a thumbs up, and then made a jabbing-upwards motion with her finger.

Obliging her, Erin started raising the volume bit by bit. But Tilly kept on with her insistent gesture, inducing Erin to crank it up so loud that it was borderline painful for her ears. Tilly knew this wasn't ideal, but she also knew that Erin would need the total immersion to make it through this particularly trying section of their little odyssey. The idea was that by force-feeding Erin's mind this deluge of white noise, of scrambled junk data, it might clog it up enough to keep her from grabbing onto the whirling tail of the next hysterical panic-spiral. That was the hope, anyway.

"Alright, you can still hear me, right?" Tilly asked, her voice incredibly faint and distorted against the wall of noise crashing against Erin's consciousness.

It took Erin a few extra seconds to process what Tilly had actually said. When she had pieced it together, she just gave another very subtle nod.

"Good to know. You're doing so great, Erin. And now's the easy part. The driver isn't gonna try to talk to you with those in. You can just keep looking down at your phone. Maybe pretend you're watching something. Or you can just close your eyes if you like. Either way, you don't have to pay any attention to what's out the window. Just be here with me. We can just stay in our own little world together. Does that sound good?"

Erin closed her eyes.

"Awesome, now just relax and let the journey pass by. I'll be right here, right next to you the whole time. I'm here if you want to talk. And if not, that's fine too. Just do whatever you need to do."

Erin did *not* want to talk.

She needed to just sit there in the darkness and isolation of behind her eyelids, to let it enfold her in its heavy black swaddling. It was also somehow tranquilizing to, as a background sensation, feel the steady vibration of the car's forward motion passing through her body. The combination of the two was soothingly womblike.

By giving herself over to this cocoon of comforting sensory overload, she was soon starting to feel moderately calmer. And when she noticed this, she was so surprised and so pleased that she tried not to notice it, to pretend she had never noticed it, lest she scare this new development away like approaching a skittish little bird.

Tilly was staring intently at Erin, allowing herself an expression of naked fear and worry.

It had, of course, been obvious beforehand that ferrying Erin through the world outside her apartment was going to be... problematic. But Tilly also believed that Erin - *especially* an Erin motivated by potentially reuniting with her beloved - had reserves of strength and resilience she didn't even know about. These would surely kick in and temper the otherwise enormous strain on her...

Alas, as far as Tilly could tell, even if they had indeed kicked in, the strain was considerably greater than she had even anticipated.

Right now, enduring what she was enduring, Erin was a creature of incredible fragility and incredible volatility. A powderkeg dangling by a single, fraying thread over a flickering sea of lit candles, as heavy gusts rock it to-and-fro. So that any clear-eyed analysis could only deduce that combustion was not only inevitable but probably imminent.

Nevertheless, Tilly was going to do everything she could to delay it, to keep Erin together. Because if Erin did explode, creating some big scene out here in the real world, she was going to get scooped up by people who'd be anything but kind or sympathetic to the crazy-woman going berserk in the middle of the street. And who knew what would happen from there? Well, nothing good anyway. Erin would be adrift in a system that was going to take a long time to understand her, if it ever did, and which was more or less inimical to her survival.

Not a minute went by where Tilly did not remain painfully aware of this great danger she was exposing Erin to. She felt terrible for putting her in such a precarious predicament. But there was no going back. This would all be worth it in the end if they could just make it there safely.

Totally oblivious to this fretting over her ultimate fate, Erin was still just relishing the safe space she found herself in. Presently, the repetitive, forceful pitter-patter of the rain was affecting the darkness she saw in strange and intriguing ways. The noise was translating itself, upon the blank canvas her closed eyes were presenting her brain with, into something visual. For a flittering blizzard of what seemed akin to sparkling television static was drifting across the black backdrop. She was enraptured by this odd phenomenon, concentrating on how it looked, how its pulsing corresponded to the rhythm of the rainfall in her ears. Again, she tried to ignore her sense of gratitude that this was absorbing her and helping pass the time. Because good things sometimes have a way of deserting those who actually appreciate them, yet sticking like magnets to those who couldn't care less. An inexplicable mechanism. That is, unless one employs the most reliable heuristic for understanding the universe: always assume you're just seeing but part of an unimaginably elaborate and exquisite Rube Goldberg machine for pointless cruelty.

Although Erin would have guessed that it had been longer, she had actually only been in the taxi for ten minutes now. And, given the hospital is on the other side of the city, that meant she had a little over the same to go before she would arrive there.

If only this latter half of the journey could have gone so well...

Just a minute or two later, the taxi went over a speedbump. And then even her meagre succor was revoked.

Erin was jolted upwards. Her eyes shot open in surprise and one of the earphones slipped out, dropping into her lap.

She was abruptly thrown back into reality, the outside world inflicting itself upon her with redoubled vividness and malice.

They were passing through a part of the city she didn't really recognise. There were so many unfamiliar buildings looming large through the window, boxing her in from both sides. And there were so many people walking along the sidewalk, whose faces she barely had time to see as the taxi zipped by. And the racket of the other cars zooming along beside them was oppressive and disorientating.

Her face became very pale. Her nostrils were flaring rapidly as her breathing sped up. She pressed her fists down hard into the leather car seat, trying to stay in control.

"Look at me, Erin, look at me."

Unheeded, Tilly floated in front of Erin, trying to monopolise her view.

"Just breathe, kittycat. Just breathe. You're okay, you're fine. Just breathe. Stay with me, stay calm."

It descended upon her so quickly, this mix of intense motion sickness and panic-attack. She was resisting it mightily, but it was no good. It had her. It *definitely* had her. It was making her body feel like it was being spun around in a centrifuge, bubbling up a violent nausea. The tips of her ears suddenly became very hot and her stomach was apparently flipping itself over and over in cramped somersaults.

She started greedily sucking in breaths through her now wide-open mouth. But none of them seemed to do anything. It was like there was no oxygen left inside the car, like she was trying to inhale pure vacuum and thus collapsing her lungs.

Her head was spinning and she was blinking a lot to shift the blurriness from her vision.

She had to get out. She had to get out. She had to get out. *She had to get out.*

Tilly slid out of the way as Erin lurched forward and knocked frantically on the plexiglass divider.

"Air! I need air! I need to get out! I need to get out!" she shrieked, wild-eyed.

Judging by his face, the banging startled the driver and pissed him off, but as soon as he heard her frenzied pleas, he seemed to grasp the urgency of the situation. It was likely not the first time that this had happened in his taxi, which must have given him some sense of what the priority had to be right now.

So, rather than scold her, he just called back, "alright, alright, hang on a second!"

A moment later, he had pulled out of the traffic and parked up by the sidewalk.

And when the car came to a stop, Erin yanked the handle and threw open the door, rushing out through it. Her phone, still attached to her by the wire, was dragged out too. It clattered, unnoticed, onto the road, taking the earphones with it.

Erin had just a second once she regained her footing outside the car to scan her surroundings. Naturally, there wasn't a trashcan or bush close to her, or even a little patch of grass, or *anything* remotely suitable really.

She didn't have time to stop and fret about this, however.

There was a tree embedded in the pavement somewhat nearby. It caught her eye. Staggering and nearly tripping, she sprinted over to it.

Just as soon as she dropped to her knees in front of it, she spewed out a thick slurry of vomit onto its exposed roots.

Then she tried to stay perfectly still, desperately willing no more to come.

Her body did not care about her appeals to it. A few seconds later, it made her heave again and out came more vomit.

She once again held still, trying to judge whether it was over now, trying so very hard to make it so. She was tensing her entire body, hoping to regain dominion over it and force back down whatever else might want to come up.

Yet another heave convulsed her all of a sudden, but she threw up very little this time.

And then she knew it was finally over. She didn't need to wait to feel it out, she just knew.

She crawled on her hands and knees around to the side of the tree trunk that wasn't vomit-splattered, and sat against it, breathing deeply. With the back of her hand, she wiped her mouth and chin. She also grabbed the front of her sweater and shook it, to remove the tiny chunks stuck there.

"You've got to be kidding me with this shit. What is it? Drugs? You on drugs?!" the driver, standing a safe distance away and looking on, irately demanded to know.

Erin glared at him, indignant fury burning in her eyes. All else seemed to fall away, so aghast was she at his callousness. If there had been any rocks of decent heft close at hand, it was a certainty that she would have taken aim at his head. With enough patience, one of those pot-shots is bound to land. But much to her chagrin, with her eager throwing-arm deprived of ammunition, she could do little more than hug her knees and focus on her breathing.

A few of the nearby pedestrians who had stopped to look at her awkwardly unfroze and walked on, unwilling to indulge in any further voyeurism now that the subject could stare back. She glowered at them as they went on their way. That they too were so easily escaping their due thrown retribution was additionally galling. She would have settled for pinging pebbles off backs at this point, but the little ring of dirt around the tree didn't even have those.

In this moment, she hated the world and all its peoples with a renewed passion. She felt like some unlucky soul who has ended up hopelessly trapped behind enemy lines.

Tilly materialised next to Erin, sitting down against the tree too.

"I'm so sorry you had to go through that," she offered softly.

"Yeah, me too," Erin despondently thought back.

Choking up, Tilly shook her head sadly. Her voice wavered with emotion.

"I wish... *so much*... that I could hug you, Erin."

Erin couldn't even bring herself to reply.

She turned sideways slightly, and they just looked at each other tenderly. They were merely a couple inches apart, but separated by an impenetrable existential divide.

Speaking in the faintest whisper, Erin finally managed to repeat, "yeah... me too."

They leaned their heads together and just sat there with one another.

The puzzled taxi driver seemed to give up on waiting for a much belated response to his question. He threw his hands up in the air and tutted exasperatedly before starting to walk back to his car. This fare wasn't worth the headache.

Though loathe to interrupt their moment together, Tilly was watching the driver leave with concern seeping into her expression.

"Uh... Erin... our ride seems to be going... We might want to do something about that," she suggested gingerly, with an apologetic tone for having to say it.

Erin breathed out a long sigh.

Through gritted teeth, she muttered, "yes, I suppose we might."

There was a brief pause as she soaked up the last dregs of emotional support from their closeness.

"Hey!" she then shouted over to the departing figure, suddenly having no trouble finding her voice.

The taxi driver stopped and looked over his shoulder.

"I'm going to the hospital for a fucking reason, don't you think?!" she bellowed sharply. "So, leaving a sick woman high and dry half-way there isn't a very good idea, is it?!"

The taxi driver now turned around fully. He looked her in the eye, trying to get a read on the honesty of her claim. There was a begrudging deliberativeness shown upon his face which suggested that he resented the conundrum he had been placed in, but was nonetheless considering how best to resolve it with minimal repercussions.

Passersby were once again gawking at the scene unfolding there. But now Erin had very loudly and unambiguously provided them with a specific lens through which to view the standoff. So, this time the rubberneckers were mostly looking at *him*, throwing glances laden with judgmental disbelief his way.

At last, the combined pressure of all those stares bearing down on him forced his hand. He rubbed the back of his neck uncomfortably as he protested half-heartedly.

"Look, I'm real sorry that you're, uhhh, ill and all. But I can't have you yakking up the rest of your breakfast in my car. I'm just renting it. And there's the deposit and... everything..."

Several jaws fell open upon hearing this weaselly response. One of the onlookers actually scoffed loud enough for them to hear.

The driver quickly stared down at his shoes, both to evade all of the accusatory eyes and to hide his grimace of discomfiture.

Erin, leaning against the tree for assistance, gradually pulled herself up to her feet and said irritably, "yeah, yeah, I'm all puked out, don't worry. Your precious upholstery will make it through unblemished."

She was brazenly calling his bluff.

As he resumed walking over to the car, the driver just grumbled out a terse, "alright, let's go."

She dusted herself off as best she could, though both the seat and the knees of her jeans were stained with dirt now.

Something rather strange happened then.

Upon following him back over to the car, she felt incredibly childlike all of a sudden. She had an intense disgust for the intrusion of this ridiculous emotion, but her mind would not relent. It had chosen, for some unexplainable reason, to superimpose upon this moment the ersatz feeling of being some bratty kid sulkily trailing her father back to his car after causing a scene out in public.

It was in this deeply weird, jumbled mindstate that she found herself replaying what had just occurred. And she re-experienced the humiliation of it very, very acutely. Her cheeks burned with shame and embarrassment. Most of all, this made her so furious that she'd had to go through it at all. She could feel the tears trying to come, but bit down on her tongue and balled her fists as hard as she could to keep them at bay. She fucking detested that her body tried to make her cry when she was actually just angry.

Weak, disloyal shell! I want to be as warrior, not as victim!

She wished to stare down this uncaring world and give it the finger, not allow it the victory of making her blubber like a baby. She had a feeling that it was once again trying to test her, to break her, and she was dead set on denying it the pleasure.

The acrid taste of vomit still lingered very strongly in her mouth.

When she reached the taxi, she noticed her phone and the pilfered earphones lying by the curbside beneath the car.

"Well, fuck," she mouthed in frustration.

For about fifteen seconds, she just stood there with her eyes closed, massaging her temples to try and dissipate some of her impotent rage.

Then she bent down and scooped them up. Holding them up to the light, she scowled as she saw how they were speckled with the gutter grime.

Throwing open the car door, she slid into her seat and slammed it closed. The driver did not speak, he just pulled off.

Tilly re-appeared and said, "ouch, what's the damage?"

Erin turned the phone over in her hands, checking it out. The casing had accrued dings at the corners and various scratches all over, but the screen itself seemed to have miraculously escaped any noticeable harm, which was good enough for her.

"Could have been a lot worse I guess," Erin answered mentally.

"Oh, that's something at least."

Erin didn't care to credit this look-on-the-bright-side optimism with a reply. She just started in on cleaning the phone and the earphones by thoroughly rubbing them with the bottom of her sweater. Afterwards she brought the actual earbuds close before her eyes to inspect them. They definitely were not 'clean', not by a long shot. And she was also now reminded that she was getting a stranger-to-stranger ear-wax transplant. All in all then, rather disgusting. But she was not exactly flush with other options.

She snorted air through her nose in vexation and slotted the earphones back into her ears. Immediately the rain-noise greeted her again, having evidently just gone on playing this whole time. She turned the volume way down, not finding it blaring against her eardrums particularly bearable or necessary anymore.

"So..." Tilly began tentatively, "how are you feeling? It was, like, pretty impressive how you really told that guy off back there..."

"I don't know. I guess I'm not all that scared or anxious now. I mean, things can hardly get any worse than puking my guts out in front of a small audience, right? So, right now, I'm just... fucking *mad*. Mad I had to endure that, mad at this taxi driver being such an unbelievable prick, mad that I have to be out here at all. Hell, hopefully this anger sticks around long enough to see me through the rest of this shit. That way, I might just have a chance."

Tilly just nodded along understandingly, for she was thinking it all over and still unsure of how to reply.

She couldn't help but find new cause for concern. Though it was good that Erin had been invigorated by this sudden influx of anger, it was obviously also mostly just a masking agent. And to the degree that it was indeed fuel, it was only providing the same erratic, junky energy as a child's manic sugar-high. Similarly, it would not have a very long half-life. This meant that when the anger finally degraded into something like hopelessness and self-pity, instead of propelling her onwards it was going to bring everything to a halt.

"And how are you feeling, like, physically? You know, after..."

"Needless to say, I've definitely felt better. My throat was already kind of hurting a bit when I woke up today and now it burns like a motherfucker. Who'd have guessed stomach acid wasn't the best salve?..."

Tilly *was* comforted by the little flicker of a smirk which twitched the corners of Erin's mouth as she thought up this little quip.

She laughed and said, "good to see that your messed-up sense of humour is still functioning just fine."

Just then the car turned a corner. Erin moved her head closer to the window, staring out it solemnly.

"Yeah, well, let's hope that everything else makes it through this day intact too. We're about to arrive."

The driver pulled up by the hospital's main entrance, slipping into the designated drop-off bay. He glanced at her significantly in the rearview mirror. His lips were moving, but she couldn't hear what he said, and she didn't care. She just wanted to get out of this damn car. Retrieving her purse, she fumbled with the zip in her hurry. Then she crammed a few banknotes - which was sure to be more than enough to cover the charge - through the little plexiglass aperture, and bundled out of the door.

The taxi speedily departed, just as Tilly delicately pointed out, "um, Erin, you set it up so the app would just bill your card...."

Erin spun round, but the taxi was already far off in the distance. She turned back and laid her hand over her forehead in frustration.

Under her breath, she said, "fuuuuucccck. I *really* overpaid that asshole then."

"Yeah... that sucks..."

That was all Tilly could think to offer.

Rubbing her eyes, Erin tried to just shake it off, thinking, "okay, shit, whatever. We're here now. That's what matters."

Other people were getting out of cars behind her and going past her as they walked over to the doors. But she just stood there and looked up at the hospital's frontage.

"Nobody ever just stops and looks at stuff. I mean, look at this thing. Fucking weird looking building, really."

Tilly gazed upwards too.

"I think they were going for, uh, a 'modern' appearance. You know, avoid that blocky, drab thing that most hospitals have going on."

"Well, it looks like... Shit, I don't know... The headquarters of some new company trying too hard to be hip and unique or something like that. The aesthetic really isn't going to age well."

"No, I suppose it won't."

Erin remained planted there, still caught in a contemplative reverie, taking in a building which couldn't possibly merit *this* much contemplation. Tilly did not have to be in Erin's head to know that she wasn't lingering here because she was thinking about architecture. That would have been apparent to anyone with eyes.

Tilly wasn't at all unsympathetic to Erin's very understandable stalling, and didn't want to truncate it too brusquely. But she knew she had to step in.

"Once more unto the breach, huh?" she prompted quietly, with a little nervous smile.

Erin kept on staring up, her expression unchanged. But a slight flaring of her nostrils betrayed that she had gotten the message.

After a few moments, she just replied distantly, "aye."

The sheer gravity of whatever was about to happen was immensely intimidating, yet there was no more putting it off. This was one of those scary chokepoints life sometimes erects very blatantly in your way: there's no path forward but through the *event* and out the other side. So you'd better just get going.

She swallowed hard and deliberatively rapped her fist on her chin several times, like boxers do as a nervous tic before a bout starts to simulate getting hit. Then she set off towards the big automatic doors.

When she got inside the entrance area, a row of vending machines along the wall caught her eye. She made a beeline for the one selling drinks and bought a bottle of flavoured water. Surveying the room to find the nearest of the trashcans dotted around, she wended her way through the large but sparsely filled seating area to get to it. It was a little strange, given

473

the rain was still playing in her ears, to be passing all these people without being able to hear their chatter. She liked it though. It felt like she was merely a spectral visitor drifting through their world, separate and untouched.

At the trashcan, she swilled the water around her mouth and spat it out a few times. She was vaguely aware that the people sat nearby were sneaking judgy glances at her. This should have made her very self-conscious, but she now found it remarkably easy to ignore them and their disapproval.

"Screw 'em," she thought wryly.

Tilly actually chortled in surprise.

With an amused expression, she cheerily concurred, "yep, screw 'em."

Finally, Erin took a few actual sips of the water and then threw the still half-full bottle away.

"Do you know where we're actually supposed to go?" Tilly asked.

"Well, they just said the sixth floor, and assuming it hasn't changed to something else... that's got the coma ward on it."

"We should probably double check that before we head up. There's a big sign over there which has all the floors labelled," Tilly advised in response, pointing over by the reception desk.

Erin nodded and, navigating through the rows of seats again, went over there.

No one was currently queueing at the reception desk, so she stood a fair distance away from it, to avoid the people manning it thinking she was coming up to them.

She looked up at the sign mounted on the wall and read down the color-coded list of floors.

"There you go. *Sixth floor*. Still the same," Erin murmured to herself.

And as she looked back down, she saw that one of the receptionists was waving to get her attention.

Erin tried not to let her annoyance show on her face. She was debating whether she could just walk away. It would be rude, sure, but she wasn't going to see this guy ever again, so who cared?

The receptionist began saying something at Erin, which was, of course, inaudible to her. Before she could stop herself, she just automatically pulled out one of the earphones and stepped over towards the desk. It was like some instinctual polite reaction hardwired into her.

She just caught the very end of what the man was saying.

"-with that. Or do you have an appointment?"

Seeing Erin remove the earbud, the man smiled embarrassedly and quickly appended, "oh, sorry about that, I didn't realize you couldn't hear me."

Although she wanted to smile back, to ease the awkward feeling that arose, Erin couldn't bring herself to do it fast enough. And then the opportunity had passed. The awkwardness only intensified.

She strained to at least try and keep her tone somewhere in the ballpark of cordial as she responded, "I'm... good, I don't need any help... thank you. I was called in to meet with a doctor on the coma ward."

Erin had stumbled over her words a bit, and the man seemed a little confused.

"Sorry, you said a doctor called you in? The doctors usually don't call people directly..."

At this point, Erin was *very much* regretting the fact that she had allowed herself to be entangled in this pointless conversation. She let an extra instant pass before answering, to inconspicuously take a deep breath through her nose. When she spoke again, she tried to slow herself down and enunciate more clearly.

"It was a nurse who called me. To come see Dr. Vance on Ward B. He's overseeing my partner's case."

Irritation flared up anew inside her. She really resented having to explain herself, having to say all this aloud to a stranger. She reminded herself that she could just walk away from this exercise in frustration, and was just about to do so when the receptionist replied.

Erin providing these details had evidently checked out, because the man gave another little smile and said, "oh okay, no problem. Just go on up and tell them at the desk there. They'll fetch him as soon as he's available."

It took a conscious effort for Erin to fight the urge to inject some sarcasm into it, but she managed to just flatly say, "thanks."

Then she strode briskly over to the elevators and slapped the call button.

"Hmmph, goddamn busybody wasting our time," she thought pettishly to herself as she put the earbud back in.

Tilly came beside Erin and playfully mimed punching her on the shoulder.

"It's alright, it's behind us now. No big deal, right?"

Erin glanced away, and mouthed, "sure."

Without any noise heralding its arrival, the elevator simply opened. They both stepped inside it. It was one of those really spacious elevators, made to accommodate multiple hospital beds at once, which was nice.

Erin quickly tapped the sixth floor button. Then she tapped the 'close doors' button, just *once*.

Noticing this, Tilly let out a soft little giggle.

"Not about to make the same mistake twice, huh?" she asked in a lighthearted way.

But Erin just coolly said back, "nope."

The doors closed. And the elevator began to ascend.

Tilly decided she had better give up on trying to break the tension. It just wasn't going to happen. More than that though, she knew deep down that she was also doing it for herself, to assuage the trepidation and guiltiness she felt.

They were standing side-by-side. Suddenly Erin looked over at Tilly and breathlessly rattled off a bunch of worried questions aloud.

"What if she *is* awake? What if that really is why they called me in? What... do I say to her? And, holy jesus motherfucking jesus fucking christ, what if she... knows... that I left her?!"

Tilly took a moment to really think about her answer.

"Firstly, you'll know what to do when the time comes. And secondly... let me put it this way... would you forgive her if the roles were reversed and she had done the same?"

"Of course. I'd forgive her anything."

"Well then, you'll... merely have to trust that she loves you as much as you love her. Not too much of a stretch, is it?"

Erin didn't answer. She just stared down at her hands and began nervously rubbing her thumbnail with her other thumb.

The elevator doors opened.

They came out at the start of a very long winding corridor, which had entrances to all the wards on this floor.

Instantly she was assaulted by that awful, sobering smell which permeates all hospitals. It was the heavy chemical stench of *sterilisation*. Not just an unpleasant odour, but a disquieting reminder too. These buildings meant for housing the diseased required a daily sisyphean battle, an attempt to slosh around enough biocide compounds to stop their germs from taking up residence there too. It was a never-ending struggle which, with the passage of enough time, was only going to immunize the enemy against the means of their extermination. There had never been a war like it in the history of the human species. And there was going to be no more wars, among *other* things, once it could no longer be waged effectively.

Erin tried not to think about this.

"Do you know where we're going from here?" Tilly inquired.

Staring down the corridor with dread plastered on her face, Erin nodded.

"I remember. Down here. Then round that bend. About halfway down the next stretch, there are these big swingy double doors on the right."

Her hands were shaking. She tried to tense the muscles in them to keep them still, but to no avail.

She took a step forward. But then stopped again.

She bit down on her bottom lip, and her eyes became wide and unseeing and ruminative. The shaking had spread, sowing a subtle jitteriness across her body.

Tilly was watching carefully, weighing how long to let this go on.

But soon a doctor came out of a doorway up ahead and went up the corridor. The movement snapped Erin out of her pensiveness. Her eyes refocused on the doctor, tracking him until he went around the corner and out of view.

Another thirty seconds passed, and then just as Tilly was about to say something, Erin began walking slowly up the corridor. She jammed her hands as far as they would go into her shallow jeans pockets, to try and forcefully smother their quivering.

Dotted along the walls were generic landscape or still-life paintings, whose subject matter was so impossibly bland that it was forgotten as soon as one's gaze left it. These examples of artwork from local people were meant to liven up the dull space, but they somehow managed to be more depressing than the plain walls could have ever been. And the reason for that was obvious. It was not just that these dabblers were untalented, or even that their ill-smeared canvases were boring, it was mostly that their creations were so devoid of *any* artistic spark whatsoever. This made them seem like what an AI tasked with the job might pump out to decorate a mental asylum's common areas. Precisely psychologically neutral pictures which couldn't possibly arouse any strong reaction. Things to merely look at, not to wonder about. The mental equivalent of serving watery oatmeal or only having nailed-down furniture with rounded edges. This was, ironically, quite upsetting. A desire to deface this perverse non-art arose in her and was promptly quashed. After all, she didn't have... any means to do it. More's the pity.

Despite all that, she still briefly inspected each painting with mild disdain as she went by, to give herself something, anything, else to focus on. And to surreptitiously prolong her walk to her destination.

But, alas... eventually... she got there.

And when she did finally come before the double-door entrance to Ward B, she stopped again. She just stood there, still as a statue.

"You did it, Erin, you made it. The summit of the mountain," Tilly cooed in encouragement.

Erin slowly looked round at Tilly with a cynical expression.

She replied morosely, "the entrance to the fucking underworld, more like."

She pulled out her earphones and, pausing the rain-noise, jammed them and the phone into her sweater pocket.

Then she took a few deep breaths, and went through the doors.

It was so quiet, as well befit this polite antechamber to death. All that could be heard was the occasional sound of talking and unhurried footsteps. Urgency was just not the name of the taskmaster cracking the whip in this place. Things simply moved at a slow pace, much as they did for those poor souls stored herein, who were each trapped in their own private limbos.

There wasn't anyone stationed at the sign-in desk, and just a few people sat in the small waiting area in front of it. There was an older and a younger woman sitting together, giving off a mother-daughter vibe. They were leaning in close over a phone and having a surprisingly giggly conversation in hushed tones. And there was a very elderly man - who looked about a hundred and forty years old if he was a day - sat by himself. Two things about him were impossible to miss. The first was that a conspicuous prosthetic ear was affixed on the left side of his head. The second was a slight yellow hue to his skin. One had to try hard not to stare, which she dutifully did. He was engrossed in reading a beat-up paperback whose print was nearly large enough to be visible from space. She went and sat opposite him, but he didn't even look up.

The minutes dragged by. She took to slowly tapping each of her teeth with her tongue, as though performing a dental inventory, to try and assuage her boredom. It did not work. She was only getting more and more uncomfortable and antsy.

She looked over at the desk, to see if it was still empty, *very* frequently. And each new confirmation that nothing had changed managed to bristle her incrementally more than the last time. This upward trend could not go on forever; it had a rapidly approaching ceiling.

"Goddamn it! I can't believe the inconsiderate fuckface who's supposed to be manning the desk is just leaving us waiting like this!" she thought after fifteen minutes had passed, now thoroughly aggravated.

Tilly was sat opposite, next to the old-timer, and had been paying close attention to Erin. She was about to speak, but Erin's next thought popped up first.

"Man it's fucking warm in here!"

Erin stood up and yanked off her beanie. Then she clumsily peeled her sweater off, for a moment having a hard time tugging it over her head.

As she was smoothing out her t-shirt where it had bunched up at the bottom, she was positively seething.

She ranted silently to herself, "not only are they rude enough to leave us sitting here like chumps, but they crank up the heat so we can boil in our own sweat too. God I wish I had kept that water now. Though, surprise surprise, that shitty vending machine gave me a room temperature one. Still, sometimes when you're overheated, drinking any water seems to cool you down. I mean, if they're going to keep you waiting like this, they should at least have a fucking water cooler or some shit, so you can-"

Tilly could see that Erin's hyper-concentrated anxiety, which had no outlet, was being transmuted into this bitterness and ire.

She jumped in and cut off this rambling train of thought by saying soothingly, "it's okay, Erin. Everything's going to go just fine."

Picking up on what Tilly was doing and why, Erin scrunched up her face in displeasure at seeing that the root of her tantrum was so transparent from the outside, and yet so opaque to her. She felt silly. With a huff, she dropped back into her chair. And she now tried to tamp down her ill temper because she was embarrassed by it.

Yet after a few drawn-out, calming breaths, she gave up the endeavour halfway through, too impatient to go on. Just the remnants of her incensed mood remained.

She got up again and mentally declared, "alright, I'm good, I'm good. But I'm not sitting here like some compliant idiot anymore. I need to get things moving. I'll just, like, go find someone and let them know I'm here. Then hopefully they'll go notify the Doc for me."

Tilly got up too, offering no protest.

She simply said, "sure thing, I'll be right behind you."

Erin resolutely marched past the desk and into the actual ward.

There were a lot of comatose patients in hospital beds just out there in the open, lined along the walls. She tried not to look at them. It was a *deeply unsettling* sight. And there were various people, a mix of doctors and nurses and visitors, moving around the ward, going into rooms and behind drawn privacy-curtains. None of them paid her much attention.

Up ahead there was a nurses' station, where a tall, bespectacled middle-aged woman was bent over the countertop filling in something on a clipboard. She had dirty-blonde hair pulled into a tight, high ponytail. And the circular retractable-ID-badge holder which was clipped onto her scrubs was adorned with a smiley-face and the caption 'a smile costs nothing'. The choice to buy and wear this customized item was a bit like stapling the results of a magazine personality test to your forehead. A more dire omen of imminent frustration one rarely finds.

"Alright, there you are. I suppose... that's as good a place as any to start," Erin warily thought to herself.

She walked over and, not wanting to puncture the quiet too harshly, ventured a soft "h-hello?"

The nurse, facing away, didn't seem to hear. At any rate, she didn't look around.

Erin cleared her throat and tried again, louder and more confidently.

"Hello?"

This time she succeeded in getting the nurse's attention. The woman swivelled around to face Erin, a little taken aback.

"Uh, hi? Can I help you?"

Erin gestured back towards the waiting area and started to explain, "sorry... there, like, wasn't anyone at the desk. I'm here to see-"

The nurse's face suddenly lit up with warmth, and she interrupted to say, "oh, I'm sorry I didn't recognise you! Jeez, really took me a sec, what with you... I mean, you... Well anyhow, it has been a little while, hasn't it?"

Now was Erin's turn to be taken aback, though she did her best to hide it. She was very confused. But she made herself adopt some meagre facsimile of the nurse's happy, surprised expression, even if she doubted it was anywhere near as warm or convincing.

"Oh darn, I'm sorry about this too," the nurse went on, cheerfully. "But I'm *sooo* unbelievably bad with names. It's this friggin' job, I'm telling you: your poor brain gets crammed with a million new things each day and then flushed as soon as you step out the door. Although, okay, wait... wait... hmm... don't tell me. I know it. I know I know it... ummmm..."

The nurse rhythmically rapped her knuckles on the countertop and looked up at the ceiling as she strained hard to remember. She was making a deliberative humming noise.

Eventually she slapped her hand down in triumph and exclaimed, "wait, wait, wait! I got it! Ummm... Ellie... isn't it?!...."

Erin was trying not to let her little faux-smile fade, and replied in an even tone, "it's Erin."

"Oh, yes, yes, sorry about that! Erin, Erin, of course! And you remember me, right? Genevieve?"

"Uh, yep, of course... Genevieve..." Erin said quickly, falsely. "Like you said, just... takes a second."

Erin felt so uncomfortable that she had to break eye contact, so she tried to just nonchalantly glance around the ward, taking it all in. She was searching her mind for this Genevieve, trying to place her. Certainly she had had to interact with a whole bunch of hospital staff. And she felt like - *maybe* - she did have the faintest shadow of a memory of having spoken to this woman in the past. But it was hard to tell whether this was authentic or just her brain seeking to play along with her grasping for any corresponding recollection.

"It's good to see you again. You know, I missed our conversations about trashy TV shows when you left. I've never heard anyone tear them apart quite as passionately as you."

Erin winced at the reference to her leaving.

"Oh... yeah... sorry about that..."

Genevieve seemed a little perplexed by this, but more so bemused. She laughed lightheartedly, replying, "ha, you don't have to apologize for that, silly goose."

Just then, another nurse called down from the far end of the ward. Despite the fact that he wasn't even shouting, his raised voice still cut through the relative quiet rather arrestingly.

"Yo, you got my C22 over there, Gen?"

Erin was so on edge, so focussed on getting through this conversation, that she damn near jumped out of her skin. Her head whipped around to look over at him, like a startled owl.

For her part, Genevieve just rolled her eyes dramatically, as if to apologize for the interruption.

"One sec!" she called back, whilst holding up a finger to Erin to signal the same thing.

She turned back to the counter and rapidly moved about all the papers messily amassed atop it, taking stock of what was there.

"Some of these kids would lose their heads if they weren't screwed on, I swear," she said with a chuckle as she went on searching.

Erin had a sense that this comment was meant for her amusement too, and was glad that she wasn't being looked at as it was said, so she didn't have to force out a fake laugh.

She shot a baffled look over at Tilly, who was by her side. Tilly just offered a minute shrug, as if to say 'ahh, what can you do?' Still, she wasn't looking at Genevieve or the loud male nurse. Her watchful gaze was, and had been, only locked attentively on Erin.

The rustling of paper went on for a few moments more and then Genevieve gave up her search. She relayed her findings.

"Nada! Umm, you know what? Check Carly's tray, it might've got swept up there with the other stuff from this morning."

"Will do!" the other nurse shot back, hurrying off somewhere else.

Turning back to Erin, she resumed in the same friendly tone.

"Sorry about that! Anyways, dear me, where was I? Oh yeah. How are you? How have you been? Dish the deets, girly!"

As these questions left Genevieve's mouth, her gaze incidentally drifted down. And Erin saw it linger on the faded but numerous track marks on her bare forearm. Despite their faintness, Erin could not possibly kid herself that, especially under these fluorescent lights, a trained nurse was going to mistake them for anything other than what they were. The only change this sight elicited was a flicker of surprise in Genevieve's countenance, which was instantly stifled. Somehow it was worse that she felt she had to conceal her reaction to be nice.

Erin's insides now felt like they were shrivelling up.

She cursed herself for forgetting about these telltale blemishes, for forgetting to keep them covered up. Combined with her gaunt, sickly appearance, they probably made her look like a heroin addict or something. The interaction with this nurse was already so confounding and vexing, but now she felt so unbearably exposed as well. Paranoia began to creep in. It seemed as though all her secrets could be figured out by deductive reasoning once this unsightly clue had been glimpsed.

How she wished she hadn't taken the sweater off now. But there it was, hanging uselessly in her grasp. As she replied, she instinctively shifted her stance, without caring about subtlety, so that she was holding the balled-up bundle of sweater and beanie behind her back with both hands. This at least served to turn her forearms away from view.

"I've been... just fine," she distractedly affirmed, now feeling so self-conscious and discomposed that going back to the tedium of the waiting area seemed infinitely preferable. She summoned the courage to be bold and, segueing ungracefully, made to wrap up the conversation.

"I, uh, don't mean to keep you from your work. I'm sure you're very busy. I'm... just... here to see Dr. Vance, he wanted to speak to me. C-can you let him know I'm here?"

Genevieve was rather disappointed that Erin was intent upon cutting their reunion chitchat short, and made no effort to hide it from her face or her voice.

"Oh... yes... sure. I'll find him and let him know. He's around here somewhere."

There was now a palpable awkwardness hanging in the air between them.

Erin knew she should just say thank you and leave. But *the question* was still there before her, fast becoming the regnant factor in her decision-making. It had only ever been expanding within her mind and consuming everything else around it, like a whale somehow swallowing its own ocean and ballooning colossally. She tried to remind herself that she only had to wait a little while longer for the actual doctor to come over and talk to her. But in the end she really couldn't help but ask now anyway.

"Do you k-know what's going on with this whole thing? Is she... okay? Do you know what the... change... means?"

Thinking for a second, Genevieve tilted her head and said, "sorry for being a ditz again, but who is it you're referring to?..."

Displacing the expression of plaintive eagerness-to-know that had just previously been there, a scowl descended upon Erin's face. This resulted in a rather stark juxtaposition, to say the least.

Her voice was positively dripping with indignant disbelief as she replied, "uh, the girl whose room I was always, you know, 'hanging out' in?..."

The sarcasm seemed to miss its mark. A flash of pleased realization spread across Genevieve's face.

"Oh, gotcha, gotcha. Someone you befriended here?"

Erin could not believe how stupid and befuddled Genevieve was proving in this moment. She suddenly felt such contempt for this foolish woman, who apparently remembered their small talk about TV shows but not the name of the person who meant everything to Erin. There was an insult in there somewhere, *surely*.

Before Erin could go about issuing a correction - and, she thought spitefully, hopefully causing Genevieve much embarrassment - a scornful comment slipped through her lips first.

"I was just a little bit too preoccupied to be making friends while I was here," she said, impatiently throwing glances around the ward to express her exasperation.

Genevieve was clearly nonplussed by what was going on. She could sense that there was a subtext she must be missing, but was nonetheless stumped. The whole thing had become very uncomfortable. She smiled nervously and uncertainly.

"Umm, sure, of course. I meant when you moved wards, during *your recovery*."

Right away, Erin's eyes locked back onto Genevieve. She was staring directly at her mouth, wanting so badly to see the words being said again, to make sure she had heard them correctly.

The moment seemed to stretch out like a drooping glob of molten glass being pulled at either end by pincers. Time itself was slowing down to keep her trapped there.

Then Erin felt everything - her world and her self - come apart.

But in this state of disassembly, she became privy to the hidden workings of the machine that so few ever glimpse. It was as though she could see *who she was* and *what had happened to her* thoroughly anatomized before her eyes. Each piece was suspended in mid-air for easy inspection, like in an exploded-view blueprint. And all of them, no matter how small, vibrated with purpose, being indispensable in making up the whole.

Though she felt overwhelmed and frightened by the sight to a degree she had never thought possible, she made herself stare unflinchingly at it. There was so much she wanted to know, so many specific elements she wanted to focus in on. Yet it was hard not to just get lost in the spectacle of the thing.

She marvelled not only at the sheer number of floating pieces, but also their diversity. Then she progressed to puzzling over the complexity of how they meshed together into some fine-tuned symphony of personhood. And finally her attention was drawn to the entire swaths which were grayed out like redactions on classified documents. Those were things she *should* be able to see, but couldn't. It felt like an unbearably egregious deprivation. She anguished over what they might be, and why they were even hidden in the first place. And her anguish was only deepened when she saw that they had been superficially obscured by counterfeit replacements. These sullied the harmonious aesthetic of everything else, being ugly and misshapen because of their falsity. She longed to know their origin. And how to obliterate them.

But, abruptly, the split-second of profound clarity ended.

What she was looking at recohered into a whole with blinding speed, integrating together with such precision that she couldn't even make out any seams from the reunification.

She was back in the hospital again. A surging, concussive headrush disorientated her. It produced a halo of blurriness around the very edges of her vision and walloped away her equilibrium. She wobbled backwards and, losing her footing, fell down onto her butt.

Genevieve jumped into action quickly. She dashed over and crouched down beside Erin, holding her head at the back so that if she passed out it wouldn't hit the floor. She was asking a lot of concerned questions, but they did not penetrate Erin's stupor even a little bit, like needles bending against concrete.

Erin just sat there, unresponsive. She was staring dead-eyed straight ahead, right over Genevieve's shoulder as if the woman wasn't even there. Her mouth hung open and her breathing was shallow and raspy.

Bringing her other hand in front of Erin's face, Genevieve repeatedly snapped her fingers.

The noise and the motion of this, so close before her eyes, succeeded in attracting Erin's notice. And, akin to the slow repositioning of a satellite dish to inspect some incredibly distant object in space, she very slowly turned her head until her unseeing gaze alighted upon Genevieve.

It took more than a few seconds to zero in her vision on a certain target, but as soon as she really saw the fingers, she was pulled out of her obliviousness.

Unfortunately, now that she had her senses back, a heavy delirium of fear and confusion and panic descended upon her.

Startled to find herself on the floor, she involuntarily yelped and scooted away from Genevieve with her hands. Then she scrambled to her feet and frantically looked around. The bright lights were dazzling. They further distorted her eyesight as though it were splattered all over with oil streaks. And it certainly didn't help matters that she suddenly had what felt like a brutal, throbbing migraine.

Tilly drifted right in front of Erin. Her eyes were wells of utter sorrow and her voice caught in her throat as she said softly, "we... should talk."

Erin *tried* to focus on Tilly's face and figure out what she had said. But her mind, as if its power cable had suddenly been unplugged and then plugged back in, was still coming back online. So she couldn't think straight, or at all really. And in that darkness where there was no thought, there was just the lone lighthouse keeper, who stands watch in the recesses of every animal's mind. This primal instinct spoke to her in a language which does not even need to be processed to be understood. A sort of morse code of emotion. It told her in no uncertain terms: go! go! fly from here! get away! flee! regroup elsewhere! This was the only counsel she had, and she heeded its message well.

She roared in a hoarse, unintelligible voice, "get away from me!"

And she tried to push Tilly away, but her hands fell short.

Pivoting around, she broke into a sprint down the ward.

All of the people nearby turned to look at the commotion.

She faintly registered that Genevieve was yelling something after her. And then she saw a young, stocky female nurse up ahead, who was pushing along a line of bare IV stands to take them somewhere, yell an answer back. With a speedy sidestep, she moved herself and her haul into Erin's path, stretching out her arms wide to get ready to intercept.

Erin saw this obstacle to her escape, and shrieked like a banshee. It was a noise of pure, animalistic ferocity, entirely unlike any one might expect *could* come from such a slight woman. But in that instant, she was not herself, she was blind rage incarnate.

The nurse's face showed that she was rattled by this wild battle-cry. Still, to her credit, she stood her ground nevertheless.

As Erin came close, she juked to one side, causing the nurse to reposition there to meet her. But when Erin got to the impromptu barricade, she dipped back over to the other side again before the nurse could react. Although she was now out of reach of being grabbed, she did still have to get past the row of IV stands. Without actually stopping, she just reached forward and shoved the two that were directly in her way to either side as hard as she could, creating a gap to dart through.

The nurse had just turned towards Erin and went to leap at her to try and get close enough to grab her. But she was also unwittingly jumping right into the path of one of the IV stands that Erin had just thrust aside with great force. Before she even had time for her neurons to spark and make her register the danger, the metal pole smashed into her face. She instantly crumpled to her knees whilst clutching her nose, which was already trickling blood down across her lips. In a few moments, it would escalate to a full-blown crimson waterfall.

Still running at full-pelt, Erin didn't even see the hurt she was leaving in her wake. She was just laser-focused on making it to the double-doors and getting the hell out of here.

Not too far away from the ward's entrance was a janitor who seemed to have only just noticed the chaotic scene taking place behind him. He'd stepped away from his cart to start moving into position to make his own interception attempt. But after seeing the blood pouring from the nurse's flattened nose, he was frozen in indecision. And by the time Erin blew past him, he had retreated back to his cart with his back turned to signal his pacificity, intent upon not incurring the wrath of this crazy waif's blitzkrieg too. It was suddenly a very easy call to make.

Erin flung open one of the doors and it banged loudly against the wall. She came out into the corridor where a few startled people stared at her in bewilderment as she whipped past. She ran all the way back to the elevator and hammered the call button with her closed fist, anxiously shifting her weight from one foot to another as she waited. Thankfully the elevator came almost immediately and she jumped inside.

As she was about to hit the 'ground floor' button, she hesitated. She was just now beginning to regain the ability to actually think, though for the most part her mind was still foggy and overloaded. It occurred to her that if Genevieve concluded that she had had some kind of episode, it followed that apprehending her 'for her own safety' must be the protocol here. And so, if Genevieve phoned down quickly enough, a human blockade of hospital security would probably be waiting for her down there at the exit.

This situation was so horrible. Why were they trying to get her? She hadn't done anything wrong. She didn't want to hurt anyone. She just wanted to get far away from this place, to get home.

Having only a second to think it over, she impulsively hit the 'fourth floor' button instead. The doors closed and the elevator began to descend.

Erin was rubbing her eyes hard, trying to clear her vision. Before she could finish, the doors opened. With no actual plan for what she was going to do, she left the elevator and found herself at the start of another corridor. There was luckily no-one walking along this first stretch, and Erin began to jog down it. Unexpectedly, a door labelled 'Custodial Supplies' soon caught her eye and she skidded to a halt in front of it.

Though she figured it must surely be locked, she tried the handle anyway.

It wasn't locked.

Her eyes shot wide in relief and gratitude. She pulled open the door and leapt inside.

It was a small room, but its cramped confines were actually comforting to her. They put her in the headspace of being back in her apartment and soothed her simmering agoraphobia.

Unfortunately, it also smelled absolutely awful. There were a few janitor carts and mop buckets taking up most of the open space. Along the walls were tall shelving units filled with cleaning products and general hospital supplies.

Having taken stock of where she was, Erin turned back towards the door and took a firm grip of the handle with both hands. If anyone tried to get in here, she was going to hold this door handle still with all her might.

This was to be her sanctum while she got her head right and figured out what the fuck was going on. She had commandeered it, under the ancient natural right of securing for oneself a safe place when *in extremis*. For as long as she needed it, it was hers. No one else's. No one was getting in here, and she'd fight them off if they tried. She considered what could function as a defensive weapon should the need arise. There were, unsurprisingly, slim pickings. But... a cart could perhaps be used as an improvised battering ram if it came to it. So too... maybe one of those wooden mop handles could be snapped in half to create some kind of pointed stick. And it was possible she might be able to...

Without a sound, Tilly appeared behind her.

"Nice digs," she joked sadly.

Erin let out a little cry of surprise and spun around with her elbow raised to smash her ambusher.

Startled in turn, Tilly raised her palms to Erin and made a 'settle-down' gesture with them. In a soft, sympathetic voice, she said, "it's okay, it's just me, it's just me."

Alas, this did nothing to calm Erin down.

"You scared the shit out of me!" she barked testily.

Tilly nodded in concession and apologetically offered, "yeah... umm, sorry about that. Maybe not such a good idea in hindsight. I was just... I just thought it might help break the ice. You know, ease the tension..."

Erin passed over all of this. Still livid, she clutched her head and cried, "what the hell is happening to me?! That stupid fucking nurse... said... said..." - she couldn't bring herself to repeat it - "and now... I can see all these jumbled, hazy... *memories*... from somebody else's life!"

Taking a deep breath to prepare herself, Tilly said, "those aren't... Wait, first things first, I just want you to know I'm sorry I had to shanghai you here like this. But there was no other way, please believe that. You *had* to return to this place, and let it touch you again. If there had been some painless way to expose you to the truth, to trigger these memories..." She trailed off, her eyes glimmering with a sheen of teariness. "Well, I would have gladly riven myself into pieces if that was what it took to give it to you."

As she turned her face away, meaning to clear away the tears, she inadvertently took in the janitor's closet. It was as grubby and as dingy as could be imagined. She saw the discolored walls and the filthy mopheads and the giant packs of cheap toilet rolls on the shelves. There were cobwebs in the corners of the ceiling and, ironically, various dead bugs in the corners of the floor. Truly, a more sordid setting would be hard to find. With a little whimper of sorrow, she looked down at her feet.

Then in a quiet, broken voice, she said to herself, "oh god, I never wanted it to happen somewhere like *this*."

Erin was only getting more impatient and more mad as she listened. Firstly, it was cold in here, and she had started to shiver a little bit. Frustratingly enough, her sweater and hat had been left behind on the floor of the nurses' station. So she was rubbing her bare arms, now covered in goosebumps, to try and warm them up. Secondly, she didn't care one jot about Tilly's cryptic apologies, or anything else whatsoever. She just wanted answers, and she wanted them now.

She erupted, hollering, "I don't care about any of this bullshit! Just tell me what the fuck is going on!"

Tilly looked up. Her eyes were no less teary than before, but her gaze and her countenance now bespoke a certain newfound determination. She knew she had to be strong for Erin, had to steel herself to carry out her awful duty.

It was time to give Erin the worst gift she'd ever receive.

"You... you fell, Erin. *It was you who fell that day.* There is no Tilly. Or, at least, not as you think of her. She's just you. Who you were before the accident."

Erin's eyes widened and her pupils dilated. Her face became blank with terror. She stepped backwards towards the door, shaking her head slowly, until her back came up against it.

"No," she answered simply.

Taking a step closer, Tilly went on carefully. It seemed so surreal that this moment was finally upon them. In the past, there had been so many idle moments where she'd thought about exactly how she would say all this. Hopefully that preparation would now prove worthwhile.

"You... were... in a medically induced coma for three weeks. They brought you out of it once they managed to reduce the brain swelling. And then this hospital became your home for a while. The recovery process from the *traumatic brain injury* was intensive and arduous. And... unsurprisingly... you hated every minute of it with a burning passion. You could barely walk more than ten paces, Erin, and *still* you made three separate escape attempts. You wanted out so badly that you started lying to your doctors: playing down the symptoms they could detect, hiding the ones they couldn't. You were so very committed to the act and, hell, you had a laptop, so you could look up what they wanted to see. Eventually they concluded that you'd only suffered a relatively minor TBI and it was healing nicely. And once you had made it through all the basic recovery protocols, they couldn't stop you from discharging yourself."

"No, no, it's n-not true. None of it is true," Erin whispered, staring through Tilly. Her face was white as a sheet. And she was pressing herself up against the door, as if trying to get as far away from these revelations as possible.

Tilly had a pained expression from compassion and sadness. She didn't want to go on. She didn't want to force Erin to take in anymore. But the thing had been started, and it had to be seen through. She had to get the whole story out, handover the *entire* cache of forgotten secrets, if she was going to equip Erin with the knowledge and understanding needed to survive the coming wilderness.

"When you got home, you just hid yourself away in your apartment. But soon... the medications you were supposed to be taking ran out and you weren't about to go pick up more. Without those or the support system at the hospital, you had only the oppressive loneliness of your solitude. And so the effects of the TBI on your psyche began to assert themselves in their true magnitude. This made the knowledge of what had happened to you become unbearable, causing your mental state to rapidly disintegrate over the next few months. Finally... it all came to a head... and you suffered a... *catastrophic*... breakdown.

"Your mind, as a last-ditch self-preservation measure, sealed off all recollection of your accident and the time following it, and hid this stark gap in your memory from you too. They call it scotomization, Erin, I looked it up. It reset you and you went on as if nothing had ever happened. Amazingly, you lasted about a year and a half like that. But, ironically enough, the gigantic strain of self-deception was itself corroding your sanity. So... well... you had your first dream about 'Tilly'. That was the truth fighting against its bondage, trying to seep out through the cracks however possible."

Erin had gradually slid down the door and now she was sat at its bottom, holding her knees and staring up at Tilly with defiant, tear-brimmed eyes.

This situation was utterly bizarre. And she refused to dignify it by engaging with it as if it were real. It *couldn't* be real. And what Tilly was saying *couldn't* possibly be true. Much like that moment during a particularly horrific nightmare where you're actually willing yourself to wake up from it, Erin just wanted this to be over. She just wanted out.

"It's a lie. All of it, all lies. It *can't* be the truth..." she hissed in response.

"I'm afraid it is true, Erin. Besides, I know that you can now faintly remember at least some of this. A few of your quarantined memories are beginning to reappear, aren't they? They're blurry and incomplete, but they will become clearer and clearer, and in time they will be joined by all the others too. Still, even the glimpses you have right now vouch for what I'm claiming, don't they?"

Although Erin could not deny this, she could not admit it either. She just clenched her jaw and looked away angrily.

"This is all just grade-a horseshit! And Tilly proves it! I have so many vivid, detailed memories of my time as her lover, my time at her bedside! They prove she's real!"

"Hmm... This is the part you're really not going to like," Tilly said unhappily, grimacing in anticipation. "*Your mind completely fabricated Tilly and the life you shared with her.* You were starting to become more and more curious about your dream-girl's inexplicable arrival. So, in order to... uh, palliatively... sate that hunger for answers, you were given a backstory which let you creep a *bit* closer to the truth. And because that false epiphany made you feel like you had gotten to the bottom of things, your mind concocted some fake memories to help prop it up. But the mind is not the expert storyteller it believes itself to be. It just hastily threw together a... hodgepodge of random invention, guesswork... and distorted fragments of what really happened.

"And yet... well, okay, let me put it this way. When dreaming, the mind's creative faculties run amok. It places these fantastical scenarios before you which, umm, tumble chaotically into one another, and it expects you to just go along with them anyway. Funny thing is, you do. Because they're all you have in that moment. Likewise, in Tilly your mind also gave you a story a little too disjointed, a little too crazy to easily believe, but you did anyway. After all, it was the only story you had. And when it comes to trying to understand things, we will always choose a bad story over no story at all. Because... nature doesn't abhor a vacuum half as much as one's sense of self."

The tears were now falling down her cheek, but Erin was clinging onto her anger and would not give herself over to the crying. So the tears just went on trickling down, unacknowledged, from her scowl.

"This... this d-doesn't make any sense! If I was able to force my brain to give me *some* answers, I would have just jumped straight past those stopgaps to the whole truth!"

Tilly shook her head sternly. Inside, however, she was glad Erin was actually starting to grapple with and think about these new truths.

"Listen, you *needed* a story which made the accident about somebody else. You simply couldn't live with the reality that it happened to you, or that you had to deal with its aftermath all alone. And most of all, you couldn't deal with the fact that it... happened for no reason. With no one else to blame, you wanted a way to blame yourself for the death of who you were. So your mind deluded you into looking at it as if you were merely an outside observer. That allowed you to grieve over the tragedy happening to someone you could love unconditionally, because with all your self-loathing you never let yourself grieve over it having happened to you. And plus it enabled you to express your confused sense of guilt. You didn't abandon Tilly, you abandoned yourself. You ran away from what you needed to get better."

The words were at last penetrating Erin's disbelief. She was weeping freely now.

With her cheeks wet and her upper lip slick with snot, she blubbered out, "no, no, no! I n-never... I could have n-never...! I-I... *can't*... have been Tilly. She's... so different from me!"

It took Tilly a few moments to respond. She was staring at Erin, overcome by enormous pity. Despite how many times she had practiced these explanations before, anticipating what questions or objections would arise, delivering them was so much harder than she'd ever feared. Especially when seeing firsthand exactly what this was doing to Erin. She couldn't help but feel that it was her fault Erin was crying, which was crushing. She felt so bad it was making her resolve waver. Presently, she wanted nothing more than to cut everything off here and just go over to comfort Erin. Yet she knew that this was merely her selfish desire to run away from doing this incredibly unpleasant thing. If she genuinely wanted to act in Erin's best interest, it was impossible to spare her the emotional toll of hearing these crucial truths.

She sighed miserably and resumed talking.

"In some ways that's true, yes. The most important difference is that the brain trauma caused your personality to radically shift when you woke up from the coma. The doctors had no way of picking up on that, of course, because... uh, there weren't any visitors to point out how you were before. As for appearance... well, you lost quite a bit of weight languishing in that hospital bed. And then even more when you got home and your eating disorder popped up. There's not that much else to it. I mean, sure, you were younger and you used to have long, dyed hair, but beyond that, you look pretty similar to me. You just... stopped looking at yourself in the mirror, Erin, and your self-image became wildly askew. And then your mind, keen to preserve its subterfuge, did the rest."

Erin's head was now between her knees and she was hyperventilating as she sobbed uncontrollably. The sounds she was making reverberated around the small room horribly. She was so desperately trying to suck in deep breaths, but it felt like a boulder lay upon her chest, suffocating her.

The garbled words she managed to wail out under these circumstances were basically incomprehensible, but luckily Tilly didn't have to rely on actually hearing them.

"No! You don't get it! Fuck appearance! Fuck all that stupid shit! S-she was... so much... *better* than me! She was h-happy and kind and... g-good!"

Tilly nodded understandingly. The statement was untrue, but she knew exactly what Erin meant.

"You have to come to terms with Tilly being someone *you* used to be. To that extent, she'll always be a part of you. But that *person*? She's gone, Erin. She died in the hospital bed where you rode out your coma. And that really sucks. And that's really fucking sad. She didn't deserve her untimely ending. And I get that you want to... revere her now to make up for it, I really do. However, you're not honouring her memory by obsessing over her and pretending she was perfect. Yes, she had a lot of positive qualities, just as you do, but she also had her flaws and her problems and all the rest of it. You need to truly mourn her, which means letting her go. And when you've stopped... worshipping the idealized ghost of who you were, you'll finally... be able to decide who you want to be now."

Erin pulled up the bottom of her t-shirt to dab at her eyes and wipe her dripping nose on. The tears were still flowing, but now the despair was beginning to give way to a resurgence of rage. She felt an intense hatred towards Tilly, for these things she was saying and for the deceit she had evidently engaged in for so long.

"Take your advice and cram it up your fucking ass!" she spat furiously. "Why the hell should I listen to you now?! How could I ever trust you again when all you've done is lie to me and manipulate me! You even tricked me into coming here!"

Tilly exhaled wearily.

"Please try to really think about what I'm about to say. I'm not somebody else, some stranger. And I'm not your enemy. I'm the part of you that wants to live, that wants to heal. Though you didn't realize it, it was *you* who deputized me to make the choices you wanted to make but couldn't bring yourself to. Look, you may not believe this, but I actually can't *really* force you to do anything. You wouldn't be here if you didn't want to be, deep down. Don't you see that? If you really wanted to just give up and die, you would never have made me, let alone made me how I am."

"B-but... you were... *her*... and you were-"

Here Tilly interjected, saying gently, "only ever what you needed me to be, each step of the way. Something to love, something to hate. A mirror this time, a canvas that time. Whatever you required, I became."

Looking away sulkily, Erin scoffed. The tears had stopped altogether now.

"Oh you've got a fucking perfect answer for everything, right?!" she threw back bitterly. "You're so wise and you're so kindly, such a benevolent guardian angel. So why didn't you just tell me all of this as soon as I manifested you? You could have spared me all the awful, awful shit I went through!"

"Well, I think you're probably not going to enjoy this answer all that much then. Not that you've been overly fond of any of the other answers so far...."

Tilly gave a little nervous smile here. But Erin pointedly just went on staring at her with the same hostile gaze.

"So, uh, anyway. It's pretty simple really. We're both running on the same... uh... malfunctioning hardware. I'm sorry to put it so bluntly, but it's really kind of a mess in here. The lingering effects of your TBI definitely don't help, but mostly it's the fact that when your mind sealed off the traumatic memories which were tearing you apart, it acted with a... certain reckless haste for the sake of self-preservation. Its erasure spree was rather clumsy and overzealous, leading to an element of... *scattershot*. Collateral damage, Erin. Superfluous gaps in your memory.

Yet, just like blind spots in your vision which you can only see once trained to notice them, you couldn't even sense any of these absences. Which meant that for a while neither could I. Then, when I finally could, it took time to sort through them all, to figure out what was relevant and why. And, given that you weren't at all ready to re-learn the truth yet, I had to move slowly and carefully. Even though I was operating from the inside,

I couldn't risk just... openly vivisecting your memory banks, so putting the story together took time."

Notes of horror swam across Erin's face. She was picturing her mind ineptly hacking away at itself, haphazardly chopping out whole swaths of her life. What else did she not know about herself, about what had happened to her? The possibilities were endless, and absolutely terrifying. She held her head in her hands.

Tilly picked up on this brewing fear and jumped in quickly to add, "the memories aren't gone. They weren't, like, deleted outright. Your mind... just kind of buried them for when you're in a better state mentally. So please don't worry. When you get the treatment you need, it'll all come flooding back I'm sure."

This did technically serve its purpose: Erin *was* no longer caught up in her fretting now.

Because she was once again too pissed off instead. Her expression soured and she wrinkled her nose in disgust.

"Oh, you're *sure*, are you? You're sure?! Based on fucking what? You mess around in my head a bit - from the inside, I might add! - and google some medical mumbo-jumbo and now... you think you have a fucking neurology PhD? Your 'assurances' aren't worth a thimble full of shit!" she snapped.

There was a pause as Tilly tried to collect herself. This verbal attack had rather blindsided her. She wasn't certain it had really been a worthwhile trade: exchanging fear for another bout of anger. It was definitely a thankless one, at any rate. And having to flip between comforting mode and fending-off-beratement mode at the drop of a hat was very flustering.

"I-I'm just saying that... that... it stands to reason that you'll probably get all those things back once-"

"Ah yes. And that will be just great, won't it?" Erin butted in to mutter darkly. She roughly wiped her face with her palms, dragging away the wetness. Then she reached up overhead and grabbed hold of the door handle to shakily pull herself up to her feet.

"You just don't get it, do you?" she continued, as she dusted herself off. "I have this fundamental idea about who I am, which is my fucking everything. But, oh look, it's incomplete. So here you come, with your... chirpy insistence that I just let a mysterious influx of... shitty old puzzle pieces slot into all those gaps. Now the whole jigsaw looks totally fucking different, doesn't it?! And what if I don't like this strange new person I find out I actually am?! What if I hate her goddamn guts?! There'll be no going back! I'll be sentencing myself to living my life out as her! I'll take on all her sins, all her awfulness, forever!"

"Erin, you may have done things you'll regret, but you were unwell, you weren't in your right mind. As much as you may not want to believe it, you *are* a good person. Yesterday, today, and tomorrow."

"Yeah, and how the fuck would you know? You're just the immaculate babysitter my damaged brain is making me hallucinate. Just a ridiculous byproduct of unprocessable grief, that's it. You only exist because I was too scared to just go ahead and kill myself. Because I wanted to pretend someone was always arguing me out of it. God... how stupid I've been..."

Erin grimaced and shook her head in embarrassment to punctuate the sentiment. She was so unbelievably mad at herself, and yet somehow even more so at Tilly. Petty as it was, the strength of that resentment meant Erin was not above trying to reflect back some of the hurt she felt.

She went on by saying, "so you know what? No more of your fucking explanations. For all I know, you're just telling me what I want to hear again. For all I know, you're actually trying to fuck me over. This could all just be another line of red herring nonsense to keep me occupied for another couple of months. These new memories unfurling from hibernation for me could be just as phony as the others!"

Tilly was hoping not to look wounded by what had been said. This was not easy. She just tried to maintain eye contact and seem unruffled as she thought Erin's point over. She needed to retain control over this situation, to dictate the flow of things. That meant being above useless quarrelling. The bait for which had been plainly laid at her feet. But, no, she had to be the calm authority here, or at least play the part well enough.

"Your mistrust is understandable. And... to be totally frank... you *can't* be absolutely sure that what I'm telling you is true. Not yet anyway," she said, giving a little shrug of concession. "Maybe there *is* another trapdoor, another floor further down in these twisty catacombs housing the moments that were taken from you. I'd ask you to trust me when I say that you're already at the bedrock, but" - she glanced away sadly - "I get why that wouldn't count for all that much anymore. So I suppose I'll just point this out: at the very least, you must be closer to the final, whole truth than you've ever been, right? It's the best you've got right now, so why not run with it as far as it goes?"

Erin was barely listening. Her eyes were downcast and she was lost in reflection.

When Tilly had finished, it seemed to pull Erin back. But there was something changed about her now, something unsettling. She looked up and let her head loll around on her neck.

"There was no point to any of it," she declared plainly, as if to no-one in particular. "To *us*. How I... felt. All that we had, all that we went through together. All the... suffering... I put myself through."

A deep melancholy infected her gaze and she started massaging her temples despondently. It was really starting to sink in at this point. And the implications were torturesome. She looked shell-shocked.

"Good god..." she whispered, again really just to herself, in affirmation. "There was no fucking point to any of it."

This was scarier to Tilly than the crying or the shouting. It was so much more dangerous. This dire-seed could not be allowed to take root. The sense of hopelessness which sprouted would sap away all of Erin's will to fight. Because, starved of oxygen by that competing growth, the crucial fire in her belly would be smothered and extinguished. And the resulting apathy would wrap around her like vines erupting from her skin, becoming an irreversible paralytic.

With a voice heavy with emotion, Tilly exclaimed, "don't say that! There was a point! You're here, aren't you?!"

Galvanised by Tilly's intensity, Erin stamped her foot and gave a little shriek of frustration.

Jabbing a finger towards the door and fending off the speedy return of tears, she yelled back, "I won't make it in their world! Don't you see that?! I w-won't be able to take it! T-this is my end!"

Stepping closer still to Erin, Tilly's eyes were serious and tender.

She lowered her voice and pronounced with utmost certainty, *"this will not destroy you."*

Erin took a step back, away from Tilly. She was shaking her head, her face awash with despair. She didn't want to let the emotion overcome her again; she wanted to maintain a feisty, steely facade. But despite her resistance, it had her in its clutches once more.

"I can't do this! I can't survive it alone!"

Tilly's composure did not desert her. She went on staring into Erin's eyes, and wearing a sincere and compassionate expression.

Her tone was no less sure as she replied, "this self-pity isn't the Erin I know. It's merely the costume you put on when you want to give yourself an excuse not to try. Because heed me when I say: you have an immense strength that you do not permit yourself to acknowledge. I mean, you made it through *hell* alone! Most would have perished under a quarter of what you've endured. And now all that's left is the last few steps out of the inferno. It will be a cakewalk in comparison."

This tough love only incensed Erin.

"That's easy for you to say! *I'm* the one who will have to go through it! That's what you don't get! You've thrown me into this, whether it turns out good or fucking godawful!" she barked in breathless succession.

Then she disdainfully walked straight through Tilly. With her arms folded, she started pacing up and down the small stretch of free space along the middle of the room. She was both thinking it all over and trying to work off this new flare up of animosity.

Tilly let a few minutes pass, watching from beside the door, and then ventured softly, "how are you feeling?"

Erin glanced over at her with eyes that were incredibly tired, and hard, and still smouldering with the embers of anger.

She whispered fiercely, "fuck you forever."

Tilly didn't speak for a moment. She couldn't. She just looked away. Her chest rising and falling betrayed the big, deep breath she was subtly taking.

"That's... maybe fair," she returned at last, nodding sadly.

Ceasing her pacing, Erin planted her feet and ranted exasperatedly.

"You wanna know how I feel?! Well, I'm all cried out I guess. I don't have anything else to give. I feel empty, spent. At this point, I'm just... *done*. I'm so done. I give up. Tomorrow I'm probably going to find out that Tilly's actually my long-lost twin... or that I'm Tilly and you're Erin... or that I'm just dreaming all of this from inside my coma or some other stupid shit like that. And then the day after, I'll find out some bizarre new bullshit which supersedes *that*. So what is the fucking point? I obviously have no say in any of this, just the urge to pretend I do. Meaning that... fighting against it is just... like, adding to its power to torment me. I'd rather deny it the satisfaction. Might as well just give myself over to it, right? That's the smart play, right?! Just throw myself headfirst into the woodchipper! Maybe there's some final modicum of fucking control in that!"

Now flushed and puffing, Erin took a few seconds to catch her breath.

"So... what does that mean exactly? What are you planning to do?" Tilly used the opening to inquire cautiously.

Erin huffed and rolled her eyes, as if to chide Tilly for not 'getting it'. Then, trying to do it as nonchalantly as possible, she unfolded her arms and furtively lay her hands down by her jeans' pockets. Then she switched to holding her hands together behind her back, resting them on the rear pockets.

A tiny flicker of annoyance minutely disturbed her expression.

But then she had it back under control.

"You know what we're doing. Back up to the sixth floor. Back to the fucking storehouse for the barely-living dead. Sidle up to Nurse Airhead again. Tell her what the deal is. And... whatever... just go from there," she explained with haughty impatience.

Tilly was taken aback, her eyes widening slightly with surprise. But she saw that Erin was evidently in earnest about this intention. She felt a certain disquieting mix of conflicting emotions. She was, of course, pleased that Erin seemed to have come around, yet there was also a lingering wariness she couldn't shake.

Still, who cared if this somehow felt too easy? All that mattered was getting Erin where she needed to be.

"Shall... we... go then?" she said, with a nervous glance towards the door.

Taking a deep breath which morphed into a sigh, Erin nodded and went over to the door. There was a moment of hesitation as she reached for the handle.

With her back still to Tilly, she carefully adopted a neutral tone and asked, "the phone call, that was... your handiwork?"

This caught Tilly very much off guard. It seemed such a strange thing to care about, what with all that had just transpired. Now it was her turn to hesitate.

There was no good way to say this. No way to make it sound like anything else than what it was.

"Um... no... not as such. Though I did hope that certain... acts... on my part may perhaps start a... domino effect, leading to something like that manifesting itself."

Erin's head tilted forward slightly and she closed her eyes momentarily. She lay her hand upon the handle and squeezed the unyielding metal hard.

"*Tinkering,*" she muttered disgustedly to herself before she re-opened her eyes.

Leaving the room, she stepped out into the corridor with Tilly and carefully shut the door behind them.

Then she took a second to scan the corridor and make sure there were no security guards around, or anyone else paying special attention to her. Although there were a fair number of people coursing up and down the corridor, comprising both hospital staff and patients, they were too absorbed in their own business to really notice her.

Satisfied that the coast was clear, she walked down to the elevators. As she got there, one had just arrived and let out a very chatty, animated group of visitors. Unfortunately, there was a man standing next to her, waiting for the elevator too. Puffing her cheeks up, she blew out a very long exhalation in frustration. Then she just gestured to the one that had just come, offering it to him. He seemed confused for an instant but did indeed step inside and take it. She waited for the next one to arrive, tapping her foot impatiently. This one let out a teenage boy with a leg cast densely covered in messages and doodles, being pushed in a wheelchair by a female orderly. He had a big floppy silver faux-hawk.

The boy saw Erin's band t-shirt and actually squealed with glee. He grabbed hold of the wheels to stop the orderly from pushing him out into the corridor.

"Oh. My. God! You *cannot* be serious! I ab-soooooooooo-lutely love 'Bush Baby Death Cries' too! Oh man they rock! I've never even... I haven't even seen anyone else... Like, anyway, that tee is so rad!"

Erin just looked at him impassively with bloodshot eyes, almost looking straight through him as if he wasn't even there. She was staring at him like one impotently stares out of a window at a blaring car alarm which won't shut up. Not *just* wishing it would stop, but wishing it had never even appeared in one's own little universe to begin with. A desire for retroactive erasure. It was, to say the least, very unnerving to be on the receiving end of this.

Fifteen awkward seconds passed.

The boy looked side to side uncomfortably and said, "ummm... okay?..."

Then the orderly cleared her throat and started pushing him out of the elevator, murmuring, "let's... head on, why don't we?"

Erin hopped inside it before the doors closed, and hit the sixth floor button.

As the elevator ascended, Tilly was trying to think of a way to dissolve the tense silence that had arisen between them. But she was finding Erin so hard to read right now, and would no doubt incur her wrath by choosing unwisely. This was a weighty disincentive against even trying.

Erin just stood there, powerfully lost in contemplation.

She suddenly felt she could just barely perceive, hidden in the portrait of her life, the few faint brushstrokes which tauntingly hinted at all the pentimenti wherein her story unfolded differently. Especially maddening was the fact that no matter which configuration she pieced together these fragments of possibility into, she could only ever discern the same thing. Over and over and over. It was always an ethereal other-Erin who had chosen *not* to venture out-of-doors that one icy morning and whose unlived life was consequently one of happiness and ease.

Could she really be the *only* Erin, of the immense multitude there could have been, who was doomed to this tragic path? There was an all-pervading existential loneliness entailed by that proposition which made her bones ache. It was unthinkable. And it was profoundly improbable. And with galling certainty, she somehow knew it was true.

She so dearly wished that she could just take a scalpel and, with judicious incisions, cut out even one of these hypothetical Erins. It would free that girl from her bondage behind the Erin who had ended up glaring out so forlornly from the canvas. Even if it meant trading places and allowing *herself* to vanish behind the paint, she would do it. But this was, of course, impossible. No matter how fervent or selfless the desire to do so was, abstract traces of could-have-beens cannot be heaped into a pile to make a person.

The elevator doors opened and presented the familiar sixth floor corridor.

Whilst the two of them strolled down it together, Tilly finally plucked up the courage to ask, "why don't you talk to me about what you're thinking right now? This is a... heavy situation, Erin... to put it mildly. It's not good to keep it all trapped inside."

"Why don't you just snoop inside my mind and see for yourself," Erin responded slowly, contemptuously.

Tilly didn't reply straight away. Over the course of the next few moments, her face became more serious.

At last, she quietly mumbled, "I... can't."

Erin replied in a quiet tone also. But this one was infused with a distinctly spiteful satisfaction.

"No, you can't."

When they entered through the double-doors of Ward B once more, Erin went right past the waiting area. In the ward itself, she saw the same janitor from before setting out bright yellow 'wet floor' signs around where he had just cleaned up the blood. The poor nurse whose nose had supplied it was nowhere to be seen however.

When the people who had witnessed Erin's rampage noticed her return, they just stared frostily at her as she went by, but said nothing. One of these was the male nurse who had misplaced his form. Upon recognising her, he hurriedly departed to elsewhere on the ward.

Erin was thankful that no one was currently at the nurses' station. She strode up to it and saw that her sweater and hat had been picked up and neatly piled on the countertop. She snatched up the sweater and slid her phone out of its pocket, letting the earphones fall to the floor without a second glance. They were a silly expedient she no longer needed. She even stepped on them, cracking the plastic casing of the earbuds... just to do it. After unlocking the phone and checking it had enough battery, she tapped on the taxi app.

Then she turned to Tilly and emphatically held the screen up before her face.

"This is all I wanted. To get my ass out of here," she said aloud, her voice cold and defiant. She smugly waggled the phone like a trophy.

Tilly's eyes were black fury.

Her jaw was clenched and her fists were balled tight. She was disappointed and livid and somehow unsurprised. And, most of all, entirely out of patience. This really was the last straw.

"Erin..." she began slowly, through gritted teeth, "you said you were going to-"

"Yeah, that's exactly what *all of you* want, isn't it?! God, you're just the same as these motherfuckers," Erin hissed to interrupt, making a sweeping gesture towards the whole ward.

She put on a mock-serious doctorly tone, all pompousness and condescension, and continued.

"'Oh yes, goodness gracious young lady, just turn yourself over to us! Let us coerce and manipulate you! Let us incompetently *tinker* with your brain! We'll be careful! We've only got your best interests at heart, we swear! Pinky-fucking-promise!' That's them! That's you!"

Tilly had no idea how to respond. She just glared at Erin as she went on.

"I can't claim to know how to fix this shit, but... hell.... at least I now maybe understand the problem at last. Whatever it takes, I'll figure it out! And it'll happen on my fucking terms, nobody else's! Not in their captivity, or yours!"

"This *isn't* something you can fix by yourself!" Tilly exclaimed, belatedly finding her tongue again.

Erin shouted back, "we'll fucking see about that!"

At this, Tilly straightened, and her demeanour sobered.

"*'We'* aren't going to do anything of the sort. If you leave this place, when you're so very close to finally getting the help you so desperately need... you'll be leaving it alone. I won't stick around to help you suffer through yet more needless self-destruction. I won't do it, Erin."

There was no way for Erin to hide the effect of this blow. A threat of abandonment was something she was particularly sensitive to, a hidden vulnerability only a mental roommate would know about. So it really hit her hard and her face told the story all too plainly. First there was shock, next a certain wounded look of betrayal, and lastly the mixture hardened into a thick armour of resentment and feigned disregard.

"That's... fine with me!" she blurted out. "You said this is where *she* perished, right?! So I guess it's only fitting that her fucking insolent ghost takes up residence here too! You think I can't make another one of you as soon as I get home?! A new version who won't stab me in the back the whole time!"

Now it was Tilly's turn to look surprised and hurt.

This shouting-match bridge-burning was not at all what either of them truly wanted, but they were locked into their respective stances now. Even if the prospect of separation alarmed them both, there just could be no backing down. This had to come to a head.

"Please, think this through. Don't let your hotheadedness lure you into making a terrible mistake! You're exactly where you need to be. You know this *has* to happen, you know this was always the inevitable endpoint for you! Stop fighting it, just let it happen!"

Erin did not concur. She did not concur at all.

She had a very different conception of the matter, one she was willing to embrace to the hilt. It was, she felt, the only thing she had to fall back on now.

Even when fate had her inescapably trapped in its net, she meant to writhe and struggle against it. Even if that's futile, even if that's foolish. Because the defiance itself is what matters. It's what grants one some semblance of dignity. A middle-finger to the suffocating, mummifying fabric of the cosmos. And that's the all-important distinction between the slave and the captive. The slave kowtows and accepts. The captive bellows and resists. Thus the slave has relinquished something precious which the captive still strives to protect. That little 'fuck you' makes all the difference in the world.

"Yeah, yeah, like I said, I guess we'll just fucking see about that! Won't we?!"

"This hostility is just a defense mechanism, you know that! You're just a frightened little girl running away from something difficult and scary! That isn't who you want to be, not really!"

Erin's nostrils flared with rage. She scoffed and, turning to leave, scornfully retorted, "that's funny, because here I am, walking right out the goddamn door."

Genevieve, evidently notified of Erin's return, appeared around a corner at the distant end of the ward and came jogging down to the nurses' station.

As she got close, she called out, "Erin?! What the heck happened?! Why'd you wig out like that?! You broke Debbie's friggin' nose! Where have-"

Erin stopped to look round at her. But she had precisely no interest in even pretending to care. She just rolled her eyes disdainfully and interrupted to say, "save it, you fucking insufferable bimbo."

The consternation on Genevieve's face only intensified further. And her eyebrows shot up in shocked indignation at having her concerned questioning rebuffed in such an aggressive way. The whole thing was mystifying. What had happened to the timid, taciturn woman who first approached her? Who was this erratic body-double brazenly spouting insults? It made Jekyll and Hyde look like bumbling community-theatre bit players with tepid commitment to the roles.

This reaction was lost on Erin, however, because she was now too busy processing what she had just learned.

She had broken that other nurse's nose? But how? She had never even touched her!

She quickly replayed her escape in her mind, and the only opportunity for it to have happened became painfully clear. The would-be tackler had *put herself* in the exact wrong place at the exact wrong time. Crappy for her, even worse for Erin. Perhaps the most galling thing was that this unbelievably bad luck should not even have been surprising at this point.

Erin groaned. Her face scrunched up in frustration and she smacked her forehead with her palm.

This made things so much more serious. It escalated everything. She was now not only the madwoman who had freaked out and caused some big scene, she had also injured someone. Plus, its accidental nature was obvious only to her. If she had been worried that hospital security might try to grab her before learning of this development, now she was *sure* they would. And as she'd no doubt be 'considered dangerous' now, they were likely not going to be terribly gunshy about the level of force they employed. She had seen many humiliating videos online of people being tasered, where they drooled and flopped around like fishes washed up on shore. That was *not* going to happen to her.

She had to get the fuck out of here, and fast.

Yet again, she broke into a sprint down the ward.

Behind her, she heard Genevieve aggravatedly yell, "come on! Again?! This day just keeps getting better and better!"

She had managed to get about ten meters away when running suddenly became incredibly, inexplicably difficult.

It was like she had been enclosed in a private sphere of slowed-time. Each laboured stride took her several seconds, as though she was trying to run through waist-high molasses. The spectacle of it must have looked both ridiculous and disturbing to the onlookers, but she was much too flummoxed and infuriated to care about that.

As Erin struggled to keep moving, to break through this invisible restraint and pick up speed, Tilly was airily drifting alongside her as though she were a tethered kite. She was wholly past her anger now. Indeed, it was easy to shed her ire from this vantage, surveying Erin like a bug trapped helplessly in a jar. She just looked on with distant pity.

"I'm sorry I got so mad, and said things I didn't mean," she offered softly. "I had just really hoped that" - she breathed a heavy sigh - "well... it doesn't matter. I see now that this... whole thing is just too... unbearable for you. And it's not right to blame you for the way your mind works."

Erin scarcely even registered this, so intense was her focus on muscling through the conjured impediment slowing her down. Her face was turning red with exertion and the vein along her neck was raised and bulging. She was summoning up every iota of strength to fight onwards, drawing upon the extraordinary might of the cornered animal.

"I'm afraid you'll have to suffer my help one last time. It seems I'll have to be your... emissary. Ferry some important information. Get the ball rolling for you."

This too Erin barely paid any attention to. But some usually dormant watchman-function in the language processing area of her brain did wake up and start to take notice. Lines were just begging to be read between here.

As had once been the case previously, it all happened very quickly then.

But not *quite* the same as before...

With blinding speed, Tilly drifted forward to float in front of Erin.

She whispered affectionately, "I hope you'll always remember how much I love you."

Then she started to raise her hand up towards Erin's forehead.

This was, of course, all happening a little too fast for Erin to consciously apprehend in the moment. But it didn't get past the pattern recognition filter in her mind, which now had the very worst sort of déjà vu. It screamed out an alarm and flipped the emergency circuit-breaker.

That constituted one of the mind's most sublime defensive talents: reaction before reaction. After a millisecond glimpse of an arrow soaring towards you, it doesn't waste time telling you about the arrow, or about why an arrow passing through flesh is bad, or how best to avoid arrows. It just makes you duck.

And duck she did.

Just as Tilly's palm was about to touch her, Erin instinctively jerked her head down out of the way.

Leaning forward like that did throw her way off balance though, and she tripped and fell face-forward, crashing through Tilly.

But as soon as she was about to hit the floor, she managed to use the momentum to clumsily roll over her shoulder.

On the other side of the roll, she was roughly catapulted back to her feet and she stagger-ran a few meters to keep upright.

Her face was now the very picture of mid-combat concentration and malice as she spun around to see where Tilly was.

This was easily done. Because Tilly was exactly where she had been, staring at Erin agape with pure astonishment.

At the other end of the ward, two security guards were coming through the big double doors. Obviously, word had reached them that their quarry had resurfaced.

The noise of the doors clattering shut after them attracted Erin's notice. She was still dizzy and a little discombobulated from her tumble, but her head instantly swivelled around to them.

She was now essentially boxed in, blocked in either direction.

Distractedly cracking her knuckles, she mouthed, "oh, you've got to be fucking kidding me."

The two men, spotting her, stopped short to look her over before engaging. Erin looked them over too, appraising her potential opponents. As human obstacles go, these guys were not *particularly* fearsome specimens. One was a weedy young man. He wore an ill-fitting uniform and just somehow had the distinct air of being a trainee. The other was short, paunchy and surely fast approaching retirement age.

Erin glanced around frantically.

There.

Closeby, there was an IV pole not currently in use, or even equipped with a bag, next to a comatose patient's bedside. She leapt over to it and grabbed it, roughly detaching the wide wheeled base with a kick.

Stepping back to where she had been, she held it out with both hands like a bo staff, ready to swing or jab with. The weightiness of it felt good. She was confident that she could wreak some serious havoc with it if things came to that. After all, apparently this was fast becoming her signature weapon.

She made a show of turning from the security guards to Tilly and back again, and then bellowed, "stay the fuck away, all of you!"

The other people on the ward, who had been frozen in silent awe whilst watching this drama's second act play out, all took more than a few steps back. With violence so palpably imminent, they were keen to give this lunatic a *very* wide berth until the showdown was resolved.

The two men eyed her carefully. They saw the grim determination on her face, and her pre-battle poise. They also looked at the pole she was wielding, and its not inconsiderable heft. Subsequently, they didn't need to confer or even exchange glances. It was clear to both of them that this wacko was absolutely ready to become a whirlwind of swinging steel, doling out some formidable damage. And their paltry salaries were not sufficient encouragement to blithely wade into that, not by a long shot. Nor was there enough hazard pay in the world that could have been.

"For the love of god, lady! Just put it down, would'ya?! Ain't no-one here to do you any harm! So just go ahead and take it easy, yeah?" the older security guard shouted over to her in a weary voice.

"Please don't do this, Erin," Tilly called from afar.

Erin looked back at her and snarled, "they *aren't* taking me..."

Tilly started to very slowly drift over.

"And neither are you!"

Erin turned around fully and jabbed out with the pole to signal the very sincere threat underwriting her certainty about that.

Coming to a sudden halt, Tilly said, "you're not thinking straight right now. Fear and anger are clouding your mind. And I can't let you do something really stupid that you'll really regret."

"That's not your fucking decision, you-"

The sound of slow approaching footsteps behind her got Erin's attention and she spun around abruptly.

Both men stopped in their tracks, having sneakily ventured a couple paces closer while Erin was distracted. They held their hands up to reiterate their peaceable intent.

Erin slammed the outstretched end of the pole as hard as she could down onto the floor, which produced a tremendous *crack*.

"Back the fuck up I said!" she screeched at them.

The older man hurriedly mumbled, "alright, alright, just take it easy."

Nudging his colleague, they both took several steps backwards, ceding the progress they had just made.

"I don't want to hurt anyone! So you rent-a-cop fuckers just keep your distance and everything-"

Again Erin sensed something behind her. She swivelled around in time to see that Tilly was just ten feet away, speedily drifting up to her.

Tightening her grip, Erin swung the pole like a bat, aiming at Tilly's fast-approaching midsection.

The blow was just inches away from landing when Tilly blinked out of existence and instantly rematerialised on Erin's left.

After sailing through empty space, the pole's remaining momentum yanked Erin off-balance and she had to stumble along with it to stay on her feet.

This inadvertent repositioning allowed her to very narrowly dodge Tilly, who after reappearing had surged toward Erin with an outstretched hand.

Having both missed, like unlucky jousters, they each span back around to face the other.

Erin wasted no time in executing her counterattack. She planted her feet and went about repeatedly stabbing the pole out like a spear. But each time Tilly would vanish and reappear slightly to the left or right with infuriating speed.

Actually growling in frustration, Erin stopped and switched tactics. She span on the spot to swing the outstretched pole around herself with great force. The intent being that even if Tilly blink-dodged to one side, the pole's follow-through motion would catch her there too.

But Tilly *didn't* teleport in this way. Instead, drifting incredibly fast, she circled around Erin, staying just slightly ahead of the pole's path.

Unfortunately, the senior security guard had been progressively creeping up closer and closer behind Erin as she played this game of mutual-keepaway. He was right behind her when she unwittingly spun around towards him with her improvised bludgeon whipping around too.

Tilly passed right through the man. The pole chasing right behind her did not.

The very end of it whacked into the thick meat at the side of his thigh very hard, eliciting a pain-stricken yowl. That leg completely failed him and he dropped to one knee. Then he fell back onto his butt, and quickly scooted away from the radius of Erin's whirling, indiscriminate fury in case it started back up again. He stopped up against a patient's bed some distance away, leaning his back against it and clutching his tenderised thigh while wincing and sucking in air through his teeth.

His young partner had not dared to follow alongside during this doomed ambush-attempt. He was still frozen where the two had previously been and was now staring at the hobbled man, wide-eyed and fearful. It had just happened so mind-bogglingly fast. This chick had chopped down that poor bastard like it was nothing.

"I-I'm gonna, uh, g-go get some help," he murmured faintly, awestruck with fright.

Then he turned and ran, bursting through the double doors as he beat a hasty retreat.

Standing there stunned, pole held limply in her hands, Erin was dumbly fixated upon the security guard she had just felled.

"Erin!" Tilly yelled, horrified by what just transpired.

Though this roused Erin out of her appalled entrancement, she could still only hover a thousand-yard stare over Tilly.

The shock and sheepish remorse which abruptly transformed her expression was very childlike. Swallowing hard, she said meekly, "w-where did he?... I didn't... I didn't even see... I wasn't-"

Tilly bullishly snorted air through her nose. Aflame with a correspondingly parental wrath, she proclaimed, "this ends now!"

In the blink of an eye, she shot forth, floating up to Erin and then right through her.

Erin had no taste for belligerence anymore but this was all happening so quickly that her animal instincts reacted for her.

As she swivelled about-face to track Tilly, she was holding the pole horizontally in front of herself. Without time to reposition her grip, she was only able to thrust it straight out in the hope of pushing Tilly away.

Of course, she caught only a fleeting glimpse of Tilly ducking under this attempted parry. Because Tilly had cut back once more and thrown herself right through Erin again.

Then when Erin span around one last time, she saw only a palm held aloft before her lights went out.

She simply crumpled to the floor like a building neatly demolished down into its own footprint. The pole slipped from her grasp and went skittering across the floor until it hit the wall.

And as Erin faded, in that split-second before she had totally ceded the helm, she knew in her heart that... she was glad to go. She saw it all so clearly now. She had been exactly what was needed. She was the hardy mortsafe - however unwittingly so, however unwillingly so - which had protected the dead part of herself long enough for it to finally seize a chance at resurrection. It was self-sacrifice in the truest, noblest sense. She had weathered what the soft creature she had once been could never have endured.

Laying there in an awkward heap, her body was perfectly still. The ward was now deathly silent. People didn't even dare to breathe.

Then, after a long moment elapsed, her eyes shot open.

With some difficulty, she untangled her limbs and pushed herself up to a sitting position.

She looked blearily around at everyone staring at her in wary bewilderment.

As the weight of their probing gazes accumulated, she rubbed the back of her neck in embarrassment. The uncomfortable quiet was solidifying like drying cement. She nervously bit at the inside of her lip as she deliberated.

Then, at last, in a soft voice she abashedly offered, "yeah... uh... sorry about... all that. She can just sometimes get kind of... ferocious when she's scared, but it's not-"

Upon spotting Genevieve in the distance, her face lit up with recognition and eager excitement. All trace of her momentary unease was erased. The elixir of purpose now lent her a commanding confidence as she beckoned the woman over. She watched as Genevieve, despite herself, took a few uncertain steps forward.

Wreathed in this new aura of resoluteness, she started getting up to her feet.

And, employing a let's-get-down-to-business tone, made another request.

"Grab a notepad, would you? There's... quite a lot I need to tell you about Erin."

ABOUT THE AUTHOR

Ryan Finch is the author of *Whence, Simulacrum?*, which is his debut novel. (He fully accepts that the only way it was ever going to be able to retain its supremely impractical and self-indulgent title was by self-publishing.)

He lives in England, with his gorgeous and appallingly talented girlfriend/editor/fellow-author Samantha and a surly housecat named Rudy. He loves them both dearly. However, he must admit, he *is* a little bewildered that Rudy still occasionally savages his forearms and shins despite all the fatherly affection he has shown him over the years. Possibly the mysteries of feline aloofness are destined to forever elude him.

In his spare time, he plays video-games, wages the sacred but arduous daily battle of trying to make himself write, unashamedly only ever eats one or two flavours of ice-cream, and is steadily working his way through the daunting backlog of unread books on his shelves. One time he tried to stop himself from buying new books until that backlog was cleared, but quickly succumbed to temptation. He considers it the books' fault, for being so pretty and so full of vast, amorphous promise.

He's surprised to discover that he does indeed feel pressured to make the customary quirky non-sequitur jokes which are peppered throughout author bios nowadays. He feels this pressure because he, too, wants you to know he's irreverent and witty and - he cannot possibly stress this forcefully enough – really *very* super chill. To that end, he's contemplating telling you that he lives off of stardust sandwiches or collects bullet-ants and paints them yellow or has an extra earlobe on the back of his knee or some other whimsical made-up shit like that. He is no more immune to the wanting-people-to-like-you instinct than anyone else.

Also, he sure does hope to have some other actual recognisable writing credits to mention in sections like these sooner rather than later, because, golly, is this bad boy looking *thin* in that regard.

You can find his other writings, including personal posts and political/cultural essays, at **ryanfinchwrites.com** and follow him for updates on Twitter at, you guessed it, **@ryanfinchwrites**

You can also find the podcast, *After Rambling Through All That...*, he does with Samantha at **ARTATpodcast.com**

And, lastly, he has no idea why the fuck he's adhering to that stuffy tradition of writing the author bio in third-person. *He* knows that you know this is him writing this, *you* know that he knows that you know he's writing this, and... well... it's all just a bit disquieting. He asks that you forgive him this lapse into orthodoxy. Perhaps he'll have more nonconformist moxie to apply to the back matter when it comes to releasing his next novel...

A SMALL REQUEST
FROM THE AUTHOR
(PLEASE DO NOT READ THIS UNTIL YOU HAVE FINISHED THE BOOK)

First of all: don't be a stranger. And, yes, I really do mean that. Seriously, you just read something which took me more than three years to write, something which I really poured myself into, something which is incredibly special and precious and personal to me. So, if there's a better starting point for reaching out to someone, you'd have to cite it to me, because I'm downright flummoxed.

Basically, I want to hear from you! (Even if you just want to say hello.) Shoot me an email at **ryanfinchwrites@gmail.com** and, as long as it's not malware and/or dick pics, I promise I'll reply. Tell me what you thought about the story. Tell me what you thought about Erin. Tell me how that one chapter affected you. Tell me about the really weird thing that happened to you while you were reading the book in a coffee shop or on the train or in a Yakuza hangout spot or in that underground cave. Tell me all about the theory you've been nursing, the one which posits that *A&F* is actually Erin's dead mom using spectral IM to look out for her from beyond the grave. Whatever it is, I want to hear it. And feel free to ask me whatever the hell you like. I'm an open bo- yeah, no, you're right, that would be way too on the nose.

And then secondly, I hope you won't think this somehow uncouth, but may I ask a small favour? I would *really* appreciate it if you could go onto **Amazon** and leave a review. (And maybe even recommend the book to someone you know, or post about it on social media, if you woke up feeling extra generous today.) I would love for as many people as possible to be able to read this book, and little visibility-bumps like that help make it happen.

So... pretty please? And if that doesn't work, then how about this: do it or I'll ugly-cry. I'm not bluffing. I'll do it. I'll make everyone in this room uncomfortable as fuck. Listen, in this modern paradigm of ruthless self-promotion, you gotta be willing to do whatever it takes. I already got the URL for the book's website tattooed onto my forehead, so... believe me... this would be small potatoes in comparison.

Lightning Source UK Ltd.
Milton Keynes UK
UKHW012233070222
398344UK00002B/159

9 781838 532895